THE DETECTIVE

ALSO BY RODERICK THORP

INTO THE FOREST

The Detective

RODERICK THORP

THE DIAL PRESS · NEW YORK

For Noel

IN this breathless pause at the threshold of a long passage we seemed to be measuring our fitness for . . . the appointed task of both our existences to be carried out . . .

—*The Secret Sharer*

PART ONE

CHAPTER ONE

■ ■

". . . AND NOW, RECAPPING TODAY'S HEADLINES," THE NEWS broadcaster continued, "the search in Port Smith for little Mary Shoftel goes on. Grim spokesmen for the Port Smith Police Department this morning released the information that since last Friday evening, more than five hundred men have been diverted from other duties to hunt for the seven-year-old girl. No evidence of kidnap or ransom notes has been revealed. The little girl, who had been playing in front of her home in the Westlake district of Port Smith on Thursday afternoon when she disappeared, requires daily medication for the treatment of a rare form of anemia. In an interview with WTOU's Bill Phillips, health officials here in Manitou stated that the lack of the medication would weaken little Mary, but in no way would it prove fatal. The search goes on.

"In a related story, the Port Smith police this morning announced the arrest of twenty-two-year-old Donald L. Harrow, Jr., in connection with a series of obscene and threatening telephone calls received at the Shoftel home yesterday. Young Harrow is being held on charges of obscenity, disturbing the peace, and obstructing justice. Other charges are forthcoming. It was reported that Mrs. Edna Shoftel, mother of little Mary, has been under heavy sedation since yesterday afternoon, when the crank telephone calls began."

The announcer paused. "Now, at nine thirty-four A.M., WTOU and WTOU-FM bring you the official United States Weather Bureau forecast for Manitou, Cuyahauga County, Upton County, and vicinity. Cloudy today with possible snow flurries late this afternoon, tempera-

3

ture in the low thirties, dropping to the twenties tonight, five to ten degrees colder in the mountain areas. Tomorrow, Tuesday, November sixteenth, cloudy and seasonably cold again with possible snow. Present humidity, sixty-eight percent; barometer thirty point two inches and steady; wind out of the west at eight miles an hour; and the temperature now, at the observatory atop the Manitou Life Insurance Building in downtown Manitou, thirty-one degrees . . ."

Joseph Leland, in his shirt sleeves, turned the radio off. Puffing on his cigarette, he hurried with the buttons of his cuffs. He had awakened with his mind racing. Usually he had time to stop over coffee and get things aligned, but not this morning: as of this moment he had been awake seventeen minutes. He hoped that he could get the taste of toothpaste out of his mouth with cigarettes while he rode downtown. He hated the taste of toothpaste, and for some reason it always made him feel that he was wearing the clothing he had slept in. He puffed again. Now he shivered; somebody stepping on his grave. It was the shock of getting going. The reaction of his body reminded him of a dog shaking water off his back, and he grinned as he returned to the bedroom for a tie.

The newsman's words followed him through the apartment. Leland had turned on the radio for the weather and the international news; he had forgotten the Shoftel case. He did not want to hear about it, for he knew that Mary Shoftel was dead. The responses of the Port Smith Police Department after the failure to find her quickly, the number of men working on the case, the cooperation with the press, and the lack of an announcement of a kidnap, all pointed to a rape and murder. On the face of it there was some piece of evidence, perhaps the report of a neighborhood man suddenly moving from his boarding house, that gave the P.S.P.D. a direction in which to go. The men who were in on the search were looking for the girl's body. They knew it. The only thing they had going for them was that most child-rapist-murderers had no taste for the act once it was done. They cleaned up after themselves the way cats scratched at their droppings.

The newspapers and radio and television stations had turned the case into the circus it had become—"hoping against hope" was a phrase Leland had heard. Leland usually read three or four news-

4

papers a day in the attempt to find out what was really happening, but he had passed them over on Saturday and yesterday. He knew that in a case like this what was really happening, if anybody knew it, was unprintable in newspapers. On Friday night, without a picture to run, one of the Port Smith papers had gone with a front-page editorial sketch of the weeping parents, captioned "Why?" Leland wondered why. The newspapers knew the truth almost as well as the police. Before the end of the week the father would be escorted through the corridors of the police headquarters basement to view the freshly decomposing body of his daughter. Leland had seen enough doctored victims of crimes of violence—one would have been enough. They were stripped and bathed down with alcohol, the wounds cleaned and tucked together for the official photographs. After death, before it sank back into the skull, the human eye had a strange shine. The oldest corpse Leland had seen in that basement, a man over seventy, had looked like a child surprised. Having been kicked to death had been only part of it. Death itself seemed to have put the expression on his face. They all looked young and surprised, those whom death had overtaken quickly. Mr. Shoftel would see his own child, and Leland, who had always had the role he had been playing to hide behind, could not eagerly wish Mr. Shoftel a long life. Every man had his nightmares, and it was not hard to imagine Mr. Shoftel's. Setting his jacket on his shoulders before the mirror. Leland could not conceive any experience for Mr. Shoftel that would not be clouded by the memory of a dead daughter. Mr. Shoftel would have something to remember after he saw her body, and if he read the newspapers, he was being set up for it nicely. Leland started to fill his pockets.

Leland was thirty-six, five feet ten, and weighed one hundred and forty pounds. His hair was dark brown, thick and cut short. He did not part it. His skin was fair and had a faint translucent quality, so that he had to work hard to look closely shaved. His lips were dark, the kind that seemed moist when they were not. His brown eyes were his most attractive feature—and most expressive, too, for he had had to practice drawing other people into talking, which required staying silent and conveying impressions, true or deliberately mis-

5

leading, with the eyes. There was a scar, the result of an automobile accident, in his left brow, and there was another, from a different kind of accident, along the side of his jaw. Both scars were small, thin, and white; most people did not take much notice of them. It was only in recent years that Leland had begun to pay attention to his appearance —until two years ago he had parted his hair on the side and allowed it to grow as long as the barber would allow—and the impression that he made now was as crisp and conservative but at the same time as energetic as that of a young congressman still learning his job. But not quite: there were the scars which, if they blended in, nevertheless had their effect; and the eyes, which perhaps had had to mislead too much and looked tired. The young-congressman presentation was created in fact by habits that Leland regarded as bad: his suits ran to sober browns and grays—all of them two-buttoned, medium lapeled —today's was a brown worsted—and he used bow ties. He had more than thirty of them. He liked them; they were easier for him to tie and more comfortable to live with than four-in-hands. Today's tie was dark brown with dot-sized white doodads resembling blighted cloves. It had been a gift in celebration of nothing, and he liked it.

He came out of the bedroom with his topcoat over his arm and a five-dollar bill in his hand. The money was for the cleaning woman, Mrs. Walsh, who was due in the afternoon. This was the last thing he had to attend to before he could leave. Out of simple habit of living alone, Leland took a last look around.

The telephone rang. He knew who it was. "Relax, I'm on my way," was his response into the receiver. The crisp impression that his appearance made was ruined when he spoke. His speech was city speech, roughly enunciated and slurred. His own thought was that it was no worse than the twang they spoke up here.

"This is important," his secretary, Florence Cline, said. "You could have been asleep. I think you'd better hurry."

"Where are you? At my desk?" She called him from there when she thought there was trouble.

"Yes. There are some people outside, there's something you have to handle, and the phone will start to ring as soon as people have their second coffee."

"Why?"

"Your picture is in the Port Smith *Herald-Press*. They've started a series on famous old crimes, I guess because of Mary Shoftel, and they have the Leikman case today. Your picture is on the bottom of page one, over the caption 'War Hero Cop Who Tracked Down Leikman's Killer . . .' "

"Say no more." The Shoftel case was more than the depraved circus he had thought; it had moved into ritual. The *Herald-Press* had run a similar series during the Leikman case. Now one of the papers had to start a fund. There had been none six and a half years ago, because nobody had cared about Leikman or his family, but a fund really was standard. When one of these things happened the public waited and looked for a place to send its money. This added to its sense of participation. Leland asked, "Who are the people in the office?"

"Schwartzwald, for one," she said. "He's seeing Mr. Petrakis now."

"Swell. Keep your voice down." Leland and his partner, Mike Petrakis, had adjoining offices, separated by a plasterboard wall. "What does Schwartzwald want? I told him on Friday that I'd call him."

"He likes it here, I think."

"All right, who else?"

"Mrs. Colin MacIver."

"Don't know her. What kind of a looking woman is she?"

"Early twenties, small, brunette, cute, and pregnant."

"No kidding? Okay."

"With her is a Mr. Miller. Fred, he said. He's—"

"I know him," Leland said. "Heavy guy around fifty."

"That's him. Mr. Petrakis doesn't know who he is. He gave him that polite look as he came out to greet Mr. Schwartzwald."

Greet Mr. Schwartzwald. Mike still had a lot to learn about handling people. Leland said, "Mike wouldn't know Miller. He's an agent for Manitou down in Port Smith"—in the proper contexts, the name of the town was sufficient to identify the insurance company—"and he's another pest, like Schwartzwald. The last thing we need is

7

him drumming up trade. I haven't seen him in years. Does he still have that tweed overcoat?"

"Brown, with raglan sleeves," Florence said. "He kept his hat on when he sat down—"

"He's bald."

"I sort of knew that," she said.

"Okay, what is it that I have to handle?"

"Hugh Thoms called. He thinks he was spotted last night on the custody case. It was late and the woman seemed to be on her way home. She turned around and went by him and looked him straight in the eye. He'll explain it to you."

Leland did not like that. The case was a lawyer's referral and a man was trying to get his child away from his ex-wife because she had a boyfriend. The lawyer would not have a case to take to court, but that did not devalue this work. Being spotted would; it would devalue Leland. There was a very good chance that Hugh Thoms was wrong because he was an extremely cautious man, but they could not risk it. It was something to handle, as Florence had said. "Did you tell Mike?"

"I haven't been able to."

"If he wants to get going on it, tell him that I said to see if he can't pull someone out of Bonney's who knows how to tail, and we'll put Hugh in the store for the duration."

"Hugh was very upset," she said.

"He would be. When you're sixty-eight we'll let you get upset, too."

"Yes, sir." Her tone indicated that she was not bothering to listen, which was all right. Leland was still not awake. A directive on how to treat Hugh Thoms was something she did not have to hear. Leland knew that she liked Hugh in her own way, even if Hugh made it clear that he did not understand the faith Leland had in her, a girl who had just turned twenty.

"Was there anything else?" he asked.

"No, sir."

"I'll be down in ten minutes."

It was enough of a goodbye, and they hung up.

His apartment was in a new building in the Clifford Heights section, looking down on the center of commercial Manitou. On a bluff over the river, to the right in his picture window, was a cluster of old mills and factories, some a hundred years old, and in their center, rising like the tomb of an Aztec king, was the square, buttressed, fourteen-story home office of the Manitou Life Insurance Company. In spite of a population nearing three hundred and fifty thousand, Manitou was still a company town, and that was the company. Twelve thousand people worked there, and many others depended wholly or in part on the business it made. When Leland had come here six years ago to take the job the company had offered, he had not known what to make of the location in the heart of the industrial district. But it had been no mistake; Manitou, the town, which had suffered terribly in the depression, was prospering in the postwar boom, and planned to rebuild from there, on the spot on which it had been founded. In six or seven years a score of apartments and commercial buildings, the home office among them, would rise from a grassy plain and command a view thirty miles down a river that surely was one of the most beautiful in the world.

When he could, Leland still went down to the executives' dining room under the rooftop observatory. The paintings there showed that the vista had hardly changed in the three centuries since the fur traders had come up the 170 miles from Port Smith. Leland had a business here now, and many deep attachments, but he still saw himself as a guest and, when he was near that view, a stranger. Deer were still being taken within sight of downtown, nothing so remarkable. But Leland had spent his first thirty years in Port Smith; he had never shot at an animal in his life. When he saw the river, it made him aware of how far he had come. This was his home now, but he knew that he would never feel completely comfortable. He was not unhappy, and it was not an unhappy feeling; he knew, too, that this was the most fruitful and rewarding period of his life. It was just that he would not say that he was going to be here in ten years; he refused to decide. Ten years from now he probably would still be here, but it would be because ten years of living one-day-to-the-next had passed, nothing more.

He took the five-dollar bill to the side table on which he left money for Mrs. Walsh. There, folded on a candy dish in the way a servant delivered mail, was a note from Karen. Leland knew her neat, small writing better than he knew his own. He brought the note into the light.

Midnight

Dear Joe,

Sorry. I should rouse you to say good night properly, but you're flat on your back, not to be moved. You're smoking too much. I can hear it in your breathing.

Tomorrow I have a meeting with the Superintendent and then lunch at twelve-thirty with a hysterical woman—I'm not the one who should talk, I know—who wants to take some books out of our curriculum, and then in the afternoon I go down to the Teachers' College to speak on "The Emotionally Unstable Adolescent." Don't laugh.

At night is the presentation to the School Board, which is why I have to see the Superintendent in the morning, to get our stories straight. I'll be home to cook dinner for Steffie and then back no later than ten-thirty. Can we get together? Any way you want. If you want to come over for dinner, let me know. You probably won't catch me at the office, but leave the message. I just want to see you, but I really hope you can be there later.

I had a lovely time this evening. The things we don't discuss make the others much more difficult to express. They go unsaid for too long. I had a lovely time. I mean it.

I'm looking forward to going to Montreal for the weekend. Maybe I'll get a book from the library so we'll all know what to look for when we get there.

I love you,
Karen

Leland read it again. He wished that she had awakened him. He had awakened by himself at four-thirty and had felt a pang of fear before he had seen the clock and realized that she had gone. He felt it again now, diminished but more lasting, and for a better reason: the note. Except for the dinner invitation, it was a pointless thing that only repeated what she had told him at various times during the day. Somehow she had forgotten, which was not like her. It had been midnight when she had written the note; earlier she had been asleep herself: perhaps that explained it. He knew that he could be wrong in looking too closely, but it was on something like this that their trouble usually started. It had been a good day yesterday, as she had written, but last night while he had been asleep she had been awake, unwilling to waken him, and obviously wanting to talk.

Leland folded the note and slipped it into his jacket pocket. He could not tell about dinner; Florence's call had promised another kind of day. Karen had said ten-thirty, but knowing her schedule, he could easily imagine getting a call from her later, begging off.

He put on his topcoat and started out. There was nothing he could do now. He began to sift the things that Florence had told him.

The newspaper belonged to the cabdriver.

> . . . The investigation was led by Detective Lieutenant Joseph Leland, at the time the youngest man to ever hold that high rank in the Port Smith police department. A career cop who had distinguished himself as a patrolman before the war, Leland had come back from Europe with a chestful of medals, including the Distinguished Flying Cross, collected for shooting down (Turn to p. 5)

Leland turned.

> LEIKMAN SLAYING (Story begins on p. 1)
> 21 Nazi planes. Now a private detective upstate, Leland is credited with uncovering singlehandedly the shreds of evidence that revealed the whereabouts of Leikman's killer . . .

Leland closed the newspaper, glanced at the headline, WHERE IS MARY SHOFTEL? and the newly discovered fuzzy photograph of the seven-year-old beneath, and returned the newspaper to the front seat.

"Had enough, hah?" the driver said. "I could have made a dollar on you. When we saw you coming down the hill, one of the fellows said that you'd get a kick out of seeing yourself in the paper. I said you wouldn't bother to go all the way through the article."

Leland drew on his cigarette. "You should have taken his money."

The driver's name was Everett. "To tell you the truth, I wasn't too sure myself. I shouldn't tell you that, should I? How was it? The article—was it accurate?"

"As far as it went. Sure, it was all right." The cabdrivers in Manitou worked at getting steady customers. Even when he was late, Leland rode with Everett, if Everett was around. The responsibility for keeping faith was the customer's, and you had to have a reason if you wanted to change drivers. Everett, a moonfaced farmer's son in his forties, was all right. Leland had talked him into voting Democratic in the last election.

"Do you know anything about that little girl? It's a hell of a thing. I can't even talk about it with my wife."

"Just don't build up her hopes," Leland said.

"Yeah? Shoot, I had hopes of my own. She'd better not ask me if I saw you. Did you ever work on a case like it? I guess not, it would be in the paper."

Leland flicked his ash out the window, then rolled the window up again. "I saw one, before I went into the service. A teen-ager killed a little girl, then hanged himself. The girl was nine. Her parents knew him, or knew that she had been seeing him, I forget now how it went." He had seen it by accident; he had been downtown when the bodies had come in. He had been told to go downstairs to take a look.

Now he glanced out the window again. They had reached Senapee Street, the center of the shopping district. It was a broad street, practically empty at this hour. The sky was overcast and boxes of trash were piled at the curb for collection. The street looked bleak and once in a while a neon sign was on, making the sky seem darker than it was. The wind came up the side streets from the river, buffeting the taxi.

Everett steered around a trolley car stopped to pick up a single passenger. "I guess those girls are pretty bad off," he said. "Before they're killed, I mean. My wife doesn't understand how a man does it. Physically. Neither can I, for that matter."

Everett was curious. "The girls are dead or unconscious before the action begins," Leland said.

"Dead? I don't understand that at all."

"It's called necrophilia," Leland said. "I don't understand it, either."

Everett glanced in the mirror, saw Leland watching, and looked away guiltily. "Hey, what about the Leikman case?" He was trying to be casual. "They've always talked about the crazy stuff that went on in that one. What was that about?"

Leland grinned. He couldn't let Everett con him; there would be no end to it. "You don't want to know about that," he said.

Everett stayed quiet. They passed Bonney's, which had a new enameled-metal front, covering four stories of aged gray stone. More and more of the stores were going for new fronts, but the ornate wooden eaves remained, the overhead wires, and the trolley tracks, to show the age of the town. The cab rocked again in the wind, and the suspended traffic lights swung. Leland blinked; he was still working the sleep out of his body.

CHAPTER TWO

■ ■

PAST THE SENAPEE THEATER AND THEN, DOWN CLARK STREET, THE
Gem. At the six-way intersection of Senapee, Otis, and Broadway
there were three hotels, a restaurant, two coffee shops, two more
movie houses, a second-floor ballroom, a new caffè espresso, and
three storefront strip clubs. Leland's office was on the next block, over
a furniture store, a loan office, and a law partnership.

"I hope you're wrong about that little girl," Everett said.

Leland didn't answer. There was no question about what Everett
was aiming for. Everett made the U-turn over the trolley tracks
and braked the taxi smartly before the building entrance. Leland
opened the door and handed a dollar over the top of the front seat.
Everett didn't take it right away. He looked troubled. Leland was
going to wait him out.

"Listen, how does a fellow do it? I mean, how does he get in a
little girl? They aren't developed or anything."

"Well, Everett, the one I saw was ripped open, back to front,
skin, muscle, cartilage and bone, the same way a butcher dresses a
turkey." Leland pushed the dollar toward him.

Everett took the dollar and tucked it into the breast pocket of
his jacket. He looked back at Leland unhappily. "Will I see you
tomorrow?"

"I don't know. I don't know what I'll be doing."

"Listen, I'm sorry. Are you sore at me?"

Leland patted his arm. "No, no. Don't be silly." He got out; he
couldn't wait for a response. He hadn't lied about his plans and he

14

wasn't angry. As he headed into the building he had to wonder how Everett abided the emotional scramble in which he hoped for Mary Shoftel and at the same time tried to wring a vicarious excitement out of the worst that could happen to her. The question had been phrased in the abstract, which was supposed to make it different, but he had been too nervous to pose as a man on the search for knowledge. Leland had told him that the girls were unconscious or dead and he had known that they were not developed. It did not take much to put them together and see it for the atrocity it was. Everett had not wanted to give up. Leland could not hold his hand like a child's. If Everett was going to worry about the dollar a day as well, then it ceased to be Leland's business.

Leland stepped into the elevator. " 'Morning, Charlie."

"Not a moment too soon," Charlie Scott said. "You've had three up and one down and the delivery boy just got in with the coffee." Charlie Scott was a retired cop, like Hugh Thoms.

"The one who's down," Leland asked, "a skinny guy with glasses?"

"Looks like a chicken," Charlie Scott said. He was sixty and had all his hair, in white waves, brushed like a boy's. It was something to see.

"We're ahead of the game," Leland said. The one down was Schwartzwald. He had come in on Friday convinced that one of the booth men at his drive-in was stealing. It was a stupid situation, for he had only to put in ticket-takers, as in the movie houses, to check the men who handled the money. Leland had been sure that Schwartzwald was afraid of the additional salaries and Leland had wanted to conclude business as quickly as possible. Five cars, twenty people, all three nights of the weekend: the best way, Leland had assured him, of doing the job. It could have been made to last for weeks, for a lot more money. Mike had brought the people together and had handled the generalship, but Leland had not escaped entirely. The exit gates had been in plain view of the admissions booths, and Leland had been compelled to sit through *The Fang of Blood* and *Captain from Corsica* three full times. Leland did not even know if the booth man had stolen, because he had not stolen from him. Now Leland took off his topcoat in preparation for getting past Fred Miller.

With the topcoat over his right arm, Leland pushed into his office. Not pausing in his stride, he let his eyes fall on Miller. "Hiya, Fred. This is a surprise." With a beefy grunt, Miller struggled up, extending his hand until he saw how Leland was encumbered. With his other hand Leland leaned on Miller's shoulder. "Stay there. I'll be with you in a minute."

And he kept going, through the gate, on to the door of his office. Around on the left, the two girls exchanged whispers that were just too obvious. He signaled Florence to follow him inside.

She closed the door. "Schwartzwald's gone."

"Charlie told me." He went to his desk for the waiting container of coffee. "Thanks," he said, lifting the cup to her. She had her notebook, which meant that there had been more calls.

"You had a long-distance call from Port Smith. Your father. He asked if you had seen the paper. I said that you would call him back."

"Did you try to set a time?"

"He said that he would be in his office all day. The Manitou *Star* called. They didn't say what they wanted. They'll call back. Hugh Thoms called again. He's on the job in spite of last night. Max at Bonney's called in sick and Mrs. Freeman, too. She works this evening, four to nine, but she was sure she wouldn't make it. Upset stomach."

Leland Associates handled the store security at Bonney's by contract.

"What was the matter with Max?"

"He didn't say."

"Have you talked to Mike?"

"Not yet."

"Okay." Leland drank more of the coffee. Florence was a big girl; in heels she was almost as tall as Leland. She still carried some of her baby fat, which made her clothes fit her badly, and even now her blouse was beginning to creep out of her skirt. At four in the afternoon she could look pretty ragged, and Leland presumed that

Hugh Thoms registered that fact along with her frosted hair in forming his poor opinion of her. Hugh was a wonderful old cop, but Leland had to look the other way when he shook his head after Florence left them alone. What Hugh didn't know was that Florence was drawing the higher salary and that Leland thought she was worth it, or more. She could do any outside job and she ran the office with the assurance of a floor nurse. Leland had tried to talk her into going to college in the evenings, but she thought that that was beyond her —and so it probably was. Her father was a drunk and her mother had drawn into a shell years ago. Florence had become engaged last summer to a young fellow who picked her up on Fridays, a tool-and-die apprentice. They were to be married next year. She had asked Leland to recommend a marriage manual, which he had done, but he did not know if they had read it. He hoped that their luck would hold until she felt more certain about living the life of a woman. The urgency of her telephone conversations and the way she had to take possession of her fiancé when he came to meet her were disheartening. The little she said about the hours she kept suggested that she still needed the effect of long and late Saturday nights to beat down the last of her defenses. She wasn't a cold person and it happened often. Leland wanted her to have a start in life before she became pregnant. He did not want to see her tripped up by something she would outgrow.

She said, "In the mail today were the usual checks, some ads, a brochure from Piper Aircraft, which I saved, the report, and the expense sheet from Florida—"

"Have they got anything?"

"Shots of him in his bathing suit on the beach. No brace or elastic bandage."

There was nothing to say. The two men were on a casualty claims case in which the claimant swore that he was one hundred per cent disabled, but he was spending his days fishing for marlin. A lot of money was involved and the company wanted to try for a settlement. One of the parties to the policy contract was trying to cheat the other, but Leland did not know which, or care. As often as not in these cases it was the contract that was bad, but that didn't concern

17

Leland, either. He had never lied for a company, and a company had never made a statement to a client only to learn that the information Leland had supplied was in error.

Florence said, "There's a strange letter from R.F.D. One, Fayetteville, which I looked up on the map. It's down in Franklin County. A man says people are breaking into his house at night."

"Throw that out."

"Shall I tell Mike you're here?"

He said, "You have to talk to Sheila and Patsy."

"I saw that when you came in."

"The important thing is, did Miller? I couldn't hang around to find out."

"I took a look," she said. "He didn't, but she did. Mrs. MacIver. She was a little confused."

"She could be a little confused, anyway," Leland said.

"Don't judge her too quickly," Florence said. "She's not stupid. I've been watching her. She doesn't enjoy Mr. Miller's company. She keeps her responses to him short—Yes, Please, and No, thank you."

"She's about six months along, isn't she?"

"You know as much about it as I do. For her sake, I hope she is."

Florence didn't care for her. Leland said, "What's the matter with her skin?"

"I've been thinking about that. She had acne, but she's had her skin treated since. It's possible that she had her face planed. That's a mild plastic surgery where they shave off the scarred layers of your skin."

Leland grinned and toasted her again with the coffee container. *"Your* skin, maybe, but not mine."

"Did you ever see such dark eyes? Her hair is naturally jet black. She has it on her wrists. Her wrists are delicate, but they're hard, too. She's worked hard."

"Enough. How did you like *Captain from Corsica?*"

"Mention it again and I'll quit, I swear."

"Did he steal from you?"

"Oh, yes, all three nights. What about you? He didn't take from Mike the last two times, but he did the first, when Joan was driving and Mike was sitting over on the other side."

"He didn't take from me," Leland said, sorry that the man was a thief.

"Do you know what you have to do this afternoon?" she asked.

"Three o'clock, Bonney's. We're going to talk about the High View Shopping Center. Does Mike have the figures?"

"He was able to tell me before Schwartzwald came in that he needs another half hour, then he'll be able to spread them out for you. Do you want to see the *Herald-Press?*"

"No, I had it in the cab coming down. Were there any other calls?"

"No. No, there weren't."

He hesitated, realizing that it wasn't the casual question he had thought. Florence had known it right away. He didn't expect Karen to call. He had her schedule; she couldn't. He would play this scene again today if he wasn't careful. He said, "I'm going in to see Mike while I drink my breakfast. Give me a buzz in five minutes."

On her signal he made his way back through his office to the waiting room. Miller rose, removing his hat, and tried to take Mrs. MacIver by the elbow. She had been dreaming and, startled, she pulled her arm back. She saw Leland's interest and she looked away as she stood up, brushing at her coat. It wasn't a natural, spontaneous act. He wanted to see what would happen if he stared. When her eyes came up she flushed and tried to look away again. It wasn't shyness exactly. It was a kind of curious, misplaced intensity. Now Leland knew more about her than he would have if she had ignored him.

She had unbuttoned her coat in the warmth of the office and underneath she had on a white-trimmed navy blue smock suit. No hat; her hair had been blown by the wind. Her hair was as black as a cat's. It came halfway down her neck all the way around and was parted on the side and combed almost straight: it made her look like a little girl. She was little, five feet one or two. She had an annoyed expression, almost sulking. A better disposition would have suited her

19

unlined face. It had occurred to Leland that she could be Miller's cousin, whom he had fetched here on a stupid errand, but the action between them now made him reject that. Her husband could have abandoned her, but Leland did not think much of that, either. She was not the kind who got abandoned—he was trying to be objective. She was a very pretty young woman, and her prettiness did not have much to do with being pregnant. She had a casebook full of problems—her youth, her skin, she was probably flat-chested—but there was something interesting and difficult about her.

Miller let her through the gate, staying close to her side. He stuck his right hand out for Leland.

"Hello, Fred," Leland said. Miller was the shorter of the two, but he outweighed Leland by fifty pounds. Under the raglan coat was a brown pinstripe suit with wide lapels. He had gained twenty pounds more since he had ordered it. The tips of his shirt collar were turned up from absorbed perspiration.

"Hello, Joe," he said. "I should have dropped you a line first, but I figured that you kept regular business hours. This is Mrs. Colin MacIver, of Port Smith. This is Joe Leland, Norma."

"How do you do?" Alto and soft, like a touch of adenoiditis. She did not want to shake hands.

"How are you?" Leland said. "Shall we go inside?"

"I was wondering," she said. She looked back at Florence. Leland beckoned to his secretary. He had been wondering himself how Mrs. MacIver had lasted.

"That's right," she said. "Thank you."

"Flo, see that Mrs. MacIver has what she wants. We'll be in my office." And as soon as Miller was inside, Leland closed the door.

Miller wrestled out of his coat and hung it on the clothes tree. "What was that about?"

"A trip to the bathroom. Have a seat. Took the train up, eh?"

"That's right. How'd you know? Boy, we were up early."

Leland thought that he could let the question go. Miller had been wearing his shirt for hours; if he had taken the plane—there was a plane every two hours—he would still look fresh.

Miller eased into one of the armchairs in front of Leland's desk.

The desk was clear but for the telephone, intercom, and the brochure from Piper. On either side of the door to Mike's office were bookcases containing law, police, and criminology textbooks. Against the opposite wall was a green vinyl-covered couch, and above it, two citations from the Port Smith Police Department. One was dated 1940 and had *Valor* printed on it, and the other, dated 1948, simply showed Leland's name. On the bookcases, across from the citations so that a rough symmetry was achieved, were two model airplanes, in attitudes of climbing, a P-47 Thunderbolt and, nearer the outer office, a P-51 Mustang. Their builder—not Leland—had arranged them to point to a vertex near the ceiling, but somehow the Thunderbolt had become twisted around to face the window. The furnishings were so simple in total that this irregularity disturbed the balance of the room. Leland gathered up the Piper brochure and slipped it into a lower drawer.

He took his time lighting a cigarette. He had not forgotten that a conversation with Miller was a heavy task. "Tell me how you've been, Fred. Let's just bat the breeze until Mrs. MacIver gets back."

"I'm doing all right. I'm a Chartered Life Underwriter now, you know. Got my Million Dollar Award."

"Very nice," Leland said. "Very, very nice."

"You seem to be doing good," Miller said, looking around. He had a graying horseshoe of hair above his ears. "I guess you're doing about the same kind of thing you used to do for the company." When Leland nodded, Miller said, "Did you see the *Herald-Press* today? This is the first time I've had the chance to read up on it—"

"Excuse me," Leland said. He got up, gesturing to the Thunderbolt. His mind was working and he wanted to find his ground. Mrs. MacIver wasn't close to Miller, so Miller's presence probably meant insurance, a lot of it, for fives and tens usually did not bring an agent this far. The more Leland thought of it, the more his curiosity was aroused. The one other time they had done real business together, when Leland had been chief of Manitou's Investigations Division, Miller's suspicions had led to a doctor who had been encouraging bribes from policy applicants. When that had ended, Miller had kept coming back, clouding Leland's memory of the case with long, boring hours of following the company policy of being nice to agents. Mrs. MacIver could still be a cluck, but Leland found it increasingly hard to believe. When he returned to his desk, the light on the telephone was flashing.

It was Hugh Thoms. He wanted to deliver a report but Leland told him to save it. Leland outlined the plan to move Hugh into Bonney's while Harry McLeod took over the custody case. Leland told Hugh to hold his ground until McLeod came to relieve him. When Hugh said that he understood, Leland said good and pushed the disconnect button.

"Small difficulties," he said over his hand to Miller.

Miller nodded, with a gentle smile. He had a face that was in the process of collapsing into his neck.

It took Harry McLeod a minute to get to the telephone. Leland swung his chair around to the bookcase. McLeod reminded him that, as an ex-insurance man, he had never worked on a custody investigation and that showing old Hugh Thoms around the store would swamp the few people who had reported to work today. Now the door to the outer office opened and Florence and Mrs. MacIver entered. Florence gave Leland a signal with her hand and he waved her off. For Mrs. MacIver, Leland pointed to the other armchair on the bookcase side of the desk. Florence took her coat. Through the telephone McLeod asked if he could have Mrs. Agnew, another Bonney's-experienced operative, from one to nine. Leland said distinctly that he would have Florence call Mrs. Agnew and ask her to report at one o'clock. Now Mrs. MacIver sat down, not taking her eyes off Leland. Leland gave McLeod the location and the make and model of Hugh Thoms' car. Hugh would give McLeod the details of the case. Leland put down the telephone and looked to Florence, where she waited at the door.

"I'll make that call," she said in a tone that was unnatural, and went out.

"I'm sorry about these interruptions," Leland said to the others, "but I can't say there won't be more. My partner is doing some paperwork that requires his strict attention, and one of us has to pick up the telephone."

"Your partner," Mrs. MacIver said. "Wasn't he a football player at Jefferson a few years ago?"

"That's right," Leland said. "He was an All-America quarterback, 1949. Mike Petrakis."

"Then he had that automobile accident," Mrs. MacIver said.

"Either you went to Jefferson or you're a football fan," said Leland.

"Neither. I went to Port Smith College. My husband was the Jefferson graduate."

"Was?"

"He's dead."

"Oh. I'm sorry to hear that," said Leland. The intercom buzzed; it seemed to jolt Miller. "Yes?" Leland asked.

"Joe," Mike Petrakis said, "would you step in here a minute?"

"I'll be right there." He stood up. "Excuse me." Miller gaped. Mrs. MacIver leaned forward a little, looking up. Her eyes met Leland's as he moved around the desk. Before he reached the door he thought to ask her what she wanted, but when he looked around, she was sitting back, brushing at her skirt.

Mike was at his desk with his cuffs turned up. There were papers spread out and an account ledger braced against the telephone like a missal.

"What's up?" Leland asked.

"Search me," Mike said. "I—"

The door to the outer office opened and Florence stepped in. "I asked Mr. Petrakis to buzz you, Mr. Leland. I wanted to tell you something without alerting Mr. Miller."

"Miller?"

"Yes. Mrs. MacIver had to make the trip to the rest room, all right, but when we got out there, just before she went inside, you know, the john, she turned to me and said, 'I was hoping that I'd be able to speak to your boss alone.'"

CHAPTER THREE

. . . .

"ANYTHING ELSE?" LELAND ASKED.

"Just that," Florence said. "I timed combing my hair so she would have to wait for me when she got out, but then she seemed to look straight through me. I don't know, there's something funny about her."

"She seemed like a nice kid to me," Mike said.

"I'm not sure of that," Leland said. He was trying to encourage Florence. Mike was so generous with people that he intimidated practically everybody. It was hard even for Florence to be critical when she knew that Mike would object.

"It's just a feeling I have," she said, looking at Leland. "She's not sure of herself—very unsure, in fact—but there's a kind of hardness deep inside her, and she's close to it now."

"She connived this," Leland said. "She saw the intercom on your desk and figured that you could work something."

"That's what I mean," Florence said. "She's capable of it. Her mind is really going."

"I think you're both reading too much into it," Mike said. "She wants only what she said."

"No," said Leland, "you have to be with her to see it. Flo, you did a good job. If I call you, come in on the double. Her husband is dead, and in her condition, she might be more upset than we can see. Miller wouldn't know."

"Shoot, I don't like this at all," she said.

He didn't want her going too far. "That's not for you to say," he said.

"I'm sorry."

"Don't go yet, Flo," Mike said. "You can direct the calls into me now. I'll be having lunch here, so I'll have the extra time to work on these figures."

On Mondays Mike had lunch with Joan. Leland waited until Florence had closed the door. "Is everything all right, fella?"

"Oh, sure." He leaned back. "She just called. Her stomach's upset. She doesn't want to leave the house."

"Oh. Well, tell her to take care." Something needled Leland; he couldn't make it out. "I'd better get back," he said.

Their heads turned as he re-entered. He didn't try to read anything on Mrs. MacIver's face. In his chair, he swiveled to her and asked, "What did your husband die of?"

"That's why we're here." That soft, controlled voice. It didn't fit her.

Leland scratched the back of his hand. "Would you care for a cigarette?"

"No, thank you."

The pack was on the desk. "Fred?"

"Thanks, I will."

He directed himself to Miller and waited while Miller got comfortable. "Let's see what we have, Fred. When did MacIver die?"

"August twelfth."

"How old was he?"

"Thirty-two."

"Was there a coroner's inquest?"

"Yes, there was."

Leland glanced at Mrs. MacIver: she was checking Miller's answers.

"What was the verdict?"

"Suicide." Miller leaned toward the ash tray.

"How much insurance?"

"A hundred and eighty-seven thousand, but—"

Leland nodded. "How much was paid off?"

"Thirty-seven thousand."

"The rest was protected by the two-year suicide clause?" Leland asked.

"That's right," Miller said.

"Don't you think it was suicide?"

"I don't know."

"What do you think it was?"

"I don't have an opinion, Joe. I knew Colin for nine years, and I didn't think this of him."

"How long did the clause have to run?"

"Even the longest was less than a year."

"Say he had been thinking of suicide, was he the sort of guy to have waited?"

"Oh, yes," Miller said.

"Tell me why," Leland said.

"Well, for one thing, he was a very good man with money."

"He never mentioned suicide to you?" Leland asked. "Never talked about others—Carole Landis, James Forrestal?"

"No, he never did."

"Okay," said Leland. "Did you see the autopsy protocol or the inquest proceedings?"

"No, just the death certificate."

"Give me the cause of death."

"That's getting rough, Joe."

"I'll stop you if I think so," Leland said.

"Death was caused by a frontal skull fracture. That's not it exactly."

"Close enough. Where did he jump or fall?"

"From the roof of Flatlands Racetrack."

"Give me the time of day."

"Four twenty-eight exactly. They were able—"

"The horses were running," Leland said. "Okay. You write all the insurance?"

"Every cent."

"What did MacIver do for a living?"

"He was an accountant, a C. P. A."

26

Leland turned away from Miller. "Did your husband leave a will, Mrs. MacIver?"

"Yes."

"Who is the executor?"

"I am. Executrix."

"Who are the heirs to the estate?"

"I am—just me."

"What sort of condition is it in—debts and so forth?"

She repositioned herself in the chair. "There were the funeral expenses, the lease on his office, the salary for that week for his secretary, the utilities bills and things like that. The court approved a month's severance for the secretary. I wanted to give her that."

"Then everything has been cleared up except taxes?" Leland said.

"Yes, that's right."

"You don't mind telling me how much was left, do you?"

"No. It came to two hundred and thirty-two thousand dollars."

Leland sat back and scratched the back of his hand. There was no sense in concealing his surprise. Her husband had bought his insurance in increasing amounts over nine years, which meant that he had earned his own money. He had done very well. Fred Miller had been his insurance agent: *that* was interesting. "How was his money invested?" Leland asked her.

"Stocks—six or seven different firms—our home, some undeveloped property north of Middleford in Clausen County, forty thousand dollars in cash, the cars, and the other personal things."

"That was it?"

"Yes." If she thought that he was hinting at something, she did not indicate it. She stared at him, waiting. One thing: she had not been Mrs. MacIver all the nine years Miller had known him. She looked to be in her early twenties, but if she said she was just twenty, he would believe it. Leland turned to Miller.

"Fred, you knew MacIver through writing his insurance?"

"Yes." He pursed his mouth grimly and nodded. "Yes," he said again.

"What kind of a guy was he? How did he strike you?"

"He was a nice guy—thoughtful, cheerful. Doing business with him was always a pleasure."

"Um. How old are you, Mrs. MacIver?"

The intercom buzzed.

"I'll be twenty-six tomorrow." she said.

"You look younger," Leland said. "Yes?"

"Excuse me, Mr. Leland, but there's the reporter from the *Star* on the telephone and he says it's urgent. He sounds it, too."

"All right. Excuse me," he said to the others. "Hello?"

"Mr. Leland? This is Larry Becker of the Manitou *Star*. There's a story going around Port Smith that you've made a break in the Mary Shoftel kidnapping. What about it?"

"What about what? Why is it a kidnapping now?"

"Then you do have a story?"

He should have thought before he answered. "I don't know if I do or not. I haven't been out of Manitou in a month."

"That doesn't matter. Let me ask you one question. Did you get a telephone call this morning from the Port Smith Police Department?"

"I don't know. Did I?"

"You certainly did, Mr. Leland."

"Let me make you a deal," Leland said. "You tell me how you got your information, and I'll tell you what the call was about."

"I have to protect my sources, Mr. Leland."

"Then I can't help you."

"You refuse to cooperate?"

Leland swung his chair around toward the windows. "Listen, kid, if you really knew your job, you'd have been able to figure out what that call was about without bothering me, but because you're such a dimwit, you don't even have a so-called source anymore. I'll see you around." He hung up and pressed the intercom button. "Flo, come in here a moment."

"Yes, sir."

When she came in, he said, "Don't sit down. First, no person-to-person calls from Port Smith. No more from the *Star*. I'm up in my private plane." Mrs. MacIver giggled. "Second, write me a little note and stick it under my phone, to the effect that the guy on the switchboard in my father's precinct is shooting off his mouth to reporters. Third, tell Sheila that any reporter-looking guys are to be told that I'm gone for the day, she doesn't know where. If they want to hang around, she's to buzz Mike. Then tell Mike that they think I'm working on the Shoftel case because my father called me about the article in the *Herald-Press*. For the time being, anyway, we don't want to be disturbed."

"You'd like me to come back?" Florence asked.

"Yes, and bring your notebook. Please."

He waited for her to go out. There had been a pattern to the questions that the reporter had interrupted. Leland was certain now that Miller did not know anything about Colin MacIver that Mrs. MacIver did not know far better. Of Mrs. MacIver he asked, "Did you know that your husband went to the track?"

"Yes, he went fairly regularly. Most of the time I went with him."

"Are you sure that it was most of the time, and that he didn't go other times that you didn't know about at all?"

"No."

"No what?"

"No, I'm not sure."

"All right." He thought he could work with her. He turned to Miller. "What about you, Fred? Did you know that he played the horses?"

"He mentioned once that he had been to the track, but that was all." He was trying to match her precision: perfect.

"Did he say whether he won or lost?"

"No, he just said that he was having a good time. I asked him. It was before he remarried." He glanced at Mrs. MacIver. "He was living alone and I said that it was a lonely life."

"After he remarried, did he continue to run around? Did he keep up with his girl friends?"

"Not that I know of," Miller said.

"Mrs. MacIver?" Leland asked.

She shook her head, shrugged, and finally, before he turned away, looked toward the bookcase. It made Leland pause. Perhaps it had been Miller's use of the word "remarriage" that had unstrung her, but she was suddenly and literally quite unable to handle herself. Leland said, "Just a couple of more questions for you, Fred. Did you ever see MacIver drunk?"

"No."

"Hung over?"

"No."

"Did you attend parties with him, see him in bars or nightclubs or at a golf course or tennis court?"

"No."

Florence had returned through Mike's door during this last exchange. As she went to her chair at Leland's right she had to turn her head to hide her smile. Leland had overdone it. It had not been necessary to make Miller himself see how little he knew of Colin MacIver. But perhaps it solved the next problem. Of Miller, Leland asked, "Did you have plans for the rest of the day?"

"No—no."

"Well, I want to talk to Mrs. MacIver alone. We'll be at least an hour, maybe a lot more. If you want to make plans to meet—"

"I don't see how we can," Mrs. MacIver said to Miller.

It seemed quick. She was grabbing the opportunity.

"Can you get home all right?" Miller asked her. "I'll go down to the company and—"

"Of course I can get home all right," she said, and laughed. There was a cruelty in her laughter and Miller looked hurt. She turned away from him calmly: it had been an accident. Leland was fascinated. Miller had brought it upon himself, looking for a way to hang around. Now it seemed as if she were trying to remember to be tough with him. Miller did deserve it; the clumsiness with which he had handled the mention of her husband's remarriage had taken its toll of her—and it had been the clumsiness, Leland was sure, not the stating of the fact.

"I'll call back later," Miller said to them all, unhappy.

"That's a good idea, Fred," Leland said. "If we're still busy, you can check with her in the morning. Wait, I'll walk with you to the door." He got up and went around to the left and put his hand on Miller's shoulder. When they got to the outer office, Leland said, "Thanks for your help. I don't know where this is going, but there might be something to it."

"You don't know if you're going to take the case?"

"I don't know if there is a case," Leland said. "Why did you come all the way up here to me? There are plenty of good people in Port Smith."

"She wanted you. She called me to ask about you. If you take the case, will you keep me posted? I liked him. She's a nice woman—"

Leland cut him off. "She'll be the client, Fred," he said.

"Sure, but, you know, give me a ring. Reverse the charges."

"Okay," Leland said, clapping him on the back.

"He didn't know your husband at all," Leland said as he crossed the room.

"No," she said simply.

Leland sat down and turned toward her. Her eyes, her lashes and brows, were very dark but clearly defined, so that they contrasted sharply with the finely pitted texture of her skin. Her lips were thin, her teeth small and white: she did look like a child. She was sitting very straight, prepared—or even braced. Leland said, "Miller told me that you were the one to first mention my name. Why did you bring him here with you?"

"I didn't." She tugged at her skirt. "He wanted to come." She wasn't satisfied with that answer. She looked up at Leland. "He had met you, he thought he could make things easy. I don't think he was wrong, really." That did justice to Miller. She sat back.

"Why did you want me?" Leland asked.

"At one time, my husband knew you." She watched him, trying to measure his reaction, whatever it was. Leland felt one, something physical, like the wrench of a parachute when it caught the wind. "You wouldn't remember," she said quietly. "He told me that he himself might have forgotten, if your name hadn't come up in the papers."

"When was this—when he knew me?"

"During the war. He was in the One hundred and sixty-first Fighter Squadron, too. He didn't speak of it often, but when we were first going out, when he was trying to identify for me where he had been and what he had done in the war, he said that the One hundred sixty-first had been your squadron. He arrived ten days before you went home and someone introduced him to you. You shook hands. He knew that I would remember you because I have a memory for things I've seen in the papers. For instance, when I had to, I remembered the item I saw in the *Examiner* about you opening this agency. That was two weeks ago, just before I called Mr. Miller to find out more about you."

"Does Miller know that your husband knew me?"

"I know that he doesn't," she said. "On his office wall he has a letter from you, thanking him for something he did in connection with a fraud against the insurance company. Colin saw it one day and told me about it. This was when we were married, after he had told me about being in the same squadron with you. I asked him if he talked to Mr. Miller about that, and he said no. I thought that was strange, but after I met Mr. Miller, I understood. Colin never would have heard the end of it."

"Your husband could have taken his business elsewhere if he felt that strongly about Miller."

"I don't know how he felt about Mr. Miller," she said. "He had started with him, that much I found out later. Maybe he felt loyal. Or sorry for him. For years my mother did business with a milkman she couldn't stand."

"Mm. That article in the *Examiner* you remembered appeared over three years ago. It was just a paragraph on an inside page."

"Well, Colin had mentioned you twice in conversation, once before and once after I saw it. I had an important association."

Now he could begin to believe it. "Still, this is a Port Smith matter. You lived there, and Flatlands is in Clausen County. I don't remember your husband at all. I don't have any special knowledge to bring to the case."

"Colin was born in Manitou, Mr. Leland. His mother and his

first wife still live here. After the war, he and his first wife moved back and forth several times. There's a lot that happened here that I want to know, too."

"Then you're not just interested in the circumstances of his death," he said.

"I'm interested in everything you can learn about him," Mrs. MacIver said. "We were married a little over two years. There was a lot that I never learned. I never met his mother. She didn't come to our wedding."

"Quite a bit of that you could do yourself."

"I'm not capable of it," she said.

Leland scratched the back of his hand. He hoped that Florence was not so shocked that she would allow herself to stare.

"Mrs. MacIver," he said, "I may as well tell you now that, for something like this, we have to charge a hundred dollars per man per day, plus expenses."

She went to her sulking expression again. "I have the money." She took a deep breath, as if she could not believe that it was so difficult to understand her. "I never had money before in my life. It was his money. Until eight o'clock on August twelfth I thought that I was going to have a life with him."

"Excuse me, what time?"

She frowned. "What do you mean?"

"What time do you say you learned of his death?"

"Eight o'clock. Why?"

"Put it down, Flo, if you don't mind."

"I have it."

"What's wrong?" Mrs. MacIver asked, looking to both of them.

"Were you anywhere you couldn't be reached until eight o'clock?"

"No, I was home. I had been to the doctor's, but I was back from there by four o'clock."

"Did your husband have proper identification on him?"

"Yes, a wallet, his car keys with his name attached, and I think his sports jacket had his name sewn inside. Yes, that, too. Why?"

"He died in a public place three and a half hours before. You should have been called by five—five-thirty at the latest. This is something that I would like to know more about. Was anything said about it at the coroner's inquest?"

"I don't know. We were late getting there, and it was over."

"They took no testimony from you?" he asked. "Did you get a transcript?"

"No. This is the next thing I've done."

He felt Florence look up. He was thinking of today's date, too —three months had passed—but for the moment he was more interested in the coroner's inquest. It was incredible. "Who is we?" he asked. "Who went with you?"

"A neighbor, Dr. Wendell Roberts. He lives next door. Should I say the address?" Florence had been writing again. Leland nodded. Turning to Florence, Mrs. MacIver said, "He lives at Two thirty-six Collegeville Road, Port Smith Nineteen. My address is Two thirty-eight."

"Is he your doctor?" Leland asked.

"No—we're good friends, that's all. He was Colin's friend as well as mine."

"Collegeville Road is near the Jefferson campus. What is he? A teacher?"

"Yes, he teaches, but he's a medical doctor. A psychiatrist."

"Was Mr. MacIver under his care?"

"Oh, no. I was. I was in therapy for three years, but it ended almost a year before I met Colin."

"Does Fred Miller know anything about it?"

"Absolutely not, I—"

"Excuse me," Leland said, "but could you tell me why you had to see Dr. Roberts in the first place?"

"Not right now, if you don't mind." She glanced at Florence, who had her eyes on her notebook. Leland nodded understanding.

"It isn't my business," he said. "I'm sorry."

"That's all right. It's your business if you're going to do this for me."

He had apologized to put her at ease. He thought that he had

34

already indicated that he understood that she would tell him after Florence had gone. She had not grasped it—but not, he knew now, because she was stupid. He said, "Now, about Dr. Roberts again. Did he have any comment about the time it took to contact you on the day Mr. MacIver died?"

"If he did, he kept it from me. We both reacted when we found that the inquest was over before we got there. The room was cleared. We had to learn from a clerk what the verdict was. Dr. Roberts was curious, and so was I. There are some things that he's fairly innocent about. I'm quoting him now. He had never been to a coroner's inquest before."

"Most people pass them up," Leland said. That had been a slip; he didn't want to be smart with her. "Now, why haven't you met Mr. MacIver's mother and why didn't she come to the wedding?"

"She thinks that Colin wronged his first wife. That's only my own guess. It was Colin who divorced her, you see. Her name is Betty. They had no children. Until he divorced her, there never had been a divorce in his family. Before our wedding, Colin came up here to ask his mother to attend—he never told me what was said or done, but I know that it wasn't pleasant. That was the last time that she saw him alive."

"Does she know that he's dead?"

"Yes, I sent her a telegram. There was no answer, but she did receive it. I checked."

"Do you want to meet her?"

"Definitely not," she said. "If she knew I was pregnant, she might try to take the baby from me. Or else she would try to be my friend. I don't want her near our baby."

Leland had heard this before. "Do you know anything else about the relationship between your husband and his mother?"

"When he made the trip up here, he wasn't happy about it. That seems to tell it all. All the things Mr. Miller said about my husband were true, Mr. Leland. He was thoughtful and fun-loving, but he was also moody and quiet and withdrawn. He kept his life to himself."

"Maybe he wanted it that way, and didn't want you to do this."

"He *died*, Mr. Leland. Listen, he knew why. I don't, and if I don't find out, his child will never have the chance to know who his father was. I was a sick woman for years, and I'm not going to get sick again over this. It would be too easy. Do you have any idea of what he cheated us of?"

"I think so," he said.

"Well, I've had the chance to think. He did it for a reason—if he did it. If for some reason it was murder, you know what I want then. An accident—he was on the roof of a *racetrack*. I want to know why. Mr. Leland, the dead have no rights—that's a point of law. Colin's privacy isn't sacred anymore."

"I think you're absolutely right, Mrs. MacIver," Leland said.

"Then you'll do this for me?" she asked.

"Yes, I think so. We'll start right now." He leaned forward. "There are a few things you have to understand. In this state the death of a man is taken very seriously. If we find evidence that refutes the coroner's verdict, we have no choice but to bring it to the attention of the authorities. No choice, do you understand? If we find evidence that corroborates his findings but sheds light on misconduct by him or the police involved, or even the ambulance driver, we must bring that to the authorities, too. The law is perfectly clear on what must be done when a man is the victim of a homicide—homicide meaning any unnatural death, including suicide—and you can be sure that these officials do not want to be accused of malfeasance or negligence. It would be extremely ugly for both of us if we brought accusations. If we have evidence, we'll be amply protected by the law but there are other ways to bring pressure to bear. We won't be protected from the press, for example. The newspapers can be manipulated. If you have anything that you don't want printed, you had better give thought to it now." He paused, and she said nothing.

"Here's something else for you to think about," he said. "I work very closely with the police. Although our communications are privileged in court, I'll be obliged to discuss certain of them with the police, both here and in Port Smith, to gain access to records that are not public. You have to trust me not to reveal to the police or anyone else something that clearly isn't their business."

"I understand that," she said. She was sitting very straight again.

"And finally, since we will be working together, you're going to see me do things that you won't like or understand. You should be prepared. It will seem as if I'm doing business and passing the time of day over your husband's body. I'm not. If I stop to consider your feelings, you may not get the job you're paying for. Do you understand that?"

"Yes."

"Now, on the matter of reports, there won't be anything in them that we haven't discussed in advance. I don't know how often you'll get reports; that will depend on how fast the information comes in. It will take only a couple of days to know if we're going to get a run for your money. We'll review what we have and decide if we should go on. I'll tell you if I think you ought to drop it. That will mean the end, as far as I'm concerned. We won't take your money if we can't earn it." He did not know if he had forgotten anything. He swiveled toward Florence, who looked up from her notebook.

"Payment," she said.

He turned again to Mrs. MacIver. "I told you the fee. We accept a retainer and bill you for the balance. We'll take care of that before you leave. Any expenses we have will be itemized and, as much as possible, documented. Do you have any questions?"

"No, it seems all right."

"Flo? What time do you have?"

"Eleven-five," she said.

"Mrs. MacIver, I think we ought to see your husband's mother and former wife first, as long as they're so convenient to us." He wanted to hear their side as quickly as he could. "I'll use a cover and keep you out of it. Do you have his mother's address? I'll get the other from her."

"Colin gave me both of them. Neither would have moved since we were married." She searched her purse and drew an address book from the welter of stuff inside.

"How long were you married?" Leland asked her.

"A little over two years. Two years and a month."

"How long was your courtship?"

She looked up from the book. "A year and two months."

"Now, the article in the *Examiner* appeared just over three years ago—"

"It was in the summer," she said. "We were just beginning to see each other steadily. He had already mentioned being in the same squadron with you. When I saw the article I thought of telling him, but it slipped my mind. It wasn't important, then."

Now he had a clear picture of the sequence of events and a better insight into the workings of her mind. "Now his former wife: has she remarried?"

"Yes, five years ago, just six months after Colin divorced her."

"What was that? Adultery?"

"No," she said, "Colin was very clear on that. He went out to Nevada and got it on mental cruelty. They had made an agreement by which he was to give her money, and it terminated when she married. He didn't want to talk about why he wanted a divorce or was willing to pay her to get it, and I had sufficient reasons of my own, I thought, not to question him too closely. He wanted to be fair to her in what he told me. He didn't want me to regard her as a hateful person when he didn't regard her that way himself. Very rarely some little bitterness would come out, but he was always desperately ashamed of that. It was no act; he had no reason to act with me. He held himself responsible for a share of the failure of that marriage, and there was an astonishment he showed over things I would do or say. Those things would be perfectly normal, in terms of what I've been led to understand about normality—and I *have* been led to an understanding, believe me. What I mean to say is, there were things that he should have gotten from his marriage with Betty Ford that he simply didn't get, and he couldn't help showing it when he got them from me. It was as if he had given up hope of ever getting them. They were simple things, gifts of love, mostly. We had success, and the success seemed, among other things, to revive an opinion that he had held about her and had forgotten in the process of giving up his hope— that she, for whatever else could be said about her, was unstable. I'm not the one who should talk, I know, but that was the impression I received—"

She stopped—she was finished—but for a moment Leland was afraid that she had noticed his reaction to something she had said. He didn't know what she could have seen; the feeling had been like being torn out of a fantasy. In fact, however, it had been exactly the opposite of that: he had been intensely interested in what she had been saying; but then she had said, "I'm not the one who should talk, I know"—word-for-word what Karen had written in the note this morning. He had been able to see Karen's handwriting—everything. He wanted to remember the context in which she had used the phrase. He had to suppress the urge to take out the note and reread it. Of the two strange physical shocks he had sustained in this conversation, he wanted to think that this was the stranger—at first. Really he had brought them both upon himself, with no sane reason for feeling either. During the war he had known scores of men, and many more had known him. And as for this: it was as if he were trying to keep that fear he had felt, the sense of danger, in the forefront of his mind. It did not make sense. His memory of yesterday was telling him something more rational than he had wanted to believe when he had found the note. Karen wanted to see him, it was that simple. If he was afraid that something was going to happen, it was because he wanted to be afraid. Still, he could not forget the pointlessness of so much that she had written. At the least, he intended to ask her about it.

Mrs. MacIver began to read off the names and addresses of her mother-in-law and her husband's first wife. Leland felt as if he had just come back from answering the door. More subdued, he said, "If there were any friends or relatives he was in touch with here, let us have their names, too."

"No, there weren't any—I don't think." She looked up from the little book. "I mailed all the letters that were written at home. There could have been somebody he wrote to from the office."

Leland smiled. "I don't think so."

"Why not?"

"If it had been a man or a relative, there would have been no need for caution; if it had been a woman and he had wanted to be cautious, he could have telephoned. He could have afforded it."

"Do you think there could have been another woman?"

"Certainly not up here. He didn't come here, you said, and certainly she didn't go down there. Not continually. A person would give up if he or she received no cooperation. I'm not sure that we'll find one who lives down there, either."

"Why?"

"Why would he have married you? Or stayed married? He established that he was capable of divorce. If he was as secretive as you've suggested, he made attachments slowly and firmly. The two go together. If there was another woman, you would have known about it, one way or another, long ago."

"Yes, I see. You're right." She turned back to the address book.

Florence glanced at him. Florence had never met anyone like Norma MacIver, and she did not know how to react. Leland had to think of Mrs. MacIver as one of those people who were stronger than they realized. Often they said more about themselves than they had to, and tried to draw people closer to them than most people cared to go. Leland guessed that Florence was still bristling over the incident in the ladies' room, when Mrs. MacIver had made such good use of her. It didn't count for much, actually, because Florence would have disliked Mrs. MacIver anyway. Mrs. MacIver's desperate scrabbling was beyond the comprehension of a girl who thought she had little difficulty finding ways of doing the things she wanted to do. To Leland it was apparent that Mrs. MacIver did not figure her native talents in the equation of her goals—she did things because they had to be done. Perhaps the figuring was done in the same clumsy, shattered way she had got herself here this morning—but here she was, and if she had asked for a lot from Leland and Florence —and Miller—she had not asked for sympathy. She wanted love, that was clear, but she did not expect to be liked. Leland liked her, but he did not know if he could have her around for long. The interesting, difficult thing about her drained him.

He had been talking about himself when he had said that a man who was closemouthed made his attachments slowly. He had known men who told nothing about themselves and had emotional lives as tangled as international law. Looking at the man's wife, Leland could not believe that MacIver was one of these; but Leland had to hold the reservation that a certain kind of honest man, in the psychological upheaval that might have preceded a death like Mac-Iver's, could have deeply misled a woman who seemed to need to be dead-honest with men.

Leland turned to read upside down the names and addresses that Florence had transcribed.

"Mrs. MacIver," he said, "what we're going to do now is get a couple of things in motion." Florence was reaching for the telephone. "We'll start with Manitou and get a look at the file," he said to her, and she began to dial. He took the handset. Over it, he said to Mrs. MacIver, "This is the file the insurance company began on your husband when he took out his first policy. With all the insurance written on him, the file should be as thick as a telephone book, with every document and piece of correspondence connected with his business." The line opened before he was finished and he asked the operator for an extension. "You came to the right place," he said across the desk, skipping on. "Normally, to see these papers, you have to get a court order."

The extension was picked up and Leland identified himself and told the clerk what he wanted. Someone would have to go down to the home office after one o'clock to pick it up. Leland said thank you and goodbye. He had repeated the information for Florence, who was still copying it on a fresh page in her notebook.

"Who now?" she asked.

"Warren Johnson," he said. He lit another cigarette and looked at his watch. Almost eleven-twenty. "Johnson is the Chief of the Manitou Police Force," he told Mrs. MacIver. She nodded.

"Ready," said Florence. Leland picked up the handset again.

"Warren? It's Joe Leland."

"Well, well. I was just about to get a warrant for your arrest. Why are you trying to screw me out of my job?" He laughed. "I was just going to call you, Joe."

"What's wrong?" In spite of the laughter, Leland was alarmed. This man would help him only as long as it did not cause him trouble.

"This is it, kid," Warren Johnson said. "A reporter from the *Star* just called the Mayor and asked him when there would be an announcement in the Shoftel case. The Mayor wanted to know what the hell he was talking about and the fellow said that he had learned that you were working on the case but that you weren't talking about it because of instructions you had gotten from me, which he, the reporter, assumed came from higher up."

"You can see that he's trying to make trouble," Leland said.

"Of course I can see that," Warren Johnson said. "Now what is it all about?"

Leland told him that his father had called about the article in the *Herald-Press*. Mrs. MacIver was smiling again. She had no idea how serious a thing like this could become. All public officials were prima donnas in their dealings with the people who needed them. Leland said into the telephone, "You tell the Mayor that I'm sorry that this happened. You know how I work. If I had anything, you'd be the first one I'd call."

"That's what I told him, but he found it hard to believe that your father would take time out to call you on a day like today."

"What does today have to do with it?"

"Where've you been? It's the worst-kept secret since the atom bomb. When the time comes, they're going to move everything over to your father's precinct. They don't want trouble and the Eleventh is far enough from the scene to take the energy out of the people who want to stand around outside. They've had crowds off and on all through the weekend at the Fifth Precinct. Your father has the job of setting everything up. I guess they're running the usual weirdos through the Eleventh now."

"There you are," Leland said. "I don't even know that."

"Well, the next time your father wants to talk about police work, you answer the phone," Warren Johnson said. He knew Leland's parents. "I saw the *Herald-Press* today. Let me ask you a question. After Leikman's uncle threatened to sue you, did you hear from him again?"

Leland laughed. "No, he knew I had him by the short hairs."

"I thought it was something like that. I thought that maybe he wrote some letters. Okay. What did you have on your mind?"

"I have a client, Warren, whose husband jumped, fell, or was thrown from the roof of Flatlands Racetrack last August. The verdict was suicide. No notes, no business difficulties. He was very well off. He was born and raised here and he lived here off and on with his first wife. I want to know all I can about him."

"If you get anything that concerns me, Joe, I want it right away, personally," Warren Johnson said. "Give me the stuff. I'll shoot it back to you within a half hour."

When Leland had begun to talk about the case, Florence had asked Mrs. MacIver for a picture of her husband. Now Leland reached over the desk to take a large color print. "Here we go," he said to Warren Johnson. "Colin—" He looked to Mrs. MacIver for the middle name, and she whispered it. "—William MacIver, capital M, a, c, capital I, v, e, r. W.M.A. Deceased August twelfth, this year. Age at death, thirty-two. About six feet tall, one hundred and seventy pounds, light brown hair, brown eyes, small white scar, size of a nickel, under the left ear. Last address—" He read it from Florence's notebook. "And could you check out the traffic court, Warren?" he asked. "It's just a flyer, but I want to know my man."

"Sure. Say hello to Charlie Scott for me. How's he doing on that job, by the way?"

"Oh, having his ups and downs."

"Sometimes you disappoint me, Joe. I'll have somebody call you back."

"Half an hour," Leland said to Florence as he hung up.

"Now I understand what you meant before," Mrs. MacIver said. She brushed her hair away from her forehead. "Are there going to be any more calls like that?"

"Just one, to my father in Port Smith." Leland motioned to Florence. "You can see that I'm trying to gather as much as I can. If we draw nothing from these calls it doesn't mean that we've learned nothing. On the contrary, we've cleared the air. The same will be true for the insurance file. When your husband made applications for his policies, he was investigated and reported on. His personal habits and so forth. I started to tell you that. At least we'll have the reports, no matter how trivial the information on them."

She moved forward on the chair. Her hand jerked aimlessly near her skirt hem. "The whole thing makes me so unhappy suddenly. I don't want to look that closely. I'm reacting, I know, but now I don't want to think that I'm betraying him."

"Look at you," Leland said. The call was going through. "Truthfully, Mrs. MacIver, you were the one who was betrayed. Perhaps by your husband, perhaps by the man or men who killed him, certainly by the officials of Clausen County. At several points along the line there were attempts to strip you—and your child—of your hope. You knew that when you came in here, didn't you?" She nodded, like a child. "Well, it's obvious what you're suffering. It simply isn't fair."

She nodded again and stood up. "I have to go to the bathroom. I'll be right back."

Leland took the handset from Florence. "Go with her. See if she needs anything."

Mrs. MacIver stopped by the door. "Mr. Leland, if you're going to ask your father about police records, you'd better ask him about me. My maiden name is Colucci. C, o, l, u, c, c, i."

She closed the door behind her. Florence looked back at Leland, as if to say, "See, didn't I tell you?" Leland waved her out, angry. He felt like a moron.

The suspects in the Shoftel disappearance, all the known sex offenders, were being run through the Eleventh Precinct. Warren Johnson's information, in fact, was twelve hours old. More than fifty men and six women had been in and out of the station, and the roundup was still going on. The theorists and armchair detectives downtown were guessing that the child had never left her neighborhood. Yesterday they had been saying that the case would never be solved. Leland's father, captain of the Eleventh Precinct, had no ideas. He had been on the job since Saturday afternoon. The scheme to use the Eleventh had come from downtown, and John Leland, although he would not say it on the telephone, felt vindicated once again. The Eleventh was a dead-end assignment, not a punishment but an area that attracted no natural attention and required a consistent high effort. It belonged to John Leland because he did not advertise himself, and because he could not browbeat his subordinates for the sake of creating a record. He was interested in the man on the switchboard who was talking to reporters, but it would take him days to move on him.

It was the way he worked. The man would be checked out of the house to the most remote post on the foot patrol. If he didn't figure out why, he would hear about it—after a time. It would come down from the captain through the lieutenant and the sergeant, and it might be distilled to a simple, "Oh, and keep your mouth shut when you're on the board, will you?" If the captain liked him, the man might be brought back inside where he could be watched. A man with good qualities who could learn a lesson soon had nothing going against him. John Leland knew every man in his precinct, and he thought that it was part of his job to be a teacher.

He had no argument with the men who had quit working to be more than patrolmen. He had helped teach nearly every man of middle rank downtown, and they knew that he in his own turn was frozen where he was. His situation was as much a part of the Department lore as the name of the first commissioner, and his inability to resign and draw his pension told the beginning and the end of the story of his career: he had wanted to be a cop, just like the patrolmen. He had said it often: he would not change a thing.

The Shoftel disappearance was Port Smith's most sensational case since the Leikman killing, yet there was still nothing to show for the hundreds of thousands of dollars' worth of police work that had gone into it. Late Thursday afternoon, a candy store owner three blocks away had served a little girl he had not seen before, but the owner could not be sure of the girl or furnish a description of the man. It was being kept quiet. Captain Leland was beginning to despair for the young men who had been put in charge of the case. His son knew some of them. If the crime did prove insoluble, the young men would wear it around their necks the rest of their professional lives.

Using Florence's notebook, Joe Leland told his father that he had another matter to discuss. His father thought he remembered reading in the newspapers about the man who had gone off the racetrack roof. Joe Leland told him that he did not want to go into the finer points now, but he thought that there was something worthy of his interest. He gave his father the name and address of the dead man and then, remembering, the maiden name of the dead man's wife. His father said that he would try to have the information for him before lunch.

They said goodbye and Joe Leland swung away from the telephone and stared at the door to the outer office. He drummed his fingers on the desk. Finally he picked up Colin MacIver's photograph and turned it into the light.

CHAPTER FOUR

■ ■

COLIN MACIVER WAS SMILING. HE WAS STANDING WITH HIS WEIGHT
on his right leg, his hands on his hips. The scene was a park and the
time was autumn or early spring. He was wearing a light blue pullover
sweater and chino pants. Some kind of plaid sports shirt poked
from under the sweater at the collar and cuffs. On his right hand was
a school ring and ID bracelet, and on his left a wedding ring and, to
be seen faintly as a bulge beneath the sweater, a wristwatch. MacIver
looked younger than thirty-two or thirty-one at first glance. Tall,
handsome, and slim, if he had made it to his fifties and had turned
gray and added fifteen pounds, he would have become an impressive
figure; which formed an interesting contrast with what was going to
happen to his widow: she was too small to gain many pounds without
looking plump, weary, and domestic. MacIver's face was thin and it
was composed of planes rather than curves and bulges. His temples
were almost at right angles to his forehead, which showed no deep
creases. From the neatness of his clothes, the careful trim of his
haircut, the amount of jewelry, and the shine of his shoes, easily
discernible through the matted yellow grass, Leland reckoned that
MacIver had spent a fair amount of time at his grooming. Leland
tried to add that to the rest of what he had learned about handsome,
successful, deceased Colin William MacIver: accountant, two marriages, fighter pilot. How had he done in the war? It was a thing
Leland could check quickly. A man who had played the horses and
had had his name sewn into his sports jackets, Colin MacIver had
divorced one woman for her instability—maybe—and married an-

other for hers—maybe again. The second Mrs. MacIver still had a lot of talking to do. Leland picked up the telephone.

Florence came into the office and Leland put down the telephone again. "Mrs. MacIver told me to come back," she said. "She's combing her hair. There was nothing she wanted."

"How is she?"

"All right." Florence slumped into her chair and crossed her ankles. "Did you take her seriously? Are you checking on her?"

"It seemed like the thing to do. I don't think you should be here when the call comes in. We won't draw a blank, that's certain, and there's no point in embarrassing her."

"I'm sorry if I've done anything wrong," she said. "She makes me nervous, is all."

"You've done all right," he said. "It doesn't have anything to do with your conduct. She didn't plan to tell us about whatever she's done. For a wife—a widow—a mission like this has a similarity to going through the man's pockets. She's trying to make it up to him. She knows that she has something to hide. If we learn anything about her husband, she'll be on his level, in our eyes, because we will have learned about her, too."

"Then she really expects us to learn something about him," Florence said.

"In some ways. She's running away from the idea." The telephone light began to flash. "She loved him, there's no doubt in my mind about that. Half the reason for her being here is to see us fail. She's gone this far believing in an accident or some sudden, inexplicable death wish. She can go the rest of the way, believing it, if she learns even a little more than she does now."

"I told Sheila which calls to let through," Florence said. She sat up and took the receiver and put her hand over the mouthpiece. "How do you feel about an accident or what you said?"

"It's nonsense, and when she's using her head, Mrs. MacIver knows it, too."

She said hello, and reached for her notebook. As she began to write he swung his chair away from her and stared at the door. He could bring up the image of Colin MacIver at will. The face looking

48

into the camera had the mark of a dead man on it, which was Leland's own doing. He had seen too much sudden, violent death for his own health's sake and he knew it—but he would have been dishonest if he had avoided this case. Six months ago he had checked out a life insurance claim upstate in which a truck driver had gone off a mountain road, had been thrown clear, and then had his truck roll over him. The State Police had had beautiful pictures.

Mrs. MacIver entered now, turning to the door as she closed it quietly. Leland could see the lines of her thighs against her blue skirt. She had short, shapely legs, slender ankles, and small feet. She walked to her chair lightly, watching Florence writing in the notebook. Leland did not try to conceal his gaze; the mood pressed on him like a tidal current. He recalled what Florence had said about the hard-seeming wrists. The black hair was on her forearms, even and fine. Mrs. MacIver was wearing some kind of charm bracelet, and no rings. Her hands had the hardness, but they were delicate, too—or just thin; either way, they did not appear to be strong. She was watching Florence as she sat down, and her skirt slid up over her knees. Her knees were round and smooth; her bones were heavier than Karen's.

Norma MacIver moved back on the chair and shifted her legs and Leland got a look above her knees. Her thighs were well fleshed, almost heavy. The stockings were stretched taut. Leland wanted to know what she looked like when she was not carrying a child. With her small breasts and doll-like face, probably a lot like a child herself.

Leland picked up his cigarette pack, not daring to look in her eyes. He was still conscious of her movements, but for another reason. She sat still, not bringing her hands toward her hem. He had been obvious, staring, but if she had seen him, she was not going to hit at his ego by showing that his interest had been unpleasant. It was a nice thing to know about her. With elaborate slowness Leland put his burnt-out match in the ash tray. The understanding between them, if there was one, was adult, but he could not help feeling a little like a kid who had got around the corner with a palmed Baby Ruth.

Florence put down the receiver. "That was Mr. Johnson's office," she said. "There was nothing in the criminal index, but for the summer of 1946, the last half of 1947, the summer of '48, and all of '49, there are notations for twenty-three parking and minor traffic tickets, all paid in full. That was before the point system went into effect on drivers' licenses."

Leland drew on his cigarette. "What do you think, Mrs. Mac-Iver?"

"Why—he drove fast, but not like that. He never got a ticket while I knew him."

Florence stood up. "Mr. Leland? I'll type up these notes and put the addresses on index cards for you."

"Go ahead. Thanks for your help, Flo."

"There's paper and pencils in your top drawer if you need them. You have that appointment at three o'clock, and you have to see Mike before you go."

"I haven't forgotten. Okay."

Assembling her papers, Florence moved around behind Mrs. MacIver's chair. Leland waited until the door latch clicked.

"Do you drive a car, Mrs. MacIver?"

"Yes, I do. I went to a school after we were married." She cleared her throat. "Colin gave me the lessons as a present. Then, when I had my license, we shopped for a car for me, a two-door sedan with automatic shift. I have to sit on a cushion to see over the wheel. I picked it, but after a while Colin used it when he went down to the office and left me his car—it has a power seat. He thought I was an excellent driver."

"What kind of a car did he have?"

"A Dresden-blue Cadillac convertible with power everything. Did you plan for your secretary to leave?"

Leland said, "You know, I asked you if you had anything you wanted to keep to yourself. You would not have told me to check for a record on you if there weren't one there. I don't know where this will lead, and neither do you, and I want to be sure that you know what you're doing."

"I was going to tell you anyway," she said. "I was upset when I let it out like that. If you want your secretary back here to help you, that's all right. I know that she will find out about it later. That doesn't bother me; it's just that I've found that with some people, life is less of a strain when they don't know, or if they do find out, they don't hear it from me. It doesn't really apply to her because you wouldn't have her around if she didn't know how to take things. She doesn't like me, but she doesn't let it interfere with doing what you want her to do."

"What makes you think that she doesn't like you?"

"A certain crispness in her voice when we're outside. You know, for a while I thought it was a proprietary interest that she had in you—that the ring on her finger was yours."

Leland smiled. "Oh, no. She's a baby. So are you, really—but never mind. I could say that I got her to leave so I could ask you to lunch, which I plan to do, but that isn't true. I just didn't get around to asking you while she was here. We have more to discuss, you and I, and it will be easier over something to eat. I have another reason to go out, though. If you accept, I'll want to take us to a place where I may be able to transact some business of my own, personal business. It won't take long."

"It seems to be important to you," she said.

"The point is, I can do it on my own time, if you prefer. We can go to a place other than the one I have in mind."

"No, the way you want. Mr. Miller told me that you never mentioned your personal life."

"No, that isn't right. I—well, you're seeing for yourself. Anyway, I'm taking you to the best restaurant in town."

"He volunteered that information about you," she said. "I didn't ask."

"That's what I expected," he said. He wanted to prepare her for what he was going to ask at lunch. He thought he could see a real break in the tension she had brought in this morning and he did not want to spring any surprises on her. He was reminded of the careful look he had given her a moment ago. Florence could have seen it, too; he had not thought of that. Now a lapse was spreading in the conversation—he felt a near-panicky urge to pick it up again.

Norma MacIver had completely forgotten her skirt, and with a genuine guilt he kept his eyes up. He did not care for thinking of how easy she was to abuse. He had called her a baby: she wasn't, but he wanted her to be. The telephone light blinked, cutting through the web of thoughts, and as he picked up he could feel a relief. Another moment, she would have offered him a penny.

The call was from the P. S. P. D.

"It reads like this, Mr. Leland," the rasping, tired voice said. "MacIver is clean except for a lot of parking and minor traffic summonses from '46 to '49. Do you want the figures?"

Leland had his paper and pencil. "Just tell me how many there are."

"Let's see. Fifteen, sixteen, seventeen. Seventeen, that's the bundle. Now we go on to Miss Colucci."

"On December fourteenth, '45, she was picked up in Northport riding around in a stolen car. No disposition on that.

"On April third, '49, she was Drunk and Disorderly in a gin mill downtown. There were additional charges of malicious mischief and disturbing the peace. She was put on two years' probation on condition, and ordered to make full restitution for the damage she did. They hit her with the book on those charges."

"Okay, thanks a lot." Leland put down the receiver and swiveled to Mrs. MacIver. "It's not so bad. If it's where you came from, you traveled a long way—and very well, too."

"That's what I keep telling myself." She smiled, flushing a little.

"Did your husband know?"

"Oh, yes. Sometimes, when he wanted to tease me, he called me 'Dragon Lady.' I was supposed to have mysterious criminal connections. One time he came home with a cheongsam, but that was something else again."

"You'll have to tell me what a—cheongsam?—is."

"Chinese dress. Slit up the side. Oh, it's very nice," she said, affecting a little melody in her voice. It was his turn to blush, a bit, while he grinned. With mock gravity he coughed, then thought better of sustaining the mood.

52

"Listen," he said, genuinely earnest, "on your husband, they had a list of seventeen parking and minor traffic tickets, which completes what they had here. You say he never got a ticket while you knew him, and the record bears out that he didn't conceal any from you. I don't know what such a wacky thing could mean in relation to his death, but we ought to try for an explanation of what it means by itself—if anything. Can we talk about it with your doctor friend?"

"Dr. Roberts? Yes. I don't know if he'll have much to say about it. To him, it would only indicate something. He wouldn't want to make a judgment on the one thing alone. I've seen him at work."

Leland said, "We can say for ourselves that all those tickets would indicate a certain hostility or antisocial attitude. But I want an authoritative opinion. That's why I want to talk with the doctor."

"Yes, of course." She moved her hand toward him nervously. "The tickets shouldn't be a complete surprise to me, looking at them in those terms. You heard how he treated Mr. Miller—from a distance. He was that way with many, many people. Well, you'll hear about it at lunch."

"That's right," he said. "That's what I hope lunch will be all about." He picked up the telephone again. "One more call, and we can go." He put his finger on the disconnect button. "This concerns you, too. I have a book from the squadron, a souvenir book that some of the pilots published when the war was over. Whatever your husband did will be in there, the number of missions, any planes he shot down, and so forth. You can read it for yourself."

"Yes, all right. Thank you."

He dialed. There was a ring, then a second. At the third he moved to hang up, but the line opened and a small hello could be heard through the office. Leland brought the handset up again, turned toward the bookcase, and rocked back in the chair.

"Hello, Steffie, it's Daddy. Why are you home from school?"

"I have an upset stomach. Were you trying to get Mommy? She stopped in for coffee, but she just left. How did you know she'd be here?"

"Sometimes she stops off at home before a lunch date. How are you feeling? Are you all right?"

"Oh, sure," she said. "It's just annoying. She'll be at the Flamingo for lunch, if you want to go meet her, but she has a woman with her."

"I know. You can do me a favor if you will, honey. Do you know my souvenir book from the war? The one the men put together?"

"It's on the shelf in the hall."

"That's the one. Would you mind if one of the girls from the office stopped by to pick it up? She can get you some magazines, if you want."

"Okay. Tell her to get about a dozen. She'll know what I want. I'm going crazy with this television."

"All right," he said. "If I miss your mother, what time did she say she would be home?"

"Four-thirty. She has a meeting later and she has to be out of the house at a quarter to seven."

"I know about the meeting, too, sweet. Will you see that a place is set for me? I'm going to accept her invitation to dinner."

"Gee, it took you long enough," Stephanie said.

"The invitation was in a note, smarty. You'll be nice to me if you want revenge at rummy." He looked over at Mrs. MacIver; she was smiling.

"Who says I want to play with you? Wait—I take that back! I want to go to Montreal, too. Are you going to stay this evening?"

"Yes, I think so. Listen, Stef, how was Mommy feeling this morning? She seemed tired last night."

"Tired is right! She was *exhausted!*" There was silence. He had made up the business of Karen being tired to give his question less consequence.

He asked, "What's the matter?"

"Nothing. I was going to ask you something personal."

"Are you sure?"

"Yes, Daddy."

"It's just that I wouldn't want you to keep something from me because you think it would upset me." That was enough; he could hurt her badly if she thought that something was wrong.

54

Steffie said, "I got carried away. I was going to ask what you were doing to her to make her so tired."

"Oh." She thought she was intruding. She was thirteen and the only thing she did not know was that he had been told she had heard it all, officially, over a year ago. He wanted to swivel around toward the window now, but didn't. "Honey, would you laugh if I told you that I didn't get up myself until after nine o'clock?"

"Oh, *yes!* It's wonderful! Daddy, sometimes you're an absolute terror."

"If you tell her I said anything to you, I'll break both your legs." Mrs. MacIver laughed aloud. He said to Steffie, "I have to get off the phone. The girl will pick up the book after lunch."

"Okay. Don't let her forget the magazines."

"Right, honey. I love you."

She was gone. Sighing audibly, he swung around to Mrs. MacIver. "You heard? We can leave any time."

"I heard. Will two hundred dollars be enough to start?" He nodded. She said, "On the train coming up, Mr. Miller said that he didn't know if you were married or not. He couldn't even guess."

"Well, when I saw him regularly, I wasn't so sure myself. Steffie and her mother were still in Port Smith. It's been complicated."

"It doesn't seem that way now," she said. "You aren't living together, but you see each other—you want to see each other."

"It's still complicated." He stopped there, thinking of what he had done on the telephone. Only a little while ago he had thought that he had had no reason for what he had felt when he had found Karen's note; now, at this first chance, he had indulged in it with Steffie, chancing God-knew-what damage to her. Even the wildest fears had anticipated nothing happening, just an ugly incommunicado in which things ran downhill: it was a well-charted territory in their lives. The other mistake he had made, in telling anything to Mrs. MacIver, was in trying to be honest. He didn't know why he hadn't lied. The result was that he had looked back. He had tried it rarely in the past and never did it now. In the fourteen years he and Karen had been married they had been separated by the war for three years and by their own actions for more than six: almost ten years in total and, on the face of it, unbearable. It had not seemed that way, and he still refused to believe that the arithmetic was going to weigh them down. Since she had followed him to Manitou they had lived one day to the next in a hopeful circling of a normal life; but finally, together, they were too frightened by the past to take the single necessary step. One consequence was that they were more sensitive to each other than most couples; another was that each lived with an irritation that had been covered, layer by layer, by the need and understanding they shared: loneliness, a pearl seed.

He would see Steffie tonight. He hadn't been fooling about the rummy match. He said, "If you look behind you on the bookcases you'll see two of Steffie's creations. She made those airplanes for me when she was nine."

Mrs. MacIver twisted around. "Oh? Why, they're very good. They were the planes you flew in the war." She smiled. "Is she Daddy's girl?"

"Mommy's, too. With us she's very adult and sophisticated, but when she's with other people—we hear about it—she's still quite shy."

"That's sweet. Your complications don't seem to have bothered her."

"We can't tell. We'll have to see how she does with her own marriage. Wait a minute." His thoughts had leapfrogged in another direction; he touched the intercom buttom. "Mike? What did Joan eat at the movie last night?"

"Let's see. We skipped dinner and filled up there. I had chow mein sandwiches. She had a hot dog."

"So did everybody else who is sick today, I'm sure. Steffie had two hot dogs and she can't leave the house. Do you want to call Schwartzwald or shall I?"

"I'd better. If I tell him that your daughter is sick, it will scare him more than if you tell him yourself."

"You're right. Okay." Leland released the button. To Mrs. MacIver, he said, "That skinny character you saw this morning is trying to beat us out of our fee. We did the work and now he wants us to settle for less. His iceboxes probably broke down and he's been selling bad meat. You and I will have better luck at lunch. On the way out I'll tell Florence about the souvenir book and, if you care to come back to the office, you can have it then. I'm going to look at it myself."

She stood up. "We'll see. How did you know that I saw that man? He was gone before you got here."

"We have a Distant Early Warning System in this office. I knew you were here before I left home."

She knew that he could have said that he had guessed. Her eyes shined. "You needed a warning for me?"

"No," he said. "For your chubby friend."

She put her hand on her stomach, then pulled it away quickly. "Oh, *Mr. Miller!* I'm so conscious of this." She shook her head, blushing. "Tell me, is the restaurant far? I have to know before we leave."

He laughed. "You'll make it, don't worry."

Of the people who were ill today, the one who had Leland's least sympathy was his partner's wife, Joan Petrakis. Under normal circumstances days would pass and Leland would not hear of her or give her a thought. Twice this morning he himself had mentioned her name, and perhaps, indirectly, Mrs. MacIver had been the cause. She had brought Mike Petrakis' background into the conversation at the beginning and she was close to his age—a year or two younger. For his own amusement Leland wondered how Mrs. MacIver would react to a close-quarters encounter with the woman who was the wife of All-America '49—who had had that automobile accident. It was impossible for anyone to come out the victor in a skirmish with Joan, let alone Norma MacIver with her slowballer's assortment of social assets. Joan was simply overpoweringly concerned with her own welfare and as talented in the infighting as a crippled tiger. What Leland entertained himself imagining was Norma MacIver's unhappiness after the fact, as she compared the wife to the husband in the light of her own bannerless intentions. Mike Petrakis had the maddening positive trustfulness of many football players—men who had broken others' bones strictly by accident—but not his wife. Joan Petrakis could take one look at the swollen-bellied Widow MacIver and conclude that she was plotting Mike's seduction in a revolving door. Down deep, it was the way Joan was. She suspected everyone, including Karen and Steffie, and not in the least Leland himself, if not of a plot then some knowledge that could hurt her, and the end product of the suspicion and her desire to stay better than even was that she was more guilty than anyone she knew of the offenses she pretended to condemn. She knew it; she was not stupid. She turned every meeting into a skirmish, so that any pleasure that could have been derived was swept away, and all the people involved—except her husband, whose mind was a blank when it came to perversity—went away with the sense of having done battle for their dignity, if not integrity. Leland was curious about the questions Norma MacIver would ask after such a meeting, how she would react to the answers, and the way she would measure them against her knowledge of her own struggle.

Joan came from a successful family and she had always had some money; where Norma MacIver showed no awareness of money as a tool, Joan knew money's uses as the poor could never learn them. Her first years of marriage with Mike had been made easy by her father's gifts, and if Mike principally had accepted the gifts as a way of pleasing her, he had endured them over a longer period through what he believed was her need. Joan understood his temperament and worked it to her advantage. The game was for petty stakes, and Leland and Karen had watched it with deepening sorrow. Joan was a pretty girl with a quick mind. She had married a young man who had made a good start. What she was doing, posing as a person with near-uncontrollable anxieties, was so wildly, indiscriminately destructive that Leland had to stop telling Karen what Mike told him about Joan. He evaded the dinners and double dates that Mike suggested, to Mike's confusion. Once Mike mentioned that Joan was pressing him to accept a gift from her father to repay the interest-free loan that Karen had made when the partnership had been started. Joan "didn't want to be indebted" to Karen. Leland never spoke of the offer with his wife. Later, he realized that what mattered was that the loan predated Joan's arrival in Manitou; it was something that she had had no voice in. When Leland told Mike later—without ever having consulted Karen—that Karen saw no point to the idea, Joan went after Karen, through Leland. One night at a dance while they were alone she asked him why he and Karen had stayed married so long when religion was not a factor, and then later that same night, all of them more tired and less sober, she leaned her hips into him during a fox trot, with the natural result—reminding him at once of the Mae West line, "Is that your gun, officer, or are you just glad to see me?" Because of Mike there was a limit to the terms in which Leland could put her right. She wasn't making an offer, just testing and perhaps attempting to get what she would not use but threaten with, if only with the eyes, to get him to do what she wanted. High as he was, he had sense enough to try to play it as farce—"If you tilt your head downward and slightly to the left, Joannie baby, you'll give me the chance to drool in your ear"—and that had finished it. It was clear to her that he understood—at the lowest level—that she was a woman of absolutely no follow-through. With her there would never be any telephone calls and quick dates downtown. He showed he knew it, and it made her hate him more.

Mike never learned that the strain between her and Leland had reached such intensity. He must have wondered why he and Leland could not seem to be closer friends—he had to assume that it had to do with Leland's own life. They had casual friends in common, but they never stopped for a beer by themselves. Mike did not know it, but it was something that Leland had grown up with and missed badly.

Still childless, Mike coached a football team and Little League baseball, and Joan traveled back and forth to her family in Port Smith. For her part, Karen did not know yet about the attempt to buy her out, or the escapade on the dance floor. Karen would not start something on a dance floor or with the hands under a tablecloth without expecting an early good night. It was a matter of ethics. She had not seen Joan Petrakis except for one collision in the office in almost two years, and that was as she wanted. The things she did not know would infuriate her and perhaps impel her to take action even now. She would believe that she had been purposely protected, that Joan's willfulness had been in her life even though she had not known it—no difference in the morality—and the action she might take would be only what she thought was long overdue. Probably it would come down to a telephone call. Joan was not the kind to hang up a telephone, no matter what was being said. Leland knew his wife: Karen would go to any cruelty to be assured that she had finally driven Joan out of her life. Karen Widener Leland was not a natural fighter; fighting was something she had had to learn. Of the sixteen years her husband had known her he could fairly say that she had never bitched or sought a fight. She would not agree, he knew; she would point to instance after instance in which she was sure she had looked for trouble. In his estimation she would be using a standard of judgment that could not apply. There had been circumstances that neither of them had understood. Those things still weighed on them, Karen having to bear the greater burden, and she felt—rightly—that she could do it even with a certain style if she had no trouble with people like Joan.

When Mike had had his knee shattered by a taxicab in New York four years ago, Leland had gone there to offer him a job as his assistant in the Investigations Divison of the Manitou Life Insurance Company. Leland had seen Mike on the football field and had judged him to be an audacious and inventive man. In the hospital he told Mike that it was his hope that Mike could eventually bring those qualities into business. What Leland had to offer in return was a job at less than eight thousand a year—not much, in relation to the other offers that Mike was receiving. It was not a matter of Mike's fame, but the qualities that had led to it, and Leland expected him to give them in full amount. In a week Mike called long-distance to accept the offer and explain why. He knew from the newspapers of what Leland had done, and could not believe that there was deception in what he had said. The sporting-goods firms and tobacco companies wanted to put him on display. He wanted to think he was better than a man who needed a break.

Ten months later, when the department was pulled out from under everyone in an economy move, Leland asked Mike if he was willing to go into a partnership. Mike wanted to know if Leland thought he still owed him anything—not long before, he had promised a future. Leland could remember thinking of the hustle to get new jobs, and how they were all a part of it. "I'm putting up my life's savings. My wife is lending me four grand she had to sweat bullets to save. What do you think I owe you out of that?"

Mike went in with him with the money he had collected from his accident.

The final courtship of Joan Wellman of Port Smith coincided with those events. From Mike's behavior and the bits of information he dropped in conversation, Leland gathered that, over the previous three years, the romance had been governed pretty much by Joan's immaturity and caprice. Twice, in disgust with her, Mike had walked out. The first time they had resumed, it had been at his instigation; the second time, at hers. The second resumption had come just before the start of the partnership, and in the new office Leland observed Mike wrestling with the decision long after he had made it. He had never had difficulty with women in the simpler situations of seduction and shacking up, and if there never had been a game called football, his good looks and easygoing manner would have attracted both the jelly beans and the more complicated women whose lives precluded all honesty save that over the coffee and after the hotels and trips out of town. He gave in to Joan in spite of what he thought was going to be the futility of it all. It was something Leland could see. Mike seemed to be consciously accepting a degree of unhappiness the way a snake slowly swallows a frog. After three years, there could be no meaningful concessions from Joan; yet, apparently, she and Mike were only beginning to have intercourse. By the expression on Mike's face, she was crying afterward, reporting the lateness of her periods when they were only a day overdue, calling him long-distance in the late hours of the night and having nothing to say—all extensions of what she had done with him before. Her trouble did not have much to do with sex; if she had little taste for sex, Mike's torment would have been of another kind, and far worse. Her trouble was her trouble, a child's reaction to her own desire. She had to have Mike, and she didn't like it; she didn't like the feeling of need, which had finally left her vulnerable. Then things happened too quickly, their engagement, parties, a wedding—a promise grimly and hopefully kept—a house given, furnished; in the excitement nothing was settled except the fact of their marriage, which they had to accommodate however they could. Love was what a man made it; what they had decided gave Mike little cause to suspect that he did not love his wife, or that she did not love him. With love believed—as Joan, too, believed it—the rest began, the two altered but not changed by believing; and because they believed, basically they were satisfied. The act of marriage itself was the continuing unconscious testament of good faith; unconsciously it created love. Many marriages began in more bitter and imperfectly resolved crises—only a few men did not know that—but the parties thereto were right if they remembered just the decision they had made: that settled it, whatever each of the parties was and had to be. Mike never would be interested in someone simpler—it did not figure, because he saw only the good in Joan, however inadequate, just as he saw it in everyone else; and Joan never could begin a search for someone to match her, scheme for plot, because that would mean having to battle for the control over her situation that she already possessed. Meanwhile their decision remained in force and the testament continued: it *was* settled. The sacrifices were small. When they were not faced with the effect on them, Mr. and Mrs. Joseph Leland knew that as well as anyone.

For a young woman like Norma MacIver, who had been arrested as a teen-ager in a stolen car and then later as drunk and disorderly, and who had gone into psychotherapy as a condition of parole, the trouble a Joan Petrakis brewed for people would be heartsickening for the opportunities it wasted. The attempt to ease Karen away from the partnership would be outside her world of ideas. It was not just that she did not understand the deployment of money. In the same situation she would know that Karen would not think much of her—Karen was the kind who stepped up and said hello; she had a natural, admittedly unreasonable aversion to quiet women. But if Norma MacIver could not have Karen as a good friend, she would know that she could have her as an ally. As much as the next woman, Karen enjoyed having people for dinner, chatting on the telephone, meeting downtown for shopping jaunts. As Leland understood them, these things did not require women to be very close. Leland thought that Norma MacIver would not understand Joan Petrakis' rejection of such offerings, small as they were, for an objective that would bring her no nearer to people. That was the key. Norma MacIver wanted to learn about her late husband not only because he had died, but because she was not sure that she had really known him. Under the same conditions, Karen might have come to the same conclusion. It would not have taken her so long to get going and she would not appear to be suffering as greatly, but the result would be the same. Again, it was a question of ethics.

Mrs. MacIver wanted to tell things in order, as well as she could. She had decided it in the taxi, and Leland had had to agree. For as long as he stayed with this, he wanted to get as many versions of things as he could, and it was more than simply justice that prompted him to hear her out completely. MacIver's mother and first wife were going to contradict and possibly discredit her understanding of MacIver's history. If only to establish a place from which to start, Leland wanted to enforce his sympathy with his client's point of view.

Sitting in the Flamingo and going through the fruit salad—her obstetrician had asked her not to drink—he realized that it had taken him too long to see her desire to do it this way for what it was. It was the level on which she knew she could make a contribution. So there was another reason for him not to interfere: on her own terms, she was relaxed and doing well. He saw no point in determining if she had made her decision consciously or intuitively. She had had a relapse in his office when he had been checking the police file—reacting, she had said. The thing was that she had put it behind her and was trying to work on any terms. Perhaps she had even forgotten. It didn't matter; she wasn't leaving it to him to find his way as he could. She would tell him everything she thought would help him to see her husband, starting with the woman he had made his second wife.

Karen had not yet arrived. The Flamingo was a long sunken room to the side of a large foyer that also gave access to a half-dozen catering rooms upstairs. Like the rooms overhead, the public restaurant was finished in a softly lit stippled coral. There were no pictures on the walls, but a pair of gigantic whitewashed birch branches mounted above a bordering of artificial ivy. These were the new decorations and nobody liked them. Leland had taken a table by the wall where he could be seen from the entrance, but he had decided at the last moment to sit with his back to the entrance so he could give less divided attention to what Mrs. MacIver was saying. He had hedged: Mrs. MacIver could see the entrance and she had a description of Karen.

"I went to Franklin Pierce High School," she said in her soft voice. "It was bad, and we had trouble, but nothing like what they have now with the race problem. There were fights, but nobody was ever killed. When two fellows had an argument, they settled it themselves. Maybe that's romanticizing it, but I never saw anything like the picture they ran in the *Herald-Press* last week of that colored boy with the blood pouring out of his head. Did you see that?"

"There was a film on television," he said.

"I saw that, too. I was in a tough crowd, and some of the fellows were out of school and working. A couple had prewar cars and when my parents thought I was at Gloria's house or Anne's or the confraternity, we were out bombing around town. We'd go to June Island or Northport, and once in a while we'd go down to Joytown and the boys would look for fairies to beat up."

"I've always wondered who you troublemaking kids were."

She laughed. "Oh, yes. Joytown was your district then, wasn't it?"

"Fifth Precinct. It didn't take you long to get picked up in the stolen car, did it?"

She shook her head as she swallowed. "One of the fellows came around with a car that he said was his and I, dope that I was, believed him. Three of us. We were picked up at Northport. Don't ask me what we were doing up there in December."

"You just glide over that, if you want to," he said.

"Dr. Roberts used to say that I shouldn't. People would hold fewer surprises and I would feel better getting rid of it. That was true then, when I was in therapy, and saw a lot of people who were in therapy, too. It isn't true now when I meet all kinds of people, so-called healthy people. It makes them uneasy, as if I had cancer. Am I getting through?"

"Perfectly."

"Listen, sometimes I call him Dr. Roberts and sometimes Wendell. He was always Dr. Roberts to me before we moved next door to him, and then I started calling him Wendell. I'll say both when I'm not thinking of it."

"I won't be confused. How did you happen to move next door to him?"

"An accident. I'll tell you about it, but I want to go on. Funny, I probably wouldn't if your rates were less, so Colin was right."

"You'll have to explain that," he said.

"Colin was sure that cost had something to do with the amount of effort a person would put into thereapy. The more you paid, the harder you worked. This is similar—the success of it depends on how much I contribute. I want to tell everything so you can help me get value for my money."

"I see." Leland thought it was a curious, cynical insight for a man married to a woman who had been in therapy. MacIver had passed this crack and he had bought her a car. They seemed to be on opposite ends of the scale. And this man had died a violent death.

"The night we were arrested," she said, "my father came up to the station. My mother couldn't. She couldn't face it. As soon as he saw me he hit me, hard, across the mouth. They had to tell him not to do it again."

"Is he from the other side?"

"Oh, no. Sounds that way, doesn't it? His parents were, and so were hers, but they both came from Bay Slope. Do you know where Our Lady Mother of Heaven Church is? On Roswell Avenue?"

"Yes."

"They were married there. That night I was arrested, it was too late to find a judge and have bail set, so the boys were sent upstairs and Gloria and I were taken into the city to the women's jail. In the morning the police were able to convince the owner of the car not to press charges. In those days the police did what they could to keep new kids out of court."

"They still do," he said.

"So nothing was done, but they frightened the hell out of us, which was right. When I got home my father made me take off my skirt and and he beat me across the legs with his belt. I've never screamed as I did that day."

"Okay," Leland said. He did not want to see it, even in his mind. The waiter came for the empty dishes. Her hands clasped in her lap, Norma MacIver took the moment to think of what she had said. She had her head back and the skin on her neck was sallow. She had stayed close to home since the death of her husband. She looked at Leland.

"They watched me pretty carefully after that. I wasn't allowed to go out after dark, but that didn't make a difference. It didn't take me long to fix on a fellow, and he and I would use Gloria's apartment. At first he was just fooling with me, I know, and seeing another girl at night. Then he stopped seeing her and there was just me. Of course that was gratifying, even though he was getting something from me that he didn't get from her. We didn't last long, a couple of months. It had to be that way at our age—and we were Catholic. I had my qualms, but he had worse. He went back to the church and confession and the whole business. It hurt me when I found out. I hated him sneaking behind my back and letting the priest call me a whore. We knew what the priests said about the girls.

"I decided that it was wrong to restrict myself to one fellow. Once I got past the second, the rest were easy. I had my needs—I mean it; I needed sex. I never felt a fall from grace. I was different from the other girls in other ways, too. I was shy—believe that?— and I had my complexion problem, but none of the fellows ever abused me. Oh, they swapped stories, but they did that over all the girls. They knew that I had a mind, because in that lousy school I had almost the highest marks in the class. Even the biggest, ugliest characters—I didn't have anything else to do with them—" She stopped, smiling. "Yes, I did, one or two of them—even they would ask me about World History and say, 'Gee, thanks, Norie.' Now *that* embarrasses me. I wanted to be called Norie then." She took a drink of water.

"I didn't have mean trouble because I liked men and enjoyed making love. One of them told me that what he liked was that I just didn't lie there and moan. I was horrified—my own *friends!* I felt good after hearing that; I felt like a woman because I thought I screwed like a woman, which was a stupid conclusion to come to. There's your wife."

She had said it without a breath or change of inflection and he turned toward the entrance as naturally as she had told him that it was time to do it. But it was like getting up from the floor. Norma MacIver had completely disarmed him. The sensation of having lost track stayed with him, so that Karen saw him before he could wave to her, and then when he did wave the action felt so needless and strange that he was sure that she would notice something wrong. He stopped, swallowed suddenly, and waited. He felt blood coming to his face. It was a cheap trick on himself. He had been caught paying attention to another woman.

Karen said something to her guest, a plump woman in her forties, then she spoke to the headwaiter. The woman and the head-waiter went straight down the aisle as Karen came toward Leland and Mrs. MacIver. Leland got up. Karen's smile was directed at him, mock-weary and mischievous. She wrinkled her nose at him. Out of the corner of his eye Leland caught Mrs. MacIver's reaction: she had expected something else. There was another thing—the same trick: she knew, too, how much she had had his attention. She looked away—she didn't want Leland to look at her. Karen moved her purse under her other arm and brushed at her short, light brown hair.

"Hi. If this is a surprise for me, you know me too well."

"How do you feel?"

She rolled her eyes and made the motion of whistling through her teeth. There was nothing the matter. "Steffie is home today," she said. "Her stomach is bothering her."

"I know. I called, trying to catch you. It was the hot dogs. I'll tell you about it later."

"All right. Are you coming to dinner?"

"I'll be there at five o'clock. I may have to go out again to relieve some people—oh, we have a lot of sickness today—but I'll be back."

"Good," she said quietly. "Did you see the *Herald-Press?*"

"Yes, don't remind me. We have a new client," he said turning to Mrs. MacIver. "Karen, this is Mrs. Colin MacIver, of Port Smith. Mrs. MacIver, I'd like you to meet Mrs. Leland."

"How do you do?" Karen liked to shake hands. Mrs. MacIver reached up. She was still nervous. It took her time to get in stride.

"Hello," she said, and smiled.

"I have to get back, dear," Karen said to him. "This woman came in with her list of books just knowing I was one of the enemy. The list *starts* with *The Grapes of Wrath.* I could use a drink, but I don't dare." She kissed his cheek. "I guess that's allowed. See you later. Mrs. MacIver, perhaps we'll meet again."

"Yes," she said. "Goodbye."

Leland sat down. Norma MacIver waited a moment. She said, "You know, when I was sick, trying to get better, I used to watch other women to see what was expected of me. I would have watched her."

"That's very kind of you to say, Mrs. MacIver."

"Could we use first names?"

"Sure—Norma. Call me Joe."

"Joe," she said. Then, "She's tall, isn't she? She doesn't look like she has a daughter—how old?"

"Thirteen. She's five-six. It's not really tall."

"I can't wait to see myself after this baby is born. I know what it's going to do to me."

"You don't know about that."

"Your wife has real charm. I wish that I had been able to tell Colin as much as she told you just now. The message was on every wavelength."

"You sound as if you're tired. Relax."

"It's catching up with me," she said. "I was up very early this morning. What the hell?" She rubbed her forehead. "Excuse me, will you? I'm just being my old neurotic self again. 'Could we use first names?' " she asked, parodying herself. "Who am I kidding? Now all

68

of a sudden I'm tired. I guess I didn't want to meet your wife after all. I like you. If I had a brain—shit. I'm sorry."

"Suppose you just try to relax," he said again. "It wouldn't help if I said that I like you? That I've taken my looks at you?"

"No," she said, "it wouldn't help." She picked up her glass of water. "Not really," she said. "You see, I'm taking my own looks at me right now. I'm wiser to me than you are. I see things that you just can't."

CHAPTER FIVE

■ ■

AFTER HIGH SCHOOL SHE WENT TO WORK. SHE THOUGHT OF COLLEGE, but not seriously. She liked the money she was making more. At a dance on the Port Smith campus she met a liberal arts sophomore named Jimmy, aged nineteen. They ended the evening in a hotel downtown.

He had never slept with a girl but he knew female anatomy; he asked and she told him that there had been only one before him, a sailor. Jimmy believed it. It hurt him but he took it bravely, and eventually he felt proud of his maturity and understanding. Things went smoothly. She moved away from home and registered in a night class in Freshman English in Port Smith. The affair went on into the next year, more intense and more complicated, more satisfactory to her, and she felt sure that she and Jimmy would be married. She made a B in English and started two more courses in the spring. When it became obvious that she was going to make A's, Jimmy began to act badly. He was jealous, he admitted it. He said that he wanted her to quit school, even mentioning marriage, but when she tried to make certain that he would marry her if she quit, he would not give her a direct answer. By the summer he was saying that he could never marry her, that he did not love her enough. She wept, got sick, but could not bring herself to break off. By September he had done it. She resolved to keep her life in good order.

"I did, for a month," she told Leland. "Later in therapy I told Wendell that I hadn't been able to stand not having sex, and he asked me why I hadn't masturbated. I've never done that, but that wasn't what I hadn't been able to stand not having. It was that and all the rest of sex, do you understand?"

"I think so. Did you realize that Jimmy was only looking for a way to get rid of you when he asked you to quit school?"

"You saw that? That it was too important to me?"

"Of course. I haven't been around psychiatrists, but I've been around."

She smiled. "I lasted the month, then I met a man at the Castle Gardens, that dance hall on State Street. I didn't know it at the time, but he was even more infantile about his needs than I was. He had a job, a car, decent apartment, and he spent everything he made on himself. He went out to a cocktail lounge or a movie every night, and at the age of thirty, that sort of thing should have worn thin. I don't know, it has with me already. Anyway, we went around, and then I moved in with him."

It was what Leland should have known, but had closed his mind to: a woman working toward a breakdown. He saw her as she was now, whole, even if pieced together, and it did not seem that a full-scale coming-apart really was possible. It had been; it had been the only way she could have come to be as she was. She had to be close to people, apprised, unreserving, firmly established. There were things that she missed; they came up so often, it was as if the piecing together had been a make-do job. The whole experience had not made her a different person than she had been. Therapy had not provided her with a new birth certificate, only with another diploma.

She had missed his surprise with the easy telling of Dr. Roberts' suggestion. Leland had had no intimate contact with therapy, only what he had heard from acquaintances and what he had read in a few books, but he understood that public policy could be left at the doctor's door—which was right when public policy had been a destructive influence on the patient right along. It was also possible that Roberts had not been making a suggestion, but asking a question about her behavior. The answer was interesting and it showed another thing about Colin MacIver. Their marriage had been a success; the man who had cracked about getting value in therapy had been able to fill her needs.

"With Jimmy at least I'd been able to get nine credits at night, but while I was living with this man, I wasn't able to do anything—anything. Finally I had an idea, and I put it to him: either we marry or we break off. He laughed. At last it came to me: he thought I was an idiot. We were in a bar and I started to yell at him. He threatened to hit me and I told him to go ahead, that I would have him arrested. He said something about picking up my clothes and then he walked out. I couldn't move. I got drunk and a man tried to pick me up. Have you seen a sober man try to take advantage of a woman who is falling-down drunk? Leering and sneering and waiting, you can see the sadism written on his face. I was so furious with him and the other bum, I started to curse, you know, muttering to myself. All I wanted was someone to love me. I remember looking in the mirror and calling myself a little shit, over and over. I had to get it out of my system. The stool I was sitting on had a top that came off. I got up, pulled off the seat—it was heavy—and threw it over the bar. It barely got over the bar, and it went off like this—" with her hand she traced an arc to the right. "It hit a pyramid of bottles and glass shelves and managed to touch the bottom of the mirror, four by six feet. Glass came down in an avalanche, and there was the bare plywood underneath. We all stared at it, and the bartender looked at me as if I had pulled off his toupee. Then some man grabbed my arms and they called the police."

She stopped for a sip of milk. They were having the roast beef. She had seen venison on the menu but he had told her to forget it. It was commercially prepared frozen deer meat brought up from Pennsylvania because people expected to see it during the season. Her milk was more doctor's orders. She had told Leland that it was richer than the milk in Port Smith. He had forgotten.

"Women's prison again," she said, holding the glass. "They ran some tests and, as I learned when I faced the judge, field workers checked on me. My parents had had enough. The first time I saw them in, I don't know, six years, was at Colin's funeral. I see them regularly now, I guess: I went there for dinner once and they visited me once, that's all. Hold it."

She opened her purse and looked through it, Leland thought, for a handkerchief. Out came a bottle of red capsules. "Iron and calcium. If I don't take them my teeth will fall out."

"Are you all right?" he asked.

She nodded. "It was too early for medicine when I left Port Smith. In the morning all I can eat is a breakfast-type breakfast." She took the capsule with a swallow of water. "One of these days I'm going to be a woman of the world." She dropped the bottle into her purse and snapped the clasp shut. "I guess I had the toughest judge in Port Smith. 'Young lady,' " she mimed, deepening her voice, " 'for the life of me I can't see what happened to you, but I've been told that you'll respond better to treatment than you will to jail. Would you be willing to see a doctor?' I said yes before I realized that he meant a psychiatrist. Then he explained what probation was and what violation of it would mean—I would have to serve a full sentence, ninety days, with nothing off for the probation time I had put in. Talk about mixed emotions. I hadn't realized that I had sunk so low in the opinion of society. I was that close to jail. I knew I needed help, but I didn't think I was sick. I didn't want it put down on the record. I wanted to tell him to shut up, all I had done was break a mirror—just over seven years ago, by the way. You're supposed to have seven years' bad luck, but they don't tell you which seven. My luck for seven years was nothing but good. I wanted to tell him I'd rather go to jail than be humiliated by what he was saying. But he could send me to jail and say what he pleased, anyway. So he assigned me to a probation officer."

She went to the probation officer, a woman, and arrangements were made with a psychiatric clinic for an interview. The interviewers were oily and patronizing; her fees were adjusted to her ability to pay. She had no voice in the decision. Finally when she was dropped into Wendell Roberts' office, in her anger she said, "This shits. I should have gone to jail."

"That can be arranged," he said, and reached for the telephone.

"Don't!" she cried.

From her salary, sixty dollars a week, the clinic took twenty, and from her free time, two evenings, then three, every week. In six months she was registered again in Port Smith College, and all her evenings were filled. She continued to see men, many of them, whenever she could. If anything, Dr. Roberts encouraged her to go out. She would come in on a Monday evening with a tale of spending Saturday night and Sunday sleeping with a fellow in her history class.

"Do you want to tell me how it was?"

"It was all right," she said.

"No better than that?"

"You have to get used to a person."

"Did you get used to him?"

"A little. He would wait until the last minute, then he was always hurrying. I wanted him to stay but he wouldn't."

"I hope you told him," he said.

"I did. But he didn't say anything, and then the next time he did practically the same thing all over again."

"Are you going to see him this weekend?"

"He mentioned something," she said. "I haven't made up my mind. If I decide not to see him, I'll probably have to cut history. It will be the only way to avoid him."

"I thought you said you had a book review to turn in."

"I know, I know. Listen, if I go to class and this fellow asks me out, can I tell him that you want to give me a test Saturday night— that you've scheduled other people and this will be the only chance you'll have to give it?"

"That's a complicated lie, Norma," Dr. Roberts said.

"I know, I was thinking of it Sunday when he was in the bathroom."

He stared at her. "You could tell him that whether I knew or not, couldn't you?"

"Yes, sure, but it would be easier for me if you went along with it."

She wanted to show Leland a snapshot of Dr. Roberts that she had taken at a barbecue in her back yard at the beginning of the summer. It had not been posed, she said as she passed it over the table. It had caught Roberts in the middle of a leap high into the air for the shuttlecock in a badminton game. He was wearing a sweatshirt and a pair of chinos of the sort that MacIver had been wearing in the picture she had given Leland back at the office. Roberts looked tall and thin, almost spidery, and in excellent condition for his age, around fifty. He had an even tan, which meant a sunlamp at that time of year—and he worked out to keep in shape. He had not seen the camera, his eyes squinted up into the sun. His hair was white, the little there was, and it looked as if he had the barber trim it with the machine. The fringe above his ear was no longer than a two-day growth of beard. He looked like a man who would adjust to being innocent about some things. Apparently he knew how to play and enjoy himself, but he made such good use of his time teaching, maintaining a private practice, and putting in hours at a clinic, that Leland wanted to see him as a man who did not forget himself at the wrong times. As an analyst Roberts himself had been through psychoanalysis—Leland knew that much. Leland had heard of analysts on whom the process had not taken, but this man did not seem to be one of them. He could be innocent, but he was not easily fooled. Leland returned the photograph.

"Has he seen this?"

"Oh, yes. I had an eight-by-ten print made and framed. He has it on his desk at home."

"He must be quite a character," Leland said.

"He is. You'll like him, I know you will."

After a year in therapy, she wanted to accept the offer of another student to live with him. Now Roberts did not like it. He did not say no, but he insisted that she go home and think it through a second time. When she came in the next week she told him that she had gone out and picked up a sailor to test her feelings for the fellow who wanted her to live with him.

"The next morning, I was in love with the Navy. I like them both, I really do, but I couldn't possibly love either of them. How could I? They're both attractive enough for me to sleep with, but I don't have to live with anybody for sex. I can get all the sex I want. In a way, I want all the sex I can get, too. That's normal, isn't it? I mean, it is for me. I don't have to wreck my life for it."

"Norma," Roberts said, "I think it's time I bought you a beer. I owe you a beer, collectable when you're discharged."

What she had succeeded in doing was getting sex separated from love, she told Leland. She had had to do that so she could finally put them together again in a meaningful way. Dr. Roberts didn't think it was necessary for her to know precisely why she was willing to endure a variety of abuses for the sake of maintaining an emotional attachment; it would be enough for her to remember that she was liable to do it. She saw that sex was only a device in her relationships; her enjoyment of it only promoted her desire to get into and stay inside a basically secure relationship, regardless of other penalties. Roberts asked her to try to enjoy sex without becoming entangled emotionally with the men she chose. She wanted to make a ground rule: never the same man on successive weekends. If she thought she needed a ground rule, he said, all right. He gave her his home telephone number to use if she thought she was going to slip. His wife could always locate him if he was out. He would call Norma and they would see if they could not talk their way through it.

She called him once, on a Saturday night at three in the morning. He sat up with her, via the telephone, for two hours, until she was too tired to call the fellow she had wanted to see. She heard Mrs. Roberts bringing him coffee and turning on the radio for herself. She had to compare it with what she could expect if she did make the other call: eventually, a hysterical argument. When she hung up she went to sleep, and when she reported on Monday evening, she could report that there had been no accidents.

First, because of her rule, she had to realize that sex without the hope of developing a relationship was something that she could imagine so carefully that, on most occasions, she could dismiss it from her thoughts like an extra portion of dessert. When it wasn't a thought, but something physical, it became another matter. She had Roberts' approval to handle it as she wanted, but when she could look at a man in her room and know that there would be someone else before she would see him again, the pleasure of the act was diminished to a simple throe she was glad to have done. Second, the desire not to break what amounted to a promise to Dr. Roberts gave her a strength with men that she had never used before. Sometimes she told them about it, asking them to respect it and her, and interestingly, the few who said they were willing to try raised serious doubts about themselves in her mind. In the eight months the rule stayed in effect, she was able to generate a wariness that served her, but also began to frighten her. Roberts released her from the promise, but she did not release herself for another two months. She met a fellow she liked and went with him for nearly a month, then broke it off when he mentioned something he wanted them to do in the following summer. "I don't want to get serious," she told Roberts.

She was twenty then. Her life stayed in good order, as she wanted to put it, through her twenty-first birthday. One evening in the cafeteria at Port Smith College she met a boy of eighteen, who asked her to go out. At the next session she told Roberts about it, and that she wanted to see the boy. Roberts told her to go ahead.

It lasted until July, and for the first time since Jimmy, she felt something she wanted to call love. The boy moved in. He was majoring in math—he didn't know why—and worked in a pathology laboratory downtown. There was no question in her mind about his age: he would set the alarm so he could read before breakfast, and on the weekends he took them incredible distances in search of particular movies, and once he suggested a trip to New York to see a Charlie Chaplin double bill. She began to have her doubts when she saw in his devotion to her much of what she herself once had tried to bring to love. She promptly began asserting herself to the point where there was nothing left of him. She told Dr. Roberts that she would break it off if the boy proposed marriage. When that came, she kept to her word.

"It wasn't a pretty scene," she said to Leland. "He wasn't just too young for marriage, he was too young for abiding by what I had to do for my own health. I was still so involved that I wanted to forget why I had to do it, even though he was telling me again by fighting me. He was willing to do anything to keep it going. It wasn't healthy for either of us. He was too young for me and there was no telling which way he was going to change. I wanted somebody older. Not only that, I didn't want to look at him and see myself as I had been. He telephoned me off and on for almost a year, until I told him that I was going to marry Colin."

A month before Dr. Roberts planned to discharge her, while they were still talking about what she thought she could expect from a relationship with a man, Dr. Roberts' wife died of a stroke. In the next weeks he gave up all hope of doing his job with Norma. She was his only patient near discharge at the time and he needed to talk to someone about the things other doctors would expect to hear and which his friends—his wife's friends, too—would not be able to bear.

"Tonight while I was cooking dinner I remembered a time up in Maine, three or four summers ago. We were walking in the woods and she slipped and grabbed my hand. I held her arm so she wouldn't fall. Simple thing." He was sitting back, Norma told Leland, his hands clasped at the back of his neck. "Tonight while I was at the stove I relived the entire moment. I could feel the pressure of her hand again, and the fear in her eyes. Her voice rang out inside me. It's so curious, Norma. I miss everything about her. There was so much I never gave a thought to. Do you find that shocking for someone in my position to say?"

"No, no, no."

He said, "She puts her nightgowns—pink, sleeveless, ordinary nightgowns—on a hook on the inside of the closet door. The closet is empty now. I cleaned it out the first morning. I looked in there anyway last night. That doesn't say much for me as a doctor, does it? I stood there staring at a coat hook, Norma. I was thinking, 'I should have saved something, at least.'

"I still talk about her in the present tense," he said. "I don't want to accept the fact that she's dead."

"All that time," she told Leland, "he had been working to help me build the confidence I needed to act on my own. I'll never be a woman of the world, but there are some things that I can do now that I couldn't do before. I know that I could have made it here to Manitou alone. Dr. Roberts believed that I could change from what I had been to what I became. After his wife died and he took me into his confidence, I saw how deeply he believed it. He told me later that he wouldn't have done it if he had been thinking clearly—he didn't say so in those words. He was afraid of what it could have done to me. Anyone could have seen that he was beside himself. I did. He didn't think about what he was doing—but I did; I couldn't help being proud of myself."

For the rest of the year she lived on her own, changing jobs, trading her furnished room for a larger apartment in the same building. At Christmas she sent Dr. Roberts a card and he telephoned her in return. He was giving a party and wanted her to attend. She went, and an assistant professor of physics took her home. In late January, she had another call from Dr. Roberts, who had heard that his friend was seeing her. He asked if she was all right, and she told him that she was. He had not heard from her, he said, and he wanted to be assured that there was nothing she wanted to discuss. There wasn't. He asked her if she planned to be married. She said that she hadn't been asked.

"Norma, I think I just called you to snoop, like any friend."

She laughed over the telephone. "I'm friends with him, too. Just friends—loyal friends, I think. God, I hope!"

"You've made me feel ashamed," he said. "Are you going to be angry with me?"

"Of course not," she said.

"You know, last summer when my wife died and I leaned on you as I did, I lost track of what I was doing and saying. You can understand how I could worry about having impaired my usefulness to you."

"You haven't, Dr. Roberts."

"Can we stay in touch? No matter what happens in the physics department. Whether I've lost an ex-patient or not, I'd like to gain a friend."

She did not fail to see that he was very worried, and after she told the professor that she thought she had met the man she wanted to marry, she did not forget to call Dr. Roberts, too.

"My professor is still single," she told Leland. "The last time I saw him was a year ago at Wendell's house. He went to Caltech in July. When he learned about Colin he wrote to me, but I haven't answered it—yet. I don't know if I will. We weren't what you'd call a ball of fire together, and I don't want to start something that will lead me to settle—well, just settle.

"Colin came into the office in the early spring, before tax time. You saw his picture. The men who come into the office of a wholesale electrical supply house don't look like him—or dress like him, either. I was the secretary to the office manager and because I knew the operation and how to run office machines, I was assigned to work with him. It took us until lunch time to set up in an empty room. We hadn't exchanged more than orders and acknowledgments until then. He asked if I knew of a good place to eat. I told him where the bosses went and he asked me to join him. I said no, and he said all right, perhaps tomorrow. I had second thoughts. I had said no because I didn't want to go where the bosses would be, for one thing—it's a matter of the way things are done—and for another, I didn't know him when he asked. But he was so gracious and at the same time so disappointed in the way he accepted my refusal, that I came right out and asked if I could change my mind. I tried to make myself pretty. Can you understand that?"

"Yes."

"Well, you had to see his smile," she said. "I swear I wish I didn't have the memory of it. I had let go with him, and he let go in return, taking me in without embarrassment or hesitation. You can't tell now, but I don't have a bad waistline—and I do have a big can. He looked me up and down and then he sort of looked around me, all the while smiling the most natural way, warm and fresh. He said, 'Sure, you can change your mind.' He was just delighted and he wasn't afraid to show me, but at the same time he made it clear in the way he looked in my eyes that he was going to treat me with dignity."

She sipped her coffee. There were a few crumbs scattered between their coffee cups and water glasses. The restaurant was still crowded. Some of the faces had changed and Leland's view of Karen was blocked by a man who had shifted his chair to face the man sitting beside him. Leland said to Norma, "I don't want you to knock yourself out telling things that will hurt you."

She shook her head. "Talking is the best thing I can do. I'll sleep tonight. I won't worry about something I've held back."

"How do you feel?"

"Tired, genuinely, but I'm all right. I want to go on. I found out during lunch that he wasn't married, but it didn't help a whole lot. I was feeling all the things I had felt as a kid. I was just that attracted to him. We had lunch again the following day, and the day after that, and that evening he took me to dinner. He was reserved and very, very gentle. He talked about what he was doing and what he thought, rather than what he had done. He wasn't keeping anything secret; it was just that the conversation stayed in the present. I mentioned that I had been in therapy and he seemed interested, but not avidly curious. He asked about the next night, which was Saturday night, but I already had a date. 'Then I guess I'll see you Monday,' he said.

"Sunday I looked him up in the phone book. He lived in one of the white sections in Bay Slope and I wondered if he had lied to me about being married, because that isn't an area where single men with money live. I wanted to call, or go over and check, but I didn't. That was a rough day for me.

"Monday was going to be his last day, but we went to lunch just as if he were going to be there for weeks to come. He asked if I was busy that night, and I had one of my classes until ten o'clock. He offered to pick me up afterward and I said yes. We went for coffee and a ride. We drove for an hour or more, west and south—his driving was perfect, by the way—and I remember that we passed the government arsenal at Holly Hills. Finally we pulled into one of those roadside rests."

They had a cigarette. The car was a big one, a Buick or Oldsmobile hardtop; she couldn't tell. The night was mild, and the window on her side was part-way down.

"I hadn't planned to come so far," he said. "You'll be home late. Tomorrow you'll be tired."

"I wanted to see you, Colin."

"These aren't the terms you would have set," he said.

"Don't be sure." She told about looking him up in the telephone book. "I'm not a baby. I know what I'm doing here."

"There's no such thing as an uncomplicated lay," he said. It was as if he thought she was a virgin and he wanted to shock her.

"I'd want to see you again, of course," she said.

He looked at her. "I'd want to see you, too. Tomorrow. It's the way I am."

"I'll take good care of you," she said. It sounded lewd. "Of your feelings," she added. "I know who you are." She didn't know why she said it or even, really, what it meant.

"He just closed his eyes," she said. "He put his head back and looked so relieved. I kissed him and got up on my knees and held him against my breast. We never did make love. We kissed a little, made ourselves comfortable, and fell asleep. Later we drove home. It was close to dawn. The dampness was in the car.

"The next night we had dinner before my class and afterward he drove me home. He didn't come up. We were tired. We were teasing ourselves, but it was playful. We wanted to play."

Leland nodded. There was a lot that she didn't know—as she had said. MacIver's tension at the time they met was interesting but probably not meaningful, three years before his death. Two and half years had passed since he had divorced his first wife. Leland would try to learn why tomorrow. Perhaps there would even be something in the insurance files. Leland wanted to know the other women MacIver had seen steadily, regularly, seriously—however one wanted to express that. MacIver had been free the Friday and Saturday nights of the week he had met Norma, and Monday and Tuesday. Leland made a note to get the address of MacIver's bachelor apartment.

"He told me that he had been married before and that his first wife had remarried. They had been married three years and it hadn't worked out. He made such a confession of it and told it with such difficulty that I didn't want to make him discuss it with me. I had to go by what I knew of him on my own. I did want to know if he had cheated on her; I was thinking then of the way I thought I was finally going to give myself to him. I didn't want it thrown away stupidly. He told me he hadn't—and that she hadn't done it to him, either. I told you he was careful about that. He still didn't like her, but he kept it quiet. But because of her, he didn't expect a lot from me. It crept into the way he treated me. We'd go to a crowded bar and he'd wait for me to say something about being knocked around by the other people. One night he had to work late and called to cancel a date. He asked if he could come up later, at eleven o'clock. It seemed silly, so I said no. He didn't sound sincerely interested in dragging himself up to my place for an hour after a long day. I wasn't disappointed about having our date broken, and that confused him. He wasn't hurt by my reaction; he just didn't understand it.

"When we were talking about a thing and he had no more that he wanted to say, he wouldn't say anything, just drift off. Most people can't sit and do absolutely nothing for half an hour, but he could. He never thought about her, though—Betty, his first wife. Once, in the beginning, I asked him. He didn't lie. I don't like to think that she knew him longer than I did. At least, it wasn't important to him when he knew me.

"There were women in between. I don't have anything to prove that except what went on with us, but I have the feeling that he had had a lot of women before he met me. I mean a lot."

"Just a minute," Leland said.

Karen had stood up at her table. She glanced behind her once and then, when she saw that she had his eye, gave him a little signal to go to the lobby. "Excuse me," he said to Norma. He saw Karen say to her companion, "I'll be just a minute."

On his way out the bit of lipreading gave him a curious pleasure: she had been too far away for him to have actually heard her, but her voice had sounded perfectly in his ears, soft and close. He waited near the checkroom.

She came up the steps from the restaurant, looked to the left and right, saw him, and walked over quickly.

"What is it?"

"I overheard a conversation at another table," she said. "Did you see where I was sitting? It was the table to my left, two men in gray suits."

"I'll take a look when I go back," he said.

"One man told the other that he heard that you were working on the Shoftel case. Are you?"

He was too startled to laugh. "No, I'm not. What else were they talking about? I'd like to have an idea of where they got the story."

"I heard something about land clearance. I didn't begin to pay attention until I heard your name."

"Maybe one or the other was in the Mayor's office this morning." He explained that. She was wearing a tailored tan suit he had seen many times. For some reason she had on no jewelry. He liked her in earrings, the small ones, and a single strand of pearls. Her freckles were showing, and he liked that. "The trouble is, I'll probably be going down to Port Smith late tomorrow or Wednesday on this thing that came in today. I'll go in to see Pop and he's up to his ears in the Shoftel case. I've already talked to Warren Johnson about what I'm doing, but the Mayor, if he wants to, will think that I'm double-crossing them."

"Is there anything I can do?" Once in a while she saw the Mayor at a dedication or a school board function and he made it a point to call her by her first name. She had never tried it, but she probably could get him on the telephone.

Leland said, "If there is, you'll hear from me. This may be a good one. Mrs. MacIver's husband went off the roof of Flatlands Racetrack three months ago. It could be murder, suicide—anything."

"The poor kid," she said.

"Poor is not what you'd call her. He left a quarter of a million. He was thirty-two and he earned it himself."

"Does this mean that we should forget about Montreal?"

"No—I don't know. It's too soon to tell. If it comes to that, would you settle for Port Smith?"

"Let me think about it," she said honestly. She looked over her shoulder. "We're taking more time than we should."

"You're not upset, are you? I'm not sure yet myself."

She smiled. "No, I'm not upset."

He took her arm. "Listen, what was that note about last night?"

She moved closer. "Do I have to tell you *now?*"

"It gave me a rough morning," he said.

"All right, I started to invite you to Manitou State Teachers College to hear my talk, but I changed my mind because I didn't think you would want to come."

"Did you read what you left? Why didn't you just write another note?"

"Not *now,* Joe. This woman is—"

"To hell with her." He was squeezing her arm. He let go. "It will only take a moment."

"You're getting yourself worked up over nothing," she said. "I only had that one piece of paper and I didn't want to start rummaging around in your desk for another. What would you have thought if I had crossed out a dozen lines? I just wanted to tell you something, that's all. I thought I had. I'm sorry."

"*I'm* sorry." He stroked her arm where he had held it.

"Are you all right?" she asked. "I don't want to leave you now if you don't feel right about something." She kissed him quickly, her lips dry and warm. "Joe? Please? Maybe I was stupid."

"No—no." He shook his head. "I did this to myself. Go back inside. I'll see you later."

She touched his cheek. She didn't want to kiss him again here. He was going to wait a moment. He remembered that he wanted to take a look at the two men who had been talking about him. Karen went down the steps, watching what she was doing. She *looked* as if she had had a working-over. All morning, he had known what he had been doing. If this had not been a public place, he could have made it much worse. Certainly he didn't want to think about what he had forced her to carry for the rest of the day.

When he returned to the table there were fresh cups of coffee. "I took the liberty," Norma MacIver said. "I hope you don't mind."

"No, not at all."

"Is everything all right?"

"Oh, yes. Another result of the trouble that that reporter made for me. My wife overheard a conversation at another table."

"On the way up in the train today I read the article in the *Herald-Press.* Indirectly, that's been the cause of it all. Your father wouldn't have called you, would he? What was the point of running an article like that? I mean, besides selling newspapers?"

"That's right. It was truth to no good purpose." He stirred his coffee.

"Are you sure everything is all right?" she asked.

"Excuse me?"

"Your personal business," she said. "Were you able to get it transacted? Don't answer me if you don't want to."

"No, that's all right. The truth is that I transacted my personal business when my wife came to the table. This is something else. I wish you weren't so sensitive to people's moods. You bring a mood to the surface and make it more acute than it might be otherwise."

"Perhaps that's truth to no good purpose," she said.

He wanted to keep talking. "You have it backwards. You're an extremely honest person, but the trouble is that your honesty demands honesty in return, even from people you know as little as you know me. Most people, including me, get so used to the ease of lying when it doesn't seem to count that the truth becomes as difficult to handle as flypaper. It's awkward. But you happen to be right, and the rest of the world is wrong."

"Thank you." Her eyes fluttered. Maybe he had gone too far. He had thought that talking would put what he had done to Karen behind him. He stirred his coffee again. For some reason he was still walking a tightrope over utter confusion. The note had started it, but now it had a momentum of its own. In the past ten minutes he had tried to solve two problems by creating new ones. He knew from experience that he would never solve anything by running away.

"He said in advance that his mother was a very stupid woman. Those are his words, not mine. He made the trip mostly to observe the social graces, and that alone was a big concession to her. The MacIvers are supposed to be a very old family up here."

"Never heard of them," Leland said. "There is an old families crowd in Manitou, but they don't carry much weight."

"All right, let me tell you. She married a MacIver, her maiden name was Newton, and her mother's maiden name was Clifford—"

"That cuts a little ice. I live in Clifford Heights, and a John Clifford made a pact with the Indians. There's a statue of him overlooking the rapids."

"I know, Colin told me. Anyway, those are the names. Colin's father died of a heart attack when he was forty-three. Colin was fourteen—something like that. Mr. MacIver was in real estate. He didn't own any, or very much, and he was an associate with his organization, not a partner. I don't know very much about those things, but when he died, they didn't miss him. Those are Colin's words, too—succinct, aren't they?

"I said in the office that there never had been a divorce in his family. If there were other reasons why his mother opposed our marriage, I didn't hear them. By that I mean she may have objected to my religion—the religion I was given—or my Italian background. She did like Betty; Colin never told me why. He came back to Port Smith from the trip with just the statement that she wanted nothing to do with us. She would have no idea how angry or unhappy she made him. It took him weeks to get over it. I don't know why he bothered to go, for he had predicted the outcome. But in no other way, in nothing he ever did or said, did he show an interest in her.

"He had no mementos or medals from the war, not even his pilot's wings. He never said that he had shot down any planes. I knew that it had been a fighter squadron and he told me he had flown a Mustang. Is that right? He had been in combat, he did say that, and that's all."

"The Mustangs came in toward the end of the war," Leland said. "In the souvenir book I asked my daughter for is a day-by-day account of what the squadron did. Your husband's part will be there for you to see."

She reached for the pack of cigarettes. The crowd had thinned out. Karen had gone, giving him a wink as she had passed on the far aisle. Norma said, "I know that he didn't go into the war until late, and that he had finished a year at the University of California before he went in. When he came out he was able to start at Jefferson in the spring of 1946. He switched to accounting—what from, I don't remember, something in liberal arts. He married Betty in 1946, too. That was the summer. The summer of 1949, he was in Nevada. He didn't go right through college, because there was a time of eight months in 1947 when he lived up here, and he was here again in

1948. He told me these things. In 1949 again he came back; from here he went out west, and returned to Port Smith.

"He went to work for Benson, Philips and Stratton, and then went out on his own. When he came into my office he had just landed the account, a very big account. I understood his work a little, but he didn't discuss it with me. He was capable of setting up an accounting system and teaching office girls how to run it. His way with me when we worked together was very competent and cool, so very cool, in fact, that I thought he didn't like what he was doing, as if it were all a lot of paper-shuffling. He set it up, though, carefully, and for the rest of the year I continued to work, it was perfect. The bosses were extremely pleased. I *know* that they had been afraid that they would have to hire an accountant full-time. In any case, they helped him get new clients.

"He had an office, but he could have just as easily bought a jacket with larger pockets. The day after he died, for something to do, I went down and closed it up. I hadn't been able to sleep, so I got there at six in the morning. Colin didn't have a car trunkful of papers. The janitor and I got it all downstairs in two trips in the elevator. When I got home I pushed it all into the crawl space over the garage. It's there for you to look at."

"I'll want to do that," Leland said.

"He had a secretary, Miss Enid Alma—that's her whole name. I have her address at home, if you want to see her. She thought Colin was a sweet young man. She typed his letters and took the calls. Colin said she wasn't bright, but that she could do the jobs he wanted. I think she was married at one time, but I don't know. She had no dependents. I know that because I sent off her social security for the last quarter and made out her withholding slips for next spring's filings.

"Colin's personal books were at home. He wasn't a grind. At home he never worked more than twenty minutes at a sitting. He could work at his desk and follow a television program at the same time. He did it all the time. Once at a party someone said he saw another person add a list of double numbers—twenty-nine, forty-three, eighty-six—as someone else read them aloud. Colin said that it was a stupid trick and that he could do it, too. The other man wanted to bet him ten dollars. Colin made it fifty and then he did the trick, without ever having tried it before. He told me that later. The man got upset and the party could have been wrecked then if Colin hadn't told him to split the fifty between his wife and me. We saw that Colin was trying to save the evening and took the money. At other parties people would try to talk Colin into doing it again, but he wouldn't. He was that sort of person; he could say no and make it stick.

"With Colin there were people who could do no wrong and others who could do no right. He would say hello to them, but I knew the things he could pretend to do, and one of them was that he could pretend to look at people. He would smile and nod, but his eyes wouldn't be focused. I know that because he would tune me out in the same way if I bored him with some trivial crud. I got out of that habit.

"But I was one of the people who could do no wrong. I told him what I've told you, maybe more, and he said that if I ever had more trouble, I could do whatever I had to do. He said that once and never again, never mentioned other men, never asked me if I was happy. See? I do know all about it. The things my old boyfriends would say or do would stop you in your tracks. I took Colin to meet Dr. Roberts. He was wonderful. He didn't try to horn in—I mean, my business with Dr. Roberts was my own. He knew a little bit about everything in a conversational way, and that evening he and Wendell talked about the popularization of Freud's discoveries. Colin convinced Wendell that the magazines and the movies were all making it seem too easy. It wasn't helpful to the people who were on the verge of seeking help to talk about hopeless cases, but they did exist, and nobody mentioned them. He meant the cruel people, the people who are numb to everything, the people who even use psychotherapy to support their illnesses. It wasn't an argument, just a discussion over dinner. We went to the theater and had a fine time. When we drove Wendell home they talked about cars they had owned. Colin had just bought the Cadillac convertible. Wendell once had had a supercharged Auburn Speedster—used; I remember him saying that. And Colin saying that the Cadillac wasn't in that league. I remember that night very well. The next day Wendell called me to say that I had done very well for myself and to thank Colin for him for the fine evening. I made sure I did.

"After we were married I moved into his apartment. We were there three–four months. He didn't want to live in a development, or too far from the city, or in a place where all the trees had been cut down. When Wendell called and said that the house next door to his was available, I had my doubts at first, because it isn't always wise to live so close to one's friends. Colin didn't think it would matter, because the houses aren't jammed together out there, and Wendell— another quote from Colin—is a civilized man. He wouldn't be in for breakfast every morning trying to find out if we'd been well laid the night before. End of quote. We went out to look at the house and decided that, all in all, we liked it. It's Tudor and looks small on the outside, but the rooms are large. We wanted a place that looked warm and comfortable. Styles didn't matter. They—I've always had the feeling—excuse me." She took a drink of water. Her hand was shaking. As she put the glass down, Leland saw that she smeared the lipstick on her upper lip. He gave her a sign, and she took a mirror from her purse. With a tissue she wiped away the smear, then put the mirror down. "How's that?"

"Fine."

"I stepped in quicksand. I began to see things again."

"I know."

"I've decided to go to a hotel and stay overnight. I'm going to live it up. Tomorrow morning I'll go shopping before I catch the train. Maybe I'll see a movie tonight. I'll see how I feel. After all, I'm a woman with a little money now."

"That's the ticket."

"I have a fully paid-up house and two cars," she said. "If I'm careful with my investments and don't change my habits too much, I can live on my money until the baby is done with high school. Of course I'll go back to work. No matter what, I'm going to finish college. Only thirty credits to go. Did you think that I'd finished? In your office I told you that I had gone. I *went,* is what I said."

"I was going to say that if you're willing to wait until tomorrow afternoon, I'll take you to Port Smith myself. If nothing new comes up and I have no trouble with the two ladies I'm going to see, I'll be ready by three o'clock. We're supposed to have a little snow, but I think the weather will hold."

"For a while I thought you were kidding when you mentioned your plane. I've only flown once before, down to Bermuda last winter. It was like being on a bus. If you don't mind having me, I'd love to come with you."

"Fine. This afternoon, after I've had a look at the souvenir book, I'll send it over to your hotel. You don't have to come back to the office for it."

"Don't trouble those girls," she said.

"It's what you're paying them for. When we get down to Port Smith, I'll need some names and addresses. I'll want an appointment with Dr. Roberts."

She laughed. "He's not that difficult to see."

"All right, whatever you think is necessary. Now, what do you recall about the day or days before your husband died?"

"I was getting to that." She cleared her throat. "If there was anything out of the ordinary, I didn't notice it. He was not more quiet. There was no unusual mail, I heard no telephone calls. At the office, Miss Alma was as stunned as I was. Colin had his own habits and ways of doing things, and I didn't question them. He was a good husband and I know he loved me. When a woman who has as little to offer as I do is loved the way he loved me, she is just very damned glad, and behaves accordingly. I didn't question him.

"He used to go to the track without telling me, but often, just as unexpectedly, he would tell me in the morning or even call from the office to find out if I wanted to go with him. Just as often, I couldn't, because I had classes or I was working in the house. I tried not to let that job get in our way, but twice I remember not wanting to leave a room half-painted. I wanted to do it for him. He spent a couple of weekends on it, because he couldn't completely let me do it myself.

"When I was home he would call to say hello—not to check on me; please, *please* don't get that idea—and once or twice a week we would meet for lunch. He was not a publicly demonstrative man, holding my hand or breathing on me in the way some men do with their women. He saved it all for when we were alone. There were times when he surprised me with little presents. We were never separated overnight—never more than ten hours. We were so close and constantly in touch with each other—I don't know, among our friends, there are women and men who don't seem to relate at all. There's one woman whose husband doesn't get excited until after he falls asleep. Then he wakes her. She hates him for it, because it wrecks her *sleep!* She wanted to get even with him; she was looking for someone to put her up for one night, to punish him. I never mentioned it to Colin, not because he would have said no, which he would, but because it would have upset him. He wakes me up all the time—

"He *woke* me up, and I was glad to be there. I woke him more than once." She waved her hand to keep Leland from coming to her aid. "He—he—there's another couple. They don't love each other. They just have their social lives in the same living room. They haven't done it in years.

"I said that he had a lot of girls. He didn't say anything, as I said, but he would say what he had seen and where he had gone, and there were many, many places and things that he would not have gone to alone. He knew how to handle dating situations, how to pay for things, open doors—oh, let's face it: he was slick. He knew everything there was to know, and then he invented a couple of things. I'm talking now about his social skills, but you might as well hear it all. We never missed a night. We missed a couple of days because of our nights, sleeping around the clock. He had an appetite, and it was for loving, not going through the motions. Now I've had enough. Joe, order me a drink, please. A martini, two to one with a drop of orange bitters. I feel like spitting in somebody's eye, and it might as well be that damned doctor's."

Leland was already motioning to the waiter. He wanted one for himself.

CHAPTER SIX

■ ● ■ ● ■ □ ■ ■ ■ ■ ■ ■ ■ ■ ■ ■ ■ ■ ■ ■ ● ■ ● ■

"BETTER NOW," SHE SAID. "I HAD THOUGHT I HAD FINISHED WITH these scenes. Probably I'll be doing it—not very frequently—for the rest of my life, no matter what happens to me or who I marry, wondering about the what-might-have-beens. People's lives take such severe turns. Once I made a conscious effort to associate a song with a person—Jimmy, as a matter of fact. The song became a standard. Even when Colin was alive and I heard that song, my mind would respond on cue. We do so many stupid, sorry things.

"The day he died. No, the evening before. We went to a movie. I wasn't in production clothes then. We met downtown, under the Proctor marquee on State Street. He had the car and I had come down by bus. It was warm and we put the top down. There was plenty of time before the last show, so we drove through town out to the Point. We parked on the ocean side, with the sun at our backs. There were some people there, a couple of them rolled up in blankets. We necked. He talked a little about his day. He had seen two clients, a jeweler and a wholesale produce man. He told me he had seen the biggest, darkest strawberries. I asked him why he hadn't asked for some. It wasn't the season and they were hard to come by. He said he didn't want to be bothered—it would mean a debt, even if only a small one. He was like a baby about strawberries in heavy cream. I made a note to look for some. We necked some more and went to an Italian restaurant near my old neighborhood for dinner.

"We both had veal parmigiano and drove back to—*wait!* There were kids in the car! That's right, in the parking lot outside the restaurant. I wanted to go right over that. I haven't thought of them in months. There were three of them, fifteen or sixteen, big kids, sitting in the front seat. One of them had his knee up on the dashboard."

"Stay where you are, Norma," Colin said. She stood by the trunk, behind him. The three boys turned to them, the one behind the wheel grinning.

"Nice car, Dad."

Colin opened the door. "Get out—fast."

The boy made a face and moved slowly. "Don't rank me, Dad. I like the car."

Colin grabbed him by the collar and jerked him out onto the ground. Colin put his foot on his neck and pressed his face into the pavement. "I could kill you now, you little bastard."

"Okay! Okay!"

"Tell your friends to stand clear."

They moved toward the gate.

"Norma, get in the car."

The boys hustled out of the tiny lot. When he got in, she patted his leg.

"How do you *like* that?" he asked her.

"It's all right. They didn't take anything."

He started the car and turned it around and pulled onto the narrow street. The boys were standing on the far sidewalk. As the car came by, the one Colin had manhandled stepped off the curb between parked cars, and spat. Colin threw up his arm and jammed on the brake. It happened so quickly that Norma was thrown toward the dash. The boys were running the other way. Colin took her arm and pulled her back in the seat.

"Are you all right?"

"Yes," she said. "What did they do—oh! Those little pigs!"

He wiped the side of his face with his handkerchief. He put up his elbow to keep her away from him. He rubbed his face hard so that his skin reddened from the pressure. "Did I get it all?"

"Yes. Oh, I'm sorry, honey. I'm so sorry."

"Forget it." He started forward, still holding the handkerchief.

He threw it over the side of the door. After a block he turned on the radio, then snapped it off again. She sat quietly. When they got out of the neighborhood she reached for his hand.

"Don't touch me," he said. "Wait until I wash."

She looked up from the table to Leland. "After a while we stopped and I waited in the car while he went into a cocktail lounge and washed. When he came out he said, 'I still feel crummy. I can smell him.' We sat through the movie, but he was uncomfortable. He couldn't sit still. When we got home he showered and shaved. The shave was unnecessary. I sat on the toilet seat, watching him. He kept staring at his face, in the mirror. 'Ah, Christ,' he said. 'For Christ's sake.' I made him come to bed. Funny, but my memory of this tried to twist itself around. I wanted to think he was tired and just a little depressed. Your wife has tried to make you forget something by doing something special, hasn't she?"

"Sure. If I'm not too tired, I usually take over."

"Yes, yes, that's it. That's what I mean, and that's what happened. He took his time. Who says, 'I like a man who takes his time'?"

"Mae West. She's one of Karen's favorites. When she wants to, Karen can do a pretty fair imitation of her."

She thought about that. "Colin said that it was no great trick to make love three times in an hour if you're in good health and you've had a day or two off, but it was something if you could make one— the first one—*last* for an hour."

"I couldn't do it. I don't mind telling you, either."

"Neither could he. That's why he thought it was such a trick. That night, I sort of half woke up. I remember rolling toward him and making a lunge, and I got my hand on him, but then I fell asleep again. The sheet and the blanket were too heavy for me to move under. I think he moved and said something—he never said anything that was clear—and that was it. The alarm clock is the next thing I remember.

"In the morning he had orange juice, bacon and eggs, and two cups of coffee. Except for Sunday pancakes, he had that breakfast every morning for two years. We didn't say much—I never heard of anybody who talks at breakfast. He kissed me goodbye and gave me a feel and kissed me again. I heard the starter motor of the Cadillac in the driveway, then I did the dishes and went back to bed. He didn't call during the day, so I made dinner. At seven o'clock I called his office and there was no answer. At eight o'clock the telephone rang and it was the police."

Leland sighed. "All right. There are a couple of good hotels near here, so we'll walk over and get you settled. The girl will come over with the souvenir book. I'll give you a number where I can be reached if something comes up. I don't think I'll be talking to you again until tomorrow. I'll have my office take care of Miller when he calls."

"What do you think so far?"

"There's a lot more I want to know. A lot, Norma. I don't want to venture any guesses when I see all the things I don't know."

She nodded. If she was unhappy, there was nothing he could do about it. Her husband's apparently leisurely approach to his business prodded Leland: certainly it didn't account for the estate that MacIver had amassed. His dealings with people were interesting, too. A young man, capable of saying no, who could calmly roll a sucker bet from ten to fifty dollars. Norma had called him slick. Yes. And cool: yes, that, too. This had been the man who had married this little girl. Slick, cool characters usually installed girls like her in apartments and bragged to their friends. Colin MacIver had not been one of these. Leland could not forget what Norma had told him about the night in the car when MacIver had fallen asleep against her breast. Dr. Roberts had liked him. MacIver had known a little about everything in a conversational way. Thoughtful and fun-loving, but quiet and withdrawn. If Colin MacIver had been murdered the reasons would show themselves—but how, really, was a man thrown off the roof of a racetrack on a meeting day? Leland would have to see. If MacIver had killed himself, why had he made such a spectacle of it? He left a pregnant wife. An accident? Why had he been on the roof of the track? There was a lot that Norma did not know, because there was a lot that Colin MacIver had concealed. Leland was very interested in a meeting with the mother and the first wife.

At the office, he tried Mike on the addition trick. Even slowly, Mike could not handle the figures. He could do it, he thought, if he practiced picturing the moves of the beads of an abacus. Leland thought that it might be the way MacIver had done it, and if true, it was an interesting look into the workings of MacIver's mind.

The souvenir book and the insurance file arrived before Leland left for Bonney's, but there was no time to look at them. Sheila reported that Steffie was dressed and feeling better.

There were three telephone messages on his desk when he returned. For the fourth day in a row a tool-and-die man at the Kelso Chain Works was out sick. He had a history of short illnesses and Personnel suspected alcoholism. In a matter like this they had to have something substantial to take to the union. Leland had done a half-dozen jobs for them in the past and there was nothing to negotiate.

The second message was Hugh Thoms' report for the weekend, a diary of the ordinary business of an ordinary woman. He had included last night's incident, when the woman had walked by him. The report would be phrased in the third person. Leland added the note that the operative was subsequently replaced. If, in a day or two, the woman's movements showed no change, he would strike the item and forget about it.

The third message was brief: "Everett (?) called. He apologizes again for what happened this morning. You would understand, he said."

Leland laughed and put the message in the wastepaper basket. He signaled Florence.

"This is ready," he said, giving her Hugh Thoms' report. "Ask Mike if he wouldn't mind handling the Kelso thing. I'll be relieving Harry McLeod for dinner."

"Do you want me to do anything?"

"See how they're making out at Bonney's. If they need help and you want to work, put yourself on for a couple of hours. I'll be there after eight o'clock. Everett is my cabdriver. There's a taxi shack down the block from my apartment. See if you can look up the number there and leave the message that I probably won't see him until

Friday, if then, and no, I'm not angry with him. Who is going to take the souvenir book over to Mrs. MacIver?"

"I am."

"Tell her I'll call first thing in the morning. She knows that, but it won't hurt her to hear it again. You're putting in a long day. If you decide to go down to Bonney's, be sure to eat a good dinner first. I don't want anything happening to you."

"Yes, sir."

"Buzz me at ten to five. I have arrangements of my own about dinner."

"Yes, sir," she said, and went out. He reached for the souvenir book.

161st FIGHTER SQUADRON
EIGHTH AIR FORCE
E. T. O. 1943–1945

He looked for the index. He had not been through the book since he had received it, in 1947, and as he went past faces he thought he recognized, it struck him for the first time that Colin Mac-Iver had been one of them. He had made himself a part of the statistics that anyone in the insurance business knew just too well. The youngest of the faces was now thirty, the senior officers well into their forties. Leland exchanged cards with some of them and letters with one: he heard things. Myocardial infarction. Carcinoma. In the insurance files were certified photocopies of the death certificates, as innocuous as licenses to drive. In time they would be stapled to every one. Leland did not like this, looking at the young faces and wondering who, and how, and when. The records said that MacIver was their suicide, that he had brought it upon himself. Perhaps. Through him, whether he wanted or not, Leland could see what awaited them all.

SECOND LIEUTENANT COLIN W. MACIVER, beside a formal portrait of a tense young man wearing his overseas cap, followed by the date of his birth and his home town, Manitou, and then a little history:

Colin MacIver arrived late, March 14, 1945, after a year at the University of California. Like so many of us, he did his advanced fighter training at Lake Charles. He flew seventeen missions over Germany until V-E Day, and is credited with two kills and two probables. Lt. MacIver's gun cameras produced some of the first pictures of a German jet, which are shown on page 54. As for the speed of his reflexes, which enabled him to get such pictures, Mac said, "He made his pass and I clipped his arc, that's all. Anybody would have done the same." We know better, Mac. It was nice going.

Leland looked at the photograph. Probably MacIver had not been called "Mac" before or since. He looked very young. Not much of his hair was visible, but it seemed to be cut more severely than had been the style in those days. The jaw looked not as sharp, and there was a puffiness—the tension, perhaps—around his mouth. He looked toward the floor, as the photographer had instructed him to do; he looked stolid, humorless, immature. Photographs were no way to judge such things. The left side of his neck was visible and there was no scar. Leland turned to the day-by-day account.

In the paragraphs for the sixteenth of March he found his own name. "Leland got his nineteenth today, a Focke-Wulf over Regensburg. Billy Gibbs, watching from above, said it went like this: 'Joe spotted a loner on the deck outside of town, after a bust of an afternoon. After a little Alphonse and Gaston he won the toss and went down for him. He crawled up on his tail and blew him up with the first burst. There was no plane left, just wreckage, for a mile. They're building them cheaper and flying them stupider.'"

Leland could remember. A chill of disgust went through him. The plane and the man—boy, probably—had torn apart in less than a second. Leland wondered how Billy, who had been his wingman, would feel about his language now. Billy ran a hardware store in Eureka, California. His weight had ballooned to two hundred and ten pounds and he had four children. By the look of the snapshots he sometimes sent east, he was a long way from killing. Leland kept turning pages, reading for MacIver.

March 20: "Joe Leland got a double today for twenty and twenty-one! The 161st's leading ace and wingman Billy Gibbs spotted four Focke-Wulfs twenty miles north of Regensburg, at seventeen thousand over heavy clouds. 'They were absolutely green,' Leland said. 'Billy and I went at them together, hitting the third finger and Charlie. One, two, and four broke for the cloud. The man in the middle flamed. He bailed out. Number one reached the cloud but I caught number two and blew him up. Billy chased four all the way into the cloud. We saw smoke, but we couldn't hang around.' "

On the next page was MacIver's name: "2nd Lt. Colin W. MacIver broke the ice for himself today with a kill of an FW-190 over the Danube. 'I caught him in the rudder at thirty degrees. He couldn't turn and there was nothing but clear air ahead. I poured it in until he broke up and fell. The pilot must have been dead in the seat.' " Leland thought he had a vague recollection of having heard about it. He read on; he did not want his memory playing tricks on him.

There were no other mentions of MacIver until the 29th, two days after Leland's name had been in the "Going Home" list: "Colin MacIver got his second kill and a first probable this morning at the Czech border. At 0900, after an uneventful search for targets, MacIver and his wingman spotted a crippled Lightning dodging for home on the deck, with a 190 in pursuit. 'He wasn't watching his tail. I caught him in the wing and he dipped and hit a tree.' MacIver's wingman, 2nd Lt. P. J. Matthews, of Vineland, New Jersey, added, 'Colin had closed on Jerry so fast that he was on the other side when Jerry blew up. Colin's backwash was making a wake in the trees like a speedboat. When he came up again I ducked under to look for branches in his scoop, but how he got away clean I'll never know.' The probable came a few minutes later. MacIver says, 'The Lightning was making about two hundred. Before I came up I closed in on him and gave him a waggle. He was all right and understood that we would watch his tail. We lined ourselves up in the sun while he played around, trying to catch the light. P. J. spotted three ME-109's closing on him from the north, so we went after them. They broke and turned to engage us and I caught one underneath while he was going for P. J. and he began to smoke. He started down but we lost sight of him and the other two ran. We continued to follow the 38 to his base. Apparently he couldn't get his gear down and he slid off the runway into an ambulance, flipped, and exploded.' "

100

The second probable was recorded in a tally at the end of a description of a brief, confused dogfight. There was no other mention of MacIver in the diary. Leland marked the places for Norma and turned to page 54. The pictures were a fine series of views of the top and tail of the jet to an elevation of forty degrees, showing the jet twisting out of the camera's field. MacIver had gotten an excellent shot at the plane and it was a tribute to his ability to fly. Leland wrote this opinion on the piece of paper he put over the page as a mark, then put the book in the center of the desk and reached for the insurance file.

He could tell by the thickness of the file, about an inch uncompressed, and the color of the papers, mostly white, that the Manitou Life Insurance Company had found little that it had thought unusual about Colin MacIver. Across the tab of the cover was a string of numbers indicating eight or nine policies collected inside, but Leland already knew that MacIver had compiled his policies over a period of time. The way to read these files was from the bottom, because each new sheet was pinned over those that had come before.

Nov. 1, 1945: "Preliminary application, $2,000 Whole Life. No physical examination requ'd. R. L."

Nov. 5: "App. $2,000 W. L. beneficiary, estate of the insured." MACIVER, Colin William, 163 Park Lane South, Port Smith 11. Agent, F. Miller. Single. Employer: Bedell, Quade, Lewis and Byrd, Stockbrokers. Occupation: Clerk. Veteran (Officer) Honorably Discharged. "No additional remarks or comments. F. M." (That was Miller.)

April 13, 1946: "This is to inform you that I am changing the beneficiary of my policy to Betty Ford, my fiancée. Very truly yours, Colin William MacIver." It was a note written in a kind of lopsided, childish script.

April 15: "Kindly sign the enclosed form to accomplish the change in beneficiary you desire. Sincerely yours." This was initialed P. T. It was an onionskin copy of a letter sent by a correspondent in the Beneficiary Division of the Policy Change Department. The company had a form for everything, or could make one. The company never agreed to anything expressed in language it had not written or advised. The form, filled out by the company and signed by MacIver, followed.

Aug. 9: "Please send me the form to change the beneficiary of my policy to my wife, Betty Ford MacIver. Thank you." He had learned quickly, Leland thought. The reply and the signed form followed.

Sept. 22: Preliminary application for $5,000 Whole Life. Agent Miller. New address for MacIver, 1643 Marshal Foch Boulevard, Port Smith. "Physical examination required. Secure appointment with company doctor. R. L." A routine decision made by a junior underwriter. Same day: Change of address letter sent. Leland could quote it from memory: "So that we may keep our records properly for your protection, kindly notify us promptly when you change your address."

Sept. 24: "Appt. Pt. Smith. Dr Kelleher 10 A.M. 9/28/46. F. M." (Miller.) The company examination form came next, dated September 28: name, address, age, date of birth, sex, race, height six feet, weight one hundred and seventy pounds, brown hair, gray eyes, no blemishes or distinguishing marks, teeth good, lungs clear, vision twenty-twenty, reflexes sharp, tonsils and adenoids out, heart and blood pressure normal, no obesity. Had the insured had: thirty diseases and afflictions. All no save whooping cough. "To the best of my ability I can determine no reason why this person would be uninsurable with the Manitou Life Insurance Company. A. J. Kelleher, M.D." On the next page, the new application, with one change: OCCUPATION: G. I. Bill Student at Jefferson U. College of Business Administration. And under remarks and comments: "Subject holds two jobs, evenings and weekends, and has been doing so since the beginning of the year. Must be considered a good risk. F. M." After that, address changes: Port Smith, Port Smith, Marigold Drive, Canby, which was a suburb of Manitou, Port Smith, Canby a second time, returning again to Port Smith.

Mar. 13, 1948: Preliminary application for $10,000 30 Payment Life. "Physical examination requ'd. Secure appt. with co. dr. R. S."

Mar. 15: "Appt. secured Kelleher 3/21/48. F. M."

Mar. 20: "Subj called today to postpone appt. Resched. 3/30/48. Kelleher." By the look of his handwriting, Dr. Kelleher had aged.

Mar. 28: "Subj called to cancel appt for 3/30. No new appt set. Referred file back to Miller. Kelleher."

Apr. 2: "Have spoken to subject on telephone twice. Has lost interest in policy at this time. Maybe next year. Says he is not getting a better deal from anyone else. Do not close this number. Miller."

Dec. 8: "Subj entered office today unexpectedly to discuss policy pending since spring. Wants to designate bene estate and change bene's on previous two policies to estate. Says he wants to do it unobtrusively. Apparently he is experiencing some marital difficulty and is contemplating divorce. I told him that he could designate beneficiaries as he wishes. Can I make an appointment with Kelleher for a new physical?"

Dec. 11: "Dear Mr. Miller: You may instruct your client that the company must be furnished with a document executed by him affirming that no separation or divorce agreement with provisions concerning the disposition of his insurance exists between him and his wife. Then he may use the properly worded forms I have enclosed for his convenience to change the beneficiary as he desires. I am holding an open file. Sincerely." At the bottom of this onionskin copy: "Consulted Law Dept. Wording okayed on telephone by Darnell. Company policy to absolve itself of responsibility in cases where irate wife may want to sue us for manipulating property to which she has a claim. A letter from the insured taking responsibility will hold up in court, except, of course, if we have prior knowledge of insured's competence. Not case here. G.V. Alexis, Chief." Leland knew Alexis well, a man who did not believe in assuming any responsibility on his own. Leland knew the law concerning MacIver's contracts, and MacIver had been entitled to make the monkeys in the zoo his beneficiaries if he had wanted, and without any prior statements—at least at this stage.

Dec. 14, 1948: "Appt. secured Kelleher 12/19/48. Miller."

Dec. 14, 1948: "This is to inform you that no agreements exist between my wife and me concerning the disposition of my life insurance policies. Colin W. MacIver."

Dec. 14, 1948: ". . . in a mode acceptable to the company, I hereby designate as beneficiary to the above policy (policies) THE ESTATE OF THE INSURED . . ."

Dec. 19, 1948: Another physical, signed Kelleher. Changes of address: Port Smith, Reno, Port Smith.

Florence opened the door. "Time, Mr. Leland."

"Thanks."

There was still no sign of the snow that had been predicted. The file in a manila envelope, Leland crossed Senapee Street toward the six-way intersection to search for a vacant taxi. The sky was turning dull. He breathed deeply, quickly, unconsciously making use of the patrolman's trick of gathering new energy. He wanted to get ahead of himself and try to weigh what he had learned. The facts swirled around inside him, an old, familiar sensation; and in the old, familiar pattern, he wanted to nail them down. He had only himself, no squad to send hustling. He had MacIver, who emerged now and then from the swirl of facts. He was like something you could see only out of the corner of the eye. You tried to look directly, it disappeared. A fighter pilot, as brave as a man was ever called upon to be, and the coroner of Clausen County had said he had committed suicide.

The house was on the other side of the river. Later, to relieve Harry McLeod, Leland would have to call another taxi to get back here. He wasn't thinking: Karen was headed in this direction for the School Board meeting. It was on days like this that Leland felt the lack of a car. He could not bring himself to buy one. For the little pleasure they gave, cars were as burdensome as house pets. It was his opinion, and on days like this he was stuck with it.

Rolling toward the bridge at the foot of Otis Street, Leland got out the file and turned it toward the light of the window.

On February 17, 1950, MacIver had made another preliminary application for insurance—a Whole Life policy of five thousand dollars. In the space for scars and other identifying marks Dr. Kelleher had made note of a "circular scar on the left side of the neck."

Apparently the old man had concluded—as Leland had—that the scar bore no resemblance to the lateral, razor-thin "hesitation marks" of potential suicide. However, the scar was dated. MacIver had gotten it sometime between December 19, 1948, and February of 1950. Allowing time for healing and the lividness to disappear, it could be more closely dated to the first six or nine months of 1949. It would be interesting to know how he had acquired it.

Once again, the beneficiary of the policy was MacIver's estate, which was also interesting. At no time since the war had MacIver considered making his mother the beneficiary of his insurance. Many single men named their mothers—most agents, and probably Fred Miller, suggested it.

Oct. 9, 1951: "Prelim. app for $25,000 W.L. DISAB BEN." Leland skipped ahead. The physical examination was conducted this time by a Dr. Rosenberg.

Oct. 18, 1951: "Six interviews with neighbors and business associates, all favorable. Two neighbors and janitor report no immoderate habits for a single man. Keeps company with one young woman, said by one neighbor to be quiet and friendly. Janitor thinks marriage is imminent, said subject had many girl friends with no favorites until this one. Subject is whiz C.P.A., according to clients. Good business sense and knows own worth, meaning fees are high. Personable, good-natured. One termed him 'ruthlessly efficient.' All see big future for subject, estimate personal worth at thirty–forty thousand dollars, securities and cash. Modest apartment indicates nothing, for it is convenient to downtown Port Smith area. McLeod." "O.K. Leland."

No one had mentioned MacIver's gambling. Perhaps they had not known; perhaps they had thought nothing about it. In any case, MacIver had not plunged so deeply that he had gotten into noticeable trouble.

The next page was the application itself, and the beneficiary designated was "my fiancée, Norma Colucci."

In October of 1952 MacIver informed the company that he was living on Collegeville Road, and in January of 1953 he applied for a fifty-thousand-dollar Whole Life policy, took another physical examination and passed, and designated his wife, Norma Colucci MacIver, as his beneficiary. At the same time he made her the beneficiary of all his earlier policies. The investigation this time was conducted by the Eagle Investigation system, of Port Smith, whose work Leland did not know.

"SUBJECT: Colin William MacIver ND880345718

"DISPOSITION: Generally favorable impressions. In connection with the matter of Mr. MacIver's application we interviewed three of Mr. MacIver's neighbors and five of his business associates. Their cooperation made a further investigation inadvisable in this case.

"PERSONAL: The first of the neighbor interviewees is a psychiatrist and professor of high standing. He gives the subject the highest rating as a family man and other moral qualities. Describes habits as moderate. A light social drinker. Spoke admiringly of the subject and said he knew him well.

"The second neighbor, also a professor (neighborhood borders Jefferson University campus) has a slight acquaintance. Describes subject as 'very bright and affable.' Never saw him drunk, etc.

"The third neighbor is an executive of a leading manufacturing concern. Describes subject as 'a moderate man with a fine sense of humor.' When asked if he would hire him in some capacity or other, neighbor said, 'most assuredly.' However, this neighbor reports having once driven on a Saturday to a gas station with the subject. The subject paid his bill from a 'wad of paper money—big denominations —too thick to fold, maybe five thousand dollars.' The subject did not explain this to the neighbor, and in subsequent interviews when the question was raised, no one had ever seen the subject with unusually large amounts of cash. Neighbor describes him as dutiful and affectionate husband.

"BUSINESS AND FINANCIAL: Three of the five business associates were clients of the subject, who is a C.P.A. All regard him as highly competent man, thorough and efficient. They said that he did not underprice himself and they respected him for it. When asked about his personal worth, all of them used his personal appearance as a yardstick and they reckoned anything from twenty-five to a hundred thousand dollars as his total assets. At the bank, the credit officer states that all of the subject's personal financing is done through the institution. The subject has not committed himself to large loans at high interest. The bank's vice president stated that the subject has in his various accounts an amount in excess of forty-five thousand dollars. He also has the largest safe deposit box available, and the vice president assumes that it contains stocks and bonds. He also regarded the subject as a 'clever' man with money."

Clever was an understatement, Leland thought as the taxi crossed the bridge. The house and two cars, now, a year and a half after the report, were free and clear. Leland had to see MacIver's investment portfolio. He marked his place and closed the file. He wanted to stay with it. Colin William MacIver: son, husband, bedmate, businessman, pilot. The night before he died he had put his foot on a boy's neck and threatened to kill him. Leland, with his policeman's sensitivities, did not like that. Or the rate at which MacIver had made his money. Leland had directions to go and dozens of leads to follow up, if necessary. He did not want to tear a hole in Norma's money. At the same time, he could not see leaving the job undone.

Harry McLeod walked down the hill to the luncheonette for his meal and left Leland standing in the cold across the street from a four-story sandstone apartment house. Report: the subject had gone to the delicatessen and returned. Leland had a sweater, scarf, and gloves, but there was no holding out the blowing cold. The woman would be wearing a green coat and kerchief. The building was not unlike the one in Port Smith in which Leland had grown up and where his parents lived—as they chose. This one, unlike the other, could be run-down and even infested with vermin, and Leland could not understand a man who would be glad to see the woman he had married living in such circumstances. Now he wanted their child. In a business in which the satisfactions were almost always in the execution, this particular aspect was the most unpleasant. Leland took his deep breaths, stamped his feet, and waited.

At seven-thirty a teen-aged girl entered the building, and five minutes later the woman emerged. She was dark-haired, busty, in her late twenties. She walked down the hill and crossed in front of Leland, who wanted to give her a good lead. She was good-looking and neat about herself. She turned the corner and Leland stepped up his pace. Harry McLeod was in the middle of the block and had to be told.

She was waiting at the bus stop on the next corner. In the luncheonette, McLeod, with his long face and white crew cut, was spooning up soup.

"I'm going for a bus ride," Leland told him.

"I'll take it. I'm too cold to eat."

"Follow us in the car," Leland said. "I was going downtown anyway."

McLeod had already settled with the counterman. Leland had to think that if he was bright enough to do that without police training, he could take on more of this work. Leland gave him a lead out the door, then picked up a copy of the Manitou *Star* to take down to the bus stop.

The woman took a middle seat. Leland went to the rear and read the paper. The Shoftel case had moved over to the left side of the front page. The roundup was still on and the day had been rife with wild rumors. Leland looked over the rest of the page, turned to the sports section, saw that the lead story was an A.P. feature on track and field, and folded the paper.

The subject had brown bangs and a turned-up nose. The air had freshened her cheeks. She was a domestic, warm-looking woman, sitting quietly glancing at the small billboards over the windows. The jogging of the bus glazed her eyes. She was a million miles from the corruption her ex-husband wanted to pin on her. Leland wanted to get up, introduce himself, and say, "Madam, for your own protection, get in touch with your lawyer." He had had the thought on other cases. It was not that he was in favor of giving the game a sporting chance; it was that he thought that deals like this were simply stinking.

She got off downtown, three blocks south of Bonney's. McLeod tapped the horn as he rolled past for a parking stall. The subject walked back, stopped at a shoe store window, and Leland went by her. The street wasn't crowded and he could tail her from the front. She crossed at the corner and Leland, still in front, was getting the feel of her moves. When she went into a lingerie store he was pausing to light a cigarette. He went back. She was at a counter. He could see McLeod walking up quickly on the other side. REPORT: the subject went to buy a brassiere—D cup?—causing the operative to wonder in passing how much the subject's continuing normal sexuality was preying on her ex-husband's mind.

Leland went on to Bonney's. Florence had signed herself on and was working the main entrance. Max, she said, was moving between the entrance and the mezzanine, Mrs. Agnew was in the women's shop, and Hugh Thoms was on the fourth floor. Mrs. Carter had gone home with stomach trouble. Leland told Florence to take over the mezzanine and send Max downstairs. In a moment Max rode the escalator down and strolled through the record department on his way over to Leland. Max was a squat, squared-off character with a moustache that made Leland think of Jerry Colonna. He wore a billowing, paper-thin topcoat to make him pass for a customer. He stood next to Leland while he spoke so he could keep watching the shoppers.

"We've a quiet day," he said. "During the five o'clock rush we had a known booster come through. Negro man. Got his picture from D'Arcy's. He had just about wiped them out when they got him. He went around with his coat open and I covered him man-to-man. I let him know me. Jack Bonney himself saw us playing tag through the mezzanine. He seemed to like it. At least, he saw that he was getting his money's worth."

"Don't let him kid you," Leland said. "His father told me today that their losses stayed even these past two years while their volume went up twelve per cent. And that's not figuring the big drop their losses took when we came in."

"So we have the High View project," Max said.

"We had it all along. It was a question of agreeing on the cost."

"Excuse me."

"I saw him," Leland said. A kid at the portable radios.

Leland left the store at ten to nine. His legs were getting heavy. He stopped for sugar doughnuts for Steffie and found another taxi. He nearly fell asleep during the ride across the river. Going up the walk, he could feel sleep nipping at his ankles like a dog.

"Steffie?" He closed the door. The television set was blasting and Steffie was not in the room. The house wasn't large, a ranch model that ran to the back of the lot, but it was possible to stand in the living room and hear nothing of someone in the bedrooms. "Steffie, where are you, honey?"

Now she answered. She was putting up her hair. Leland lowered the television sound and went into the kitchen. Karen had bought the house before they had begun to see each other regularly again. She had told him of it one Sunday at the old apartment when he had gone to see Steffie, and he had had to be surprised with her choice. Karen had never owned a house before, and she had spoken often of wanting the bedrooms upstairs. The lot under this house rolled up, then down again, and the bedroom floor was seven feet off the ground. The effect was the same as a two-story. Still, he knew that it wasn't the house that she would have bought if she had been with him; but it had been important to her a few years ago, and because it had been a success, he was fond of it, the way one was fond of anything that had served. She would not feel the same way; the way she was, once the need was gone, the house would be something she would want to put behind her. She would be thinking about dealing for something else.

Steffie had done the dishes. Leland heated the coffee and brought a tray into the living room.

"Come on, I have a surprise for you!"

"I'm coming!"

She was too old for this. She liked it, but he would have to find another approach. He stayed on his feet; a soft chair would anesthetize him. There was a panel show on the television set. Leland turned away and stretched, brushing his knuckles against the low ceiling. While his arms were in the air Steffie tiptoed behind him and pulled his shirttail out of his pants.

"Hey! What's the idea?"

"Some rummy game," she said.

"What's the matter now?"

"After I have a couple of these," she said, "I'm going right to bed. I'm very tired, I really am." She bit into a doughnut and cupped her hand under her chin to catch the flakes of sugar. "Mmf. Fresh."

"Get over the table, lady."

"I said they're fresh." She licked her lips and bit in again. Her hair was in rollers, covered by a pink kerchief, and she had on her nightgown and robe. She was thin and long-legged and she looked like him, with his hair and coloring, and oddly, she did not seem to be turning out badly. It was her mother's influence. When she wanted, Steffie could affect her mother's carriage and grace, light and quick and seemingly effortless—when she wanted. She was still too young and did not care.

Karen had said ten-thirty. He sat down on the couch and drank his coffee. He had not heated it enough. Steffie had taken the chair in the corner, folding her legs Indian style. She was holding a napkin under her chin while she watched the panel show. He leaned back. His energy was running out of his body in a flood. He opened his tie, unbuttoned his collar, and stared at the wall. Karen favored bright colors and vivid contrasts. The Clifford Heights apartment, though sunlit and airy, was done in walnut and beige. He had started with a few pieces of walnut furniture four or five years ago and now he was stuck with it. If he ever moved back here, he would have to get rid of the lot.

"Good night, Daddy."

"What, did I fall asleep? What time is it?"

"Ten-thirty. You dozed."

"Oh. All right. Good night, baby."

The coffee table was cleared, the television set was off. She had done it. He tried the front door. It was open; he left it alone. The kitchen and dining room lights were out. There was no point in waiting for Karen.

He showered and put on a pair of pajamas. At five to eleven he padded out to the living room to pick up a couple of magazines.

Karen came in, cradling her briefcase against her chest. "Hi. Look at you. I'm sorry I'm late, honey, but the Superintendent had to have coffee and talk over how it went." She kissed him on the mouth, her lips cold.

"Steffie might still be awake. There's a doughnut for you. Do you want coffee? I'll have another one with you."

"Too much, I won't sleep. Let me say good night to Steffie." She went past him. He would have taken her coat and things, but she had moved too fast for him.

They collided in the hall as she came out of Steffie's room. "Can I get you anything?" he asked.

She looked at his eyes. "Are you so tired? Steffie told me you had fallen asleep. I'm sorry, Joe. I wouldn't have put you to this if I had known."

"Don't be silly. I'm all right. I'm waking up again."

"Get into bed and relax," she said. "I'll turn off the lights and check the door."

"I meant to do that," he said. He went into the bedroom. The MacIver file was on the night table, but he wasn't going to open it now. He had read it through one time; he just wanted to get it clearer in his mind. He turned on the switches regulating both halves of the electric blanket, propped up his pillows, and got into the bed.

She came in, opening her coat. "I'll be as quick as I can. Let me get into the shower. Did you get to look at the file again, at least?"

She went to hang up her coat. He had told her what he had hoped to do when she had driven him back into town. "No, I didn't look at it. Now I'm thinking I'll let it go until I see his mother and his first wife."

She came out of the closet in her stocking feet. "What about your custody case?" It was still a surprise to him to see how much shorter she was without her heels.

"The subject went shopping," he said. "Come over here and I'll unhook you."

She opened her jacket and went to her briefcase. "I bought a fresh *Herald-Press* so I could keep your scrapbook up to date. Are you going to hate me for wanting to be just a little bit of an idiot?"

She came over and sat on the edge of the bed. "I'll leave it here to see if you sneak a look while I'm in the bathroom." He held her sleeves while she pulled her arms out. She turned her back to him and he undid the bra snaps with a deft pinch-and-twist. A shrug and her bra fell into her lap. There were red welts under her arms where the straps had rubbed. When she slumped as she was doing now, he could march his fingers up the bones of her spine. She had freckles too thick to count on her arms and shoulders, but her back was so white it gave hints of blue. She looked over her shoulder at him. "I'm glad you're here tonight. We won't knock down any buildings, but we'll make it worthwhile."

"Let's just see how we do," he said.

She smiled. She was weary and her lipstick was chewed off. "Do you want to knock down a building? I don't suppose I can interest you in another shower."

"Nope."

"Will you dry me?"

"Nope."

"Come on, when was the last time you did that?" She kissed him. He wanted to take a little squeeze, but she had his arm pinned. The taste of the cold was still in her mouth, but she was getting to him. She sat up. "I'm sweaty and if I sit here for long, you're going to have to put me to bed like a drunk."

"Go get ready, a shower will make you feel better."

"You're subdued," she said. "I see that now."

"I didn't like falling asleep in front of Steffie. She'll think I'm getting old. I had told her we were going to make a night of it."

"You were tired. She knows that." She unfastened her skirt and sat there.

"I pulled a beaut with her this morning—maybe." He patted her thigh. "When I called to get you, I asked her how you had felt at breakfast. She didn't want to tell me that you had been showing the effect of last night. I said something on the order of not wanting her to judge what I should hear. Then she told me the truth, but maybe because she got the sense of my thoughts—that I had reason to believe you were upset. That damned note."

"Joe, we went through that at lunch."

"I know, I know. I'm talking about Steffie now. How was she when you checked?"

"All right."

"Mrs. MacIver was in the office when I was telling Steffie that I was coming over. She asked about her. She said Steffie sounded like a sweet kid. She asked me if I thought the way we're living has worked on her."

"And you've been thinking about it since," she said. "Therapy didn't teach her anything."

"No, I haven't been thinking about it," he said. "And what she said was all right when she said it. I told you about her."

Karen stood up and stepped out of her skirt. "Steffie knows who her father is. I don't want you ever thinking that you've let her down. You *know* that you haven't. Go in her room sometime and look at the pictures she has of us." She went to the closet to hang up her suit. "She started that whole business because of the pictures we had saved from the war."

"I know." The frames on Steffie's dresser were stuffed with every kind of picture of both of them. Buried beneath the snapshots and newspaper clippings on his side was an eight-by-ten of him holding one of the four blades of the prop of the Mustang. She had first learned who her father was from pictures like it and all the things her mother had told her.

Karen pulled up her half-slip and undid her garters. "Steffie might need us more than some other children need their parents," she said quietly, "but we'll never know how much of that is due to the war. It might have happened anyway, we've said that. We haven't let her down. Look at her. Would you want her any other way?"

"Look at you," he said. Her slip was hitched up and her stockings were falling down.

"For God's sake, Joe. I thought this was bothering you."

"I just wanted to hear you talk to me, I think," he said.

"I'll cut you a record to take to Port Smith," she said. She pulled off her stockings.

"Come on, Karen. I meant it."

114

Now the girdle. "I'm sorry. I don't need that little pussy trying you on for size."

"Where do you get that?"

She wasn't looking at him. Nude, she shook out the girdle and the half-slip. "You're not naïve, Joe. I saw her in the restaurant. I'm just glad she's as big as she is—although I don't think it would stop her."

"Karen, I *told* you. Do you want me to drop the case?"

"Of course not." She went to her pocketbook for her cigarettes. She was so slender that she seemed to float. "Let's just be straight on her." The cigarette pack jumped out of her hand and bounced on the floor. "She may have been sick, she may still be sick, but when I came over to you in the Flamingo, she had the expression of a kid who had just pulled her hand out of the cookie jar." She got her cigarette lit. "If she can't sleep with you, she'll settle for less. I know what I'm talking about."

"Come over here. Please? Karen, please."

She sat down beside him. The softness of the mattress made her slump again. She folded her arms across her stomach. He said, "Remember before the war when I was on plainclothes patrol on State Street? Remember what Marty Harris used to say?"

She nodded.

"I want you to say it."

"I'm not a baby, Joe."

"Come on."

"He would look at the girls, but he would throw the action to his wife."

"Are you going to come to Port Smith this weekend?"

"You know I don't like to go there."

"I know. You go for my parents on the holidays. This time do it for me."

"I'll see." He tried to caress her. She sat up, to look better. He didn't care.

"I've been rocking along all day," he said. "I've been waiting to take it out on you."

"It was that note."

"It was everything. Everything."

She smiled. "Now you're ready to get laid."

He sat up. "Not tonight. Tonight I want to make love to you."

"That was nice. Thank you." She kissed his forehead, then got up and turned around so he could pat her bottom. He made sure not to watch her cross to the bathroom. She would think that he was judging her mood, figuring how to act. When the door closed, he made a pawing grab at one of the magazines, then left it where it was. The cigarettes falling out of her hand had told him where he stood. He hadn't seen Norma MacIver's expression as she had seen it, but he knew that she was right about what had been going on. Norma had all but said it. And he had spent most of the morning, it seemed on reflection, thinking about Norma as a bedmate.

The shower started. He looked at the ceiling. The walls were done in a pale lime green, making the ceiling the softest white imaginable. He wanted Karen to come to Port Smith. More honestly at this moment, he wished he could insist on an end to this. When they had begun to see each other again, more than four years ago, she had said that he could not come back to live with them only to leave again. If he came back, he came back to stay, and if he left, they would have to divorce. She was right. No one, particularly Steffie, could live in such confusion. Karen was as hard on herself as a monk, but she thought it was necessary; if he wanted her, he had to accept the conditions she felt she had to impose on herself. He knew that he could not argue. He had seen the results.

People assumed things about him because of the war and the Leikman case, and if they heard stories about her—it was still possible, and she never forgot—they assumed other things about her. They had to know her. Few people ever got it right, even then. Up here, if they knew her but had only met him, they guessed that he had something that could not be determined in the equation of their marriage. The people she worked with were in awe of her competence with people and her crisp rationality. In her five years in Manitou she had advanced to Assistant Superintendent of Schools, in charge of the junior highs, and if she were a man, they would be grooming her as the Superintendent's successor. That was part of what made the

116

people she worked with look for an indeterminable factor in him. He had been too close to the blood and despair of life. He had had his hands in it. Her friends did not want to believe that she had carried the child of a man who had done what he had done.

She wanted to carry more. In the bind they had achieved, she had to hope to. All through their marriage, however their circumstances had shifted, they had tried to be equals—something *he* never forgot: inside, he had always had to strive to be her equal. Tending children negated the feeling of equality in her, a fact they had learned to their sorrow. Currently, she could not turn her back on what her work had done for her; she could not take the chance. She was afraid of what would happen to the competence, and more, the crisp rationality. He saw it more clearly: she was doing something useful and important while he was in a business he could take no pride in. He was a businessman, a moneymaker. She would not be able to lean on that for her sense of worth. Neither could he. If she gave up her job, his own sense of worth would all but disappear. As it stood, it was through her need and his inconvenience that he felt useful. In that they were alike; they wanted to feel that they were not only taking.

They had come to this separately, achieved this logjam of hope, but she wanted to share the responsibility for what he had done to himself. He had wanted to be a cop, and had given it up on account of what she had done in Port Smith. He would not have that. There was no responsibility to share and no need for guilt. She fought that, but he was right. He had made his own decision. If anything, it proved how much he had to have her.

He could move in tomorrow if they were willing to surrender the idea of having more children, but then there would be nothing to work for or aspire to. This time she would not feel it alone. It was true that while he had been a cop he had had a sense of direction. He could settle no more than she for a life in which the goal was money. While they had this apparent impasse, they had the illusion of direction: they could believe that they were getting closer, closer to being able to do it all. The hope was that he could make his business big enough and important enough to fill the needs of both of them. Then she would not be afraid of what tending children could do. They had agreed on it long ago. She was thirty-seven years old and having children now would shatter her youth. Yet she looked forward to it. They *were* getting closer; beneath the illusion was a very real hope. It was still too soon to think about, much less discuss again. They stayed half in illusion, half in fact, and involved in a necessary myth they never discussed. He loved her more than ever, she loved him. They had accomplished that. And they were not worried about Steffie. From where they had found themselves, it was a long way to have come.

The shower stopped. He thought of her drying herself in the clouds of steam. He grabbed again at one of the magazines, then reached for the newspaper. He looked at his picture, "WAR HERO COP WHO TRACKED DOWN LEIKMAN'S KILLER." That was enough. He put the newspaper and the magazines on the floor.

She came out. She was wearing a long flannel nightgown and she had brushed her hair back from her face. Her skin, the little he could see of it now, was pink from the hot water. Her powder and eye makeup were gone, and her green eyes seemed pale compared to the way he was used to seeing them. She opened the window. She could not sleep without fresh air; the nightgown was a guard against catching cold.

She got into bed and made herself comfortable on her back. She looked up at him. "Share a cigarette with me?"

"I thought I was smoking too much."

She smiled mischievously. "You're not afraid of a little cancer, are you?"

"There's a joke about that."

"You told me. That's why I said it." She watched him light the cigarette. He offered it to her. Her body radiated warmth. He could smell the soap mixed with the oils of her skin. "I didn't check on you," she said. "Did you look at the paper?"

"At my picture. If I had any sense, I'd send them a new one." He took the cigarette.

"Turn out the light."

He did. "The shower make you feel better?"

"Yes. One more drag and that's enough for me." There was a

118

convulsion on her side of the bed. She was arching her back and pulling up her nightgown. He held the cigarette to her lips. "Good," she said. "You finish it." She rolled against him, lifting her knee over his thigh. He put his arm around her and pulled her gown up more. Her back was still damp. He tucked the covers around her. She opened his pajamas slowly and rubbed his stomach with the tips of her fingers. "Do you love me?" she asked.

"I always have," he said. He snubbed out the cigarette and put the ash tray on the night table. He groped around: the ash tray went on the MacIver file. He cradled Karen's head against his chest and kissed her hair. "I've always loved you."

"Do you think you'll do anything in Port Smith?"

"I don't know."

"You can still do whatever you want," she said. "You know that."

"I know."

"Have you thought about it?"

"What?"

"Doing things with her."

"A little." He wanted to stop her. He turned her head up and kissed her on the mouth. She moved up, kissing him deeply. When he opened his eyes, she was looking at him. The window was near her side of the bed; the light from it let him see her eyes. She was almost sitting up.

"This is our business, isn't it?"

"Of course," he said.

"I never think this way out of bed anymore," she said. "You know that."

"Yes, I know that."

"I had to say it. I had to get it out of my system. I don't want you to do anything with her."

"I know that, too."

She smiled. "What I want doesn't matter, does it."

"No, it doesn't. I'll do what I want."

"That's right, that's right. I love you." She kissed him, kissed his neck. He tried to move her toward him. She breathed steadily, deeply.

"Come on," he said.

"I'd die for you, Joey."

He smiled. "I'm not asking for that, Freckles."

It was a litany they had started in college, one of many ways they could say they were happy.

"I love you," she said again. "I've been waiting all day to be with you."

"I'm sorry I was rough on you this afternoon."

She shook her head. "I'm still your baby, aren't I, Joey?" He said yes as her eyes got heavier and she buried herself against his neck. He said it again and they began to move. She kissed his neck and pressed herself against him more. She hurried, trying to stifle the sound she made. She squeezed him, crying, kissing her way to his mouth. The bed rattled. She drove him on, running her knuckles up over his ribs suddenly; he started, he couldn't stop. She made him keep going another full minute, then she threw herself against him. She stayed quiet, pressing her lips to his lips.

Slowly, still together, they rolled onto their sides. He ran his hand over her back.

She kissed his chin. "My leg will go to sleep."

He let her straighten out. He was the one who was falling asleep. As always, it was like going over backwards, perfectly safe.

CHAPTER SEVEN

■ ■

JOE LELAND ENTERED THE ARMY AIR CORPS IN 1942 WITH A RANK IN
the Port Smith Police Department of Detective Second Grade, the
middle rank in detectives, three steps up the ladder of promotion. He
had attained that rank in two and a half years, very rapidly by the
standards of the Department, which worked on a test-and-merit system, but by no means as rapidly as some men had moved during the
days of spoils and patronage. Leland's good fortune had come as a
result of the action that had also led to his citation for valor, five days
after he had got out of the Academy grays. He had been promoted the
next day by the Commissioner to Plainclothes Patrolman, and a year
later he had scored high grades on the test for Detective Third Grade.
Before his enlistment in the Army he had taken the test for Detective Second Grade and, by nothing but a fluke, had made the highest
grade of that year. He had been first on the list and had served a total
of eight days in the new grade when he had been advised that he was
subject to the draft. He and Karen had decided to use his freedom of
choice while he still had it. He had been in the Air Corps a year and
a half when, under political pressure, the Port Smith City Council
passed a measure permitting servicemen to compete in civil service
examinations. Thus, in England, Leland became a Detective Lieutenant in a police force he did not work for; and in 1946 when he was
discharged, he became, at twenty-eight, second in command of detectives in the Fifth Precinct, the toughest and busiest precinct in the
city.

On the North Side, the Fifth covered the lower part of Westlake, a rundown section of brownstones, walk-ups, and neighborhood stores. Its social problems were small and crime rate low. The half of Westlake that the Fifth took in occupied half of the Fifth's territory, but less than twenty percent of its men and time. Westlake, after the war, was still a place where social workers never went.

The rest of the Fifth was beyond the aid of those not armed. That included the entertainment district, embracing State Street, and the repository of the city's gravest ills, known to the Post Office as Port Smith 3, but called Joytown by the population or, less openly, Port Smith 69. It paralleled State Street down to Lewis Park, a cuff of grass at the edge of the bay.

Joytown was a mile long and six blocks wide, centering on Pleasance Street—the name since Colonial times, and the butt of countless bad jokes. The buildings were old, two, three, and four stories, most with mansard roofs. They were cold-water flats, rooming houses, and hotels. Some were simply condemned above the street floor. In spite of the disruption to commerce of the area, the fire laws were strictly enforced.

On any Wednesday afternoon with ten men on sick call, the Fifth Precinct could clean out Joytown: prostitutes, pimps, homos, junkies, pushers, vagrants, and bums; but that night and Thursday morning ninety-five percent of them would be rightly on the street again for lack of evidence. On Thursday afternoon the newspapers would attack the police for having sought headlines, which the papers had given eagerly. On Friday, a whore or pimp would complain of police brutality, and the Commissioner, following the law, would suspend the implicated officer until a hearing could be convened. Commercial and entertainment interests in Port Smith had a use for Joytown, and this was the context in which the police enforced the laws.

The pushers and pimps remained their fair game. Brazen whores were run in for sentences of sixty days. Sex offenders were handled with dispatch. There had never been a kidnapping in the modern era, and the last murder case in which the killer had not been found with his victim had occurred in 1944, when a soldier on leave had strangled a prostitute. Burglaries took most of the time of the Fifth

122

Detective Squad, collecting evidence, interviewing, waiting for breaks. Brawlings in which no complaints were made were not counted in the squad's statistics. The rest of its business required speed. Muggings and heists were solved in an hour or two, or not at all. Rapes, those that were reported, generally took a few days: most were the result of bad pickups. The Fifth detectives, and more particularly the men not assigned to burglary details, were called the Bucket Brigade. On busy nights they did nothing but answer the phones and run.

In 1948, night tour still began at six P.M. and ran twelve hours. On the third Friday in March, Joe Leland checked in feeling quite chipper. It had been a blustery day but a pleasant one. The cool air had helped him sleep well after his tour the night before, and in the afternoon he and Karen had taken Steffie to the playground and then to a restaurant for dinner. He had left them outside a movie—Greer Garson and Walter Pidgeon in something or other—and Karen had asked to be awakened when he came home at a quarter to seven the next morning.

The early hours were quiet, as always, but the men braced for a big weekend. The weather had been bad the previous two weekends, when the hooples, the troublemakers, had hoped to come out of their winter shells. This was going to be a hoople night; the men said it as they came in.

Leland, in charge, wanted the pending paperwork cleared up quickly. At nine o'clock there was a stickup of a delicatessen in Westlake. At nine-thirty a patrolman found a man exposing himself in Lewis Park. The man was without identification and refused to give his name. He was put in the squad room tank while a description was circulated and the cars around Lewis Park were marked. Cars that did not move in twenty-four hours would be checked for owner-ship. Leland was confident that the man would be identified this way, if his family did not submit a missing persons report first. At ten o'clock, near State Street, a man approached a lone woman, punched her in the face, called her Clara—not her name—and ran into the crowd. It seemed to be a case of mistaken identity and Leland thought that they had better forget it. In the meantime, a burglary was reported on Annadale Avenue, one of the better blocks on the fringe of Joytown. Two men went over to get a list of what had been taken. At ten-forty a suspect in the delicatessen stickup was brought in, newly drunk, and thrown in the tank with the sex offender. A plainclothes patrolman brought in a whore for soliciting on State Street. When the two men came back with the burglary list it was eleven-thirty and the police buff who assisted the desk sergeant downstairs was sent out for sandwiches and coffee.

At one-thirty when the call came in there had been quiet for an hour. The whore was in the women's jail and the stickup suspect had been identified. The sex offender watched them all interestedly, entertained and calmed. Six men were on duty, three in a whispered conversation by the windows, Schoenstein, Leland's partner and second lowest in seniority, handling the calls, and Leland juggling the schedule for April, when Quillan, one of the senior men, was taking his vacation to get married again after three years of widowerhood. He was marrying his son's mother-in-law, variously "to give my kid a break," "to keep my feet warm," and "to give myself a heart attack." He had the good humor of a man who considered himself lucky.

Schoenstein took a call, listened, and reached for his pad. "Yes, Robbie. All right. Forty-seven Forster. Right. Thanks, Robbie." He hung up. "Joe?" He looked at Leland as if stricken. "Murder. It's a mess."

Leland was getting up. "Put on your coat. That was Robbie Loughran?" Schoenstein, a handsome blond young man, nodded. Over his shoulder, to the men at the window, Leland said, "Reynolds, take over the phone. Curran, get the camera, the lights, plenty of film." He looked to Schoenstein for more information.

"Robbie was pretty upset."

"Never mind that stuff. Get the kit. Reynolds, start calling from the bottom of the roster. Get four men. Leave the Captain alone. If he checks in, give him what we have. Unless I tell you otherwise, we're on top of it. Get a medical examiner over to Forty-seven Forster. As we need men, start with Tanner and Maule. You stay on the phone no matter what happens."

Downstairs, they picked up a uniformed officer to drive. In the car, Schoenstein reported that Robbie Loughran had said that he had

124

never seen anything like it. Loughran was not a very emotional man but he had been doing his best to control himself. He had touched nothing and he had called from the landlady's apartment. The landlady had discovered the body. Leland took it in, trying to clear his mind for all the jobs he had to do. After a while Danny Curran suggested that they pin their shields on their lapels. It was a little thing, but it showed that he was getting ready, too.

There were two prowl cars nosed in at the curb on Forster Street, and a crowd stood buffing on the sidewalk. The red flashers on the cars swept the first-floor windows on both sides of the block. Inside the red brick building, the landlady's apartment door was open and she could be heard crying within. Loughran was waiting for them.

"Hiya, Robbie," Leland said. "Making work for us?"

"Finding it, Joe. You're not going to like this. Carl is up at the apartment door. I'm the only one who's seen it—and the landlady. She didn't touch the body. She says she needs a cup of tea, and she does, too."

"Have someone give it to her, Robbie, and you come up with us. Dave, tell the guys outside not to let anybody without a badge in or out. They're to be held. The man who flubs this one can kiss his career goodbye, and that's no kidding."

Schoenstein nodded and went up the hall. Leland and Danny Curran waited for him and then for Loughran. The four went up the stairs. Loughran said, "The landlady is Mrs. Agnes McFee, a widow. She says that the body is her tenant, Theodore Leikman, L,e,i,k,m,a,n. She thinks it is, anyway. Lived alone. The body is mutilated, Joe. She found him twenty minutes ago, after she heard some noise. I was around the corner when I heard her screaming."

"You did a good job, Robbie. Thanks." Carl Schultzer stepped aside for them and they went into the apartment.

There was a little foyer, six-by-six, and the main room spread off to the left. The kitchen was at the back. The bedrooms would be off at the right. The place was not a cold-water flat; it seemed, in fact, to be a place most people would find desirable.

On the foyer floor, beyond the swing of the front door, was a lump of white pottery, a hollow broken piece of something, about the size of a softball. It was smeared with blood and gray slime. Loughran, just behind Leland, said, "Mrs. McFee doesn't think she kicked that or banged it with the door. The door was ajar when she came up. She's pretty sure she kept her hands off of everything. She goes to the movies a lot. The body is in the bedroom on the right side of that hall."

The living room had expensive, handsome furnishings, which were now in disarray. The contents of an ash tray were scattered across the top of the coffee table; there was some more broken china, lighter and thinner than the chunk in the foyer. From across the room the pieces appeared to be clean. Opposite the sofa and the coffee table was a liquor cabinet, doors open. On top was a phonograph. A record was on the turntable and there were other records, unjacketed, on top of the cabinet. A couple of highball glasses were beside the records and a cigarette butt floated in the liquid of one of them. If there had been any ice in the glasses, it was melted.

"Danny," Leland said, "take a series of overlapping views of this room. Move in on the obvious things. Get a couple of shots of that thing in the hall, then fish it up onto a newspaper and put it in a place where it won't be kicked."

"I'll tape off the room, too," Curran said.

"Just the foyer," Leland said. "The rest has to be dusted. Give Dave a hand with that when you have the pictures. Dave, is there a piece of chalk?"

"Yes, Joe."

"Give it to Danny and let him do the marking as he goes around. Let's have a look in the bedroom."

There were other doors off the hall, all closed. Leland said, "Dave, check out those knobs so we can have a look at the rest of the place. Robbie, do you have anything else to tell us?"

"Just that the landlady said that Leikman lived alone, he was a designer of some kind, and was in his early twenties—you may not be able to tell. She heard voices up here from about six o'clock on, but Leikman was a quiet tenant generally and she left him alone. It was

126

quiet awhile and then there was more noise, more or less continuous from eleven o'clock, and then at one o'clock she heard the door bang hard, but not so that it caught—as if the bolt had been thrown first. She didn't hear anyone on the stairs, she was very clear about that, because she was alerted by the strange sound of the door. She waited for someone to come down. Then she got an 'eerie feeling,' she called it, and decided to come up. The door was ajar."

"What kind of noises? Did she say?"

"Shouts and banging around, like a violent argument. But not a brawl. Then there was just banging around. I didn't press her, Joe, because I didn't think she could take it. After I saw the body I thought of the roof but decided too much time had passed—she said about ten minutes—and I called in."

"Okay. She gets along with you, so go down and keep her happy. Don't say anything about further questioning. Stop out front and tell them to get two men up here with flashlights. And tell them to call the squad and get Maule and Tanner over here. This takes top priority. Anyone who wants to come in or out—run them into the landlady's apartment until we've taken statements. She'll let us use her place, I think."

"Knobs are clear, Joe," Dave Schoenstein said. "There's another bedroom here with some things you'll want to see."

"Okay. Anything else, Robbie?"

"Just him in there," Loughran said.

"We'll handle him. Ready, Dave?"

"Sure—"

Leland did not know if Schoenstein saw the body first or if the wind only seemed to go out of him because Leland's own reaction affected his hearing. His eyes reacted, he knew, and his stomach, and his heart. His heart seemed to jam. In 1940 as a rookie he had seen three healthy men die in the interval of two minutes, and during the war he had seen airplanes explode and unmistakable pieces of flesh fall through the air, but those experiences had not hit him with the calculated, terrible cruelty of this.

Theodore Leikman stared back. He was naked, sitting on the floor, his legs spread. His body, gray now, was smeared with finger-marks of blood. His right hand seemed to end in a pool of blood. The hand, at first glance, seemed shredded. The eyes had that dry, soft shine; they stared at Leland because they had rolled up and the head had tilted down. His tongue protruded from the corner of his mouth, which was encrusted with blood. Above his eyes, like a forelock, was a gray mass like something boiled over. The back of his skull was dented in like a punctured rubber ball. There was blood four feet up the wall behind him, on the dresser beside him and, Leland saw in the corner of his eye, in splatters on the bed. He looked again at the hand. The thumb and forefinger had been removed. There was blood in the crotch. The penis had been cut off, in the same shredded way.

"Oh, Jesus," Schoenstein said. "Joe, I'm going to be sick."

"No," Leland said. "Tense your muscles. Swallow and hold it." He stepped into the room, his skin prickling. There was the dank odor of blood. He stepped carefully over the body and walked around the bed. The shade on the night-table lamp had been knocked awry, which accounted for the harsh light. The bed was a double with both pillows impressed and one darkly soiled. Schoenstein was watching him like a boy. Leland went around to the other side of the bed, careful where he put his feet. "Get out your notebook, Dave."

"What is it, Joe?"

"One of the missing parts. I want to have an idea of where it was in case somebody gets sloppy."

"Want the tape?"

"No, I'll use my hand. Go tell Danny to watch his step in here." Like many detectives, Leland knew the measurements of his hand. He could reckon distances to a thirty-second of an inch.

When he was done he made his way to the pillows, not touching anything, talking as he looked around. "I want a lab report on Leikman's hair tonic, a list of the contents of the medicine cabinet, and I want to know from the autopsy when Mr. Leikman had his last ejaculation."

"There's a bed in the other room."

"Okay. I want the pillow cases analyzed for hair tonic and the sheets checked for semen stains. The same for that bed, too. We'll look at that in a minute." In the ash tray was a cigarette butt with far more ashes than even two or three cigarettes could have made. Leland passed the information on to Schoenstein.

"The men with the flashlights are here."

"Keep them outside. We're still missing the thumb and the index finger. Don't forget that. Tell everyone to watch where they're walking. I'm coming out."

In the living room he told the patrolmen what they were looking for, and what to cover. When they were done with the roofs and the back yards, they were to search the sewers and garbage cans for four blocks in every direction. Maule and Tanner came in and were told to take over the job of dusting for prints. Leland wanted Schoenstein for collating data.

The second bedroom, smaller than the first, was as stark as the rest of the apartment was finely furnished. Leland's shoes crunched on the bare floor. When he took another step his shoes crunched again, grittily. He rocked his weight back and forth and stared at Schoenstein. "Too coarse for sugar."

"Sand."

"Scoop it up. Maybe we'll be able to place it."

The bed was a single with a folding metal frame, loosely made. The pillow had the same dirty stain as the other. The dresser, a cheap one, had been cleaned out, for the drawers were open and Leland could see inside them. He nudged open the closet door with his foot. On the floor, in the corner of the closet, was a lump of dark material—it seemed like wool. From the middle of the floor Leland picked up a quarter-inch crumb of black shiny material. Patent leather. He held it in his palm until Schoenstein stood up. "Something for an envelope. It might be helpful."

Danny Curran's flashbulbs were going off in the big bedroom. Leland waited until he came out. "I got everything. I saw that thing on the floor, too."

"We'll wait for you to work through here. Don't miss the thing in the corner of the closet."

"More?" Curran asked.

Leland shook his head. "It's a sweater or something." He stepped back for him. "Dave, labels on everything."

"Right, Joe."

Curran took his pictures and slipped the plates into his shoulder bag. "We don't need these right away, do we?"

"No," Leland said. "Put the bag out in the hall with Carl and give us a hand here."

The sweater, a medium-sized bulky-knit navy blue, was taken from the closet and labeled, and Schoenstein made a note to have it checked for hair tonic and hair. The sweater's owner probably was headed out of town, but there was no way to stop him. He had lived here almost secretly, because the woman just downstairs had had no knowledge of his existence. A sweater of this type and hair tonic made him a young man. Light-haired men rarely used hair tonic in large quantities. In a change of mind, Leland told Schoenstein to reverse the sweater here and now and go over it for hair. Leland could feel himself becoming impatient. He wanted to work on the other room, but he was forbidden to disturb the body in any way until the medical examiner had made a preliminary inspection.

"Hair," Schoenstein reported. "Dark brown curly. You can see it. The sweater smells of body odor and all the spring is out of the wool."

"Okay. Maybe we can get some more. Dan, let's you and I turn down this bed. Dave, watch the bed while we turn, in case we start to disturb anything we can't see."

These sheets, too, were splattered with semen stains. The sheets were limp, as if they had been slept on many nights, and the bottoms of them were smeared with dirt. "Tape off the bed," Leland said.

It was seventy-two inches long. The smears of dirt did not come closer than three inches to the bottom of the bed. The pillow was squared away with the top. "I make him to be a little guy," Curran said. "Five-five or five-six."

"Short, but not little," Leland said. "The sweater says he's broader than you or me. If he took our friend in there, he's strong as hell."

"If?" Curran asked.

"I'm not thinking anything yet—but I do want to talk to the guy."

"Who's in charge here?" a voice in the living room demanded.

"In the bedroom."

There were two men, one the assistant medical examiner, a wry young Irishman Leland had met two or three times before on suicides. The other was a surprise, Herbert A. Davis, whom they all knew. He was active in public affairs, not a politician or a representative of any special interest, and over the years he had been appointed to a dozen committees and authorities. "Are you in charge here?" he asked Leland. He was a large, fleshy man in his late fifties, six feet two inches tall and over two hundred and twenty pounds.

"That's right, Mr. Davis. What's your business here?"

"I have a badge from the sheriff's office."

"This is beyond his jurisdiction. I have to ask you to leave. You're not qualified to handle evidence."

"I think I can lend a hand," he said. He had a voice trained in public speaking, full and intimidating.

"Dave, show Mr. Davis to the street. I'll take the responsibility."

"You're making a mistake," Herbert Davis said.

"Dave, if he gives you trouble, cuff and frisk him and run him down to the station. He shouldn't be up here in the first place."

"I'll be back," Davis warned. "What's your name?"

"My name is Joseph Leland. There's a procedure for making complaints. Dave?"

Schoenstein followed Davis out of the room. The medical examiner turned away to laugh. Curran stared at Leland as if there had been a lapse in his sanity. Public figures were treated with deference at fires and crime scenes. There was too much to do here for that silliness, Leland was sure. The evidence was scant enough, and there was a good chance that things would get worse before they would get better.

"There were reporters downstairs," the medical examiner said. "You've bought it. Your war record may get you off, but he's still going to make you dangle."

"Get the reporters, Dan," Leland said. "They'll be more interested in this, anyway."

"Show me the stiff," the examiner said. "I don't want to get caught in the crossfire."

"In the other room."

Leland told him what he wanted to know.

"Swell," the examiner said when he saw Leikman. "He's dead. You can quote me. He didn't commit suicide, either."

"The faster you give us the stuff, the faster we'll get our man," Leland said.

"Stop kidding yourself. From now on, in Sunday supplements across the country, you're 'The Hapless Detective.' "

With Curran and Schoenstein, Leland met the reporters in the hall. "Davis says you're stumped," said one. "What about it?"

"We're in good shape. I'll give you a quick briefing on what we have, then you can come in and take a few pictures. We're going to restrict you, but you'll understand why. The victim is Theodore Leikman, the tenant. Early twenties, white man. He was bludgeoned to death around midnight with a china bookend or bric-a-brac. It would kill anybody. The corpse was found mutilated and nude by a woman in the building, who found the door ajar and the lights on. You can't talk to her yet. The mutilations are sexual. Although Leikman passed himself off as living alone, he had a roommate, on whom we have a very good fix. The roommate cleared out quite suddenly, and we're looking for him."

"How soon on an arrest?"

"Not long."

"Leikman a homo?"

"He had a secret roommate. That's all I can tell you for now."

"What about Herbert Davis? What was he doing here?"

"He came as a representative of the sheriff's office."

"The sheriff has no jurisdiction here," a reporter said.

"You have the ball," Leland said. "Run with it."

"How soon can we get in the murder room?"

"We have a lot to do. Sorry."

"What about the mutilations?"

"That's all I can give you now."

"Pictures?"

"The murder room when we've been in there. Forget the body. If we turn up a snapshot of Leikman we'll pass it to you."

"Pictures of you, Lieutenant?"

"Headquarters has shots of us all. What you get downstairs and so forth is up to you." He turned to Carl Shultzer and nodded, then went back into the apartment. The appearance of Davis had forced him to see the reporters, because Davis had a way of making anyone or anything opposing him look incompetent, shirking, or corrupt. Leland had been obliged to protect the Department, the Precinct, and the men on this case, including himself; but now he had to realize that he could not conduct the investigation itself in response to bullying tactics. False steps could wreck a case. Still, a statement would come from Davis' office tomorrow, obscuring the facts and pressing Leland's superiors—Davis would go a long way to cover his own sudden embarrassing exit here tonight. For the sake of all, Leland had to appear to be making important moves. Davis' ego and influence were that powerful, as all those who had had even the most remote contact with him could testify. Davis had a public following that was not interested in his personality. It respected him as a figure of unstinting, expert beneficence. Weighing it all, and still wondering why Davis had come here in the first place, Leland made his decisions.

He asked Maule and Tanner if they were getting any prints.

"We peeled some beauts off the liquor cabinet and the glasses. One of those drinks is nonalcoholic, by the way," Tanner said.

To Curran, Leland said, "We're going to issue a call for a John Doe, white, middle twenties or early thirties, five-five or five-six, heavyset or broad build, dark-brown wavy hair. Conscious of his appearance. May be carrying suitcases and bearing the marks of a fight. Wanted for murder. That will go out to the counties and the State Police as well. He may be on the roads."

"It's slim, Joe."

"You think we're plunging? We could have given that to the newspapers. All I want is a little luck."

Curran shook his head and went out. Leland, with Schoenstein in tow, went around to the master bedroom. The body had been moved, slumped down and twisted on its side. The eyes bulged and the jaw hung ajar. On the wall against which it had rested was a smear of brownish red and dirty gray, surrounded by a spotted outline of Curran's chalk. The medical examiner, on one knee beside the corpse, looked up with his mouth twisted unpleasantly. "He's been dead about two hours, perhaps two and a half. Figure eleven-thirty to midnight. There are chips of china in his skull, so that fixes that crockery you have there. The blows on the head did kill him, very little doubt of that. He was hit a dozen, fifteen, maybe twenty times. Needless to say, the man who did this is capable of practically anything. The mutilations—well, I slept through my psych courses." He stood up, looking down at the corpse. "Junior, here, was a homosexual. He had a liaison shortly before his death. He's wearing some kind of fruity perfume, but it doesn't solve his problem." He began to pull off his rubber gloves. "The mutilations were done with a dull knife—dull edge. That kind of home surgery really requires a razor. I didn't see the fingers. I'll just take smears of the matter on that piece of pottery." He coughed. "The contents of his stomach will be analyzed—that goes without saying. I'll call my boss now, so you'll have your report early tomorrow morning." He sighed. "Ever have a fairy sneer at you? They do it all the time. The next one who does it I'll kill myself."

"An interesting attitude, Doctor," Leland said, deadpan.

"Sure. I checked the fingernails he has left. They're clean, no foreign matter under them. They've been professionally manicured and painted with clear polish. Is there anything else I can help you with? If not, I'll call the office. I have to go down to the wagon for a jar and some slides. What a mess. It's so uplifting to learn about the way other people live." He stepped between them to get out.

When Curran came back Leland told him to get Robbie Loughran and go through the building for tenants who knew anything about Leikman and his habits. Leland and Schoenstein went downstairs to question the landlady. Because of the configuration of the first floor hall, her small quarters were under Leikman's room only in certain areas. Mrs. McFee was an old lady who followed the radio programs and she was very certain of her times. The noise had started around six o'clock and had stopped between seven-fifteen and seven-thirty, when she had been listening to Smilin' Jack Smith. It had begun again at eleven o'clock, when she had heard voices, but the walls and floors were too thick for her to have made out any conversation. She had heard some other sounds, like things being pushed around, and then, at one o'clock exactly, while she had been waiting for the remote broadcast from the Travelers Hotel because they had Les Brown and that lovely Doris Day singing "Sentimental Journey," she had heard the door slam in that funny way. She knew nothing about Mr. Leikman except that he was a quiet, well-mannered boy who paid his rent on time. He was studying to be a clothes designer. He had been living in the building fourteen months.

Automatically Leland asked her to get all the rent receipts for that period, thinking that Leikman might have met and befriended someone who had since moved out. While Schoenstein made that list, Dan Curran brought in a young girl wearing a housecoat and slippers. Her dark hair was up in curlers. Curran introduced her as Carol Linjak.

"What's this about Teddy?"

"Soon enough, Miss Linjak. We'd like you to help us with a few things first—"

"At this hour? You people go around waking people up just to casually ask questions? I insist on knowing why you're doing this."

"Your friend Teddy was murdered," Leland said.

"I don't believe you."

"Take our word for it. You may be able to help us find his murderer if you cooperate."

She stared a moment, deciding. "All right," she said brusquely. "What do you want to know?"

"When was the last time you saw him?"

"Tuesday evening in the hall. I was coming home from a date and Teddy came out of his apartment. We bumped into each other. It was about eleven o'clock."

"Can you tell us how you're sure of this?"

"My date was with me. I went out with Teddy, too. I had to introduce them, and it was difficult—strained. For me, anyway. Do you want my date's name?"

"Yes, I think so."

She gave his name and address. "We're friends. Teddy and I were friends, too. I knew he was gay. He never said it, but I think he thought I knew. Anyway, he didn't care. At least, he didn't try to prove he wasn't. He would come upstairs and ask if I wanted to go to a dance or something and if I said yes we would go. He had to make an appearance at his job and he used me for that. We could talk about movies and books and so forth. Some of the men I met at these affairs asked me for my telephone number but I said no so that he wouldn't be, um, you know. I can't think of the word."

"Cuckolded. It doesn't strictly apply. Where did he work?"

"Western Union. In the central office. He was a teletype operator."

"What about his designing?"

"That was something he talked about. He said he was saving his money to go to a fashion school, but he wasn't saving quickly. You saw the way his apartment is furnished."

"What about his friends? Did you meet any of them?"

"No."

"Did he ever say or do anything to indicate to you how he made his other contacts?"

She regarded him. "That was well put. No."

"And all the time you knew him, he lived alone?"

"No. For the past couple of months or so, he had a roommate, companion, boyfriend, whatever you want to call him. I saw him once and heard him another time. A short, stocky fellow. Very muscular."

"What color hair?"

"Dark brown. It was long and he had sideburns, like an actor. The time I saw him I was coming down the stairs and he was going into their apartment with the mail. He was wearing a T-shirt. The other time I rang their bell and Teddy answered and I heard this fellow and when I apologized for interrupting, Teddy said no, it was just his roommate. I didn't ask."

"When was the last time you went out with Leikman?"

"Before Christmas. That was the time I rang his bell to find out what time he was going to pick me up. It was an office party, December twenty-third."

"You're not very upset by Leikman's death, Miss Linjak."

She looked at him coldly. "I'm not going to show you whether I am or not. That's clear, isn't it?"

"Absolutely," he said. "You've been a very big help. I must ask you not to discuss any of this with anybody, especially the newspapers. Don't speak to them at all."

"I'll be hearing from you?"

"That's right. Good night."

Curran moved to escort her back to her room, and she said to him, "I know where I live, thank you." Leland gave him a sign to let her go.

"Cop-hater," Curran said when she was gone.

Leland shook his head. "She was right. She didn't have to show us anything."

"She got us off the hook with that description," Curran said.

"Maybe that's our little bit of luck—a rattleproof, trustworthy woman. Was there anyone else?"

"No. I wish I knew how you figure trustworthy."

"Leikman trusted her. By her account, she didn't let him down. As a matter of fact, I kind of like her myself. Let's see what's cooking upstairs."

"I'm getting an education," Schoenstein said before they went into the Leikman apartment. "I feel like the dumbest cop alive."

"Don't let it throw you, boy," Curran said. "We're all doing only what our daddies taught us."

"I think I'll put you on report," Leland said.

"I meant in the general sense," Curran said, flustered. "That we were playing it by ear." He had forgotten about Leland's father.

"Relax," Leland said. "I'm needling you."

The uniformed patrolmen he had put on the search returned to report that they had found nothing. The fingerprint men finished the living room and the small bedroom and went on to the bathroom. Leland wished he had more testimony than he had: he was wary of laboratory evidence, not because he himself doubted its veracity, but because juries could be convinced that scientific methods were only so many steps of guesswork. As clearly as the scant evidence pointed to the roommate, Leland had not dismissed other ideas. There was too much that was not clear about the evening. Leland wanted to know exactly what had happened. There could have been another person—say one of those men who beat up homosexuals for the fun of it. How much trace of himself could he have left in one visit? By the landlady's account, people had been in and out—noise and silence. It was also possible that the landlady had entered and run out while the roommate had been packing his clothes. While she had run out he could have gone over the rooftops. Even so, Robbie Loughran probably could not have got him. How long would it have taken a man of the roommate's size and apparent condition to hurdle two-foot walls and find an unlocked access door? The slam of the apartment door could have been an accident, or the wind, or the invention of a nosy old woman who had come up in curiosity over the general noise. Leland decided to put all the ideas away for a while, and he told Schoenstein to note that they were to canvass the shops in the area to find someone who had seen Leikman and the roommate together.

While the three detectives dismantled the living room they played Leikman's records. There was a chance that some of the records weren't what their labels said. Under the cushions of the couch were two hairpins and an earring snarled in lint. The cigarette butts scattered out of the ash tray were all one brand, and again the ashes were too thick for the number of cigarettes. Curran said that many people flushed their cigarettes down the toilet. Leland thought it was a long walk to take in this apartment, and he was not satisfied until he remembered a girl he had known in college who would half-empty ash trays by picking out the butts and matchsticks while leaving the ashes. They would see.

Leikman had subscribed to *The New Yorker* and *Vogue,* and copies of *Vogue* had pages neatly removed. The detectives reckoned that the pages would turn up in Leikman's bedroom.

The examiner's men came to take away the body. Leland finished the chalk outline on the wall. In the small bedroom Curran and Schoenstein removed fibers from the joints of the dresser drawers. The mattress was turned over, for no reason, it developed. Schoenstein got on a chair and looked at the top of the closet. Nothing.

The fingerprint men finished in the bathroom and the three followed them in there. The fingerprint men went on to the master bedroom. They had found prints in all the rooms so far and no signs of wiping or fouling the surfaces. In burglaries, the men responsible either wiped everything in sight, or splashed it with soda pop, milk, and once, honey. Here there were over eighty prints which had to be sorted and matched and finally checked with the prints to be taken from Leikman, the landlady, the roommate when they found him, and anyone else who had been in the apartment in the past several days. Whatever was left would be sent to the files and, if necessary, passed on to Washington.

In the bathroom were pink towels and washcloths for two, a pink shower curtain and pink curtains on the window over the tub, which was spotless, like the other fixtures. There was an expensive scale, which Leland and Curran tried out. The roommate had taken his toothbrush, razor, blades, and shaving cream. In the medicine cabinet where the blades had left their marks were longish hairs, dark and softer than the beard of the roommate probably would be. Schoenstein swept them into an envelope. In the corner under the sink, Curran discovered a gallon bottle of light mineral oil, half-full. All three men hunkered on the bathroom floor and looked at the bottle.

"Well?" Leland asked.

"Somebody had constipation?" Curran said.

"Not Leikman," Schoenstein said.

"Not the roommate, either," Leland said. "It's not likely. This is for sedentary people. He wouldn't have those muscles Miss Linjak saw if he didn't work out. If he worked out, he wasn't sedentary and wouldn't have had constipation."

"Maybe he used it to oil his pal," Curran said.

"No, the medical examiner said grease. Why should they use something greasy if they have a vat of this stuff?"

"It's too thin, anyway," Schoenstein said. "It has to be thick, like Vaseline. Even Vaseline breaks down and gets viscous."

"How do you know?" Curran asked.

"Men and *women* use Vaseline," Schoenstein said.

"I wouldn't know," Curran said sourly.

"Neither would I," Leland said.

"Congratulations," Curran said to Schoenstein, who blushed. Leland laughed loudly. "So it isn't for that. Okay."

"Some people like to drink it," Schoenstein said.

Curran looked at him again. "Keep it up and you're going to be a suspect."

"Dave," Leland said, "maybe we ought to check the drugstores in the area to see if anyone remembers selling a gallon of mineral oil. Maybe Muscle Boy had a prescription filled out in the same store."

The other team finished with the dusting. Leland told them to return to the Precinct and draw up a preliminary report as concise as they could make it. On the way out they were to tell Carl Schultzer to stay at the apartment door until relieved. Robbie Loughran was to stay with the landlady and a third man was to cover the front. All other uniformed men could go back to their posts. The photographers could come up for their crime-scene shots; the buffs, if they were still there, were to be cleared away. Leland figured that he would have been called if the work at the Precinct had increased, so he said nothing changing the order bringing in additional men. He also figured that he would be back at the Precinct before the end of the tour, so he said nothing about who could go home at six o'clock—or later, if that had to be the case. The chief of the Fifth Detectives, Bill Richardson, followed the rule that the older men went home first, and until nine o'clock, when Richardson came in, Leland would follow that rule.

The photographers were allowed to shoot from the bedroom

140

door. They wanted to see where the "secret roommate" had stayed, and Leland let them have shots of the little bedroom. They asked if there was anything new, and Leland said that progress was being made. They were not happy with that. One of them grabbed a shot of Curran opening a dresser drawer and then the others had to have it, too. They had heard that there was a girl witness and they wanted pictures of her. Leland said not now and got them out of the apartment.

Apparently Leikman had put away the clothes he had worn that day. There was nothing around and all the hangers in the closet were in use. The hamper was in the closet, too, against the back wall, and on top of the small pile was a relatively fresh shirt, a set of underwear, and a pair of socks. Next was a set of pajamas and, under them, another shirt and more underwear and socks, one more set of pajamas—and then the bottom.

"I never saw a hamper in a closet before," Schoenstein said. "I don't think it's healthy."

It sounded right to Leland. Schoenstein was trying to get his head up. Leland said, "The important thing is, he put everything in here after one wearing. I get two wearings out of pajamas and sport shirts. In a nutty way, he was trying to be clean. It's a good thing to know about him."

"The poor bastard," Curran said. "He sent his stuff out, too. All of it. The things in the drawers show that."

"See his wallet?"

"It's in the top drawer. I didn't want the photographers to catch it."

"Nice going," Leland said. "I think we're doing all right."

"We have our problems," Curran said. He was in his late thirties and had several more years' experience than Leland. "You're doing a good job, Joe. You've made some fine catches, but when Davis put the buzz on you I thought it was going to get away from you. Don't let him make you wind up holding your ass."

That was a Department expression for failure. "Not on *this* case," Leland said.

Curran laughed. "Just take your time, that's all."

In the wallet they found fifty-seven dollars in paper, eighty cents in ordinary coins, four three-cent postage stamps, and an 1859 Indian head penny, the value of which they were not qualified to determine. There was a dentist's appointment booklet, a local dry cleaner's receipt, a ticket from a Chinese laundry on the next block. In another compartment was an assortment of business cards: a doctor's, one from a home furnishings store, another from a Chinese restaurant on Pleasance Street. On the other side of the bill compartment was an address book, a slim, expensive leather version of the kind sold in candy stores for a dime. Leland put it aside until he was done emptying the wallet. In the pocket under the change purse was a receipt from a U-drive-it dated February 3 and a small piece of pink cord. Leland recognized it as the kind used to attach pencils to dance cards and said so to the others. He opened the picture compartment. The first was a formal high school graduation photograph of a pretty, bird-nosed blonde, dated June, 1942, and inscribed "To Teddy," and at the bottom, "All my love, Susan." Behind it, wedged in the same celluloid folder, was a snapshot of Susan and Theodore Leikman in bathing suits beside a lake. There was no date, but the youth on the subjects' faces and the length of the skirt on the girl's suit indicated to Leland a time between 1940 and 1943. The next photograph, backed to the other two, was dated 1941, and was of a 1936 DeSoto Airflow sedan. In the second folder was a formal portrait of a woman of thirty or thirty-five years wearing a cloche hat and what appeared to be a plain black suit. There was no date. The next photograph, the only one in that folder, was a wedding shot, circa 1919 or '20, of the same woman and a man of about thirty. His haircut was of the bowl type and in his cutaway coat he looked as if he were realizing that his fly was open. In the next folder was Theodore Leikman's Social Security card and driver's license, which gave his age as twenty-three, and bore this address. In the last folder was his Selective Service registration card and two classification cards, giving Leikman's status as 4-F. The identification card in the wallet bore another address, in Wokoma Lake, upstate.

The address book produced more than thirty names and numbers, some with addresses, most without. Carol Linjak was listed, and so was a Susan Starrett, no address, with an exchange not in Port Smith. Leland gave the book to Schoenstein, who knew what to do. "Tell the operator to check the books for Pettit and Carter counties for the numbers outside the city."

"Some of these numbers will be discontinued or recently changed," Schoenstein said. "We'll have to wait while they check their files."

Curran said, "How are you going to work this?"

"A lot of these people have something to hide, that's certain," Leland said. "I don't think they're going to start running. We have a break with the time. It's three o'clock now and the newspapers won't be on the streets until six. We'll take the people in this area first, men and women, then we'll work out, men first, then women. No one leaves the city. Pull in anyone who gives us trouble. Our first call will be to the Wokoma Lake authorities to determine who lives at the home address. We want Susan Starrett to stay available for interrogation, if necessary. The sex part of this is not going to be pleasant for the women who knew him. Susan Starrett will be getting an ugly surprise, I think, and so will some of the others. That's not our problem and we'd better get it out of our minds."

"That's right," Curran said. "We have to stay sharp. What do you think?"

"Nothing yet, but I want to see that roommate."

"That's about the way I shape it up," Curran said.

Wedged between the mattress and the counterpane of the bed they found a sticky, crushed tube of ointment. Lifting it with a set of tweezers, Curran dropped it into one of the specimen envelopes.

The rest of the room provided little more. In the closet were books pertaining to Leikman's job, and in the dresser were scrapbooks and sketchbooks relating to his interest, fashions. Leikman had been skillful with pen and ink. A steel box that Curran pried open with Leland's penknife produced grammar and high school diplomas, copies of income tax returns, and a birth certificate. Leland and Curran finished with the room before Schoenstein, who had marshaled two operators, had completed securing the addresses for the names in Leikman's little book. Schoenstein had the names and addresses on index cards spread across the top of the coffee table, and Leland looked them over. He had a prescience of weariness and distaste. One by one he gathered the cards, following the plan he had described to Curran. Schoenstein spelled still another name into the telephone. He was up to the R's.

CHAPTER EIGHT

■■■■■■■■■■■■■■■■■■■■■■■■■■■■■■■■

EIGHT HOURS LATER IN THE SQUAD ROOM LELAND, CURRAN, SCHOEN-
stein, Tanner, Maule, Quillan, and Captain Richardson reviewed what
they had. There were reporters downstairs, and the morning three-stars
had spread the case across their front pages with banners and photographs of the death scene. On the windowsill the radio was playing;
since seven o'clock the half-hour newscasts had given the killing the
lead spot, abbreviating and reworking the material carried by the
papers. The announcers were still talking of the secret roommate, the
dragnet, the mysterious mutilations, the equally mysterious and
somehow spectacular appearance of Herbert Davis, who was still not
available for comment, and finally that Joseph Leland, the World
War Two fighter ace, was leading the investigation for the Police
Department. On page 3 of the Port Smith *Press* was an old Eighth
Air Force photograph of Leland in the cockpit of his Thunderbolt,
grinning and giving the "thumbs-up" sign that all was well.

Leland conducted the discussion and Schoenstein had pencil and
paper in his lap. The desk tops were littered with coffee containers.
The tank was empty; the exhibitionist arrested the night before in
Lewis Park had identified himself. His sister had been called and he
had been taken to headquarters to be held over until Monday
morning.

Leikman had been killed between eleven and eleven-thirty the
previous night by person or persons unknown, who had crushed Leikman's skull with more than twenty blows with the piece of china
found in the living room. The piece of china had been identified, or

classified, as a free-form piece of bric-a-brac or bookend. The assumption was that Leikman had not been hit from behind. His left cheekbone bore a bruise and the inside of his lower lip was cut. Leikman had been nude at the start of the fight: his clothes had been found clean. The condition of his body showed that he had had homosexual connection immediately prior to the fight that had led to his death. For purposes of identification, the semen stains on both beds were useless; the protein compounds broke down and, in a sense, died, soon after contact with the air. Another fact the detectives could bear in mind was that no woman was involved. The bed bore none of the usual evidence of a woman—powder, long hair, and so forth.

Richardson wanted to know why women were being mentioned at all.

"Leikman had it both ways," Leland said. "We interviewed his girl friends late last night."

"Go ahead," Richardson said disgustedly. He was a big man, fifty-five years old, and so long a leader that he could say a thing without thinking about it and make his men feel what he wanted.

Leland said, "Some of Leikman's women friends either knew or suspected he was a homosexual, and either didn't care or, for want of clarification, we'll say suffered in silence. But no woman made a discovery about him last night and killed him for it, then mutilated his body. All of them are firmly alibied. One who didn't know about him guessed this morning while we were questioning her—a sophomore at Jefferson. She had had intercourse with him. She came all to pieces." He paused without wanting to. "There's nothing we can do about that. We didn't kill him and we didn't live his life."

"That's the only attitude we can have," Richardson said. He looked around. "All of you who are on this: keep your heads up on that score. Go ahead, Joe."

"The lab report is in on some of the items. The stains on the pillowcases on both beds match and are from a common brand of hair pomade. The grease on the body and that in the tube we found haven't been compared yet, but we can assume that they're the same. The hair found on the sweater is definitely as it appeared last night:

dark-brown wavy. Matching the grease on the pillowcases with the grease on the hair will take some time because of the size of the samples. We'll have the evidence that the man Miss Linjak saw in the hall and whom Leikman identified to her as his roommate slept in both beds.

"We stopped back at her apartment before we returned here and she's sure she can pick him out of a lineup. The Chinese laundryman and the dry cleaner can't even remember Leikman. However, the laundry did turn up clothes that definitely did not belong to Leikman—already washed. Large T-shirts and shorts, two dress shirts with sixteen-and-a-half collars. The dry cleaner had nothing. The U-drive-it receipt shows that the car Leikman rented six weeks ago was driven forty-seven miles in one day and returned. We haven't hit the U-drive-it yet, but it doesn't seem likely that Leikman would have rented a car just once to ride around town. There's only this one receipt, so the records at the U-drive-it have to be checked. My opinion is that if we turn up nothing more there, we don't go on to other places. I've rented cars myself and one of those outfits is the same as the next. One thing, Leikman put the receipt in his wallet. He would have shoved it in his pocket if the experience had been a common one. Dan Curran and I think he took a twenty-three-and-a-half-mile trip that day. We have no clues as to where he went.

"In the bathroom we found a gallon of mineral oil, half full. It seems as if our missing friend drank the stuff because Leikman didn't. The contents of Leikman's stomach still have to analyzed, but the coroner assures us that the effects of mineral oil are visible to the eye and he didn't see them. Also in the bathroom was some hair the lab says came from the body of a human being. That's as opposed to the face. Leikman bore no evidence of shaving his body, so we can figure it's the roommate. Why is anybody's guess, but we'll know we have our man when we check his legs."

"Sounds exciting," Richardson said.

"Dan," Leland said, "what did I miss?"

"The fingerprints," he said.

"I was saving that." Leland looked at Tanner.

"We had a break," Tanner said. "Western Union had Leikman's

prints on file from the war. In the apartment were over eighty prints and fragments, and matching up, they reduce to seventeen different. Eight belong to Leikman and two are the landlady's—they were on the front door and the door frame. We have seven left, so we're waiting for the roommate.

"One of the seven is a fragment, a very small partial, that we lifted from the ash tray in the living room. It's unique, with no brothers anywhere else in the apartment. We're curious about this one, because it's the only one of the eighty without brothers. In any case, it's much too small to take into court and the lab says that any use we try to make of it would be poorly advised. That's the way they put it. There aren't enough points to work with."

"Let's not anticipate anything," Richardson said.

"For all we know," Schoenstein said, "it could be a toe. People put their bare feet—"

He stopped as the others stared at him. They began to laugh. They were laughing when the telephone rang. Richardson, red-faced, reached for it on the desk behind him. He raised his hand for quiet, but two of the men were laughing so hard they were coughing and getting out of their chairs. "Joe," Richardson said. "It's your wife." To Schoenstein, he said, "We'll tippytoe across that bridge when we come to it."

Laughing, Leland went to a telephone in the corner.

"Seventeen, Joe," Richardson called.

Leland pushed button seventeen and lifted the receiver. Richardson hung up. "Karen?" Leland asked.

"I wasn't going to call until I heard the news on the radio. I was going to ask if you wanted me to bring some fresh clothes, but it sounds like a beer party in there."

"I'll explain it when I see you," Leland said. "I didn't call you so you could sleep. Don't bother about clothes. I think I'll get a break soon. For a little while."

"Darling, it sounds horrible. There's no danger, is there?"

"No, none at all," he said. "I'm all right."

"Do you want us out when you come home? We'll let you sleep, if you want."

"No, it isn't necessary," he said. "Relax, Karen. This is just a little overtime."

"I'm sorry," she said. "I'm trying to help—"

"You're doing fine," he said softly. "Round about seven o'clock—well, let's just say I knew I wasn't where I wanted to be."

"I love you. If you can't get a ride home, take a taxi—" The telephone rang again, one of the other lines. "What was that?"

"Another extension, that's all." He saw Richardson take this one, too. "I can't discuss the case with you, honey." It was something he had to say; the way he said it, she knew she would hear about it when he got home. Richardson went into his office, stepping briskly. "The heat's on us, Karen. The laughter you heard was the result of Dave letting loose another of his wild ideas."

"You sound distracted," she said.

"The call that just came in was important. I may have to hang up in a hurry. I'll be home as fast as I can, but don't you plan to go out unless there's something you want to do."

"Joe," Richardson called from his door, "get on sixteen. It's the Commissioner."

"That's it," he said to Karen. "I'll call you later if I get the chance."

"We have to do the shopping—okay. Take care and hurry home. We'll—oh, okay," she said. "We'll see you later."

"Not long," he said, and pushed the sixteen button. "Hello, sir."

"Lieutenant Leland? Joe?"

"That's right sir. What can I do for you?"

He wanted Leland's personal impressions of the case and a synopsis of what had been done since last night. He wanted to know what kind of a person Leikman had been. It was just curiosity, and he made no effort to hide it as he asked Leland to tell him what Leikman had been doing in Port Smith, what kind of life he had lived, and the people he had seen.

Across the room, Schoenstein was telling the same story, that Leikman had come to Port Smith in 1944 for the job at Western Union. Some of his homosexual contacts dated back to 1945, and for a while he had made no attempt to conceal his homosexuality. One of the men questioned last night reported that he had met Leikman at a party in the fall of 1945 and that Leikman had been wearing eye shadow. Two other men admitted having had sexual relations with him in 1946. Leikman had had a girl friend, a Susan Starrett, in Lake Wokoma—no one had seen her yet—and sometime in 1946 he had begun to see women again. The police had seen four of them and one, the sophomore at Jefferson, had said that she had been intimate with him. The others regarded him as a friendly date. One had thought that he had been effeminate, but had not taken it seriously.

Two of the numbers in Leikman's book had been those of men at work. One, married, had said that he had not given Leikman the number and had had no idea that Leikman had considered him more than a business acquaintance. The other man seemed to have been more involved. He had behaved guiltily, and there was a plainclothesman assigned to him now. Last night he had been to the movies alone. It was such a flimsy alibi that Leland believed it. If the man tried to leave town or his fingerprints at Western Union matched any of those found in the apartment, he would be picked up. From him and the first man they had taken a list of the people who had worked with Leikman but were no longer with the company. There were seven. The forty-nine people still with the company and not in Leikman's book would be seen on Monday.

In all, they had been able to pinpoint a dozen men with whom Leikman definitely had had homosexual connections. There were three others on whom no decision could be made. Two of the flagrant homosexuals had stated that Leikman had had many, many contacts. One had seen Leikman go off with three different men on three nights in 1945. The other had heard Leikman say in 1946 that he had been with "at least thirty." Leikman had kept no diaries or records, so there appeared to be no way to trace all these people, and through them, the roommate. Only three people, including Miss Linjak, had had any idea of a roommate. One man had said that Leikman had spoken in November or December of having met "a person with interesting possibilities." The other, who had known Leikman for years, had met him during Christmas week on Pleasance Street, and

Leikman had said, in a conversational, newsy way, that he had a roommate. That was it on the roommate so far. Unless something turned up first, Leland planned to go up to Lake Wokoma tomorrow to see Leikman's aunt and uncle, by whom Leikman had been raised. Leikman had been on good terms with them, and there was a chance that they had something to lead to the roommate. Leland would decide there if he would see Susan Starrett.

"Okay," the Commissioner said. "It sounds right. Now, Lieutenant—Joe—there's a couple of things I have to tell you. You have that little airplane, don't you?"

"A J-3. That's right, sir."

"Under no circumstances are you to use it tomorrow. Take one of the Department cars. I'll explain why. Now you've done a good job with the press. You have your own reputation and popularity helping us all. No matter how this goes, the chances are even we're going to get our brains beat out. If we wind up holding our asses, it's guaranteed. Have you guessed why Davis showed up there last night?"

Leland said no.

"You couldn't know. He's made plans for Joytown, to tear it down and put up some kind of housing project. He's been waiting for an opportunity to turn on the heat and get his way. He had his secretary listening to the S-W band, if that doesn't beat all. This murder is the opportunity, follow?"

"Yes, sir."

"If we wind up in the bag, the Mayor is going to kill us. He's not any more responsible for conditions down there than anyone else, and he won't stand still to become Davis' target. He'll have to kill us to protect himself. Firing me and shaking up the Fifth doesn't sound nice, but he'll do it just the same. You don't deserve to be a First Grade again and I don't deserve to be looking for work. So.

"On the other hand, if we break this—and the faster, the better—we have our fifty-fifty chance. Most people know why Joytown exists and that the job we've been given is that of keeping the lid on the garbage can. Still, if any criticism is directed at us, even though we've broken the case, we can sit tight and take it. You know we can't defend ourselves. We're out of order if we make policy statements. We have to take it.

"You offended Davis last night, Joe. Don't worry, I'm not going to tell you to eat turd. I have only myself to judge these things by, but the people and the newspapers know you and like you. Until now, anyway, you haven't made a public mistake. If you make one now, I don't think you'll pay for it as heavily with the papers and the people as you would if they didn't know you. If I took you off the case, *I'd* have to answer for it, not you. 'What are you doing to our boy?' they'd want to know. Follow me?"

"Yes, sir."

"I don't know if all this has occurred to Davis, but maybe it has. He hasn't said anything yet about you. I don't think he will. When he hits, he'll hit the administration and the Department. The newspapers will seek you out. Don't figure that because he's letting you off the hook, you have to defend us. Do your job and treat the papers as you have been. You're a sophisticated and intelligent man, and I know that if I give you a free hand you won't abuse it. I have to say no to the flying because some people might think that you've been doing it right along and drawing your expenses when it's something you would do for pleasure anyway. Not that you ever have done it or that I care much. I'm telling Captain Richardson that you're to handle whatever goes out to the press. Consult him on the moves you want to make. If you're in agreement, the two of you can have pretty much what you want. The two of you are good cops, and I respect you both. Now let me speak to him, please."

"Yes, sir. Captain—sixteen again."

Richardson returned to his office, and when he was on the line, Leland put down his receiver and went into the office and closed the door. In a minute Richardson said goodbye, hung up, and looked at Leland.

"He's scared, Joe. This is between you and me, but he's evading his responsibilities. If we fail, this will get tied to our tails, and he'll help them tie it. It's a hell of a thing, when you think of commissioners who would be here right now, taking charge. So you handle the press. Have you figured out why?"

"He spelled it out for me."

"Jesus. He's not backing you up, he's hiding behind you. Maybe the Mayor put him up to it. Now *there* is a man full of confidence. But we're supposed to go out and do or die, eh? What makes me so sick is that they're willing to engineer a man as young as you are into a position where he'll draw the most fire. How old are you—thirty?"

"I'll be thirty this year."

"What do they know about you? Maybe they even resent you for having become somebody without having indebted yourself to them. Frankly, I wouldn't want to be you for anything. You know that. They don't figure that you're a man with troubles of your own, but a dumb kid they can feed to that—madman. A housing project. Why, we may come up looking like we're against it because we don't want to get squashed. The Commissioner is kidding himself if he thinks Davis won't try to hit you. He'll try to make you look young, clumsy, impetuous, and even crooked. Somehow he'll do it. Before he's done with you people will be checking your pants to see if you're wearing diapers."

Leland scratched the back of his hand. "I've got a wife and little girl. I'm not going home to them with my ass dragging because of a guy like Davis. My wife is bright, but that isn't saying she isn't going to be hurt and ashamed if I don't hit back. And you know there's no explaining things to little girls. If I don't slay my enemies, her heart will be broken. But for more than that, I reserve the right to defend myself."

" 'Atta boy," Richardson said, and stood up. He looked around, as if sniffing the air, and then, with a little frown, stared straight out, as if, as his men sometimes believed, he was looking into the future.

The next day Leland and Schoenstein made the four-hour automobile trip to Lake Wokoma. They stopped first at the town police station, where they picked up the Chief of Police and a uniformed officer, and then they drove in one of the local cars up the mountain overlooking the lake to the home of Mr. and Mrs. Walter Howard, Leikman's aunt and uncle. The house was a two-story white-frame about forty years old, moderately gingerbreaded, with a wraparound porch. The driveway was a pair of sandy tracks worn through the unkempt lawn. The March air was drier here, although the lake itself was visible down beyond the back of the house, and Leland, in his topcoat, felt overwarm and edgy. As he made his way over the lawn, the soil soft and uncertain under his feet, he saw the curtains hanging in the front room and had an anticipation of the very dry coal-fire heat in the house in which the rooms would be too small for the four men coming inside.

Now, thirty-six hours after the killing, practically nothing had panned out. The U-drive-it had produced only a duplicate of the document the police already possessed. The autopsy and the lab tests had confirmed what the police had presumed. The rest of the people in Leikman's book had been less helpful than those who had been seen first. The names of the seven people who had once worked at Western Union had led nowhere. One man was dead, and three were too old or sick to understand what this was about. The real problem was still the roommate, of whom there was still no trace after all these hours. It was as if Leland has shot his bolt of luck with the early description.

He recognized the young woman who met them at the door. Susan Starrett.

Timidly, baring her teeth slightly in her nervousness, she glanced at them all. Her face was thinner and more pinched than it had been in the high school photographs. She looked as if she had had a bad day and night.

"This way," she whispered. She led them to a room to the right of the narrow center hall. The room was as Leland had imagined, small and dark. In the center was a polished round table with a doily, and on the doily, a cream-colored fruit bowl, and in the bowl, a paper clip. Mr. Howard, a fat dark man with his black hair grown long on one side and slicked across his bald crown, rose from the high-backed love seat. He blinked at the four men. He was fat enough for Leland to wonder if he ever denied himself anything, and the part in his hair, barely an inch above his ear, made Leland think that he was too vain to take himself any way but seriously. Miss Starrett slipped onto the seat beside him. When the Chief introduced Leland and Howard looked at him to see if it was proper to shake hands, Leland produced his badge, let Howard just get his eyes on it, and then he put it away.

"This is Miss Starrett," Howard said, sitting again. "She lives across the road there." He waved vaguely at the curtains. "Sit down, sit down, all of you." He looked at Leland. "Want a beer?"

"Not while we're working, thanks."

"How about some coffee?"

"We came a long way. We'd appreciate it."

Miss Starrett got up and Howard expanded into the extra room on the seat. He was wearing blue pinstripe pants and an off-yellow sports shirt with a blue knitted tie. "My woman took to bed yesterday when she got the news. She couldn't have children and that kid was like her own. Her sister's child. Married again and went to California and that was it, never heard from her again. What are you going to do with a kid? Put him on the poor farm?"

"Can't do that," Leland said agreeably. He was sitting on Howard's left, on a small Gay Nineties chair as soft and comfortable as a medicine ball.

"That's what I say. Well, he made up for what my wife missed." He folded his hands across his belly and eyed Leland. "Something the matter with him, wasn't there?"

"Well, he was murdered," Leland said.

"No, I mean down in his drawers. He was a faggot."

"I'm not free to discuss that," Leland said.

Howard nodded. "Well, he was. I caught him jerkin' off in the garage one time and I beat his ass. He never did it again, that's for sure. He did other things, though. I don't see how I can help you, mister. He left here five years ago and all we ever learned was what he wrote in his letters."

"We'd like to read them," Leland said.

"All of them?"

"Every one."

"Jesus, if you say so. My old lady saved every damned one—" he grinned "—just for you. How do you like that?"

"I like it very much," Leland said.

Howard didn't move. "You're the one who shot down all them planes, aren't you? I read about you in the paper."

"I'm the one."

"Now that's my idea of doing something. The country ought to set you men up so you never have to work again. I'd help pay for that, I think. You men deserve better than you got. So did the ones in the first war. My cousin got gassed in that one. But he gets checks for it."

"May we see the letters?" Leland asked.

"Why, sure. They're upstairs. Wait here." He stopped at the door. "Hey, if my wife comes down, don't say anything about Ted being a faggot. She's not a strong woman."

The four men sat there, staring at separate sections of the room, waiting for him to return.

Miss Starrett, entering by the side door, preceded him by a minute. She put the tray bearing the cups and saucers on the edge of the table, took the bowl from the center and, not letting go of the tray, put the bowl on a small side table behind her. She was a girl who looked older than she was, and Leland could not help wondering why. When Howard re-entered carrying a messy stack of letters and torn envelopes, Leland said to him, "I'm going to have to ask you a formality question. Where were you Friday night?"

"I was down to Halsteader's Tavern, here in town. All night."

"Anybody see you?"

He grinned malevolently. "Old Halsteader himself, for one. Billy Swan. Frank Gilfoyle, he's head of the volunteer fire department."

Leland laughed. "I told you it was a formality. Give the letters to my father there. He's the one who reads."

Howard gave the letters to Schoenstein, laughing at him. "Get yourself up to the table," Howard said.

"Read backwards, Dave," Leland said. Schoenstein had to be wondering why Leland had not volunteered to take half the work. He would see soon.

The cups of coffee came around. Leland caught Susan Starrett's eyes and stared at her, longer than she could stand. She did not know what to do. He backed off.

156

"You know," Howard said, "you ought to write a book about your experiences. I bet you'd make a lot of money."

"I had an offer," Leland said. "That was three years ago, and I doubt if they'd be interested today. People are tired of hearing about that now."

"Oh, no," Howard said. "You'd be surprised."

Leland knew that the local cops were thinking he was crazy, coming so far for social chatter. "To tell you the truth," he said to Howard, "I hate to write even my reports. If I didn't have Dad here to do my dirty work, I'd be pounding a beat."

"I know what you mean," Howard said. He moved on the settee to make room for Miss Starrett.

"Don't sit down, Miss Starrett," Leland said briskly. Howard blinked at him. "If you have a coat, get it. It's time you and I had a little talk."

She stood still, frightened, her eyes drawn toward Howard.

"You didn't say you wanted to talk to her," he said. He hated Leland now. He knew that he had been taken, but he didn't understand how it had been done.

"I didn't say we didn't," Leland said, getting to his feet.

"She hardly knew Ted."

That clinched it. Leland didn't look at him. He said to the girl, "Get your coat. All I'm interested in is the man who killed Teddy."

It was out now, and the others could only gape. Schoenstein, Leland could sense, was stunned. "Teddy" had done it to him. It was the first time Leland had used the name. Later he would want to know how Leland had felt so sure of what he had suggested. It had been more than a feeling. Susan Starrett had moved through the house with authority. Mrs. Howard, who had saved her foster son's letters, would not have encouraged his former girl friend. Howard would not have promoted the girl out of goodness of soul. Not him. He had brought her along and bided his time. Perhaps it had taken years. His behavior settled it. It had taken Leland too long to recognize it for what it was. Howard had been playing bull of the herd. Some men did it with all women, but the way he had treated her had shown none of the sly self-consciousness that would go with pretense in him. For Leland it had been a question of believing what the others had not wanted to believe. It was a mistake to forget how many kinds of people there were in the world. Now what Leland wanted to see were the letters from Leikman to her, after he had learned of what had happened with Howard. Leland felt less sure of this ground, but it was still worth crossing.

She had her coat. He followed her to the porch. "Just over there," she said, indicating another two-story frame diagonally across the blacktop. The house needed paint and repairs. "My mother's down to church, so there's nothing we can't talk about. Good thing you came in a police car and it's in all the papers. People here peep around the curtains all the time."

"If it will help, I'll pin on my badge."

"They don't know about me and Walt," she said. "We've been careful. He doesn't know that I have letters from Ted. I'm glad you didn't say that in there. I saved mine, too. How do you like that?" She was mocking Howard now. She must have listened at the kitchen door.

"I like it very much," Leland said, mocking himself.

"Look at that shack. You'd think Walt would paint it for us, for what I'm giving him. But he says people will get suspicious. He's not fooling me. You men are all alike. My father was the same way. My mother's told me things," she said, believing it. "Even Teddy. There's no such thing as love, I learned that much."

It wasn't Leland's job to argue with her.

"When Teddy went away," she said as they went up the walk, "I thought my heart would break. He ruined me for anyone else. I guess this is *his* reward—I'll never get a decent man. Now he doesn't have anything, so I guess it's fair. I have to say you got that fat old man good back there. I thought his eyes would jump right out of his head. It'll be something for me to think about for a long time to come." They went inside. "My father died three years ago. We bought new furniture with the insurance. I have a job downtown, so we get by. Sit down and I'll get the letters."

They were innocuous little notes, and while Leland looked through them she went on talking. "We were seventeen when we went

158

together. I thought he was going to marry me, and then he up and went to Port Smith. He had it in his mind all along. Walt told me about him one time. At least Walt doesn't want a lot of things from me I don't—" She let it lie. Leland looked up.

"What kind of things?"

"You know—things." She made her mouth small and unpleasant. "Teddy had a dirty mind. I don't want to talk about it."

Leland nodded and went on reading. He was looking for a name, any name, he would not recognize. She said she had an album and would get it and he nodded again.

She put the album, open, beside him as he continued to read, the thought recurring to him that if Schoenstein found anything he would come running across the road.

"We took some real funny pictures," she said. "There's one of me in a Betsy Ross costume for a party and Teddy had on a leopard skin. I rented mine but he bought his. He made it over into briefs for some pictures we took for a strength and health magazine." She turned the page. "The pictures came back because Teddy wasn't built well enough, so we put them in here."

"Stupid," Leland said.

"Excuse me?"

He shook his head, staring at the shots. They were five-by-sevens of Leikman at about seventeen, in a sort of leopard-skin bathing suit, posing, insanely, as a muscle man. His skin was shining as if he were in a heavy sweat, and every hair on his head was carefully in place.

"How well do you remember these?" he asked.

"Oh, very well," she said.

"What did he use on his skin?"

"Stuff from the drugstore. All the weight lifters use it. You wash it off with alcohol."

"Mineral oil," he said.

"That's right. That's what it was."

"I need these pictures," he said. He tore them out of the album. "Under no circumstances are you to tell anyone what we've discussed here. Do you understand?"

"What about me and Walt? Are you going to bring that out?"

"That depends on you."

"Can I have the pictures back?" she asked.

"When we're done with them." He stood up. "Close up the house, Miss Starrett. Put away the album. I'll see you across the street."

He went quickly over to the Howard place. The Chief opened the door. "Where's Miss Starrett?"

"She'll be here. Dave?" he called. "Come out here, if you will."

When Schoenstein came out on the porch Leland handed him the photographs. He looked at them all. "So?"

Leland told him about the mineral oil. "When we found Leikman he didn't have a muscle to his name. The bottle under the sink belonged to the roommate. It explains why he shaved his body—for pictures. Our boy is a muscle-builder."

"Now all we have to do is find pictures," Schoenstein said, troubled.

"You're doing things the hard way. First thing we have to go on is that he didn't carry weights out with him Friday night."

"No, of course not."

"So he never had them. He went to a YMCA or a gymnasium. Our lousy description will help us now. Somebody will remember him."

Schoenstein grinned. "It's a good thing I didn't go with her. I wouldn't have made the connection."

"Don't kid yourself. It hit me right between the eyes."

Schoenstein looked over his shoulder. "You had him worried in there. He figures you're a pretty sexy guy."

Leland pursed his lips. "Tell me about the letters."

"Pure bullshit."

"That's the way I feel about the whole dump. Let's get out of here."

In the squad room they made a list of gymnasiums and YMCA's. The names of the weight-lifting and muscle-building clubs

160

would be gathered from their personnel, who would be told to keep quiet.

Richardson endorsed Leland's plan and put through a call for additional men on the Monday tour. The gym workers had to be encouraged to tell everything they knew about men who even remotely fitted the description. To know that one was married and that another had been with witnesses at the time of the killing would save a lot of legwork. Richardson did not want to engage in a wholesale roundup. It was bad public relations and worse police work. He would do it if he had to, of course. The case was getting too cold for them to let opportunities slip through their fingers.

The next morning, as the plan went into effect, Herbert Davis issued a statement attacking, in the main, Lieutenant Joseph Leland. Leland was an authentic hero, deserving all the honor tendered him, but in this matter he was serving as a willing dupe of the city administration and the higher authorities in the Port Smith Police Department. The administration and the Department were in concert in using Leland, a courageous but naïve man, as a shield to cover the incompetence and malfeasance that not only had allowed a situation such as Joytown to generate, but a vicious murderer to commit his crime and make good his escape. Evidence had been mishandled and facts misinterpreted. In the seventy-two hours since the police had entered the case not even the name of the so-called "secret roommate" had been learned. Yet instead of looking for the murderer, the Port Smith Police Department concerned itself with its public relations. Leland, because of his personal reputation, had been selected to "handle the press" for the duration of the case. Yesterday, Sunday, playing his role, Leland had taken an eight-hour motor trip to Lake Wokoma to conduct a meaningless twenty-minute interview with the aunt and uncle of Theodore Leikman. Right now the uncle was consulting his attorneys about the possibility of suing the Port Smith Police Department and Joseph Leland personally for the anguish he and his wife had been made to suffer in the cause of political expediency. Why Leland wanted to lend his name to covering and obscuring the lines of responsibility in such a tawdry matter was a question the

161

Lieutenant would do well to answer before his reputation was further tarnished.

"It's a feint," Richardson said in his office. "He doesn't know how you're going to respond, but he's willing to lose a little to gain a lot. Maybe his informant in the Department thinks you're naïve. Davis is willing to take the chance to mousetrap the people he wants. What he wants most of all is that housing project. Take your time now when you talk to the reporters."

"He's still giving me my lumps for bouncing him Friday night."

"Of course he is," Richardson said. "But don't lose your head."

"He thinks that I'm Lucky Lindy or somebody."

"Some people figure you're all like that."

Leland grinned. "Come on. He's going to wish he'd been hit by a truck."

The reporters and photographers saw them before they reached the bottom of the stairs. Flashbulbs began to shoot off. Leland took a breath. "Save that stuff for later. You know Captain Richardson, I think."

Some of the men nodded. "Do you have a statement, Lieutenant?"

"Was I supposed to?" he asked. "When they made me press officer they didn't tell me I'd have to do that."

A few smiled. "You are handling the news releases, then," one said.

"Just as I'm doing now. Questions and answers. There'll be no releases as you know them. We don't have men or time for that."

"Who gave the orders, Lieutenant, if you don't mind?"

"I've been on top of the case from the start," he said, evading the question. "The decision was made on the theory that you people would be most interested in the murder."

"How do you feel about Davis' charge that you're being used as a shield?"

"I'm giving the information, not concealing it."

"Is the Department concealing evidence?"

"For the moment, of course it is. It's intelligent police work. When the time comes, we'll reveal what we have."

"Davis says that the trip to Lake Wokoma was a smoke-making expedition."

"The trip to Wokoma was confidential. Davis did our case a disservice by revealing it at this time." He wanted to draw the reporters into asking about Friday night. "There's more to police work than flashing around a badge."

One was caught. "Why was Davis there on Friday night?"

"He was buffing."

"Buffing, did you say?"

"That's what I said. Buffing."

"A buff is a fellow who hangs around the police, isn't he?" one of them asked.

"That's right," Leland said.

"You disapprove of buffing?"

Now Leland had his chance. "Oh, no. We have buffs here at the Fifth all the time. They run errands, get cigarettes and coffee and so forth, and generally make themselves helpful."

"Can we quote?"

"What are you here for?"

One of the reporters wanted to play the game. "Did you send Mr. Davis out for coffee?"

Leland grinned. "Oh, no. We were too busy."

Another reporter cut short the laughter. "What's the progress on the case?"

"Considerable. We have to keep it confidential. I'm certain that there'll be something for you in the next forty-eight to seventy-two hours."

"Nothing now, though?"

"Sorry," Leland said.

"Has the Commissioner or the Mayor spoken to you about the case?"

"The line of responsibility isn't changed in this case. I answer to Captain Richardson. He's my boss. He has his superiors, and so forth."

"Did you speak with the Commissioner, Captain?"

"A table of organization is available at headquarters," Leland said.

"Perhaps I wasn't heard—" the reporter started.

"Yes?" Leland said to another.

"I wanted to ask Captain Richardson how well he thought you were handling the case."

"If there's a citation awarded in this case, Joe will get it," Richardson said. "Excuse me, I have things to do." He turned upstairs.

"What do you think of Joytown, Lieutenant?"

"A housing project is an idea I've heard kicked around."

"Do you think Mr. Howard will sue you?"

"We'll have to see what happens," Leland said, and smiled.

"A personal question, Lieutenant. We've been led to understand that there's some sort of difficulty between you and your wife."

"You've been led wrong—very wrong." Unnerved, he looked at the others. They, too, thought that the question had been improper. "Is there anything else?"

"No. Thanks for your help, Lieutenant."

Pictures were taken, then Leland went upstairs. Richardson was waiting for him. He had had to get away; he had seen that he didn't know anything about dealing with reporters. He wanted to see how they worked over what Leland said about Davis.

The afternoon papers gave it front-page coverage, and one ran a picture of Davis beside a picture of one of the buffs of the Fifth, a simple-minded man who had been loitering in the station for thirty-five years. JOB STEALING? ran the headline, and under both photographs, "What I do is I go for coffee and stuff, and sometimes I sweep a little. The cops are nice guys. I don't know what I'd do if I couldn't help out." By four o'clock the story as it was running in all the papers was hanging on the bulletin board in the squad room, but at that hour Leland, Dan Curran, and Dave Schoenstein were at the Springfield Street YMCA, questioning the desk clerk, Frederick Jensen, about the man he thought they were looking for. The man was a regular member of that branch and had given as his residence, a year and a half before when he had joined, an address in Westlake which the detectives knew was a rooming house.

164

"He used to come three or four times a week, just for the weights. I'm not always behind the desk. I saw him in there. He looks a lot shorter than he is because he's so wide. Very well built. A quiet fellow. One of the other members spoke to me about him once, saying that his personal effects were dirty. We don't like to speak to the men about things like that if we can help it."

Leland looked at a sign over the desk that read *Swearing is lip filth*. "Can you recall anything else?"

"He doesn't come in so much anymore, once a week or once every ten days. Last summer, he didn't come in at all. When I saw him in September he was very tanned. I didn't inquire where he had been, but it was obvious that it had been the beach. I'll ask around for you, though, and see if he told anybody else."

"We'd appreciate that. Keep it among the personnel. Unless we call you in the meantime, give us a ring when he comes in."

Schoenstein had the information from the membership card. Felix Tesla, twenty-six, born in Winnipeg. At the rooming house the detectives learned that Tesla had moved out last June and had left no forwarding address. He had not had a car. Nothing unusual had been noticed about him. Leland asked about the condition of his sheets. The landlady had no way of knowing, because she subscribed to a linen service and the tenants delivered their dirty sheets in little muslin bags.

The telephone company had no numbers, public or unlisted, for Felix Tesla. At a newsstand Leland bought copies of all the weight-lifting and muscle-building magazines and returned to the YMCA. Frederick Jensen saw Tesla in none of them. Leland called the public library. It did not collect issues of the magazines he had in mind. The detectives returned to the squad room.

By nine o'clock every gymnasium, YMCA, and health club had been covered, and Tesla's was the single name that had been drawn. Richardson approved, for the morning, long-distance calls to the magazine publishers to see about files on Felix Tesla, and perhaps a return address.

Leland did not attempt to go home until midnight. Herbert Davis made no additional comment. Leland read the papers, which had treated him kindly. There was no mention of his private life. One editorial, in the *Herald*, which was reasonable but colorless, assured its readers that the police were making progress. No editorial criticized Davis, but Leland had not expected it. Leland went home approximately satisfied, for another idea about the case had begun to develop for him.

The telephone calls to the magazines produced two files with photographs. The most recent address was of no help to the police in their search for Tesla, but it settled another, more important question. The address was Leikman's, and it fixed Tesla positively as the man who had lived with Leikman to the time of his death. Leland asked the magazine publishers to deliver the photographs to the police headquarters in their respective cities for transmission by radio to Port Smith.

Richardson let Leland proceed with his new idea. It was a bad one, he thought, but worth a try because it was cheaper and quieter than a public city-wide dragnet. Richardson was sure that Tesla had beat it back to Canada. Leland agreed that Tesla was seeking safety, but he was certain that Tesla had returned again to the beach where he had worked last summer. In February he and Leikman had driven there in the rented car: it was an explanation for the sand in Tesla's room. The sand had fallen out of the clothes Tesla had worn that day as he had been packing them on the murder night. A man who went to bed dirty would leave sandy clothes hanging in a closet for six weeks. Richardson was willing to accept that. Leland's plan was to check the beaches inside the twenty-three-and-a-half-mile radius the mileage on the rented car indicated.

The map showed that there were three beaches inside that area. Richardson let Leland have six men. If they produced nothing by the end of the day, they would review the entire matter.

Leland sent Tanner and Maule to Northport, a city beach, Curran and Quillan to Piantic Bay, thirteen miles south of the city, and he took Schoenstein with him to Clarendon, eighteen miles south. His feeling was that Clarendon was the best choice. The largest and most expensive resort, it was developing a reputation similar to Joytown's. After checking in at the Clarendon Borough Police Headquarters, he and Schoenstein went about their business. At two o'clock, Tanner and Maule joined them. They had found nothing at Northport. In the afternoon paper Herbert Davis accused Leland of flippancy and grandstanding. Joytown was a serious problem. Leland's remarks were a disservice to the Police Department and Port Smith. For the city's sake, Davis hoped that Leland's actions would erase the terrible impression of his words.

At four-ten P.M., at 18 Furnast Place in South Clarendon, a small, paunchy man in his fifties opened the door to Leland's ringing.

"Port Smith Police Department, sir. Last summer did you have a roomer here by the name of Felix Tesla?"

"That's right. What about him?"

"Have you seen him recently?"

"This morning, when he went out for breakfast. He's up in his room now. Why do you want him?"

Leland raised his hand to quiet him. Schoenstein went down the steps to signal Tanner and Maule on the other side of the street. They came running. "Now, quietly," Leland said. "Who else is in the house?"

"No one. Just me." He looked frightened.

"Which is Tesla's room?"

"Number three. Up the stairs."

"Get across the street—we want him for murder. Tanner, cover the alley. Maule, on the boardwalk. Dave, back me up. No shooting. Ready to go in sixty seconds."

Leland and Schoenstein went up the stairs softly. They could hear nothing at the door. Leland glanced at his watch when they heard, faintly, "Hey! Out here!"

It was Maule's voice. With Schoenstein in front, they raced down the stairs. Maule was not in sight as they headed up the ramp to the boardwalk. Two heads bobbed on the other side of the sand. Tesla broke free of Maule. Tesla was barefoot, wearing a T-shirt and slacks. He was terrified. He headed down the beach toward the water with Maule in pursuit, topcoat flapping. Schoenstein ran parallel to them on the boardwalk, pulling his coat off as he ran. Leland let the coat go and tried to keep up with him, beyond the two men running awkwardly on the sand. Schoenstein ran down a ramp onto the sand and cut an angle of interception. Leland was fifty feet behind him when Schoenstein let go a flying block from a distance of what seemed like ten feet. Tesla went down and struggled to get up, but Maule was upon him. Tesla screeched and tore at Maule's clothes. Schoenstein scrambled at Tesla's kicking legs. As Leland came up he drew his gun and dropped his weight on one knee across Tesla's chest. He hit Tesla once across the top of the head to no effect; a second blow and Tesla, still conscious, quit fighting.

Clearing Tesla out of Clarendon alerted the press, which waited in force at the Fifth Precinct. Cameras flashed as Tesla was hustled past. Barricades had been set up to keep back a crowd that had gathered; there were shouts and cheers, indignant and larking by turns, that could be heard inside the house at the sergeant's desk where Tesla was booked on suspicion. More pictures were taken there: Tesla, sullen and unshaved, flanked by Leland and Schoenstein. The cuffs on Tesla's wrists were identified as Schoenstein's.

Three hours later, when the first editions of the next morning's papers came on the stands, they led with the story of Tesla's capture. The *Herald* ran an editorial congratulating the Department for the speed with which Tesla had been brought in. The *Press*, while agreeing with Herbert Davis that the Joytown situation needed correction, chided him for "reacting emotionally" and "leaping to unwarranted conclusions about the Port Smith Police Department."

Around the time the first editions came out, Tesla gave in a little and changed his story. At first he claimed that he had not known Leikman well at all, that they had been only roommates, and that if Leikman had been a homosexual, he, Tesla, had had no knowledge of it. Then he gave it up. He had had an "affair" with Leikman, it was true. Last Friday evening they had had an argument—about money—and he had packed and left at seven-thirty and had not returned. He had wandered around the city until he had come to the decision to return to the beach. By then it had been too late to travel, so he had spent the night in an abandoned car on Pier Twelve. At dawn he had walked across Harbor Bridge, then had caught the bus to Clarendon.

168

The hair was identified as his. The bit of patent leather fit the corner of his wallet. All the unidentified prints from the apartment save the small fragment on the living room ash tray matched his hands. Tanner and Maule were assigned to work with the lab on the final report; Leland heard from them that the men of the lab did not give much importance to the unidentified fragment. There were other parts of the hand that could produce prints that could resemble fingerprints over an area as large as their fragment. In that sense, Dave Schoenstein had not been wrong by much with his suggestion. What the fragment was, really, was a classic example of the rule that disallowed bits and pieces like it to be admitted as evidence in a court.

Tesla admitted to Richardson that he had gone back to the apartment "around midnight." He talked excitedly, stammering, shouting, gesturing. He had seen the body on the floor in the bedroom. He had panicked, thrown his clothes in his suitcase, and run. Richardson, following the story, asked if he had not been curious about the china object on the floor of the foyer. Yes, Tesla said, he had picked it up when he had come in. Richardson wanted to know how he had cleaned his hand. With his handkerchief. He had thrown the handkerchief off Harbor Bridge. The rest of the story was as he had told it.

The next morning the Commissioner had Leland tell him about the capture. On the questioning, there was nothing new to report. Tesla was sticking with his last story. He was being given rest periods and meals and being carefully treated. No one was satisfied. On the matter of the china object, there had been no prints on it; it had been thoroughly, almost deliberately smeared. The Commissioner interrupted and asked to speak to Captain Richardson. When Richardson came out of his office later he looked annoyed.

"He still wants to play football. We can't release a confession until he says so. He's giving out the full story on your detective work. The Mayor wants to undo what he thinks Davis did to his administration, so brace yourself."

For the afternoon papers the Commissioner gave out the details of the developments that had led to Tesla's capture, and for the next morning's editions, the news of his confession. The papers that afternoon carried the details of the murder and what they could print about the mutilations. Twenty-four hours after that, there was the story of Richardson, Leland, and Schoenstein receiving special citations in the Commissioner's office.

Tesla's confession was more a step in his collapse than a confession, not the first step or the last in the disintegration of his personality. Richardson and Leland saw it in the report they received from Canada. Arrested Toronto, 1939, auto theft, no disposition; 1941, Toronto, auto theft, sentenced two years suspended conditional to military service; discharged dishonorably RCAF 1942, sent to Grande Soule Work Farm; arrested 1945, Montreal, public nuisance, sentenced ninety days; 1945, Montreal, public nuisance, sentenced one year; 1946, Montreal, malicious mischief, no disposition. His entry into the United States was not recorded, and there was no file anywhere in this country attesting to a continuation of the patterns he had set in Canada. By his own statements Tesla had come almost directly to Port Smith and had worked temporary jobs. He had met Theodore Leikman in November of 1947 and had moved in with him the same month. In response to questions, he said that the furnishings in the small room had been selected and paid for by Leikman. Leikman had kept both keys to the apartment. Quillan asked him if Leikman had not kept him prisoner. Tesla said no. Quillan asked again and Tesla said no again.

Richardson thought that Quillan had caught something, and told them all to keep at it. To Richardson it seemed to fit into the contrast between Leikman's pretensions and his actual life: the fine apartment —and Tesla. Leland told Richardson of Leikman's uncle, and that Leikman had not had to go far to have learned cruelty.

The confession came that afternoon. Leland had told Schoenstein to sit in and listen to Quillan when he could. Schoenstein had fallen into the pattern of the questions, and when he had begun to see the break, he had pressed the button that signaled Richardson's office. Richardson had picked up Leland in the squad room.

Tesla was sitting in the armchair facing the desk. Quillan was behind the desk, his hands clasped on the blotter. Behind him the blinds were pulled up halfway. The triple windows gave view of the brick wall of the garage behind the station. Quillan waited until Richardson and Leland had taken chairs near the door.

"Okay, Felix, tell me about Teddy's body again."

"You mean the way I found it?"

"No, no. What you liked about it."

Tesla glanced at Richardson and Leland.

"No, no, Felix," Quillan said. "Over here. Tell me."

"It was nice."

"How nice?"

"Like a girl's," Tesla said.

"You mean soft?"

Tesla nodded.

"No, no, Felix. We always talk. We always *say* the words."

"It was soft."

"Louder."

"It was soft!"

"Did you kiss him?"

"Y-yes."

"You used to pretend he was a girl."

Tesla nodded.

"Felix?"

"Yes."

"What did you do with his pecker after you cut it off?"

"Nothing. I didn't cut it off."

"He used to tease you, didn't he?"

"Yes." When Leland had left, four hours ago, Tesla had not been willing to admit this.

"He used to call you names. What names?"

"Bull. Stud. Names like that."

"He used to tease you in bed. Tell us how."

Tesla shook his head.

"Now, Felix, we're not going to have that."

"He used to make me beg."

"On your knees?"

"On my knees."

"What else?"

"I had to kiss his foot."

"You wanted to hit him."

"Yes."

Quillan scratched the back of his head, a signal. This was something new.

"You wanted to punish him."

"Yes."

"He used to tease you."

"Yes."

"He called you names."

"Yes."

"He thought you were stupid."

"Yes."

"And he laughed at you," Quillan said.

"He called me names," Tesla said.

"You hated him, didn't you?" Quillan asked.

"I hated what he did to me. I wanted to hit him."

"Now, that Friday night, what did you fight about?"

"He wanted me to leave. He didn't want me living there anymore."

"You wanted to stay."

"Until I found a job," Tesla pleaded. "But he wanted me out right away. I had those few dollars saved—I didn't want to spend it. I didn't have to, but he wanted me out."

"So you went out."

"To calm down. That's right."

"And when you came back later, the argument started again, he was just as insistent as before, and he called you names again. He went too far this time, and you hit him."

Tesla stared at him. He began to bang his fists together furiously.

"He teased you," Quillan said, leaning forward. "He teased you and called you names. He teased you and you hit him. You hit him on the head until you killed him."

Tesla moaned. His eyes closed, but before they did, Leland could see the pupils roll back.

"You killed him, Felix. You cut him with a knife and threw the knife and his fingers off the Harbor Bridge. That's *really* what you did, isn't it? You *did* the killing, Felix. You smashed in his skull. How many times? How many times did you keep hitting him?"

Tesla nodded.

"*Say* it, Felix!" Quillan screamed.

It came out, hardly audible.

"*Louder!*"

"I killed him," Tesla said softly.

"And you threw the *knife* off Harbor Bridge?"

"Yes!" And he bent forward and vomited.

Richardson caught Quillan's eye and gave him the sign of the circled thumb and forefinger. Quillan's mouth twisted—he was not happy. Richardson tapped Leland's elbow and they got up and went out quietly.

"Do *you* think it will stick?" he asked Leland in the squad room.

"I have no idea."

"Well, when Quillan is finished, tell him to take twenty-four hours. I have to make some calls."

The assumption was that the confession would be retracted at the trial, but it was not. The defense argued that Tesla was insane at the time of the crime. Two psychiatrists testified to the fact of his disintegration—and by the end of the trial, Tesla had developed a facial tic. The district attorney presented the State's case with care and detail, and Leland was made to testify for two days, cataloguing every step he and the others had taken. The testimony of three psychiatrists was offered in rebuttal to the defense, and at the summing up the district attorney argued that Tesla's criminal record was an indicator of the violence and social irresponsibility that had been part of him for many years. In two hours the jury found Tesla guilty of murder in the first degree, with no recommendation for mercy. The judge, following the law, sentenced Tesla to death.

Six months later, appeals rejected, Tesla died. Two months after that, when it seemed that it could be done with a minimum of publicity, Leland submitted his resignation from the Port Smith Police Department. It had been a move he had been contemplating since the middle of the summer. The newspapers were interested, but Leland kept himself unavailable to reporters. The resignation was accepted "with regret," and the Department issued a statement that Lieutenant Leland had resigned for a variety of personal and business reasons. It was vague, but correct. Leland's arrangements with the Manitou Life Insurance Company, made before the resignation had been submitted, gave him time to conclude his affairs in Port Smith and make the move north. No announcement concerning his employment by Manitou was made until the day he began working. As much as possible he wanted to maintain the appearance of having located at Manitou after he had resigned from the Port Smith Police Department. It was not a matter of deception; the Department knew the truth. The Department had helped him move without drawing public attention where it would have been drawn, and he was not disposed to return embarrassment for kindness.

CHAPTER NINE

∎∎∎∎∎∎∎∎∎∎∎∎∎∎∎∎∎∎∎∎∎∎∎∎∎∎∎∎∎

"COME ON, DRAGON LADY," COLIN MACIVER SAID, "TELL ME WHAT you're thinking about."

Norma Colucci stretched. "Really want to know?" They were at Piantic Bay in the early evening and there was still light. She raised herself onto her elbows on the beach blanket and looked over her toes at the water. "I'm thinking that my father should see me now. How well I've done." She looked at him, squinting in the warm breeze. "You're the kind of man he calls 'Mister,' and you love me."

"It's not really surprising," he said. "The woman you've become since he saw you last, most men would love you."

"Do you mean that?"

"Yes, I do."

"Well, I don't care about that." She sat up. "I'm happy. Content. Languid?" She laughed. "I don't know how to say it. I love loving you. I love this. That's what I was thinking when you broke in on me. You broke in on a variation of the theme. My parents can't help me. There's no way to better what I feel." She rubbed her ankles. "The old griefs are gone. I want to do good things. Okay?"

"Okay."

"This is the first time we've mentioned my trouble since I told you."

"It was because I said 'most men.' I'm sorry."

"No, no, not at all. I don't want you to think that."

He grinned. "Okay. I'm full of 'okays' tonight. You have me feeling content, too. Very content."

"How did you get that scar on your neck?"

"Changing the subject?"

"No, silly, I—"

He laughed. "I got it when I was a kid. Another kid knocked me off my bicycle."

"All right. Do you want to go in the water again? I want to. We can go back to my place and take a shower and maybe we can go out for a sausage pizza and a beer. I feel like putting on weight tonight."

Which must have been the way it happened, Leland thought as he waited for Norma MacIver to return to the telephone. She hadn't broken down; it was only that room service had arrived with her breakfast. She hadn't broken down last night when she had studied her husband's picture in the souvenir book and had seen no scar. He had lied to her. In a way, she had just said to Leland, she had expected it. She hadn't known where the first lie would appear, and it was interesting that it would come up over something she had all but forgotten. Leland hadn't mentioned the insurance file to her, and now he was thinking that he would wait until they left for Port Smith. She picked up the receiver again.

"Norma, I think that I'll have more on this for you this afternoon after I see his mother and—" He didn't want to say "first wife"; he checked the card on his desk—"Betty Kaminsky. If I get any cooperation from them, I won't have trouble bringing it up. Until then, I don't think you and I should try to discuss it. Do you think you can agree with that?"

"Yes. Yes, I think so."

"It's hard for me to tell over the telephone if you're all right."

"Oh, yes. I could have called you last night if I had been really upset."

"That's the ticket. Now, listen. I've called the field where I keep my plane and they say we'll be able to go any time after eleven o'clock. You better figure two-thirty or three. I'll call you in plenty of time."

"You're in a much better mood today than you were yesterday."

"I guess I am. Part of it has to do with the fact that I'm going to do some flying."

"I see," she said. "You'll call me?"

"That's right."

"Goodbye."

"Goodbye, Norma."

He had to remember that she didn't know even approximately when MacIver had acquired the scar. For all Leland knew, she could be thinking that it predated the first marriage. He doubted that. Although MacIver had assured her that there had been no adultery, she would not be able to think of anything else. What stuck with Leland was the facility with which MacIver had lied—long after she had embraced for a certainty the idea that his knowledge of her background shielded her from lies from him. He had spun it off with stunning ease. "Let's face it," she had said yesterday, "he was slick." Yes, Leland thought. It was too soon to stop jumping from point to point: Leland thought of the small fortune MacIver had left. "Another kid knocked me off my bicycle." When Leland had been in the Police Academy he had known a fellow who had told all his women that he had never been in love before. This wasn't on the same order. It was something else.

Leland had to call the lawyer on the custody case and the personnel man at the Kelso Chain Works before he could get going on Colin MacIver. Last night, Mike had rung the absentee's bell on the pretext of asking directions, and as soon as the door had opened he had known the cause of the problem: the wife's drinking. The odors of alcohol and neglected children had hit Mike like the stink of a brewery. The man had answered the door and had given the directions graciously. In a case like this Leland could only tell what they had seen, heard, and smelled. The man could have been sick during the day, too; it wasn't for them to say. The family was obviously in trouble and there were places for it to go for help. If all of that had to be shown to the man by outsiders, then that was a problem he had made for himself.

The snow flurries that had been forecast for yesterday afternoon had come during the night, leaving a veil too thin to measure, much less clear away, and it had been disappearing fast by eight-thirty, when the traffic across the river had been heaviest. Karen had said that she would be in her office most of the day. He would call her before he left for Port Smith.

Leland had to go up and down Crestview Road in Canby twice before he located the home of Mrs. William MacIver. It wasn't what he had been looking for. Sitting in Mike's black two-door sedan at the curb, Leland had to think that perhaps Mrs. MacIver's sense of tradition wasn't as deeply rooted as he had been led to believe.

The house was new. It was a single-level contemporary design of fieldstone and white shingling, squatting in the middle of a carefully tended quarter-acre of lawn. Leland did not know his landscaping, but he thought he could see at least ten different kinds of shrubs around the house and bordering the flagstone walk. At one end of the roof was a very complicated television antenna, and at the other, on top of the chimney, was a lightning arrester of the latest configuration. It had been heavily advertised in the area last spring.

It was possible that she had married again. Leland hadn't even thought of that. The house showed a woman's influence but a man's work. Leland got out of the car and went up the walk.

There was only one name on the plate: MacIver. Leland tapped the brass door knocker lightly.

"Yes?"

A chain on the door; he could see a pale blue eye.

"My name is Joseph Leland. I knew your son during the war." He passed his identification through the crack. She took it and the door closed slightly. It opened again and the chain banged taut.

"A private detective? Did that little Guinea hire you? What do you mean you knew my son during the war?"

"We were in the One sixty-one together over Germany. In Mustangs."

The eye relaxed. "And? What do you want?"

"There's good reason to believe that Colin was murdered. Another of Colin's friends asked me to look into it."

"Just a minute." The door closed and he heard the chain fall slack. The door opened.

She was in her fifties, neat, beginning to put on weight. Her hair

178

was blued and combed up. It was eleven o'clock in the morning and she was fully dressed, from expensive daytime dress to pearl earrings. She was elaborately made up, and her skin was very fair under the rouge. It was rouge, too: old-fashioned, carefully applied.

"Come in, come in," she said. "I don't want to be seen talking on the doorstep."

He followed her into the sunken living room. The furniture was all new, contemporary; for all the use it showed, he could have stepped into one of the larger displays at an exposition in Grand Rapids.

Mrs. MacIver had an upright, shoulders-back walk that belied her age. She seemed to be in good health. Her legs were knotting up, but there were no marks—varicose veins, blemishes—on the skin. She turned to him now, shifting her weight as if she had been to charm school. It was interesting. "Excuse me. Are you the Leland who shot down all those planes?"

"That's right."

"Colin mentioned you in his letters. Let me have your coat, please. Do sit down. Would you like some coffee?"

"No. No, thanks."

He sat down and waited until she returned from the hall closet. Little Guinea: that explained one thing—perhaps. The pictures on the walls were pastoral views of never-never land. As a child Leland had had a storybook filled with line drawings in the same style. These pictures were thirty or forty years old, the only old things he had seen so far. It did not promise much.

He remembered to rise when she returned. "The letters you mentioned. Did you happen to save them?"

"No, I'm sorry. Sit down. When I moved out of the big house I took only what I thought I would want. I didn't think that Colin would die. Do you know anything about Colin and me?"

"I've been told that you weren't in touch."

"That's right." She sat like charm school, too, her legs under her and her hands clasped on one knee. The schools taught women never to face a man head-on, lest her hips give him the impression of a battleship about to run him down. After the war Karen had bought a

179

book by one of the authorities; when she had seen that, she had put the book away.

Leland said, "Mrs. MacIver, I was hoping that you heard from him before he died."

"No."

"The man who contacted me said that you hadn't seen Colin since before his second marriage."

"That's right."

"Can you tell me why that was?"

"A family situation. You haven't bothered Betty, have you? She's been ill."

"I'm sorry to hear that."

"She's had difficulty for years because of Colin, and I don't think it would be helpful if you bothered her."

"Yes, of course. Let me change the subject. Did your son ever tell you anything of his business affairs?"

"No. Should he have?"

"I don't know," Leland said. The game was over. He was learning nothing and she was tightening up anyway. Lines had appeared across her brow and her upper lip like the soft shadows of a sunset. "Let me ask you this, Mrs. MacIver: are there any questions that you have about your son's death?"

"No. No, I think I know less about it than you do, Mr. Leland. You haven't told me of anything you knew about him. You didn't know him at all, did you?"

"We were introduced," he said. "He was very young then."

"He was very young when he died," she said. She smiled; she thought that he was securely in her trap. "Can you tell me when you met Colin?"

"February or March of '45. I went home shortly after that. Another thing: before his death, Colin had a scar on the left side of his neck. He didn't have it when I knew him. Could you tell me how he got that?"

"I could but I won't."

"I beg your pardon?"

180

The lines were deeper now. "You understood me. I won't discuss it with you."

"Well, could you tell me if it had anything to do with the collapse of his first marriage?"

"I'm sorry." She got up. "This is a waste of time. You can tell that little Guinea that she needn't ever come around here, if the mood strikes her. I'm not interested in her or whatever she thinks she's up to. I'll get your coat."

Leland waited in the living room. He could get in another two questions if he made her show him the way to the door. When she returned and saw him holding his ground she let out an audible sigh. Her face looked as hard as cast iron. "Goodbye, Mr. Leland."

"Do you feel that the scar had a connection with his death?"

"Goodbye! Please!"

"Mrs. MacIver, I feel that you do have information that could help me. A man doesn't fall to his death for no reason. If you do know about that scar—"

"Of *course* I know, but I'm not going to tell *you!*" She let her eyes go over him as if his presence brutalized her. "Would you leave? If you come around me and mine again, I'll have to take action against you."

Leland took his time buttoning his coat. "Mine?"

"A figure of speech. Leave, *please!*" She went ahead of him.

Leland stopped in the foyer. "Did your son contribute to your support?"

No answer. The door was open. He nodded, stepped out, and the door slammed so suddenly, so close behind him, that the rush of air slapped his coat hard against his back. If he had hesitated, he would have been hurt badly. She had taken that chance. He hurried out to the car, not looking back. Mrs. MacIver wasn't as sane as she thought she was. She was sane and the rest of the world was mad—even her son? Leland meant to find out.

The quickest way from Canby to High View was over high-crowned secondary roads that cut through the last truck farms in Cuyahauga County. Every half-mile or so was a small tract of houses, occupied or still under construction. In five years at the most, the area would be just another suburb. The population of Manitou was supposed to double as soon as the war babies began to marry—that meant Steffie, too. He could be a grandfather in another five or six years. It frightened him but made him more than a little happy.

He stopped at a roadside shack to call in and try to get his head up for the interview with Betty Kaminsky. Florence had nothing new. There was no one in the office and the girls had the radio playing. He asked about the news. She said that she had heard nothing on the Shoftel case. He hadn't been thinking of it. He hadn't been thinking of anything; the question had just come out of him. He was beginning to see what talking to the senior Mrs. MacIver had done to him.

Over coffee he tried to memorize what she had said. It wasn't much, but he thought he had more than he had before. Simply having seen her had advanced the work, but he had to do better with Betty Kaminsky. He had not forgotten that Mrs. MacIver had said that she had been ill. All it meant to him was potential trouble. This time he would be on his guard.

There was no difficulty with the Argyle Road address. He had been prepared for the house by the preceding half-mile, threading through a maze of bright cracker boxes exactly like it. In the shadows the pockets of snow clung with a grimness the owners could not have foreseen in the springs and summers they had come here househunting. These places were built and sold like automobiles, and the bright warm months were their showrooms. Leland could feel the mountain wind whipping up the slope; no child's coat could cut such a wind—in this good place to bring up children.

A man opened the door. Leland presented his identification again. "I'd like to speak with Mrs. Kaminsky, if I may."

The man was plump, in his mid-thirties, blond, balding, and he wore horn-rimmed glasses. He had a small mouth and the beginnings of a double chin. "Well, I'll have to see," he said, pleasantly enough. "She's been sick."

"I know," Leland said. "Mrs. MacIver told me."

The man stared. "I don't understand."

"I'm looking into the death of Colin MacIver."

"What did you say?" In his shirt sleeves he tried to step out onto the stoop. The wind hit him and he looked around. "Come in, come in, but speak softly. This is the first we've heard." He closed the door and led Leland to the foot of the stairs to the second floor. He held Leland's forearm. "When was this? How did it happen?"

"Over three months ago." Leland decided not to fox around with this man. "MacIver jumped, fell, or was thrown from the roof of Flatlands Racetrack in Port Smith on August twelfth."

"My God! What a terrible thing!"

"Who is it, Murray?"

"A man, dear! He wants to ask me some questions!"

"Say I'm an insurance investigator asking about a neighbor, if you want," Leland said quietly.

"He's a private detective!" Murray Kaminsky called up.

"What does he want?"

Leland realized that he had no idea of what she looked like.

"I'll tell you," Kaminsky called. "Just relax." He turned to Leland. "All she's had is a touch of flu. She's better now, but I don't know whether you can see her. She isn't going to take this well."

"I understand. But maybe you can help me. There are some serious questions about MacIver's death."

"I guess there are. I'll see what I can do. What an awful thing. You want to come into the kitchen? She won't hear us there. Let me see if she needs anything."

Leland opened his coat while he waited. The kitchen had a northern exposure and needed light. The walls were a vivid yellow, so intense it hurt the eyes. After a moment the muffled voices upstairs stopped. Kaminsky appeared. He flipped the wall switch and an overhead fluorescent light blossomed. It left Leland blinking.

"Have a seat," Kaminsky said.

They sat down on opposite sides of a white Formica table. "Cigarette?"

"Thanks. Take off your coat. Put it over the back of the chair." Kaminsky moved a glass ash tray to the center of the table.

"I appreciate this help, Mr. Kaminsky—"

"Murray." He took Leland's light.

"Call me Joe. Murray, I appreciate this, so I'll level with you.

MacIver's death was ruled a suicide, but we want to be sure. Did you ever meet him?"

"No, but I saw pictures of him. I would have known him anywhere."

"Are those pictures still around?"

"No, Betty got rid of them." He looked at Leland a moment. "Maybe you know it, maybe you don't, but Betty's had a rough time since their divorce."

"I'm getting that idea."

"I want to help you. I don't like to see any man die. If I tell you things in confidence, I want you to understand."

"I will."

"It took Betty a while to get rid of those pictures, okay?"

"Thanks."

"I mean that she had them around. In the bottom of a drawer."

"That's what I thought you meant. *He* married again, too. Did you know that?"

"Sure. A little Italian girl."

Mrs. MacIver kept them informed. Leland wondered what Kaminsky thought of her. "By his second wife's account, they were happy together. Coming when it did, his death doesn't figure at all."

"He was a complicated man," Kaminsky said. "It shouldn't be a surprise to us—to Betty, and through her, to me."

"Can you explain that?"

He tapped his cigarette. "It's hard. I should try. I'll tell you, Joe, I'm still rocking from the news. I never liked what I heard about the guy, and all of a sudden there you are telling me he's dead."

"I understand that, Murray."

"You working for the widow?"

"That has to be confidential."

"You answered me. She deserves to know. How is she fixed, by the way? Did he leave her anything?"

Leland asked, "What do you do for a living?"

"I'm an electrical engineer."

"She doesn't need anything," Leland said.

"Why did you want to know what I did?"

"Professional ethics. I like you, but I can't get in the habit of giving out information for free."

Kaminsky laughed. "You want a cup of coffee?"

"I just had one, but I wouldn't mind another."

"Does the old lady know? Mrs. MacIver?"

"I wanted to ask you what you thought of her," Leland said.

"Let's go in order. You answer my question first."

"She's known since August."

"And she never said anything." Kaminsky nodded to himself. "We shouldn't be surprised by that, either." He paused, staring at the coffeepot on the stove. "Mrs. MacIver is a funny kind of woman, Joe, very proper, very refined. Something happens to her as you get to know her better—she comes apart before your eyes. Maybe—*we* think—she's getting senile, very slowly. It's hard to explain to someone who hasn't experienced it."

Leland told him about the near-miss with the front door.

"There," Kaminsky said. "So maybe you do know. Let me put it this way: you were dealing with a woman who had none of her dreams come true. Her dreams are unrealistic, to be sure, but there they are. She still has them. She comes from what she thinks was a fine old family and she was raised with the impression that she was going to live the life that went before—you know, during the eighties and nineties. She married a scuffling kind of guy and he died young. That wasn't supposed to happen. She couldn't understand her son— that wasn't supposed to happen, either. In justice to him, she doesn't understand anybody. For all we can tell, she may not be bright enough. I don't mean to attack her. She hides behind her propriety and refinement. She doesn't *want* to know things. We just can't tell if she's bright or dull."

The coffee was ready. He stayed quiet while he served it. "Betty's a tea drinker," he told Leland. "That's why I didn't ask if she wanted any of this."

Leland tended to his cup.

"You want to hear about Colin MacIver. There's no point in talking about his mother." Kaminsky removed his horn-rimmed glasses and began to clean them with a paper napkin. His face looked harder and more tired. "Betty met him at a party at Jefferson in 1946. I have no reason to doubt anything she's told me. I'm telling you the truth as I understand it. She was smitten with the idea of him having been a fighter pilot. I was in the Engineers myself." The glasses went on again. "Anyway, she was twenty-two. She had just finished her undergraduate work in teaching. She went for him like a duck to water. There was a time when she could tell me these things. It's all dead stuff now—or it was until you showed up. Betty and I both know that she married me on the rebound, but we've made a good thing of it. You married?"

"Fourteen years," Leland said.

"Love your wife?"

"More every day."

"That's the way I feel. Madness, isn't it? So you know that relationships change. In the beginning, MacIver was very much a part of us. The point is, it would have gotten you nowhere to have tried to discuss this with her. She wouldn't have been able to talk for long without thinking back and having to stop.

"MacIver must have been a terrific character in those days, at least to be acquainted with. Betty married him in less than six months —the same with me, but for different reasons. People get to know their friends, but they marry acquaintances. It's more a question of relief than love, don't you think?"

Leland sipped his coffee. "This is no time for an argument. I married my best friend."

"You're one of the few. A lot of people don't learn about the people they marry until after they've married them, and some never get to know them at all."

"You've done a lot of thinking about it."

"Let's just say that it's been worth my while."

"Okay."

"He wasn't the same person afterward. She told me that it was like learning a secret. He was moody, depressed, angry—even violent. For a long time he seemed to be riding on the lip of hysteria."

"You're going to have to explain that."

"They were married. They had a honeymoon—a time of honeymoon, do you understand?"

Leland nodded.

"They calmed down a little," Kaminsky said. "For about a year they drifted along quietly. He was going to Jefferson for accounting while they taught. GI couple, skidding their way through, movies every other week, a double date once in a while, and that was it. Then he started to pull into himself. He never hit her, but he was capable of it. He did things that took the place of hitting her, threw dishes and deliberately broke things."

Leland nodded. There was no way he could get around talking to Betty Kaminsky now. To some degree, it was a case of the old saw about love being blind, and Leland could not take Kaminsky's word that he was not still hypnotized by his wife. He was an intelligent man, but by his own admission he had married foolishly. Leland liked him but did not know him, and it was possible for Kaminsky to have an opinion of himself that would cause him to marry badly and be "very damned glad"—as Norma had said. And what did this say about MacIver? Leland was in sympathy with MacIver in his choice of Norma, but it could have been that MacIver had chosen her for reasons utterly different from Leland's own.

No. She was an honest person. She had described her marriage reasonably well. She had said things about herself that Leland could check easily with Wendell Roberts. No, MacIver was still the man who had loved her as she had described—and in spite of the lies he had told her.

Kaminsky read something in Leland's eyes. "This isn't what you've heard from other people, is it?"

"No, it isn't."

"It's true, I assure you," Kaminsky said. "And it gets worse. I know the toll it's taken on Betty. It's going to hurt her even now to know that he's dead. A human being doesn't give up on another after they've lived together for years. Not completely. A little part of her still wishes him well.

"I'll tell you what I know. He had a girl friend while he was married to Betty. They weren't married a year when it came out.

187

Chances were, he started with this girl very soon after he and Betty were married. One night he came home all cut up. Bleeding. He wouldn't say anything about it. It made no sense. The kind of cut it was wasn't the kind of thing you get falling. His girl friend must have done it."

"Describe it to me," Leland said.

"It was on his neck, a kind of a gouge. It was the kind of thing a woman would do."

"When did this happen, did you say?"

"I'm not sure of the date," Kaminsky said. "When Betty told me, she said that they hadn't been married a year."

Leland nodded.

"He had been using the dodge that he had been studying late at the university library. He never said a word about it later. If he had regrets, he never expressed them."

Leland said, "They came up here several times to visit his mother. Is that how your wife and Mrs. MacIver became friends?"

"They're not friends," Kaminsky said. "Don't be mistaken about that. Betty will call her once in a while—she did it this weekend because she had nothing to do—or she'll drive over and look in on her, or she'll be invited, once in a very great while, for an evening. In the beginning Betty tried to get her over here, but Mrs. MacIver never came, so Betty stopped asking."

"Do you think that has something to do with your religion?"

"I'm not Jewish," Kaminsky said.

"Does Mrs. MacIver know that?"

"I'm sure she does. She knows all about me, what I do, maybe even how much money I make. Betty tells me that the old lady likes me."

"The impression I got from her was that she would think you're Jewish, and that would be the end of it."

"She's a bigot, you mean? Sure she is, but it's so ingrained in her that she's not even aware of it. She says 'boogie' and 'kike' as easily as we say 'Negro' and 'Jew.' They're perfectly acceptable terms to her. The important thing to remember is that the people they refer to aren't acceptable themselves. She simply wouldn't have them in the house. It's the way she was raised, and the way she'll go to her grave.

"I'm all right to her, probably mostly because Betty married me. My father was Jewish, but my mother was an Episcopalian, and she was the one who prevailed on the issue of my religion. Betty and I thrashed this out long ago about Mrs. MacIver. Mrs. MacIver is—and was—alone in the world. She's always been fond of Betty. Before Betty married me, her reasons for staying in touch with the old lady were more complicated than they are today, but she did feel sorry for her. Mrs. MacIver's loneliness is her own fault, mostly, but Betty can't help continuing to feel sorry for her. After the divorce and Mrs. MacIver's objections to it, Colin MacIver took the opportunity to unload her. He never came back here, as far as we know. Betty can't abide that, and neither can I. She's his mother. Or was."

"I have information that says he was here three years ago to tell his mother that he was marrying again," Leland told him. "He came here specifically to ask her blessing."

Kaminsky regarded him a moment. "Now see, that's the way the old lady is. She told Betty that she received a long letter informing her of the marriage. And she hasn't told Betty that he's dead, either. Maybe she thinks that Betty shouldn't know, or that as long as Betty's resentment of MacIver is alive, she's on good ground emotionally. I have trouble understanding it myself, but it's the only guess I can make about this. As I said, she doesn't understand anybody. Maybe this is the way she's worked it out—and maybe not."

"She's gotten worse in recent years," Leland suggested.

"That's right. She used to belong to clubs. She doesn't anymore."

"Did her son contribute to her support?"

"Not that I know of. He didn't have to, that's for sure."

"Why is that?"

"The old man left her a bundle twenty years ago. Maybe she's down to the scraps, but Betty knew exactly what was there when she was married to Colin, and there was plenty."

Leland had to think of the description of the senior MacIver that

Norma had related to him. He said to Kaminsky, "You called him a scuffler."

"He was, but he made a couple of good scores. So have I, for that matter. In the market. He made his in real estate. I hear things in my business—you know, the exotic stocks."

"Do you know any more about the father?"

"Just that. He made his money in the real estate boom here in the twenties. He wasn't alone."

Leland asked, "Now, what about the divorce?"

"Colin asked for it, and eventually did the filing. He sprung it on her one night. 'I want a divorce.' She was in love with him. He had been out of school a while and they were beginning to get ahead. She'd thought that they would begin to live. He wanted a divorce and she said no. She said no for half a year, and then gave up. In a little while she met me and we were married pretty quickly. It cost her a lot of money to marry me. He was paying her enough to make some women think twice."

"I'd like to have the figures," Leland said.

"He gave her four thousand dollars not to contest the suit and sent her four hundred a month after that. There wasn't any real agreement, but he sent it. She had letters and bank statements that would have looked good in court. That doesn't do him justice. On money, he could be counted on. If he said he was going to do a thing, he did it."

"He could make a thing like that clear enough for her to believe it?"

"He wasn't a scuffler. He didn't tell her anything, but all the time they were married, he handled the money, and they never had trouble for a minute. He worked it up into quite a little bit, considering their savings. It was the way he conducted himself around money. He made the right moves. That's really all I can tell you."

"Okay. Thanks. Did you hear from him when you were married?"

"No. I expected a telegram or something—after all, he was getting off the hook—but nothing came."

Leland drank his coffee. What kept sticking at him was Betty's

190

lie about the time MacIver had come home bleeding. The insurance file placed it around the middle of 1949, nearly three years after the marriage. Leland wanted to believe Kaminsky on everything else, but he couldn't. He couldn't take the chance. Kaminsky was a likable, convincing man, but he had admitted too many weaknesses for Leland to think that even he believed everything he had said. This is the truth as I know it: *these are the lies Betty told to me. I try not to think about them.*

Leland had gained very little for a morning's work. There were things to tell Mrs. MacIver, but he had hoped for more: that there had been a previous attempt at suicide, that what MacIver had told about himself was at direct odds with what his mother and first wife could prove. Proof: no one thought to keep records anymore. It was too much work. Leland had only to look at his own memory to know how fallible memory was. It took work to capture things as they had happened. Kaminsky had talked off the top of his head, so had Mrs. MacIver. Norma had come prepared, but all she knew was the tail end of her husband's life—and just the things he had done, never what he had thought. He had never told her his real thoughts. What Leland had heard today indicated that MacIver had had good reason for never telling. Still, there was the suddenness, the unexpectedness, of his death, the hurried verdict of the Clausen County coroner, the handling of the afternoon of August 12 by the Clausen County police. Leland had not even moved toward that yet. He could not help thinking what no detective ever wanted to think: that a man could make his moves without leaving a trace. The chance of failing was strong enough for Leland to feel it, like the shock of anger he had felt when the door had slammed at his back.

Upstairs, a door opened. "Murray? Are you still down there?"

"Yes, honey. What is it?"

"I'm coming down."

"No, stay in bed."

They could hear her on the stairs. Kaminsky couldn't turn his eyes from the doorway.

She entered the kitchen, wrapped in a pink wool robe. She had had more than a touch of flu, Leland thought at first. She was very pale and drawn. She had pinned back her hair, but Leland could see that she had not combed it, as if she had been in bed for too long. Her hair was dark red, thick and shoulder length. She had a thin face and what Leland would call a long neck. The robe was belted tightly. She was slender and she looked tall, though she was not as tall as Karen. Her legs and especially her hips were longer in proportion to her upper torso. She had a larger bosom than most women with the same slight bone structure, and with her narrow waist and shoulders she gave an impression of lightness, softness, and extraordinary delicacy. She was an extraordinary woman, interesting to look at but somehow not exciting to think about. Part of it was her illness and part of it was her eyes—round, open hazel eyes. They made her look like a stranger here. Leland wanted to think that she knew it and did not care. Her eyes were so bland that they offered no clue to who she was. He wanted to see into her, but for some reason the inability to do it only annoyed him.

"Betty, this is Mr. Leland."

"How do you do? Excuse me, I haven't been feeling well. Murray, I'm going to have a cup of tea."

"I'll get it."

"Would you?" She let him move away from the table; she was going to take his seat, too. She wasn't wearing a brassiere; as she pulled the collar of her robe together her breasts moved up, yielded, soft. "What is it that I can't hear until Mr. Leland is gone? Sit down, Mr. Leland. I'm sorry."

Leland sat down.

Kaminsky was at the sink. "Betty, it's about Colin MacIver."

"What has he done now?" She put her elbows on the table and picked at her long, clear fingernails. "Murray?"

He hesitated. Finally he looked at Leland. She did not see herself in the terms Kaminsky saw her. Of course she was taking advantage, maybe even seriously. Her eyes played a role in this, too. Leland had to remind himself that she was thirty years old. She did not look or act it. MacIver's second wife was carrying a baby, but even normally she would not move as lightly as this woman moved when she was sick. Now Leland remembered irrelevantly that today was Norma's twenty-sixth birthday.

"You might as well tell her," Kaminsky said.

She sat back, guessing, but waiting to be told. She looked like a child about to be struck for the very first time, unable to believe that it was going to happen to her. The muscles in her temples twitched. Leland said, "He's been dead since August twelfth." Her brow furrowed. Her face seemed to sag. "He jumped, fell, or was thrown from the roof of Flatlands Racetrack."

"Oh, dear God." She bit her lip and then reached into her pocket for a handkerchief. "Excuse me," she said. Leland waited while she tended herself. She turned away from them. "Go ahead," she said.

"The coroner ruled it a suicide—" Leland said.

"Are you all right, Betty?"

"I will be, honey." She swallowed. "Oh, dear God." She shook her head slowly, her mouth pulling down in the corners. The tears shimmered in her eyes. She wiped them and blew her nose again. "You didn't know before this, did you, Murray?"

"No, dear, I didn't."

"What about his mother?" she asked Leland.

"She was notified at the time."

"Oh, the poor woman. Murray? The past couple of times I talked to her I thought there was something the matter, didn't I?"

"That's right. Mr. Leland is here to find out what he can about him."

Leland let a moment pass. "You see, Mrs. Kaminsky, there was no warning of suicide—" He stopped as Kaminsky brought over the cup of tea.

"If you're all right, Betty, I'll give you a chance to talk to him alone."

"All right. Thank you."

Leland preferred not to watch him leave. He was going to sit somewhere and wait until he was called.

"Who hired you, Mr. Leland?" She sniffed.

"I have to keep that confidential," he said.

"I read about you in the *Herald-Press* yesterday. If you were just anybody, if you hadn't once shaken Colin's hand, I don't think I could talk to you." She looked away, staring. She had to go slowly. She tasted her tea, used her handkerchief on her eyes again, and helped herself to one of Leland's cigarettes. "I know your wife, too." She lit the cigarette herself. The skin around her eyes was in blotches. "Not to speak to, just by sight. I substitute-teach up here once in a while. I'm from Port Smith, too, like the both of you."

"I know."

"I remember when you got the scar on your jaw years ago. When was that?"

"1940."

"I was sixteen. There was that picture of you with the blood running down your neck. How many men died that night?"

"Three."

She nodded. "Did my husband recognize you?"

"I don't think it matters to him."

"That's right, it doesn't. After me, everybody is treated alike."

"I gathered that."

"I thought you had. It's the way Murray is." She blinked and the tears ran down her cheeks. "Colin is dead?"

"Yes. I'm sorry."

"When we were divorced I wondered how much I would know about his life from then on. I didn't want this to happen to him. I didn't."

"I can see that, Mrs. Kaminsky."

"Did Murray tell you much?"

"Very, very little," he said.

"What did you hear from his present wife? I mean, his widow? Can you tell me what she is like?"

"You'd get along." He didn't know if they would or not. "She knows practically nothing about you. In the last phase of his life, Colin MacIver said very little about himself to anybody. It's why I'm here, why I'm involved at all."

"I suppose she's in the same position I was in. I had no one to go to. I never had many friends, and after Colin left, I had no friends at all. The poor girl, I feel so sorry for her. I see myself in her place."

Leland stayed quiet.

"When Murray came along offering his kindness I leaped at him. I had to. This is worse for her, but it *is* the same, in a way."

"She'll be all right," Leland said.

"The degree isn't the same, but the quality of the thing is. It's strange that the last thing Colin should do should hurt someone badly. He died as he lived—it's disgusting to say, even to think, but it's true. He hurt people all his life."

"I'm very interested in that, Mrs. Kaminsky."

"I mean his family," she said. "His mother. And me. And now this little girl he married."

"While you knew him, did he hurt anyone outside the family? Did he ever hurt anyone badly enough to evoke a threat you heard of or learned of later?"

She stared at him, incredulous, almost angry. "You mean, did he ever make anybody mad enough to kill him?"

"Yes, that's what I mean."

"Colin was a coward, Mr. Leland. He wasn't capable of making enemies on that level."

Leland let his eyes drop and had to regret it at once. He wasn't going to get her to cooperate and he didn't want to tell her anything through his reactions. It was past the time to change the subject. "What did you know of his financial affairs?"

"Affairs? All but a year of the time I knew him, he was in college."

"He did work," Leland said.

"Yes, that's right, and we made ends meet. Well, more than that. We were able to save steadily. He was very careful with money. I don't mean to say that he was cheap. He didn't spend foolishly or impulsively. Murray does that. We're the only people we know with a shortwave receiver. He bought it because it was a good one."

"If it's any consolation, I bought my first airplane on an impulse."

She smiled. It wasn't what he had expected. He let his pleasure show and she took it happily, but uncertainly. In her own way she was as complicated to understand as MacIver's second wife. He wanted to think that she was ready to defend herself, always, but it wasn't as simple as that. He said, "I'd like to ask about the settlement between you, if I may."

"Did Murray tell you about that?"

"A bit. I knew of it before I spoke to him."

"Please don't lie to me," she said. "Remembering Colin brings me close enough to lying."

"When you asked me who I represent I told you that it was confidential. I could have given you a cock-and-bull story, but I didn't."

"Yes, I suppose you're right."

He had to press. He saw that he had been pressing for some time, instinctively. As lightly as she carried herself, she was the victim of an inner inertia. It made Leland think that she would be married to Colin MacIver yet if he had not taken action. He had cheated on her and even had come home bleeding and she had done nothing. Since the divorce she had had a difficult time—it was no wonder. Leland said, "My understanding of what happened is that he sued for the divorce and made a rather large settlement with you."

"He didn't buy me out, Mr. Leland. It never came up. In one of our final arguments he dared me to stay unmarried for more than a year. Before that he agreed to give me four thousand dollars—all our savings and then some. It was what he projected would be half of what we would have made over our minimum standard of living in the next two years. According to him, I was entitled to that."

"Are you quoting?"

"Yes, as a matter of fact. The other part of the settlement, four hundred dollars a month, was the result of our argument. It was what he would pay as long as I stayed unmarried. If I were the kind of woman he wanted to think I was, I could have collected for years. A woman doesn't have to get married. She learns that quickly, after a divorce."

"I'm interested in the kind of woman he thought you were," Leland said.

196

"A leech. All take and no give."

"Is that a quote, too?"

"Not precisely. I said that he was a coward. I said it to him—'Is that what you think I am?' And he didn't answer."

"And you took that for agreement," Leland said.

"What would you take it for?"

"The same as you. You're right. Why did he think you would marry again?"

"From his own point of view, he thought he understood me. He said that I would be unable to control myself—that I would marry the first man who was nice to me."

There was nothing for Leland to say. Betty Kaminsky sat back, slumping, staring at her cup. "Of course I did exactly what he said," she half-whispered. "Murray knows it. We had some terrible fights in the beginning, at least as terrible as those I had with Colin." She looked up. "One of the differences between Murray and Colin is that Murray doesn't quit. He knew me better than I knew myself. He saw that I would come around—that I would change.

"One of the things that kept Murray and me from being really married for so long was that I stayed under the influence of Colin's opinion of me." She sat up. "I don't mean *physically*. You didn't take it that way, did you?"

"No, of course not."

"Good. God, I'm not as bad as that. —See? That's an expression of Colin's influence. I'm not bad at all. I'm not a leech or a bitch or anything like that. You see, Colin was right as far as he went in saying that I would marry the first man who was nice to me. He didn't go far enough. I've never been close to people. I've never had a lot of friends—this weekend while I've been sick, I've heard from no one. No one's called. It's the way I've always been, to my sorrow. People aren't drawn to me. I have the same needs as you or Murray or your wife. When Murray was nice to me, I just responded, the same way as I tried to respond when I met Colin."

He asked, "Was MacIver lucky with the horses?"

"Horses? While I knew him, he never gambled."

It seemed impossible, but he could not challenge her. He had to wonder how well she knew anybody besides herself. Her marriage with MacIver had only encouraged her self-involvement—she had just said that it was the way she had always been. If Leland wanted to assume things about MacIver's character, he could understand how MacIver had gone outside a marriage with her. Then Leland had to explain the lies to Norma—who obviously would have understood. MacIver had had the insight to accept her on her terms. Leland had to remember what Norma had told him about Colin MacIver and what he had done. This woman had described him as a coward. From his own experience in the war Leland knew better. And finally there was the fact of MacIver's sudden death. The closer Leland tried to get, the more MacIver skittered away. Leland could not believe that he knew more than he had at this same time yesterday.

"Another thing," he said. "Do you know any reason why he would try to create the impression that you and his mother were closer than you really are?"

"It was the way he saw it," she said. "For him, it was the truth. He hated that woman when I met him. I tried to be nice to her. He drew the inference that we were friendly."

"Do you know why he hated her?"

"You met her. She's not an easy person to get along with. Like me."

She wanted to talk about herself. Leland said, "His father didn't get good marks, either."

"All I've heard about his father tells me that he was a good man. He simply did not make history."

"He was a plugger, you mean?"

"A plugger who earned enough in his short life to support his family long after he was gone. How do you think Colin got to the University of California before the war? On money earned by his father's investments. In spite of the social position she thinks she has, Mrs. MacIver would be very poor if it had not been for her husband. He was a quiet, retiring man. I know the kind of things Colin must have said about him. Colin could have disparaged anyone. *That* was a thing he could do well. He didn't know what he wanted for himself. That's something I've had to learn, too. I still haven't learned it, and

198

he's dead and buried." She smiled, baring her teeth. "He made some mess during the short time he was on this earth, Mr. Leland. I think you're beginning to see that."

Not precisely; Leland was thinking about the man who had done the trick with the numbers for fifty dollars and had given the money to the wives. Murray Kaminsky appeared in the doorway.

"I think that's about it," he said. "Betty, I don't want you getting upset."

She hesitated before answering. "Yes, I think you're right."

Leland got up. "Thank you for the help you've given, both of you. I appreciate it."

She nodded. Leland adjusted the collar of his topcoat and let Kaminsky show him to the front door. Kaminsky stepped out onto the cement stoop.

"I had to cut it short," he said. "She's going to have a rough time."

"I know, and I sincerely regret it."

Kaminsky offered his hand. "Good luck to you. I'll be interested in hearing what you learn."

"Sorry. Ethics again. I won't wish you good luck. You're doing fine."

"More every day." Kaminsky grinned. "So help me."

Leland remembered what he was referring to. He had to think that Kaminsky really wasn't the man for the job he had chosen, and that Betty Ford MacIver Kaminsky would never be whole. Leland couldn't be casual about it, or joking. He nodded goodbye pleasantly, turned, and went down the walk.

In the office after he dictated his notes on the mother and Betty Kaminsky, Leland gave Florence a list of things he wanted her to do while he was gone. She read it back to him when he had finished.

"I'm to search the titles of Mrs. MacIver's houses, the one in Canby and the one they lived in originally. The address for that is in your souvenir book. I'm to get the files from the insurance company on MacIver's father and record the terms of the settlements of the policies. If there's a copy of his will, I'm to summarize the provisions."

"Good. I want you to try to get an idea of her current worth. Call the Credit Bureau—you know. See if she has a charge account at Bonney's or any of the other big stores. I'll be calling you, so don't send anything unless I tell you."

She got up to leave. "Where will you be staying?"

"I'll let you know." He had to go down to his apartment and pack a bag before he picked up Norma at her hotel. When Florence closed the door Leland reached for the telephone and dialed Karen's number. Her secretary put him through.

"It's me," he said. "Are you busy?"

"No, no. How are you doing?"

"Not bad. I'd like you to do me a favor, if you will. Would you check on the employment record of a Betty Kaminsky?" He spelled the last name. "It's Betty, not Elizabeth. She's a substitute teacher."

"It may not be easy for me if she hasn't been in junior or senior high," Karen said.

"That's all right, do the best you can. She was MacIver's first wife and I want to know what people think of her. There isn't much chance of getting hold of anybody who knew them when they were married."

"How was his mother?"

He told her. "And as far as this Betty goes, she has traits in common with his mother and his second wife, but I don't see that the second marriage is a case of a man trying to marry the same woman again. Physically, she's on the other end of the scale, willowy, graceful, and fair. She's a redhead. And where Norma MacIver is friendly, this woman knows that she's ingrown, and doesn't care."

"Maybe she's become that way."

"No, she told me otherwise. MacIver must have known it when he married her. Apparently he lost interest quickly, but stuck it out as long as he could—in his own style." Leland told her about the scar. "Finally he said that he didn't love her and had to have a divorce. They fought for a while, but she gave in." He recounted the terms of

200

the settlement and then told her about the lies both of the principals had told about the scar.

"Joe, it's possible that they didn't want to remember the truth. There are things that I don't want to think about and don't remember correctly. You've done it, too."

"I just wish it were as simple as that. By Norma MacIver's account this guy was slick as hell. He gave her a story that was pure fiction. He lied to his first wife—he was an accomplished, polished liar. There's no way to get around that. His mother might have something to do with that—I can understand how he would get into the pattern of lying to her. There are a lot of questions still unanswered. I want to know how he got that quarter of a million. Betty Kaminsky didn't have any idea that he had accumulated so much."

"All right," she said, "let me ask you a question: how are *you* doing?"

"I'm in great shape," he said.

"I can't help believing that this is very unpleasant for you. It's not the same as one of those divorce or custody things. You're closer to it. You *were* upset yesterday."

"That was something else. Don't you worry about me."

"How did your client react this morning?"

"She did her reacting last night when she saw the souvenir book. I decided to let it go at that until I could see her. She did say that she had expected something—which is logical, because she's been able to live with his death only on the assumption that there were things he didn't tell her."

"Please be careful of her, Joe."

"She was calm this morning, Karen. I think that the thing you saw yesterday in the Flamingo was the result of the state of nerves she had built up before she saw me. It had nothing to do with me."

"That's as good a reason as any to be careful. You can provide an immense relief for her—you know that I'm putting it delicately."

He wanted to get off the topic. "What have you decided to do about the weekend?"

"You don't even know if you'll still be there, Joe. Let's talk about it later in the week."

Her tone had turned harsh. He didn't know how to answer her.

She said, "I can't get excited about going to Port Smith under any circumstances. Call it an aberration if you want, but it's the way I want to keep things."

"It's hardly an aberration when you put it in your head deliberately. You know that better than I do."

"Please don't try to push me into anything. I said last night that I would think about it—isn't that enough? I don't want to fight."

"I don't want to fight with you," he said. "I wasn't trying to push you, either. You know that."

"Don't let anything happen," she said.

"No."

"Joe?"

"No, nothing will happen. I promise you, Karen."

"Are you all right?"

"You can bet on it. You seemed all right this morning yourself."

"I was. Still am. Do you love me?"

He thought of Kaminsky. "More every day."

"That's right. Be careful, honey. Don't take chances."

Those days were over. He said that he wouldn't take chances and they made their goodbyes. Putting down the receiver, he realized that he hadn't given her a message for Steffie. That was something to regret. The conversation had come apart and he could not tell who had made the first mistake. He was sure she knew it now. There was nothing he could do and he did not see himself staying bothered by it. For the first time in years he was too absorbed in the job he was doing. He pushed the button on the intercom.

"What's the number at Mrs. MacIver's hotel?"

"It's on your desk," Florence said.

"Where? I don't see it."

"I'll be right in," she said.

The slip of paper with the telephone number was under the photographs that had come from Florida. While Florence called the hotel Leland slipped the photographs into the file. That alone cleared his desk of clutter. Florence gave him the receiver.

"Give me room four twenty-one, please," he said.

"I'm sorry, but four twenty-one checked out at noon. May I have your name, sir?"

"Hold on." He covered the mouthpiece and said to Florence, "She checked out at noon. She didn't call here, did she?"

"No, sir. I'm certain of it."

"My name is Joseph Leland," he said to the hotel operator.

"There's a message for you. Just a minute." Leland turned to Florence and made a sour face. He tucked the receiver against his shoulder and scratched his knuckles. The cold air of yesterday and this morning had caused the skin to crack. "Hello? Here's the message: 'Your book is with the desk clerk. I've taken the twelve-thirty train and will meet you at the airport with the car.' "

"Anything else?"

"No, sir. That's it."

He hung up and repeated the message to Florence.

"Does she know which airport?"

"Of course not. If I know my client, she'll be at the International wondering why my Cessna isn't up in the pattern with all the intercontinental jobs. I ought to land there so she can pay the fee."

"You'll be going to Phillips," she said. "I'll send the telegram, if you want."

"Good. Make the call to the airport, too. Tell the line boys I'll be ready to go at three o'clock. She left the souvenir book at the desk at the hotel, which was good of her. Pick it up when you get a chance. I'm going in to get things squared away with Mike."

CHAPTER TEN

■ ■

AT FIVE THOUSAND FEET HE TRIMMED OFF, ADJUSTED THE CAR-
buretor heat, and throttled down to ninety miles an hour. There was a
tail wind that let the plane slip along without struggling. Under him,
flat as glass in the sunshine, the river rolled swiftly rearward. Instinctively he waggled the tail and looked back. Clear. It was clear
ahead, too. A flotilla of cumulus was anchored harmlessly in the east.
On that side of the river the railroad track stretched as straight as a
cable, and two miles down, a freight train moved toward him. He
opened his collar. If Norma had wanted, he could have shown her
how to fly. He had taught Karen and Stephanie and Mike and Warren
Johnson, but he never tired; he loved flying, and it had taken him
years to become accustomed to that development in his personality; it
was part of him now and he enjoyed it. He had learned to fly; he had
made it a happy thing; he wanted to share it.

Perhaps Karen had been more right than he had thought in her
suggestion about MacIver and Betty Kaminsky not wanting to remember. By the time MacIver had met Norma he could have told the
lie so many times that he had begun to believe it himself. There was a
myth that Leland let Karen believe because it helped her—he had
begun to believe it, too, a little, because it flattered him. MacIver's
story would have flattered him, too, measured against the truth. Mac-
Iver had been slick, but he had not used the lie in a malicious way. At
lunch yesterday Norma had said that she had told her college boyfriend that there had been only one lover before him. In all three
instances—if the suggestion about MacIver was right—the truth

would have been a burden to the people who would have had to bear it. Leland had to think of the night in the car with Norma when MacIver had been so emotional: remembering that, the suggestion had a certain validity.

For entirely different reasons the suggestion fit Betty Kaminsky far better than it fit her first husband. She was more than involved with herself—she was lost in who she thought she was. Her second husband had told Leland that she had been worse. Leland had no choice but to believe it. The facts bore it out. There was no question about her ego, and MacIver had given it a terrible beating over three years' time. With her, it was simply a matter of saving face.

At the heart of it Karen had been talking about what happens to people when a marriage fails: sometimes, a kind of insanity. It was possible that Leland's current custody case was only another example, compounded. The ex-wife could be taking on a boyfriend to prove to herself that she could give love; the ex-husband could be hiring private detectives to establish that she had not been worthy of his love in the first place. In custody cases Leland couldn't entertain such considerations. He rarely had more information than he needed to do his job. Colin MacIver was different. It was exactly into this area that Leland had to press. In this job the justifications and self-appeasements were more than simply lies to work past, they were factors subtly operating on the truth. MacIver had lied to Norma because of who they were, both of them. Leland knew who she was. MacIver was the thing. It was only possible that he had had no malicious intent. There was the way he had treated his first wife— with his reservations, Leland generally accepted her account of Mac-Iver as her husband. She had called him a coward, an apt enough name for a man who came home bleeding after three years of marriage and wouldn't explain why. Her story made things of her, too— and not just another liar. Leland wanted to know what kind of man divorced a woman like her and then turned around and made little Norma happy. There was Kaminsky, but Leland did not think he could look at Kaminsky and see an image of MacIver. For one thing, Kaminsky wasn't so interesting, and he did not wear well. Leland liked him less for not knowing his wife as well as he had thought, and for leaving her in the kitchen—there was something despicable in that. The most important thing about Kaminsky was that he was there. He was there because MacIver was not. There was just that much difference between them. No, Kaminsky told Leland nothing about Colin MacIver.

And this was only one facet of MacIver's life. He had died. He had been on the roof of a racetrack. He had had business up there, and it had been concluded when he had come down.

And the quarter of a million. There was definitely more to Colin William MacIver than a glimpse of the mechanics of guilt. Leland was drawn to that, as Karen had pointed out unconsciously, but very clearly. *You're closer to it.* He had not thought of it, but he was drawing on parts of himself that were not usually for hire—and never in custody cases. What diverted Leland now was not the separate reasons for Karen's concern—Norma, Port Smith, the idea that he had been thoughtlessly dredging through his own life for the keys to another—it was that the basic motive was so near the surface, and that she had made the necessary associations so easily. In point of fact he had forgotten that what was myth to him was reality to her, and however close he thought he was to the way things were between them, he was never as close as she was. She was the center, and his understanding came through her good grace.

Down below, like a string of beads being pulled over a piece of lace, the freight train moved along the lightly snow-covered ridge beside the river. In the airplane, the steady sound of the air-cooled engine had almost the same effect as silence. Leland felt isolated, and he wanted to believe that he was over a very quiet world—he knew he was deceiving himself. On both sides of the river, as far as the ground haze allowed, he could see farm buildings and wooded sections and snowy fields, brown and yellow and vivid, gusting white. Winter and summer, this was the route he flew to Port Smith, down the river without radio, charts, or landmarks, to the crooked X of Phillips Airport in Clausen County. By car he was still within an hour of Manitou; the radio stations reached here, and even some of the stronger transmitters of Port Smith. Delivery trucks brought the newspapers morning and evening. There was no such thing as isolation; this was very much the world in which MacIver had lived and died. He had traveled on those railroad tracks down there. At the northern terminus of the line, Leland had his wife and daughter—his entire existence. At the southern end was a grimy and blighted city of three million, still diverting itself with the search for Mary Shoftel—Leland had heard that while he was packing—and in a very few minutes, because the weather was so clear, Leland would begin to see the inverted dome of soot and smoke that rested permanently on the area. After the war when he had returned from his stay at Lake Charles, Leland had felt the sensation of coming home. Now he was indifferent—removed. He had learned that there were other cities and that each had its own character and charm. The memory of the happiness of his ignorance was like that of a man thinking back on an old girl friend, punishing himself with fantasy. He was not deluding himself. When this was over he would turn and walk away. If he did not feel comfortable in Manitou, then he knew he could never live in Port Smith again. His reasons were not the same as Karen's. They had to do with her. One time, before the war, he would have never believed it would come to this. Then, too, he would not have believed he would ever walk out on her. His old captain, Bill Richardson —he was dead now—had had a way of staring off into space, as if he were reading the future. Most people agreed that they did not want to know what was coming. The way most people lived their lives, and Leland was among them, they did not want to know what had passed, either.

"I don't think I've seen you before," she said as they started to dance.

"This isn't my neck of the woods," he said.

Her green eyes sparkled. "Sounds as if you don't like it." It was a party at a sorority house on the Jefferson campus; one of his friends had asked him to come.

"I didn't say that," he said. "I like it fine. My name's Joe Leland."

"Karen Widener. I'm a guest here, too. Hello. Do you always talk so tough?"

"I didn't know I did. You're not from Port Smith, are you?"

"All my life," she said.

"Well, we all sound the way I sound—except you."

"I didn't know I sounded different."

"Your voice is more musical," he said. "More polished. It's hard to believe."

"Are you saying I'm a phony?"

"Of course not. I don't even know you."

"Why did you ask me to dance?"

"I wanted to see what drew the crowd. You've had characters around you all night. I could see that you were attractive. It's the voice. The voice cinches it."

"Maybe it's saying something."

"In this context it doesn't matter."

She looked at him. "You like to tease, don't you? You want to get my goat."

"No, not at all. I want to hear you turn phrases like 'get my goat'—tell me how you do it. Tell me your secret."

"Okay, okay. Now I'll have to think about it. You may have spoiled my evening." She leaned back against his arm. "How old are you?"

"Nineteen," he said.

"I thought I was older than you. I'm twenty. I'll bet you work."

"It isn't supposed to show."

"Some people around here work, too," she said. "I know you people from P.S.C. never believe it."

"I guess that means you," he said.

"I have two jobs," she said. She watched him. He didn't know what she was getting at.

"You have only one," she said after a moment.

"I'm not trying to get rich."

She said, "All my money goes toward tuition and expenses. I'm not getting rich, either."

"You're not getting help from your family. I see. Sorry to hear it."

"There isn't any family," she said.

"You'll have to explain that."

"There never was," she said. "I moved out of my last foster home two years ago. I've said something now, haven't I?"

He stopped dancing. She pushed him until he started again. She said, "I want you to know right off. God knows why. You wanted to hear a secret—sort of. I've never sprung it on anyone like that before. And you've tried to keep my attention with a trick right out of *Huckleberry Finn*. You're not even handsome."

"You're out of order. Settle down."

"I'm settled. I apologize. Don't be angry. Let's have a good time. I want to, I think."

"I can't remember our house when there wasn't talk about cops," he said. "I'm as familiar with the precinct houses in this town as any civilian, save a few old buffs." They were in a cafeteria across the street from the department store where she worked on Saturdays. He had asked her where she wanted to have dinner and she had said a place where she could kick off her shoes and maybe put her feet up on a chair.

"It's not a question of any one thing or some nasty subconscious motive," he said. "For me, being a cop is synonymous with what's good and useful—at least, within my reach."

"Okay."

"Fully satisfied?"

"Yes." He had frightened her. She had asked about his politics and he had assured her that he was not a Fascist. She was certain that there was going to be another war. Although she had no time for the political clubs on campus, they had her sympathy. They weren't going to stop the war, of course. She did not know how it would interfere with her own life. She wanted to do something important—what, she did not know. She enjoyed work; she was most happy when she had more than she could do. So far, since she had been on her own, she had done well. Her friends said that she was going to have success.

She did not know who her parents were. There were reasons why children were passed over in adoption centers. She could have been a sickly baby or she could have been adopted and then taken back because the parents had been unfit. When a child reached the age of three or four the market for her disappeared. The records were kept secret, but she had no interest in that time of her life. She had been in three foster homes and had been treated well. She was in touch with the families, but that was all. She did not think about it much. All her life she had had her own room—the state required it in foster homes—and her habits and attitudes probably were her own. The past two years had helped her find herself. She really did not know how she was going to spend the rest of her life. She hoped that it would go well. She hoped it very much.

"Are we going to see each other again?"

"I'll call you next week."

"That's sort of diffident," she said.

"I *will* call, Karen."

"Do you always say what you mean?"

"Relax," he said. "Forget what you've told me. I've put it away. You do the same."

"I'm saying other things, too," she said.

"I know. I like you. I can't say more."

"I see. Yes, all right."

That Tuesday, when he called her, she was out; and when he did get her the next night and tried to make a date for Saturday, she was busy. He settled for Friday. They made their arrangements, said goodbye, and did not talk again until they saw each other.

It was as if they had not had the intimacy of the weekend before. She came down to the foyer of the dorm with the same nervous vivaciousness that had attracted him at the party. It was something she used on strangers, and now he knew it. They went to a movie on State Street, sat through it silently, and then stopped at a coffee shop. She talked about what she had done during the week. The date had taken most of his money, but he was not going to admit that to her.

On the sidewalk he took her by the wrist, like a child, and hailed a taxi.

"What are you doing?"

"I'm sending you home." The taxi stopped in front of them and he opened the door. Perhaps she had not heard him properly, because she got in. He passed two dollars over the front seat. Karen turned to him, frightened. "You've been nothing but a pain in the ass tonight," he said. "I'll let you figure out why. Maybe when you want to stop kidding—" He let it die, because it would be a confession. He closed the door and gave the cabdriver the address. The cab moved out to the traffic and Joe Leland, who had never done this before, watched it go, so scared he was shaking.

She called the next morning.

"I'm sorry."

He had to brazen it through. "And?"

"I'd like to see you again."

"I don't want a repetition of this week," he said.

"Can we have lunch today?"

It meant traveling downtown to meet her at the store. "I have work to do."

"What about tomorrow?"

"All right. There's a bank on the corner of Franklin and Kenmore. I'll meet you there at one o'clock."

"I'll be there."

He was there first, wondering if she had outsmarted him, but then the trolley came and he saw that she was on it. He watched her get off, unaware of him. It was a cold, raw day. Bundled up, she looked around for him. He had never seen her by herself, and for a moment, before she saw him, it was a pleasure he could not have imagined. He wanted them to be themselves today. She saw him and waved. He did not know what he was going to say first and he stood there happily watching her as she crossed the street to him.

"God!" she cried. "It's *cold!*"

"All we can do is walk. There isn't a place open for blocks."

"Then kiss me hello. I need a reason for coming this far."

"I thought I was the reason," he said, still very nervous.

"You are. That's the idea."

He kissed her. "Your nose is cold."

"So's yours. Come on, let's walk."

He headed them toward State Street, as if the lights there could beat back the wind. Finally he told her that he was broke. She did not want to go back to the dormitory, she said, and opened her purse. He argued lamely and took the three dollars she could spare. They went to a movie and sat in the last row of the balcony and necked. He found out that she knew how to soul kiss. He became too excited and halfway through the second feature he had to move away. Out of the corner of his eye he saw her smiling and she took his hand and squeezed it. She was happy, and for all that he did not understand about her, he was happy, too.

Three nights a week he was the admissions clerk in the emergency ward at the City Hospital on Division Street. On the night Karen came down without calling there were three people on the benches waiting to see the intern, two drunks who had scuffled and fallen, and a man who had walked over from his job after something in his dinner pail had disagreed with him. Leland was interviewing a middle-aged woman who said she had a foot on her chest. She would not give her correct age. As Karen came in Leland said to the woman, "Then I won't let you see the doctor. The paper can't read twenty-one plus when you have a pair of lungs in their forties. The X rays will show that. Suppose some doctor upstairs thinks you're only twenty-one? A look at the X-ray and he'll send out an ambulance. Think about that." He turned to Karen, standing behind her, smiling. "Are you losing blood?"

"No—no."

"Have a seat, please."

"You won't let me see the doctor?" the woman asked.

"Definitely not."

She leaned forward. "I'm fifty-three," she whispered.

Leland pretended to write it small. "Now if you'll have a seat over there, the doctor will call you." He wrote, "Complains of difficulty breathing," and put the sheet to the side, under the others. "Next, please."

Karen came up and sat down. "I have heart trouble," she said.

He wrote it down. "You'll have to explain that."

"There's a young man I know—"

"Do you love him?"

"I don't know. He's the only real man I've ever met."

"I'll bet you say that to all the admissions clerks," he said as he began to draw triangles around her name.

"I had nothing to do," she said. "I hope you don't mind."

He leaned back and patted his stomach. "It's fine, but what am I going to do Thursday night at this time, when you're not here?"

"Don't think I wouldn't like to follow you around," she said.

"Are you going to wait until I'm through?"

"Yes."

A policeman came in. "We need a stretcher with restraining straps, fast."

"Right." He got up. "Get behind the desk, Karen." The litter was in the other room. When he had wheeled it out, the police had brought in their man, a little Negro bleeding profusely from the face. He was screaming, cursing, and kicking out. As the officers tried to maneuver him onto the litter, he broke away. The police grabbed him again and threw him onto the litter. "Sit on him," Leland said. He fastened the ankle straps. "Left arm," he said. "Now the right." Then he locked the chest strap. "What happened to him?"

"He went through a window. Don't know his name." The cop looked down at the man. "You son of a bitch, you're lucky we didn't pump a couple into you. Look at this overcoat. Who's going to pay to have it cleaned?"

"We'll get his name later," Leland said. "How about you? Are either of you hurt?"

"I skinned my knuckle on his teeth," the cop said.

"First door on the right. Wash it off. There's a bottle of iodine on the shelf. Leave your name and shield number on my desk and I'll do the report. I'll get the doctor," he said.

When he came back, Karen was gone. He went to the door, but she was out of sight. He had another half hour before relief.

She was waiting for him at the corner. "I'm sorry. I couldn't help it. I had to get out of there."

"That doesn't happen every night," he said.

"I don't know what made me run. Life is like that, I know it, but I had to go for the door. Maybe it was seeing you in the midst of all those flailing arms and legs. One thing, you're brave enough for the police."

"You didn't notice the protection I had. You shouldn't concentrate on me so much."

"You ordered them around, too. You told him to wash his cut and he did it."

He laughed. "He saw that I knew that he wouldn't get his sick pay if the thing infects and he hadn't availed himself of treatment. He was protecting himself. They check those things."

"It frightened me," she said. "I can't explain it. I know that there was no real danger. Maybe I'm not ready for that side of you."

"There's nothing to be ready for."

"We have different ways of seeing it," she said.

"You're being foolish."

"I don't think so! There was something about it that *upsets* me!"

"Come on, I don't want to fight."

"Neither do I, Joe—"

"Okay, forget it."

"You asked me something in there."

"I remember," he said.

"I don't know the answer yet. I came here. And I waited for you after I ran out. I'm sorry I ran. I'm ashamed of it. Maybe that's love, too. I don't know."

He put his arm around her. "I don't want you to think about it anymore."

He opened the door. She looked over his shoulder into the apartment. "Is the coast clear?"

"I wasn't kidding you. They know you're here tonight. I had to restrain my mother from buying a cake."

She stepped in. "Why? I like cake." She unbuttoned her coat.

"You look normal. On the way over I thought of you with a pipe and smoking jacket. I couldn't help it, I laughed aloud. People turned around and stared."

"Okay, what would you like to see first? You have to be shown around."

"Your room, of course. I've never been in a man's bedroom, I want you to know."

"I don't mind the advertising, but keep the false claims to a minimum. I'll find out if you're lying or not."

"The hell you will."

He had been trying to tease her. "Just for you, I didn't touch a thing. When I was a kid I knew another kid who tacked headlines and news pictures to the wall. I did it, too, for a while. Anyway, I thought it was smart. They're still there."

She wasn't listening. He watched her looking at all the junk of his childhood. He realized that there seemed to be no phase that he had not gone through. She appeared to like what she saw, but he could not help being afraid that she was trying to remember it for her own amusement later when she was alone.

His father was on the night tour and his mother had gone up to Northport to stay with his aunt. For the first time this year she had picked a Wednesday, the one night when both Joe and Karen were free. It had seemed that the days would never pass. They had whispered about being alone, but when he was honest with himself, he saw it as part of their lovemaking and not the promise of more.

"I wish I had this," Karen said.

"You will. You'll have your daughter's, too."

"Thank you for saying that. I want a family with all the other things. I don't know what I want—that's the truth."

"There are very few people who can do what you're doing. Remember that."

"Put a job in front of me and I'll do it, whether I have any feeling for it or not. I'm still in college, so I'm preparing myself, but when I get out I know I'll just take the best job I can find. It won't matter. I want to know myself better than that."

"Don't ask so much of yourself. Don't think about it for now."

"It's easy for you to say. You know what you want. You've advised me more than once to stop thinking. Do you like me brainless?"

"I like you when you see yourself as you really are. You're an accomplished, polished young lady. I saw that the night I met you. You have a right to be proud of yourself."

"Do you know that you terrorized me that night?"

"So?"

"Tough guy, I feel safe with you now."

"That's a hell of thing to say tonight."

"I'm not going to have sex with you, Joe. Don't try to make me. I don't want to get started on that."

He said, "I think we ought to change the subject. And get out of this room."

In the living room he tuned the radio to a dance band broadcast. She had lit a cigarette, and when he turned to her, she put it in an ash tray. He took her closely.

"I'm not going to spoil this for you," she said.

"Don't talk that way," he said.

"You know, there are times now when you still frighten me."

"Now?"

She kissed his neck. "Yes. I had a dream about that fellow at the hospital that night. You didn't see your hands. They looked so strong." She put her arms around him. He had not stopped taking pleasure from how soft and supple she was. Before he had met her, he had not thought that anyone so slim could be so soft. He kissed her ear. "Let's try to finish this one dance, anyway," she said.

"I was thinking that."

"I haven't done much, Joe. I really haven't."

"I wasn't thinking about that."

"You're the first one who's ever excited me," she said.

"Is that what made you afraid?"

"I guess so. Yes."

"Don't think about it—there I go again."

"Sometimes it's good advice," she said. "Sometimes I just want to hold you and not think anything."

216

"Now?"

"No."

She was afraid. When the number ended he let go of her and turned out the light. His palms were wet. He loved her. He was sure that there was nothing about her that he did not love. In the darkness she took his hands. "We might as well sit down," she said.

They went to the couch. On the radio the dance band began again. He kissed her on the mouth and she kissed him back. They tried to press their bodies together, awkwardly. He reached down and pulled the laces of his shoes. She saw what he was doing and slipped out of hers. They kissed again, leaned back, and wrapped their legs together. He felt the sharpness of her garter against his thigh. She shifted back a little, not moving her legs.

"You should see your eyes. You've been through this before, probably right here on this couch."

"Don't talk like that," he said.

"How many girls have you slept with?"

"I haven't asked about what you've done," he said.

"You don't have any trouble," she said. If she had meant that there had been mischief in his eyes, she could not realize what her own were like. She picked at the button on his shirt. "You're so damned gentle."

"And you think that gives me away?"

"There are times when you're not. That's what gives you away. You know what to be—and when."

"Okay."

"How do I rate?"

"How do you think I'm going to answer that now?"

She looked at the shirt button. "Do you have hair on your chest?"

He nodded.

"Really? That's wonderful."

He put his hand on her blouse over her breast. She watched his eyes and he let the pleasure show in them and he moved his hand as he thought she wanted him to do now, not gently. She bit her lip, happy. He reached for her blouse button.

He stared at her. Her eyes changed; she was not angry. He got to his feet.

"Where are you going?"

"To lower the radio."

She sat up straight. "I don't want to go to bed with you, Joe."

"You're the one who keeps mentioning it."

"Can you blame me?"

"Yes," he said. "And you know it."

"Let's not fight!"

He didn't answer. She rubbed her hands against her knees. Something made him stop before he sat down again and he took her wrist to bring her to him. She misunderstood, and twisted her legs onto the couch and lay back. She brought her arms up to her breasts as if that gave him room beside her; it was girlish and it made him smile. He got beside her.

She put her face against his neck. "Are we safe here?"

"Nobody will bother us."

"I'm terribly excited, Joe. My leg is shaking."

"I'd like to see that."

"Go ahead." She moved and raised one knee and waited.

With his fingers he lifted her skirt and slip. Carefully he pulled them up all the way around. She wasn't wearing a girdle. Her legs were very slim and her stockings were pulled up high. He put his hand over her garter.

"Do you like my legs?" she asked.

"Very, very much."

"There aren't any freckles where you wouldn't want them. They start above my knees and work down."

"None on your hips," he said.

"No."

"Your bottom?"

She laughed. "I don't know."

"What about on top?"

"Birthmarks. Hold me, Joe. I love you."

"I love you, too. You've known it."

She pushed him back. "Does it hurt?"

It took him a moment to understand. "No."

She was watching him. Now she smiled. "I'm going to help you," she said.

He kissed her. "Do you mean it?"

"No—no. Stop it, Joe. I can't."

"Are you afraid of getting pregnant?"

"No, that's not it, I—"

"You have to make up your mind about what you want to do."

"I won't have the burden put on me!"

She was right. If they didn't go on, their frustration would leave an anger they couldn't control. He knew her and he was learning himself. "Go into my room, Karen."

She looked afraid. "I don't want to, Joe. Please."

He stroked her hair. "Go ahead."

She got up slowly. She bent over to get her shoes, then changed her mind about them and stood up. Her hand reaching for the button on her skirt, she walked unhappily across the room to the other door. The dishevelment of her clothing pulled at him and made him want to tell her to stop. She had believed him and her belief had made it just this simple. His astonishment with the simplicity of it kept him still until she was in his room, and then he got up to follow her. He was afraid not to be near her.

She stood by the chair at the window. As he entered she stepped out of her skirt, silent and light, and what he could see of her face was as beautiful and calm as anything he had ever seen. She turned to him, looking as if she were surprised and really pleased with what they were doing. "I do love you, Joe."

"I know. Don't take off your slip. I want to do it."

"Let me do the stockings. I don't want to get them snagged."

"Okay." He got out of his shirt with his eyes away from her. He didn't want to spoil it for them by seeing her in awkward postures of undressing.

She presented herself, barefoot, in blouse and slip. He was so happy with her it played tricks with his eyes.

"Do you like the way I look?"

"Yes. Very, very much."

"You're not lying now, either," she said. "I can see it." She hugged him tightly.

"Turn your back," he said.

"All right." She giggled.

"We don't have to see each other wrestling with our clothes," he said.

In a moment he heard the bed jounce. "Okay," she said. "I made room for you on the right side. It's the side you always want in the movies."

"We're going to have a long and happy life," he said.

"Aren't you going to take off your shorts?"

"Not yet." He had tried not to look at her until he was ready. She was sitting on her side of the bed, half-turned to him. He had never seen anything so beautiful. He sat beside her, kissed her and caressed her breast.

"Joe, I'm scared."

"Don't be. Just relax. Kiss me. Relax. I love you, Karen, you know that."

"I know. You're not disappointed, are you?"

"No. You'll see."

"You're gentle. Kiss me. Oh, Joey, I do love you." She put her arms around him and kissed his chest. She rubbed her face against it. "I knew I'd like this. Thank you."

"For what?"

"For being the way you are."

"Hush up. You're the only one I've really wanted for this, do you know that? Everything about you is wonderful. I don't think it, I know it. You're all I want."

"I want a lot of this," she said.

"We haven't even started." He stroked her back. He needed her and she did not know it. If they married and she bore his children, all the gifts of love would still come from her. "Do you know all the things I'm going to do to make you happy?"

"I'm happy now, Joe. I really do love you. I'm just learning how much."

220

He held her against him. He had no idea of the time, but it was not late. He ran his hand over her back and she twisted and lay down. He patted her bare bottom. "Karen?"

"Do you still want to marry me?" she asked.

"Yes." She hugged him, kissed him. For a moment he thought that she did not know that he was waiting for her to say it, too.

"If I don't marry you I'm crazy," she said.

That winter, the next spring, and the following summer, they saw each other every weekend, and late at night during the week. She changed jobs and they had to find new places to meet. They went to parties and down to Joytown, and when they were broke they went to Young Communist League meetings, put their names to nothing, and helped themselves to cake and coffee. She gave him André Malraux to read. One afternoon at a departmental reception one of her professors saw him squeeze her bottom and he laughed aloud; another time, quite late, she was locked out of the dormitory and had to spend the night at his house, and in the morning his parents found him on the couch and her in his bed in his pajamas.

In August she moved out of the dormitory to a room and a half downtown. He contributed to the rent and had a key. She thought it was smug of him, having a woman downtown at his age, and so did he. He had never been happier, and he did not keep it a secret from her. He adored her, she understood that better now. He was willing to do the shopping, pin the hems on her skirts, shampoo her hair, and let her shampoo his. He would not tag along to push a cart for her in a supermarket while she made the selections, or stand around in a department store while she looked at dresses. She could calibrate the strength of his feeling about a thing by the amount of obscenity in his speech, and she learned that he did not like to hear her go beyond "hell" and "damn."

His method of learning was memorization. He was not a bad student, but through practice he had become capable of retaining thousands of pieces of information that did not interest him. When she told him that the way he worked made her feel like a waste, he did not understand why. She said that it seemed that he could do anything he put his mind to, but she was wrong; there were some things, like mathematics, in which he could not do well. If she felt he was better disciplined, he felt that she had the greater natural intelligence. Her interests were wider-ranged. She did not believe that, and when he began to study for the policeman's examination she offered to help, to see how he did it.

"Defensive wounds," she said.

"Cuts on the hands of a victim from trying to fend off a knife."

"I'm going to skip around," she said. "How long can you use a search warrant?"

"Ten days."

"What's the telephone number of police headquarters?"

"Crown Seven, six thousand."

"Where is the Eighteenth Precinct station house?"

"There isn't any. It burned down in 1918 and wasn't rebuilt." She closed the book. "I've had enough. Fix me some coffee."

"Full of piss and vinegar, aren't you, to order me around?"

"Well, who's taking this damned test, you or me? I think you ought to do something for me."

"You're right." And he got up to fix the coffee.

They were graduated from their different colleges on the same day in June, 1940, and on the next day they were married. The part of the ceremony asking who gave the bride away was omitted, and afterward her three foster families met at his parents' home to exchange polite, stilted conversation about her childhood. Pictures were taken, cocktails accepted or declined, and the affair was over by early afternoon. The schedule called for dinner downtown as guests of his parents, but he decided that an early train would be better. In the coach going north, Karen cried. It had not been the day that she had hoped for, although she could not say what that had been. She fell asleep after a while, her head on his shoulder, and when they arrived in Manitou, there was still light.

They had to find a taxi to make the trip to the cabin they had borrowed from one of his father's friends. The fare was three dollars, and after a half hour of riding, the groom began to have his doubts about what they would find. Karen was in no mood for something primitive, gritty, and uncomfortable. He wanted to tell the driver to turn around and go back to a hotel.

They came to the lake and found the cabin. In the dimness they could see one lamp down the road, swinging in the wind. The porch didn't creak, he could feel no heavy dirt under his feet, and the door swung in easily. He felt along the wall for the light switch, then he turned to her. "Ready?"

She nodded. She looked terribly unhappy.

"Well, put the packages down," he said.

"Why?"

"Did you forget?"

"What?"

"Put them down." He took them out of her hands, then moved to pick her up.

"Joe, you're a fool."

"Tonight you're a bride," he said.

When he put her down again she kissed him. "Are you going to treat me like one?"

"Yes."

"I'm so scared. We could have undone it any time until this morning. Now we're—something, anyway."

"Trapped, do you think?"

"Joe, you've been so good to me. I don't know."

"I would have had some things another way today. There have been a few things we're going to like later on. You'll see. Give yourself a chance."

She stood still a moment. "Give me a kiss." He did. She said, "A girl in the store told me about a friend of hers who spent her wedding night in the bathroom. One look at her husband and she was gone, screaming. What do you think of that?"

"What are you trying to tell me?"

"That I'm going to take my medicine." She kissed him again. "I love you. I hated last night after you'd gone home. I didn't sleep. It was so lonely. Today would never come."

"Don't think about that. You're the lady of the house now."

She hugged him. "You'll be happy, you'll see."

When they returned to the city they had another two weeks before he started at the Academy. She went back to her old jobs and he finished at the hospital. When his first department check came she began to look for full-time work in earnest. For a while she had bad luck and it got her down. There were jobs on assembly lines paying nearly twice as much as she was offered by offices and the department stores. One evening he found her in tears. He was helpless. What she felt was more than a desire to have a job she could be proud of. His salary would remain under fifty dollars a week for the next two years and she was sure that this was the one period in their lives when they would have the chance to get ahead. There was nothing he could do; his classes ran from nine to six and he could not even have his lunch outside. The assignments in the Department came on the basis of grades, and he didn't want to spend the next four years in Northport or Bay Slope. These things made her feel worse. She could not help him, and after she had gone through the newspapers, there was nothing for her to do but prepare herself for the morning.

He would awaken her gently. Their lovemaking had a fulfilling harmony that impatience could be no match for. Sometimes he would awaken her again later, excited, and he would put his arms around her. If she awakened enough she would try to help, but mostly she slept too soundly. He would caress her until she pushed herself against him suddenly and tried to kiss him. Sometimes she moved to make him kiss her breasts. Once she asked if he wished there was milk in her, and when he said no, she said she did. He did not fully understand that. For her part, she could not understand his fascination with her bottom. Neither could he. But he had it, and at times he could make her jealous of herself.

She found a job: at the Port Smith Hotel, as assistant to the banquet coordinator. It was interesting work and the salary promised to pass his within a year. She would have to attend many of the dinners, working late in the evenings, but he wanted her to give it a try. Remembering the impressions she had made on him when he had met her, he thought that she could make a success of it. If it led to important contacts for her, all the better.

The job was more of a grind than they had anticipated, and for a while she made plans to work at it only a year and go on to something else. The Friday before Labor Day she got the afternoon off to see him graduate and be photographed for the newspapers with the twenty-four other rookies. That evening they took the train to Manitou again, this time to stay at a resort. That night, or the next, or the one after, he made her pregnant, and even if there had been no war, the course of their lives had begun its irreversible turning.

CHAPTER ELEVEN

∎ ∎

TUESDAY AFTERNOON, HE REPORTED EARLY TO THE FIFTH PRECINCT for briefing. Uniformed officers worked three shifts, the one advantage they had over the detectives and plainclothesmen. As a rookie, Joe Leland drew no permanent assignment. His education wasn't completed. On-the-job training in a precinct as busy as the Fifth had to be accomplished any way it could be fitted in.

The first two evenings he was taken around on patrol in a few mild blocks in Westlake and on the third night he covered the beat alone. The feeling of newness was wearing off, he recognized many of the faces, and later, when the streets had cleared for the night, he investigated some of the things he had noticed in the two nights before. He wrote a couple of parking tickets, waiting until his relief came at a quarter to twelve, and by twelve-thirty, he was on the streetcar home.

The next evening he read on the board that he was to replace a sick man in one of the cars. It was a choice assignment and he would not have drawn it if he did not need the experience. Probably he would wait six months before getting a car again.

His partner for the night, Carl Krolevich, drove. He was an overweight, curly-haired man in his forties, pleasant and a little shy. He knew Joe's father. There was not much to a prowl car, he said. All they had to do was ride around, watch, and listen to the radio. Leland took a more serious view and felt uncomfortable with Krolevich because of it. Nothing happened and the time seemed to drag. Slowly they covered the streets of Westlake up to the precinct border.

At seven-thirty they had a call about a disturbance in a building on Florida Street. The wife answered the door. She looked as if she had been fighting, but said that there was nothing the matter. Going down the stairs again, Krolevich said that he had expected it. Experience would show Leland that there was nothing to these calls ninety-nine percent of the time.

An hour later they took their turns having dinner in a cafeteria on Pleasance Street. The sky was dark when they started rolling again. The September chill was in the air. Routine calls rolled out of the radio, none for their car, and Leland began to feel his legs numbing. There was no conversation now, and with his elbow on the windowsill, he watched the passing stores. On Palmetto Avenue, a business street on a slight hill, Leland thought he saw something in an auto supply store. There was one car on the block, at the corner in front of the store.

"Pull over," he said.

Krolevich did. "Come on," he said, setting the hand brake. They walked back to the car. Leland put his hand on the hood.

"It's hot."

Krolevich looked around. There were no places the driver could have gone to which he could not have parked closer. Krolevich unbuttoned his holster, then hesitated.

"Joe, go around the side. Keep low as you pass the windows and the displays will cover you. Identify yourself loud and clear. We'll flush them in this direction."

Leland nodded. His mouth had gone dry. He unbuttoned his own holster, got below the window displays, and moved to the corner. He looked back to Krolevich, waiting near the wall. Krolevich gave him a wave. Leland turned the corner. A little distance up the hill the wall ended, and ten feet beyond was a wire fence. There was no light between, and instinctively Leland wanted to draw his gun. He had only thought he had seen something, and he had to wish that the car hood had not been hot, or the car had not been there at all. He stood still and listened. Nothing. He drew his gun and disengaged the safety. He tried to put his feet down lightly. At the end of the wall he peered around. Garbage. Litter. Crates. The crates were piled head-high, and as his eyes adjusted he saw a passage between them to a little stairway down, and then a door to the back of the store. There was nothing to see inside the small panes of window. Leland picked his way along.

Something crashed inside the store, there was a shout, and Leland was about to alert Krolevich when the door before him flew open. A man stood there, staring, then tried to shut the door. There was another shout inside, an explosion, and falling glass. "Carl!" Leland cried. The door opened again as Leland started moving toward it, and this time the man raised a pistol. His eyes glazed with fear, he fired.

It was like a flame along Leland's jaw. Not stopping, he fired back. He had not thought of aiming, but somehow the man reacted as if he had been hit with the blade of a shovel. Before he reached the stairs Leland fired again into the darkness. There was more breaking glass. "Carl! I'm coming through!" No answer. He went into the darkness running, and pitched over the body of the man he had shot. The light from the street poured through the windows of the store. The front door was open.

"Carl!"

The car went into reverse and came into view. The driver shifted quickly into forward gear, and leaning crazily, the car pulled away from the curb. There was a crash of metal and glass. Leland ran down the aisle to the front of the store. The glass in the door was shattered, and on the sidewalk lay Krolevich. Leland reached the sidewalk, still running, and leaped over him. The car had not straightened from the collision with the rear of the police coupé. On one knee Leland aimed for the left rear tire. With the first shot the car bucked back and swerved. It leaped the curb and turned a store front into a shower of glass. Leland was up and running toward it. The car door opened.

"Throw down your gun!"

The driver raised it toward him. He was fully in the light, thirty feet away. Leland stopped, braced himself, offering his profile, and took aim. He fired first, and the man slid out of the car. Leland ran up. The man's head was on the seat. The bullet had entered under his eye. Leland reached over him and turned the ignition key, then, beginning to tremble at last, ran back to Krolevich.

Krolevich had a bullet in his heart. Bent over him, Leland saw his own blood pour onto the sidewalk. He felt faint now, and he got up and hurried to the radio.

He sat still in the car until help came.

His father had been a policeman seventeen years and had never drawn his gun. Before that night, Krolevich had never drawn his. Most officers went from rookies to retirees without calling on their weapons for more than practice. Without having completed a week Leland had shot and killed two men and had reported the death of a partner. The percentages had had to catch up with some rookie, his father had said sympathetically. He had offered the best help. There was no answer or explanation. He had said that some of the men were upset for Joe because he had lost a partner. Lieutenant Leland knew that his son was too new to the job to have had a full understanding of what that meant. He was right. Joe Leland had not known Carl Krolevich.

No one could explain what had happened. After the first noise Krolevich had become curious and had made himself seen. The burglars had raced to the back to find Leland and had panicked. When the one who had shot Krolevich had fired, the other had tried to shoot his way past Leland. At the sound of the first shot a man on the next block had gone to his window and watched Leland come running out of the store. Leland had never hesitated; the man had never seen anything like it. He would never complain about the police again.

The man at the back of the store had been hit twice in the chest. The bullets had entered within the diameter of an inch. Leland was able to tell his father why. He had seen the man go back and had estimated where he had fallen. Still, his father was astounded. He told his father that the second man, in retrospect, had seemed dazed by the crash.

"Oh, you had to shoot," his father assured him.

"I know that I couldn't take the chance. What do I tell Karen?

229

Does she understand what happened, that there wasn't the time to think?"

"She doesn't want you to worry. Tell her everything. Show her that the thing isn't preying on you."

"Who said it isn't? I killed two human beings, didn't I?"

"I know. Don't shut her out, that's what I mean. She wants to help you. Give her the chance."

"It didn't take her long to get here when they called her," he said.

"There you are," his father said.

"One thing: no more uniforms for her to get ready."

"She took your uniform out with her that night. It's all cleaned and ready to wear. Even the brass is polished."

"She didn't tell me that."

"That's the way she is," his father said. "I figured that out about her a long time ago. You have a hell of a girl there. Oh, yes. The newspapers are all over headquarters. They're sorry about Krolevich, but they can't help thinking and talking about you. What you did makes them glad they're policemen. You read the papers. A lot of people got a lot of things out of the way you handled yourself. Think about it."

He watched his father go out. He wanted to hide. He wanted Karen to hold him like a baby. This was not the first time the desire had come upon him, but now it was what he wanted more than anything. He felt frightened and cold and he didn't care who knew it.

When he came home she took the week off, and except for his trips to the clinic, their time was their own. He could not turn his head and the bandage extended from his temple to his neck, but he did not want to stay home. On the fourth night a family in a restaurant recognized him and would not stop staring.

"Do you want to leave?" Karen asked him.

"No, I'm all right. I—maybe Krolevich didn't believe me when I told him I saw something in there."

"What? How long have you been thinking this?"

"I don't know. Maybe he didn't believe me. I had only met him

230

that night and I didn't even like him. Maybe he felt that. When he told me to go around the side I even thought for a moment that he was taking the easy part for himself. Why did he expose himself? Why didn't he get a shot off? What the hell *was* he thinking? I've been wondering if he didn't panic, like the other two."

"Did you panic?"

"No. At least, I thought I had my wits about me. I didn't shoot until I saw that the man in the door was going to shoot me. It happened so quickly that he did get the first shot. Then I shot to kill. I could have aimed low, but I was afraid for myself. He would have killed me. The other one, too. I had to stop them both. I would have to do it again exactly the same way." He stopped. "Well, what do you think of me?"

"The same things I thought before. This is a side of you I saw a long time ago. I know that you're thinking of it for the first time. It keeps you away from me."

"And?"

"I'm unhappy. You aren't the same anymore. I'm not crying. I'm waiting for you to learn to live with it."

"I'm still wondering how Krolevich threw his life away. Come on, let's get out of here."

At home she had things to do. He turned on the radio. It would be a week before he could return to work. He could still feel the responses of his body to what had happened. He was not an unusual man. He had not wanted Karen's mothering until he had been frightened. She had said that he wasn't the same. He wasn't a thoughtful person, he knew, and he would let his mind lose its hold on what he had seen and done. That itself was curious and terrifying.

Karen brought him a cup of coffee. He made room for her to sit beside him.

"How do you feel?" she asked.

"Better. I'll be all right."

"Are you comfortable?"

"Sure. What's on your mind?"

"I don't know how you're going to react. I don't know what it means yet, but my period is late. It doesn't mean I'm pregnant for sure. A lot of women are late all the time."

She was so concerned for him that she was trying to wish it away. "You are. You'll see," he said.

"You're glad?"

"Am I?" He put his cup and saucer on the table. "Come on. I couldn't be happier. It's fine, honey."

"You're not kidding me, are you?"

"Do you think I am?"

"I don't know," she said.

"I'm not. Karen, I'm not."

"I don't know what to think. It changes so much. Why should you take it this way?"

"Ah, to hell with that. How am I supposed to take it?"

"That's it," she said. "You're doing what you're supposed to. Don't fool me, Joe. If you're not happy, say so."

"For what? What would I do that for, anyway?"

"So the truth will be out. We're not dishonest with each other. I want things going right."

"I'm glad, Karen. I really am."

"I was careful. I tried to be."

"Don't talk like that."

"I'm not the mother type," she said.

"That's not the way you tell it when the lights are out. Look at me. Is it?"

She kissed him. "That's different. I'm not the real mother type, a skinny thing like me."

Now he thought he understood. She wanted to be told and told again. She didn't believe him. If they had tried for it, it would not have mattered as much to him. It did something to him that he needed. "Karen, I'm very happy. You have to believe it."

"I hope you are. I've hated this. I've been afraid to tell you."

"It was exactly the right thing to do, honey."

She started to pull away, angry. "Don't overdo it, Joe."

"I'm not. I mean it."

"All right." She got up.

232

"Where are you going?"

"To wash my face. I'm all right."

When her second period was due and did not come they went to a doctor. They had done no damage staying away; everything appeared normal. They told his parents and her foster parents and their friends, but she went on working, saving money. His promotion to plainclothes patrolman meant an increase of two hundred dollars a year, but they had spent almost as much on uniforms and equipment he did not need anymore. He had a regular partner, a man almost his own age, named Marty Harris. Marty was married and lived on Bay Slope. Six nights a week, when they were not otherwise assigned, they covered State Street and the Joytown area. They were known to the saloonkeepers and theater owners, and simply circulated. When they met friends who wanted to know what they were doing in that part of town, they were on their way in or out of a movie or had just come out of a bar. They were in a hurry, late, or not in the mood to join other people. Mostly they arrested brawlers, prostitutes, pickpockets, homosexuals, drunk-and-disorderlies, molesters, exhibitionists, masturbators, creators of public nuisance, and once, a car thief. It was easy, safe work. Bartenders offered cigarettes and bottles, theater owners offered cigarettes and candy, restaurateurs offered food, whores and homosexuals offered themselves, and the rest offered money. It was part of the work and forgotten. Cases in court were only complicated by charges of attempted bribery or lewdness. Marty's previous partner had gone to bed with a really pretty whore, and from then on he had her peddling herself under his nose. Putting one's duke in the tambourine, one way or the other, could only lead to grief. Marty had run into pretty girls, too, but, he said, he gave his wife all the action. It was part of the job, too, like sore feet, and the trick was in not thinking too much about it.

In December, Karen's boss asked her if she was pregnant, and when she said yes, the woman fired her. The job was not for a woman with a stomach.

"That was the way she put it," Karen told him the next morning.

"Just as cruelly as she could. It was loathsome to her. I wanted to slap her face."

When she had come home the evening before, he had already left for work. Now the sun had been up two hours and he was aching for bed.

"It was all I could do to get home," she said. "I wanted to come looking for you. I just came home and cried. What are we going to use for the money I could have made? Oh, damn it, Joe!" She stopped, curled her lip at her cigarette and dropped it, from the height of a foot, into her coffee cup. "Tomorrow I'll call those people who pay you to address envelopes."

"Let's see what happens," he said.

"Well, maybe I'll call them. Look at the mess I made," she said.

He finished eating and got up to clear the table. When he was done she said, "I'm sorry I'm in such a bitch, Joe."

"Hell, you were hit by a brick. I understand that."

She reached for another cigarette and, after fumbling with the matches, got it lit. He went over to her and put his hand on her forehead. "I'm all right," she said.

"Come to bed."

She shook her head. "I'm wide awake." She stood up. "You're being nice. I'm trying to be cruel."

"I didn't hear it."

"It was there. The funny thing is, I would like to go to bed—and pull the covers over my head."

He kissed her cheek. "I need my sleep, Karen. I really do."

"I know. Okay."

Later, when he awoke, he found her asleep beside him, on top of the bedclothing, still wearing her slip. He left her alone, and later still, when he was ready to leave for work, he put a cover over her. She murmured something and he kissed her cheek. In the evening he called her and there was no answer. When he came home again the following morning, she was in bed in her nightgown, asleep. That afternoon he opened his eyes as she entered the bedroom, her coat unbuttoned and her kerchief undone.

"How are you feeling?" he asked.

234

"All right. I've done the shopping. Let me warm my hands and I'll get your breakfast." She slipped out of her coat and sat beside him. She had on one of her maternity outfits. "I've decided to get used to these. I wore one to the movies last night." Color came to her face. "Make way for the pregnant lady."

He rubbed her stomach. He was still trying to get used to the hardness of it. She leaned over and he kissed her. Her lips were cold from the outdoors.

"I take it you want to do me more damage?" she asked.

"That doesn't sound cooperative."

"Try me."

"I am."

"It doesn't seem enthusiastic," she said.

"Angry with me?"

"No. No, I'm not."

"I know you've had a bad week, Karen. I'm trying to help."

"And so am I," she said. "I don't want to rattle around here with my belly hanging low."

"You're not. You've been home exactly one day."

"I'm going to call those envelope-addressing people tomorrow."

"Why did you hesitate now? You still haven't answered my question."

"Fine," he said.

"It took me a moment to remember what you were talking about. And why tomorrow? Yesterday you seemed ready to do it today."

"I was hoping I'd get more encouragement from you."

"I want your promise that you won't try to do too much. They pay by the piece, and we can use all the money we can get, we both know that, but I don't want you making yourself sick about it."

"I won't." She stood up. "Then it's settled. Come on, I'll get your breakfast."

He grabbed her arm.

"Stick around," he said.

"Have your breakfast first. We've talked too much."

In the next week she called all the places offering work at home, even some regular employment agencies, but could turn up nothing. She did not stop looking; she kept her reactions from him and he knew she could be not less depressed, only more resigned. Without telling her, he asked at the Precinct if anyone knew of a job, but more and more he could see how he and Karen could get by on his income alone, so that when she mentioned taking a twelve-dollar course at Jefferson in the evenings, he urged her to go ahead. The baby was due in early May and she could not possibly finish the course, and that defeated the idea at last.

She felt she needed something good and useful to do in the months before it became impossible for her to do anything but wait, but as the months passed the problem settled itself. Her moods shifted more quickly, and he could not tell when to get close to her and when to stay clear. At times she would not let go of his hand, and at others she would not even want to talk. Physically, everything was supposed to be perfect, but she looked and acted more tired, and found herself more disabled. She had to keep her legs up and her back had to be rubbed. She watched the veins in her legs, but none of them popped. Of course he had to tie her shoes, and later, fasten her brassiere. He liked the shape of her even in the last month and he told her so, but she could not believe him. He would come up from behind and put his arms around her, and no matter how receptive she was, she would challenge the pleasure he got from it. On the other hand, she was not afraid of letting him see her undressed, and while he was terrified, a little, for her sake, he was still very pleased for his own. He did not challenge the pleasure she got from finding that she still excited him, but her pleasure was changed: harder, less consequential, not truly satisfying to him. He knew these things and could not deal with them.

They had quit making love in her sixth month, not stopping suddenly, but after having tapered off. The act of love had become of less consequence to her. She was still willing to please him in the ways she could, but he would not let her. It was gratification without the giving of love and he did not want it. She was hurt anyway. She was his lover in spite of what they did not do, and he did not get his fill of caresses and finding her in his sleep. If she did not understand him, it

236

was because she was not capable of understanding him at this time.

She asked him three or four times if he was a conspirator in a baby shower planned for her. Such things worried and occupied her. She had to have his opinion on purchases she made for herself or the baby. It was as though she still wanted to know that she was loved and thought about, and her mind found new ways for her happiness to replace the old, in which she had somehow lost her confidence. The lapse made him love her more, and in some way, it made her more appealing to him. There was a baby shower and he was a conspirator in it, and enough of her college friends came to make it a success. She cried, and she was not a woman who cried. In the next days she showed him that she had been made genuinely happy, and her guilelessness was something he knew he would not forget. She modeled the dressing gowns she had been given and asked which ones he wanted to see, and she worked on ideas to make his life easy the week she would be away.

Stephanie was born on May 5 in the afternoon and he saw Karen that evening during visiting hours. She could not keep her eyes open.

"How do you feel?" he asked.

"Empty, done—I don't even want to eat. I tell you, Joe, I don't want to do it again tomorrow. Or next year."

"Of course not."

"Promise me. I may change my mind, but let me have that privilege. Just promise me now."

"I promise. Don't think about it. You have to take care of yourself."

She relaxed. "Did you see her? Did she look all right to you?"

"She looks fine," he said. "I hope you don't mind the dark hair."

"No." She smiled tiredly. "Do you love me?"

"Yes, very much. I love you very much." He took her hand. "I'll go, if you want to rest."

"No, stay with me. We'll have more children. I have to get that out of my system."

"Sure." He kissed her hand. "I'm so glad you're well. I've been scared to death—dizzy half the time."

"You? The nurse told me not to let you open your jacket because your gun would frighten people. She knew who you are—what you are. She remembered."

He kissed her hand again. "I wasn't exaggerating. I loved you when we got married, but I had no idea that there was so much more to it."

"Joe, I love you the same way."

"Thank you." It was barely audible.

When his vacation came they went up every day to Northport. During their courtship they had never gone to the beach; now, with Stephanie on the blanket under the umbrella, they took turns in the water and going on errands, and had a better time than any of the teen-agers they saw. Karen began to believe what he had been telling her, that motherhood had improved her figure. He knew from his own experience that she would not believe him alone. He had never been convinced or flattered when she had told him that she thought he was handsome—she had lied that first night. Now, after trying to assure her about her appearance, seeing both sides, and knowing he was right about her, he had begun to feel some of the pride she said she felt in him. It was an exhilarating feeling; and at Northport, when she was admired by other men, it was a pleasure for her of which he knew he was a part. They felt satisfaction with each other, gratitude and deeper affection. At the end of the two weeks they were much closer and they were rested. They were able to say that the confusion seemed to have been taken out of their lives.

They had people over in the evenings and they alternated going to the movies. By the end of the summer there was still not much to Stephanie; she ate and slept and looked at things at random. The radio did not attract her attention and they had to prove to themselves that she was not deaf. He clapped his hands behind her and she cried, and then he regretted having startled her. He was not very good with her. Karen was good and looked good with her, holding her, cuddling her. It was an element of Karen he had not anticipated. She was a good mother and as time went on she became a better one. It was not in him to see and give as much as she did, but he felt no mystification, only pride, and while his own love for the baby grew, he simply imitated his wife, as happy about it as any of the expected parts of fatherhood.

Their first attempts to make love again were failures. They should have been prepared for it, they realized later. Part of the trouble was their tension; they kept listening for the baby, first in the bedroom with the crib six feet away, then in the living room with the bedroom door closed. The other part was the hurried, thoughtless way they tried to get to each other. It occurred to him on the second night that they had solved nothing by moving to the couch; it intensified their single-mindedness; it was more like a scrimmage than an act of love. With the baby asleep they moved the crib into the living room, near enough to the bedroom door, and went to sleep themselves. When she got back into bed after the early morning feeding, it was not a failure. Later, when the alarm went off, he woke up to find her sitting beside him, smoking a cigarette.

"Good morning," she said.

"Something on your mind?"

"I had to think about it. It was the daylight, I'm sure of it."

"Don't get yourself into any habits. We have to take it when we can get it."

"No, I don't mean that. All last fall and winter you were on the night tour. Whether we did it when you came home or before you left, there was daylight. I did like it. Maybe it was all I needed to solve my problem."

"You thought you had a problem?"

"No, not really." She smiled.

"Okay. Get out of the bed. Fix me something to eat."

She kissed him. "You're a good husband."

They prepared for the examination for Detective Third Grade, and the day after the Saturday he took it, the Japanese attacked Pearl Harbor. The Joseph Lelands were at his parents' apartment for dinner. His father went through the building telling the other tenants. They crowded into the apartment to wonder and listen for later bulletins. A few of the women cried and the men tried to guess what would happen. Leland hated it. He hated the idea of it, and after a while, he heard none of the jabber around him. There was no question that he would be one of those who would have to fight. He didn't want to go away from home. That was all that it meant to him. He had to think of the kind of war it would be and how long it would last, but what he felt most, like a charge of poison in his system, was the disruption of his peaceful life. He was sitting in the kitchen thinking these things and Karen came in and sat across from him. He gave her a game smile. Some teen-agers entered, making noise. For more than a year now, he had been their hero.

"Joe? What are you going to join, Joe? They're going to take you, too, so you might as well enlist."

He looked at them. Karen was watching him. These were his first thoughts on the matter.

"I'll go into the Air Corps, probably."

"Hey! That's great! No kidding! Hey, why?"

They were drunk with the idea of fighting. "So I can turn around and run if I have to," he said, laughing. "I want to come home."

CHAPTER TWELVE

■ ■

THEY READ THE NEWSPAPERS AND IN THE MEANTIME THE EXAMINA-
tion grades came through. His grade was high and he was in the
first group to be promoted. The Philippines fell and in the darkness
that followed there were predictions of defeat. There were stories of
the Japanese plans for invading the United States, murder, rape, and
enslavement, and the misery changed, among the people he knew,
into a hatred and anger he could not have imagined. The war was to
be a war of vengeance. The absurd conception of America as a
peaceable nation that had never lost a war was given broad, welcome
circulation. One evening he and Karen tried to project, carefully,
thoughtfully, the course of the fighting. There was a good chance that
the Germans and the Japanese would achieve all their war aims. The
Russian spring offensive could have any outcome, and the attack on
Tokyo by the Mitchell bombers looked like a very brave show. No
one could reckon the resources of the enemy. A series of swift blows,
if they could be delivered, could put America out of the war.

He committed himself to the test for Detective Second Grade
while he waited. He made the highest grade and his name was placed
at the top of the list. The week after the promotion he learned that he
was going to be drafted, and impulsively he took the step that he had
mentioned casually, bitterly, on Pearl Harbor Day. That night, he
was able to tell Karen, too, that his police rank would be frozen for
the duration of the war. He would pick up where he had left off.

"I'll get a chance at flying. Probably my reflexes aren't fast
enough. It will be bombers or transports, if I make it at all."

She had looked for work in the morning and found a job on the first try. She would be inspecting valve guides on an assembly line. His mother would mind Stephanie during the days. There was no choice; no one they knew was not somehow involved. Now she bit her lip.

"What is it?" he asked.

"You'll do well. You know you will."

"I wish I did."

"Your eyes are better than perfect, you know that. And as for your reflexes, they'll have to go some to find a set that are faster. You're alive because of your reflexes."

"I'm not sure. We'll see what happens."

She was proved right on both counts. Still, he started with a handicap, for the college boys of his class had followed the barnstormers and air shows and a few had even built airplanes of their own. More, he was the oldest man in the school, twenty-four, and the only one of the three who were married who had had no flying experience. Until his first flight in a Ryan Trainer, he was willing to write himself off.

If the Ryan could forgive the abuses of a novice, he still flew it well. He knew it. Watching the others, he knew he was better than any of them, and soon they recognized it. He could fly better than anyone in the class, tighter, faster, closer to the design limits. His instructors granted that he was a natural pilot. He was as proud as a boy and he was willing to try anything.

He was sent on to Advanced Fighter Pilot Training at Lake Charles, Louisiana. In the spring of 1943 he arrived in England with the bulk of the Eighth Air Force, and like most, absolutely fresh. The Fourth Group, the Wolfpack, had already seen action in British Spitfires, but with the Eighth Air Force becoming fully operational, they were switched with the rest to Republic Thunderbolts, and a lot of what they had gained in combat experience they lost in having to learn the new airplanes. Heavy and faster but less maneuverable, the Thunderbolts looked like flying milk bottles. They weighed seven tons, as much as a crosstown bus. They had the most powerful engines in fighter aircraft at that time, Pratt and Whitney supercharged

Double Wasp engines, eighteen cylinders, two thousand horsepower, capable of pulling the Thunderbolts at speeds in excess of four hundred and thirty miles per hour.

He wrote to Karen, "To some of the men I am the leader because I am the oldest and presumably the most experienced. Not all of them have to shave every day. They want me to play the role of Raoul Lufbery for them and I do like it. Most of the boys can sense how close I am to you and although they will probably never meet you, they would like to marry women like you. What I mean is, the man I am is a reflection of what you have done for me.

"This last thought is one of many like it that I've had recently. Absence makes the heart grow bolder, if you will indulge that. I have the desire to do a lot of loving through the mails. I just want you to know that I love you and that you are here with me."

Later he wrote, "We have been working out like football players. More than most people want to realize, aerial combat is a team effort, and the men have to know each other well. In our exercises I have been working with 2nd Lt. William P. Gibbs, of Oakland, California. Billy will be my wingman. He'll have to protect me. I am the offense and he is the defense and counterpunch. He is twenty-one and single and a cheery character. He is an excellent pilot and I am in good hands. Where I will be going he will be, too, protecting me. It is something to think about—there are a lot of things on that order over here."

Karen wrote to him: "It is hard to believe that only a year and a half has passed since the start of the war. Three windows out of five display the flags to show someone in the service and I have seen a few gold stars, too. Ration books, red points, and V-mail are part of our lives. There is not much complaining. There is more comradeship, if anything, as a result of the sacrifices we are making—and little enough, most of us find ourselves adding. There is absolutely no doubt in our minds that we are going to win this war. We are working like hell in the plant and it is like that day and night everywhere in town. It makes me want to cry and I have cried—you and Billy are not alone. You aren't, and we want you to know it. Our love goes out to you.

"P.S. I am rolling my cigarettes on a little machine. What do you think of that?"

"We went into action today," he wrote. "I am safe and sound. The mission was as escort to our big friends—the bombers—and that's about all I can tell you. We were attacked by a pack of Messerschmitts, so I have had a taste of combat. I have never seen such a confusing mess in my life. No one could have a clear picture of what happened. I got on the tail of one, shot at him and maybe hit him, but he shook me off as easily as a man shrugs a fly off his neck. One got on me, but Billy chased him. It was over as fast as it began, but I had my eyes open—I mean this, Karen, or I would not have written any of it—and I think I have the hang of it. Billy feels the same way. We won't have trouble again."

The next time she read of his combat experience was the next Wednesday morning. On the front page of the Port Smith *Herald* the headline of a small, boxed item near the bottom of column eight read: "P.S.P.D. HERO GUNS DOWN THREE NAZI PLANES."

On his third mission they were jumped halfway to the target area by a pack of ME-109's. He was on the perimeter with an unobstructed view of the thirty or forty fighters bearing down from one o'clock high. As soon as he had the command he turned into them and kicked in the supercharger. The ME's had gained an equality in the first pass in having acquired the height; going downhill, the Thunderbolts could eat them alive.

"Are you with me, Billy?"

"Right behind you, Joe. You're out in front."

"Shut up, the two of you," the squadron leader called.

In finger threes and fours, the 109's spread out as the distance closed. Leland seemed alone in the front, burning fuel at the rate of a gallon a minute. He sighted in on the lead three-finger group, kicked the rudder pedals left and right, and sprayed. Instantly, by insane luck, the middle plane exploded. The outside ME's broke left and right. Pieces of the middle plane splattered against the Thunderbolt as Leland powered through the black smoke, terrified. A man had

244

died because of a lucky shot that could be in store for him, too. He was clear on the other side.

"Going down, Billy. Cover me."

"I'm with you, fella."

Leland skidded around to the left and followed the second ME down. He was already lifting into his first pass at the bombers. Leland crossed the arc, found him spread-eagled in the sight, and split his fingernail pushing on the button. The Messerschmitt flopped over and fell.

"You picked one up, Joe. Don't show him much."

"Right."

Slipping back and forth, he looked over his shoulder and saw Billy lining up on his pursuer, and another lining up on Billy. Leland feinted left, pulled up hard right, rolled, turned, and leveled as Billy's pursuer pulled up to intersect Billy's arc. Leland fired into his exposed underside. Bits and pieces tumbled away, then smoke appeared. The pilot rolled the ship and pulled on the canopy. Past him now, Leland looked back and saw him tumble out. Someone else had engaged the 109 that had been on his tail.

Overhead, one of the B-17's burst with a flash. Another churned smoke from two engines. Chutes opened. Debris rained out of the sky. Pushing his airplane in the attempt to get back to the fight, Joe Leland could feel nothing but horror.

The next day, in the same place, he made his fourth kill.

Two days after that, over Holland, he made kills five and six.

The *Herald* had followed its boxed item by recording the fourth plane on an inside page. Numbers five and six rated page one in all the Port Smith papers, and editorials in two of them. He had become an ace, the first in his squadron, the first from the Port Smith area.

Karen sent the clipping to him. "You can see now that you can't protect us from what you are doing or the dangers that you are facing. There are some functions as a wife I can still fulfill, and if you feel you want to, write all that you have on your mind to me. You're older than you were after the robbery at the auto store, but I know you and what you're thinking about. Perhaps better than you I know why you have done so well over there, and it isn't only because of your eyesight or nervous system. You couldn't do the same outside the frame of public service. Think and see if I am not right. No need to tell you we are all very, very proud. Please, please take care. You know me, too, and you know what is in my heart—all the time, every day and every night."

There was nothing he wanted to put down in writing. He had seen bodies and fragments of bodies falling out of the sky and he did not want Karen to have a picture of it. The newspapers liked to write that the fighter pilots were the last soldiers fighting man-to-man, and more than in any other part of the war it was true, but the net effect, day after day, was more like that of a gigantic killing ground. It showed them all that daylight bombing was a disaster of the first magnitude. That the war in the air was not the romantic tournament the newspapers were saying it was, was reason enough not to try to correct the impressions at home. If the Port Smith papers had fixed on him as the personification of a lie, and he hated it, he had to be glad that he was being protected from having to tell the truth. Karen could see into him, but only if he helped her. He did not want to write about the truth, so he did not, and he wrote about the things that came to him readily when he sat down to write.

When the Port Smith City Council passed the emergency bill allowing civil service employees to take their examinations while in the military, Karen did not simply inform him of the fact and wait for his reply. The forms, old tests, and all the study books he needed came in one package. "Now I'm inspired," she wrote. "With your permission, I'd like to go back to college in the evenings. Your parents are willing to mind Stephanie. The more I think about it, the more I feel that this is my big chance. After the war the colleges will be jammed with ex-servicemen. Also, one field with real opportunity for women will be opening up wide after the war—education. I will want to work even if we have more children; you know that. The success I've had with Steffie makes me think that I will like teaching and be good at it. I can do well, Joe, so please say I can try."

He said yes, amused and curious about her asking his permission so carefully. In his letter he treated the issue seriously, because it was important to her and she would be straining to see if he really meant yes. If she knew him, he knew her better. She had to see that he was satisfied with her, and she had to know that she was doing her share.

In September, in an action over Holland, he and Billy Gibbs, separated from their squadron and assisting a crippled Liberator back to England, fought off a half-dozen Messerschmitts and Focke-Wulfs, shooting down two, damaging two, and sending the others running. For the action they were awarded the Distinguished Flying Cross. They were interviewed by reporters from Port Smith and Oakland, a syndicated columnist, a commentator for the Mutual Broadcasting System, and a camera crew from Movietone News. All three Port Smith papers ran on their front pages a wire service photograph of Leland with his arm through a hole shot in the wing of the Thunderbolt while behind him his mechanic painted the ninth swastika on the fuselage. In a letter he received later Karen reported that all of her conversations concerned his exploits and that he had become a public property. People wanted to know what he was like and if she had had any idea that these things were going to happen when she married him.

"I answer no because it's less complicated. The truth is that the answer is yes, as well as anyone can predict the future. I have tried to tell the truth once, in psych class, where the professor, a very gracious old man, started the hour by saying he'd never had as a student the wife of an air ace. He congratulated you and said that I must be very proud. I said I was. He asked the question and I said yes. I told him—the class, really—about your strong sense of duty. Some of them hadn't known about the robbery. He said that he'd always been curious about the personal lives of men like you, and I said yes, that's too bad—very quickly, you know, and without malice, and we all laughed. He laughed, and said something very nice to me. You've said it but I am showing no modesty in telling it to you. Very casually he said, 'Your husband must need you very much.' Of course he meant that I had your interests at heart."

At the end of the year he went up to the American Embassy and took the examination for Detective Lieutenant. The results came back quicker than they would have under normal conditions. He had passed. In January, at the end of the month, he went home for thirty days. It was his first trip home since Christmas, 1942.

She met him at ten o'clock in the evening at the downtown railroad station, her hands in her pockets, her kerchief loose around her neck. He had changed, he realized, as he saw her face. Her eyes filled up and she had trouble speaking. He put down his valise.

"Hello, Joe."

"Hello, honey. You look fine." He took her in his arms and kissed her. He sobbed as he held her. When he moved back she took out her handkerchief for both of them.

"Stephanie's with your parents. We can go there or home, whichever you want."

"Let's go home."

She unbuttoned his coat. "Let me see the ribbon." She touched it with her fingertips. "They know how to make them impressive. Joe, I hope you're proud."

"This is no time to talk about it. Come on."

In the cab they kissed and held each other. She had put on a little weight. It was the starchy diet, she told him, and he would see many people who had been affected by it. He had put on another five pounds. He had put on ten pounds in training, all muscle, and he was at the highest weight of his life.

The small talk ended abruptly and she put her head on his chest and he looked out the window. The changes in the city were as she described them in her letters, and there was a bleakness on the streets, fewer cars, and in two gas stations they passed there were cars up on blocks. In a first floor window of their building was one of the rectangular flags, and upstairs, in their own, another.

Karen went up the steps without waiting for him, and as he paid the cabdriver he watched her. He wanted so many things now, but most of all to protect her from this. It was too much to ask of her, and he wished there was more for her that he could do. The war was hurting them more than they could guess—he could see it in the way she put the key in the lock.

She led the way up the stairs. "You can call your folks if you want to. They said it wasn't necessary, that we could wait until morning."

"Let's not make any decisions," he said. "I don't want to call them."

She turned on a light and removed her coat. Nothing in the apartment had changed. He took off his coat and began to unbutton his blouse. She looked at him and smiled. She undid her skirt. "I put in the diaphragm before I went down to the station. I didn't know what you'd want, but I thought I wouldn't keep you waiting."

"I love you, Karen."

"I love you. Let's go into the bedroom. Did I tell you how much I missed you in there?"

"No."

She took off her blouse. "I have." She finished undressing. He had been watching her and was not done. When he stood up she looked at him. "In my own waiting I haven't thought of what waiting would do to you."

"I've tried not to think about it."

She moved to him. "I'll make it worthwhile." She kissed him on the mouth. He put his arms around her slowly, touching her smooth skin with his fingertips first, drawing her to him so her breasts just touched him. They stopped kissing and looked into each other's eyes. She looked vulnerable and small. He drew her to him again and kissed her neck. At first she did not move, and then she breathed deeply and locked her arms around his neck tightly. She pressed herself against him. "My baby. I love you," she said. "I love you so very much."

"Hold on," he said.

"Are you going to carry me?"

"I want to."

She made herself ready. As he lifted her he felt her body shudder, and instinctively he thought that she was going to cry. He did not think he understood it. She held him tightly as he carried her to bed, and then, as he put her down gently, she looked up at him, teary, smiling. "I missed you. I love you. Are you going to tease me?" He shook his head. "Give it, then," she said softly. "Let me be your good wife."

They were different with each other and knew it and did not try to force themselves. Four weeks was not enough time. They were careful but not like strangers. He did not know if she really looked and smelled and tasted different or if his mind had altered the things it had had to remember. But she loved him somehow, and somehow his happiness in being with her was real. It was a joy settled on a very strange sorrow, and he knew that if it troubled him, it troubled her, and he said nothing about it. What she had to overcome to be a wife to a changed man was enough to make him weep; it made him love her more. They did not have the time to clear away the tension of all the things they needed to discuss, yet they gave to each other. It seemed to him that she gave more than he did. The idea that he was on a rest from risking his life was an unrealistic way of seeing it. She saw it that way, and thus had no rest herself. In no sense were his needs subjugated, while hers were. He had had the option of transferring to the United States and had turned it down. Now he wished he had taken it. She had written nothing about it; perhaps she had been as blind as he had been to their needs before he had come home.

Two nights before he was to leave he told her he was sorry. She said he was being foolish. He didn't answer. In the next days they seemed further away from each other than they had been at the start, and at the railroad station the last afternoon, there was the feeling that nothing had been accomplished. She knew it as well as he did, and she broke down and wept bitterly. Holding her, he could not help thinking that there was a limit to what people could take, and that they had reached it. The discovery gave him no satisfaction, because he could not tell how much of the damage they had done themselves, separately and together. He kissed her again and held her tightly. The act itself became its own meaning, and he could not let go of her. He held onto her as if she were the only luck in his life, not knowing if she could feel what was happening to him, not caring, either. He held her until the desire, for that was what it was, was fulfilled. She stopped crying, and after she kissed him in return, she smiled.

He was assigned to transporting one of the new long-range P-51 Mustang fighters to England. It put him on his guard. The Mustang had the capability to protect the bombers all the way to Berlin, and to him, who believed at least in the inevitable effectiveness of saturation bombing, the turning point of the war had come. The war would end soon after the creation of the second front. He had to be careful. At the start he had set out to live, and if he returned to the fighting not remembering that because he could see the victory, he would be dead.

The nature of the war in the air changed very quickly, and even the 161st, one of the last squadrons to be equipped with the Mustangs, was able to feel it. The Thunderbolts, loaded with bombs and rockets, were sent across the Channel to attack small targets in France and the low countries. The formations were smaller and the successes greater. The enemy was less formidable, and the old hands were the ones who could see it best. The only answer was that the finest that Germany had been able to put in the sky were dead. It was horrible.

Something had come over him. If he relaxed he went numb—static. When it happened he had to use his strength and will to get going again, and a mission required hours of preparation inside himself. He was not flying less well; he could judge that. He was doing something wrong while he was in the air, omitting that thing that had made him an ace. What it was, he did not know. He knew he was not right, and he had to wait for the mood to pass, like a sailing ship waiting for a wind.

On May 18, while returning to base, they were attacked by a group of FW's and Leland shot down two of them.

"By the time you read this you will have known it for several weeks because the newspapermen were here again and perhaps as I sign my name here the story will be going into print in Port Smith. I became a double ace today—plus one, to bring my total credit to eleven. One of the reporters told me that my record is now among the top ten in the E.T.O., eighth or ninth—well behind the leaders, anyway. I have to tell you that although the reporters are good guys I am sick of their jobs. Do I sell newspapers? The new men coming in who want to meet me expect something that I am not. I tried to explain to you months ago. Billy and I have talked it over, and I do have to be something for these men. 'He's a man like me. If he can do it, so can I,' is their attitude. That part would have been required of me, anyway, but in addition I have to show that the attention I am getting is a pleasant and worthwhile thing by itself. In the process the fact that human beings are dying is lost. I don't like it and I do feel that the newspapers are greatly responsible. As you may have guessed, I have been in a kind of depression these past weeks, but now I have snapped out of it, I think. I am interested in my job again—this job. Somehow who I really am must become clear to these kids, or literally it will kill them. For the first time in my life I am forced to find words for myself—the opposite of 'don't think about it,' that I used to say so much. I have to show that I can handle who I am and what I've done, and that I have an accurate perspective on the attendant and irrelevant nonsense. I used to think that a man grows up and that was that. But situations change and he is required to give something more or different and how much he gives is the measure of what he is. Today I told the papers exactly what happened in the air—that will confuse you until you read this. I've come to the conclusion that the more said about aerial combat, the better. I am still just trying to do my job, but now my job is different from what it was. What the professor said about my needing you was true. You knew it. I do need you, now more than ever."

"I know that I missed a couple of letters, Joe, but I've been very busy these past three days. I put off writing my term paper in education, and when I set aside time to do it, I had to put in extra time at the plant. You can take some satisfaction in the fact that there is no coasting at home. This summer I will work on my thesis exclusively, and by January I will have my degree. I have no news, really I don't, and I am still bone-tired. This is a rotten letter to receive, and as soon as I can snap back I will write a better one. I will send this nevertheless, as I know you want it . . ."

"See? I am having my breakfast and writing to you again. I mailed the last one before I went to bed last night. Sleep helped. I had a dream, and this morning I woke up believing that I was five months pregnant—I actually looked for my stomach. I felt very let down when I really woke up. We should have talked about it, at least. We *are* living in a sort of suspended animation, but we should have somehow reaffirmed what we got married for. Maybe I want you to tell me again what you are going to do to me. Do you remember? I loved that kind of talk. I did, Joe. I want to hear it again from you."

Her next letter, dated two days later, had a different tone. "The announcement came late this morning over the public address system. Everybody felt the gravity of it at once and there was no cheering. Down at the other end of the shop one of the men got up on a bench and said, 'I think we ought to pray.' It was superfluous. We were thinking of all of you. I know you're in it and I pray to God that you're all right. We aren't getting much news but we don't think that they would hold anything back. There is that desire to talk to strangers. I heard one woman say as we were leaving tonight, 'Just wait until they see our production figures tomorrow.' That's about the attitude. Of course the churches are open. People are afraid for the country and what will happen to it after the war. In so many ways America is irretrievably committed. This is our proudest moment, but there is a deep fear about our national destiny. We will have to be something after the war, and none of us knows what it is. We are ill-prepared, or too young, or confused. But we do not want to see bad things happen after all that we have worked for. D-Day may someday be a national holiday, but today is a very sober day, serious and prayerful."

The tone of her letters did not let down again, and when he shot down the twelfth and thirteenth she sent him the clippings from the papers and detailed the reactions of the people she had come to know since he had been away. The letters were fuller, as if she understood better what had happened to them after his leave. She seemed to be working at holding them together for the time the war would last. He did not believe that it would end by Christmas, as so many were saying. He was too busy to give to her as she was giving to him and he said so, and later her answer came back: that it had not entered her mind.

In July the squadron was moved to France and in August it was given the Mustangs. At the end of September he had ten days and he went up to Scotland with a camera. The country was much like the upstate area where they had spent their honeymoon. He enjoyed himself, and wrote telling her so. When he returned to France a bundle of her letters was waiting, the last teasing him gently but frightenedly about how he was going to spend his leave. Her next letters were in response to the ones he had sent from Scotland. He had conveyed the freshness and pleasure he had gotten from the countryside. She was glad that he had been able to rest.

During the German counterattack in December there was nothing that airplanes could do until the skies cleared. The Nazis were making their last effort, and the battle among the fighters was as fierce as Leland had ever seen it. In the next month he shot down five more planes and after one mission he found the lip of the Mustang's air scoop shot away. He led half the squadron in an attack on a small airfield, and the later photographs showed that seventeen aircraft had been destroyed. He was promoted to Captain. Unofficially he learned that he was going to be sent home as an instructor, and for the rest of the tour he flew as wingman to Billy, who in the process became a double ace. They alternated after a while, and Leland brought his total to twenty-one. His orders came through, he went to England and caught a ride on a C-54 for Mitchel Field in New York. He had ten days before he was due at Lake Charles.

CHAPTER THIRTEEN

. . . .

WHEN HE SAW HER HIS FIRST THOUGHT WAS THAT THE FOURTEEN months he had been away hadn't happened at all. Then he saw that they had, because she was pale and she had lost the weight she had gained in the previous year. As he crossed the station she raised her hand in a gesture she could not seem to control, and she ran toward him, as unhappy as he had ever seen her, and pressed her face against his shoulder.

"There, Karen. Take it easy. We're all right now."

"I hope so," she said. "I hope we are."

"How is Steffie?"

"Fine. Everybody's well." She straightened up and sniffed. The strain still showed. "They'll see you tomorrow. I—have to work tomorrow but I'll have the next day and the weekend and most of next week—"

"Let's get out of here," he said.

"You haven't kissed me hello."

He stopped and kissed her. She broke away hurriedly. After she had asked, he had looked for something better, and now he showed his surprise. She laughed. "Don't worry, Captain." She glanced at the valise. "Is there anything I can carry?"

"No—no, there isn't."

In the cab she asked if he had brought her anything. He said that it was only something small. She wanted to know what it was anyway.

"All I could find in Paris. I thought you might think more of where it came from than what it was."

"I didn't know you had gotten to Paris," she said.

"On my way to England."

"So? Did you have fun?"

He laughed. "I was there two hours."

"I'm sorry, Joe."

He was shocked. "For what?"

"Nothing. I'm glad you're home." She put her hands around his arm and her head on his shoulder. In the way she did it, not out of loving urge, but some wifely duty, it was wrong. It felt wrong to him, loveless and pretended, like something she had learned at a movie.

Outside the apartment she asked him if he wanted to go for something to eat. He turned her around to him.

"Are you hungry?"

"No. I thought you might be."

"Is anything the matter?"

She shook her head. "No." Her animation was faked.

"Are you having your period? Is that what it is?"

"No." She said something he couldn't hear. He asked her to repeat it. She said it was nothing.

"Let's go upstairs," he said.

She went ahead of him. The way she was acting, she wanted him to find out what was bothering her. She unlocked the door and turned on the light. It was four o'clock in the afternoon and the blinds were drawn and the house was dark. It was the way you found a house when there was sickness.

"I decided to make a scrapbook of your clippings," she said as she went into the bedroom. "It's on the coffee table. I even got a clipping service in case I missed any."

He didn't answer. He took off his hat and coat and sat down on the sofa like a guest. She came back wearing her slip, carrying her dress. "What's the matter?"

"I don't know, Karen. You tell me."

She removed her stockings. "I have nothing to tell you."

"Then stop treating me as if I were your third cousin from Tennessee."

"I'm doing nothing of the sort." She took off her slip.

256

"A customer, then," he said frightenedly. "Karen, I didn't pay for this. If you'd rather do something else, say so."

She smiled mischievously. "How do you know how a customer is treated?"

"It doesn't take much imagination," he said more ruefully than he had intended. Now she put her hands on her hips in a parody of the pinup photographs. As parody it was sharper and more brutal than she could have wanted. They had lost control of themselves, both of them.

"Come on, Joe. Come inside."

"I want to know what's going on, Karen."

"Can't you guess?"

"I don't believe this," he said. "Something's wrong."

She came closer, her eyes bright. "Like what?"

"I don't know."

"Then come inside." She hesitated, then turned away from him, giving him no choice but to follow. The bedroom was almost as dark as it was at night. "Now you can kiss me," she said. He did. Her skin was moist with perspiration, and he could smell it, unhealthy and sour. She saw the bewilderment and unhappiness on his face as he moved away from her.

"You're lying," he said. He pushed her away. "You're lying and you know it. Your clothes are in the other room. Put them on. I didn't come home for this nonsense."

"You had it in Europe, you mean."

"That doesn't deserve an answer," he said.

"You weren't faithful," she said. He didn't look at her. "You weren't," she repeated, faltering. "Don't try to tell me you were."

"I'm not going to try to tell you anything—" He looked into her face. She was frightened to death. "Now I get it," he whispered. He could hardly see. "Thanks." He waved his hand at her. "Get away," he said quietly. "Go away from me."

"Joe—" She took a step toward him and he pushed her back violently. He regretted it right away. She fell against the door and there was a sharp crack. She stood up holding her elbow, trembling and pale.

"Joe, I'm sorry—"

"I didn't mean to hurt you. Get out of here a minute. I have it coming to me—at least."

She went out. He closed the door. The room could be anyone's, he felt so strange, sick, and hurting. He turned on the light and looked harder at the bed, not getting nearer, wondering if she had used it. There was no reason to think that she had kept faith on any level. He did not know what to believe, even that she had let Stephanie see her—he could not finish the thought. He turned to the dresser, untied his tie, and retied it as perfectly as he could. He knew that he was trying not to think. When he was done he picked up her brush and brushed his hair. He was afraid to look at his own eyes; it would be like stepping off the world. He thought of how close he had come to sleeping with her now, and that it was likely that he never would have the chance again. He considered it, as witless as Punch. He wanted her. His desire for her was as heavy and naked as a stone. He turned out the light and opened the door.

She was not finished dressing. He went to the kitchen and set out the cups and saucers. When he had the coffee hot he sat down and waited, and finally she came out.

"Thank you," she said.

He did not know where to start. He did not even know if he wanted to learn what had happened. He could feel his mind evading the name she had put on him and the things that could have been seen by people who knew them. Instinctively he did not want to make it worse. He did not want to attack her. Even now she was the only person who could protect him from the pain of this thing—but he did not want to ask her if he was still in a position to help her.

"Do you want a divorce?"

"I don't know, Joe. I don't know what I want."

"Are you going to tell me about it?"

"There's nothing to tell. I was attracted to him."

"You're right," he said suddenly. "There's nothing to tell."

"You—"

"I know, but be quiet. I don't want to hear that stuff. Not now."

"I *thought* I was attracted to him."

"Are you still seeing him?"

"I told him I'd call him after I'd seen you. Spoke to you. But I wasn't sure that I was going to speak to you about it. Or call him. I don't know."

"Who is he?"

"A professor from school."

"The one who said I needed you?"

"No, he's an old man. Another one."

"When did it start?"

"Last spring—May. Joe, do we have to go through this? What do you want to know?"

"The idea of you screwing some other guy while I'm getting my ass shot off doesn't exactly thrill me, Karen. There are some things I want to know."

"Or what?"

"Or nothing. I'm not going to threaten you. Does he want to marry you?"

She swallowed. "Yes."

"And what have you said?"

"I am married."

"I see." He paused, and she misunderstood him.

"That amuses you? I didn't just fall into bed with him. It took a bit of time—"

"Shut up!"

She stopped.

"All right, when did you say you'd call him?

"I'm not one of your criminals, Joe."

"When?"

"I won't tell you—I didn't give him a specific time."

"Call him tonight." His voice thickened and he felt afraid. "You call and tell him what happened here. You're not going to see him anymore—at least, until I've had a chance to think."

"About what?"

"I'll tell you, damn it! I'm entitled to something!"

"Joe, you can't punish me for this. I won't be punished."

"I didn't say anything about punishment! For Christ's sake, I don't think you know what you want, and I don't want anything to happen that doesn't have to."

"How do you know what I want?" she cried.

"I know you better than you know yourself! In this case, I'm right and you're wrong, and you're going to call him!"

She was silent, cowed because he had outshouted her. She said, "All I can think of are the things you can do to me—in court, out of court. You could hurt me any way you want, and no one would blame you."

"That's in your mind, Karen."

"What am I supposed to tell him?" It was a plea; she wanted to be told what he wanted.

"That I'm home and you're going to Louisiana with me. That you want to."

"You expect me to say it?"

"I don't know. I don't know."

She stared at him. "You love me?"

"You know the answer to that. What do you want to believe?"

In a few minutes she carried her cup to the sink. "I'm going to call him now," she said. "I want you to hear." He sat still, not believing that he had understood, until she turned to him. "Come on." He followed her to the telephone. "You won't have to hear his voice," she said. "Only mine." She had to wait after dialing. "Hello? It's me, that's right. I told him what happened and we've talked it over. . . . Yes, just now. I don't want to see you again. . . . Yes, I do mean it. It's final." She listened a moment. "No, it's final." She took the receiver with both hands. "It's not your business. It never was. I don't want to be cruel with you, but it's true. I was wrong—no, I won't say your name. . . . Yes, he's standing right here, but it's just that I don't want to say it. I'm not doing anything I don't want to do. . . . I understand that, and I appreciate your concern." She was quiet. "All right, goodbye. I wish you the same. . . . That's childish. . . . I'm sorry if it hurt you, but you knew a year ago that you could get hurt. . . . That's your opinion. . . . That's right, goodbye." She put down the telephone. "Joe, I'm sorry."

"No more for a while. Please."

"I told you it started in May. He was involved long before I was. When you were home I wasn't even aware of it."

He didn't answer.

"Are you hungry? I'll fix you something."

"All right. Call me when it's ready." He sat down, not like a guest, but a man come home from a graveside.

He had said he would think, but he did not know what to think about. There were many things that he would have to learn and face, if he was going to stay. He wanted to stay; even if he could not tell her properly, she knew it. The call settled nothing; it could be undone with another call. She might not think that both men could see it that way. He did not want to face the fact that she had slept with someone else, but she had acknowledged on the telephone that she had talked in a way that was worse. The thoughts multiplied each other so that the core of the pain and shock extended and penetrated to the palms of his hands and the tips of his fingers. She came into the room with a sandwich and a glass of milk. She put them on the table beside the chair and sat down before him. She pressed her cheek to his knee.

"Thank you," she said.

"No, Karen. Get up."

"I want to say this. I couldn't handle it anymore. As soon as I saw you I knew what would happen. I don't know why I did it. I pitied him. I even hated him. I did, Joe."

"Get up. Come on." Even as he said it he understood the reservation of trust inside him. He wanted to help her, but he could feel a fresh, strong withholding of belief. For the first time since their courtship, he was measuring her. In her own torment she did not feel the change in him. She would as she improved, and then she would be hurt again. The change made him not care. He could not help thinking that he had the right to tend to himself first. The horrible reactions worked onward like the reflections in a house of mirrors, and at the end, like stepping outside again, he still blamed her viciously for having started it all.

This mixed with desire. As he wondered at his thoughts he had to see that he had to try to keep a rein on all the thoughts that could hurt her; he saw again just so quickly that this was what he wanted. He bade her once more to get up. Her face was blotched from the emotion she could not expel. "I want you to lie down for a while," he said. "I'm not going to bother you. I'm going to call my mother and tell her to keep Steffie until tomorrow evening or maybe the next morning. If she wants to know why, I'll tell her you're not feeling well. You stay home from the job, too, needless to say." She nodded. "Is there anything I ought to know?"

"You say it so innocently," she whispered.

"I mean, did anybody see you with him, or anybody guess that something was wrong?"

"No. Would that change your mind?"

"Why ask a question like that?"

"I don't know," she said.

"Why do you think I want to know?" he asked.

"So there would be no surprises like that," she said.

"That's all," he said. "That's all there is to it."

While she slept he made the call and then called his father at work. He listened carefully for something in their voices. He could not hear it, and felt perverse for having tried. In the bedroom he stripped to his underwear and lay down beside her. Her back was to him. He kissed her neck and her cheek. She smelled like herself. She awakened and rolled to him to kiss him on the mouth. Her body was so hot it seemed feverish. "I love you, Joe."

"I love you."

He made no move toward her and she stared into his eyes. He wanted her, but only half from love. He did not want to abuse her. She seemed to be waiting for that, not for him. He did not want her to whisper encouragement she did not mean. He did not want her sympathy. And he could anticipate the defeat of finding her not ready for him. He kissed her again and put his head down on the pillow.

"Do you want to put your arms around me the way you used to?"

He didn't answer. He was sorry she knew him well enough to

remember his pleasure with such things. He loved her, and he was sorry about that, too.

He awakened later in the darkness and, not thinking, rolled toward her and found her. For him, it was over as quickly as it began.

"Did you make it?"

"Yes," she said. "I was ready. I was dreaming about it." She kissed him. She kissed him again.

"I don't want to know what happened, Karen. Do you understand? There's nothing about it that I want to hear. I don't want to know."

"Someday I'll tell you," she said.

"Not now."

After a while they moved away from each other. She got up from the bed and opened the blinds. The lights from the street gave him a clear view of her face. She came back and sat on the edge of the bed. "Were you faithful to me?"

"I'm not going to tell you," he said. It had been an impulse, but the words had come out convincingly.

She got closer. "You've never told me about any of your girls."

"That's right."

"I hadn't thought seriously about that side of you until this year."

"Remember what I told you, Karen."

"I am, sweetheart." She kissed him. "Do you know what I think? I think your silence is the best line any man ever gave a woman."

"I'm listening."

"Scotland, for example. I would have believed that if—well, I would have believed it. I understand that Scottish girls are supposed to have very firm bodies."

"And?"

"And the way you've always been, you could fall in love with a girl and I would never know."

"Tell me, do I love you?"

"Yes," she said.

"Then there's nothing you have to know, is there?"

"Did you have a good time in Scotland?"

"Yes."

"That hurts a little—but you know that."

"That's right, Karen. It's gone far enough."

She got up. He did not watch her. He wondered how much of this she had gotten from her boyfriend. The thought seemed to smother him. There was nothing he could do about the past. He had to believe her and live as if nothing fatal had happened. It didn't have to be fatal. The more he thought about taking her to Louisiana the more it appealed to him. If she thought that he did not trust her he would forget the idea. He had begun to make plans for after the war, but he had to let them rest. He could hear her in the kitchen. This was not the first time the sounds she made in that place made him yearn for her. She was the same and his desire for her was unchanged. Quietly he got out of bed and went toward the kitchen light. She was wearing a cotton robe. She looked over her shoulder and smiled, unkempt. After Stephanie had been born he had come to the thought that he would not hesitate to lay down his life for either of them, if it had to come to that. Had he changed? He loved them. He loved her. But he did not know.

She stayed in Port Smith while he went to Lake Charles alone. She had saved money while he had been away, more than they had ever had before, and they could not believe that conditions after the war would let them recoup what it would cost to travel. They could not be sure, either, that he would stay in Louisiana until the war's end. No one knew what the Japanese had saved for the defense of their islands. The longer the assault took, the better were his chances of becoming part of it. He did not even discuss it with her.

Very little had eased between them. He strained away from the idea of having to trust her. It repelled him. There never had been a current of desperation between them, and she gave the indication of wanting—something. She had asked again about "his women." He had not forgotten that she had been the one to say that it hurt. He

264

was afraid to speak of it. The parts of their marriage came away from each other; the roles of the night were removed from the roles of the day.

He came home on leave for Christmas, 1945, and then, two months later, for good. He was not ready to go back to work. It was too cold to take Stephanie to Manitou so they went by train to Miami and by bus to Key West, and after two nights in a hotel he found a bungalow they could sublet, dearly, for a month. They needed time. Both of them had trouble believing that it was really done and that he would not be forced to go away again. He told her what he had not put in his letters and it did not purge him of the experience. He still felt locked in when it no longer existed. It was in his dreams; he could feel it in the footfalls behind him. She asked if he wanted to hear what she had done. Without thinking he gave an evasive reply, and then it was too late. Her silence was nervous and sullen and what she felt inside it was entirely his fault. Since he had come home the games between them had stopped, but it was as if she had only misplaced them in her mind. There were times when telling her he loved her was wrong, and others when she wanted to be held, cuddled, and protected. He gave it all willingly and even guiltily and kept still about it at other times. He awakened once to find her making love to him as he had done with her at the beginning; as she had done with him he pretended to stay asleep. The next day she was in a happy mood, but he did not ask why, because he was afraid he would lie badly. In the evening after Stephanie went to bed Karen seemed nervous, and he wanted to take her down to the beach, but she did not want to leave Steffie alone.

"If I ever wanted a divorce, would you give it to me?"

"Sure," he said. Now he saw: she wanted to fight.

"Will you promise me that?"

"Yes." He had to go slowly. More than wanting to fight, she wanted to be cruel. If he asked her if she wanted a divorce now she would say no and be left unsatisfied. She would change the subject but her intent would stay the same. It would not be harmless, then.

"Can I sit on the porch?"

She wanted to talk nonsense. "Sure, if you want."

"I mean alone."

"I know."

Later when they were preparing for bed, she said she was sorry. "I don't know what happened."

"Do you want to see him again?"

"No—no. I know what it would be like. I feel all right now. There's never a time when I don't regret it, but when I get in a mood like the one I was in tonight I want to go wallow in—something. I want to wallow in anything."

He had to encourage her to keep talking. "What was he like?"

"He was young—older than you in years, but young. You heard me on the telephone that day. He wanted me to say his name. It upset him, yet he wished me good luck. It was false magnanimity. He honestly didn't want to see you get killed, but when you did something good it depressed him. I think he knew better than I did how it was going to turn out. He wanted to marry me. He wanted to talk to you himself, but I knew what would come of that."

"What?"

"He couldn't have handled himself with you. All you would have had to do was open the door and tell him to get out. He would have obeyed you. He was the sort of person who could be trussed up that way, only to get angry—impotently—later. It was something I read in his eyes. He wasn't a bad person. He was bright and very witty. If you had thrown me out I would have gone to him. It wouldn't have worked out, but I would have gone just the same. He loved me and needed me."

"What did that teacher tell you?"

"I know."

"Is there any beer in the icebox?"

She nodded. "That's another thing. He liked beer, but not enough to remember to have it in the house. He wanted it and it wasn't there."

"Neither were you," he said.

"After a while I tried to be. I would be less than honest if I told you otherwise. I liked him but I never could admire him. I knew what you would think of him. You would have laughed at him—not cruelly; you wouldn't have been able to help it. There was nothing to look up to. There always is with you, and that's the difference, for better or worse."

He sat on the edge of the bed, thinking about this. Perhaps dignity had nothing to do with it. He seemed to have no dignity left. She got on the bed behind him and touched his back with her hand. "There aren't any comparisons in my mind. I shouldn't have said it. I love you. That was something inside me, something I had to get out. I hated it and myself and all I could think of were the dirty words I knew for myself. I didn't act clean and I didn't feel clean."

"What about now?"

"I'm forgetting. Slowly but surely I'm forgetting. I tried to wreck the only family I've ever had, and I want to forget it. Do you want that beer now? We can drink it quickly and take a cold shower and then make love on top of the sheets with the windows open."

He grinned. "I'll sleep for a week."

She kissed him on the back of the neck. "You'll remember why just as soon as you wake up."

In Port Smith he returned to work while she looked for a larger apartment. It was impossible. Barracks for veterans had been put up on the lots on the north side, and landlords of permanent buildings wanted hundreds of dollars in fees for the vacancies that turned up. She kept looking. Stephanie took over their bedroom and they moved onto a daybed in the living room. Steffie would not be of school age until September, and until then Karen could not work. The job was there and she was eager. He told her to stop looking for an apartment and shop for a car. The waiting lists for new cars were months long. Through a friend Karen located a LaSalle convertible, expensive for such an old car, but too much like a Cadillac for them to refuse.

That summer on his vacation they drove to Canada. She had taken driving lessons with a girl friend and had developed into an excellent chauffeur. Driving did not interest him and he took advantage of her desire to drive. The car became hers completely and he took the trolley to work and she picked him up in the evenings. Once, when they were going to spend his forty-eight hours at the beach, she came by at the end of the night tour, six in the morning.

When the schools opened in September she had almost as little free time as he did. She had to learn her job. Their hours had to be organized, and in the mornings, whether he was coming in or going out, he kept quiet and let them sleep. If that was an inconvenience, he did not believe it, and it was the only change he had to make. No part of the household suffered; there were things that distressed her, she said, but they had to be pointed out to him. He was proud of her. That did not please her much, because she had become determined. The job was not what she had been led to expect and she was disappointed with the lack of freedom inside it. She came home angry or tired. There was no way she could fight back. He had to keep still. The money in the job became more important to her, and when she said casually that she would transfer to another school for the next year, he tried to find ways to keep it in her mind.

At the end of the year he drove out to Phillips Airport in Clausen County, the largest private airport in the state, and he learned there that he was not the first ex-pilot to turn up. Some had come to learn what had happened to the old airplanes. Leland had read that the Government was selling off as many as it could, but he did not know that thousands of others were rotting where they stood —bombers and fighters, of no interest to commercial users. The man he talked to had seen a Liberator bought, stripped of its wings, and converted into a diner. P-40's and Aircobras were showing up at amusement parks. They were inadequate as private aircraft, too expensive, too limited in use. They were not even good for crop dusting.

That evening he told Karen what he had seen and heard. They had a party to attend and as they crossed town he gave her an idea of what it would cost to own and operate their own airplane. He thought that they were restricted to a two-place plane, something like a Taylorcraft, and he wasn't happy about it. She was driving and she listened, thoughtful.

"Have you thought about becoming a commercial pilot? You're not too old to change careers."

He said no. "That's not the way I feel about it. It's more a case of 'I love my wife, but oh you kid.' "

She laughed. "Oh, really? Tell me about that."

"You know what I mean—" But something harsh had come through his tone. He had betrayed himself. In the afternoon, when he had entered the apartment, the telephone had been ringing. He had picked up in time, for the line had been open, but when he had said hello, no one had answered. He had heard no breathing, but for as long as he had held the receiver, no dial had come on. He had touched the button, and the dial tone had sounded at once. There had been nothing wrong with the telephone. He had decided not to ask if someone was bothering her; if there was and she chose not to tell him, she had her reasons. If he was wrong he could hurt and embarrass her. But the more he had thought, the more he had wanted to find out about it. She could want to protect him. If that was the case, he wanted it stopped. He kept quiet now as she concentrated on her driving, her face set hard.

"I've never said anything about what you did overseas," she said.

"I know, Karen—"

"Then why did you get so rough?"

"No reason, I—"

"Come on, I know when you're lying."

He could not think of an answer. She said bitterly, "I'm sorry, but I couldn't take it lightly if something were going on now. I've got too many other things to worry about."

"All right, there was a telephone call today. Whoever it was wouldn't answer when I said hello."

"And you think I'm up to something? You've had this on your mind all this time?"

"No. For God's sake, Karen, I thought he might be bothering you."

"And I was protecting him?"

"No, that you were protecting me! Watch what you're doing—" She did not hear or see. The car went through a light as another car started out from the side street. He reached for the steering wheel as she saw the car and tried to brake. They could have made it around if she had used the accelerator. The other car hit them solidly in the side and they bounced once, sliding toward the far corner. The brakes were not grabbing. She turned the wheel to the right as they skidded and he tried to help her, but it was too late, the car hit the lamp post head-on with a resounding bang. He had underestimated their speed and had not braced himself. He rose out of the seat and struck his head on the rearview mirror.

In two hours a squad car was taking them home. He had a headache, a gash on his brow with six stitches, and a sore elbow; she had cuts on her knees and a long scrape on the inside of her calf. She was still in mild shock. He had been knocked out, no more than a second or two, but the sight of him slumped on the seat had scared her badly. He had had to push her out of the car and direct a passerby to call the emergency squad. No one in the other car had been hurt. He had promised the driver that the damage to the car would be paid for. It did not seem as if there was going to be a suit; the other people had been glad that the accident had not been more serious.

The LaSalle was a loss. When the car had hit them her foot had slipped off the brake pedal and she had not been able to move. He told her not to talk. The shock did not help her. She had to talk about the car and how close she had come to killing him. She had not been able to help even when he had been unconscious. She had failed him in too many ways.

The car pulled up to their door. They got out and went up the steps. Suddenly she looked back.

"What is it?" he asked.

"They heard what I said."

In the apartment he asked, "What did you say?"

She threw her purse onto the couch. "I told them everything. They know everything."

"That's not true. You were upset, they know that."

"You didn't see their faces. I did."

"Take it easy, Karen."

"Don't give me that." She turned to him. "How can you be so calm?"

"I don't see anything to get upset about."

She turned away again. "No, I guess not."

"Does that mean anything?"

"Not what you think!"

"I'm not thinking anything, Karen. What's the matter with you?"

"I hope to God you never find out." She was undoing the clasp on her collar. Her stockings were in tatters and smeared with blood. "I hope to God you never feel this way—this thing, this awfulness."

"I don't understand."

"I know you don't, and I don't hold it against you." The dress fell to the floor. She didn't pick it up. "Everything seems to go well for a while, and then the bottom goes out for me. It's happened again and again."

"Like when?"

"Like tonight."

"What other times?"

"Am I a suspect? Are we going to play policeman?"

"What other times, Karen? I'm not going to fool with you."

"The day we got married. You remember how I was. I cried on the train. I got scared. Before, I could feel things going along well, but the ground underneath me seemed to get thinner and thinner. I couldn't do anything after you left the night before. It collapsed. I didn't recognize it then or the next time, when Steffie was born, but this time I could almost chart its progress. It happened another time I know of, too."

"When?"

"You know."

"I want you to tell me."

"After your leave. During your leave. Before I took up with what's-his-name. It's not you. It doesn't have anything to do with you. It's all inside me. I can't say it, can't touch it, but it's there. I get afraid and angry and I don't see how doing anything will help me."

What he could not say was that he did not understand. He could not help but feel that it did have to do with him—that she did not love him. "Look, do I make you happy?"

"Sometimes."

She had given it another meaning. "Only sometimes?"

"The rest of the time I pretend."

"What about before we were married?"

"It was perfect. I didn't have trouble until Steffie was born."

"I remember that morning," he said.

"It didn't happen then. That's when I decided to pretend. I sat up working it out. It didn't begin to happen again easily, like before, until we went to Florida."

"Oh, Jesus, Karen."

"Don't you want to know about him?"

"No."

"He never did it. Never."

"That's a consolation," he said. It was, childishly. He sat down. He did not know what to think.

"I love you, Joe."

"Not the way I love you. That's clear now."

"I'm not like other people—normal people. I'm just trying to get off the roller coaster. There are times when I can't control what I do. I can't forget myself. I thought we'd never talk of these things. Joe, I do love you. I'd do anything for you. I'm the way I am, but I'm trying to help myself. Maybe there'll always be nights like tonight when I start wrecking everything. The bottom goes out and eventually I feel this awful poison in my system. Listen, I always get pleasure out of going to bed with you. I do, honey."

He could not say that he felt it was ruined. "Don't ever pretend anything—*anything*—again. Just be what you want and do what you want. Say you'll do that."

"You do love me that way," she said.

"Say it, Karen. Please."

"I promise."

She meant it, it was in her tone and her expression, yet it was no relief to him, only a burden. She had said roller coaster. To him it was a treadmill that he had been on before. He had forgotten it, and now he felt as if he had indulged himself all this time.

Still, he did not see the danger signals. She kept speaking of the accident; months later, without warning, she asked him if he had heard anything about what she had said that night. He didn't know it, but the problem she had told him about had returned. He did not think of looking for it. Rightly she thought that it would obsess him. She made plans to stay home for the next school year. She equated it with being a good wife, which in turn she equated with "making up" for what she had almost done to him.

By summer, he felt squeamish about what was happening.

"What did you do with yourself today?"

"I window-shopped. I saw some dresses I liked, but I don't think I really want them."

"Oh."

"Why did you ask?"

"Just interested in you, that's all."

"Well, maybe I will get something for myself."

Neither could take the chance of accusing the other of lying.

By her own account later, it took her until mid-October to remember that somebody might have been trying to reach her the afternoon of the accident. When she could retain it, the idea of seeing him again was the most exciting, thrilling thing she could think of.

She met him one night when Joe was working, faking an excuse to leave Steffie with his parents. She knew that she was not fooling herself, but that did not turn her around. She was trembling when she stepped out of the elevator. When she pressed the bell her legs were shaking violently. Inside, she needed twenty minutes to regain a semblance of composure, and then she was bitterly ashamed. It did not stop her. It was only a matter of facing herself once, then she could tend to the reason she was there. Sickened with herself, she could even take charge.

Later, with her help, Leland learned why she was able to fool him. She succeeded because the affair made her curiously more eager for him. It was his real if obscure triumph over her lover, who did not see it. She knew her husband better. She did not have to lie to him except for her lover's sake, and her actions made her have to lie to him, who was still trying to gain possession of her. Sooner or later her lying and his possessiveness would have annoyed her, and with nothing to lose, she would have hurt him more cruelly than she could have hurt the man who was innocent of her faithlessness. Midway through this stupid set of victories, Leland accidentally discovered what she was doing, and upset things a little.

The night after Thanksgiving, on his way in a car from Police Headquarters to the Fifth Precinct, he saw them together on Washington Avenue. His first impulse was to scream. "Go around the block!" he shouted to the driver, and then, "Go back about three blocks. When you come down again open up the siren and I'll tell you when to stop."

They were still on the street. She was supposed to be playing cards with her girl friends. As he passed, drawing everyone's attention, he didn't turn his head. But he was sure that she had seen him.

Blocks ahead, he had the driver pull to the curb. In a candy store, he called Richardson and asked for the rest of the night off. "I have a good excuse. I can't tell you what it is. I'm not sick."

"I'm sorry, Joe, I have to know. I'm not a book man, but it's a lot to ask."

"Something's come up. That's all I can tell you."

"Calm down. Whatever it is, calm down."

"I'm not going to do anything. I'm just going home to wait."

"I see." Leland had told him earlier what his wife's "plans" were. "Listen, Joe, don't do anything you'll regret."

"It's no problem." He didn't care. "I've been through it before."

"Okay. I'll see you tomorrow. If you want anything, call me."

At home, he called his mother to tell her to keep Steffie overnight. When Karen arrived to get her, she was to get the message, and that was all.

Her key went into the lock at twelve-thirty. He was sitting in the living room. "What is it, honey? What happened?"

"Don't con me. I saw you tonight."

"I saw you, too," she said sullenly. She took off her coat.

274

"I went around the block a second time."

"I figured you did. So?"

"So, is this the same guy? How long have you been seeing him?"

"I won't play that game. It's none of your business." She started into the bedroom, trying to look unperturbed. There was no color in her face. He grabbed her arm.

"Now listen to me, you miserable bitch. If you want a divorce, say so. You can have anything you want. You're no good to anybody this way. You have to decide one way or the other."

She tried to wrench free. "I'll think it over."

He wanted to knock her down. It did not seem possible that someone he could subdue so easily by force could generate such viciousness. As he moved to hit her with the back of his hand she seemed to step into it, exulting in having drawn it out of him. Her head snapped to one side and, when she turned to him again, she was bleeding from the lip.

"Happy now?" she asked.

"Are you?"

"Yes. You see, things have changed."

"You made love to me this morning."

"I don't see what that has to do with it."

"Who is he?"

"The same. You guessed it. I've been seeing him for a month."

"And things have changed," he said.

"That's right." She was trying to make him hit her again. Her heart wasn't in it, and neither was his.

He said, "Sleep in Steffie's bed tonight. Tomorrow, too. I don't want you near me. I just don't want you near me."

"You're a nasty bastard. That's what Jerry said tonight, and he's right."

"Oh, he knew it was me."

"He recognized you from the newspapers. Does that inflate your ego? I would think so."

"Get away from me, Karen," he said, and walked away himself. He sat down in the kitchen, and when he came out again, she had gone to bed—in Steffie's bed. He was not tired—it was the middle of his working day—but he opened the folding couch and lay down upon it. She awakened him. The light came through the door from the other room.

"Joe? Take off your clothes. You'll mess them up."

He had a headache. "Okay."

She gave him his pajamas and he got under the covers.

"I'm sorry, Joe. I am sorry."

"Stop it, Karen."

"I want you to know it."

The next morning she did not want to go to his parents' for Steffie. His mother wanted to know what had happened, and he told her that he had no explanation. She pressed him for one, but there was no plausible lie to fit, so he said nothing. There was a certain amount that she could guess, but the way he felt, he didn't care.

That evening Richardson said that he could take a leave of absence if he wanted. Leland thanked him and said that he would think it over. It was pointless. In a year or two there would be the same thing all over again.

The next afternoon, Steffie went to the movies with a friend.

"Listen," Karen said. "She wants to know what's going on."

"Tell her whatever you want. I trust your judgment."

"Joe, I don't want to start up again."

"I don't care what you want. As long as you have anything to do with him, you're on your own. I didn't tell my mother anything, but I'm sure that you won't be able to use her again, at least until I say so. You can go out on my nights off, but the kid will see you and you'll have to explain somehow. You can see him when she's in school, of course, but it's not so good in the daytime—"

She walked out of the room.

She told Steffie that she could no longer sleep on the folding couch. It was a flimsy story, but she could think of nothing better. The next week Jerry Palmer telephoned him at the station. He believed the lies Karen was telling. He wanted to know why Leland was willing to wreck her life, his own, and probably Steffie's for something that could not work. Leland hung up on him.

There was nothing between Karen and him now. He did not want to talk to her. She tried going out on the nights he was home, but then abruptly quit. Once she said she was going to the movies alone. When she returned she threw an empty popcorn box on the couch beside him.

Without telling her, he spent his afternoons shopping for an airplane. In the middle of December he found a prewar J-3, a two-seater, in excellent condition but not much good for anything but sport. He bought it and told her about it afterward. He asked if she wanted to see it and she said no.

She came in early one afternoon while he was having breakfast. It was the week before Christmas.

"Is the coffee hot?"

"Help yourself." By the stiffness in her face he knew that he had to wait until she worked around to what she wanted to tell him.

"Who knows about me at the Precinct?"

"Richardson."

"You told him?"

"The night I saw you. I wanted to come home."

"How did it feel?"

"When you look him in the eye you'll know."

"Thanks." She stirred her coffee and threw the spoon into the sink. "You win, after a fashion. We broke up today."

"There's nothing I can tell you."

"Don't gloat, you bastard. I'm going to stay in Steffie's room. I don't know what I'll be doing now. I want to be left to myself."

"Can you tell me what that means?"

"No. Let's not talk. I don't feel very well."

They left it at that. He did not hear from Palmer. With Christmas so close he hoped Karen would soften a little. In Steffie's presence she was civilized, but nothing more. He did not want to endure the preparation for Steffie's holiday in such misery. Still, he could not discuss it with Karen. If there was going to be anything left he could not give in to her, because it meant giving in to what she had done.

Christmas went by. After the New Year he got out of bed one

afternoon and found her in the kitchen, her face red from crying. "Leave me alone," she said.

"I'd like to have something to eat."

"Oh, go ahead." She went inside. Alone, he had to think that this did not have to mean anything good. Palmer could want to see her again. The further Leland carried the thought the more he realized how bitter he remained. If she thought that she had had enough of his bitterness, she had no idea of what was still choking inside him.

She came out again, her face washed. "Can I ask you a question?"

"Shoot."

"Where are you getting your sex?"

"None of your business."

"Are you getting it?"

He sat back. "You know what my appetites are."

"Joe, if you bring home a disease, that will be the end."

"Don't worry about it."

"You know your way around those whores. You could be doing anything."

"I told you not to worry about it."

"Would you be willing to have sex with me again?"

"For its own sake? On those terms?"

"That's the way it would have to be. I wouldn't hold back."

He regarded her. "You don't have any more trouble?"

"Once in a while. I'm all right if I don't start worrying about it. Then I lock up."

"I think I can understand that. Okay. Go inside."

"Joe, I don't mean now."

"I don't either. I don't want to talk anymore."

"Do you hate me?"

"Inside, Karen."

He had had to chase her. They had accomplished something and then it had seemed as if she had wanted to kill it. Even striking the bargain, promising not to hold back, she had tried to make it too clear. Where they were now, a sex agreement was a step forward.

Strangely, it could make them more humane. He had been willing to take it for what it could lead to, but she had asked if he hated her. In the autumn she had courted disaster; now she wanted more security than it was possible to have.

They made love the next morning. She kissed him awake, warm with powder and perfume. She loved him, she said. He couldn't respond. Afterward, she wanted to know if he was all right. He said yes. He was certain that she had not pretended. She stayed close to him, affectionate but not happy, and quiet. He knew what was to come and was afraid because he could not deny her for long. She was sick with herself, but without the terror that had followed the previous times. He knew he was seeing the worst part, but he could not control his reaction to it. It was not what she really was, what she had been when he had met her. Thus he felt part of the blame being thrust upon himself, and he struggled to deny it. Yet he could not accept the idea that all this had been in her when they had met. If he had known, he would have married her anyway—he had to accept that fact. There was nothing he had done to help her because he had not known how she could be helped; even now it all came from her and, mostly by choice, he took it. There were words for him, and the way he was letting it go once more, he had no right to protest.

A week later she asked him if he wanted to know the real purpose behind the shopping trips. It was like a kick in the stomach. She could not look into his eyes while she said it. She had been trying to meet men. A man. She had conceived of seeing Palmer again simply because it would be less complicated. She had made a compromise with what she had really wanted.

"I wanted the excitement. I was testing myself—I wanted to see what I was capable of doing. Don't ask me why. I want you to know what I did, Joe. I'd just go downtown and walk and look at people—men. I'd think about going someplace for a drink. I never talked to anybody, just looked. And thought. Oh, yes. Thought. I don't have any idea why I did it.

"The last time I said I was trying to hurt the only family I ever had. This time I was able to convince myself that I could get away with it without hurting you and Steffie. I hurt you anyway. It didn't matter whether the sex with him was satisfactory; the other thrill was there. It is a thrill, a deep, dirty thrill, and that's what I did it for. I'm sorry now—involuntarily sorry, if you can understand that. It's not like after the automobile accident, when I could close my eyes and see us heading toward that pole again. I've tried to keep my mind clear, just so I could be of some use to somebody—myself. But it's as if I were getting physically sick. I feel it coming up inside me, a sick feeling."

She was not saying that she would not do it again, and because she wasn't he had to believe what she was saying. He wanted her to tell him when and if she felt it coming again, but even as helpless as he was, he could see that that was futile for them both as well as humiliating for her. The way she described it, in the beginning she would be safer and kinder in lying to him. As long as he was unwilling to explore his misgivings over the final meaning to or even the use of what they were going through, he had to take his chances.

Twice before the end of the month she called him at work to ask him to come home. The second time, he was out of the building and not expected for an hour, and she broke down. It frightened the man with whom she was speaking and Richardson heard the commotion. He cut in on his extension and she hung up. There was no controlling it now. In a week Captain Leland was asking Richardson if he knew anything about his son's wife. Richardson played dumb. Some of the men Leland saw infrequently quit asking about his family. Leland had only Richardson's word about what they knew. The reporter who asked about his private life during the Leikman case had gotten the story easily. By that third week in March she was doing better and most of his doubts were put aside. Her resistance to the jolts of everyday life was lower; she was quicker to say what displeased her. He could not tell if things were going to ease. She was trying. She was suffering with the effort she was making, even if it was largely misplaced. She was trying to be a good wife, which took no trying from her. He was waiting to hear her express some interest, even dreamy, of going to work again. She was at her best when she was working, and he was surprised that she did not know it herself.

She returned to their bed. She had to lie again to Steffie, saying that there must have been something the matter with her back, and the girl seemed to believe it. Steffie was closer to her than him and really, now especially, he was glad. If Karen ever thought of Steffie learning of Palmer, she was not intimidated, and her husband had to wonder if it were not the girl's confidence that kept Karen going. His own relationship with her was as taut as a wire.

In the late spring the School Board informed her that a job was open for the next year, and she ignored the letter. A month later, without previously speaking with him, she went looking for work downtown. He decided to see what was going to happen. She had trouble, but she did not tell him much about it. The first week in June, she started work as an assistant buyer in a department store. He was sick over it. It was a terrible job for her. It was a waste of her abilities.

It did not make her happy. It drained her emotionally; she resisted him more than before. The salary was ten dollars above what she would have made as a teacher but far below his salary as a detective lieutenant. There was no pooling of money as there had been the previous year; he paid the running expenses as he had been doing and she put most of her money into improvements in the apartment or clothing for Stephanie or herself. One evening he saw her making a list of the things she had bought. He had to keep still. Another night, he started to make love to her and she put him off.

The next night, when he kissed her, she would not open her mouth for him.

"What's the matter tonight?"

"I don't feel like it, that's all."

"Are you having trouble again?"

"No. No."

"Then what is it?"

"I'm not in the mood. I just don't feel like putting in the effort." She reached for her cigarettes. "We're beyond the honeymoon stage, anyway."

"We'll both decide that," he said.

"Are you going to push me around again?"

"When have I pushed you around?"

"Oh, come on, Joe, I don't want to fight. I don't even want to talk. I want to be left alone. I'm doing all right."

"The hell you are."

"What does that mean?"

As clearly and calmly as he could, he tried to indicate his objections to her attitude toward him and the way she was handling herself with her money. The two of them were living lives that were proximate and parallel, but nothing more. In the darkness he could feel her growing angry.

"Do you want me to quit?" she asked at last.

He did, but he could not bring himself to say it.

"All right," she said. "I know what you want. I'm going to stay there. You're jealous of the things I've been able to do for us, and I've been waiting for you to pull this. So far as saying no to you is concerned, I'm expressing my true feelings. It's just not worth it to me as often as we've been doing it."

"What do you think is fair?"

"Once a week."

"You're kidding."

"No. I'm not."

He couldn't control himself. "I was better off when you were cheating on me."

She said coldly, "I won't forget that."

"Do you want a divorce? Is that it?"

"No. I didn't say that."

He got up from the bed, thinking that maybe he wanted one. There was nothing he could do for her like this. More and more, there was nothing he wanted to do for her at all. He had to be honest. He had to think it all over again.

"Where are you going?"

"To the kitchen," he said. "Now *I* want to be left alone."

CHAPTER FOURTEEN

∎∎∎∎∎∎∎∎∎∎∎∎∎∎∎∎∎∎∎∎∎∎∎∎∎∎∎∎∎

THE OFFER FROM MANITOU MADE HIS DECISION FOR HIM. HE TOOK IT without telling her and waited, hoping that things would change. They did not. At the end of the summer he told her that he was resigning from the Police Department and taking a job in private business in another city. He wasn't taking her. He didn't want her.

"What are we supposed to do?"

"Karen, I don't care. You have your job. I'll send you what I can."

"'I could sue you. I could get a judgment against you."

"That's your decision. I don't figure that there's anything between us anymore."

"I had the right to be told that you were doing this!"

"You think so? I wanted you to come around by yourself, not under pressure. We both know you could have done that—for a while. What's the use of threats? They're not what I want from a marriage, what I think I should get."

"I stopped. I've tried to be honest since I stopped."

"That's not all, Karen. What did you go to college for? You're not bettering yourself, you're just being important. These things you've bought—it's as if you wanted them around as proof that you are part of the world. You know you're not really putting in the effort. You're like a kid feeling sorry for yourself. You're trying to show the world—or me. It's just stupid."

"What about Stephanie?"

He had known while he had been speaking that he had not been saying the thing exactly, but that she wanted to change the subject was her admission that he had come close. He said, "I'm not out to destroy you. You're a fit mother, and she does belong with you. I'd like to see her, but under the circumstances, that's up to you."

"You bet it is."

"Karen, that's just why I'm leaving. Your attitude right now is just an extension of what it was yesterday. You don't know how you feel about me anymore. Inevitably, somehow, you get down to hurting me. You wanted to do something good when I met you. What happened to that? You've got yourself on a merry-go-round, doing the same things again and again. You're back where you started from. Instead of that hotel, where the woman hurt you when you became pregnant, it's a department store. Instead of being all bound up inside, you're just not making love at all. You've done good things —Steffie, the war work, getting your Master's, teaching—but you've also had two affairs with the same emotional cripple, and you'd just as soon have a third—"

"I probably will, when you're gone."

"Don't you see?" he pleaded. "You took a grisly satisfaction in saying that. I don't know what's made you like this. The world doesn't owe you anything. It did once, but you're even with everybody now. You're bitter about something—me, maybe it's marriage, or even life itself. It's as if you want something that isn't here. You're full of hate, for me, your boyfriend, most of all for yourself. As long as you stay this way, you're going to keep doing the same things again and again. None of them is going to get you the prize, whatever it is you want. Think, Karen. You've carried some of these things as far as you could, and they've given you no satisfaction. You're on a merry-go-round, don't you see? It doesn't go anywhere, and least of all to where you want."

"You can leave whenever you want."

"I haven't changed my mind."

He flew down to see Steffie every other Sunday, and on most visits he took her places while Karen remained at home. He had nothing to say to Karen, and if he could have arranged it, he would

284

not have seen her at all. She understood that she could have a divorce whenever she wanted, but she made no move. She was seeing Palmer again, as she had promised. If anything, it was only what it had been before; some lie or other was holding Palmer off, but Leland tried to keep his thoughts away from it. He felt relieved, unhappy, lonely, and not curiously, ashamed. His progress in Manitou was good and he was invited to spend the holidays with two families. He was able to decline and go to Port Smith. Karen wanted them all together for Christmas. The day was a success for Steffie, as much as success was possible. Karen was tense, but she tried to be pleasant. He followed her lead. On New Year's Eve, in Manitou at a party given by one of the men under him, he drank himself unconscious.

Another man, thinking he was divorced, arranged a date with his sister, a pretty brunette twenty-nine years old. Leland straightened out the misunderstanding quickly and at the end of the evening, knowing just that he and his wife had been unable to make it work since the end of the war, she agreed to see him again. By April, he was taking too much of her time for her to know less than the truth, and he told her. She did not know how she felt about him, but she thought she had a right to know if he was determined not to divorce his wife. He said no, but inside, he was not certain. He was still attached to Karen and a part of him wanted to stay accessible to her. It was an exercise in vanity, for when they had been living together, she had not thought of him. She was miserable, and he kept thinking of it too often for it to be good for him. He liked this girl, but he was so used to Karen's ways, her faults not excepted, that what was unique about the one only brought the other clearer to his mind. Anne's virtues and accomplishments had no value to him, for while he was attracted and sometimes intrigued, because he was distracted, he was never in love. He knew it and, he thought, so did she.

Early in September Karen moved to Manitou. In the summer she had told him that the affair with Palmer was done and she was going to apply for a teaching position in Manitou. She did not say what had happened or what she expected of him now that he was seeing someone else. He said that he did not want trouble. It was cruel, but she did not seem to feel it. She said that she would not be in his way.

Anne was suspicious. He told her that he did not intend to see Karen more often or let her interfere with his life. She was not assured, although she tried to hide it. One evening in November they ran into Karen on Clark Street. After the introductions she excused herself quickly. He told Anne that she had been nervous, even afraid. Anne said that he would hear from her, and not about his regular visit.

She was right. Karen called him the next morning.

"I'm sorry it happened, Joe. I didn't want to meet her. It was an accident."

"Take it easy, kid. It doesn't mean as much as you want to think it does."

"She knows about me, doesn't she? Do you want to marry her?"

"I can't discuss that with you."

"I deserve whatever I get, I know. Listen, I'm sorry about what I did to you. I'm trying to put myself together again. I came here because I wanted to get away from that town. You had a right to see Steffie. There's nothing more to it."

"There shouldn't be. I hope you know that."

"Some day I'll tell you what happened to me," she said.

"I don't want to hear it—"

She knew that she had gone too far. Perhaps it had been a slip, but it did not matter. He had reacted as if she had tried the cheapest trick, and she could see it, too. She hung up.

Later, what she might have intended was lost, for he could not help staying angry with her for having gotten to his feelings, and he distrusted and even disliked her more. He had the feeling that she would know that she had made him want to be closer to Anne, but he had to wonder if she was going to see that Anne's insight into her did not enhance Anne in his eyes. Doing what Anne had predicted made Karen the more pitiable, and he was too distorted and confused by pity, apprehension, and lack of love to be of much use to someone who had the right to make strong demands upon him. He did not like

286

it, yet he could not strip himself of his confusion to do something about it.

The following spring, Anne broke off with him. He had let it run out of his hands and she could not help being bitter. If his shame made him think that he really wanted her, it was too late. She was too smart for that. He found himself trying to forget that his feeling for her had not been strong enough to make him take the steps to marry her. The self-pity made him cautious. He kept away from Karen. He thought that if he found her willing to start again, he would blame her for what had been his own fault. He wanted to blame someone besides himself, and the way he felt, he could resurrect old issues no matter how much he did not want to. Far down, he did not want to do it to her.

It came up months later on a Sunday evening after she had started her second year in the Manitou schools. She had guessed what had happened to Anne and she was sorry. She thought that she probably had had a good deal to do with the breakup.

Steffie was in bed. Karen had asked him to stay for coffee, but, he hoped now, not to hear her comments on the curious bonds between people. On second thought, he wondered if she was going to come right out and flatter herself.

She said, "Next spring I'll be able to apply for an assistant principal's job. I'm going to. My record is perfect. I've been getting on committees and making myself known."

"Then you intend to stay," he said.

"I have a good chance here."

"What's on your mind, Karen? I wouldn't like to see you building toward something impossible."

"I'm not." She could have hurt him. The egotism of his remark would have been hard for most people to resist. She asked, "Do you think you're ready to hear what happened to me?"

"Like what?"

"You'll find out. I thought today about doing this. If I start to tell you things and you stop me, I may never be able to talk about them with anyone. I'm not kidding. I want you to promise me that you won't stop me."

"All right."

"I'd *like* you to promise me. Please."

"All right, Karen, I promise you."

"I called him after you left, as you said I would. I told him that you and I had fought since I had last seen him and that your going away was the compromise we had reached. The story was confused and his attitude was about the same as yours is now, except that he went through the motions of believing. He wanted things to work. As soon as I had him I was sorry. I was still filled with the anger that I had tried to take out on you. I didn't want to make love with him, but I had to, if I wanted him to keep coming around as long as it was convenient to me."

"Is this the truth?"

"Yes. I swear it is."

"Why didn't you say anything to me?"

"I couldn't. I couldn't talk to anybody. There was nothing you could have done, anyway. You couldn't have helped. I was too sick to be helped."

"Did you know it?"

"I had some idea, but I ignored it. I wanted to. I'm still sick in many, many ways."

She stopped. He had not been looking at her at that moment, and slowly he raised his eyes. She was wearing dark slacks and a little short-sleeved blouse. Her hands were clasped between her knees, her knuckles white. She was staring at him, just staring. For a moment it was actually insane.

"What is it, Karen?"

She faltered. "I loved you, do you know that?"

"I think so. It was a long time ago."

"When, do you think?"

"Karen, I don't want to play a game—"

"It's no game, Joe. Please. Let me do it this way. It's hard for me. When did I love you?"

He shook his head. "Before the war. Afterwards, for a while. I can't be sure of what you felt. I only know what I felt."

She said, "You stopped loving me the night you saw me on

Washington Avenue. That was the start for you. You could have been brought back, if you had been given the right treatment. It would have been difficult, but it could have been done. Not by me, not by the person I was. By the time I got home that night, I didn't want to. After your mother told me that she was keeping Steffie for the night, I thought you would kill me. I twisted everything you had done in the war and before. I expected you to punch me as soon as you saw me."

"I wanted to."

"But you didn't. I had to goad you into hitting me. Anyone would have wanted to hit me. I knew the kind of man you were, that you wouldn't unless I dared you, but in spite of that, as I went home and thought about you having seen me, I couldn't stop imagining you hitting me. When I came up here to Manitou I could feel it inside me as I wondered how you would react to me being so close. What you would do to me. I honestly didn't want you back. I needed a clean start and this was the place, considering your rights with Steffie. I didn't want you back because the same things would have started all over again. I know that far, far better than you. I just wanted to be myself and do the few things I was certain I could do well, yet I had fantasies—still have them—of you punching me and knocking me down. I've never been really punched, I don't even know what it feels like, but I keep thinking about it."

"Why?"

"When I know you won't do it? That's very wise of you."

It wasn't wise. He had only asked a cop's question. Now he was sure that he didn't know what she was talking about. She was sitting there in the same way, waiting. It seemed as if she were studying him, but he knew better. He wanted to believe that she was remembering the things they had done, that he was still her husband, but what it came down to, he knew, was that she was waiting for herself, for some reservoir of strength inside her to fill again. She needed it to talk—she had said that she had planned this.

She looked away. "I told you once that I was trying to destroy the only family I've ever known. That was right. If our family had been a good job, or a lot of money, somehow I would have thrown it away. Believe me, I was trying to hurt myself. I don't know why. I think about you hurting me because I want you to do the job for me. By the time I get to that, there are specific reasons why you should hurt me, things that I've done. I've made the reasons for you.

"I cheated on him, too. I did the things I told you about. I actually did them. Do you know what I mean?"

He sat back. It was like something materializing out of a fog. It was there for him to see, but he couldn't make the proper connections to identify it. He made them, remembered, and it was as if the room moved. It made him physically dizzy. She did not notice at first, then she did and closed her eyes. He heard the breath run out of him in a rush. He didn't know what it was supposed to signify—outrage, indignation. It hurt her and he was sorry. He didn't understand where it had come from, perhaps the breaking of the last unhappy illusion. He felt helpless, as if desperately ill. His skin prickled, his stomach contracted and doubled up.

"I'm sorry," she said.

"I don't know what to say, Karen." His voice had broken; what he had said had been hardly louder than a whisper.

"Just listen to me, that's all. I won't say anything if you decide you've had enough."

He wasn't sure that she wasn't trying to do something to herself. He didn't think he could make that clear; she would think that he was questioning her motives for his own sake. He saw that there was nothing for him to risk and she had already surrendered every advantage over him. He shook his head, then he said, "You keep going."

"With you I tried to pick up men. With him I succeeded. You would think that after the first time I would have turned myself in at a hospital. I didn't, I only thought of it. It happened four times. I tried to tell you of the thrill in it, the sick, delicious thrill. He never found out, fortunately for him. I told him I was leaving Port Smith for a fresh start but I didn't tell him why I needed it. I didn't owe him anything. He took his chances."

"So did I."

"No, no. Listen, Joe, there are a few things you don't have straight—lies I told you. I told you lies about what happened after

Steffie was born, that I pretended. That's true, as far as it went. Most of the time I did pretend, but not always, as I wanted you to believe. There were times when I wasn't faking, usually if you caught me when we were just waking up. I had orgasms then and other times. I had no trouble all during Christmas, 1942. You probably don't even remember. And the night you came home from England the first time. In the railroad station, when I saw you, before we even got near each other, it happened a little."

"Then you didn't have trouble with Palmer, as you said."

"No."

"Why did you lie?"

"I wanted you to help me, but I thought that I didn't want to hurt you with the truth. That really wasn't it. I couldn't bear having anybody know the truth—even me."

"What about now?"

"I'm telling you the truth as well as I know it. You can't help me, Joe. I can only help myself. There's no reason to lie."

"Then why tell me at all?"

"You're really the only one I can talk to. I want to talk. I know it will be good for me."

"You could have had Palmer," he said.

"No. I can't explain why—it has to do with me."

"Don't con me, Karen."

"You're my husband. You trusted me—you still do, with Steffie. You let me know things about yourself—your fears, what you thought. I didn't want that from him. I've always come back to telling you the truth. I believe that. I'm not trying to con you."

"Did you ever have trouble with him?"

She knew what he meant. "Yes. And one other time, too. I'm not sure it has very much to do with sex—why I have trouble, or even what I've done."

She became silent. His body felt drained, as if he had endured a bad electric shock. He couldn't think—he didn't know what to think about. He was on the edge: he could go to a lawyer and see how he could get Steffie away from her. There wasn't a mark on Steffie but he was on the edge of closing his eyes to that and doing what he wanted for himself.

"Nobody but me knew about any of this," she said. "I couldn't have been trying to hurt you or Steffie or even him. It was all me, for me, directed at me. I still won't admit that I've failed with myself. I came here for one last chance with myself. It almost happened again after I bumped into you with Anne. I was in that mood for weeks—angry, sulking. Only I know how close I came to losing my job. Those men in Port Smith were married. You know what would happen to a teacher caught in a hotel."

"All right, Karen."

"You loved her, didn't you?"

"Why do you want to know?"

"Just tell me," she said.

"I could have made a good thing with her." He thought of something. "Did you *pick* married men?"

"Yes. I was afraid of the others. I thought married men would understand, and I was right. I'm sorry. Joe, it's the truth. They were on the prowl—I don't mean that as an excuse. They were looking for the same thing. It worked, too, with Jerry Palmer, and with three of the four others."

He looked at her.

"There's something you have to understand. I'm trying to face up to myself. This has to be part of it. I can't talk as if I'm still living in a dream. I wanted something and that fourth man wouldn't give it to me because he had an attack of conscience. I had to use this language to keep reminding myself that this was the way I wanted to see it. Maybe this is what I am, all I am, as a human being.

"With Jerry Palmer the first time I let myself believe that I needed sex and he took advantage of your absence. It wasn't like that. I had already let you down long before Jerry Palmer appeared. I was a rotten wife and a lousy human being. I had my good moments, but nothing had turned out the way I wanted. I was jealous of you— oh, of course I was. I didn't like being stuck at home. I didn't like being pregnant. And I'm sure that none of this is a surprise to you.

"Jerry used to take me home from school—that's how it started."

"Was this before or after my leave?"

"After. I swear, honey. Then when I realized how far I was actually willing to go, I thought about where you were and what you could learn. I made myself believe that I was safe. But even then I made him wait."

"I don't want to hear any more, Karen."

She touched his hand, then withdrew. "Can I ask you something? When you were with Anne, did you hold anything back? Did you show her who you were, the way you did with me?"

"Why do you want to know?"

"Maybe I want you to tell me that I'm not anybody you remember."

"Stop it. For God's sake—no, I didn't hold back, but yes, I remember you."

"Was she better than me?"

"You're smarter than that. In any case, *I* was the one who couldn't satisfy *you.*"

"That was *my* fault!"

"Do you want me to leave?"

"Do you want to?"

"You wanted to talk. I'll listen. I'm going into the other room. When you're calm, you come out."

He sat down on the couch. The door to Steffie's room was closed. He still didn't understand why this had happened. Now, from the kitchen, Karen called him. He got up and went to the door. She was standing at the sink, her back to him.

"Are you all right?"

"Yes. Joe, please listen. It's the only thing I'm asking."

It felt like a merry-go-round again. They were saying everything a second, a third time. "I'm trying, Karen. Why did you ask me those things?"

"I don't know. That's the point. There are things I want to say and I can't say them."

"Like what?"

293

"Like what I did. Like asking what you did. I don't know why. I want to know if I killed everything between us."

"You'd have to kill Steffie. Are you willing to do that?"

"Of course not." She glanced at him. "I don't believe I'm insane. Why haven't you divorced me?"

He took a breath. "I'm not sure myself."

"Do you know what you're married to?"

He wasn't going to answer that.

"That's exactly what I am, you know." She turned, slowly. She looked so pale and sickly in the fluorescent light that it frightened him. "Once I started with Jerry I decided to do things that would make him fall in love with me. You have to do that. I consciously tried. I pretended and acted and planned things. There was a part of me always thinking of a new way to go further. I couldn't really forget myself, so that was the way I got around it. I mean this, Joe. It was the same with the others. All of them wanted to see me again."

"A job well done? Any woman could do it."

"I know that. Don't you think I know it? That's what it's all about. I knew these things in advance and I went ahead and courted them anyway.

"On second thought, you're wrong. Any woman couldn't have done it. The night I went back to Palmer I was so frightened I could feel my legs buckling under me. It was the same with the other men those afternoons in the hotels. Most women couldn't have gone against themselves that way. All the selecting I did was in picking men who were physically attractive. That's all. One time I didn't want to do it at all and I didn't let that stop me. It was a question of getting it out of my system."

"Why didn't you go to a hospital? Why didn't you call me? You could have gone to a psychiatrist."

"I didn't want to admit that I'd failed—in spite of all the evidence. It's really comic. That was important to me. Do you remember? I was going to have success. There were always men around. You saw that the night you met me. I was a flirt—I didn't even realize it until you were in the service. Jerry Palmer couldn't keep away from me and I tormented him. I would let him kiss me but when he put his hand on me I would push it away—but *very* slowly. I never did it with you or any of the others when I was further along. He begged for that kind of treatment and I was the person to give it to him. *Just* the person. He thought that that was what love was all about."

"Are you excusing yourself?"

"No—no! I told you how I was after I decided to go with him. My legs were buckling then, too, but I made no attempt to stop—other than pretending for quite another purpose. I did want to stop, I didn't like it, I didn't like him, but I went ahead in spite of it. What it was doing to me was too important. The sick thrill of it was too important. The next day I felt ashamed when I thought of it, but when I didn't think, I felt relieved. In some ways I was glad I did it—every time. Even after the afternoon with the man who didn't want to play my game. I'd wanted to lose myself in it. I always thought hard about what I was doing, closing my mind to the things I didn't like for the sake of the things I did."

He sat down at the table again. He couldn't look at her.

"That's only the half of it, Joe. I couldn't *help* thinking and feeling ashamed. It made me afraid to go out of the house. I couldn't help feeling that people could see I was dirty. I'd call in sick at the job. That last summer, I did it too often. They fired me."

"You didn't tell me that."

She bent down beside him, putting her hands on the edge of the table to brace herself. "How could I? It was proof of what I was. It reminded me of how much I should feel dirty and ashamed. That's how destructive it is—the whole thing. I'm still expecting you to hit me—and if I succeeded in making you do it, I'd be indulging myself."

"That's a way of putting it."

"I *would*. Life would be simpler if I could be punished once, like a child. I want it even though I know it won't work.

"I still want the things I wanted when I was going to college. I want to have a success and be somebody." She sat down on the floor and looked up at him. "Is that insane? I still want to be useful."

"No."

"I know now that I never fully *gave* myself to that idea. There was always a part of me that held back. At first I didn't know why. I found out. It was something I couldn't control. It held back and even acted up on the day we got married. I wanted to marry you more than I've ever wanted to do anything, and I've never, ever regretted it—although you have—but it was there that day, something repugnant and calculating. Do you know what it is to really *hate* yourself? To know that a part of you is willing to throw away everything of value and behave in an absolutely uncontrolled way? I did everything with those men, men I never saw before. That's why I want to hear that you didn't hold back with Anne. I don't want to know that you saved anything that belonged to us."

"That's the same as being punched, isn't it?"

She looked up. "Yes." He waited for more. She searched his eyes. She asked, "Did you?"

"You really *can't* control yourself, can you?"

She shook her head. Her face was blotching; he thought that she was going to be sick. "I loved her, Karen. There are times when I wish she had become pregnant. I wouldn't have hesitated, then."

"I'm sorry."

"That wasn't what you wanted to hear. Now try to put the whole thing out of your mind. Forget it. Don't ask again."

She stayed quiet. Then, "When we first met I was full of dreams about what my adult life was going to be like. They weren't clear, but I was going to be in the world, valuable, not necessarily important, but valuable. People were going to be pleased that I was doing my job, whatever it was, and they were going to be grateful. That was what growing up meant to me. It didn't change because I met you. You were filled with the same dreams—but they were better founded. You didn't *plan* on things happening to you. When they did, you were sensible enough to react to them. You did what you had to."

"I remember. I remember how you carried the ball after the night Krolevich was killed. I needed it. But I never had any idea of what you needed."

"Don't start that, Joe. I didn't know myself. I do know myself now, better than I did then. I could disgust you with the things I think."

"Like what? Go ahead and say them."

296

"Like I've taken to wondering whether you were ever faithful to me."

"I was."

"But things happened in Europe," she said.

"We've discussed that."

"Not really—"

"You know enough. That's the way I want to keep it."

She started to get to her feet. "I only wanted to give you an idea. I wonder about you because it makes what I did more tolerable." She cleared the table and rinsed out the cups and saucers. "I could insult you now. Shall I add insult to injury?" He waited. With her back to him, she said, "I could do it with you now."

"I know—but I'm not going to let you."

"That's right. That's what I need more. Talking about it changes it, anyway. See? I know all the tricks. I don't really want to start up with you. Tonight made me want to do it. I'd start giving you the rights of a husband. I'd want to, but I know I'm not ready. It's too soon for you, too. What if Anne called you? You'd resent me if you were all tangled up and wanted to see her. Live your life and enjoy yourself.

"I don't even want to *think*," she said. "It's one day at a time for me. I won't go to bed with you until I can really let go. I don't want to *plan* ways to go further. I don't want to worry about cheating on you. We *have* had really good moments. I'm not looking for it to happen all the time—oh, no. I know what to expect from an adult relationship.

"The hell of it is that I always did know. I've never been able to do anything about it until now—and maybe not even now. I have to be honest, with you and myself." She looked over her shoulder. "Listen, if Anne does call you, you make up your own mind. I won't kid you about the way I feel. I'm not capable of loving a man. If you decide to marry her, you won't be hurting me."

"All right."

"I mean it," she said.

"I think you do."

"I'm sorry to have to put you through this."

"No. It took courage to tell me." He hesitated. "I want you to call me now if you want to talk to someone."

"I can't call you about anything else, though."

"I know that, too. Karen, you'll never be able to bullshit me again. That's what you succeeded in doing tonight. I remember the signs. I'll know if you go off again. You can't go back. You have to be honest."

"You'd divorce me and take Steffie," she said.

"I think I'd have to."

She nodded, then looked up. "I've been good all the time I've been in Manitou."

"I thought that."

"I'm making that offer again. I'll just take care of you if you want that."

"That's no good for you."

"I'll be able to think about it later. I will, anyway—you know?" Now she sat down. "I guess that's everything. Have I left anything out? Is there anything that you don't know about me?" She turned away. "Do you want to know how often I put myself to sleep that way at nights?"

"I didn't ask. It's your business. Anybody living alone has that kind of tension. You don't have to be ashamed of it."

Her body shook. She was crying. "You'd better go. This isn't going to do us any good."

"Are you all right?"

"Yes. I'll call you when you get home, if you'd like. Steffie's clothes aren't ready for school tomorrow. If you want to talk—just talk—from now on, call me."

"I was waiting for you to say that."

"Oh, yes, I want you to call." She turned to him. "*I* need it. Before we were married and we had that little apartment we both paid the rent on, I used to wait for you. *That* was the happiest time of my life. We did a lot of talking then." She stopped, almost hopeful. "I want to talk to you. I've needed what happened here tonight. All my life I've really wanted it much, much more than the other thing."

"What other thing?"

"What I was looking for. Excitement." The word was not right. She closed her eyes and shook her head from side to side. Her lip trembled until she bit down on it. "Adventure. I was looking for that. My dreams," she said softly. Tears spilled down her cheeks. "I wanted romance."

He leaned over and kissed her lightly on the mouth.

PART TWO

CHAPTER FIFTEEN

∎ ∎

THE PALL OVER PORT SMITH, A PERMANENT INVERTED BOWL OF soot, dirt, and dust, rose stiffly and precariously in the red air like smoke over a smoldering fire. An airliner dropping from the holding pattern southwest of the International Airport slipped down deeper into the murk, nearly vanishing, its running lights trailing clues. Below was the bay and beyond was the spit of land Port Smith called the Point, and beyond that was the ocean, an oily expanse without surface or definable end. Nearer, the lights of the city glittered and swam in the smoke and shadow, and directly underneath, the roads of Clausen County slashed the hardening gloom in every direction. Cautious in the presence of the heavier traffic in the air, Leland raised Phillips Airport on the radio, identified himself, and received permission to land.

On the downwind leg he looked among the Quonset huts and service shacks for Norma, but could not see her. He made the final turn. On the highway at the far end of the strip, six lanes of cars, all alit, slid quickly to the left and right. Leland could pick out the letters on the neon signs along the road as the buildings rose above the black horizon. The strip came up faster; the tarmac appeared, racing, making the beams from the lights in the nose of the plane converge and sharpen. Now a gentle easing back and the wheels touched softly, chirped, and took hold on the ground. Like a car, the plane rolled along the strip. He was down; as if he had put on another topcoat and a pair of hip boots, he could feel the pressure of the bottom of a sea.

She was in the office. As he crossed to the counter he directed her to keep her seat on the orange plastic couch. He wanted to order gasoline and service. She came over anyway while he signed the sheet.

"Why didn't you wait for me in Manitou?" He watched the mechanic check the list. She didn't answer. The mechanic said all right and Leland picked up his suitcase and motioned Norma toward the outer door. She stayed quiet until they were outside. Her coat was unbuttoned and she held it closed with her hands in the slash pockets. Today's smock suit was light blue and she had a little jeweled pin on the collar. She brought out a set of car keys. The wind was stronger at ground level and it blew her black hair back from her forehead and made her have to squint to see. "I had an attack of nerves. I wanted to get out of that hotel room. Until your telegram came, I hadn't thought of there being more than one airport in Port Smith. I know that I should have called your office, but I wasn't thinking. I just wanted to go."

"All right, no harm was done, but you have to get it into your mind who we're working for. It's not only a matter of making our job easier. You'll know where you stand. Florence would have told you that I was working on your case. You would have felt better and there would have been none of this running around and missed connections."

She nodded, then shook her head. "I'm not sure."

He was coming to her, not the other way around, and because of it he found himself trying to hold down an increasing desire to be rough with her. He said, almost involuntarily, "Let's forget it. It was one of those things."

She came up smiling. "How was the flight? Did you enjoy it as much as you expected?"

She was trying to be pleasant. "Yes. It was fine."

"I'm sorry I missed it. There's our car."

The color in the sky gave the blue finish of the Cadillac a purplish tinge. The painted metal was so deep with a wax and cornstarch shine that it looked brighter than the chrome plating on the wheels and bumpers. If the car had ever been in bad weather, no one could know. It was the way Colin MacIver had kept his car. Norma would not have tried to make it look better after his death. She was doing what he had done because it was what he had taught her to do. This was a way a man continued to live through his widow, the style he had established. It never worked the other way; widowers unraveled everything their wives had done.

Norma unlocked the door on the passenger's side and Leland put his suitcase on the floor behind the front seat as she went around the front of the car. She looked over the convertible top. "Do you want to drive?"

He wanted to try the car, but he said no. They got inside.

She said, "Some men are uncomfortable when a woman is driving. Do you have enough room for your knees? I had to move the seat back again to accommodate our new, straight-arm driving style—the baby's and mine. This is the way the racing drivers do it, to get leverage. Colin told me that."

"Is it the way he drove?"

"Oh, no. He sat up high and close, right hand on the wheel, left elbow on the windowsill. He drove this car with one hand and one foot. And he diddled the directional signal with his left index finger. That's what he called it, diddling." She turned the starter.

"Maybe he drove the other way when he picked up all those tickets," Leland said.

"Maybe," she said coolly. The car rolled almost silently to the exit of the parking lot. She had taken what he had said as an attack. Maybe it had been stupid—because he had said it, Leland didn't want to think that—but he had wanted to focus her attention on their business. Now he had to begin again. She turned the steering wheel hand-over-hand to position the car for the entry onto the highway. There was a wait for an opening in the traffic. "Where do you intend to stay?"

"One of the hotels downtown. They're all the same. I'll call you when I get settled."

"I was thinking that you could stay with me." She had been looking over her shoulder at the passing cars; now she turned to the front and floored the accelerator. The car reared back on its springs and, with a screech of rubber, roared into the break between cars. There was nothing silent about the motor now and Leland could feel the automatic transmission struggling under the sudden, immense strain. Then, almost as suddenly as it had begun, the acceleration eased and the transmission thumped into high, and the car cruised apparently peaceably in the traffic flow at a speed of fifty miles per hour. "There's plenty of extra room at my house," she said. "I'll only have to pay a hotel bill."

"I've invited my wife to come down for the weekend," he said. "That is, of course, if I'm still here myself. It wasn't going to be on your time, but—"

"Suppose we say that you'll be my guest until Friday or when you're done with the case, whichever comes first." Her voice lowered. "I won't pay an unnecessary bill."

He was curious about when she had decided to do this, but she was so tense that asking would only start an argument. "All right. Remember what I said about getting an honest count. When I think we have all we're going to get, I'll tell you. I won't hang around."

"Then you don't have much to tell me now," she said.

"I didn't say that." He moved on the seat and took out his cigarettes. She was driving smoothly, staying in the right-hand lane. He could not remember the traffic ever having been so heavy. She seemed to know what she was doing. This car weighed five thousand pounds, more than a light truck, and it did not intimidate her. He might have expected this compulsory arrangement of staying at her home. When he had learned that she had left Manitou he had not called Karen again to tell her—it had seemed childish, and Karen really had been more upset over the prospect of coming to Port Smith herself—but now he wished he had called. They would be talking tonight on the telephone and it did not promise to be easy. For them, talking long-distance was always bad. The line of cars slowed. Norma looked over her shoulder quickly—here it came again, that neck-wrenching acceleration—and she moved the car into the center lane.

He wanted to begin with the souvenir book. She stopped him. She knew that five kills made an ace and what he had done; how could he write in the note he had enclosed that he respected her husband's record of two planes destroyed and two probables? "You tried to make me think he did something special. I don't understand that."

"He did do something special. Scores don't mean much. The character of the war kept changing. It wasn't possible to make a high score in Europe in 1945. There was a lot of the luck of circumstance in what happened to me. The accounts say that your husband flew very well. There were men who ran away from the jets. He didn't."

She was silent.

He said, "The book is the best evidence available. It was gotten together when the events were fresh. We could go to Vineland for confirmation from Matthews, his wingman, but probably he would do what I did, go to the book. Unless we get something that contradicts what we have, we ought to leave it where it stands."

"I see."

He went on to the Manitou file, skimming over the way MacIver had bought his policies, the amounts, the kinds of insurance—all the things she had learned when she had made her claim. The changes of address verified what MacIver had told her about moving back and forth between Port Smith and Manitou. She had not known that he had made her the beneficiary of his insurance before their marriage.

"He did the same thing with his first wife," Leland said. "You can say that he wasn't afraid to commit himself."

"Or that he was seeing that I got what he gave to her," she said. "The first time you do a thing like that, it's an act of love. The second, it's a decision. Be honest. That's the way it really is."

"That may be the way it was with him—we can't judge—but just as easily he could have forgotten what he had done with his first wife. It's possible. The important thing for you to remember is that he married you after he had been burned once. What I learned this morning tells me that he loved you, loved you as he had never loved anybody."

"I don't want to hear that now."

He had to let it pass.

"I don't think I ever want to hear it," she said suddenly. "Maybe I'll wonder about the might-have-beens, but I don't think I'll cry again. That's over. I've thought a lot about what I've done by hiring you. In a way I can't explain, I've begun to pay my last respects. I know that sounds brutal, but I have a right to some bitterness. He lied about who he was and he died without leaving a note to explain why. If I gave away the money, I would have my feelings straight. I'd be bitter and nothing but. I'm glad to have the money and that makes me feel guilty."

He stayed quiet. It was not just that a comment by him would upset her more; he was sure she really did not want him to speak. He doubted that she believed everything she had said. She was too far into this to see what had moved her to do it. As a way of getting to MacIver's mother, he said that MacIver had never named her as beneficiary to his insurance. He, Leland, had thought that curious until he had met Mrs. MacIver for himself.

He described the home in Canby, exterior and interior, then its occupant. As well as he could, he transcribed the conversation that had taken place. Finally he told Norma about the door being slammed against his back.

"It didn't actually hit you, did it?" she asked.

"Oh, no. I would sue her if it had. I just want you to have an understanding of the person who thinks of you as 'that little Guinea.' "

"I never did hear what she thought of me—what she thought of the things Colin told her." She looked at Leland. "Suppose she finds out about the baby and tries to take it from me? If she had a smart lawyer, she could make a lot of trouble."

"I don't think so. You have your Dr. Roberts and I'll testify to what happened this morning. She's a lot older than her years. Maybe even Murray Kaminsky would say that in court. In his estimation, she's senile."

Now she saw that he was trying to direct the conversation. She asked about the way Betty Kaminsky lived. When she heard, she asked what her husband looked like. Leland told her and she said, "I don't think he's my type."

He regarded her. "That isn't an issue, is it?"

"In a way. I was jealous of her when Colin was alive, but because she was never a subject of conversation, my feelings didn't matter much—or I never had the opportunity to explore them. You can guess what I want to know now."

"If she was pretty," he said.

"That's right."

"Norma, you know you're an attractive woman. I won't lie to you, so is she, but you're both such different types that I don't think the question of looks was a concern to him."

"He told me that," she said. "He told me he liked women who brought out the best in themselves. Once he pointed out a very dark Negro woman who was especially well groomed. It was something esthetic with him. He said he was drawn to women who understood themselves. It was what attracted him to me, he said—which was purely an accident. I don't have any insight into my appearance, how I look when I'm walking and so forth, the way actresses do. But that's what he meant. Fashions, types, hair colors—none of that mattered. What about Betty? I want to hear about her. I don't want to say her name, but I want to hear."

Leland had to continue with what Murray Kaminsky had told him. When he came to his impressions of Betty Kaminsky, he related them truthfully, carefully, skipping nothing. He told her of the red hair, the long legs, even the clear nail polish. She did not interrupt him when he went on to tell of how well Betty Kaminsky had maneuvered her present husband. Leland repeated what she had said, without offering his own opinion. When she had known McIver, she had stated very positively, he had been a coward and had never played the horses. Leland concluded with her version of how McIver had acquired the scar. There were the notations in the insurance file and Leland offered his explanation for the conflict. "Her distortion may be at the foundation of her marriage with Kaminsky—part of it, anyway. For his own sake, Kaminsky sees her as someone who suffered deeply. Perhaps it's his way of living with her self-possession. She's at the center of her world; she makes no secret of it. She broke down today when she heard, but the truth is that before I told her, she said, 'Now what has he done?' As much as she's capable of hating a person, she hates—hated—him for what he did to her—which amounts to not staying as interested in her as she is."

"So he went outside for what he needed," Norma said. "It had to be something like that. I've thought about it since I saw his picture in the book last night. He could have told me the truth; he knew that. We weren't married when it came up, and probably he thought that I wouldn't take the chance with someone who had cheated. I even said to him once that I never cheated—slept with a married man." She swallowed.

"What I find so hard to understand now," she said, "is why he wanted my love and took it as gladly as he did, but never tried to gain my understanding and trust. I would have understood, if he had told the truth. He just kept it from me. He didn't think I was a fool. He respected my intelligence." She glanced at Leland. "He just never made use of it," she said as she returned her eyes to the road. "So he cheated me, too."

"Did he?" Leland asked.

"In that sense, he did. What about the half-truths and lies about his mother's relationship with Betty? About his father and the kind of man he was? There was no need for that. I tell you, Joe, it's not easy to face."

"Norma, all we really know is that he lied about his background. In most respects, it seems, he had reasons that had nothing to do with you. He had cut himself off from those people. Maybe he wanted to forget them as much as he could."

"Why did he lie about his father?"

"I don't know. Possibly he saw him in those terms. His viewpoint of him was different from ours, and not because he was the man's son. They were equals in the ability to make money, or your husband was even his father's better. We're in awe of that ability, whether we admit it or not, and your husband saw it clearly. He understood it, and saw beyond it to the man his father was."

She smiled. "You make an effective apologist for Colin."

"You've forced me into the position of suggesting alternatives. You've sustained a shock and it's still working on you. I want you to take it easy and remember that we're dealing with facts. The way your husband treated you all the time he knew you is a fact. Keep it in mind. The reports on him when he applied for his last insurance policies described him as a good husband. Your neighbors thought so and told the investigators that. He didn't cheat you and you know it."

She glanced away from the traffic again. "Those investigators' reports don't mean anything. A neighbor wouldn't undercut a man."

"If he had been doing something ugly behind your back that they knew about, they would. It happens more often than you think. They'll say whatever comes into their minds." He had remembered something. "For instance, one of them told of having seen him with approximately five thousand dollars in his pocket one Saturday morning. Did he do that often? Carry that kind of money?"

She frowned and her eyes darted. "No. He never did that."

"He did it once. The man wasn't lying or attempting to make your husband look bad. He gave him an excellent report."

She thought about it. The sky was a dark purple now and the headlights of the oncoming cars flashed through the windshield. She reached forward and moved a lever and almost immediately warm air began to pour from beneath the dashboard. The warmth and the car's soft springing gave Leland a sense of insulation and lack of care. It occurred to him that he was learning his man in a way he could never measure. What he was doing now, sitting beside Norma as she drove, was something MacIver had done. Leland was not seeing it with MacIver's eyes and he never would. It was a trick. MacIver was a set of things that had been. No one could guess what that set of things had seen and felt and thought—yet Leland could feel himself wanting to think that he could come close.

She said softly, "He handled money like no one else I've ever known. He carried his cash in his right hip pocket, folded once, without a clip or folder. When he bought something, he would take out all the money he had and count off. The singles were the outside and the larger bills at the center. He never used credit cards. You know when you play Monopoly, how people keep their money in severe little piles? When he played, he put it in the same arrangement he had in his pocket, one big pile but without folding, small bills on top and big ones on the bottom. He never made a mistake or got confused. He treated real money as if it were Monopoly money, and vice versa."

"You have no explanation for the amount that man saw," Leland said.

"No. Is there any way to fix the date? If it was a Saturday morning, the banks were closed. He was either carrying it from late the evening before or he picked it up somewhere that day. Do you think you could find out about it?"

"First I want to see if we have to. Think now. Could he have won it at the track?"

"Yes. Yes, if he had a really winning day. He liked to double up when he was ahead. But he would have told me if he'd done that well. He always did."

"Are you sure?"

"Yes. He was like a baby when he had a big day. He wanted to spend it on me. Before we were married he had an eight-to-one shot come in and that night we spent almost a hundred on dinner and went to another place afterward, which was more. We spent a lot."

"How much did he have on it?"

"Five hundred—at eight to one."

"I should know more about this than I do," Leland said. "I know the Internal Revenue Service ruling on racetrack winnings—"

"Oh, so do I! Colin taught me the night he had that eight-to-one shot. He wouldn't let them take our picture at the nightclub. We'd had it done on other occasions, but he didn't want any records of that night."

Leland kept quiet. He did not want her to think too much on how well her husband had known his way around that sector of life. If the Internal Revenue Service had suspicions of a man, it could easily turn up nightclub photographs as evidence of expenditures in excess of income. Most men—most tax dodgers—were ignorant of the depth to which the I.R.S. could research their finances. It had taken skill to get out of the track with the four thousand. MacIver knew more than the rudimentary elements of keeping his winning days in his pocket; he meted it out in little bits and let no one make records. Now Leland said that the things she had told him and what he had heard from the Kaminskys made him think that MacIver would have been a poor choice for a player in a game like Monopoly.

"He was too good, you mean? He was, but he played to keep the others in the game. He made easy deals and carried the ones who were losing badly. Once he won a game when the rest of us realized that he had made a series of deals with all of us that left him invulnerable to rents. By just going around the board, he would eventually collect all the money. Listen, are we really going to learn anything? I can't help feeling that we're going to get so far, and then have to give up. His mother and that woman told you just part of what they know. It isn't fair. I have a right to know."

"You have a need to know," Leland said. "We aren't done with them." He told her what he had instructed Florence to do. "I want to know how he paid for his divorce so soon after finishing school, if he borrowed from his mother, and if he did, what he told her about what he intended to do with the money. There are good questions about her finances. Did he support her before he died? If he did, we'll know that he was more involved with her than he let you know. Maybe he called her from his office."

"I don't think so," she said. "I think it was as he said. He didn't have anything to do with her."

"Did you look at his office telephone bills?"

"No."

"I will."

"Maybe he did borrow from her for the divorce," she said. "That would explain why she was so against it and why she's been friendly with Betty."

He didn't answer. He had steered her away from the night MacIver had declined to be photographed spending money he had intended to conceal. Leland couldn't help wondering himself, it was too interesting. As a public accountant MacIver had moved in business circles and there was no telling how much he had picked up about the tangles of the law. He had done his clients' taxes—Mike did Leland's and Karen's—and the law was that the accountant was as responsible for errors as the man whose name appeared at the top of the form.

Leland sat up as he felt himself trying to move ahead and gather together what he had learned. Somehow MacIver had made his start and acquired the money for the divorce settlement. And from there, he had gone on to accumulate a quarter of a million. He could have been made a loan by his mother; it supported the things Norma had just said about the mother's attitude toward her son—but Leland didn't care about that; MacIver had been an accountant, nothing more, and in five years and some months he had earned enough to save two hundred and thirty-two thousand dollars. No one had said that he had worked very hard. He had gone out, courted a second wife, married her, set up a new home. He had gone to the racetrack regularly. Leland was sure that MacIver could have won all his money; he would have been paying taxes on it right along or his estate would be tied up at this moment while back taxes were being determined. How MacIver had made his money and why he had died—if, indeed, his death had had anything to do with his money—remained as veiled as they had been yesterday when Norma had entered Leland's office. Seeing it all in these terms, Leland could feel the despair of which she had spoken. They would get so close, and no more. They would have to give it up.

Concerned with other issues, Leland hoped, Norma drove her late husband's car with sureness and visible enjoyment across the county line into the city of Port Smith. The sky was black now, and the roads were still jammed with people going home to dinner. Port Smith was no place for the scant pleasures of late autumn. It was gray and damp in the days, and in the nights it became so raw that normal cold weather penetrated shoes and leather gloves and turned toes and fingers yellow-green for lack of circulation. Every patrolman in Port Smith knew the trick of ten deep breaths. The streets averaged six feet above the water table where the land was soft. Most of new Port Smith was mounted on a black glacier-scored rock, but that provided no better insulation against the weather. One of the results of the winter cold was that the people of Port Smith, a sophisticated and comfort-conscious lot, were hardier and less vulnerable than most Americans expected. At this point in his life, Leland both disliked and was concerned with this city: the cynicism that was the product of the sophistication and toughness was enough to keep the people from demanding a direction from the government, and the increase in the numbers of colored people, creating the division of rich from poor along the color line, was building a half-rational dissatisfaction that was now of subcrisis proportions. There was increasing incidence of seemingly inexplicable acts, such as the teen-age gang wars of last week. Since the beginning of history cities had built on top of themselves, layer upon layer, and Port Smith was no exception: the old maps showed streams and marshes where now stood buildings whose construction no one remembered. Port Smith was rife with citizens' committees, study groups, and action teams composed of people who had not taken part in civic affairs before. It was Leland's own Port Smith upbringing that made him wish them well but made him wonder about the sort of people who ran out nightly to meetings that accomplished nothing. That which he thought was most sane inside him considered those people and their meetings as the city's best hope. Leland lived in Manitou now; legitimately none of it was his business. That most sane thing inside him had to view his concern as only an extension of the satisfaction he felt when he read that Port Smith College won a baseball game or two in the course of a full season.

Now Norma said, "What I can't understand is why he married her."

"That's something we'll never know. We'd better just forget about it."

"He was young," she said. "He'd just got back from the war. Maybe he needed someone."

"Kaminsky told me that his wife thought that your husband was a terrific character. I took it to mean that he was impressive, polished, and mature. It was college, but she was twenty-two at the time. Maturity is something college women look for, I think."

"He was *quiet,*" she said vehemently. "Women mistake quietness for maturity. He could have been mature, yes, but he could have been lonely, too."

"Your Dr. Roberts is the one to see on that," Leland said.

"Are you angry with me?"

"You're not waiting for the facts, Norma. Now we might just catch something on the state of his mind in those days. His wingman could give us some ideas, if all else fails. That's something to think about for later on. In the meantime, stop thinking. Leave that to me. It's what you hired me for."

"I think I'll have to see Wendell for more than one thing," she said.

"What do you mean?"

"I'm making myself sick over this."

"I wouldn't go that far," he said.

"Well, he'll know by looking at me. He knows my moods and the things that go through my mind. Don't be surprised if he asks me to go over to his place tonight—without you—for an hour."

He had picked up several things. "Then you've made an appointment," he said.

"No, no. I talked to him this afternoon. We're going to drop in on him right now. He has a class this evening, and he wanted to meet you as soon as he could."

He didn't answer. She seemed to have sprung it on him, as if she had thought that he would be displeased. Actually, he was. He wanted better warning. This made him think he was being drawn into something that was more than a job for a client whose company he enjoyed. A moment ago he had had to ask himself about the depth of her commitment to this Dr. Roberts. One thing he did not like was the idea of her surrendering her options so easily. If Roberts was to say she was sick—in trouble, more likely—she would accept it and offer herself up at the time he designated. For Leland there was something demeaning in it. It created a wariness of her he was not disposed to accept.

Leland tried to turn himself to the fact that he *was* here on a job like any other, and the job was his man, Colin William MacIver, whose recent color photograph was firmly imprinted in Leland's mind. The tall, slender, carefully dressed young man who had known the ins and outs, and now was dead. The most important single thing about his whole life was his sudden death, and Leland was having difficulty keeping attention on it. He did not like it—or the way he was handling it, either.

Now he asked if she objected to the radio, and she said no. She reached forward and pushed one of the buttons. They were climbing the hill behind Bay Slope and the lanes of traffic pulled upward before them for more than a mile. In the darkness of the boulevard he could see the aging frame houses in one of the oldest sections of Port Smith. It was a Negro neighborhood now, one and two steps up from the downtown ghetto. Where the houses were not owner-occupied, the managing agencies had them painted yellow and tan and dusty green. By some covenant in the real estate business, Negroes were to be prevented from living in white houses. Until the end of the war this part of the city had been a white area, then it had been busted, block by block, and millions had been made. When Leland's father had toyed with the idea of buying his own home, he had looked here. It did not seem as if that could have been the 1930's, so long ago. Once a neighborhood changed over, it could not change again. The banks would not extend credit to white men who wanted to live in a Negro neighborhood.

The radio came on with the traffic report. The major arteries, including this one, were normal for the rush hour. There was an accident on the Northport Expressway and motorists were advised to use Central Avenue or Shore Boulevard as alternate routes. A jingle for a loan company came on as the boulevard tightened to four lanes divided by a narrow, treeless curb. The Cadillac stopped at a traffic light. The tailpipes of the crossing cars towed banners of steam. On the corner three people waited for the downtown bus, looking quite cold. As the light changed and the Cadillac charged forward, engine sucking, hydraulic couple spinning, gears slickly shifting, the radio played a set of beeps and buzzes, followed by a very grave voice intoning that it was time for the news.

"With the discovery this afternoon of the mutilated body of the little seven-year-old Mary Shoftel, the Port Smith Police Department launched the greatest manhunt in modern times for James Scanlon, a sixty-eight-year-old drifter who roomed in the house whose basement gave up the little girl's body at three-thirty P.M. today. Just minutes ago it was revealed by Detective Lieutenant David Schoenstein that Scanlon has been missing since the night Mary disappeared. Preliminary medical examinations show that the girl had been sexually assaulted. She was found at Six forty-seven East Lincoln Street, six short blocks from her home, where her mother collapsed upon hearing of her discovery. She is in serious condition. Mary was found in the corner of the cellar, buried under rags and cardboard cartons in a makeshift grave—"

Norma turned the radio off. "You don't have to hear that, do you?"

"No, I don't think so."

"It upsets me. I can't help it. I'm very conscious of children these days. I don't know what goes through a man's mind when he does a thing like this. There are some things I can imagine—project —but not this. The newspapers call it bestiality. Maybe it really is. When you were with the Police Department, did you ever work on one of these things?"

"I saw one. I saw a victim."

"A little girl? A dead little girl?"

"That's right."

"How can you live with it?"

"Watch your driving."

"I am."

"I can't," he said. "I don't. I don't think about it."

"Can you do that?"

"Most of the time."

Her eyes were staying on the road. "Can I ask you something else?"

"Go ahead."

"Could you do it? Physically. Could you keep it up?"

It had the intense shock of an unexpected slap across the face. She was maddening. He thought he should laugh, but he was too embarrassed. It was irrational, he knew it; he knew he could expect anything from her. He said, "No. No, I couldn't."

"I don't want to believe that any man could," she said.

"This one did."

"Can you be sure? The legal definition makes it rape if he just touches her with himself. I know that much."

"The report specified mutilation. In these cases that's usually a euphemism for penetration. The newspapers will work around the details, but it may come out in the trial—if there is a trial."

"He must be insane," she said. "He'll never get to trial."

"Innocent until proven guilty, Norma. You can ask your Dr. Roberts about this, too. I'd be interested in hearing his answers myself."

The car was moving down Bay Slope toward the bay, which could not be seen because of the angling of the streets. It was not far to the Crescent Expressway, and from there, a few minutes to the Jefferson University campus. "He must have stopped talking about the killing by now," Leland said, and turned the radio on again. It was rude, but he wanted the opportunity to collect his thoughts.

Collegeville Road had not changed since he had seen it last—which might have been before the war. The sorority house where he had met Karen was four blocks away, and he knew he could get out of the car and walk to the end of the street, make a half-left turn, and cut across the campus lawn to the dormitory where she had lived.

He had never come back on a sentimental visit, and he did not know if Karen had, either. It would not surprise him if she had done it while she had lived here alone. Even in November the section was beautiful and restful, lawns, trees, and shrubs carefully tended, no fun for the children he had known in his own childhood. No children were in sight. In this neighborhood they were too jaded to play after dark. Where he had grown up the children had had to be run indoors. Even Steffie had had a taste of that. He had to think of the gulf that was going to spread between Norma and her child. In neighborhoods like this the children took dancing lessons and had cats they bred and their own listed telephones. Leland could remember the street urchins around Franklin Pierce High School. He had a picture of little girls playing jacks by an apartment doorway. Norma's child would never learn what jacks were.

She parked the car in the drive and they walked past the front of the house to a flagstone path that worked through the high shrub to the house next door. This house was larger, a two-story dark brick rectangle of no identifiable style, perhaps thirty years old. A light was on in the kitchen. Norma went up the steps, tapped twice on the glass of the new aluminum storm door, and turned the knob. Leland followed her through the double doors, then through a small pantry to the kitchen, where Wendell Roberts rose from the table, dabbing at his mouth with a paper napkin.

"Right on time," Norma said to him cheerily. "I was afraid we were going to get caught in the rush hour."

"I didn't expect to see you at all," he said. He was a tall, long-limbed man, and he looked like the photograph Leland had seen. He reached across the table, almost past Norma, and took Leland's hand. "Hi, I'm Wendell Roberts." He had a solid grip.

"Joe Leland. Hiya."

"I thought I was going to make some introductions," Norma said. She put her purse on the counter and brought a chair nearer the table.

"I told you I was eager to meet him," said Roberts. He pointed to another chair. "Sit down, Joe. I'm just having a sandwich before class. Some coffee?"

Leland sat down. "No, thanks. I know you're in a hurry." Roberts was having milk with the sandwich, which looked like sliced turkey. He had not shaved since morning and his beard looked like the first snow on a pavement. His skin still had a tan and he had the appearance of a man who spent every hunting season in the field, a gentleman sportsman. He knew it and completed the picture with a plaid tweed jacket with leather elbow patches. At first he seemed like a cheerful man who enjoyed life, but his eyes and the skin around them gave away a critical intelligence. His eyes had narrowed when he had looked at Leland in a nearly unconscious effort to take his measure, and the lines in the corners suggested to Leland that he did it very often. Now that Leland had made this observation about Roberts he wondered what observations Roberts had made about him. Leland felt himself becoming wary.

Roberts said, "Well, the coffee's there if you want it. This afternoon when Norma called I told her I could pick up enough turkey for all of us, but she said it would give her heartburn."

"I guess we can believe that," Leland said. "Mind if I smoke?"

"Go ahead. I'm sure you've heard this, but I've never met a private detective before."

Leland took an ash tray from Norma. "To tell you the truth, I don't think I've ever run into a psychiatrist."

"Not even when you were on the force down here?"

"Just psychologists."

"How'd they strike you?" He took a bite of his sandwich.

"A little damp behind the ears. The pay was no good, so they were all kids."

Roberts nodded as he swallowed. "What you deserved. That's not fair. They do good things."

"I never worked with them. On the way in from the airport Norma raised a question that I told her to put to you."

She looked surprised. She knew enough about him to realize he would not have spoken if he had not had a reason. He wanted to get out from under Roberts' questions.

She asked Roberts if he had heard the news about the Shoftel killing. He said no. She told him the police had found the body and what its condition had been, and finally, that the police were looking for a man in his sixties who had disappeared the night after the girl had been taken from the sidewalk in front of her home.

Roberts looked at Leland. "Do you think he did it?"

"I'd like to talk to him."

"Nothing else?"

"I'd have to see the evidence."

"That's right, of course." Roberts turned to Norma and a momentary glance back at Leland betrayed that he was thinking that he had not been answered. "I don't know what I can tell you, sugar. The man could have a long history of this sort of thing. We'll have to wait until they catch him."

"I see," she said. She was dissatisfied, and so was Leland, who could have no complaint. He thought that she wanted to be told what went on in a man's mind when he committed such a crime.

"How have you made out so far?" Roberts asked Leland.

"We've had progress," he said.

Roberts nodded. "I've always been curious about how the police learn all the things they do. I remember that case of yours that was in the paper yesterday. Did you see the paper? You knew what the roommate looked like before you found your witness. That was amazing."

"That was a time we took a chance."

Roberts drank his milk. "Tell you what. I like to have a can of beer at night. Why don't you join me? Norma said she was going to ask you to use her guest room."

Leland's mind was working. "Tonight is all right with me."

"Is ten o'clock too late?"

"No, I'll see you then."

"Good." Roberts got up to put his dishes in the sink. He was well over six feet three inches tall, and he could not weigh more than one hundred seventy pounds. For a man in his fifties he was in excellent physical condition, straight-backed, rangy, and lithe. He had the quick, relaxed moves of a major league first baseman or a pro football end. Leland wondered about his vanity, how much he worked out, and why.

"I'm glad you two have hit it off," Norma said.

"There's a fight on television tonight, anyway," Leland said, trying to close the matter. Roberts had her under control. She had had to come over as soon as possible, for no good reason of her own. Roberts had wanted to arrange the meeting later. He was gentle with her and perhaps all Leland was seeing was a continuation of what she had needed at the funeral. He could not help having the feeling that the conversation was not going to be pleasant. Roberts certainly wanted it badly.

He was doing his dishes now. Norma got up and took a paper napkin from the plastic holder and wiped the crumbs from the table. The napkin went into a paper bag on the counter. She picked up her purse and faced Leland as Roberts turned off the taps and began to dry his hands.

"Come on, honey," she said to Leland, "we have to go."

Leland felt it. He got up and opened the doors for her. He had to look back. Roberts, in the middle of the room, watched him with an unmistakable anger. The burden was on Leland to say something for which there were no easy words. By ten o'clock they might forget it, but the result, this impression, would not be changed. Roberts' reaction could be too complicated for Leland to assess and act on— Roberts knew Norma better than Norma knew herself. It was another thing for Leland to keep in mind, in addition, obviously, to not speaking to her about what she had called him.

"Flo, listen to me," he said into the telephone. "I have some packages here that have to get to Mike. I just called his home but he's out. Is he working?"

"Not that I know of, Mr. Leland. We had a quiet afternoon."

"All right. Actually it's a small truckload of stuff, boxes full of papers, ledgers, notebooks, some correspondence. I've looked through it quickly and making sense of it will take a better-trained man than I am. Mike will have to study it item by item and draw up a written report. Tell him that I've asked him to hurry. I don't want to go into explanations, Flo, but I thought that it would be wise to get the stuff out of here tonight. I'm waiting for a truck from a delivery service now. I don't want it in the office, so it will be going to my apartment. Flo, can you see that it gets inside?"

"Of course, Mr. Leland."

"The fellow is bonded, so you won't have to worry about him. Give him a twenty. Make sure that the place is locked up tight when you leave. If you want, spend the rest of the night there, because it's going to be late when you're done. There's fresh linen in the closet. Tomorrow, tell Mike that he's to use the apartment as he wishes to get the job done. He shouldn't take the stuff out. I want you to call Mrs. Walsh, my cleaning woman, and tell her that I don't need her services on Thursday. You may have to call her for Monday, too. We'll see. Don't volunteer information to her. On the expense sheet, write yourself down for thirty dollars and the twenty for the driver. Mike goes on tomorrow at a hundred a day. Full time. You'll have to run the office. Have we had any more upset stomachs?"

"No, we're all right on that score."

"Then call Hugh Thoms and let him sit behind my desk for the duration. He can handle the people coming in. You show him how to keep things moving. Do the rest of it yourself; I just want him there for the clients."

"I understand."

"Take good care of him, Flo. This job has to come first."

"How can we reach you?"

"I'm staying at Mrs. MacIver's. Don't give her any messages, just that I should call you back."

"Is there anything else we can do?"

"No," he said. "I'll call you tomorrow afternoon. I'm in a pay phone. That's another thing. If I call you from the house, I'll let you know. Don't start telling me things."

"I understand."

"I'll see you, Flo."

"Mr. Leland?"

"What is it?"

"I'd like to stay at your place. I'd like to have Don over, too."

Her fiancé. "Oh. Well, listen, I don't want him looking at those papers."

"He won't."

"Flo, I'd be pretty unhappy if you upset the place."

"I'll clean up, I promise. Is there linen to change again?"

"Yes. Why did you tell me? You could have had him up there without letting me know."

"You'd find out somehow. I don't want you thinking I'm a sneak. You understand that I'm not a baby. My mother doesn't understand but she's been so far out of it for years that I don't care about her. Don wants this and he'd be angry with me if he got the idea that I let the chance go by. I've been saying to him that I didn't want to go to a motel for the first time for a whole night, and we've been talking about a weekend trip, but it just makes me nervous. I still get very nervous and that's the one thing I don't like. I like to be set and safe before I do a thing."

"I can understand that, Flo. Look, there's a double lock on the door. Once the papers are inside, make sure you have the locks thrown—*I* want that—and then you don't have to worry. It will be late and no one will call you."

"Now I'm going to be nervous because it will be all right."

"Karen and I used to take a shower together. We weren't nervous, we did it to get our minds off school and so forth. There, now you know about us."

"I never thought about it and I won't start now."

"That's the girl. Good night."

She said thank you and good night and he hung up to wait for the operator to call back with the charges. He was in the corridor outside the bursar's office in the administration building of Jefferson University. He had needed coins for the call, and in this quiet neighborhood he had had to walk here, about a third of a mile, to get two dollars changed. Making the call outside was a normal precaution, he had told Norma, but in fact he had acted because of what he had seen of the contents of the cartons he was sending to Manitou. Pulling them out of the crawl space of the garage where she had put them in August, he had seen that they amounted to something different from the usual paraphernalia of accountants. Mixed with the letters, bills, and acknowledgments were canceled checks drawn by MacIver for very large sums, and in some of the ledgers and notebooks were entries that seemed like nonsense, or even madness. The figures didn't add, and in one ledger where Leland tried it, the columns didn't balance. In three of the books was a word that appeared on nearly every page, "Rainbow." "Rainbow—57,264" was an example. One book, concurrent with the others, was a record of the listings of certain stocks on the New York and American exchanges. A look in the back newspapers would show if it was accurate. A miniature looseleaf notebook was full of plus and minus figures, dated. Leland was certain that this book related to MacIver's gambling, but it showed nothing in line with MacIver's rise in fortune. In a two-month period in the spring of last year, MacIver had lost seven thousand dollars.

Norma had broiled a steak for their dinner, and after she had finished cleaning the kitchen she had gone out to the garage where she had found him sitting behind the wheel of the convertible, looking at a handful of the papers. He told her that he could make out even less than he really did understand, and that he had to send it all to his office. It was her property and he could not stop her from looking at it, but when she did not try to see what it was, he was relieved. It seemed wise to wait a day before he asked her if she understood "Rainbow." MacIver's marriage with her was beginning to come up in a different light. He had kept so much of himself from her that Leland was tempted to think that he had been using her. But why? As much as Leland liked her, he had to see that she was not much of a display. She had said that she and MacIver had made love every night. Still, the deeper into the nature of their relationship Leland found himself, the less he liked it, the less was his desire for learning more. He walked back across the campus to Collegeville Road.

The panel truck from the delivery service arrived just before ten. At ten exactly, Dr. Roberts came around to the front of the house. The truck was backed up the drive and the lights from the house and the garage gave a poor illumination to work by. As Leland came out of the garage with one of the cartons he saw that Roberts had buttoned a sweater over his shirt. The air was too chilly for that. Leland, perspiring, felt cold, and the air was biting the backs of his hands where the weather had made them raw.

"I'll be with you in a minute, Doctor," he called.

"You're really going at it," Roberts said.

Leland kept working. "Time is money."

"That's what he told me," said Norma. She stepped out of the shadows. She smiled to Leland, who waited at the truck for the driver to bring up the last carton. "My money. This way, his partner will be looking at this first thing tomorrow morning."

"I see," Roberts said. He didn't like it, which brought him up even with Leland, who had not wanted him to know so much about this. Leland walked with the driver to the front of the truck. Roberts did not have to know where in Manitou the papers were going. Leland paid the driver and apologized for asking him to work at night. The girl on the other end had his tip. The driver said all right and got behind the wheel.

"Listen," Leland said. "Be careful."

"I don't want to hear it," the driver said. "I never talked to you."

"If you stop for coffee, lock the truck."

"I didn't load it," the driver said. "I don't have the key."

"You won't have trouble, but if you run out of cigarettes or swallow your chewing gum, call me. Call me collect, but call me."

"You'll hear, all right," the driver said, and turned the key. "I won't need a telephone, either." Leland walked back to the garage.

"Do you think you'll learn anything from those books?" Dr. Roberts asked.

"We'll learn if there's anything to be learned," Leland said. The truck reached the street and they watched it go by Norma's Chevrolet coupé. The taillights flashed bright at the corner, then the truck turned and disappeared. Leland found himself hoping that Mike would not fail him.

"You're going to catch a cold," Norma said. "You, too," she said to Roberts. She pushed the button that lowered the garage door. "I have coffee ready," she said.

"Thanks, honey," Roberts said, "but I'm looking forward to that beer."

"I'll leave the kitchen light on for you, Joe," she said.

"I won't be long," he said, more to Roberts. He waited with Roberts until she was inside, then they started across the lawn toward the break in the hedge.

"I'm glad that you took this case, Joe," Roberts said.

"I'm glad to hear you say that, Doctor."

"Call me Wendell, please. Do you want a shot? A shot would warm you up."

"You're the doctor."

Roberts grinned. "I don't want to hear that again."

They entered the house. "Give me your coat. We'll go into the study." Leland followed him. "For the most part, the house is closed. My wife passed on a few years ago."

"I'm sorry," Leland said. He wanted to conserve what he knew, but at the same time he could not allow himself to be caught in a lie.

If he had said, "I'm sorry to hear it," he would be lying and, eventually, caught. The memory of the failure with MacIver's mother was still fresh in Leland's mind. As he followed Roberts to the study, he thought that he was going to let Roberts keep the lead—he had wanted this, he had something to say. Roberts certainly had other things to offer the case, and Leland could lose his chance with the wrong words.

The study was on the other side of the house, off the living room, a square, good-sized room, smaller but higher than the living room in Leland's apartment. It was furnished with castoffs and hand-me-downs, a leather couch and a pair of lounge chairs, bookcases and a desk as huge as Napoleon's tomb. There were signed photographs on the walls and a small refrigerator behind the door. "I couldn't see throwing it out when we replaced it," Roberts said. "I don't like beer all this much. As old as it is, the box located here is a very prestigious item. Sit down." He took off his sweater and put it carefully over a chair. He opened his collar. "You're married, aren't you?"

"Oh, yes."

"It's worth the effort. I'm the one to tell you."

"How so?"

"With my wife dead, I'm a pretty lonely man." He brought over a tray. "Listen, Joe, I wanted to talk to you."

"I know that." He wasn't fooled by the poor-widower routine.

"Cheers," Roberts said.

"Here's looking at you."

He pointed toward the couch for Leland, and leaned against the edge of the desk and folded his arms. "You heard what Norma called you this evening. I'm quite fond of her and she's had a rough time. I'd appreciate it if you would keep that in mind. If the situation gets out of hand, you'd do well to—take the action your conscience tells you to."

"Delicately put," he said.

"Damn it, Joe, it is delicate. She *has* had a rough time, and if she can weather the next few months, she'll have a good chance at life."

"We had a conversation yesterday at lunch," Leland said, making himself comfortable. "She told me that she was your patient once—and why. I'm not going to con you. I like her. I'm not going to pretend to understand your side—" he stopped to light a cigarette "—but I know mine. She's my client, and as long as I think I have a case, I report to her."

"Joe, that can mean anything."

"That's up to you. I need all the help I can get."

"I know you—your war record. I thought that I'd see a little more cooperation."

"Are you going to cooperate with me?"

"In what ways?" Roberts asked.

"Was MacIver your patient?"

"No."

"In your conversations with him, was there anything that made you believe that he would try to take his life?"

"No."

"Did he talk to you about his marriage?"

"Not really. I would ask how Norma was, and he would say fine or something like that."

"Did he talk to you about his gambling?"

"No."

"Business?"

"Oh, no."

"In the year and a half he lived here, you never had protracted or important conversations?"

"We were both busy. Once in a while he would come over, as you have, for a beer. We would watch television or talk sports or politics. Very casually."

"What were his politics?"

"They're difficult to put into words. He hated bureaucracy and big government. He was a conservative, but he didn't think there was any genuine conservative philosophy in this country. He despised McCarthy. He was too smart to believe that the people in government didn't know what they were doing. He saw the defense effort as so much make-work, and he was sure that it was the same with the Russians, too. He was unhappy and discouraged, frankly, over the way things were going. He thought that it was corrupt and very dangerous."

"You'd say that he had a keenly developed moral sense, in that case."

Roberts looked surprised. "On the basis of his politics, I'd say so."

"Was he moral in his private life, too?"

"Oh, yes. I'd say that was true, yes. Everything that he showed me indicated that."

It was occurring to Roberts that his questioner knew more than he was letting on. Leland's knowledge of the conversation about the cost of psychiatry at their first meeting was a low trump to hold, but as long as Roberts did not know he held it, Leland was safe while he tried to read through Roberts' lies. This stuff about sports and politics was ridiculous. Leland took a swallow of beer. "What do you know about Rainbow?"

"Rainbow?" He looked surprised again. "What is it?"

"I'll find out." Leland drank some more. "What are Norma's politics, by the way?"

"That's the amusing thing," Roberts said. "She's a gut-liberal. The poor are important to her."

Leland nodded.

"Why do you ask?"

"It was what I thought," he said. Half the truth. He had asked while his mind moved on to something else and at the same time absorbed the idea that Roberts knew about Rainbow. He said, "You went with Norma to the coroner's inquest. Didn't it strike you as odd that it would be over before you got there?"

Roberts rocked forward. "Well, yes. I had thought that they would want to take testimony from her about the state of his health. A clerk told us that the prima-facie evidence establishing the mode of death had been enough for the coroner—he wasn't interested in Colin's various conditions."

"Clausen is still a relatively poor county," Leland said. "There isn't much money for the coroner to spend."

"I suppose that enters into it," Roberts said. He wiped his hand over his scalp. "Norma felt that she had been short-changed. I'd say that if she hadn't had that feeling, she wouldn't have hired you. What are your plans now? She told me that you've already seen his mother and his first wife."

"I have some ideas," Leland said, annoyed with this new breach of security.

"Joe, I thought that we were going to cooperate with each other."

"We are, Wendell. But I don't feel that it's ethical to clear my moves with you."

"Then you put me over a barrel just now. I submitted to your questions."

"If you hadn't, I'd have told Norma straightaway."

"Do you think I'd have held anything back from her all this time?"

"Frankly, I don't know."

"You're a hell of a suspicious man," Roberts said.

"Not at all. On the basis of what you've said about your concern for her, you could want to shield her from some things you might happen to know."

"Then you've found evidence from which I might want to shield her," Roberts said.

"I didn't say that. Wendell, I've been hired to do a job, and since my employer is your friend, I would think that you would share her confidence in me."

"All I want are assurances, Joe."

"Assurances against what? That's what I don't understand."

Roberts raised his arms up toward the ceiling, and Leland couldn't blame him. It *was* a stupid question. Now the telephone rang. Roberts reached for it on the desk behind him and said hello. Leland paid attention to his beer.

"No," Roberts said, "you're not interrupting anything . . . of course." As Leland glanced up he caught Roberts taking a quick look at him. Roberts turned away before Leland had a chance to recover. As Leland drank his beer down to the bottom of the glass he weighed the expression he had seen: Roberts had looked annoyed, as if

Leland was a pest who had invited himself. Now Leland heard Roberts say, "I'm glad to hear from you and I told you why this afternoon." Leland did not look now. It was the conversation of a man who did not want to be understood. "Just a minute," Roberts said into the telephone, and put the receiver down. "Joe, I want to take this in the kitchen, if you don't mind."

"Go ahead."

"Take another beer, if you like."

"Thanks, I will."

Carefully, Roberts shut the door behind him. It made no sense; if Leland wanted to hear, he had only to pick up the receiver.

Or perhaps that was the trick. Roberts could be waiting right outside—why, Leland could not guess. Nearly everything Roberts had done so far had not made *perfect* sense. Who was on the telephone now? Norma? That would be worth knowing. Leland was on his feet. So far, all right; if Roberts mistimed and barged in, Leland could be going for more beer. Without touching it, Leland fixed the location of the receiver on the desk. Now he picked it up and listened.

"If anything, it's worse now," a woman said. "The situation is out of control. I know what he's trying to do and I won't put up with it . . ."

Very quietly Leland put the receiver down. It sounded right. He went for the beer.

The legitimacy of the call did not change what Leland had thought. There was something wrong with Roberts' behavior. Probably MacIver had discussed Rainbow with him—there was nothing the matter with that even if Rainbow was something to hide. If Roberts had been treating MacIver and MacIver had killed himself, Roberts would not have let Norma work into her present state. Leland would not be here. If Roberts was more deeply involved, he could have dissuaded her from this; but she had said that Roberts had encouraged her. At the moment there was nothing to do but wait.

The shelves were filled with fat, drearily bound psychology texts with unappealing titles. It seemed as if the authors had responded to a common urge to minimize the titillation of the subject matter, and one of the results was that a word like "Psychosexuality," set in narrow, archaic type on a binding of nubby black cloth, looked deadly dull. With the fresh glass of beer in hand, Leland gladly moved down the wall toward the framed photographs.

They were the usual unconsciously incredibly-funny posed shots of people at banquets and giving and accepting awards. Roberts photographed very well. He was, of course, in all of the pictures. Their mounting was not a display of exceptionally naïve vanity; none of them was less than four years old and all bore identifications in white lettering done in a distinctively feminine hand. Leland picked out the late Mrs. Roberts in one of the award-presentation pictures. She had been a tall, mature, and handsome blonde—real blonde, with very fair skin and eyes so blue they hardly registered on the film. In all of the pictures in which she appeared she was wearing cocktail dresses or suits with small pieces of costume jewelry; but Leland was thinking of the story Norma had told him about Maine and Mrs. Roberts slipping and grabbing her husband's arm, and Leland was picturing her as she must have looked on that day, in slacks, say, and a long-sleeved blouse. She had been one of those full-figured women who were a revelation of sexuality when they put on closely fitting casual clothes. Feeling a genuine sadness increasing, Leland walked away. There were more framed photographs by the door, men in dinner jackets.

Roberts with other doctors, Roberts with a pair of priests, Roberts with, surprisingly, Leland's old friend, Herbert A. Davis. Below that was another picture of Roberts, Davis, and a gaggle of doctors and businessmen, and this one was identified as a downtown health council. On a table was a poster depicting what seemed like apartment buildings. The last picture in the row was an autographed portrait of Herbert A. Davis. Leland grinned. A head of government or a movie star could get away with it, but not Davis. Now, at the desk, was a very small click, Roberts hanging up the extension. Leland decided to wait where he was, to let Roberts know that he had been snooping. He would leave it to Roberts to wonder how much had been learned.

He came in. "Oh. All set up, I see. That was one of my patients. Did you listen in?"

Leland laughed. "I thought of it."

"I was hoping you would. Sit down, sit down." He pulled the chair around from behind the desk to face the corner Leland had taken on the couch. Roberts sat with his elbows on his knees, the long fingers of both hands curled around his glass of beer. "I don't mean to say I planned it, it's just that as I was going out it occurred to me that the receiver was there for you, and you might hear something that would help you understand what I intended to say."

Roberts had positioned himself to work Leland over, and now Leland thought that it was time to hit back, even if he had to hurt, to let Roberts know that he did not have an easy mark.

"I thought I'd learn more about you if I looked at your pictures. I was able to pick out your wife. She was a handsome woman and I'm sorry she's gone."

"She put up the pictures," Roberts said. If he knew what Leland was doing, he was not showing it. "She was very proud of me. We met and married late, but she didn't take any of these things for granted." He looked to the pictures. "She was proud to be my wife. There's no other way to say it."

"My wife has kept a scrapbook for years," Leland said. He sipped his beer. "What was it?"

"Oh. A heart attack. She didn't wake up one Wednesday. I won't ever forget anything about it. We had no warning. I knew something was wrong the moment I opened my eyes. She always responded to the alarm and then woke me, but she was just lying there. I sat up and saw that her bladder had relaxed—that shouldn't shock a policeman—so I kissed her, twice, carefully, and called the police. 'My wife is dead. I just woke up and my wife is dead.' That's what I told them, and of course I was crying. You'd expect that I'd have done better, with my training."

"I am sorry."

Roberts took a drink of beer. "I've been living like a convict since that day. Get up and go to work, come back and go to bed. A few social obligations, but with no more enthusiasm than some of these men in prison must take to the weekly movies.

"I think it's over now," he said. "I had thought it was over

334

before, but I didn't want to face how much I allowed it to change my life. That was natural. Colin's death snapped me out of it. That's natural, too. I liked him. He was a quiet sort of young man. He minded his own business and seemed to want other people to mind theirs. He didn't have close friends—no bowling team or poker cronies or anything like that. Maybe he didn't think as much of himself as he should have. I don't know, I'm only guessing. He never did say anything that could lead me to offer that to you as a professional opinion. He loved his wife desperately. Maybe you know that he had a certain amount of personal aloofness. I never saw him touch her affectionately in the two years—more—that I knew him. But he provided for her lavishly. It was the way he was. You're seeing it all for yourself. He made her happy. The most of what I know about him I learned through what I know of her, and the effect he had on her. She's not a beauty, but she's an easy woman to fall in love with—all the men who know her are a little in love with her—but she's not easy to please. She thinks she is, but she needs an enormous measure of loving, just affection, to keep her opinion of herself high enough to keep her going. She needs a man to keep her related to life. That's not to say that she'll die if she doesn't have one, but she'll run down, slowly, like an eight-day clock. By saying that the men who know her are a little in love with her, I mean that they would sleep with her if they could. Her want to be loved seems to hold out that kind of promise. As they get to know her better, they only wish that she were that simple." He finished his beer. "Want another?"

Leland held up his glass, still half full. Roberts rose and went to the refrigerator. "What did she tell you about herself? I know your communications with her are privileged, but I do wish you'd sketch in what she said. I have a reason for asking."

He returned to his chair. Leland said that she had told him about her past and her courtship with MacIver. "The rest of it concerned circumstances of his death. You know them as well as she does."

"Yes, yes, that's right." He took a swallow from the freshly filled glass. "I was hoping you'd listen in on that call so you'd get a feel for the kind of thing I do—so that if I said I went through approximately the same process with Norma, you'd be able to accept that with little difficulty."

"You figured prominently in her account of herself, Wendell. She told me about the way her therapy went."

"Did she give you any idea of the things she's susceptible to, Joe? I don't want to go too far into my own privileged communications, but I want to be sure you have an appreciation of how much of a touch-and-go situation this really is."

Leland smiled. "I'm not going to give you any help, Wendell. I'm going to make you say it."

"Joe, I'm not playing a game."

"No, you're not." He drank some beer and looked away.

"All right, yesterday she went with that heavyset fellow, what's-his-name, Miller, to Manitou to see you. You got rid of Miller for her and the two of you went to lunch. You had a long conversation. She checked into a hotel and that was the last you saw of her until she met you this evening. Do you know what she did when she got settled in the hotel room?"

He waited.

"She called me. She was on air. She didn't want to talk for long because of the long-distance charges, but she did indicate she had been able to talk to you and that you had been interested in what she had had to say. She was very impressed with you. That was at two-thirty yesterday."

Leland was beginning to dislike this intensely.

Roberts said, "She called me again today before noon. Her emotional state was as low as it had been high yesterday. It wasn't just the discovery that her husband had lied to her. The conversation with you at lunch had become important to her. You didn't seem to show the same interest that you had. In her words, she felt nervous."

"So you told her to take the train home."

"No, I told her to do what she wanted to do. Now I'll tell you why I did. Joe, I wish I could say that she's on a tightrope, and that as soon as the baby is born and she adjusts to what is required of her, she'll be safe. I can't. She's not as simple as that. I wonder if you can see that, until Colin died, her life had had an almost perfect resolv-

336

ing. She worked very hard to get away from a world of superstition and violence. Her family is far behind her now. They're in awe of her when they come here and see how easily she lives with what they can never have. Marrying Colin MacIver was a kind of reward for that effort—in her mind. She was quite up to him when they met. She dated one of my colleagues earlier that same year—he can't forget her. He's not in the city now; when he heard about Colin's death, he called me and asked if he could help by coming east. In some ways she's a brilliant girl. The tests she took at the clinic placed her in the top two percent of all scores, and she would score even higher now because of her better situation. Some people would never believe it of her. I heard that one woman called her slow-witted. Norma is intimidated by people, crowds, strangers. She assumes they're better than she is. She knows it, she knows that the feeling is part—just part—of the myth and superstition of poverty. She wishes she could sparkle, like some women, and she knows she never will. It's not a happy thing for a young woman to live with.

"For this and a lot of other reasons I have no right to discuss with you, Norma functions best in one-to-one relationships. She does well with each of us, but did you notice earlier in the kitchen when we were all together that she had nothing to say?"

"I see what you mean." He wanted another beer, but decided against it. He put the empty glass on the table beside the couch.

Roberts cleared his throat. "Joe, I want you to take another objective look at her situation. You must have done it yesterday when you decided to take this job. She was happily married, expecting a baby. Her husband died suddenly, violently, probably by his own hand. The authorities say so. She has to be wondering how this reflects on her in the one area in which she can take justifiable pride. She's a hell of a woman for a man. He left no note, no explanations. Since last August she's been searching for an answer. Suppose you find none? You've already found something that was terribly upsetting to her. You're an attractive man—you are to her. She has you to her house, has you working for her, relating to her. She told me that you're separated from your wife. Any woman would mark you as fair game. Her feeling for Colin MacIver is dying. It had to if she's to survive. He killed himself. He willfully concealed things from her. The more you uncover about him—the worse you make him look— the more you will enhance yourself. In all frankness, Joe, she's been looking for someone to displace him. That's been part of her history with men. She hardly knows she's doing it. You could get up from here and go next door and be sleeping with her within the hour, and it would be no real accomplishment. She's not promiscuous. No matter what she told you, she never has been. She and I can't have a doctor-patient relationship anymore, but she does come over to see me. On one level she's killing something inside her that has to die, and on another she's very, very afraid to let it go. Being pregnant has helped her. A baby is a baby to her and she's not capable of thinking of it as Colin's or even her own. She would feel the same about it if it had to come by parcel post. Carrying it, the expectancy of having it, has helped her get through the worst of this. The rest she has to fight. Her friends can only give her assistance."

"You want to know where I stand," Leland said.

"I've been speaking as her friend to you as someone who could help her in a way her friends cannot."

"I think I understand you now. Crudely put, you want me to stay within a set of rules. I'll tell you what I told her yesterday when I took this case. I'm going to stay with it as long as I can see a reasonable return on her investment. When that stops, so do I. I go home. If she wants to think of other things, that's her business—and yours, if you want to concern yourself." He saw Roberts tensing. "Wait until I'm finished.

"I have my own professional ethics to uphold—and the law. I do my job and give the reports to her. If I turn up evidence of a crime, I'm obligated to report it to the authorities. She was advised of that yesterday and in my opinion she understood it perfectly. She's not a baby. If she's thinking other things—and I'm not convinced that she is—they aren't far beyond the range of normal experience. She can handle them."

"Joe—"

"I said wait. I won't attempt to suggest that I know her better than you do, but I will say one thing: I saw her yesterday when you weren't around, a condition you couldn't duplicate, and she did well enough to get by. I know she was quiet this evening in your kitchen, but there were other factors at work there. You wanted to set this up and I wanted to see what you were all about. She was eager to have us talk to each other. It was almost her place to step aside. We even overran her chance to introduce us. We took the chance away from her.

"And why do you want to fool around? We both heard her call me 'honey.' You weren't afraid to mention that, were you? You take another objective look, Wendell. The reason I'm here at all is Colin MacIver. He was in her mind tonight when she brought me to you, just as she brought him to you three years ago. She wanted us to get along in the same way. The circumstances were the same, dinner and conversation—and even the conversations had a similarity. Didn't they? Don't fox around. I saw the expression on your face as we were going out."

"You've given it a lot of thought. You have a very convincing argument, even if you are wrong."

"I'm not arguing with you, Wendell. I'm not making any deals and there won't be any rules. My relationship with my client is my business and hers, and if she wants to discuss it with you, that's up to her. I'm going to advise her not to do it. You're interfering right now, impeding my progress and wasting her money. You can explain that to her, if you want. Just continue to follow this course and I'll tell her everything you've said here. It would damage your usefulness to her; she couldn't help wondering what you really thought of her. And if she had real troubles and you tried to help, she just might tell you to get lost.

"You see, Wendell, by your own admission your relationship with her is on shaky ground. She told me that you've tried to watch her pretty closely since the doctor-patient business deteriorated. I know that you're fond of her and she has a genuine love for you, but maybe you've tried to have it both ways. She was a different person around you this evening. She was wound up and maybe a little too cheerful. Are you sure you're not just saying you're her friend and still trying to be the doctor? Maybe she's been waiting for the gifts of friendship while you've kept her saddled with the burden of proving herself to a spiritual adviser."

"I understand you, Joe." Roberts stood up and stretched his arms out sideways. "You have real insight and you aren't afraid to hurt people if you think you have to. Well." He pushed the chair around behind the desk again.

"Wendell, whether Norma and I sleep together or have a love affair simply isn't your business. If you're going to be the doctor, you're going to be hers, not mine, so don't try to discuss that stuff with me. You've already gone too far. You're too close to her. Do you think she could sell that house and move to another city? She doesn't even have the choice anymore. You took it away from her."

Roberts braced his hands on the back of the chair. "So you're going to do this the way you want, as little as you know about her. Her interests aren't a consideration."

"You aren't the person to determine her interests. You want me to soft-pedal this in some way, overseeing what I do—listen, your concern for her is commendable, but I'm not going to surrender my personal options. You're out of order. I don't want to repeat this conversation to her, but I will if I have to. She could be as strong as an ox and still fail to understand your motivation. She'll be hurt and confused and you'll never have her full confidence again."

"I think you mean it," Roberts said. "And you're probably right about the consequences. It would be your doing, and terribly cruel, and you would force the responsibility on me. You know the girl a little more than a day, you have no training professionally, and yet you're convinced that you're right and I'm wrong—"

"This has very little to do with any profession, Wendell. Norma told you that this was what she wanted, you encouraged her, and now you're interfering. And you're making an additional mistake. I wouldn't tell her just the part of the conversation that would hurt you. There's no reason to do that. I'd give her the whole thing, as another report on the job she hired me to do. You're forgetting that I only work here. I'm not hiding or faking anything and I have no personal interest."

340

Roberts stared at him for what seemed like a very long time. "You're a very stubborn, determined man, Joe. I thought that years ago when I first had dealings with you, and you've said nothing tonight to alter my opinion."

"You'll have to explain that," Leland said. It was a very strange feeling, as if all the windows had blown open and all the warmth had been swept out of the room.

"When Norma spoke to me yesterday and she had such a glowing report on you, I hoped that we would be able to talk intelligently, that we would be able to come to an understanding about her. I've never been able to make up my mind about you—you were either very shrewd or very fixed in your opinions. I didn't think you could be both."

"Never mind. You said that you had dealings with me years ago. I never saw you in my life before today. I want an explanation."

"Jerry Palmer was my good friend. He taught in my department."

"Oh." He looked back at him. "Was?"

"He died last year of cancer. Does your wife know?"

"I don't—think so," Leland said.

"Will you tell her?"

"That's not your business."

"Take it easy, Joe. I didn't want to mention this. Maybe it will give you an idea of how serious I am about Norma. You *are* involved. You're not only working here. Nobody is only working anywhere. Your wife was sick—you seemed to understand that well enough. Why can't you understand this?"

"I'm not going to discuss my wife with you." He sounded like a sulking boy. He wanted to leave. Roberts leaned forward, gripping the back of the chair. He wasn't angry; he didn't have to be angry.

"Joe, you were right and Jerry Palmer was wrong. You knew her better than he did and finally she showed it."

Leland looked at him coldly. "Did you encourage him?"

"Of course not."

"Did you try to dissuade him?"

"It wasn't possible. He was perfect for the situation. I think you know that."

"Do you know her?"

"I wanted to. We never met."

"I'll tell you what I understood," Leland said. "I understood what she told me, when she got around to it, when she was able to speak of it. Palmer might have been 'perfect,' but I don't feel badly now about the rough time he had because he happens to be dead. I don't think that way. I'm sorry he died young. That's too bad, but it doesn't alter my contempt for what he did with his life.

"And just to straighten you out, she never vindicated any judgment of mine. When I left Port Smith I hoped that I could get her the hell away from me. She wanted to wreck herself and I'm sure your friend saw it as well as I did, but he was a willing participant in it."

"He couldn't help himself. He really couldn't."

"He had a hell of a lot less to lose than she did. He saw that. Of course he did. But he put her in terrible jeopardy every time he met with her."

"That's not true. They knew you. You never went to an attorney, never called Jerry Palmer at the University. You could have had him fired at any time. The kind of man you are had a lot to do with what happened—what she did, the way he conducted himself. He knew that as long as you held your ground, she would never ask for a divorce. When you went to Manitou she believed that you were leaving the door open—she could go after you, but on your terms. Jerry saw that if anything, you had tightened your hold on her. He didn't die well, as they say. He was bitter and in anguish. He vented it on you."

Leland was horrified. "Too damned bad. You're forgetting that they got started while I was in Europe. He never gave me a thought. I'm not going to start worrying about him now." He stood up. "Too damned bad for him. I'm sorry to sound childish about it, but it's the way I have to feel. I kept myself under control for years—and I was right and he was wrong, by dumb luck. She's all right now, I think, and maybe I did help her a little, but he didn't, for sure. He was only a small part of what was bothering her—that's enough. That's all I'm going to say to you. Where's my coat?"

"On the chair behind you."

"I'll think about what you said about Norma. You win that much. It took enough doing, didn't it? You're pretty cool. You gave me all that soft-soaping bullshit about her and yourself and all the while you knew that if you didn't have it your way through that, you'd drag this out. Now I'll think about it. I don't believe it, but I'll think about it." He set his coat on his shoulders. "If you don't like it and start thinking you can go further, like talking to Karen, you'll find out how tough I can be."

"I won't try that." He looked upset.

"See that you don't. You didn't know me as well as you thought, and what he told you about her was even more wrong—"

"I knew that. I knew that when he told me."

"Forget it. Get it out of your mind. I don't want to hear you speak of it again." Leland turned for the door.

"Wait. Norma will expect you to mention something. I wouldn't bring it up if I hadn't already told her."

"What is that?"

"When I told you about the way I've been living, I wasn't exaggerating. A man is coming in to open the rest of the house and on Friday I'm going to have some people in. It's something we used to do a lot. I told Norma that I would invite you."

Leland shook his head in wonder. "I'll have to speak to my wife. I've asked her to come down for the weekend, but she hasn't made up her mind. She doesn't like Port Smith anymore."

"Yes. Well, do what you want. I'm sorry about what happened this evening."

"Thanks for the beer." Leland stopped at the door and tapped the autographed portrait of Herbert A. Davis. He couldn't resist. "How well do you know this jerk?"

Roberts laughed. "He happens to be a good friend of mine."

Leland was more than even, but that didn't matter. "Another? You really know how to pick them, don't you?"

"Norma?" Except for a small lamp lit over the kitchen table, the lower floor of the house was dark.

"I'm upstairs, Joe. Leave that light on, please."

He had to go through the dining room, a formal contemporary room with a finely oiled walnut table, to get to the foyer and the wide, curved staircase to the second floor. She had been right in what she had told him yesterday; the lines of the outside of the house made it seem smaller than it really was. She had good taste. It was possible to clutter the place and she had not done it. She had wanted to make a quiet, comfortable home and she had done that.

On the second floor the curve of the staircase created a wide, rectangular hall. There was a window over the stairwell that would vent an impressive daytime light down into the foyer. The color of the walls seemed to have been selected to subdue the sensation of space; it was a sand that worked with the darker carpet and the white enamel of the staircase molding to bring the walls more within reach. In a smaller area the effect might be oppressive. Now Norma came out of her bedroom at the back of the house. She was still dressed; she had slipped off her shoes and her hair looked as if she had had her head on a pillow.

"Is everything all right?"

"Sure. I thought you were going to be downstairs with that coffee."

"Do you want a cup? Would you mind helping yourself? It was all I could do to wait up until you were in the house."

"I'll get the coffee if I want it. I'm not finished yet—I have to go out again. Do you have a key I could borrow? I could come and go without disturbing you."

"Wait a minute." She went back to her room. "Come on, Joe. I'm in a fog. I didn't mean for you to stand there."

He followed to the door. It was a dark, masculine-looking room. She went to her purse on the night table for the key. "It's almost eleven-thirty. What can you hope to accomplish now?"

"I want to set up an appointment for tomorrow. And some other things."

"Are they my business?"

"In part. I'll tell you about it tomorrow."

She returned. "And your conversation with Wendell," she said.

"That's right. Good night. You look like you need some rest."

She smiled wearily. "Thanks a lot. So do you. I get up early. What time do you want to be awakened?"

"Seven, if that's what you mean by early."

She nodded. "Anything special for breakfast?"

"I'll eat whatever you put in front of me. Thanks."

"Good night, Joe."

"Good night, kid."

This time he went in the other direction, away from the campus, to make his calls. The public buildings were closed at this hour. There was a row of stores seven blocks to the south, he was sure of that much, and with luck, a bar with a public telephone. He was going to try to get his father at the station but not at home: at home his father would be asleep. Then he was going to try Mike again and tell him what he wanted. That would be the end of the business calls and he would be able to call Karen.

Captain Leland was at the station but had left orders not to be disturbed until morning. Leland did not want to leave a message. He thought he could conclude that the Shoftel killing suspect had not been picked up yet. No matter how he tried, his father would not be able to sleep if the man was in custody.

Mike was home. He listened and then he said he would call Florence to see if she was all right. Leland told him not to bother. He didn't understand. Leland said that she had arranged for her own protection. First Mike sounded surprised, then he started to laugh at himself. Leland told him that he was getting old.

It was after midnight now. When the telephone rang the third time he knew he was getting her out of bed, but their long-standing habit was to keep ringing until the other answered. She picked up as the sixth ring began.

"Hello? Joe?"

"Yes, it's me. I'm sorry it's so late, but I couldn't help it. Were you asleep?"

"I dozed while I was watching the late movie. Is everything all right?"

"Oh, sure. It's been a busy day. Do you mind talking for a while?"

She said that it was what she had been waiting for and asked if he wanted her to call him back because of the charges. He gave her his number, hung up, and waited. While walking over he had worked out what he could tell her about his conversation with Roberts. He had a question to ask that she could answer. The rest, all the references to her, he would skip. He had not mentioned Roberts' name yesterday when he had told her of the case, and he could imagine no reason why she would guess that the case was closer to her than he made out. He was on good ground. The telephone rang and he picked up and started talking. When he told her what the doctor had said about Norma, she interrupted to say that it was what she had tried to tell him yesterday. She had sensed something wrong when she had seen her in the Flamingo. He said, "That's what I understood you to mean. I told him I would think about it. The last thing I want to do is fight with the guy. You know more about this than I do, Karen. Is it possible that he was treating MacIver? I asked Norma and she said no. I asked him and he said no, too."

"I've never heard of it. They were neighbors and friends. He couldn't have been able to maintain his distance from MacIver. He would have been involved—not emotionally, but MacIver would have been able to see him in other roles. Arguing with his wife, for example. It wouldn't work. Do you understand?"

"Yes, I think so." He was trying to fit it with the personalities as he knew them. He couldn't make a decision, and not just because he did not know MacIver. Perhaps he knew some of MacIver's traits, and enough of them to see how he would function in therapy or analysis. The truth was that he did not know the process itself; all his information had been gleaned from hearsay: what Karen had told him about child guidance, what she had picked up from Jerry Palmer, what Leland himself had heard from others—Norma, Anne had had a brother in group therapy—and what he had read in those popular books. He had to go along with Karen. She did know this better and

346

she was not unsure. On the way over, he had been closing off the other alternatives about Wendell Roberts. His opinion of him had also settled. He would never be comfortable around Roberts because of what had happened tonight, but he could not help wondering about the range and depth of his mind. Roberts was an extremely bright and sensitive man, yet he was up to playing games—badminton: there was a file of photographs on this case—and he was capable of a shrewdness and calculation—up to the harder games, too—that Leland had encountered only once or twice before. Karen had been one of those encounters, but Leland did not think she was truly Roberts' equal.

He said to her, "Listen, I'm calling from a pay telephone because I wanted to be certain of our privacy." He told her how Norma had checked out of the hotel and taken the train. "When I got down here she said she wanted me to stay at her place. After the experience with her doctor, I'm a bit leery of extensions."

"I thought she would pull something. The plane seemed like the right opportunity. I don't like to talk like this, but you do have the doctor's word, too. Be careful, Joe. You won't be able to say you weren't warned."

"You're trying to make it worse than it is. I know this is upsetting for you, but go easy. According to the doctor, she took the train because my mood was too good when I called her this morning. I didn't seem interested in her. You know why my mood was good. I wish I was home instead of here."

"Eventually, that may prove to be the trouble," she said.

"You're not talking to a college boy, Karen."

"It was supposed to be a joke."

"She knows where I stand. Relax. Forget it."

"I think we should change the subject," she said. "You said you'd been busy."

He told her that he had sent MacIver's business papers to Manitou and that Florence was at his apartment to take delivery.

"You asked her to work at this hour? You worry about me when I'm traveling late."

"She's going to stay over. She's all right."

"Joe, she'll have her boyfriend in—more ways than one."

"Karen, she asked me if she could. This job is important. I told her I wanted her to take care of the apartment."

"Joe, what's the matter with you? I would have done it for you gladly—Steffie and I together. Now you have her and her boyfriend in our bed. I like her and he's probably a very nice boy, but I care about that place. It is ours, isn't it?"

"Of course it is. You know I don't like to ask you to do these things. You work hard enough. I wasn't thinking of the other side of it. Just that."

"Joe, is anything the matter? Is there anything bothering you?"

"I don't know, Karen. I don't think so."

"This isn't working out. Drop it and come home. Give her back the money. We can stand the loss."

"No—no, it's no way to do business. I wanted it. There is a job here."

"I don't like what it's doing to you," she said.

"I don't know if it is doing anything to me. Maybe I'm coming down with a cold. I was cold last night when I was following that woman around on her shopping trip."

"If you get sick, Joe, I want you to come home."

"Sure."

"I mean it."

"Okay. Listen, what about this weekend? I want to see you."

"I haven't thought about it, honey. You'll probably be home by then, won't you? Let's not go anywhere. Let's just stay home."

"Are *you* all right, Karen?"

"Yes. I'm worried about you."

"There's nothing to worry about. I'm all right. We're all right, you and I."

"I know that. Do you want me to do anything? I'll call Florence, if you want."

He had succeeded in really upsetting her. She wanted to do something—anything. "I told Florence I'd call tomorrow. You get

348

some sleep. That's what I'm going to do. We'll get some rest and we'll feel better in the morning."

She sensed that he was trying to take control, talking down to her deliberately. "All right," she said. She sounded as if she were giving up. They made their good nights and he gathered up his change and left the booth. They had both given up for the time being. He knew he would feel that he had control if she had really said something affirmative, even a lie they could both recognize. This was Tuesday night and the weekend was a long way off. He had not thought seriously beyond tomorrow. There were things he could do, all almost purely mechanical, that could advance this "case." He did not have to think of them and that was part of his trouble. He was approaching this like an ordinary job, not really awake, and his attitude was spilling over into the rest of his life.

He awakened during the night, thinking at first that he was starting to catch cold, which would make him too restless to sleep, but as his mind cleared he could hear what had penetrated and had brought him to consciousness. It was Norma in her room. There was a bathroom in there adjoining this room and the sounds carried. It was something he had to tell her. He could hear her sniffing and coughing. He turned over on the bed and looked out the window to the ground below. She had the light on; he could see it brightening the lawn, so she was not wandering around, half asleep. He listened for a moment, then could not keep his eyes open, and relaxed. Before he fell asleep again he heard the light switch snap. He was too far into sleep to be able to associate it with anything. In a moment it was a thing behind him, and in another moment, it was nothing at all.

CHAPTER SIXTEEN

■ ■

"COME ON, WAKE UP."

"Mf. Hiya."

"You had to remember where you were," she said.

"That's right." He sat up. "Why do you women have housecoats that look like war-surplus pup tents?"

"They're comfortable. I didn't think you wore pajamas, to tell the truth. Or is that only for visiting?"

"Every night. Get out of here."

"You're a hairy one," she said.

He laughed. "I've heard that one before. Wait. What awakened you last night?"

"Could you hear?" She glanced at the wall. "What did you hear?"

"If you had brushed your hair, I would have heard it."

"Well, I had a dream. Don't concern yourself. We're having bacon and eggs, take it or leave it."

"Okay." He watched her close the door. She had told the truth, he thought. What he had heard could have been an out-and-out crying spell, but she would have had more trouble telling him that it had been a dream. It took him twenty minutes to get downstairs. He felt ragged, as if he had moved too quickly in the shower and in front of the mirror. He hadn't gotten a good shave. In the kitchen he looked out the window. The weather was heavy and low and the one man walking up toward the campus had his chin pulled into the collar of his overcoat. Leland hated raw, leaden days like this.

She asked, "What did you find out from Wendell?"

"A little of everything." He decided to take a chance. "I would guess that he knows more than he's telling."

"I know he does," she said.

"He doesn't think so," he said.

"I know that, too. In spite of himself, Wendell tries to think that I'm stupid. You want to think so, too. Don't be offended. Colin liked going over there in the evenings. It couldn't have been for sports and so forth, as he used to tell me, because he really wasn't interested in sports. He couldn't park in front of the television set for a game, and a man has to be that interested to look forward so much to conversations."

"What do you think they talked about?"

"That's what I hope you'll find out. I used to think it was me, but I'm not that complicated. That idea, that they were talking about me, is part of my own problem." She brought the breakfast and sat down. "What did he tell you?"

"Listen, kid, I don't want you to tell him what we're learning."

"I haven't, not really. He knew about the papers in the garage from before. I saw that that bothered you."

"All right. From here on, don't volunteer anything, and if he asks, just tell him that you don't know."

"I understand. Now, what did he tell you?"

"He gave me the sports and politics baloney. My guess right now is that they indulged in that male pastime, swapping lies. Your husband told his best stories in exchange for the doctor's best— about themselves, you understand. Probably Wendell used his professional training—he wouldn't be able to help it—to probe your husband about his first marriage and his adultery, and because of the ethics involved, he doesn't feel free to divulge what he heard. And he's upset about you knowing the details of the first marriage. He's worried about you, about the way you're holding up."

"I knew that," she said. "What else?"

Leland made another decision. "He told me to lay off you. Understand?" He sipped his coffee.

"That's not his business."

"Figure it as a way of seeing how deeply he is worried. Now don't say anything to him, please. I didn't get what I wanted and I hope to be able to talk to him again."

"When?"

"I don't know."

"What else happened?" she asked.

"He knew my wife at one time. We talked about that."

"Oh. Wait. He knew that when I said I was going to see you. He didn't say anything to me."

"That's not *your* business," Leland said.

"What did she say last night when you called her?"

He thought it was bitchy. "I didn't tell her. It's not her business anymore, either."

"Oh." Now she hesitated. "Listen, I was thinking about that dream while I was waiting for you to come down. It was about the baby, but he was there. Colin. I don't feel very comfortable right now."

"Okay." He kept eating. He did not think that she would make it up.

"Wendell told you to lay off? He said that?"

"You're fishing," he said.

"I know. I want to hear something nice. I'm so far gone. Look at my stomach. What could we do?"

"All things are possible. Take it from an old hand."

"All things? Really? Could you be interested?"

"That's a privileged communication."

"I'll take that as a compliment, and thank you." She looked pretty. She had not put on makeup and the pitting of her skin was apparent. It did not change his opinion. "What's on your schedule today?" she asked.

"I'm going to start at the racetrack and the Clausen County courthouse. While I'm gone, you can go through your husband's address book, making a list of the names you know and their connection with him. Also, before I go, give me the address of his old apartment on Bay Slope, Enid Alma's telephone number, and the names of his banks."

"All his accounts are closed."

"That doesn't mean anything."

"His address book is new. There won't be many names in it. Do you think there'll be some that I don't know?"

"I have no idea. Didn't he carry over the old names into the new book?"

"Not completely, I'm sure of that. He got the new book before we were married. He didn't mention it, but I noticed. The old one was an unholy mess, full of names. The new one is still in good condition."

"Will you be home today?"

"Yes."

"I'll call you as I go along. There may be some calls from Manitou. Just take the names. What do you do all day?"

"Lately? Nothing. Mess around and sleep. This will give me something to do. You'll be using the car. It will need gas, and have the oil and water checked. I want you to use the Cadillac because I'm going to sell the Chevy and I don't want anything to happen to it."

"Wendell said something about a party Friday night."

"He asked you? Good. You have to come. His parties are part of the folklore around here."

He thought he had covered himself. "I heard the radio while I was shaving. Was there any word on the Shoftel case?"

"They're still searching. Why?"

"First I want to say hello to my father, and he's in the center of the action."

"I see. On my time," she said, and laughed.

Dr. Roberts had not distorted the truth in his telling of her calls to him yesterday. As long as she had attention, she functioned beautifully.

From the badly sprung club chair in his father's office he could look through the dusty window behind the desk over the rooftops of one-story factories to the large black sheds projecting into the bay. Without moving his head, all he could read of a sign on a wall were the orange block letters of COAL CO., INC. If he bothered to look for the rest he would end up annoying himself, because he did know whose COAL CO., INC. it was, having seen it from this seat a hundred times, but he could not put the names together. He wanted to think INGALL'S, but that was wrong. From four or five blocks away carried the dim, sporadic ratcheting of a pneumatic hammer. In his private bathroom, Leland's father was shaving with an electric razor.

"I didn't really expect you until late afternoon," his father called. "Give your mother a ring. If you catch a meal with her I'd appreciate it. I was home yesterday, but she was up to her sister's."

"Okay, Pop."

"The reporters see you?"

"Yeah. One of them asked me if I was on this thing."

His father laughed. The razor switched off and he stepped into the room. He was in his undershirt and his suspenders looped about his waist. Gray hair standing up like wire, he was an approximation of what Joseph Leland expected of himself when he was sixty. Captain Leland wound the razor cord. "Schoenstein is a good boy. He's organized and he knows what he's doing."

That was high praise. "Downstairs they said he went home for a couple of hours."

"He'll get a break soon. That fellow Scanlon had about thirty dollars when he left town. He did leave. They canvassed the rooming houses, the flops, the bus stations—the whole business. There's a drawing in today's paper. Did you see it?"

"No. I'll pick it up."

His father put on his shirt. "Do you think you have something with the Colucci-MacIver business? I had a look at what the boys sent to you."

"I have a feeling about it. He went off the roof of Flatlands last August."

"You told me. You think it was murder?"

"He was a wise guy. Mike is working on his books. What can you tell me about Clausen County?"

His father raised his hand quickly. "Come inside." He led him

354

into the bathroom, where he turned on the faucets. "Tell me what you have."

Leland told him about the police calling late and the coroner's inquest.

"I want you to be careful," his father said. "There's something happening in Clausen. Nobody seems to know what it is, but federal money is involved. About six months ago a man got drunk in a bar down here and started popping off. A plainclothesman, one of my best boys, picked up what he said. Not much, just that the Government was being taken for another ride. He mentioned Clausen. You know as well as I do that when that kind of loose mouth starts, the trouble isn't far behind. There's a good chance that it isn't confined to Clausen alone. You remember Walter Dubner, who used to live on our block?"

"No."

"Fat, pompous guy, called everybody Mister. He's living in Clarendon now, the year around. He went to Europe last summer. His son bought a trucking outfit in Arizona. A couple from the block who were out there saw the son. That's scanty, but Dubner's over his head. He's a Grade Two with Department of Finance. We know what he makes. He never had a quarter until a couple of years ago.

"Out in Clausen, they had a sewer scandal. Contractors used substandard materials and padded their estimates. Streets collapsed. The indictments will be handed up this month. They have a county fire department now and a call was missed—missed completely. They kept it out of the papers.

"That was July. By dumb luck nobody died, but there's a suit for two million coming in. Three weeks ago, two on-duty cops were found in their squad car in a lovers' lane with their girl friends. A couple of kids were there, and the boy happened to have a flash camera. He got upset at seeing the squad car and what was going on inside, so while he drove by slowly, his fiancée took a picture they delivered to the Clausen County *Mail*. It wasn't printable. What was supposed to be the only copy went to the county headquarters, but other copies were made and circulated through the city rooms. There are dozens now. We saw them. How do you think we feel?

"Your Mister MacIver could have been caught in the same deal at the track. Take a look at the ambulance records. You'll probably have trouble getting them. So would I, so would the district attorney, so you'd better forget it if the doors close. That's the way things are out there. Then again, you might be onto something big, so keep a record of the trouble you have, and who caused it.

"You know why the taps are on. The smart alecs have bugged offices before. They could have their reasons. A lot of little things have been happening for no reason anybody can see. We've been getting the needle on the Shoftel case. They want it solved in a hurry. You remember the last time we had that?"

"How is Herby Davis these days?"

"Quiet. All he wants now is to extend Lewis Park two miles in both directions. People are hoping he'll drop dead. He's over sixty-five now. The city has been fighting for years for a larger share of the East Coast shipping, and he wants to limit the number of piers the city can have. He has his reasons, too, but they're malarkey. He wants another monument to himself. They'd change the name to Davis Park.

"The other day I had lunch with Fregosi, who's over at the Fourteenth now. He told me a joke about the politician who forgot the number to his Swiss bank account. It made me ask myself, 'Where did he hear it? Who would think it was so funny?'

"Excluding Davis, who doesn't change, these are some of the things that are going on lately. The last time the department heard from Davis was at the budget hearing when he wanted a police force of his own for his parks. We'll hear it again next year. On the other thing, you see what it is. Somewhere along the line the pipe with the money in it has sprung a leak, and they're coming from far and near to catch some of it."

"I've heard enough. Let's get out of here."

His father turned off the faucets and followed him into the other room. "So say hello to Karen for us. And Stephanie."

Leland smiled. "I almost forgot. They may be down on Friday night. Do you think you can put Steffie up in my room if I ask you?"

"That's the most tentative thing I ever heard. I guess so. Check with your mother. How long do you think you'll be staying on?"

"I'm going through the lady's money at better than two hundred a day, so the middle of next week is about the limit."

The telephone rang. Captain Leland listened a moment, then put his hand over the mouthpiece. "You driving a Cadillac?"

"It belongs to my client."

"He'll be right down," his father said, and hung up. "They want to set up a barricade, just in case. I won't walk with you. Be careful. I'll be here all day if you need me."

"Thanks." It was a bit of paternal support, and it felt comforting. It had muscle behind it, the authority of a long-time high-ranking cop. If Clausen had turned as sour as his own evidence of August 12 indicated, Leland could need all the official help he could get. Any police department in the state could pick up his license on demand, and then he would have to struggle with the State Bureau of Licenses to get it back. It was not in that instance that he wanted help, but today, if he antagonized someone and jammed. Officials in Clausen, with something to worry about, would avoid making powerful enemies. In their own camp they could wield terrible power, like not providing police when they were needed. It was from outside that they were the most tender, and because of our multiple governments, most accessible.

Every public servant knew how it worked. Someone saw someone else with his mitt in the basket and was stricken by nothing more or less than envy. The money was quick, big enough and, almost best of all, tax-free. A patrolman who saw his captain carrying home a case of liquor turned up at Christmas at the same bar for a bottle or two. Someone taking the chance for bigger money incited the others that much more. Workmen saw their bosses paying building inspectors and thereupon took away everything not driven into the ground. If a cop knew of others taking and had no chance to take himself, he let down. Citizens saw him lounging against buildings, smoking on the street, hustling groceries. A fireman who saw a buddy stuffing a television set into his chief's car broke down inside. Could the chief get discipline then? A fire battalion or a station house could keep clean if its officers stayed clean and made the ranks toe the line. A little man could be broken into his job or busted out of the department. But when the money leak was big enough, there was a stampede. Even a captain's morale caved if the pressure came from too many directions. The wife of a captain earning fourteen thousand was still not very well dressed when there were school tuitions and a mortgage. Could he take her nagging, spurred by her friends' derision, for very long, when the money to be taken was floating on the surface, helping or hurting no one real, and he could look in the mirror and see someone cleverer than before and, really, not more evil? It was not so much a stampede as an epidemic, and there was no one who could not be weakened enough to succumb to an infection cultured to the size he thought he was.

At the corner Leland gave in to his own immediate temptation, and looked up and to the left. KENDALL'S. It was KENDALL'S COAL CO., INC.

The longer he stayed away from Port Smith, the clearer and more completely he saw it. A man lived fastened to his own set of details, landmarks by which he picked his way through the welter of a city. The landmarks for him had long since faded. He saw it too well to please the boy Eastern thinkers said was still inside him. Cutting from between the soot-blackened buildings downtown was a bright, unfinished expressway, ending in limp tentacles at the bay. Behind it stood a green glass tower, under construction, a derrick readied over the roof like a cannon. Spread about in no order were four pink-orange clumps of public housing. The nearest to him stood on the site of lower Joytown, its walls pressing over Lewis Park like the standards of a conqueror. The problem of Joytown had not been solved, it had turned out, only moved, and the park remained the same. There were fewer prostitutes, probably as much because of the postwar easing of moral restraints as anything, but the deviates had simply scattered to other neighborhoods. The worst were still in the park, and more women were being raped and roughed-up there every year. It could not be protected at night without a cop behind every bush. Herbert Davis would have none of that from the P.S.P.D. He wanted more park, if not with its own police force, then without it, and the

358

P.S.P.D. would have to cope with the problems created as best they could.

A year ago Leland had heard from his friend Warren Johnson that the current mayor of Port Smith was a drunk, and his wife was as well. It was the sort of story that people accepted with equanimity now, and Leland had almost forgotten it. He had to think that it was something that the egoists and finaglers accounted for in their calculations, like wind drift in the Norden bomb sight. It did not advance or retard their cause. Once they were started, nothing really mattered much.

"I remember it," the moonfaced guard said. "I was one of the first ones to him. It was over there." He pointed. "You can see the top of the roof where he started. Behind the rest rooms is where he fell." The racetrack and the empty parking lot let the wind blow so freely that their bodies rocked with it. The sensation reminded Leland of all the airports he had ever known. They were standing forty feet inside the hurricane fence surrounding the property, perhaps a quarter of a mile from the main building itself. The guard was on duty at the gate, and although there was no traffic, he did not want to leave his post. He was an employee of the agency that managed the track security. "There are five of us here the year round," he said. "In the summer we supervise the extra men. In the winter we go to the regular jobs. I could have another spot, but I like it here. One of the reasons I remember what happened so well is because, believe it or not, it's the only bit of that type of trouble we've had in the twenty-seven years I've been on the job. We have deaths every year from heart attacks, but you have that everywhere.

"Let's see. I was standing ten or fifteen feet to the left and behind the entrance to the men's room just before the start of the sixth race. It happened during the sixth; they were running it. In addition to us, the guards, there were only three or four people on this side of the grandstand. The rest were up watching the race. It wasn't a big crowd. The sixth race that day was a thirty-five-hundred-dollar claiming. We could hear the shouts from the crowd. Then over that noise I heard this cry, like, 'Oh!' and then, almost directly in front of my eyes, he hit the ground. I can't tell you what that sound was like. In spite of the shouting up front, I could hear it. If I ever hear it again behind me, I'll know what it is.

"From what I saw—and it happened fast—he came down head first. He didn't live a second after he hit. We covered the body with newspapers right away. The top of his head was crushed. You never saw anything like that. You couldn't make out a human expression on his face. We had a crowd as soon as the race was over. It was hard to get in and out. We did our best to break them up.

"At first, we didn't know what to do. I was so scared, I was shaking in my pants. I should have taken charge, but things aren't that simple. You know what I mean."

Leland nodded, drawing on his cigarette.

"I told somebody to get to a phone and we tried to clear the crowd. The blood soaked up some of the papers and made a puddle. It was ten minutes before anything happened. The man who went to call came back, and the track physician, the one they have for the jockeys, came around from the other end, the clubhouse. That's quite a distance. He took a quick look under the newspapers and that was that. The ambulance came around but he wouldn't let them touch him. He was right. The police had to have it just the way it was. I was the one who noticed that he had no shoes. 'Where's his shoes?' I said, and he, the doctor, told me to send someone up to the roof. I had to stay because I might be needed. By this time the horses in the seventh were going to the post. That's a half an hour right there. The cops showed up then. It was the change of shift for them. They had just come on duty when the call went in. The right time to pull a job in this county is at four-thirty, twelve-thirty, or eight-thirty in the morning. There are never any cops at those times of day.

"To get to the roof, the man had to go under the stand and climb back up to the last row. There's an iron ladder through a hatch. We figure your man went up there earlier when he could do it without drawing attention, during the fourth or fifth races. The press box is on the roof down at the clubhouse end, at the finish line, but if he stayed back to this side, he could keep out of sight. The man I sent up yelled down that the shoes were there and so were his keys and wallet. I said

360

not to touch them. He didn't hear me because of the noise under him in the stand, he said. He brought everything down with him. He just picked it up. The cops asked him where they had been, and he said that the shoes had been about twenty feet apart, but the wallet and keys had been close together, not near the edge, not near the shoes, either. Your man's socks had only a little bit of tar on them. It was ninety-two degrees that day and that tar was tacky. And hot. He couldn't have walked around in his socks much.

"We could all see money in the wallet, so the cops were careful. I suggested that they find out who he was, but they weren't going to open the wallet without supervision. I couldn't blame them. They had to wait for the medical examiner and a cameraman. There was the rush hour and then the jam leaving the track. The examiner couldn't get near here until twenty-five to seven. The cops called their sergeant and he came out with the captain. There was nine hundred dollars in the wallet. I signed an affadavit to that effect. They got his name right away, but they went through his papers right there. I didn't get a good look. Mostly business cards. One belonged to a building contractor.

"They had his telephone number, but they waited for the medical examiner. First they wanted to see if he had left any notes, they said. I thought that was strange, to tell the truth. What difference would a note make? They waited, just standing around, then the medical examiner showed up, the cameraman made his pictures—he needed a flash by then, because the shade of the bathrooms was across the body—and then the patrolman went to the office to make the call. The captain and the sergeant took off. That was about eight o'clock. I was here until nine, calling in my report to my boss."

Leland nodded. The caution of the police reeked of guilt. He had told Norma that the death of a man was taken seriously in this state, and the Clausen police had acted as if they had been only too aware of it. There was a reason behind their call to their superiors. Nothing had been taken from the wallet. Norma had it in her possession and its contents had seemed ordinary to her. But then, so had MacIver's books.

Leland wanted to get a better view of the death scene. The guard told him to go ahead. When he came back the guard stepped out of his little shack.

"Well, I hope I helped you," he said. "I know who you're working for, and there's no reason why she should have any questions about his death."

"How do you know who I'm working for?"

"His car. That's his car you've driving. You only have to see that car once to remember it."

It was something to bear in mind.

"I'm checking in, Flo," he said into the telephone. "What do you have for me?"

"I'm still working on the jobs you gave me. No word from Mike yet. Betty Kaminsky called here an hour ago. She wants to see you. I told her that I would call her back just as soon as I could."

"Fine. How did she sound when you told her I wasn't available?" That was the answer she had been taught to give.

"It's curious. She just said, 'I see.' I had to carry the conversation after that."

He hesitated, thinking of the expense involved in seeing her. "All right. Tell her I'll be out to see her any time she wants after eleven o'clock tomorrow. When I call later, you have the particulars for me."

"You'll tell me when to meet you at the airport?"

"Right. How is everything else?"

"Fine. Mr. Leland?"

"What is it, Flo?"

"About last night. Thank you. I cleaned up after us." She said it softly.

"Forget it. I haven't given it a thought."

"I just wanted to let you know that I haven't forgotten. Thank you."

"Get back to work. I don't want to hear any more about it." After what Karen had said, the matter did embarrass him. She had been right; he should not have done it.

At one o'clock he called Norma to tell her where he had been

362

and what he planned to do for the rest of the day. She gave her approval to the trip to Manitou to see Betty Kaminsky. He had no idea of what would come of it. He told Norma that he was going to have dinner with his mother and that he would not return to Collegeville Road until eight-thirty.

There were two more banks to cover. He had been to one already, giving a story about an insurance investigation. There had been no trouble. If someone wanted identification, there were people at Manitou Life who would protect him. Partly because of the banks' early closing, he had scheduled his appointment with Enid Alma for three-thirty. She had not found work. After their telephone conversation, Leland could understand why. He reckoned that he would be done with her in less than an hour, allowing him time to see MacIver's old apartment. He hoped to find the janitor who had talked so freely to the investigators from Manitou two and a half or three years ago.

When he was done for the day he called his mother again as she had asked him to do, and what she had anticipated had occurred: his father had come home and had gone to bed. She didn't want to leave him alone; when he woke up, he would be hungry. She asked Joe if he wanted her to make dinner for him, and he said that had not been the idea. She asked if he was angry, and he told her no. She wanted to know if he was all right. He sounded as if something was wrong.

He said he was fine and would call her before the end of the week. He told her that Karen and Steffie could be coming down and he might ask her to look after Steffie—he didn't know. It confused her. He said that he might be back in Manitou himself by Saturday; but that was not what he had tried to say originally, and he knew it. He let it go. Before he said goodbye he asked her to tell his father that it was going well—he would understand.

The sky was darkening again as Leland came out of the stationery store from which he had called. The logical thing, he supposed, was to go back to Norma's, but he did not want to do that. He was not ready to talk to her. He got in the big shiny car he had left parked at a fire hydrant—no ticket. MacIver had not had the summons bug when he had driven this car. There was nothing funny about it or about anything related to MacIver anymore; but something seemed to have happened in the course of this day, and Leland felt loose, giddy, and disjointed. Not the least of it was the cold, working on the backs of his hands. He had scratched his left hand until it had opened up. There were two small spots of dried blood now, surrounded by a swath of white cracked skin.

He drove from the foot of Bay Slope around the bay and across downtown toward the Point—one of the places MacIver and Norma had visited the night before MacIver had died. Leland had not forgotten. He had no business there; he was getting lost. He had done it after the war when he had needed it; he had done it in Manitou when he had been living alone. The logical thing was to call Karen, but he would tell her what had happened only to have to repeat it to Norma later.

The traffic thinned as he came out on the other side of the city. The Point was public land, parks and a long, curving drive past the marshland that had been reclaimed for the International Airport, and then around to the north and along the sea. The shore was rocky and during the days the parking lots were crowded with fishermen's cars; in the spring and summer nights the lots were filled with the cars of lovers. There were jokes about that. Once, while they had had the LaSalle, he and Karen had come down: once had been plenty. He had wound up with his feet sticking out the open window and the top of his head jammed against the armrest of the opposite door.

He parked the car in an empty lot near the north end, turned the heater up full, then killed the motor and sat quietly. There was a heavy breeze that caused the car to shake; the breeze came over from the bay and blotted out the crashing of the sea. He did not think about the case. Slumping down in the seat, he put his head against the cold glass of the window and smoked another cigarette. His arms and legs went faintly numb, the pre-sleep sensation, but he fought it enough to stay aware of his surroundings. He thought again that this had been MacIver's car, but it was like looking at a picture of the idea rather than feeling it. It did not matter. He could feel himself trying to reconstruct MacIver's sensations and emotions—that waste-

364

ful, misleading trick. He tried to empty his mind, but things—a dozen little things, some far from his business in Port Smith—kept pressing in, leaving him uneasy and no better for having tried to rest.

Another car rolled into the lot. The headlights swept through the Cadillac, then went out as the car continued toward the shoreside curb. Leland sat up, jolted; then, even as he realized that the lights-out was a romantic's courtesy, he watched the car come to a stop a hundred yards off, at the other end of the lot. No one got out, which was normal. Leland started the Cadillac and turned it around. A quarter of a mile up the highway he swung into the next lot. He waited, lights out. Nothing came by for fifteen minutes. It was time for dinner. He would eat at a diner he knew that was near headquarters. The food was substantial and cheap, and at this hour there would be a place to park.

Norma opened the door, brushing her hair back. "Oh. I fell asleep waiting. Wendell called. I told him when you'd be back."

"Any idea of what he wanted?"

"No. We chatted. He likes you." She pushed her feet into a pair of slippers. "Would you like some coffee? I have to have it to wake up. Come on." She shuffled toward the kitchen. "All this sleeping is supposed to be good for me, but I tell you, I feel awful. Did your wife worry about her legs?"

"All the time. Just keep your feet up and you'll have no trouble."

"I'm getting a backache, too," she said. "Don't sit down. I want to get those sofa pillows under me."

She carried the cups to the living room and he held them while she made herself comfortable. Being careful in his choice of words, he told her that the racetrack guard had been all but an eyewitness. The guard had given a plausible account of the delay in notifying her, which itself was unacceptable.

"I didn't go near the courthouse. It would be a mistake to see any of the official records before knowing what made the patrolmen call their superiors. We don't want to work in the dark. If you think Wendell is being evasive you won't believe what these people are capable of. You said that the wallet was returned intact, but you can see now that maybe it wasn't. We'd better go through it again on the chance of finding something that you wouldn't recognize the first time.

"We didn't get a break from the track employees. They mishandled evidence, disturbing the things on the roof. In spite of what the guard heard and saw, there could have been another man up there, back from the edge and out of sight. He could have made his way on the roof to the emergency door at the back of the press box on top of the clubhouse. If he had run fast enough, he could have made it through while the sixth race was coming down to the finish. In that way he would have been unobserved. For the same reason, and one other, I don't think that there could have been more than one man. Two or three would have been seen or heard as they took the two steps from the press box door to the stairs to the clubhouse, even at the conclusion of a race. The other reason is that I'm certain your husband would not have stepped onto the roof if he had seen more than one man up there. His view from the top of the ladder was unobstructed. I don't think he could have been forced by two or more men to ascend the ladder—that would have been noticed. One man, if any. We may never know if the stupidity of the track security men helped him get away with murder.

"There was no robbery, we know that, but by the account of the way his things were found, there could have been a struggle. At the banks, there was no evidence of withdrawals for blackmail payments. There is the possibility that someone contacted him for the purpose of blackmail and that the first meeting, the one up there, went wrong." Leland took the chance to light a cigarette. He was not going to state the other, stronger, alternative: that her husband, unencumbered by shoes and the items in his pocket, had waited for a would-be blackmailer with the intention of killing him. Leland had no evidence; it just seemed as if MacIver, who had concealed so many things, could have planned to conceal a murder. He could have lost a brief struggle and the other man could have blundered upon his successful escape. It explained even better than the official verdict why the shoes, wallet, and keys had been on the roof, and why they had been

366

in the positions in which they had been found. MacIver had put them all down neatly, but the shoes had been kicked aside in the silent, seconds-long fight. The exclamation MacIver had uttered could have been in his surprise at having lost. It was tantalizing. It answered all the questions the evidence asked. It felt good on MacIver—within his capacities. Yet Leland had no proof, and in the lack of it, his instincts made him keep his mind clear for the real questions. Why had the police called their superiors? Why were MacIver's books in code? Why were his movements so difficult to trace? Why did so many people, his wife among them, know so little about him?

"We're going to have to wait for my partner's report before we have the picture of the progression of your husband's assets," Leland said. "His bank accounts fluctuated wildly, withdrawals followed by larger deposits. In spite of the losses he took at the track during the two months I examined, he was able to add to his accounts. My partner will have to trace your husband's transactions on the stock market. At the time of his death his accounts came to less than thirty percent of his gross assets. Although he prepared for death with a will, he had not prepared his estate. Also, there are the insurance claims you lost.

"He could have paid outright for the cars, the house, and the furniture, assuming that liquid assets of thirty percent had been his practice. His loans were for short periods; he always paid them more quickly than he had to, and he made certain to get the interest refunds to which he was entitled. On the Cadillac it came to less than twenty dollars. He waited in the office while they cleared it for him. They didn't like it, but it was obvious he earned their respect. I asked them how he handled his cash, if they had noticed; they told me what you told me yesterday: he folded it in half and put it in his right hip pocket, without a clip. They were used to seeing him carrying several hundred dollars that way, and sometimes a thousand or more. If he was carrying five thousand that Saturday morning as that neighbor reported, that was unusual. Why did he carry so much cash anyway? Why was he carrying so much on that particular day? You can see how much we need the report from Mike. With the information in the insurance folder, maybe we can piece it all together. Do you understand?"

"Yes."

"There's something else. He always carried his cash in his right hip pocket. When they brought the things down from the roof, his money was in his wallet. Maybe there was more in his pocket and it was stolen by the police, but I don't think so. If he had carried five thousand in his pocket, he wouldn't have hesitated to carry nine hundred the same way. No, I think he transferred his money from his pocket to his wallet. It seems like something a man would do before he commits suicide—it goes with the wallet and the keys on the roof. But he might have done it for an entirely different reason. The important thing is, it's indicative of something unusual. He prepared for something."

"Let's not speculate," she said.

"That's the idea." He told her of the interview with Enid Alma, which had been fruitless. The woman seemed to be a case of arrested development with a disturbingly strict and primitive personal code. She had said that MacIver had learned to respect her feelings about "swear words." Leland had asked her what she considered offensive. "Hell" and "damn"? Yes. She had not been willing to say them. These were things which Norma had heard about, vaguely. Her husband had had a wide vocabulary and she was a little surprised now that he had endured someone that straitlaced and stupid.

Leland said, "Apparently he needed someone in the office to pick up the phone and type the letters. There wasn't that much work for her. A year ago he told her not to come in before ten-thirty."

"Really? Why, he left before nine—I told you what time he left the last day. Eight-thirty. Why should he do that, leave himself without a secretary for an hour and a half? He didn't have to. He didn't even have to go to the office until ten-fifteen or later. He could have been anywhere."

"Like where?"

She sat forward. "I don't know!"

"Keep your wits about you. What we said about other women still goes. It's a ridiculous hour to conduct an affair. Miss Alma is an insufferable person. Perhaps he couldn't fire her and knew he worked better when she wasn't around. He had those books that no one understands. She knew nothing about the items in his desk. She was told to stay away from there and she did."

Out in the hall, the telephone rang. "That's Wendell, for you. Go ahead and take it."

It rang again. He got up. "Are you all right?"

"Yes." She said, "He was doing something. We know that now."

Leland reached the telephone on the fourth ring. "Hello?"

"Joe? Wendell. I want to apologize for my behavior last night. I was upset and lost my perspective."

"No, the pleasure was mine. I had a fine time."

"I see. You don't have to talk. This has been on my mind all day. I let my concern for her welfare get the better of me. It wasn't until you were gone that I realized it."

"I didn't have a bad day, all in all."

"How did you make out?"

"Oh." He had been taken literally. "Not bad. You can't always tell right away."

"That's something I should be able to understand. Were you able to speak with your wife about the party?"

"Not yet. It has to be up to her. You know that."

"Don't put any importance on it," Roberts said. "Maybe you and I can get together tomorrow night."

"I'll have to see," Leland said.

"Let me know. Good night."

"Good night."

Norma watched him return. "What will be up to me?"

"Not you, my wife. Whether we'll make the party Friday night."

"Oh, she'll have a good time—" She watched him as he sat down again. Karen and Roberts had known each other. She was wondering if she had done something wrong.

"It's not important," he said.

She put her cup on the table and leaned back. She looked weary. "When I mentioned Wendell's name in your office Monday, you didn't react at all. He's better than anyone I've ever known at concealing the truth. I've seen him listen to the most outrageous lies without flinching. I don't have any choice but to believe what you say about what went on between you last night. Your wife knew him and you didn't?"

Leland nodded. "I wouldn't have dragged her into a lie."

"This is a complicated, confusing business for me. At every turn you discover another lie that Colin told me. Wendell is lying. How do I know who is telling the truth?"

"If I'm not, I'm stealing from a pregnant widow."

She smiled. "You would be, wouldn't you? We were talking about something before the telephone rang. Do you really think it was the way you said?"

"Not adultery? Yes. We're very interested in what he was doing in that hour, but all things considered—the hour, the fact that Enid Alma would not have worked for him if she had had to take calls from a girl friend—I've decided not to give other women very much thought. You shouldn't, either."

"I'll try." She looked at the ceiling. "I don't understand about your wife and Wendell. Maybe I'm dense or something. Was she under his care?"

"No, no. Forget it. She went to Jefferson, you know." The idea came too late to be effective. "Just—forget it."

"I'm sorry."

"Okay. If you get your husband's wallet, I'll tell you what I learned from the janitor of the building where he lived when you were going out."

She did not take long. He put the wallet on the table. "Your confidence in your judgments will be restored very quickly. According to the janitor, you were the last of many female guests your husband had. So you were right about that. The janitor saw or heard them as they went in and out."

"That's right, he lived downstairs."

"The janitor was interviewed three years ago by an insurance investigator and gave the same information—even mentioned you. I wanted to hear if he ever knew any of the others. He saw four or five, but never said hello to any but you. When you came along, you were the only one. Your husband didn't see the others when he started seeing you. That's all there is to that." He reached for the wallet, not looking at her. He did not want to encourage her to pursue this.

Actually, the janitor had told him that there had been two women before Norma whom he had seen often, and one fairly regularly for a period of many months. Leland saw no reason for inflicting this information on Norma. The janitor had no real knowledge of any of the women, including her. He had been able to say that there had been no one steady in the months just before she had come along. Leland did not feel that she had to be told even this. He wanted to keep her in the habit of thinking only of what she knew.

The wallet contained a picture of her, a photographer's portrait in which she wore a light, tailored suit, MacIver's most recent driver's license, without citations, a Social Security card, an identification card giving his last address and Norma as the person to notify in case of an accident, two postage stamps stuck back to back and, stuffed deep in a pocket, a small piece of paper on which was typewritten, "The more fun had, the more people killed." Norma had not seen it before. To Leland it looked like a gag saying MacIver had picked up from one of his clients. Businessmen loved to pass around such junk.

There was a calendar, a library card, a Red Cross card dating from MacIver's college days certifying him as an Intermediate swimmer. There were no business cards. None at all. Leland returned the wallet to Norma and told her what the track guard had said about the building contractor's card.

"There were others, too," Leland said. "The police recognized something and the decision was made to clean out all the cards. They palmed them. It looks like a precautionary move—they didn't want to connect someone with a suicide."

"There could have been a note," she said.

"The guard saw it all when the wallet was opened. No notes."

"Isn't this something we have to report?"

"We have only the guard's testimony. He would have to be willing to give it under oath. His employers could advise against it.

They have to live in Clausen County. We're going to have to wait and see what it all means."

"We're not getting any answers. It's terribly draining on me. What about that little slip of paper with the joke on it?"

"It's not worth thinking about. We would be wasting our time if we tracked it down."

"If he had been saving it for me, he forgot. It's a little grim now." She stacked the empty cups and saucers. "Is there anything else?"

"No. I'll be leaving first thing tomorrow to fly back to Manitou. Lunch with Betty Kaminsky. I'll be down here again by four o'clock."

"Take the car and leave it at the airport. I won't be needing it. Do you want anything? I'm going to bed, if you don't mind. I'll probably read; I just want to get under the covers."

"Okay. Good night, kid."

She stopped at the door. "Did you call your wife yet? If you plan to, I wish you'd do it here. I'll be upstairs, and honestly, I haven't got the strength to try to listen in."

"All right, I'll call from here. Good night."

"Good night, Joe."

He listened to her in the kitchen. In a few minutes the light went out, and then he heard her on the stairs. He rubbed the back of his hand. The warmth of the house had eased some of the sting, but there was an itching now that told him that it would split wide open if he did not put something on it. Maybe he could find something in the medicine cabinet of the hall bathroom. It was taking a conscious effort to keep him from going at the thing with his fingernails.

He had to try to keep what he knew about the case in the front of his mind. The things he had learned since he had begun to see people pushed at what Norma had told him; the papers in the insurance file, and the souvenir book. They were not less true for what he had heard from the witnesses. MacIver's income and the behavior of the Clausen police said that he had come far and fast in the years since he had arranged his divorce. Probably Leland and his own friends would not have touched him, for there was a stink about him, but there was this home, his marriage, and his war record, which all of them would have admired.

"Steffie? It's Daddy. How's everything going?"

"All right. You almost caught me in the bathtub. Mommy won't be home until ten-thirty. Mrs. Robertson called during dinner. Do you know about her?"

"Yes. Oh, yes."

"She had to have Mommy at her meeting. Mommy was mad enough to scream. She's going to be even madder when she hears that you called while she was out. Are you going to call back?"

"I don't think so, honey. I'm tired myself and she may not be home until eleven o'clock. Will you give her a message? I'll be up home tomorrow during the middle of the day and I'll call her then. Tell her I'm sorry I missed her. I'm fine and everything is going well. That will mean something to her. Now, what's new with you?"

"Mommy said that the trip to Canada is off."

"I think so. I'm sorry. This came up." He could not tell her that she might be coming to Port Smith if Karen had not mentioned it.

"Do you think we'll be able to go next weekend?"

"I don't know. We haven't talked about it. And the weather will close in soon. I wouldn't kid you about it, I want to go as much as you do. Do you have that door locked?"

"Oh, yes."

"You love me? I love you."

"I love you," she said. "Are you all right?"

"Sure."

"You sound lonely," she said.

He had been worried about her loneliness; that was what she had heard in his voice, but her comment seemed to hit a mark.

She said, "You'll be home for a while tomorrow, is that it?"

Her thoughts had jumped ahead to a check of his message. "That's it," he said. "Good night, sweetheart."

He was getting into bed when Norma knocked on the door. He asked her to wait, then he asked her to come in.

She had put on the lumpy housecoat and her hair was pinned up, covered by a kerchief.

"I started to wonder if you would give me your unofficial, private opinion about what you've learned so far." She sat down at the foot of the bed. "Now, in the pajamas you wear every night, you won't be held responsible for what you say."

He took his cigarettes from the night table. The furniture here was a red maple, neat and cheerful, but somehow—on a par with most guest rooms—less than the hostess' best effort. He said, "I don't know. I just don't know."

"I suppose a lot depends on how your partner does with the books and papers."

"Your husband used codes for a reason."

"What do you think Betty Kaminsky will have to say?"

"I have my fingers crossed."

"Do you really think Colin was faithful?"

"Yes. To you, yes."

"But he wasn't to his first wife. I'm not so much."

"Norma, you're digging yourself into a hole. You'll have to be patient. This was thrust upon you, but for your own sake, you have to stand up to it. You have a long life ahead. Don't let this wreck it."

"I always wanted to be married. It's all I ever wanted."

"I know."

"I can feel his baby kicking me. He'll never see his own child. I cry for him. I know I have to start all over, but I'm nowhere near solid enough. You've had your bad times. How did you get through them?"

"They were never as bad as what you're living with. At least I thought I knew why things had gone badly."

"You thought. But that was all you needed, wasn't it? An explanation? As long as you had a reason why you were there, you were all right?"

"I think so."

"You know how badly I need a reason," she said.

"I'm learning, kid."

In her distress she smiled a little smile, mischievous, game. "Can I ask you something personal?"

"Sure."

"You've always loved your wife, haven't you?"

"It's complicated. I mean that. It wouldn't be fair to you or her to try to explain."

"You've never been with anyone but her, though."

He was stunned. "Are you really asking me?"

She put her hands on her knees. "I think I'm telling." Her attitude was so bright and childlike that he wanted to laugh.

"One. There has been one. And for a while I loved her, too."

She looked away, smiling wistfully. "I don't know whether I like it or not."

"Would you like me to say that if I had known you then, it would have been different?"

"Yes and no. I don't know. I am digging myself into a hole. Are we going to be friends?"

"Yes, I think so."

"Come downstairs. I'll make you a sandwich."

"No, that's all right." It was after ten-thirty. He would want to call Karen but it would confuse her and she would worry about what was happening. He could not call, which would make him a liar.

"I'm hungry," Norma said. "Watch me eat. Just keep me company."

He was wide awake now; if he stayed up here he would have to worry about his sense of perspective, if not his ability to reason. "All right. You step outside while I pull on a pair of pants. If you had told me in Manitou that I would be staying here, I would have brought a robe."

She got up, laughing.

"I guess I should feel a little stupid," he said.

"It's not that. Before I was married the men I knew took every chance to exhibit themselves. They tried to be subtle, but the effect was always the same. I was supposed to be wowed."

He was sitting up. As a kid he had done the same thing with Karen. "What about your husband?"

"Him, too, in the beginning."

"Outside," he said.

She made a little bow before she closed the door. "I'll be in the kitchen."

He drew on his cigarette. She had laughed at herself, and she had been all but convincing in the covering-up. Roberts was right about her but she was more right about him. Roberts thought she was stupid. Leland was still enjoying the idea when he started down the stairs.

CHAPTER SEVENTEEN

■ ■

DRIVING INTO MANITOU, FLORENCE HAD LITTLE TO TELL HIM. MIKE
had called from the apartment to report that he was still working and,
he thought, making some progress. A memorandum would have to be
drafted; there were too many details for a verbal communication. He
had instructed Florence to tell Leland that he could understand now
how MacIver had been able to add a double column of figures as they
had been read to him.

The Manitou Credit Bureau had not had a file on Mrs. MacIver.
Florence had called the banks in Canby and then the savings and loan
associations—only one of the latter was carrying an account in Mrs.
MacIver's name.

"Manitou has a file on her husband," she told Leland. "They
were supposed to call me from the warehouse yesterday afternoon,
but they didn't, so I called them again this morning, and they told me
to send someone over at two o'clock this afternoon."

"Okay, we'll just have to wait until we see the file. Her husband's estate has provided her with an income and we'll find out from
the copy of the trust agreement in the file who the trustee is. Probably
one of the downtown banks. What about the houses?"

"The Canby house is hers outright. I've had to wait on her
previous address."

"You may get that in the insurance file, too," Leland said.
"What else has been going on?"

"There's been nothing from Florida. The subject has been staying close to his hotel. We received a check from Schwartzwald for a

hundred dollars less than our fee. Mike dictated a letter over the telephone to the effect that we were accepting the check as partial payment and would expect the balance by return mail. Mike told me to tell you that he would handle it—that it's nothing for you to get angry about."

"What about that custody case? I liked what I saw of that woman."

"Nothing. Nothing's happened."

"Good." He looked out the window. Two inches of snow had fallen on Manitou, light and wet. The snow clung to the roofs and ledges and was shoveled from the sidewalks in tarnished little heaps. The air smelled clear and fresh. It looked clear, so brilliant it was not possible to miss the difference in the air. Here you could feel healthy, alert, and eager. The atmosphere in Port Smith was something that had to be overcome.

At the office he tried to get Karen on the telephone, but she was between stops at schools, en route to High View. He asked the secretary if Mrs. Leland would be available in the afternoon. She was scheduled to attend a pageant at a junior high on Clifford Heights. He said that he had no message, and hung up.

Florence had made his appointment with Betty Kaminsky for noon in the lobby of the Manitou Hotel. Leland made sure that he was on time. Betty Kaminsky came in five minutes later, and for a moment he did not want to believe it was her. She had been sick on Tuesday, but improved health alone could not account for such a change. Part of it was her clothing, which was well made and expensive and enhanced her red hair and very fair skin. Another part was her height: although her legs did not seem quite so long, she looked taller than he had reckoned on Tuesday, as tall as Karen. Her illness, the robe, slippers, and so on, had worked to confuse him. On Tuesday she had come downstairs in spite of herself, to satisfy her curiosity. And perhaps there had been more to it. Her husband had mishandled the situation and misjudged her. It could have put some of the tiredness in her eyes. Now she looked calm and self-possessed.

She did not see him right away and he took his time crossing the lobby. She was wearing a hat, which he wanted to regard as an anachronism, but Karen had told him not long ago that hats were in fashion again. This was a small, round, flat-topped thing with a bit of net attached, the whole business a light, minted green, lighter than her medium green coat. The loose ankle-length robe she had worn on Tuesday had given only hints of the curves of her figure, Leland was learning now. As he came up she was unbuttoning her coat; she was wearing a green wool suit with three large buttons down the front. It was a tailored suit, very snugly fit, and no man would notice the buttons or color for long. Maybe she was used to men staring, or maybe staring men had helped make her the jumpy, unhealthy woman she was. It was something he never would have had the chance to learn if she had not called his office. Norma would not want to hear it, but he thought that it was something to know. The presentation Betty Kaminsky was making today compelled Leland to think that what was beneath the strong will he had seen already was a desire to be tenderly but firmly handled. He did not want to think it was in his imagination, but there was really nothing he could point out. She did not seem to fit the role—there was still a certain reserve, a coolness—but she had him thinking she could be had.

She turned to him.

"Hello," he said. "You look well. Are you feeling better?"

"Yes. Oh, yes. Were you in Port Smith yesterday? I'm sorry to bother you. I feel awfully guilty."

"Don't. I wouldn't be here if I didn't think you could help." She wore a light lipstick. Her makeup was sparingly applied, neat, a mite proper, and attractive. He saw that it contributed to her air of vulnerability. Her perfume, now, too: something mild, different. "Did you pick this place for the restaurant? I don't care where we eat."

She looked around, her hair tossing on her shoulders. "The important thing is the quiet. I'm not hungry. After a cold it takes me days to regain my appetite."

"You drink a lot of tea," he said.

She smiled. "You remembered. No, I drink tea all the time."

The hotel was old-fashioned, plush and potted palms, the style from which the old movie palaces had been derived. Perhaps Mac-

Iver's mother patronized the restaurant and her former daughter-in-law had learned of it from her.

The restaurant was nearly empty: a middle-aged couple by a window overlooking the avenue, three businessmen in the most distant corner. The room needed paint and new flooring. By modern standards the tables were too big and the aisles too wide. There were three waiters in sight, and the youngest, a hawk-faced man in his forties with shining slicked-down hair, motioned them to a table in the center section.

Betty Kaminsky said, "I didn't think you were the type to remember things. What I've seen of your wife makes me think that she's not one who cares about having her birthdays remembered, or anniversaries."

"She's not, but I am," he said. "I remember everything. Tell me, is this the lunch crowd?"

"No, no. There'll be more. You remember everything?"

"I can tell you what you were wearing Tuesday. Your husband, too."

She smiled. "You gave that and took it away. That's like your wife. When she speaks before a group she plays with them, pulls and pushes. She's not afraid of people."

Leland enjoyed hearing it. The waiter returned with the water pitcher, fine thin glass. Leland asked him, "What's good today?

"Everything, sir. Everything is good."

"Thanks. Give us a minute."

"He was a big help," she said when he was gone.

"I wanted to know where we stood."

"Did he do anything when we came in? I didn't notice anything."

"There was nothing. I didn't like his face."

"You made a decision on the basis of that?"

"I checked," he said. He gave her a friendly smile. "I did, didn't I?"

"Yes, I suppose so. I don't have the courage for that."

"You really mean nerve," he said.

380

"No. Well, maybe I do. Anyway, you're not afraid of people either."

"Sometimes I am, Mrs. Kaminsky."

"Betty."

"Betty. My name is Joe. Sometimes I'm even afraid of dead people."

"You've done better than that. Why?"

"Okay. Your first husband killed himself, or at least it's what everybody, including you, seems to think. There's no apparent reason for it to have happened. What I'm afraid of is coming home empty—not finding out why."

"I see. You're hoping I can shed some light on his death. I hadn't seen him in six years. All I can tell you is what happened until then. If that helps you, all right, but I don't know how it could."

"It might."

"You mean, pieces that would fall into a pattern? I don't think so."

"I don't think so, either," he said. "We'd better see what we want to eat."

He looked over the menus at her. She wore her hair combed above her ears, letting it fall down on the back of her neck and shoulders in a style he wanted to think was dated. It wasn't; it was a style for a little girl. Probably there were times she pulled her hair back tightly and rolled it into a bun, which would make her look more her age; but she looked very young, younger than Norma—again.

When she raised her eyes he asked what she wanted to order. She had not decided. He said he did not want a drink; he was going to have a small steak and salad. That would be all right with her. He beckoned to the waiter.

She opened her purse and took out her cigarettes. "May I ask you something?"

"Go ahead."

"Is she pregnant? His widow. I thought of it after you left and Murray said that you wouldn't tell him. With that kind of an answer, I've been thinking of it since."

"It's something I'm not privileged to discuss, Betty."

"I see." She was quiet a moment. "I made up my mind about this—meeting you—yesterday. I thought I would tell Murray last night. I couldn't. I didn't want him to worry." She took a drink of water. "I know some things about Colin that he didn't know himself. I thought I wanted to tell you, but now that I'm here, I'm scared. I mean scared. If it were any worse, I'd be shaking."

He wanted to wait her out.

"If you have to see us again, I'd be grateful if you didn't mention it to Murray. It's the first sneaky thing I've done."

Leland said, "You have my word, although I won't call it sneaky."

"Murray and I are closer than many couples. It started out of necessity and we depend on it now. I know he would be hurt."

She still didn't know that her husband had told him anything. Kaminsky had felt guilty about the violation of confidence, too. Perhaps the violations and the guilt as precisely defined their marriage as their expressions of mutual need.

Now she said, "How do you get along with your brothers and sisters?"

"I don't have any."

"Neither do I. You give the impression of coming from a large family. Does your wife?"

"There's only one of her, too."

"That makes four of us—or made. Murray has two brothers and a sister. Colin was an only child. You and your wife get along with people better than he did, or I do. If I knew how you do it, I might be better off."

"I met my wife at a party, in the center of a crowd of people. That's the way she's always been. As for me, my parents always had people in, neighbors, friends, my father's friends on the force. What was outside the family came in, and we went out. It was all of a piece. Do you understand? I played stickball in the schoolyard down the block every afternoon for five years, until I outgrew it. The neighborhood mattered almost as much as the family."

The waiter was coming. She seemed to like what Leland had

said. There had been no evasion and he did not think she could help seeing that he had tried to win her trust. The waiter put down the food, repeating the order as Leland had given it to him.

"Anything else, sir?"

"Not right now."

She watched the waiter go. "I like the way you talk to him."

Leland smiled. "I don't know why."

"You never look at him."

"I said I didn't like his face."

She blushed a little. "That's not it. You expect him to hop to his job and get away from here."

"Don't you?"

"Yes, but—I don't know."

"Your husband doesn't do it that way," he said.

"Murray goes over everything twice. He doesn't take restaurants in his stride."

"What about MacIver?"

"It's hard to remember. You're all business—you want me to stay on the job." She smiled. "We rarely ate out and when we did, we didn't go to places where you could expect good service.

"I almost never met him," she said after a moment. "When I was a junior at Jefferson my father had a very severe heart attack. I wanted to quit school and go to work, but they wouldn't let me. My parents worked together in a grocery they owned and their one ambition was to get me through college.

"Colin was the one in the hurry when we were going out. Don't misunderstand, I'd never felt anything as intense before. I didn't need much of a push on my level. My father was dying, and my mother—it's hard to believe if you haven't seen it—didn't care about living anymore. My parents had lived the same way for thirty years and suddenly it was over. All of us knew it."

It was clear that she was not going to continue without encouragement from him. "You're raising questions. I don't want to be unpleasant, but if MacIver was the one who wanted to marry originally, how was he able to say at the time you were breaking up that you would remarry quickly? How could he be sure enough of that to offer you a lot of money to stay single? You said that it was a dare. I've had indications that it was a very expensive dare for him to make."

"It wasn't just a financial arrangement or a dare, it was an attack on me. In a sense, he had me beaten no matter what I did. Following the course I did, I forfeited the money and vindicated his judgment of me. But as long as I stayed single, the four hundred dollars came in unmarked envelopes—not ever a return address on them. He bought bank checks, wrapped them in plain, cheap paper, and mailed them to me. There was never a covering letter, a greeting, a question about how I was doing. It was an abuse, after the years we had spent together, and as long as I accepted the checks, I submitted to it."

"I don't fully understand," Leland said.

"I know you don't. Your appearance the other day brought back many of the things about Colin that I had thought I had succeeded in pushing away. There's no success in that. You have to go through and come out on the other side. I didn't really want to do that with Murray five years ago." She looked at Leland. "I really haven't slept since Tuesday—you know, a few minutes here and there, a nap after lunch. I'm not afraid of death, I expect it, but since Tuesday, with all these things churning up, and not wanting to hurt Murray again by mentioning them, I've been having some terrible thoughts. I'll get close to sleeping and I'll think about the way we were at the beginning, Colin and I, and then, all of a sudden, I'll think about making love to him, the physical thing, and the fact that he's dead, both things together, and it's as if he starts dying in my arms. When my father died and the mortuary people moved him from his bed to the stretcher—I had to watch though they told me not to—his head fell back and his mouth opened. You've seen dead men. I feel Colin's dead face pressed against mine. It happens when I'm on the edge of sleep. I know it means that I'm trying to blame myself, probably not for his death, but for the failure of our marriage. Was he happy in his second marriage?"

"I don't know what you want to hear," Leland said. "My opinion doesn't mean much."

"Just tell me the truth. Please."

"As nearly as I can tell, he was very happy. It's one of the things that's so strange about his death. I think you should know that he didn't talk about you. He tried to get his first marriage behind him. Everything I've learned about his second marriage tells me he was very happy indeed, and very much in love."

"Surgery without anesthetic," she said. "I was trying to flatter myself."

"You said you knew things about him that he didn't know himself. What did you have in mind?"

"Maybe you know them already," she said.

"Try me."

"We were on our honeymoon when I told him that he was much neater about himself than most men. I was going on what I had seen of my father. Colin took excellent care of his clothes and his grooming. He was meticulous—I don't mean fussy. It pleased him to know he was that sort of person. It was our honeymoon and it pleased him to know that something he hadn't thought of made me proud of him."

"His recent pictures show that he hadn't changed his habits," Leland said.

"I'm wasting your time," she said.

"There are questions I want to ask you. This has you upset and you've drawn a blank for the moment. I'd like you to tell me about the way he drove a car."

"I beg your pardon?"

"The way he drove. In the time he was married to you, he picked up more than forty traffic and parking tickets. What can you tell me about them?"

She was staring at him, unbelieving. "Who told you that?"

"The police of Manitou and Port Smith. There's no question of it."

"I remember two parking tickets. He gave them to me and I bought money orders for them. Are you sure you have the same man?"

"Absolutely."

"He handled the money. I wouldn't have known if he had gotten

385

all those tickets or not. He did such a good job of handling our money that I never questioned him. He could have paid the fines without letting me know."

"He did. How did he drive?"

"Fast. He could shift gears by just stabbing at the clutch pedal, not pushing all the way down. He liked to drive and he kept testing his abilities."

"I want to talk about money, Betty, where he got it and how he saved it. Did he borrow from his mother, for example. Give me the figures, if you can recall them."

"We were both working. When my parents died, we couldn't sell the store. There were no takers because it had been closed awhile and there was a supermarket going up on the next block. We disposed of the stock and the fixtures and used that money and their insurances to pay their medical expenses and funerals. His mother gave us a thousand dollars as a wedding present. So we started out with over a thousand dollars in the bank and the incomes from our two jobs, let's see, sixty and twenty-five dollars a week, plus his GI Bill money. We had to finish paying for the car, which he had bought before we met, and the usual running expenses. He wouldn't touch the thousand his mother had given us for more than a year. It was a question of getting us saving regularly first.

"He bought stock with it, after he had studied the market. It scared me, I remember, and I think we made seventy-five dollars in four and a half months. I couldn't keep up with it, so I left it to him.

"The first year we lived in a furnished place, a room and a half. From my parents' apartment we had taken some things, and that summer we stored them with friends while we went to stay with his mother. We had my teaching salary coming in. What we lost from his job we saved on rent. He needed the two months' rest, anyway." She paused.

"Tuesday I told you that we saved steadily. It's true, but we really did it in a series of jumps. We didn't pay his mother rent—we bought most of the food, but we would have spent that—and we banked all the surplus, the rent, utilities, and so forth. We used the car as much as possible for our entertainment. The first two springs we had big income tax refunds. Colin did the taxes and he deducted everything he could. He was very good at that. I tried to help the first year, but it just depressed me. He took the time to read all the booklets.

"By the time we broke up, even though he hadn't worked full-time most of those years, we had twenty-five hundred dollars in the bank."

"He gave you four thousand," Leland said.

"He cashed in his insurance and borrowed the rest from his mother."

He had to be careful with his phrasing. "What did your attorney think of the terms of the settlement?"

"It was all right with him. He had nothing to do. It was worked out before we went to the lawyers. It was an easy fee for my lawyer."

"MacIver pay for that?"

"Everything."

"What was his mother's reaction to the purpose of the loan?"

"She called to tell me that she would not have given him the money—two thousand dollars—she felt that she had been duped. I was miserable at the time and she followed her sympathies. I don't know if she hoped for a reconciliation or not, but—" Her voice trailed off.

Leland nodded. Of course none of it checked out, because MacIver had not cashed his policies. Nor could Leland remember seeing any notations of loans on their cash value. He had to put it out of his thoughts, for if MacIver had hidden assets from his first wife—money she had worked with him to earn—she might try to make a claim on it now. The settlement agreement had been based on fraud. There was one more side of it that he felt he could explore safely. "Can you tell me if his mother ever said that she had been repaid the two thousand?"

"Yes. She mentioned it once, perhaps two years after the divorce. My remarriage probably helped him get the money together, but neither of us—Mrs. MacIver or I—were willing to discuss it at the time."

This was another thing Norma would not want to hear, and it was so ugly that Leland had to think of Dr. Roberts' warning to him, but the other aspects drew him away from that. MacIver's motivation, for one, on which Leland had to reserve judgment until he had the figures and dates. At the least he would be able to offer Norma more than a guess about how her husband had made his start. Leland did not know how old the papers in Mike's possession were, but it seemed safe to assume that MacIver had not brought over the detailed records of his first marriage, no matter what they proved. Leland's mind began to reach for ways to come to the facts. It was almost a reflex and he had to bring it under control. His guest was sitting there, staring at her food.

He said, "Don't do yourself any damage. All of it happened long ago. It was finished last August."

She smiled. "It won't be finished until no one can remember. When we're all dead." Her eyes were large and clear. "I wasn't thinking of that. You may be the only one who has met both of his wives. We're all involved, even you."

"What were you thinking when I interrupted?"

She smiled again. "I bored you."

"No, I wanted to know what was making you look so unhappy. I guessed wrong."

"I was thinking that I haven't helped you."

"That's not true. You've helped more than you realize."

"*That's* bitchy. If a woman said that, you would want to bloody her nose."

"You're right and I'm sorry."

"And if I want to know how I've helped, I'll have to hire my own private detective."

"He couldn't help you," he said.

"Because you knew Colin briefly? Has that helped so much?"

"Let's forget it." He had been thinking that he alone had access to information from such a variety of confidential and obscure sources that no other single individual could do the job he had done already, as little as he thought of it. This was the first time the idea had come to him, and in his surprise he had to see that it was true. And as well as he had been able to learn, he was the only living person who *had* met both of MacIver's wives. Now Betty Kaminsky put her hands in her lap. He owed her another apology, for stringing her along and cutting her down. "I appreciate what you've done, Betty, and I've been trying to be honest with you. It's hard to see in advance where the line should be drawn. I am sorry."

"I wasn't thinking about it," she said.

He waited. Something was happening. She was staring past him, frowning a little. "I know what I wanted to tell you," she said quietly. "It's impossible. His death was a great shock to me. I said that I thought he killed himself because of what he had done while he was alive. It was one of those intuitive statements. I didn't have control of the facts in a way that I could communicate them to you. I still don't, although I came here wanting to believe that I was going to get control. Don't misunderstand. I do think that he killed himself." Her chest heaved.

"I didn't come down here simply to tell you things, no matter what I thought. You see the way I've done myself up. The best clothes I have. What he called me still stings. I've been afraid that you believed it, or rather, that it was true. The whole thing is confused in my mind and I can sort it out, but I don't know if I can say it. I wanted to get you interested. I wanted you to see me in a favorable light." She regarded him carefully, waiting for an answer. He could not say that he had even a hint of an understanding.

"Do you want me to tell you what I think of you? Is that it?"

"No, I'm afraid of that. I want to think that you're enjoying my company—that if I wanted, if I tried for it, I could have you make a pass at me."

"We're not like that, Betty, either of us."

"I know. It's one of the reasons why I said impossible. It was a game I was playing. Maybe I was trying to think that you could absolve me of the responsibility for what Colin did to himself. What it really amounts to is that I want to be assured that I'm what I think I am."

"Tell me what you think you are."

She sat back. "You're taking me in hand, like a father. Do people like you and your wife pity people like me? I'm serious."

"You don't know anything about us, Betty. You wouldn't ask that if you knew us."

"You both do so well," she said.

"That's the way you want to see it. Let's go back to what you think you are."

"I'm thirty years old, working on my second marriage, but I still feel like I'm just starting out. I don't have any children and I do want them. I feel like I've just finished college, that somewhere between last June and this November the whole world went right by me. I've wasted years, but I don't feel them. I wanted to get married and love a man and have a nice home, but I'm still trying to get started on it."

"All right, suppose I had made a pass at you?"

"I'd have been disappointed with you and ashamed of myself. Men look at me, but they never start anything. I'm grateful for that. Murray and I have been to parties where we've seen people operating, breaking up clinches when we came into the kitchen, but I couldn't handle it. I wouldn't know what to do. I've never been interested— today excluded. I'd be terribly afraid. I was afraid when I walked into the hotel just now."

Leland thought of the way MacIver had treated Norma. "Today you were playing a game, you said."

"Yes." She was getting upset. "I told you. I know this much: I wouldn't have told you anything about him if I had really wanted what I had said."

She did not know the difficulty she was having, trying to convince him about herself. Norma was in many ways far less appealing, and MacIver had treated Norma like a queen. No one did anything without a reason. Leland did not like himself for what he was about to do. Perhaps what was worst about it was that he had to keep up the friendly, understanding presentation; a slip, too much pressure, and she would do what he would expect of himself, push away from the table and walk out.

390

"Betty, what I don't understand is why you have trouble believing what you think of yourself. I didn't have to be told that men look at you, because I looked at you myself. You should take it as a compliment that we don't bother you. Some women go all their lives without getting a measure of respect from men. You worry about people you don't know. You tear yourself down when you have no reason to be concerned."

"I told you I was an only child. My parents watched over me and I didn't have close friends. Part of that wasn't my fault, because the people we knew were those who brought us our livelihood. My parents were always nice to them and it intimidated me. I didn't know it at the time; I realized it later, after I was married to Colin, when we were breaking up."

She stopped to light a cigarette. The meal was over. He was hungry enough to eat, but he was too involved in what he had to do. She fanned at the tangle of smoke and said, "I've learned that there are things you discover when you're under emotional strain that are useful to know but awfully hard to apply. I know I'm not gregarious. I don't go up to people. I've seen it done and I know how to do it. I just can't. I feel ridiculous when I try.

"When I was thinking about that—around the time Colin and I were breaking up—I realized that he had been the same when we had met. He hadn't had friends after the war; I had been better situated in that respect. He developed the talent he had for meeting people. I'm not contradicting myself. He had a talent and developed it. When we met he was very good in intimate relationships. He was good with me. I told him things I've never repeated, things that don't matter much but were important when they happened. A kitten I once had. You're the only person in the world who knows I had a kitten—and you know it because we're speaking of Colin. I've never bothered to mention it to Murray.

"By the end of our marriage the people we had in were the people he had met at school or his part-time job. We had lost touch with my friends, which was my fault. We went in his direction because it was the only direction there was."

She would have continued, but he raised his finger. "I'm interested in his friends. Who were they?"

"Young people like ourselves. All married. We would visit back and forth. We really weren't close."

"Do you know if he kept in touch with any of them?"

"I have no way of knowing. We stopped seeing anybody months before we broke up. It was a long time happening. Once I suggested calling some people—at the beginning of the end—but he said no. Afterward, before I left Port Smith, I called one of the girls to tell her—actually I was looking for someone to talk to—and she was upset, but not very, which shows you how close we were. It turned into one of those newsy calls. I heard who was pregnant. I didn't send her my address in Manitou, and I never heard from her again."

"MacIver gave you no indication that he was going to start seeing them again?"

"No—no." She swallowed. "They were married and he was single. He had nothing in common with them."

He had detected something, but he wanted to continue on relatively solid ground. "Did you ever try to have children?"

"There was no chance. He was finishing school, things were unsettled."

"What about now, you and Murray?"

She smiled. "Checking on *me?*"

"Go ahead, say what you want."

"I understand. We're trying. I've been to a doctor. If you had been in the bathroom on Tuesday, you might have caught a glimpse of my temperature chart. I keep it in there to show myself that I'm unashamed."

"I don't know anything about that."

"There's a temperature change during the month. You're supposed to be able to tell when—when, okay?"

"Okay. I hope you have a great baby."

She smiled. "Thank you. I wish I could repeat that to Murray. We've just started, of course. There's nothing the matter with either of us."

"I don't have to hear that."

392

"I think you're going to hear a lot more. I—well, you will. You're married. You know that I've been talking around things."

The door was ajar, but he still felt that he had to be careful. He said, "I'm going to take it that you and Murray have waited until now because you wanted your situation to stabilize."

She toyed with her matches. "I wanted to get the poison out of my system, yes."

The waiter came to the table. "Is there something wrong?"

"No, but clear it away, please." There were a few more people in the room. "We'll have coffee *and* tea."

"Some dessert?"

Leland saw her turn her head once. "Do you have some small, fresh cookies?"

"Yes, sir."

When he had gone away, Betty Kaminsky said, "Just right. I'll eat more of them than you."

"You have nervous hands. I wanted to give you something to do."

She stared at him while she evaluated this.

"Do you want to talk about the divorce now?"

"Yes, I— let's wait until we won't be interrupted."

He took the opportunity to light a cigarette. He did not want to disturb her unnecessarily. The waiter came. When he had finished, she said, "I don't think I can say it right out."

"Let's go on to something else," he said. "A little while ago when we were talking about his mother's two-thousand-dollar loan, you said that you didn't know if she was hoping for a reconciliation. You were, though, weren't you?"

She regarded him. "You don't miss anything, do you?"

"I'm here to learn." He did not wait. "You moved to Manitou in the hope of bringing about a reconciliation."

"If I had stayed in Port Smith, even though he would know my address, I would have disappeared. This way, I was staying within reach—or so I thought. I couldn't have been more wrong. While we were married we saw her often. After the divorce he never came up, never called her, never had any contact with me, except for the

393

checks. I did exactly the wrong thing if I had wanted to be close by. But then, he fooled me. Tricked me."

"Did you try to contact him?"

"Of course. While he was out west I wrote to him, and when he returned to Port Smith, I called—twice—and wrote twice more. The first letter was similar to the ones I had sent to Nevada. The last I wrote after I had met Murray. If I had it to do over, I wouldn't. You understand that, don't you?"

"Yes. This was the period, according to MacIver, in which you would marry again, quickly, with the first man who came along."

"That's right."

"And in fact your emotional condition was such that you wanted a reconciliation, wrote to him, telephoned him, and in other ways made your presence felt so that he couldn't possibly misinterpret your desires."

"Yes."

"There are two things I would like to know now," he said. "If you don't object to telling me, I'd like to hear about your dating with your husband. I want to know what MacIver knew. The second thing is the context in which MacIver said what he did about what you were going to do."

"That's more than two things," she said. "In the first case, what Colin knew and what happened weren't precisely the same. I didn't lie to him, but what I wrote was distorted, badly. Murray and I didn't get married for several months after that, so there were more checks, but never a note, as I said. For a time I imagined that I hurt him very deeply, but I was only trying to serve myself—my own vanity.

"I don't know if you can imagine the contents of the earlier letters. I can't remember the words myself, but I won't forget the substance. I wanted to try again, I was in love with him, too much had passed between us—the years we had been married—for it to be thrown away. The last letter stays very clear to me, too. I told him that he had been right in what he had said I would do, but very, very wrong in the way I would feel about it. Those are the approximate words, so you can imagine the rest. I was trying to save something of myself. I said that even if he did want to see me again, the circumstances would be very different. And so on. The whole letter was cheap and cruel. Since then one of Murray's friends has been through an episode with his own ex-wife. He was upset not by what she did, but by the fact that he had been married to her, that he had been in love with her."

Leland said, "My own impression is that what you did may have been able to hurt a college boy, but not a man in his—twenties? Sure, MacIver was twenty-seven at the time. He would have reacted in the same way as your husband's friend."

"Then that's how cheap it was." She smiled; he guessed that she was going to try to shake it off. "Do you tell your wife when her cooking is bad?"

He had to laugh. "Sometimes." He cleared his throat. "You said that the letter was a distortion."

She sat back. "I volunteered. Is that your reason for pumping me so hard? While I can't know anything for myself?"

"Betty, look at me. You've been a great help. You aren't the person MacIver tried to say—"

"You're pushing me to keep on being a good girl."

"And you're fighting. You've gone all this way, for no reason but the desire to help. There's nothing I can offer you but that satisfaction. You keep talking; it's the only way I can have the truth."

"If I think that you're going to turn around and tell her, I'll stop. I won't be able to do it. I don't dislike her; I don't know what I feel. I can't think about you telling. It does something to me."

"Then don't think about it."

"I won't hear from her, will I? She won't bother me?"

"She's had your name and address for years. If she had wanted to bother you, she would have done it long ago."

"I didn't know she was that close. It's frightening."

"Again, Betty, that's what you want to think. She's a small dark-haired girl no one looks at twice. I like her but Murray wouldn't. After this, she'll want to be left alone."

She shook her head. "I can't argue. I'm really not a person who can put up a good fight."

"I haven't tricked you, have I? Do you feel that you're being used?"

"I don't know."

"I meant what I said about Murray not liking her. She would put him to sleep."

She smiled. "There are times when I come close to doing it myself." She stopped and sipped her tea. It was cool and she wrinkled her nose. She sat quietly, looking at the corner of the table. As he began to wonder why he was waiting, she said, as softly as he had heard her so far, "I need you to get me started."

"All right. Let's go back. After MacIver went out west, he never communicated with you again?"

"Except for the checks, yes."

"How long after his return did you send him your final letter?"

She had to work it out. "Three months."

"When had you met Murray?"

"Two weeks before."

"How did you reconcile what you felt for MacIver and the fact that you had become another man's lover?"

She winced. "It wasn't that way. There was nothing to reconcile. I told you the letter was a distortion. Murray and I had been together once. When I wrote the letter I still barely knew him. He was the first man who was nice to me, as Colin had said. We went out three times the first week, and on the third date, he—stayed. All right? He was the first—I said that. Colin had been *the* first. There had been only the one time when I wrote that letter. It wasn't for several weeks that I could try it again. I went all to pieces—I was very confused and sick.

"I want to clarify that, my attitude toward sex. Colin and I were lovers before we were married. I thought it was a natural, beautiful thing." Suddenly she looked pale. He gave her a cigarette and lit it for her. She took the cigarette from her lips and sat still. "This is what she wants to know, isn't it?"

"Norma wants to know him."

She searched Leland's eyes. "You're pressing for everything you can get."

"Only because I don't know what to look for. I don't want to punish you. You gave me a scare. I don't want you getting sick again."

"No, no, I won't do that. Her name is Norma?"

"I thought you knew that."

"Colin's mother never said her name. It's ugly. Mine is bad enough, but hers is terrible. Does she have a nickname?"

"No."

"You want me to get back on the subject," she said.

"Not until you're completely ready."

"All right. I do want a moment." She smoked the cigarette and looked around the room. He finished his coffee, not watching her, and then she put out the cigarette.

"The hard thing is keeping my perspective. I can tell you the truth, that I know that he did love me at one time, but then I start forgetting what happened afterward. I don't dare. I have to contrast what it was with what it became. I'm still living in a dream. What could you call it, when a woman of my age is waiting for her life to begin?" She paused. "I'm beginning to lose my taste for your company," she said. "I don't often speak this way about myself."

"I think you're being unnecessarily severe," he said.

"I wanted you to say something like that." She ticked the spoon in her saucer with her fingernail. "I have to stop it. I'm only making things worse." She took a breath and sat up straighter.

"I loved him, but I didn't even know how to show him I wanted to love him. There were other men who had come back from the war, but there was something special about him. He seemed glad to be alive; it shone in his eyes. I thought he was the handsomest man I had ever seen. I'll never forget the effect that looking at him had on me. I *am* older now and I've seen many more men, but none of them have had the physical impact he had.

"I've learned that I'm drawn to fair, light-skinned, light-eyed men. Latin lovers appall me. You're attractive to me even though you're dark, but I know you. Your face is marked now, but I remember when it wasn't. That picture of you in the newspaper in 1940 showed a very young man who was bleeding and frightened, and when I look at you I see him as well as all the years between. That helps explain the things that were in my mind when I dressed myself today.

"The same youth was in Colin when we met. His face radiated a love of life. He was interested and happy and, in a more important way than I felt it, he had a desire for love. He had no trouble getting girls, that isn't what I mean. After we were going together, I was on the receiving end of enough cattiness—the assumption was that I had got him by going to bed with him. The fact was that he had telephone calls on the subject from one of the girls who made the most trouble for me. I heard one of those calls; I was asleep when he answered the telephone and I woke up to hear enough of the conversation. I'm telling the truth; I had been asleep and I did wake up; I hadn't been lying there faking so I could hear. He knew what had happened when he came back. I began to cry—that's how sophisticated I could be when I really tried.

"Repairing that sort of thing was what Colin was best at. He was extremely patient with me. As I said, I wanted to be his lover, but I didn't know how to go about it. In the beginning, if he put his hand on me, I would tense instinctively. One time, he laughed me out of it, and then when I was ready, he wasn't going to bother. He was playing, and he made it obvious enough even for me to know it. I had to play too.

"That was before the telephone call from that girl, of course. From the beginning I worried a little about what he had done before, and whether I was good enough. I didn't bring it up often, although now I wonder—he did know it was on my mind. I don't know if I can explain it to you, Joe. It's just that when I'm trying to be sexy I know that I'm trying and it becomes an act. A sham. I have to relax and be myself or it becomes almost impossible for me. And what frightens me is that I'm not sure that being myself is enough. Sometimes the sight of myself in a mirror just disgusts me."

"Why?"

"Well, if I put on five pounds, without a bra and girdle, I look awful. I do."

"That's ridiculous."

398

She could not raise her eyes.

"Betty, I saw you Tuesday. All right, you didn't have that five pounds, but you had been sick, and while you looked tired, annoyed, and then, later, upset, your body never did, and I certainly noticed it."

"Murray didn't think you had. He was angry with me for coming downstairs that way. There were other things on our minds, but he did mention it. 'Please don't,' he said." She smiled unhappily. "Still, I did have some clothes on."

"You're making a mistake about yourself." For a second he wanted to tell her that Anne had had the same kind of figure, without the advantage of a very narrow waist, and she had taken a pride in her body that had thrilled him. The relationship was too complicated to explain or lie about and the bit of information was not worth telling. If at this time of her life Betty Kaminsky could want a man to attempt to cheer her, then not anything he could hope to offer would help. The subject was so basically upsetting that he slipped into fantasizing about Karen and *her* delight in herself. "Betty, what does Murray think of you?"

"He won't say anything when I've put on that five pounds. If I tell him that I'm going on a diet, then he'll encourage me. After I've lost the weight I'll ask him how I look and he'll say fine, I look just right, or something like that. Once I tried to trick him, but I found that he really does notice."

Leland wasn't here for Kaminsky. "What was MacIver's attitude?"

"*My* attitude was different. I was more afraid of him than I am of Murray. Let me put it another way. I have no fear at all of Murray. Colin always intimidated me, even at the beginning when he was so patient and understanding. I thought that the best thing to do about something like gaining weight was to keep quiet—and that worked, because he didn't seem to mind. Even at the end, when for a while I had put on quite a bit more than five pounds, he never said anything. I think that when we were at our worst he still liked the way I looked, almost as if he didn't want to and couldn't help it."

Leland said, "A moment ago when you were speaking of his

patience I had the feeling that there was a plateau that you reached, that for a while things went along smoothly, and the demands you made on each other were minimal."

"Perhaps on the surface. It's hard to separate the way we were from the things we had to do. Taking care of my parents. We had to get ourselves started. Colin had to go to school and work, I had to teach. We did go along smoothly for a while, in spite of the strain. I know that I did feel snowed under. In a year I had gone from being a little college junior to becoming the working wife of a veteran. Colin told me that it was a tremendous transition, but all around were people making tremendous transitions. The night he said that, a lot of little things had piled up and he had come home from work to find none of them done and me sitting in a chair with a novel. It was childish. Much later I did the same thing again and he wasn't so kind. He pulled the book out of my hand and tore it in half."

"Much later?" The drama made Leland skeptical. She did not get the sense of his tone.

"We had been married less than a year," she said. "Several things had happened. One evening he threw a textbook across the room. Something had happened in class. He'd had an argument with an instructor. When the grades came through, by the way—this is later—Colin had a C. He was a B-plus student. He was furious then, too, and wanted to appeal to the chairman of the department. Now that I think of it, Colin's anger at that time lasted almost a week. I don't want to talk about it; the other things will slip out of my mind if I don't get them told. I haven't thought of them in years.

"One night we were talking. I forget what the subject was, but there was a difference of opinion. The more he tried to sway me to his side, the more agitated he became. We were in the kitchen. I wanted to stop. He said, 'For God's sake, why can't you understand this? Are you really that stupid?' I felt like I had been slapped. It was actually the first time I saw an explosion of his temper. I was sulking, but watching him out of the corner of my eye, and he picked up his cup by the rim—it was half full—and looked at it, stared at it. His hand was shaking so violently that I couldn't help turning around. He looked like he wanted to cry. He threw the cup against the wall.

Naturally it was one of an expensive set we had taken from my parents' apartment."

"Wait," Leland said. "He looked like he wanted to cry?"

"Yes, that's right."

"Over a difference of opinion?"

"No. No, of course not. Later he apologized for the name-calling and said that he was tired and under strain."

"Was he? Under strain?"

"He said he was. He was very upset about what he had said and done."

"Does all this strike you as having been on the level?"

"It did at the time, although I distinctly remember thinking that there was something false about it, as if he were doing it for show. Now I think that he probably was under strain, but not the kind he wanted me to think. You see, he worked three nights a week, and on Tuesdays—sometimes Thursdays—he went to the library. I believe that that's the way it started. He met someone at the library."

"Did you ever try to find out exactly what happened?"

"Yes, I asked him twice, the second time after I had agreed to the divorce. Both times he said that he didn't want to discuss it. The second time, I thought that he was afraid I was going to insist on hearing it as a condition for going any further, but I really didn't want to know. It's involved. His mood was entirely different. And so was mine."

"You said that there were other incidents."

"Things, I said. He had moods, seizures of depression, which he hadn't had when we had been dating or during the first few months of marriage. It was possible for him to go through a day without speaking a dozen words to me. I hadn't done anything to him. He would come home from work, fall into a chair and just sit there with his head back and his eyes closed. Once I asked him, 'Don't you say hello?' and he answered, 'Is it necessary? Come on.' That's all. I had seen him come in, so saying hello wasn't necessary."

"What about throwing things? Was there much of that?"

"About six or seven incidents in all. And once he pulled the medicine cabinet door off its hinges. It was a wooden door with a small mirror in the center. I came in and started yelling at him, how had it happened, why had he done it, and so forth, and he pointed his finger at me and said, 'You just stay the hell away from me. I'll fix this.' And he did."

"A moment ago you said you were afraid of him."

She frowned. "I was afraid of his moods and tastes and habits. I wanted to please him and I was afraid I wouldn't. These things he did pushed and pushed at me. I couldn't even have a nice home for myself. I yelled because I had nothing left with which to defend my own rights."

"I understand that." He did, and he knew that he would not hurt himself if he developed the idea. He had been terrifically clumsy pointing up the apparent contradiction of what she had said. He decided to let it go. He scratched at the back of his hand, felt one of his fingernails cut into the wound, and stopped. The thing was open again. If he kept it still it would stop bleeding in a minute. "Now when he did this to the medicine cabinet, was this before or after he came home with his neck cut up?"

"After, I think. Yes, after."

"I'd like to hear about that," he said.

"I have to go back again. Months before, he began coming home late—eleven o'clock, midnight. Sometimes he came in after I was asleep, at three or four in the morning. I don't know, because if I asked he would say something that wasn't in accord with the condition of his eyes or the color of his skin. Without his sleep he could look very, very haggard. Colin was a handsome man and he took good care of himself. I couldn't help being aware of his looks, especially when he wasn't up to what he could be. He would be gray and red-eyed and his skin would look drawn. By the end of the day he would be dragging himself through what he had to do, but for reasons I couldn't understand—then—he refused to stop and concede that he was exhausted.

"He would tell me he had been walking and trying to relax and clear his mind, enjoying the fresh air. It made sense, because he worked nights and Saturdays and had to spend Sundays studying. It *was* a strain, but a strain on both of us. That was one of the things that he failed to appreciate. Before we were married he would yank me out of his apartment to drive downtown for something to eat. It would be two or three o'clock in the morning, but there was a happiness to it—we had fun. I would have been happy to be there for him on the same terms again, but he never asked me. I don't even know if he ever wanted me, if *everything* he said wasn't manufactured to keep me off the track. That didn't occur to me; I just went along, believing."

"How often did he do this?" Leland asked.

"He was out very late five or six times," she said. "I can't even guess how many times he came in after two or three hours. He was late after work, too."

"Was this regular, occasional, or what?"

"He would do it two or three times in the same week, then weeks would go by when he would be home on time."

"And how long after you were married did it start?"

"Six months. Perhaps a little less."

"And all this was concurrent with the bursts of temper and the fits of depression," he said.

"Approximately. I wasn't thinking in terms of dates and time. He was my husband and I loved him. I was most interested in him."

"Tell me about the night he came home bleeding and what happened after that."

"It was a warm night, I remember that. We had had a lot of rain. It was one of the nights he was working. When he didn't come in by midnight I got ready for bed. My period was due and I was tired. When I opened my eyes again it was because of the noise he was making in the bathroom—not a lot, he was just moving around—and I looked at the clock. It was ten after two. I called him. 'What is it, honey? Is anything the matter?' 'No. Go back to sleep,' he said. His voice didn't sound right, so I got out of bed."

He was standing in front of the sink, stripped to the waist. There was a rust-colored stain of dried blood halfway down his chest. The blood was caked in the folds of his skin under his arm and matted in the hair around his nipple. She was afraid to look all at once. His shirt and his undershirt were in a small, tight pile on the cover of the toilet. The blood was spattered on them like stains on a house paint-er's rag. The hole in his neck was about the size and nearly the shape of the tip of a beer can opener. It was a gouge, rounder, deep, and the flap of skin that had been torn out lay over the hole it had left as swollen as the cork from a wine bottle. She could feel it as a burning on the side of her own neck and as a weakness that raced through every part of her body. The torn skin was already a different color, yellow, pink, and a deadly white intermixed. The bleeding had stopped but there was no seal; she could see the layers of fat and red meat underneath. It was too much of a shock and a sound came out of her, a soft wail that she heard as if she had not made it. He turned to her and she withdrew guiltily, her body knotted in the same dis-tress she felt when she crossed a room and people stared. He was pale and his eyes looked sunken and straining in their sockets. His hair had not been combed. He was ugly in the harsh light; he looked dirty and she could smell his sweat.

"I told you to stay in bed," he said.

"What happened to you, honey?"

He turned away. He took a washcloth, wet it with warm water, and wiped the blood from his chest and shoulder.

"You need a doctor!" she cried. "That needs to be stitched!"

"Get out of here, Betty. That's what I want you to do. I'm all right."

She stared. He daubed the wound with the wet washcloth. Fresh blood began to leak out. He put his back against the wall and waited, breathing heavily.

"Honey, please let me call a doctor. How are you going to close that?"

"There is a way with adhesive tape. I'm all right. Betty, sit down. Sit down and be quiet. Just be quiet."

"How did it happen?"

He stayed silent, leaning back and drawing his breath through his mouth. When he checked the bleeding again in the mirror she was thinking of ways it could have happened. She could not help being afraid. She thought of a brawl or an assault on the street, but he would not hesitate to tell her of them. She did not want to think of

404

another woman, but the idea kept coming through everything she could put up to block it, like wind pouring through the walls of an old frame house. It poured through her and hurt and sickened her. She was ashamed of herself and angry with him for not answering her. It was not too much to give her an answer now. The horror of it spiraled, catching her up; she wanted to be let go. As she watched him clean the wound his movements became a scene she watched from behind a mirror like one she had seen in a movie. He was not aware of her and her own first concern was herself. Her body was the room from which she watched; he had thrust her in it. She could feel herself losing interest in what was happening, like lights being turned down slowly. The darkness felt cold behind her knees and in her throat; her joints seemed to spread apart. She ran her hand through her hair and it felt like another hand, other hair. He pushed at the flap of the wound; it spurted clear fluid and blood. She cried out and stumbled into the hall.

"When I came back I saw that he had taken small bits of adhesive tape and cut them into miniature bow ties, with the thin center sections pulled over the break in the skin. He had got the thing flat. I watched him cover it all with one small gauze pad and two more strips of tape. It was really ingenious."

Leland nodded agreeably. She had never seen butterfly tapes and he was not going to tell her about them. As she had gone along her words had come quicker, singsong, more and more like the chatter of a person who thought she had to fill a lull at a party. She had taken a step back, as if trying to show that the thing had not had the effect that one could expect. The stillness of her hands convinced him that it was not an act. She had done as much as she had been able, going back and telling. This was the natural defense, like shock after an automobile accident.

She had asked MacIver, she said, if she could do anything for him, and he had waved her off. She had gone into the kitchen and prepared a cup of tea. She had come out again to ask a second time about what she could do, and he had set up a bed for himself on the couch. There had been nothing to say to him then, she told Leland. She had returned to the kitchen for her tea. Almost half an hour later, she had come out of the kitchen and crossed the living room in the dark. She had been able to see his eyes following her. At the bedroom door she had paused, looking back. The window had been behind her and there had been no way for him to have missed it as a chance to speak to her.

"I stood there as long as I could. It wasn't up to me to say anything. I went on into bed and watched him. We never closed the bedroom door for any reason. I kept my eyes open until they burned so badly I couldn't see. There was light in the sky before I did fall asleep. At one point I watched him smoke a cigarette—" She looked up.

"Will there be anything else?" the waiter asked.

"No, let me have the check." To her, Leland said, "We'll be just as comfortable in the lobby." She nodded and got up. At this point he wanted no distractions and it seemed as if she realized it. As he gathered up the coats he saw her hesitate at the restaurant entrance, then go on. When he reached the door, he saw that she had found a sofa by a pillar. She helped him arrange the coats over the arm beside her, then she removed her cigarettes from her purse. He took an ash tray from a table and put it on the cushion between them.

"I remember where I was," she said. "He was awake when I got up the next afternoon. There was a juice glass and a coffee cup in the sink and he was stretched out in his chair, his arm curled up around the back of his head, one of his textbooks on his lap. He had changed the dressing on his neck, and in the bathroom there was soap powder on the edge of the sink where he had washed his clothes. I didn't want to touch his things. Finally one evening he told me he was sorry. He was sorry he had hurt me. I wanted to know what had happened but he said he wasn't going to discuss it. We were back where we started —almost. I did the things I was supposed to. He did a few of the chores that he hadn't done before—you know, around the house. We started to exchange the few words we had to.

"He had been sleeping in the living room. It had taken only a few days for the thing on his neck to get down to a size he could cover with a folded gauze pad and an adhesive strip. Later he told me that it wasn't as strong as it would have been if he had had it stitched." She drew on her cigarette, sat back, and looked around the lobby. For a second, she might have been alone. It was startling. Leland waited, trying not to watch her. She turned to him.

"I don't think I can go any further without telling you things that aren't her business. If I tell them to you, can you promise to keep them to yourself? I don't have any idea of what kind of a man he was to her, but if she has any questions, I could probably answer them. She couldn't have married him if I had not agreed to the divorce. A thing like that is all wrapped up with private matters. I can't untie them, but maybe you can in telling her. Do you understand?"

"I'm getting the idea," he said.

"If it's that we stopped making love, you're getting it exactly wrong."

"All right." It was what he had been thinking.

"Can you promise not to tell her?"

"No, Betty, you know I can't."

She looked at him, smiling a faint smile. "You may be worse than he was. You don't let up for a minute. At least he would do that."

"I don't really understand," he said.

"It's all inside me. You have me thinking of things you don't know anything about."

"No, I don't."

She closed her eyes. "I was asleep one night when he came into the bedroom and put his hand under the covers. It had been weeks and I was no problem. I asked him if he wanted me. He made me be quiet. He wouldn't let me touch him. I begged him because I thought he wanted me to beg. There was a signal he had when he was ready, a way he touched me, and he did it, but it was the wrong time of the month. I told him I had to get up, but he said no, he wasn't going to let me. It scared me. I asked him if he wanted me pregnant and he wouldn't answer.

"There's something that I don't think I've made clear. I'm afraid to talk about it without asking you a personal question. It would help me, I mean it."

"Go ahead."

"It's impossible and stupid. How much of your marriage is based on sex?"

He might have laughed another time. "All of it, Betty."

"I told you it was stupid. I meant another sense." She shifted to face him more. She tugged at the hem of her skirt. "I meant, do you really know and enjoy each other?"

"Of course." It was the wrong answer for her; he knew it when he said it.

"I'm still up in the air. I don't know who you are in those terms. People run a wide range—"

"Yes, I know," he said. "I won't tell you who is doing what to whom, but my wife and I have known each other since teen-age. We have signals that go back seventeen years." He wanted her to look at him again. He waited, but she would not turn up her eyes. "All right? Betty?"

"Shame is really a kind of anger at oneself," she said. "For being stupid. I suppose everyone wants to feel that what he has is best, even when it's painfully obvious that it's near the worst."

"I guess so." It was true enough for him to feel in things he thought he had forgotten.

"If I had thought before I had spoken," she said, "I wouldn't have tried to coerce you into assuring me." With her fingertips she traced a figure eight on the plastic of the cushion between them. "I'm so stupid that I've brought myself around full circle—a double circle. I don't want to know how sophisticated you are, what your tastes are or what you like to do, but I'm drifting again as I did when I came through those doors over there."

"Think," he said. "You were able to tell me before that you knew that that was a device for running away."

She nodded, sat up, and blinked, glassy-eyed. She tried to look over her shoulder, coughed and swallowed. "All right. Colin and I had a relationship based on sex—though I'm sure that it was very different in nature from the relationship you have with your wife. That would have to be, no matter what. My marriage with Murray is different, not because I'm an especially passive woman, but because my interaction with him is different. Also, I've changed. If Colin walked up now, I would be cooler to him, maybe contemptuous. My thoughts about him have been contemptuous—in part—even since I learned of his death. Before Tuesday, well, he was off in a corner of my mind, a mental dustbin. But I don't want to get ahead of myself.

"I told you he was my lover, he taught me about love. After we became lovers, I was eager to make my dependence on him complete. One night of petting had me thinking that I was going to be physically dependent on him the rest of my life. Does this make sense to you?"

"A man can feel the same thing."

"I don't know."

"The woman's happiness with him would generate a pride he would want to keep. He would be grateful."

"Yes, Colin had some of that. The thing I'm trying to say is, if we hadn't gone the way we had, if we hadn't married, I probably would have had a breakdown right then. I must have been very repressed before I met him—I don't know if I had real thoughts about sex. Afterward, my thoughts were about him, but they were sexual thoughts. If we were going out, I would be thinking of what we were going to do. The little love acts would start as soon as we were alone. I would do things for him while he was driving. I could get myself so worked up that I wouldn't be able to take the time to do the things I had thought about."

"What about him?"

"I was clumsy and I had no imagination. Sometimes I made myself so tense I couldn't even cry—this was in the beginning. It wasn't that I didn't want to do it; I wanted him so much I became afraid. He was very patient and didn't say what he should have. Fooling with him in the car: that was wrong. I thought I was being sexy for him. My ignorance of myself was endless. He told me the facts of life—really. He made me stop calling it 'the curse.'" She looked at Leland. "That was how he was. He was the initiator and the teacher and all I had to offer was an inarticulate puppy-dog kind of desire to please."

"How did you learn these things about yourself?"

"I knew them. I knew what I was doing but I wasn't mature or strong enough to take a critical look at myself. Later, when everything came apart, he said them in the most general way. He held back; he wanted to vent his anger without being drawn in. It was because he had already quit. No matter what he said, there was always a little more he could have said. That hurt as much as anything. He gave me only a glimpse of how he had come to feel. It was a view of how it was going to be after the divorce, but I was afraid to think about it, and the fear gnawing at me just made me worse.

"In choosing to be dependent on him for the one thing, I gave up my other prerogatives. I never had an idea or a suggestion. If he wanted to be quiet, I was quiet. I watched him for clues to what I was supposed to do. I would think about going to a movie, but if he wanted to read, I wouldn't mention it. If he told me to put on a fancy nightgown, I would do it again the next night or the same day the next week in the attempt to anticipate him. On a weekday night I would assume that we were going to make love quickly. When he came to bed, he knew what I would do. If he suggested something else, I would make the adjustment. Anything he wanted was all right with me.

"If that made him sick of me, it also gave him a tremendous leeway in his own actions. He could do what he wanted because there was nothing I wanted, and he abused it. Not just in what he did outside. His moods and temper flare-ups were abuses. When he went too far and I had to defend myself, the tension in the house afterward was so fierce that there were times I didn't know how we could start talking to each other again. In the beginning we wouldn't let ourselves go to bed angry. The way we were, the decision even about that was up to him. If he was slow in putting his hand on me and I was ready, I would be afraid to take the initiative. One time, I wasn't ready, but he didn't care. I tried to stop him, push him back. We had been arguing and I couldn't fight. It wasn't any good for me, so I just tried to make it easy for him. Later, I was ready, but I was too sore."

"Wait a minute. He hurt you?"

"A little."

"Now of course he knew that. What was his attitude about it? Did he think that what he was doing would bring you around?"

"Well, it did."

"Was he sorry? Did he say anything?"

"No. I didn't want to hear it, anyway."

Leland wasn't capable of it. A man could be fooling with a woman, wrestling, and force himself upon her, but the mood would be different, one of fun, and the playing would stop as their excitement gathered them together.

"He wasn't a sadist, Joe, if that's what you're thinking."

"No. No, it's something else." No lie—now. He had remembered what Norma had said about her husband as a lover. It seemed as if MacIver had had an intuitive understanding of the psychology of sex, but Leland had to wonder about the depth of MacIver's understanding of his women. The way Betty was telling it, she had been too immature for marriage. Perhaps MacIver had been, too. Yet he had misunderstood Norma if he had thought she would shake off the effects of his death. Leland decided to set it aside. It was only one narrow approach.

"You said there were changes."

She nodded. "We were afraid to talk to each other. We couldn't look in each other's eyes." She coughed. "He would wait until I was in bed before he would come into the bedroom, and then he wouldn't kiss me. He would be affectionate and appreciative with his hands and there was a contrition in his eyes, a kind of sorrow. Instead of kissing, he would just hold me, or press his lips against my cheek. One night when he wouldn't come in, I called out to see if he was all right. He said yes but I got up anyway. I asked if he wanted to tell me what had happened, and he said no, he wasn't like that. He wanted to forget it. The weather was getting warmer and we knew by then that we weren't going to have a baby. He said that he wanted to be married to me, that he wanted me to bear his children. Sometimes we seemed to be close to being happy, he said. I told him that I loved him and wanted to understand him. He said he knew that. Then he sat back and seemed to lose interest in the conversation. It was too important to me and I had the choice of sitting there and breaking down or leaving the room. I left. Later when he did come to bed I was still awake, but I kept my eyes closed. I admit it, I did want to see what he would do. He smoked a cigarette and rolled over and went to sleep. I don't know about you, but we had—and Murray and I have—ways of saying good night when one of us is asleep. During the night someone gets up, comes back to bed, and gives the other a kiss or a pat." Leland nodded. She said, "I had been waiting for that. If he had done that, I would have been all right.

"We had started to have the talk we needed. I don't know why, but he crushed it. When he sat back I saw something in his eyes, almost a boredom. Maybe it was disgust. I don't know. The effect was like a cut from a razor. You see your skin open long before you feel the first sensation. I tried to close my eyes. That was the thing; I didn't want to see it.

"The next morning, he started talking to me as if nothing had happened. He had to go straight to work from school and he would call me at six o'clock; he needed handkerchiefs and he wanted me to buy a dozen. The business of life. The funny thing is, I expected a change. That night we made love. It's one thing to manipulate each other and have intercourse, but another to make love. We were affectionate. We tried things. I don't know how all this was communicated in advance, but it was. When he called that evening, I did most of the talking. I don't know how we achieved an understanding of something else, but we did. I felt a kind of self-interest that I hadn't had before. The affection we exchanged wasn't love as I had known it. If I thought of the breach of faith, it hurt, but it made me more passionate. Maybe it was depraved, but I was proud of myself for having survived. And something else: he was a mystery to me again. I know that he had a similar reaction, because the way I acted was a surprise to him. I withdrew from him. He wanted to know if I was all right but I didn't want to talk, I wanted to encourage him and make more love. It wasn't pretending.

"Something like that isn't abated in a single night," she said more quietly. "During the days there's a kind of glory in knowing that someone has that kind of faith in you. And in not being afraid of the meaning of your desires. I could go home almost singing, knowing that I was going to continue to be happy—it was a happy thing, too, to know that he was interested in sharing something like that with me."

If she had talked about love, real love, it would have been as if she had been trying to describe the way it was between Karen and him. They had made the same discovery during their courtship, the joy of not being afraid of the meaning of their desires. It flowed and ebbed with circumstance; twice it had sustained them when love had broken down; in Port Smith before they had gone completely sour; and again after he had split up with Anne. On those occasions the good faith required of them had had the effect of love-in-reverse, generating the strength of ego they had needed to conduct "the business of life." Now, in recent months, with everything else going so well, they had caught themselves up in it again. There was a danger: too many telephone calls, not enough time, anxiety heading to a collision with exhaustion—their needs becoming too intense for the way they were living. It was not new to them. It did not have to go badly, either; they knew that. In the past the pressure had eased without them becoming altogether aware of it. At other times circumstances—a job like this one, a regional conference for her, even a very bad cold—had intervened. That was not a side of them they ever thought about. They had their one fiction, the myth she had created of his accomplishment with other women, but—*he* believed—there was no real honesty they could not welcome, that they were not sound enough to face.

"The moods and bursts of temper came less frequently," Betty Kaminsky said. "Later he said that our marriage had become a treadmill, and I suppose there was some truth in that. There's some of the treadmill in every part of life. We did have our goals but they were far off. I wanted children, but I had agreed to wait when I married him—it was implicit. I didn't nag or make excessive demands or have an unrealistic view of our position. I used to wonder what he wanted that I didn't give him, but I haven't thought about it lately. I believe that I was everything I could have been. If we were on a treadmill he was just as responsible for it. That was something he never acknowledged. When it had suited his purposes he had been perfectly willing to let me follow his lead and serve his whims. When it didn't suit him

413

he didn't try to tell me—he held it against me. I don't know how long before he told me he actually did quit on our marriage. That's why I called him a coward the other day. That and his failure to tell me what happened the night he came home with that thing on his neck."

"I see. Now I want you to tell me how he went about asking you for a divorce."

She did not seem to like the choice of his words. Her hand pushed at the hem of her skirt again. "I knew that there was something going on months before—maybe it was as much as a year. My thoughts weren't turned in the direction of a divorce. There was no reason to think of it. Some things actually were better, as I've tried to tell you. He was quieter generally but he seemed to express himself on outside things, like politics, more. He had a shrewd, piercing sense of humor. He never said the obvious thing. I thought I saw the man he was going to be in his thirties and forties. It made me proud of him. I remember thinking that if we had a daughter, her friends were going to be a threat to me. It was one of those things that pop into your head and make you laugh aloud.

"In some ways he was kinder and more affectionate. We had reached a kind of leveling-off physically, and there were little acts on his part *designed* to show how he felt about me. He would see an ad in the newspaper for nightgowns or underwear and point it out, saying that he wanted me to get some. I hated to spend money we couldn't spare on things like that, but he insisted. I never argued with his selections, because he had excellent taste. That's another thing—I didn't dress well when I met him. He was able to articulate the changes I had to make. He wouldn't say, 'I like it,' 'I don't like it.' At first he would say, 'It isn't close enough around your waist,' and then I taught him to say, 'It has to be taken in.' He helped me. I mean that.

"He did draw into a shell. He read more. His interest in our going out slackened; he had me make more and more of our telephone calls. On our last trips to see his mother he let me tend to more of our obligations to her. If we were to go to a movie, he would stay home and read. I saw more of her than he did. I did have an easier time with her than he did, that's true—"

"I want to go back again," Leland said. "You said that your

relationship was a physical one. Just a moment ago you said you reached a leveling-off. Was that satisfactory to you?"

"Are you interested in both of us?"

"I want to know if you were satisfied, yes." He had not forgotten what Norma had told him about MacIver and that was what had prompted the question. Betty Kaminsky looked away from Leland and sighed.

"We did it about four times a week. Tuesday, Wednesday, Friday, Saturday. More than that and we would be too tired for work." She took another deep breath. "It was always the same way, missionary-style, Murray calls it. He would slap my face if he knew I was saying these things."

Leland waited.

"You see, before, Colin and I did other things—everything. Is that clear? He taught me the variations and tricks. I don't have to have it in me to be satisfied. He wouldn't do those things anymore. He wouldn't let me do them." She turned her head away. "I feel like I've done something dirty."

"I asked the question. I'm sorry."

"The night before he spoke up he had one of his bursts of temper," she said quietly. "At dinner he picked at his food as if he were sick. I asked him if he didn't feel well and he shook his head no. I don't remember what had passed the day before, but I do remember that I didn't feel like extending myself to find out what was wrong with him. You could say that my own nerves were a little frayed. He got up and emptied his plate into the garbage, not saying anything. If he wasn't sick, I had to assume there was something the matter with the food—I suppose. At the time it was a minor thing, but I was annoyed with him for not at least telling me that the food was all right. I went on eating. Next, I heard him at the door. He was going for cigarettes, he said."

He was gone more than an hour. She had set up the ironing board in the living room, the one place she could find sufficient light for working in the evening. There were piles of clothing on the sofa and she had the radio tuned to one of the local stations that played the popular records. When the door opened she had been listening to

415

a song she had not heard in a year or two, "Sentimental Journey." It was just going off. Colin had a newspaper under his arm. He took off his coat and put it on the sofa near the piles of clothing. The radio began to play "Buttermilk Sky." Colin went into the kitchen and washed his hands. He came back and turned off the radio in mid-note.

"I was listening to that," she said.

"I'm getting a headache. It will go away if I have some quiet." The newspaper was open now.

"Take some aspirin," she said. "Where were you just now?"

"Taking a walk. I stopped for a cup of coffee."

"What was the matter with the coffee here?"

"Nothing. Nothing was the matter with the coffee or the food."

"Well, how do you think it makes me feel when you get up from a meal I've prepared?" Her voice quavered. "I have a right to know what's going on. If everything was all right, why should I believe that you stopped for coffee?"

"I don't care whether you believe it or not," he said. "I don't care how it makes you feel, either. I didn't want to eat. I don't want to talk to you. Is that clear?"

"You think you can get away with anything," she said. She went to the radio. "I'm tired of you—" He had her wrist. He held her arm outstretched toward the radio, his grip so powerful she thought she could feel the bones flexing.

"Listen, I want to be left alone. I want *you* to leave me alone!"

"You're hurting me, Colin!"

"I was off balance," she said to Leland, "and he pushed me back. I tripped over my own legs and landed on my bottom. I bounced. It hurt, but I bounced, and he looked as if he wanted to laugh. But then, just as quickly, he looked very sorry, and he pulled me to my feet. I wanted to hit him, but he turned his back and went out of the room."

"You didn't go after him," Leland said. That wasn't what was on his mind. He had remembered something Kaminsky had told him.

"No," she said.

"I've had the impression that MacIver never hit you."

"That was an accident, really. He just wanted to push me back."

"Did he say that?"

"No. Why?"

"Something that happened with Norma," he said. Of course there had been no such thing. Leland thought that the act had been intentional and he had been trying for a little more information. It was not worth the risk of being caught in a lie or misstatement. "I want to know how he conducted himself between that night and the next," he said.

"We didn't spend that much time together. He slept on the couch again that night and I was just as glad. In the morning we had to get out of the house quickly. He had a different job at that time and he wasn't due home until eight-thirty. He came in on time and I had his dinner ready. I had eaten. I had test papers to grade or something and I was working in the living room. He called me and I told him what I was doing. He said that he wanted to talk to me when I was finished. All right, I said. I had two hours' work ahead of me. I kept at it for a while and then I realized that he had to be finished eating and he was just sitting there. That's exactly what he was doing. I asked him what was wrong—nicely. He wanted to know if I was through with my work. I said no and he said he would wait. Then I saw that this was more important and I sat down.

"He wanted to question me. He wanted to know what I thought of the way we were living, if I really thought I was happy. All I could answer was that I had always considered the years we had spent putting him through school an investment in the future. He said that he had been thinking about it, about us and what our life would be like. He said that he didn't think he could see any change in the way we were living. With each other. I thought then that he was going to say that he wanted us to make a new effort, but he didn't say anything. Not for a while. Then he said, 'I think we should break up.' "

The rest was not clear. She could not remember what she said, or did, or what he said. She thought he meant a separation. She wanted to think that he wanted them to live apart, take a "breather" from marriage.

"To tell the truth, Joe, I don't know what I thought. Everything was falling out from under me. I know I did scream at him. I was sure he was seeing her again. He was sorry; he didn't want it to be this way, but it was what he thought had to be. Finally—I remember this—I said that I didn't want to talk about it. I ran out of the room and then, later, I went back to the living room and finished my work.

"The next night he said only one thing to me: that he had been serious about what he had said. He wanted to face the fact that we had failed to make a happy marriage. I had gone through the day as if he hadn't said anything, so he had gauged my mood correctly. I still don't understand how I did it, but I succeeded in pushing it down whenever it came to mind. He didn't mention it the next night—he had hoped that I had begun to think, he said later—and the following night I thought I could bring up something else. I told him that I wanted to invite some people over. He said that if I thought I could outwait him, I was wrong. I had to come out of my dream, he said. We could do this in a way that would minimize the pain for both of us, or we could go through years of hurting and punishing each other for nothing. I don't know, something snapped in me: I started calling him names and accusing him—I really don't want to go much further with this. I did everything I could imagine to resist. I sulked, tried to act as if I was glad to be getting the chance to sleep with other men. Do I have to go on? He would never give me the opportunity to take it too far—at first. He would walk away from me. If I followed him to another room, he would get out of the house. It was obvious even to me that he was trying to control himself. I tried to get him to lose control, I guess because I thought it would make him feel ashamed. Finally I told him that I wouldn't discuss anything until he told me why he wanted a divorce. He resisted—even that got ugly. I goaded him, calling him a coward and a sneak. At first it seemed as if he wanted to taunt me with the things he didn't want to say. Then it all spilled out. He was no longer sure if he had ever loved me. If he felt again what he had felt for me when we had been married, he would

418

not see it as a reason for marriage. I was possessive and jealous and my fear about my position with him dragged him down. I wasn't capable of changing and he felt that any changes he wanted to make —within the marriage—had to be made uphill, against the resistance of my personality. I was so wrapped up in my own interests that I couldn't recognize his efforts to make something of our marriage for what they were. I was not giving, and that made me a bitch. I sat there listening. He'd never said *anything* like it before. It was worse than the first shock. I couldn't help thinking that they had to be true. When I could, I asked him for examples of what he meant—I insisted —and he had them, chapter and verse. Time after time when I didn't take the initiative. Things I had missed when they had happened, other things that I couldn't remember. He went all the way back to our courtship and the time that girl called and I overheard. I should have come out to the living room, he said. What could I answer to a thing like that? He was right, yes, that's what I really should have done, but I didn't think of it. I pull into my shell—that's the way I was, the way I am today. It's almost like attacking the color of my eyes.

"What didn't occur to me than, but did the next day, was that he was guilty of an even more serious offense, harboring all those grievances instead of speaking out. He was ready for that, too. He said that I wouldn't have been able to take it, that the times he had tried to tell me things, I had reacted badly. I said that he had never let me know how deeply he had felt any of it. And so on. Bit by bit we tore down everything we might have built up. It didn't take me long to attack him on his infidelity. He answered that it wouldn't have happened if I had been a little more a woman and less a child. He had had to direct me like a kid on a schoolyard line—

"Now that, I said to you, was something I had known before he told me. I knew I was timid—in a way. He certainly knew it. What he did was, he took it and twisted it and attacked me with it.

"Nothing snapped me out of my dreams," she said. "I was going to save my marriage in spite of all. He was sleeping on the couch, of course. One night I went out to him and tried to make love. He said that he wanted me, but he wasn't going to let it change anything. I couldn't take that, either—then. I asked what I was supposed to do for sex after the divorce. That was something I would have to work out for myself, he said. I said I needed sex, hoping that I could get him started. I wanted to get him involved. I thought of getting pregnant, but that would have trapped him. He would have hated me more. He wouldn't have been afraid to show it, either."

"I see. So it was roughly in this context that he said you were going to marry the first man who was nice to you."

"Yes, that's what I was getting to. Thank you. I wanted him to advise me. It was a stupid question and a stupid trick, if I thought it would draw him in. But I honestly didn't know how I was going to live alone. I was hysterical. What was he going to do? Weren't we ever going to make love again? He didn't know what he was going to do, he didn't know if we were going to make love. I was terrified of the future. I had never handled money, paid my own rent—anything. I could think of all those things and not even be able to guess what would happen. I mean that. I wanted him to make love to me. I took his hand and put it on me. At least he was human in that respect." She turned as if she were about to get up, then she sat still. "May I have my coat, Joe? I think I should go home."

He put her coat over his arm and stood up. She smiled tiredly. "My foot didn't go to sleep," she said. "I'm trembling. Isn't that something? I just might fall over myself if I tried to get up now."

"Take your time," he said. "You've done a day's work."

"I feel it. No, it's a little different. I'm all wrung out. Now you can see why I behaved as I did when I met Murray. Or why I wrote those letters to Colin. Colin pulled the rug out from under me. Maybe it had to happen to me; maybe another man would have done the same thing." Now she stood up. He held her coat while she put it on and fitted it about her shoulders. Her perfume was stronger, mixed with something pleasant in her hair. She turned around. "Do I look as battered as I feel?"

"You look fine." He was not done and he wanted to keep her attention. "You look like you could do it all over again."

She laughed. "Don't say that." She blushed a little.

"Does the word 'Rainbow' mean anything to you?"

"No. Should it?"

"No."

"What does it mean?"

He shrugged. "I haven't the faintest idea, probably nothing at all. How did you get down here?"

"The family chariot is parked in a lot down the street. Murray went in with a neighbor this morning. I said that I wanted to do some shopping. I was thinking about it, but now I'm going to go home. Can I give you a lift anywhere?"

"No, thanks, my office is just up the hill."

He put his hand under her elbow as they crossed the lobby to the revolving door. "Do you mind if I tell you something?"

"No, of course not."

"I don't know if I can say it well. I deal with a lot of hard-nosed, selfish individuals—"

"And I'm the worst," she said, and laughed. "Okay."

"You're taking advantage of me. I want to say thank you properly—" He had to stop while they pushed out to the street. The air coming up the hill was moist and fresh. "So thank you," he said. "That's from me. My client will be grateful. You would be thinking about shopping if you hadn't worked so very hard for us—"

She smiled, a little, enough to indicate that she had heard him. She was thinking. He could see the parking lot in the middle of the next block and there was time to wait. This was a narrow old street and the sky overhead was laced with telephone wires. Trucks and cars were stalled halfway down the hill like an army convoy. The wires obscured the view across the river and at the bottom of the street was a four-story gray brick warehouse that might have been built before the Civil War. Name after name had been painted below the windows of the fourth story and the weather had eroded them all. Leland lit a cigarette.

Betty Kaminsky asked, "Is there any way at all I can find out what happened to him? I did help, didn't I?"

"You know you did. But you understand how someone paying for this would object to having it given away?"

"Yes, but maybe I can work something out with her. How much money would be involved?"

"Betty, I'm certain that that wouldn't be the consideration. I'll pass along what you've done and said, believe me. Look, you're tired. This thing's been working on you."

She took a deep breath and let it out quickly. He thought that it showed the kind of tension that could turn to anger in a moment. "Listen to me, Betty. Last August twelfth a young woman gave her husband his breakfast, saw him off to work, and the next thing she heard, almost twelve hours later, was a police officer on the telephone telling her she was a widow. There is no more to it that anyone knows, save perhaps person or persons unknown. Do you understand me?"

She nodded.

"He died instantly. There were no notes. We're still unscrambling his business affairs. We don't know any more about his family than we did on Tuesday. For a year before the war he attended the University of California. After his divorce from you, he saw his mother once in a six-year span. That's it."

"You know something about his father," she said.

"He didn't respect his father. His father made enough money while he was alive to attend to the needs of his wife for another twenty years. Period."

"Colin told me once that his father was a man who gave in on the small issues to keep the peace. He wore a jacket to the table, and Mrs. MacIver has told me that she had to train him to do that. As a child Colin thought that his father didn't like her. In a dispute his father would ask him to give in to her even though she was wrong— whether she was wrong or not; he said that she was and they had to give in anyway. It was his way of taking the edge off—Colin didn't realize it until just before his father died.

"Years later, Colin said, it occurred to him that his father had been one of those quiet men for whom people develop an affection simply because they are quiet. Under it, he had been an unpleasant man—Colin said. To Colin, his father either agreed with or was too far gone to dispute his wife's opinions. In any case, he tried to undermine her with her son. That's what Colin told me; it's not saying that I believe it."

"What do you believe?"

"Probably Colin took one or two incidents and magnified and distorted them out of all proportion. I can't believe that two people would have endured the double harness he described. There must have been something between them."

"Can you tell me any more about her?"

"She won't have a cocktail in a bar. I've heard her say that she wouldn't speak to Negroes or Jews if she could help it. When Colin was a little boy she wouldn't let him out of the yard, and while he was growing up she objected to his friends. He told me that, but I believe it. After his father died, she tried to stop Colin from playing the rougher sports. She did stop him from playing high school football."

They reached the intersection. Her analysis of MacIver's parents' relationship was already in the wastebasket. Long before Leland had become a policeman and had been brought in on family quarrels, he had heard from Karen of the foster homes in which there had been no love. They had had it in their own home; there was nothing about it that he did not know.

He did not want to check his watch. She opened her purse and got out the parking stub. Leland plucked it from her fingers.

"Oh, no," she said. "I won't have her paying my parking fee."

"Be quiet. *I* want to be a sport."

"You don't owe me anything. I don't want you doing things for me."

"Did you offer me a ride?"

"Joe, stop it. You're feeling sorry for me. I won't have it."

"If anything, I'm feeling sorry for myself. I have to fly back to Port Smith this afternoon; there are things to do before I can leave. My office is on Senapee Street, a block and a half north of Otis and Broadway—"

"That isn't just up the hill," she said.

"I know. I started thinking about the climb up and then having to wait for a trolley."

"Pay for the parking. You won't get an argument from me."

She could say what she wanted. He felt disoriented and depressed. He knew the things he had to do in the office, but he was afraid that if he concentrated on them now, one or another might slip away later. He wanted to keep himself occupied. Alone, he would have two more alternatives, letting up completely—daydreaming—or pressing the development of what he had just learned. He understood his habits well enough to realize that he had to wait before trying to go ahead. There was such a thing as absorbing the material—having the material become a tool he could use. When he was going well—in a good emotional groove—the process was automatic. On Monday when he had taken this case he had been going at ninety or ninety-five percent of his capacity. It had been a good day and he had accomplished a lot. After the poor interview with Mrs. MacIver the next day, things had become more difficult. He had made mistakes—like overlooking the conspicuousness of MacIver's car and letting the racetrack guard know his client. He had made mistakes this afternoon with Betty Kaminsky. It had been her good attitude and need to talk that had provided momentum to the interview.

The car, a Dodge sedan, came up, and while she went about positioning herself behind the wheel, Leland walked around to the other side. When he got in the car, he could not help smiling.

"What is it?" Her arms extended to eleven and one o'clock on the wheel.

"My wife has the same driving style—back straight, neck rigid. She's a good driver, but you wouldn't believe it gave her any pleasure."

"I enjoy driving," she said.

"So does Karen. She just looks like an air cadet. Are you ready for takeoff?"

She laughed. "You mustn't annoy the driver." She moved the car into the traffic, moving the lever to signal a left turn. "There were a few things that I said to you—from me, about you—that I wouldn't have said if I hadn't been upset. I don't really remember exactly what I did say, but I'd like to be able to forget them."

"It was a trick you played on yourself. It had nothing to do with me."

She glanced over. "Yes, it did. But I do want to forget it. I mean that."

"You say 'I mean that,' or 'I mean it,' a lot. Do you know you do that?"

"Under certain conditions," she said. "It goes back to when Murray and I were first married." The traffic moved forward and she was able to make the turn. "There were many things that we discussed today that I had to retell to Murray after we were married because I had lied the first time around. I did have more violent arguments with him than with Colin. I wasn't honest and I was sick and confused. It was like being locked in a closet and trying to scratch a way out. I had changed husbands like a movie star and I didn't like myself for that. I wanted to make our marriage work, as the movie stars say. Mostly—I suppose; I don't really know—I was confused about sex. Colin and I did things that Murray didn't understand. This is his first marriage. He went around with a lot of women —he slept with more women than he can remember. He had to learn about marriage and I did—and didn't—want to teach him. There was something the matter with me. I ran hot and cold—that's almost a pun. I was cruel and selfish and hurt him badly." This street was narrow, too, almost an alley. A truck backed up to an unloading ramp effectively blocked the way. Without pausing, at slow speed, Betty Kaminsky drove up onto the clear sidewalk until she was past the truck. It was a standard if illegal maneuver in Manitou's back alleys, but women usually approached it very cautiously. As she wheeled the car onto the street again, she said, "You seem surprised."

"I am, but by more than your driving. We should have had lunch at a drive-in. Since we've been in the car, you've been as free as you've been all day."

"The driving helps, but I reached a peak a while ago. Now I'm tired and I don't care much. Listen, I owe you thanks. I must have been crazy this morning. Maybe I wouldn't have been as hurt and disappointed as I said if you had worked it right—and I'm sure you could have, too. I was begging for trouble."

"I thought we were going to forget it," he said.

"I'm still wondering about myself. I don't know what would have happened if you had acted another way."

"I'm sorry to hear that," he said.

"Why?" She really didn't understand. He opened the window a little.

"I'll start thinking about undoing your underwear. I'm good at it and I enjoy it."

"All right. I see." She was flustered. "I'm sorry I said anything."

He smiled. "Women have no corner on being difficult."

"I don't follow you," she said.

"I know you don't. I'm not sorry that you said what you did. I'm not sorry at all."

"Joe, I—"

"Relax. Just relax."

She stayed quiet, upset. There were things that Karen understood perfectly and he did not think they constituted a special dialogue. Betty Kaminsky turned the car onto Otis, had the green light and a clear passage, and stepped down on the accelerator. She wove through the tangle of pedestrian islands and finally turned north onto Senapee. Her skill behind the wheel intrigued him. He told her where to stop on the next block. She brought the car over to the curb and applied the hand brake.

"You drive very well."

Her hands were back on the wheel. "I said I enjoyed it. May I ask you something?"

"Go ahead."

"Did I say something wrong?"

He shook his head. "I think I did. You're good company. I went too fast for you."

Her eyes were bright in the daylight. "You see, that's what I asked you before, how people like you and your wife felt about people like me. Now, because of it, I want to encourage you. You. Hateful, isn't it? You said we weren't like that—people who became confused. I'm confused right now. And just by saying it I'm taunting you."

"Yes, you are."

426

"The trouble is, I'm not casual about these things. Neither are you." She looked out the windshield. "I would want to fall in love."

"We're not playing, Betty. If I start touching you there would have to be a lot more. So go home. You're doing fine with your husband and I'm doing fine with my wife. You and I aren't being honest. We're forcing it."

"You mean me, and it hurts."

"I mean both of us. I have reasons. Like yours, they don't have anything to do with my marriage."

"You added that. You were afraid that I would think something about you two."

"I apologize," he said.

"Maybe I went a little farther than you." She looked at him unhappily. "I *have* been trusting you. I all but left it to you to decide."

"I know you did."

"I think you'd better go," she said.

He opened the door. "Again, thank you for the help. I won't forget the compliment, either. If it turns out that I can call you about the case, I will." He got out and stood on the sidewalk and leaned into the car. He was about to say something to keep her from going away upset, when he felt a shock in his ears as if a firecracker were exploding.

"Hey, Mr. Leland!"

He looked over the roof of the car.

It was Everett in his taxi, stopped in traffic. He waved. "When did you get back?"

"Just for the day, Everett. I'm leaving again this afternoon."

"Oh." There was a glum nod. Horns blew. Taking careful notice of Betty Kaminsky, Everett eased the taxi forward. Leland watched him until there was nothing to see but the marker on the taxi roof.

Betty Kaminsky moved across the seat. "Who is he?"

"My taxi driver." Leland looked after him again. A trolley blocked the view.

"Do you think he saw anything on our faces?"

"No. It wouldn't matter, anyway."

"It's a good thing he didn't come along a minute earlier."

Leland smiled. "Cured?"

"We'll see." She looked all right. She took the door from him and closed it. He put his hand on the windowsill and she put her hand over his. Her skin felt very soft and moist; he was used to Karen. "You have an interesting hand," she said. "It doesn't go with all the things you've done." She patted it in an almost motherly way. She looked up at him. "You *will* call—if you can? About the case."

"Of course I will."

She nodded, thinking of something else, smiling a little, and moved across the seat again. She tugged at her skirt distractedly. If he tried to stop her now—he was not considering it—he would be wasting his time. The car lunged into the traffic flow. He had trapped himself with the remark about undoing her underwear. The fantasies had poured up vividly, her arms around him, the perfume in her hair. It had not been the flattery that had started him; he had been drawn to her when she had come into the lobby. He was still thinking of sleeping with her—the very craziness of it made him try to shake it out of his mind. Norma had put the money in his pocket to pay for this. He wanted to think that Everett really had seen him. Crazy, stupid thing: he felt as if someone had given him a kind of fantastic hotfoot. The fact that it had been nobody's fault but his own made him that much more angry. There was no accounting for the things that could backfire and leave a man feeling like such a damned fool.

There was no one waiting upstairs. Florence picked up her memo pad and met him at the swinging gate. "Two calls from Port Smith." She followed him into his office. "Mrs. MacIver called. She didn't seem to be able to say what was on her mind. Then your father called. He said that it wasn't important but that you wouldn't be able to get him, so you shouldn't try to call back."

"Where's Hugh?"

"Relieving Harry McLeod. It's been quiet here. You seem upset. Didn't it go well?"

"It went fine," he said. "Did the file on MacIver's father come through?"

"They called. Four-thirty."

"What about Mrs. MacIver? What do you think was on her mind?"

"She called at two o'clock. I had the idea that she wanted to be cheered up. That's not exactly it. She wanted to know what happened."

"We can forget it. She'll find out soon enough." He picked up the telephone. Hugh Thoms had adjusted the chair for himself and it was so low that Leland felt like a child at his own desk. He dialed his apartment, tapped his fingers on the desk, and looked up at Florence. Her hair looked as if she had just rolled out of bed. He thought of something to say, but held it in.

"Hello?"

"Hiya. I'm waiting for that package."

"Didn't Flo say you'd have it tomorrow? It can't be any sooner, Joe. I have to pull it all together. I was going to ask her to come over here this evening for a couple of hours of dictation and typing."

"Can you give me any idea, Mike? I'd like to have something for the client."

"Not on the telephone, Joe."

"You're not worried about a tap, are you?"

"It's possible, but I wouldn't even want a man on the frames overhearing this."

Mike had relatives working for the telephone company and he knew how the system worked. "Well, listen, is there any danger? I ought to know."

"Just use reasonable caution. Don't worry. You'll understand what I mean tomorrow."

"All right. Register the letter. Send it to her home. I'll wait for it."

"That's what I had in mind. When will I see you?—Monday?"

"I don't know. Maybe Saturday. I'll call you Saturday. I'll probably be home for the weekend."

Mike said goodbye and Leland disconnected. He dialed Karen's office.

"I'm sorry, Mr. Leland, but Mrs. Leland has gone on to Clifford Heights, as I told you earlier."

"Then she did come in," he said.

"Yes. Oh, yes."

"Did she get my message?"

"Only that you telephoned. I left it on her desk with some others."

"Just a minute." He put his hand over the mouthpiece. "Did my wife call?"

"Oh, no," Florence said. "I would have told you."

"Okay. Hello?"

"Yes?"

"When did my wife say she'd be back?"

"She said she was going to go home directly."

"And she had no message for me," he said.

"No. I'm sorry." In the singsong of the mummified civil servant.

"Shit—ah, okay. Excuse that, if you don't mind." He disconnected again. Florence was staring at him and he knew why. He did not want to give any ground. "You might as well get your coat. They're supposed to have my plane ready, but I'm going to call them anyway."

"Yes, sir." She backed away before she turned, as unhappy as he could remember. He wanted to think that she was getting the opportunity to learn something, but he didn't really believe it himself. He was doing terribly and the flight to Port Smith was coming just in time—maybe.

CHAPTER EIGHTEEN

■■■■■■■■■■■■■■■■■■■■■■■■■■■■■■■■

FROM PHILLIPS AIRPORT LELAND DROVE INTO DOWNTOWN PORT
Smith to the Eleventh Precinct. He parked the Cadillac a block away
and walked through the deserted barricades to the station house. The
desk was manned by a sergeant he did not know.

"Does the Captain expect you?"

"No, he doesn't."

The sergeant pursed his lips and sucked his teeth. "Just a
minute." He picked up the telephone. "Captain Leland? Sorry to
bother you, sir, but your son is down here. . . . No, not so far. . . .
Yes, sir." He passed the handset over the rail.

"Joe? What's on your mind?"

"You're making me feel like a jerk. I wanted to see that you had
a good dinner."

"Oh. Wait a minute." His voice sounded again, muffled. He was
talking to someone else. "Joe? Stay there. A man will come down for
you."

"What's up?"

"Has anybody come in since I asked the sergeant?"

Leland looked to the door. "No."

"I just wanted you to get on your guard. We have Scanlon, the
Shoftel suspect."

Scanlon had been picked up an hour before in a basement of a
public school in Westlake. Unwashed, unshaven, and so badly fright-

431

ened he had not been able to walk without assistance, he had thrown up twice in the unmarked car that had brought him in.

He had not been booked, in accordance with a plan that had been handed down from some obscure quarter above. The police were to work for an admission that would let them issue a statement announcing that their work was done. That statement had already been dictated over the telephone. The object, they had been told, was a quick, clean finish to the case. It did not seem as if they could fall short: a search of the suspect had turned up a religious medal that the girl had been wearing. That was dramatic. The information that a medal had been missing had not been released.

Drama was the real object. For reasons that eluded the police, the politicians in and above the Department were choosing to make the case an opportunity to bathe themselves in publicity. Television made that possible to a degree that had been unimaginable in the years after the war. If the case broke along the lines the politicians had set down, the newscasts tomorrow evening would showcase one of their own, who would have some good words to say about the effectiveness of the police. No one watching would pay much attention to the words. The presence would all but speak for itself.

Somehow it seemed more important than publicity. There was an urgency that blew it up large. There had been no discussion of Scanlon's civil rights, none of the customary nods in the direction of principle. Captain Leland had not thought of the prisoner's rights; the correct application of the official procedures gave Scanlon all the protection he could hope to get. Now Captain Leland found himself with a prisoner who had not been booked. It frightened him. He was angry, but he was frightened more. As the senior officer, he was responsible. Scanlon was just liable to have a heart attack and die. The Captain wanted the name in the book. He wanted Scanlon's signature on the list of personal possessions.

Schoenstein and the other detectives from the Fifth had pressed for the interrogation they had been promised. From his office Captain Leland led his son down the corridor to the door off the back of the squad room.

"When I called your office this afternoon it was after I got the call from downtown. I wanted to tell you to stay away from here, but as long as I've got you, I might as well let you enjoy yourself." He opened the door.

The blinds were drawn, although it was dark outside now. Only one fluorescent fixture was lit, at one end of the room, and Scanlon sat under it. The detectives of the Fifth were leaning on desks around him. Scanlon was filthy. Dirt was rubbed into the pores around his eyes and the corners of his eyes were clogged with mucus. His beard, the mess of his hair, the dirt, and the fear in his eyes made it impossible to know what he really looked like. He was gazing up at Schoenstein as if the detective were an executioner. Leland had not seen Schoenstein in five years and now it seemed as if he bore more than a slight resemblance to Murray Kaminsky. He was taller, stronger, with a longer, thinner face. He had the same thinning blond hair and Leland knew that when he was away from both of them he would not be able to recall one without confusing him with the other. Now Leland saw Tanner, and Danny Curran. They did not notice him.

With the assurance of experience Schoenstein kept up an assault of quietly posed questions in the method he had learned from Quillan years before. Quillan was living on the west coast of Florida now and would appreciate a note telling of this. Schoenstein still had the vivid imagination that could make the technique work. His questions were intensely physical, drawn from reconstructions of the crime. Some of the men in the room were plainly revolted. Quillan had told Leland that he had come upon the method watching newsreels of the German concentration camps. Stripping the victims naked had made them easy to handle. There were many kinds of nakedness. A perverted man, unless he was hopelessly insane, would be unable to stand having his acts and desires exposed and known to other men.

In a few minutes Schoenstein stood up and made his way to the front door. He gave Captain Leland a signal to join him in the corridor.

"You'd better stick with me, Joe," his father said. "We don't know who's liable to walk in."

"Hey! Joe! Your dad told me you were in town. How've you been?"

"Good, but not as busy as you. You've done all right. You've done a good job."

He nodded. "Captain, I think he's going to give. His answers are beginning to fall over each other. Maybe another hour, hour and a half, and we'll be all set."

Captain Leland looked unhappy. "He's in our custody. We have the evidence to book him. Let's do that before we go any further."

"We only need an hour and this thing will be all wrapped up," Schoenstein said.

"You're holding him incommunicado," the Captain said. "A good lawyer could leave the district attorney holding his ass if it went far enough in the courts. You *know* what would happen to you." He had his finger under Schoenstein's nose. "You'll be putting diapers on piss clams up in Northport for the next thirty years."

"It won't get to any court. The man is crazy—"

"Who says? The law will say he's sane. He did a bad thing and he knew it. That makes him sane. Are you going to bet your career against over a hundred years of decisions like that?"

"This is the way they want it," Schoenstein said. "There's no question about that."

"What do you have in writing, sonny? What did they say they'd do if the trouble started?"

He stiffened. "All right. They *dictated* a statement. All right. Joe, what do you think?"

"Don't ask him," Captain Leland said. "He's your friend and my son."

"All the better. He'll say what he thinks is best. He saw the guy and he knows the realities."

Leland drew his breath. He did not like being played off by someone he did not really know anymore. He had an opinion; he could explain it and soothe the injured feelings, but he did not have the desire.

"Don't fool around, Pop. Book him for homicide."

"That's what I was going to do," Captain Leland said. He took a look at his son. Whatever he wanted to say would have to be understood. "I have a call to make," he said. "Lieutenant, you're the

434

arresting officer. Joe, don't go downstairs without me." He went down the corridor to his office.

"You didn't hurt me," Schoenstein said, "but you didn't help me, either."

"It's not an issue of personalities. I don't know why you're willing to stick your hand in the fire for those people."

"Didn't you, six years ago?"

"I had the book in my back pocket. I went strictly by the book."

"You don't have to live with these people," Schoenstein said. "Neither does your father—he's invulnerable, in case you don't know it."

"I know."

"Well, I'm eligible for the Captain's test myself next year. Where do you think I'll be assigned if there's any discomfort today? *You* don't have to worry about that. What the hell do you care, anyway? You can fly away from it."

"Go slow, Dave."

"Ah, let me pass. I have work to do."

Leland did not want to go back to his father's office. He waited at the end of the corridor until the squad room cleared. Two men were on duty. On any other day he would want to laugh at what Schoenstein had said and done, but today it made him tired. He did not want to call Norma yet. There was nothing he wanted to do, in fact, but wait.

Captain Leland opened the door and signaled him. He had telephoned headquarters and there had been no arguments. There was a hot plate in the office, he said, if a trespasser wanted coffee.

When they had their coats off Leland told his father what had been said in the corridor after he had gone. "This was a bright kid. He was quick and eager to learn. I worked with him for two years and he never pulled anything like this."

Captain Leland shrugged. "What did you do today?"

Leland told him that he had interviewed MacIver's first wife.

"You're all over the place. You get paid for this?"

"In a way it's like a premarital investigation. I don't feel that I'm wasting the lady's money."

"How old is Schoenstein—thirty-one? He doesn't have any excuses. This is a pressure job. If he doesn't like it, he should get out."

"I don't want to apologize for him, but this is an unusual situation." Leland did not really care if it was or not. Perhaps his father had noticed something about him, for he had taken an opportunity to probe. Leland wanted to draw him out. His father would not say what he thought until he was sure—and he did not respond to straightforward questioning. Leland had thought he had shaken off the worst of the effects of what had happened with Betty Kaminsky. If something showed, he wanted to know it.

His father sat back and put his foot in the bottom drawer of the desk. "In the old days a man couldn't dream of even being a sergeant until he was forty. There's something to be said for that way of doing things. Years of routine seasons a man. He understands himself, or he should. With this setup of test-taking and a minimum of experience, you don't really know what's going to happen under pressure. You have a man who knows how to take tests. Yet this is the way we have to do it. The force is expanding. We have to find good men and bring them up. I don't like the way Schoenstein tried to handle the arrest. All right, he was told to do it, but there is the book. It's the best way of doing things. This guy is innocent until proven guilty. You have to treat him that way. Not even all the guilty behavior in the world makes him guilty. You agree with that, don't you?"

"Of course."

"If Schoenstein were a couple of years older, with a few more years of experience under his belt, he'd have been able to tell them what to do in their hats and pull them over their ears. They can push all they want if they're dealing with mature men—that's only maybe. To hell with that. If we all stayed with the procedures, the procedures would protect us. Like union work rules." He laughed. "And I'd rather choke than see a cop join a union and surrender the little professional status he has."

One of the telephones rang. "What is it? . . . Oh, yeah? . . . Who supplies the power for the lights? . . . Okay, put them over on the far side so they won't be in your way. I won't have any interference with the police function." He hung up. "The sergeant has television people on the other line. They're on their way and they want to set up in the muster room. This is the first time for this precinct. Where were we?"

Leland laughed. "You were telling me that I was too young to have been an effective cop."

"What? Cut it out. You know I didn't mean you."

"I know."

"You were the exception. That isn't just my opinion. Exceptional, sensational things happened to you. You made a great war record. It aged you. You were still a boy when you went into the service, but you established in a lot of ways that you could stand up to the pressure. You were the exception—I don't think that ever occurred to you. Today the trouble is, everybody *thinks* he's the exception. Every guy in his early and middle twenties figures he ought to climb over everybody else. It takes those years of grinding it out for him to find out who he is. Well." He swung around to the telephones. "What do you say we call your mother? She wanted me to tell her when we got him."

"Okay, but wait a minute. Is there anything on your mind?"

"About what?"

"Me."

"No, no. What makes you say that? You look a little tired, that's all." Captain Leland picked up the telephone. "Are the girls coming down? I thought I heard your mother say something about Sunday dinner."

Leland had not forgotten what he had told Mike. Now his mood had changed. "Yes, they'll be here. I'll call Mom tomorrow with the arrangements."

While Leland was talking with his mother the other telephone rang and his father answered it, listened, and gathered up his jacket. "Tell her I'll see her later. The newspaper people just came in. You'd better wait for me here. I won't be long."

He was gone for more than an hour. After a while Leland tried to call his client, but there was no answer. He went through three issues of *The Police Chief* before his father returned.

"Joe? Come on." They went into the corridor, which reverberated with noise from below. "I'm sorry I kept you waiting, but you can hear what's going on. It's a madhouse. They have it out over the radio now and there's no question about getting a crowd. I'll have to call your mother again. I'll be putting in another night. I overheard Schoenstein telling Danny Curran that he wants to go on with the interrogation. After what I've heard him say, how can I be sure that he's going to rest and feed the prisoner? It's what I get for going along with this. I could have said no. I'd *like* to be able to see my wife."

The detectives with their prisoner were coming up the stairs. Leland tried to catch Schoenstein's eye; Schoenstein saw him, then let his eyes move away as if he saw no one. Now Danny Curran and Tanner saw Leland for the first time. Danny Curran grinned and feinted a right to Leland's ribs. Leland made a gun with his fingers and shot them both.

"They're good cops," Captain Leland said when they had passed. "They can work for me any time and they know it."

The answer, that this precinct would be too slow for them, came to Leland's lips and he held it in. "Do you want me to call Mom for you? It might be less trouble for me."

"No, I'd rather do it later. Listen, did you want to talk to me about anything?"

"I had an idea that we could thrash out my own case, but it will keep."

They were at the bottom of the stairs. One of the television people saw them and stepped up. "Captain Leland?"

"What is it?"

"Not you, sir, your son. I'm sorry."

"It's Mister, now," Leland said. "What can I do for you?"

"A little interview. You worked with Lieutenant Schoenstein on the Leikman case."

"I had nothing to do with this," he said.

"We have the film. We'd like to use it."

"Go ahead, Joe," his father said. "Even if they hurt your father's feelings."

438

"I'm sorry," the man said again.

Leland turned to his father. "What do you think?"

Captain Leland pushed him. "Go ahead, you know you want to do it. Enjoy yourself."

He was hungry now but his mind had cleared and he wanted to try something else. The building in which MacIver had had his office was an eight-story sandstone in the center of the business district, as deserted now as the rest of the city would be in the hours before dawn. Leland parked the Cadillac a block away and walked to the service entrance on the side street.

The night watchman was an old Negro man, a head taller than Leland and perhaps twice Leland's weight. He wore carpenter's overalls and a flannel shirt. Leland identified himself and said he would like to ask a few questions.

"Go ahead," the man said. His voice was a revelation, a bass as true as a musical instrument. Leland asked him if MacIver's office had been rented.

"Last month," he said. "Oh, that was all cleared out, anyway. Nothing of his for quite a while."

"Has anybody been around to inquire about him?"

"No, not that I know of."

"Was the office ever broken into or tampered with?"

"Why, yes. Yes, it was. That, and half a dozen other offices in the building. Little things were taken, a couple of dollars the girls had in their desks. Souvenirs and things. It was a funny, strange kind of robbery. Nothing was taken from his office because it was empty by then. As a matter of fact, the break-in happened the night after his office was cleaned out."

"Where were you at the time?"

"Right here. I make a tour every hour or so. It was nothing to slip in while I was up above and then wait on the fire stairs while I rode my way down. I use the elevator and only look into the stairwells."

"What did the management say after it happened?"

"To me? Not a thing. I'm sixty-eight years old."

"Did the police ask you any special questions about MacIver or MacIver's office?"

"No, they just asked how it could have happened and things like that."

"Okay." He took out his wallet. "I'd like to thank you for your help."

"I don't need your money."

"Can't you use ten dollars?"

"If you think something I told you is worth ten dollars, I'll have to think about telling it to the police."

Leland laughed. "Now if I walk out of here you'll have a reason to think that I'm afraid that you will tell them."

"You say thank you and leave, I'll figure you're willing to take your chances."

"You just don't want ten dollars on these terms," Leland said.

"Not in any way I don't understand," he said. "Good evening to you."

Leland smiled, nodded, and walked out. He returned to the car and drove away slowly. Five streets over he stopped and smoked a cigarette. Mike would be able to help. Leland's sense of order was gratified. The man who had defrauded Betty Kaminsky of her rightful settlement and who had run this office had not changed that much over the years. He had tightened his operation. That was not stating it precisely, and the long day's weariness that had Leland not caring about coming closer made him worry. This was not a cold case. A man who could break into other offices to divert the attention of the police had the most dangerous kind of presence of mind. Mike had sounded a fair enough warning. If it seemed too delicate at this point to continue, the thing to do was to quit until there was more information from other sources. Right now Leland was willing to gamble on his talent and experience.

He cut the motor of the Cadillac and got out and locked up. It was a three-block walk to find a taxi. Twenty minutes had passed since he had left the building.

He told the taxi driver that he was looking for a bar that he knew a short way across town, and that he wanted to be driven slowly. As they passed the service entrance of MacIver's building, Leland looked inside. The watchman was reading a newspaper. Four blocks beyond, Leland had the driver stop. When the taxi was out of sight, he went into a diner.

He ate well, ordering the homemade vegetable soup, roast beef, rice pudding, and coffee. When he had been with the Port Smith Police Department, even as a detective, he had sought out the good diners and ordered the substantial food. The taste of the food, the sights and sounds of the place, his own full stomach, worked in a harmony to create an impression that was years old. He could close his eyes and almost believe—almost—that he was with the Department again. There was a commotion that surrounded a man who was a policeman. "I'm on the cops," he could say, and the words themselves could evoke the scene, smells, voices, walls—a telephone in a police station had a ring that did not exist anywhere else. Now, as he worked up and out of the mood—reflection, fantasy, banal yearning, self-contempt—Leland tried to press his attention to business. There were questions he could ask that he could not have asked before. And for reasons he could not understand, he wanted to believe that the answers were not really out of his reach. He turned away from that; it could be still another trick he was playing on himself.

MacIver's death had been published in the newspapers—Leland's father had remembered reading the item—and therefore anyone who had had an interest in the contents of the office could have broken in. Leland discounted the idea of a chance burglary; too much coincidence and, as the watchman had said, only little things had been taken from the other offices. A professional would have had a better appreciation of the conditions—and would have wiped out every office in the building. Leland knew as well as professional burglars that office girls often kept items of considerable value in their desks. So it was not a coincidence; someone had been after part or all of the papers that Mike had now. There was one more conclusion that Leland could draw—he could feel it—but it stayed beyond him.

The execution of the break-in clarified the terms in which Mike had phrased his warning. If MacIver had been murdered for something he had had in his office, the murderers—this would involve professionals, too—would have made it to the office in time to get what they had wanted. Leland knew that they would not have taken such chances in the first place. Professional killings were always simple. They would have surprised MacIver in his office alone, searched the place for the thing they wanted, then picked him up and thrown him out of the window. It would have been convenient and above suspicion. Every cop knew how these people worked.

Leland was not discounting the idea that MacIver had been murdered for one thing and his office burgled for another. There was still the behavior of the Clausen County authorities. There was the matter of MacIver's rise in fortune. A man who could steal from his wife while he was kicking her out could steal from anybody. What Leland had told Norma about a man running across the roof of the track and down through the press box had been pure conjecture, but now Leland felt that he was on the edge of an understanding of what had actually happened up there. Until a crime was established, all the motives in the world were worthless, but the things that had been winking and peeping at him since Monday morning seemed to be pressing hard. The feeling that he should know more than he did slithered away under the intensity of his effort. The whole matter was still so unclear that he did not know if he was being intense at all. It could be something else, only remotely connected with the case.

Outside he found another taxi and rode back past the building to the Cadillac. The watchman was dozing. Even so, Leland took the convertible two blocks to the west before turning northward to Collegeville Road. After he passed the street that ran past MacIver's building, Leland pulled over to the side and went into a bar and called Norma.

"I called the airport," she said. "They said you arrived hours ago."

"There were a few things I wanted to do. You heard that they picked up the Shoftel suspect? He did it. They have the evidence."

"There was nothing in the news about evidence," she said.

"There will be. Don't talk about it until you see it in the papers." He should have kept his mouth shut. The information about the

442

Shoftel girl's religious medal would come out soon enough, and that was not what bothered him. He had had no reason for bringing it up.

"Where are you?"

"Kent Avenue and Grove Street."

"Well, if you want to see Wendell, he's next door."

"Why do I want to see Wendell?"

"Don't you know? You're on his block—the block where he has his office."

"Oh. It was an accident. I'll be up to your place right away."

"Joe? Listen, I'll probably be next door myself when you get here. If the light over my front door is on, that's where I am. You come over."

"Your front door," he said.

"That's what I said. What's the matter?"

"I didn't think I heard correctly."

She laughed. "You must be tired. I'm going to say goodbye before someone steals my car from you."

"That doesn't sound pleasant," he said.

"I'm teasing. I have been waiting for you."

Outside the booth, Leland opened the directory and found the listings for *Roberts Wendell MD ofc, clinic* and then *res.* The office was located at 128 Grove. Leland went out of the bar to find it.

A professional building, a restyled brownstone, in the middle of the block on the other side of the street. Four doctors had plaques mounted on the rosy brick beside the solid glass door. There was a light beyond the vestibule in the carpeted hall and next to the old polished mahogany staircase was a door that would have been for a closet but for the diamond-shaped safety plate in the center. An elevator. Leland stepped back and looked up. The windows were new. They were of the kind introduced recently in Europe, double-paned, top-hinged, with the venetian blind sealed within the layers of glass. The interior would have to be done as handsomely, anything else would make no sense, and Leland could not imagine how the entire job could have been done for less than two hundred thousand dollars.

The light was on. Leland crossed the lawn, sidled through the break in the hedge, and climbed the steps to Roberts' kitchen door. The buzzer did not seem loud enough to be heard, but after a moment there was the sound of someone coming, and then Norma turned on the kitchen light. She was wearing a white blouse and a blue skirt. For a second he wanted to believe that he had forgotten that she was pregnant, but it was really that he had stopped seeing what was obvious about her. She opened the door. She looked very pretty.

"Hi. I thought about what I said on the telephone. I *was* unclear and I'm sorry."

"Forget that. I earned your money today and I'll tell you about it as soon as we get out of here."

"Wendell has other company. It's why I'm here at all." She locked the door as he got out of his coat. He had brought in the cold with it. "I'll explain that to you later," she said. "I was hoping to hear from you."

"I was being held prisoner. Did anything come up?"

She thought it was just a wisecrack. "No, but—you know."

He didn't think he did and he kept still. She said, "How was she?"

"Very helpful. Very—cooperative."

"It isn't easy to explain one woman to another, is it?"

"That's what it is," he said. "That's just what it is."

"How did *you* react to her?"

"In some ways I found her appealing," he said.

"That's right, be casual. That's the best way to tell the truth."

He looked at her. "Do you think that that's why I didn't call you?"

"Did you sleep with her? Or maybe I shouldn't bother to ask you. I apologize."

"There's nothing the matter with me," he said.

"I wasn't trying to be snotty. I am sorry. I was trying to flatter myself. If you won't fool around with me, you won't fool around with anybody—that sort of thing."

"You're right about that, but let's go inside."

She looked back over her shoulder. "Did I understand you? Did you mean that?"

"I said it." He had thought that he had meant it as small talk. "Let's go in."

She touched his lapel. "Don't expect too much from the other company, okay?"

"Okay."

"Oh, yes. What did you think of Wendell's office?"

"Did you tell him I was there?"

"No," she said.

"Don't."

She led the way. Someone had been through the house with cleaner and polish. The air was warm but Leland's own associations with housecleaning made him think of cool Saturday mornings, open windows, and fresh air pouring in from bright sunshine and deep shade. Karen wore a little kerchief when she cleaned, blue dungarees and one of his own old white shirts. Never any underwear. Sunday afternoons, someone said, were the best lovemaking times. He liked Saturday mornings. The problem was in getting her interested, working past the sincere protests of no time, you fool, too busy, you aren't going to like me now, and undoing the button and zipper on the dungarees. On the sofa quickly, uncomplicated, vulnerable: a swipe at love, a swoop, like a bird diving into the sea after some invisible prize. Are you okay? Okay. Up then, I have to work. Smiling. Once she had staggered, as in a silent movie.

Roberts, who was wearing a suit tonight, and the other company, a woman, were in the den, where a portable television set flared soundlessly on the desk. The woman was a brunette, thin, with a thin, pinched face. Her face betrayed her. There were the beginnings of jowls, and her upper lip was marked with the small gouges of tension. She was Leland's age or younger, and she wore her long straight hair in a style that would have become her except for her face. The hair style was too young. She pulled herself up as Norma and Leland approached, as if she could look down on them from a seated position. She inspected Leland thoroughly, from shoes to hairline.

Norma made the introductions, Joe Leland, Phyllis Reynolds. Leland kept his hands clasped behind his back. Phyllis Reynolds smiled without showing her teeth and did not nod, as an older woman would do. She turned as if to listen again to Roberts, who was closing the door. To Leland it did not appear that Roberts had been saying anything that needed finishing, but he said, "I was just telling Phyllis that you're living in Manitou now, Joe. I heard that they had snow up there today."

"I heard that." Roberts was checking on him while he covered for Miss Reynolds. If he had said it, it had been so many minutes ago that it made no sense now. Leland sat down on the sofa beside Norma, who shifted her weight and smoothed her skirt.

"Snow is so filthy, though," Phyllis Reynolds said. She was keeping an eye on Roberts. "I don't know how you can live with it."

Leland said that snow stayed clean in Manitou and that it rarely caused the transportation tie-ups that occurred regularly in Port Smith.

"Drink, Joe?" Roberts was at his refrigerator.

"An easy one, thanks."

"Are you still a policeman, Mr. Leland?"

"No, I'm not."

"What are you doing these days?"

"I'm connected with Manitou Life Insurance."

"I see. Is that detective work?"

"Not really. It's on the fringe."

"Here we go," Roberts said, coming over. "Cheers." He swallowed and crossed in front of them to the desk and leaned back, partially blocking the television screen. "Do you think you'll be here tomorrow night?"

"I'm having a breakdown in communications. I'm eager to come, I'll tell you that. What do you do for a living, Miss Reynolds?"

"I don't. I don't work."

"Good for you."

"I beg your pardon?"

"Good for you. Congratulations."

446

"Oh, please."

"Joe," Roberts said. "I wanted to ask you the other night how long it would take me to learn how to fly, if I wanted to take lessons."

"You could *learn* in an hour, but getting your license would take longer. It would depend on how often you could get to a field."

"Yes. I've never been in a light plane, but I've been told they're comparable to sports cars in the way they can be handled."

"There is such a thing as a sport plane," Leland said.

"Of course! Do you remember those races they had in the thirties? You were young, but I'll bet you followed them."

"No, I didn't give flying a thought until the war."

"That's interesting. You turned an unhappy experience into a happy one."

"Not exactly. I liked flying from the start. The fighting was something else."

"Wait, Joe," Norma said. "Wendell, there's a bulletin or something on television."

Roberts moved away and turned up the volume of the sound. "A NEWS SPECIAL" faded from view.

Some of the film was less than three hours old. Scanlon being booked, Scanlon with the detectives, the detectives talking with each other. There was a shot of the school from which Scanlon had been taken. The announcer, an intelligent-looking young man with horn-rimmed glasses, leaned into the camera and reviewed the events of the past seven days, almost to the hour. He used the phrase twice. Older films were shown as he continued to talk with the assurance of a personable college instructor surveying the subject of his thesis. There were bits of interviews with the girl's parents, Schoenstein, a thirtyish balding psychologist who had published a book on child-rape.

"I could tell you some things about that fellow," Roberts said. "I should, too, but I won't."

"He looks like he's thought of it personally," Norma said.

"They have no more to tell," Leland said.

Roberts turned down the volume. "What I wanted to ask you,

Joe, was what kind of physical condition I'd have to be in to qualify as a pilot."

"Good health. Eyes are important. Good depth perception and good inner ear function—"

"Turn it up, Wendell," Norma said. "No, quick. Look, will you, please?"

Leland's own face was on the screen. He was drawing on a cigarette, listening to the man who had interviewed him. The shock of seeing himself on television was far more severe than he could have imagined. It would have to be like a heart attack. It was so strange that it would have been like a dream, but for the shock. And he could see why his father had said that he looked tired. Norma said something more—what, Leland did not know; he could not stop watching —and Roberts hushed her. Leland felt as if he had been divided into two people, and that the one on the screen was liable to say anything.

"—not with the Port Smith Police Department anymore, Joe," the interviewer was saying. "What brought you down here tonight?"

"It will give you some idea of the work that went into this. This is my father's precinct—he's the Captain. He's been home once since Monday. I was trying to see that he got a solid meal when things started breaking."

"You two were saying good night. No solid meal?"

"Not tonight. There's still too much to do. He was telling me to get lost."

"You said 'still.' Do you think this wraps it up?"

"I don't think anything and neither should you."

"Lieutenant Schoenstein said that the police have all the evidence they need." The microphone tilted again back to Leland. He had thought of it as a ping-pong ball.

"Evidence isn't a trial and Dave Schoenstein would be the first to tell you. Scanlon enjoys the protection of the law. That's why he was booked. The police announced that they had him in custody— the announcement is as important as the reason why. The wrong kind of publicity does more than jeopardize Scanlon's chances of getting an impartial jury. It puts a pressure on the police, they feel it, and by the time a case gets to court, it gets thrown out because someone's

448

rights have been violated. That's one reason why you'll see a scrupulous adherence to correct procedure in this precinct and why my father will be putting in another night's work. Many of the men in this department have studied under him and the rest of them wish they had."

"You didn't serve under him, as I recall," the interviewer said.

"I had the home course."

"That's a wonderful answer," Roberts said.

"I said it a lot when I was in the Department," Leland said.

"Shhh," Norma said. "*I* want to hear this."

The interviewer then had asked about Schoenstein, and Leland had said that Schoenstein was a professional and an example of the better-educated, more sophisticated man advancing in police departments across the country. Now Leland was looking at himself, the heaviness in his eyes, the apparent colorlessness of his skin. Perhaps some of it was the result of the telecasting; the scar in his brow looked more obvious than it did in the bathroom mirror. For a second he seemed to be able to see the image on the screen as if it belonged to someone else, and for reasons not entirely related to his appearance, he was frightened. He had been looking at men's pictures this week and he could remember what he had thought about destiny and statistics. Normally you pitted your age against the ages of movie stars, and because you held actors in contempt anyway, you always came up a winner. This was different. The sadness he felt over what he had imagined for the other men spilled onto him. Something inside him resisted and wanted to celebrate having outlasted MacIver.

"For example, Dave has a Master's degree in criminology. There's no compensation for that. The way the Civil Service Law is written, the Department can only note it on his record. The important thing—aside from that inequity—is that men like Schoenstein are still electing careers in police work. It would be tragic if these good men drifted away because of our indifference."

"Do you miss the Department? You've given it a lot of thought."

"Do you think about your first girl friend?"

"Sometimes," the interviewer said, and laughed.

"That's all I'll admit to, too. Sometimes."

The crowd that had been around, about a dozen men, had laughed loudly. The scene cut to the studio announcer, who was looking into the monitor and smiling. He turned to the camera. "For those who might not know, that was Joseph Leland, whose career as a cop in Port Smith was interrupted by a war, in which he fought with some distinction. He resigned from the Police Department a few years ago for personal reasons, and now he operates a very successful private detective agency in Manitou upstate.

"The search for Mary Shoftel covered five states—"

Roberts turned the set off and looked to Leland. "Did you know that you would be on?"

"Oh, no, they grabbed me and said that they wanted to use the film. I didn't even know what station they were from."

"Perhaps that was their way of keeping you at ease," Roberts said.

"I don't think so. There were two more questions they didn't show, and then the cameraman said, 'That's it,' and that was it, don't doubt it. They were in a hell of a hurry."

"Norma, you haven't said anything."

"I'm just floored. He comes in and sits down and never says a word. I would have been all over the place—'Hey, I was on television!' I don't think I'll talk to him."

"Terrific, Joe," Roberts said. "You were the same as you are now. Perfectly natural."

Norma slapped at his arm. "You even wanted to turn it off. I won't talk to you."

Now Roberts stretched, his long arms shotting the cuffs of his shirt out of his jacket. "Your wife keeps a scrapbook, doesn't she, Joe?"

"Yes. There's not much she can do about this, is there?" A little reminder of his marital status. He had not missed it. Neither had Phyllis Reynolds. "During the war Karen used to complain about the radio broadcasts. I don't know if I even want to tell her about this."

"Why not?" Phyllis Reynolds asked.

"Well, she's missed it, hasn't she?"

"Maybe she did see it," she said.

"Not in Manitou. This was a local broadcast."

"Oh. Why isn't she with you?"

"She's working," he said pleasantly. "I make *her* work."

"Apparently your private detective agency isn't as successful as the man said."

He shrugged. He took a swallow of his drink.

"I don't care to be lied to, Mr. Leland," Phyllis Reynolds said.

"It wasn't your business, Miss Reynolds."

"What was the point to it? These people weren't surprised by what they heard, so they must have known. It strikes me that you were trying to have a joke at my expense."

"I assure you that I was not," he said.

"I'm certain that he had his reasons, Phyllis," Roberts said. "Let's talk about something else."

"I would like to say that I wasn't as impressed as you two with his appearance," she said. "Under the circumstance, with a man's life in the balance, I thought it was in loathsome taste. I don't know what right he had there, even if his father is the captain of that precinct—"

"Call headquarters and find out," Leland said.

"All right, maybe you could be there, but first you use the circumstance to project yourself into the limelight, and second, you come out with all that gobbledygook about the glorious police. Where d-did you get that? People aren't so naïve as to believe that the police have *never* raised a hand to a prisoner. Or taken graft. If it weren't for the attention this case has gotten, no one would know that this man was in custody until a confession had been beaten out of him. Correct procedure. When the police finally begin to observe correct procedure, that's when I'll stop laughing at statements like the one you just made—and I'm not alone. There are a lot of people who are thinking right now that that's the silliest thing they've heard in years."

"I don't think that he was speaking to the public," Roberts said.

"I don't understand that," Phyllis Reynolds said.

"The police do feel pressure from above," he said. "There's nothing they can do about it, either—except occasionally."

"No one asked me to say what I did," Leland said. "Don't assume anything like that."

"The picture you painted of the police is still ridiculous," Phyllis Reynolds said.

"I think you're trying to bait me now," Leland said.

"You're not going to deny that there is such a thing as police brutality, are you?"

"Of course not."

"You wouldn't want to say how often it happens, or to whom, or when, or where, would you?"

"I don't have any knowledge of those things."

"I f-find that hard to believe," she said.

"Find what you want," he said. "If you were honest about people, you would be able to face the fact that you are going to have something like that in every organization, and that sometimes it can conceal itself from the authority—or even dominate it. You are going to have it in any department the size of the P.S.P.D. I *know* that that department does a good job of staying on top of those things, and that it is the best police department in the state and one of the top five in the country. You can't demand better men on the one hand and then tear down the Department on the other—not recklessly, not irresponsibly. You have to make up your mind—or could you be one of those people still looking to a time when police aren't necessary at all?"

"Joe, I think we can go on to something else," Roberts said.

"Mr. Leland, I wonder if you've ever tried to really look at yourself," Phyllis Reynolds said as if she had not heard Roberts. "A man's life was in the balance when you were having your jokes with that television man—"

"Jokes? You were here. Where's your sense of perspective?"

"Phyllis—" Roberts said.

"No, I'm sorry. I know this man. I d-do know you, Mr. Leland. Practically everybody in this city knows you, and a good many whom

452

I know resent you. Hate you, in fact. You're a relatively famous man, a hero, and you've achieved your lofty position over the dead bodies of others—"

"That's enough." He got to his feet, handing his drink to Norma. "Is the door open?"

"Th-think about it," Phyllis Reynolds said. "You've never been in the public eye except when other men have died. Here we have another horrible instance, and you just *happen* to turn up in front of a television camera—"

"Phyllis!"

"The door is open, Joe," Norma said. "Wait, I want to go with you."

"You don't have to." His back was to Roberts.

"I want to." She handed up his glass and her glass, which contained a soft drink. His hands were shaking. He blamed Roberts for this. He had to blame Roberts. Norma did not try to say good night to the others.

"I'm sorry," she said as they went through the living room.

"Keep it for another minute."

She let him pass to pick up his coat from the kitchen chair and then she closed the doors after them. The air seemed to have turned colder. It was the alcohol; he had let down his defenses. He had not lost his own perspective, yet he hurt. He could not remember ever having thought the things she had said. Now he stopped, opened his coat, and put it around Norma's shoulders. She smiled, shaking her head, as if he were being foolish.

At her door, she said, "Go into the living room. I'll make you a cup of coffee."

"I'm not going to say anything sensible until I calm down. I controlled myself back there. And I didn't do it only for you."

"I know. Go inside. Do as you said. I know a little about her and maybe it will help you get her out of your system. Joe?" He turned around. She said, "If you know how you were able to take it, I wish you'd tell me. I could use it."

"It's no virtue," he said.

She brought in the coffee. He had been thinking of what he had to tell her. It would take an hour and he might be weary enough to make a mess even if it needed only twenty minutes. There was no way to get around the whole truth. How her husband had acquired the scar was part of the pattern of the entire first marriage, but what Leland was concerned with at this moment was the control he could muster. There was a correct way to say anything and he did not want to hurt her because he was tired. It was his tiredness that made him want to believe that he could lead her to suspend her judgments until he was finished, and she would be able to see Colin MacIver with a measure of objectivity. MacIver had had two real marriages, two intense relationships with women; if she wanted to weigh one against the other, the one that counted was the second, because it had come after the failure of the first. It was all a question of self-judgment; MacIver had torpedoed her confidence. So far—and it was quite far—Leland had been able to find no connection between her behavior as a wife and MacIver's death. The problem—because he was human—was in communicating that fact without actually having to say it.

"She's not one of Wendell's patients, if you're thinking that," she said.

"I'm not. How does he know her?"

"It's roundabout, and I'm not really sure I understand it correctly. Her father is one of the administrative people at the University and Wendell knows her that way. She lives alone and she's in therapy at the clinic with someone else. She bumped into Wendell there and insisted on being his friend on her own, not through her father. On the one hand, Wendell doesn't want to discourage her from attending the clinic, but on the other, he doesn't want her playing him off against the psychologist she's seeing. He had a cup of coffee with her once, before he could see her psychologist, and she tried that, asking his opinion of things the psychologist had said. Since then he doesn't give her the chance to be alone with him. When he can't tell her he's too busy to see her, he calls me or someone else and we talk about baseball—that's what he calls anything that doesn't have anything to do with anything."

Leland didn't answer. The idea that people could invest time in such nonsense set his teeth on edge. "I hold him responsible for what happened, anyway. He went for my throat when he asked about my wife's scrapbook. She saw it—Phyllis—and thought she could get in on it."

"I don't follow that."

"How did he know my wife kept a scrapbook?"

"You said that they knew each other."

"I didn't say how. It's nobody's business but mine and Karen's—not even his. His connection is accidental. He knows how I feel about it. He's never even met Karen, only heard of her, but he didn't hesitate to use what he knew to get at me."

"I still don't understand," she said.

"We weren't acting as if I were working for you. Think. What did you do just before he brought it up?"

"God, I don't know."

"You slapped my arm."

"Oh. I wouldn't do it now," she said.

"He isn't sure of that. He doesn't trust me. And that goes back to the time when he knew of Karen."

"When was this?"

"Five, six, ten years ago."

"And he remembered that she kept a scrapbook?"

"You would, too."

"I can't remember what she was wearing on Monday," she said.

"It's not the same."

"You won't tell me about it?"

"I really don't want to," he said.

"Now, you think that that one remark—question—caused Phyllis to think she could say what she wanted?"

"Then she lost control. Did you hear her stammer? I gave her the ammunition when I told her I was in the insurance business. Even if I had known what was going to be on the television set, I would have lied to her. It's *your* business."

"I was relieved when you said it, yes. Thank you."

"Your check when this is over will be thank you enough," he said.

"There *are* times when I forget that you're working for me." It was a rebuke, playful.

He smiled. "If I had to do the paying, I'd try to forget, too."

"Now I will slap you. Did you really earn it today?"

"Yes, I think so. Do you understand now why I blame him for what happened?"

"He could have forgotten about how he knew your wife," she said. "He knows more about you now than just that."

He put the cup and saucer on the coffee table. "No, he's too bright and too attuned to that side of life."

"Phyllis is a strain for him, too, Joe."

"We'll see." He sat back. "I'm ready to tell you what I did today. You have to be ready to listen."

The increasing seriousness of his tone had its effect. She sipped her coffee and sat quietly. He could almost see her working to clear her mind for what he had to say. He began with his arrival at the hotel and went on to the observable changes in Betty Kaminsky from Tuesday morning. He catalogued his reactions as if they could indicate something of any man's, and as if they were a part of the woman herself. When he related the things she had told, searching his memory for the order in which she had told them, he tried to give Norma a picture of the tension that had developed. It was easy to omit the exchanges between Betty Kaminsky and him.

Norma finished her coffee and lit a cigarette. When Leland described the nights after MacIver had come home bleeding, her eyes reddened; but as he moved on to the clashes that had followed, they cleared. If she had a question or an opinion, she did not interrupt to voice them. He wanted to ask what she thought, but he was honestly afraid of what she could be hiding. Finally he told her what Betty Kaminsky had said about the settlement and MacIver's insurance. "A fraud was committed, because he never did surrender or borrow on his insurance. We'll have a better picture of all that tomorrow. In any case, it isn't your concern—"

456

"I'm not going to worry about it," she said tiredly. "She should have protected herself when she had the chance."

"I really don't think she has any interest in the subject," he said.

"I'm thinking about him now, not her. What else did you do?"

He told her that he had talked with his partner and that he expected a special delivery letter in the morning on the matter of her husband's finances. "Mike didn't want to discuss it on the telephone. We're going to get something."

"And if you find evidence of a crime, you'll have to turn it over to the police."

"We'll see."

"I won't mislead you. A lot of things are on my mind. If I have to make restitution, for example. I don't want to be broke—poor—again. After I married Colin I used to have nightmares about it. I never thought of it during the day, but when I was asleep I'd dream of being back in one of my rotten little flats. With him or without him, the horror of being broke was the same. The dreams went away, but I had them again, after a fashion, when he died. I expect to have that kind of dream again tonight or tomorrow, after I know what he did."

"Don't try to anticipate those things," he said.

"I'm growing up. Maybe I had my suspicions all along, since I learned how much money there really was." The telephone rang. "You know who this is," she said. "Excuse me." She went out to the bottom of the stairs. "Hello. . . . Yes, of course he is. . . . You don't have to tell me, you'll only have to say it again to him. . . . I don't know. I mean that. . . . I'll call him. Joe? It's Wendell." When he reached her she had her hand over the mouthpiece. "He asked me if you were hurt by what happened. I said I didn't know."

"All right. Hello?"

"Joe? Wendell. I want to apologize for what happened tonight. I had no idea. Did Norma explain how Phyllis happened to be here?"

"She told me a little, yes. She was afraid that I was thinking that Miss Reynolds was your patient." Now Norma turned away and went

457

into the living room. "This isn't at all necessary, Wendell. I know that you would have averted what happened if you had seen it."

"You're getting a rough time from me, Joe, and I appear to be powerless to control it. I want to assure you that you've been getting the effects of accidents. No, Phyllis wouldn't be my patient. If someone we know comes to us for therapy, we refer them to someone else. Joe, I want to tell you why it wasn't possible for me to try to stop her as forcefully as I should have for your sake." Leland heard Norma collecting the dishes in the living room. The sounds were sharp and solitary in the house, and Roberts' voice moved farther away. The light went out in the kitchen, then in the living room. Roberts was saying something about not discouraging Phyllis, that her relationship with her therapist was delicate, but Leland was just half listening. Norma appeared at the door, turning out the last light. Her eyes caught Leland's with a steady, almost expressionless gaze. She had his cigarettes, which she had picked up from the coffee table. Roberts said, "The meaning becomes obscure at a certain point, but I am a doctor and my first responsibility is to the sick. You happened to get the worst of it."

"I understand, Wendell. Don't give it a thought."

Norma smiled: she had been listening. She gave him the cigarettes, hesitated, then touched his lapel for the second time this evening. She held her hand there. Her eyes became heavy again. Without looking at him she turned to the stairs and started up. He fixed his attention somewhere else. The touching had signified the good night she had not had voice to say. He was closer to her than ever, but he felt almost none of the excitement that Betty Kaminsky had aroused. Colin MacIver had said that there was no such thing as an easy lay. Leland could not see what MacIver could have meant. MacIver had been tense and Leland was tired, lonely, and in need of loving; maybe the difference accounted for his failure to understand. Roberts said something about the appearance on television. For some reason he wanted to make conversation and Leland was reluctant to cut him off. Leland seemed to get along so well with reporters, Roberts said; he asked if they were friends off the job.

458

"I don't know any of them," Leland said. "Never saw that interviewer before tonight."

"You see, that's interesting," Roberts said. "The announcer spoke of you as if he had coffee with you. And you don't know him, either?"

"No, I never met him."

"Do you know what I mean, Joe? They seem to have a good time when they're with you. Maybe that's why they like you."

"I don't know anything about it, Wendell. They don't all like me. I made an enemy of one on Monday morning."

"Oh? What was that about?"

"Something else. Manitou stuff."

"All right. I'm glad you didn't take Phyllis too seriously. I'm not sure that she remembers what she said to you."

"I said forget it."

"Yes. Good night, Joe."

"Good night."

Leland looked at the handset, as if it could tell him what had been on Roberts' mind. The ending had come abruptly after so much meandering and apparently pointless searching for conversation. Leland had to wonder if he had not been exposed to a side of Roberts that he had seen and misinterpreted in others. It was supposed to be an interest in people. It was just curiosity, and when it was satisfied, these presumably gregarious types turned rude. Leland was not a patient—as Roberts had reminded him—and therefore might not require first-class consideration. It was only a thought. The other possibility was that Roberts had had a private interest in learning whether Leland had connections with the press. Leland supposed that he had those connections: the newspapers had participated in the favor the Port Smith Police Department had done him when he had left Port Smith. He felt his mind wandering. He went up the stairs.

The darkness settled him. He heard her in her bathroom and once in the hall. The light switch clicked and he looked out the window to the lawn below. Dark. His thoughts went from the case, which was impenetrable now, to what the Reynolds woman had said, and he tried to imagine the people who could associate him with killing. And then there was Dave Schoenstein, who had almost leaped at the chance to wreck what remained of what Leland had thought was friendship. Leland had to ask himself if the things that had happened to him had not insulated him from other people. He had hidden the things they might not understand; he would have done that if he had never had a public life. People thought they knew him when they did not. He had had more difficulty with it in the past, but tonight it seemed to hold him. It held him like a cage. And he had reached a depth of tiredness and strain in which he could not trust what he felt.

Norma knocked on the door. He told her to come in.

"Don't turn on the light," she said.

"How do you feel?" He sat up and took his cigarettes from the night table.

"I don't know. I thought that if I talked to you I would feel better. . . . I could talk to Wendell, but I'd have to tell him the whole business before I could get to my own reaction. I'm too tired for that. Sort of. I'm not interested in telling everything to him." She sat on the bed. "That stupid woman. If she had stopped to look at the way you were taking what she was saying, she would have seen that it couldn't possibly be true. You didn't go after her. You didn't go after Wendell on the telephone. I was in your office Monday when you chewed out that reporter who bothered you, so it isn't that you're afraid of people."

"Of course not."

"Why didn't you give it to Wendell?"

"You. You want to keep his friendship. And the fact that I'm working. I don't feel that I have a score to settle with him. I like him less for what he did, but that's all."

"What about Phyllis?"

"I can't be bothered."

"She did upset you, didn't she?"

"What is it, Norma? What do you want?"

"I don't know." She rubbed her arms. "I can't say it. I don't want to be alone. I've been trying to look at Colin objectively, and

460

I've done it, but it doesn't ease this feeling I'm getting. It's sinking in as I go along. I didn't know him and I almost imagined a past for him. This is the truth and there's no variation from it and it's so ordinary. Pedestrian. I can live with it easier than with nothing and that's what I wanted, so I shouldn't complain."

"You aren't complaining," he said.

"I'm thinking that he cheated on me, too, in the mornings. I'm thinking that again."

"No. When Wendell called I had been about to tell you that I went around to your husband's office. It was broken into the night after you cleaned it out. Stop and think. His secretary never went near his desk. He didn't discuss his business with you even though you had worked with him. You have more evidence now that he would not have stayed married to you. Learn it like a catechism. If I had any other idea on the subject, I would tell you. You're going for a small fortune for my wisdom. Take advantage of it."

"Smart alec. Wise guy."

"See?"

She wanted to know more about the break-in. He told her. His eyes were adjusting to the faint light that came from the sky through the trees and the window to the place on the bed where she sat. Her hair was loose and tousled. He decided to force her to talk when he finished. She had come to him to head off trouble and she would not accomplish that if he made the conversation. He came to the end and stayed still. It was uncomfortable but he could think of nothing else. After a moment she turned her head and the poor light showed her profile. The old painters worked for the thing he could see and he realized what courage it took to paint it. Her skin was almost the color of shale, gray and light gray and blue, not truly color but shadow upon shadow in the dark. Her mouth was small and pouting, like a child's. When Karen slept her mouth looked almost the same. Maybe that vividness that people had in the presence of others was really a low-key tension, a preparation to serve as an armor against the world. This was the way they were supposed to look.

He saw her frown. "It's so horrible, Joe. I have my memories of him, specific, solid, clear memories. We did things, went places. I told you that we flew down to the Caribbean. We enjoyed driving—we rarely talked in the car. He was a handsome man. I knew the way his fingernails were shaped. I can remember how he smelled and felt and how strong he was. These other things that I asked you to learn hurt and confused me on a level I don't understand. It's as if I never existed. He hid these things from me, so of course I played no part in them, but I feel conspicuous by my absence. Who was I to him? Don't give me a pep talk. I was his wife and he loved me and I do know all that, but the things you've found out are like a new way of seeing something. I have to wonder if I've been blind. I have an excellent memory and I know just the way he was when he was with me. I have no doubt that he was being himself. Do you understand the way I feel?"

"He did do these other things," he said.

"He loved me," she said. "He forgot himself with me."

"Maybe you're learning how important you were."

"Oh, yes. Important, but not important enough to live for."

"That's a particularly cruel thing to say even about yourself."

She was quiet. Suddenly she threw her head back and looked at the ceiling she could not see.

"What is it?"

"I am really something. Oh, yes."

"All right."

"I've been thinking about a thing you said. You said that you found her appealing. Downstairs, when you were telling me what she told you, you went right over that."

"Is that what makes you think you're something?"

"No, no, of course not. I've caught you, haven't I? What happened between you?"

"She was tense. Forget it."

"You said something to me, too, you louse. In Wendell's kitchen. Remember?"

"No." He didn't.

"You would fool around with me first. What a liar. I don't even want to know what happened, you so obviously prefer a certain type."

He laughed. "What type is that?"

"Redheads, damn it."

"Karen has brown hair."

"I thought she had red hair."

"Light brown hair and freckles," he said. "The freckles mislead a lot of people."

She was quiet again. "I was thinking before of a way of making trouble."

It took a moment. "Forget that, too."

"Why? You know what had me thinking it. I don't even think it's possible, in my condition." She looked at her belly, patted, then rubbed it. "I'm too far along. I wouldn't want you to see me for the first time this way." She looked at him. "I can go pretty far with my imagination."

"Not far enough," he said. "We could make love. It's possible."

"I wouldn't want you to see this, much less press against you."

"Your back to me, on our sides."

"That's no good. I couldn't see you or kiss you."

"You could twist around. More than you know."

She smiled. "And when you see your wife tomorrow, you'll act as if you've never been away."

"That isn't a problem yet. I'm not that old."

She giggled. "Somehow we've turned the tables," she said.

"No, I liked you right away."

"Did you lie to me last night about there having been only one other?"

"No."

"I don't understand why Wendell dislikes you."

He wanted to tell her now. "His friend was Karen's boyfriend. I wouldn't give her a divorce."

"Oh."

"Surprised?"

"Do you want me to be?"

"I want to know what you thought," he said.

"I thought that it had to do with your adventures and their effect on her. That she was his patient. Something like that. When was this?"

"During the war and after."

"While you were *away?*"

"For a time."

"I don't like that at all," she said.

"It was a long war. There were a lot of casualties."

"Are you sure that that isn't the way you want to see it?"

"It isn't the way I see it at all. It's complicated. I told you that."

"I saw the way you were with her on Monday. And her, too. I didn't want to see her, that was the thing." She smiled. "I still don't understand Wendell."

"He was misinformed. He thought I was being hardheaded."

"About the divorce," she said.

"It was never a serious issue. She never asked for one, but Wendell and his friend didn't know that."

"Oh." Then she said, "Forgive me if I can't bring myself to like her."

"As long as you don't dislike her. You don't know her. She's suffered as desperately as you. She started with less."

"I'll take your word for it," she said unhappily. She rubbed her arms. "There isn't any escape, is there?"

Her tone had changed. "From what?"

"From everything. I thought that sleeping with you would solve something, temporarily. No. There would be too many people in the bed, not even counting the dead. It's the same thing I did when I was a kid. I was looking to you for something that I had to find by myself."

"I want to kiss you, anyway," he said.

"I don't think so."

"I won't debate it like a damned schoolboy. I want to."

She laughed and moved closer. He sat up more. He did feel like a schoolboy, but she knew enough to wait a moment. "Don't think," she said. He nodded. Her hand touched the back of his neck. She smiled and then lowered her eyes to watch his mouth as long as she

464

could. Her lips were thinner and firmer than Karen's. She would not let him put his tongue in her mouth, but then she forced open his mouth. She stopped and leaned back. "That's a little idiosyncrasy."

"I enjoyed it, but you said not to think."

"I like your mouth." She put her lips against his lips, just pressed them there. "Toothpaste. Pajamas every night. Are you a square, Joe?"

"You tell me."

"I slept in the nude until I got married." She kissed his chin. "Then I put clothes on."

"You like to talk?"

"This time. I just want to go and go." He kissed her neck. The odor of her skin was milky and dark, a secret. He opened the top button of the robe and tried to slip it off her shoulder, but it was bound up underneath her. "I can't reach you," he said.

He smoothed her hair back from her forehead. She looked like a different woman. She watched his eyes as he undid the next button and this time succeeded in getting her robe open. She smiled and hugged him. He ran his hand up the back of her thighs. She kissed him twice. "You don't waste any time, do you?"

"I had to get at that."

"And?"

He pinched her lightly. "Nice. Very, very nice."

"There are things you can't do now."

"I know."

"Did you want to do them?"

"Yes."

They were kissing when the telephone rang. She broke away. "That bastard."

"You think it's him? Let it go."

"No, I can't. It might be important." She was up, pulling her robe together. The telephone rang the fourth time. "All *right,* damn it!" It was a range of her voice he had not heard before, two octaves up. He put his head back against the pillow. The ringing stopped. He could not hear her voice.

She returned. "It's your wife. You'd better take it downstairs. I'll hold the line open for you."

The light in the hall went on, but she was already gone. He was sitting up, catching his breath. It was weird; his heart was beating harder than ever. In the hall he looked back to the other bedroom. Norma was holding the telephone, waiting. She did not see him. He went down the carpeted stairs barefoot. His pajamas were twisted around. He adjusted his pants and then picked up the receiver.

"Hello?"

"All right, Joe?"

"Yes, thank you." There was a click. "Karen?"

"Yes, it's me. Hello."

"What is it, Karen?"

"You called me twice today, remember?"

"Of course I did. What is it? Is there something wrong?"

"I'll let you answer that. She just said that the phone was in her room. It took her six rings to pick it up."

He straightened up and closed his eyes. "That doesn't deserve an answer."

"I'm entitled to one. I had a call placed all evening, every twenty minutes. No answer. I called your mother and she called your father. He called me, as worried as I was. He said that you left him at seven."

"I was working."

"At this hour? Where? How?"

"I'm not going to discuss it with you."

"Your answers have me ready to throw up, Joe. You should hear your tone. I thought that we had a few things settled. More, but I guess not."

"Karen, it's after midnight—"

"Where was she? Where was she when the phone was ringing?"

"In the bathroom, for all I know. I *don't* know, I was in bed."

"Where is she now? Where are you?"

"Downstairs. I don't know where she is. Calm down, will you please?"

"The second time you called today you cursed out my secretary. I didn't hear that from her, I heard it from somebody else."

"I said one word and apologized right away."

"I know. I checked with her. She did think for a moment that it was directed at her and she was shaken. She told one of her friends and that started it going. There are people down here who have been waiting for me to make a mistake, Joe. At the least you've given them something to talk about."

"All right, this is no time to go into it. I'm not kidding you, Karen. I can't talk. It's not smart."

"Why?"

"Think."

"If she's listening, tell her to go away. You have the right to take a personal call—"

"That's not it."

"What's the matter with you? Before you left, you were insisting that Steffie and I come down for the weekend. Last night when you spoke to her you didn't even mention it. I asked her what you said about it and then *I* had to explain to her. I said maybe you thought you would be home tonight."

He drew his breath. "I was taking into account the things you had said earlier. About *you* coming here."

"Joe, you've given me nothing but oblique answers since we started talking. Don't you realize that it makes me even more aware of that girl? I saw her, you told me about her. You're flaunting her at me—"

"Stop it."

There was silence. He waited as long as he could. "Karen, you said something about calling every twenty minutes. I called here once while I was out and she picked up the telephone right away."

"I won't take that from you. I can't," she said. The line was quiet for a moment, then it clicked dead. There was no confusion with this goodbye. Leland put down the receiver. He was not going to let himself think about dressing and going outside to call her back. He was too tired. She really was the cause of this and she would have to wait. He started up the stairs again, then he looked up. Norma was standing at the balustrade, her hands in the pockets of her robe. She continued to stare at him.

"I was back and forth to Wendell's all evening. I could have missed her call, the same way I just did catch yours. I should have told you that."

"You should have told me that you were listening, too."

"I know, but I had an interest. Would you have come back after that? If I hadn't been here?"

"I would have tried. I didn't stop thinking about it."

"You lied to me about yourself."

"No."

"You couldn't even say my name when I asked if you had the line."

That was true.

"So that's the way it is," she said. "She's the cop, not you. It's too bad."

His lip curled. "Sure. Whatever you want to believe."

She turned to her room. "Good night, Joe."

He did not answer. She had been facing the other way and the walls could have played tricks with her voice. He had no doubt about the way he would sound, with unhappiness compounding unhappiness. He waited until he heard her door close. More than she—she had turned away—*he* did not want to be seen.

CHAPTER NINETEEN

. . . .

SHE PRODDED HIM AWAKE. "SIT UP. COME ON. THERE'S A TELEGRAM for you."

The room was bright. Raising himself to one elbow, he took the envelope and tore it open. His fingers were numb. EASTERN FLIGHT 341 DUE PORT SMITH 10:30. MEET ME ARRIVAL GATE. MIKE. Leland gave the telegram to Norma.

"This is a change, isn't it?"

"Yes. He was going to send a letter."

"What do you want for breakfast?"

"I don't care. Wait." He sat up, pulling the covers with him. He looked at her; he did not know what he wanted to say. She knew it. She went to the door and turned around.

"Get dressed and come downstairs."

"Listen, kid—"

"Not now. Understand? Not now."

He nodded and reached for his cigarettes. She saw him, then closed the door.

While he was shaving he examined the puffiness of his face. His body was going to feel heavy for most of the day. It had taken him hours to fall asleep. And the sleep had been shallow and restless. He had not heard her, though. Her room had been quiet all night.

Downstairs he stayed quiet and she did not break in on him until he had his coffee.

"When will I hear from you?"

"I have to see my partner first. Then there may be the problem of finding a place to talk. I'll call you when I can."

She looked at the kitchen clock. "You have plenty of time before the plane arrives. If you want to lie down for a while, I'll wake you."

"I've been up too long for that. I'm too awake."

"I don't want you to think about last night," she said. "I don't want you to be upset."

He said nothing.

"If you have time when you get to the airport, I wish you would call me."

"All right."

She got up to get the coffeepot. "What do you think you'll be doing about tonight?"

"I don't know."

"His parties start about eight-thirty, but he invites so many that sometimes people are still coming in at ten and eleven. There will be a crush, I promise you."

"I don't even want to think about it," he said. He sat back: the words had come out of him automatically. "Will you need your car?"

"Oh, no. I'll see you today, won't I?"

"That's right. Yes, you'll see me."

He started for the airport at nine-thirty. The rush hour was over. It was a rare day for Port Smith, the kind that usually came after the holiday weekends. The air was clear, the visibility so good that the horizon sparkled. There was a crisp, gusty wind that tossed and wrenched the papers in the empty streets. Days like this stayed in the mind. He had been graduated from high school and come home from the service on days like this one. He tried to concentrate on the driving. It crossed his mind that he was taking MacIver's car over approximately the same route MacIver had used—Leland felt himself resisting thinking of that, too. He had done this before recently, driving and wasting time in his mind, but at first he could not remember when. He tried to remember his dreams. The sensation—not *déjà vu*—had him feeling strange and uneasy. For the next few minutes he traced his movements in Port Smith until he recalled Wednesday,

470

in the evening, when he had driven around the bay and down to the Point. He had hidden it from himself as if it were shameful. The combination of sensations left him even more unsettled; he wanted to think about things again but he could not help feeling that *that* was running away. It occurred to him to pull the car over and sit quietly for a minute, but he did not do it. He had been tired at times in the past, and he could remember having confused dreams of combat with reality during the war. Now at least he knew a little about the condition he was in. He pressed the buttons for the power windows. The air was cold, but it was what he wanted.

No airport in the world does business in the morning. He was able to park the car quickly and get into the administration building before the air penetrated his clothing. He was on the escalator to the second-floor coffee shop when he remembered something else. The banks of telephone booths were downstairs. He went around and rode down again, sorting out his change.

"Hello?"

"Norma? Joe. You told me to call."

"Yes, I wanted to make sure you understood about last night. I thought it would be easier to explain over the telephone. Wait until I get my cigarettes."

He waited.

"I didn't hear all of your telephone call," she said. "Just a bit at the end, but I think I caught the drift. I wasn't married long, but you know what happened to me before and maybe you can believe that I can understand how those things come about—"

"What things?"

"Tension, missed connections. Don't make this difficult for me, please."

"No, I don't want to. I didn't know what you meant."

"You haven't seen her since Monday, okay?"

"Norma, I'm not any good with telephones—"

"All you have to do is listen, Joe. What I wanted to tell you was that before the telephone rang last night, you and I were playing—isn't that what it was?"

"I guess. I don't know."

"It isn't possible. I saw it first, that's all. It would have been fine until we fell asleep, but then we would have awakened all confused. If you had slept with me last night, what would you be thinking about now?"

He knew himself. He knew the way he would be, but he did not see the point of picking at it this way.

"It would be nice for me if you said it," she said quietly.

"I'd be thinking about you, Norma. You know I would."

"You took the harshness out of your voice. Thank you. You're not as tough as you want people to believe."

It seemed as if she wanted him to comment on that, but then she coughed. "I can't take the chance of being confused again. When you were on the telephone, I couldn't get it out of my mind. I could lie to you now and say that the whole thing was some sort of temporary aberration and wasn't the real me, or that I wasn't playing and you misled me about what we were doing, but part of my trouble is that I've never learned how to live with liars. I want to be able to live with myself. Someday my baby will be looking to me for clues to the way to behave, and if I really want to do a good job with him, I'd better start practicing now. It's a lousy motivation for my own personal acts, but my baby is going to have his father's death hanging over his head all his life, and I have to try to make a balance for sanity."

"Sure. Anybody would understand that."

"I could have an affair with you. I could even be your mistress, if you wanted. If I let myself. Last night I saw those things coming and I had to get out any way I could. So I said those things. I said them deliberately. I like you. You know I do."

"I know."

"I wish," she said. "I just wish. We could have a good time, Joe. We could have something wonderful." There was a silence. "I guess I've spelled it out."

"If I said that I'd think it over, you would misunderstand," he said.

"Not now. I wouldn't."

He was quiet. He was wondering what he had done.

472

She said, "Joe, if—well, I won't be waiting for you to say something. I won't be looking at you."

"That's right. That helps."

"I'm getting smarter. I never was a complainer. I won't get fat, either—I've been trying to promise myself that. Joe, when you call me later about what your partner has told you, don't talk about anything else. I don't want any more today. I really don't."

He thought that she would know that that would have the opposite effect on him, but he did not doubt that she had meant it sincerely. He had to stay one step ahead just to keep up with her—which was so promising that he had to be a little frightened. They said goodbye and he left the booth and rode the escalator again to the second floor.

He took a table by the window where he could look across the runways and the bay beyond to most of the city of Port Smith. When the wind was right it was possible to watch the airplanes complete their final turns over Bay Slope and come in straight across the water in long descents, sliding and correcting and growing larger all the way. The sun would flicker on the water and catch the metal and glass of the traffic moving up the narrow streets of the Slope; the airplanes would float into that line of sight with still a long way to come, sometimes rising, propellers shining. When the planes touched down you could see the landing-gear assemblies flex, tires flatten, rubber tailing off in smoke. Leland could see it—most people needed binoculars—when it was there; now he recaptured it as he sat by the plastic philodendron that trimmed the windows of the coffee shop. He could hear the clatter from the kitchen as things were being prepared for lunch. He felt himself drifting toward the conversation with Norma, but he could not face it seriously. He had what she had said about the two of them together in a nowhere-anywhere that did not account for her house on Collegeville Road or his business in Manitou or his family or her money. The coffee turned cold, and when the time came to leave, he paused to count the cigarettes in the ash tray. Four. Pretty good going for a man who had been at the table for thirty-five minutes.

Mike was the first passenger through the door of the venerable and now miniature DC-3. He had his topcoat over his arm and he blinked in the sunshine as if he had been flying all night. As he came across the asphalt he smiled and looked back at the old airplane.

"I could feel the wind," he said. "It came right through the body plates."

Leland laughed. "All part of the design, fella. You have to understand these things."

Mike looked around. "We have a lot of talking to do. Where can we go where we won't be heard?"

Leland told him that the coffee shop was empty.

"You were on television this morning, I'd better not forget to tell you that. WTOU-TV. They called your apartment to tell you. I stayed over last night. I called Karen. She was on her way out but she said she would wait to see you."

Leland explained how the interview had come about. There had been nothing in Mike's tone in his mention of Karen, and Leland thought that that was a good sign of how she was doing. He led the way back to the table he had had and took the same chair. The table had been wiped clean and the ash tray emptied. Mike was hungry. When the waitress came, he ordered bacon and eggs and coffee right away. Leland wanted more coffee.

Mike lit a cigarette and looked out the window. His mouth was pulled down at the corners. "Now you're going to have to be patient," he said. "Florence and I worked two hours last night trying to get it all into a report. We had to give up. What I have in my pocket is an outline—of what, you'll hear soon enough—and it's for you to use when you tell our client what her husband was up to. I pity her, Joe. You won't be able to help thinking about what he did—what he started, because it's still going on. I don't know how it relates to his death, if at all. There was no evidence of threats or violence in his correspondence."

He drew on the cigarette and looked out at the runways and the water. An old Taylorcraft was moving on the outer taxi strip. It was too far away to hear.

"I spent the first half of Wednesday going through his papers, setting aside the obvious things, office bills, copies of dunning letters.

That left a lot. I read it all, whether I understood it or not. I put the letters in sequence, and that made things clearer. There were documents or photostats of documents. Put together, the letters and documents and books are a record of his part in a mess spread all over Port Smith. He called it Rainbow because he had a sense of humor. There can't be any other reason.

"I don't know why he kept a record. Maybe he thought that someday he would change his mind and blow the whistle on all the others. It wasn't his insurance, what a man puts in a safe deposit box. And it wasn't a rat's nest; he wasn't a compulsive saver. I could see in the way the things were boxed that he had them in files and drawers in a genuine, maintainable system. He wasn't afraid, or he wouldn't have kept some of the things. The most distinguishing feature of it all is its completeness. If he had been afraid, he would have disposed of or secreted some of it, but he didn't."

The waitress was coming. Mike turned to the window again, as if he simply could not expend the energy that small talk required. He waited a long time after she was gone.

"The coded books are informal, simplified copies of other books held elsewhere, and my guess is that he worked on those other books, returned to his office, and transcribed what he could remember. In the letters and documents are cross-references attesting to his memory. Some people would say out of hand that he could not have done it, but I've seen it. Adding that double column of figures had to be nothing to him. Letters and documents refer to appliances; in his books they turn up as kitchen sinks. In the letters are references to payments; in his books they turn up as $C_{12}H_{22}O_{11}$."

"What is that?"

"I looked it up. Sugar."

"You said a sense of humor."

"Very much so. In total, the 'sugar' items run into thousands. The books don't specify where the payments went, but that can be deduced from the letters and memoranda."

"Where?"

"You name it, Joe. I'm not kidding."

"Swell."

"I believe he kept up the codes to entertain himself and to ward off casual snoopers, such as his secretary. A few of his personal papers, his gambling records, for example, had little games in them."

"How did he do with the gambling?"

"He dropped forty-six thousand in two years."

"Lost it?"

"That's right."

"What about his taxes? Maybe he anticipated having to conceal winnings."

"No. MacIver was like the little girl with the curl. At some things he was a model citizen. His tax returns show that he absorbed his losses completely, paying his taxes on them in full. He claimed the usual entertainment and other expenses that businessmen claim, and they do seem legitimate. Put it another way. He was too smart to cheat on his taxes. Under the law, Colin MacIver is absolutely clean."

"What about bribery?"

"Not him. The payments were made, but not by him. Not by any man. The payments went to bagmen as consultation fees—for example. That's the way the payments will appear on the books of the corporations that made them. MacIver kept those books. That's how he knew that it really was sugar."

"So he kept their books and they paid him well," Leland said.

"Don't try to guess ahead," Mike said. "As I went through the correspondence and memoranda, I had to start lists of names. One list is of the people in the Port Smith municipal departments who had contact with the conspiracy. Another is of the bagmen and other small fry. The third is a list of the principals themselves. There are thirty-eight names on that list and it *is* logical to assume that MacIver did not know everybody. You'll see what I mean. There is a fourth list, of people whose roles are unclear. Oh, everything is clear on the surface; it's just that the nature of the thing makes you start questioning. It makes you sick with yourself. You want to see the financial records of everyone you come across. By the way, number one on the fourth list is your old friend, Herbert A. Davis. His connection would seem legitimate under any circumstance, but there is so much dirt around that you have to ask.

476

"One more name. On the fourth list, too. Dr. Wendell Roberts, who happens to be MacIver's next door neighbor—"

"I know. Mrs. MacIver was under his care."

"He's the one. I see. You told me that she had been under treatment. His connection with Rainbow isn't through MacIver. On paper, he wouldn't know that MacIver was connected with it. They're so remote on the table of organization that you would have to give him the benefit of the doubt. Now I want to know if you understand the function of the Port Smith Planning Board."

Leland frowned and sat back. "Under the City Charter, the Board acts as an advisory agency. It makes recommendations for city development. It files reports with the City Council."

"I want to be sure that you understand it in practice," Mike said.

"Well, of the nine men on the Board, three must be Catholic. Another has to come from the liberal Jewish community. One or two downtown businessmen. Two or three places are reserved for political payoffs—ex-mayors, campaign contributors. Sometimes the Board does good work, but the determining factor is muscle—the membership shows that. All Catholic cemeteries have traffic lights at their entrances, working night and day. Traffic isn't the Board's department, but the principle is the same."

"In some ways you know more about it than I do. We're dealing with a complicated situation, so again, don't try to guess ahead. Through friendship and business association, the group that makes up Rainbow has several connections with the Planning Board, on the Board itself and at the staff level. A member of Herbert Davis' staff and an assistant secretary of the Planning Board serve on the same charity committees—I know this from my football days. The evidence that they've exchanged information is in MacIver's files. Letters mention projects that weren't proposed by the Board for another six months. This isn't a simple land speculation. The newspapers watch that pretty closely. Rainbow is infinitely more complicated and subtle, and land is only the beginning. The thirty-eight principals are shareholders or officers in twenty-three different corporations." Mike looked out the window again. "Where is Suffolk Street from here?"

Leland had to pick his way to it. It was on a slight rise north and east of the business district. From this distance it was a black smear of tar paper on the tenement roofs. Leland had a clearer sense of what was coming. Moderate rent, high-rise housing was going to be built on Suffolk Street within the next two years.

Mike said, "Five years ago, six real estate companies and four individuals descended on that area and began buying up the available land. In a few cases the companies and the individuals bid against each other. Three years ago, after these new people had acquired sixty percent of the area, it was announced that Suffolk Street was being proposed as a housing site. By that time some of the parcels had changed hands, back and forth, one new outfit to another, seven, eight times. On the occasion of each sale the price was raised significantly. By then, three years ago, the individuals who had begun in the buying were out. Three of them were officers in the companies that had taken over their parcels. All of them, individuals and companies, were part of Rainbow.

"Now follow this. The tenement at Eighty-four Suffolk sold for seventeen thousand dollars five years ago. Last year—the land still hasn't been acquired by the city—it went to the Suffolk Street Land Company for sixty-six thousand dollars. The vice-president of the company that sold the building to Suffolk Street Land happens to be the wife of that previously mentioned member of Herbert Davis' staff. They live down the block from the president of Suffolk Street Land. What they're waiting for is the city to move to acquire the land under the provisions of a Federal Housing Act. Of course they're going to realize a decent return on their investment. But that's only the first part.

"Here's where it gets difficult. The city will arrange to sell the site to the Port Smith Development Corporation for approximately half of what it will pay Suffolk Street Land. The loss represents part of the federal, state, and city stake in new housing. That's the way the law was written. The Port Smith Development Corporation will build the project, rent the apartments at fixed rates, maintain the

478

buildings, keep the grounds, and retain all rights of ownership. Obviously, the Port Smith Development Corporation has had to demonstrate some kind of financial responsibility. It has—and the Federal Government has agreed to extend to it very low cost, very low interest credit for construction. The president of the Port Smith Development Corporation went to Washington with a letter of recommendation from the office of Herbert Davis, signed by our staff member; and another from a banker downtown who is a member of the Port Smith Planning Board. The Port Smith Development Corporation is going into this with its own capital to the extent of a half-million dollars. Through one set of paper corporations, Rainbow acquired the site for less than two hundred and eighty thousand. The city plans to buy the site for three million. Rainbow will reinvest a sixth of the three million to get the federal credit and the title to a project valued at twenty-seven million. Using techniques developed elsewhere, the people in Rainbow will draw off another six million above and beyond the value of Suffolk Street Houses.

"On Palmer Avenue, where the housing is already completed, they had to move more quickly. The city was in a hurry, so they had to settle for a third of the land. When their construction company took over, they more than made up for what they had sacrificed. Remember that the old buildings were still occupied. Rainbow collected the rents. Demolition was delayed—stalled. Every month was a month to the good. Under normal conditions, slums return their investment every five years, but here was a windfall situation. No repairs, no maintenance. It was two years before the first building came down. For two years the construction company collected rents, and then, as it demolished buildings and tenants were shifted from one building to the next, the company raised the rents as much as the old wartime rental law allows."

"That takes heart."

"Not for them. After the first block came down, it was flattened and covered with blacktop. The construction company paid for that and then leased the block to the E and F Services Corporation, which Rainbow created for that purpose, at one hundred dollars a month. The construction company took a loss it applied to taxes and the cost of construction—in other words, the federal loan, while the smaller E and F Services operated the block as a parking lot at enormous profit.

"The objective was to draw as much as possible out of the construction company. In another deal it sold all the appliances in the slums to another Rainbow outfit and then leased them back at three times the sale price. On a third project, the rent collecting was farmed out to an agency—Rainbow-owned, of course—so that the construction company took a beating while the collection agency made the money."

"A moment ago you said that MacIver was clean. There wouldn't be any trouble making a case of conspiracy."

"The way I've explained it, yes. Conflict of interest is studiously avoided. The correspondence is carefully worded—you could argue that it refers to nothing but entirely unrelated transactions. The books MacIver kept have to be interpreted. If you called a grand jury, a score of innocent, maligned know-nothings would parade to the stand and wonder what you were talking about."

It was true.

"I have found one opening," Mike said. "The banker on the Planning Board. His name is Thomas Hanrahan and he's the president of the Port Smith Commercial Trust Company on Merchant Street. I told you that he recommended the Port Smith Development Corporation. He wrote a total of four letters, sending copies to the secretary of Port Smith Development, who happened to be Colin MacIver. The day before Hanrahan wrote the last letter, Port Smith Development acquired, for stock, the Gordon Holding Company, which was a real estate company involved in another project. It had a tax credit that made it valuable. Thomas Hanrahan, Jr., age twelve, had five hundred shares of Gordon Holding that were exchanged for one hundred and fifty shares of Port Smith Development. As I say, the transaction was completed the day before Hanrahan wrote his last letter. The first letter contained the usual document attesting that he had no personal interest in Port Smith Development. As his son's guardian, he executes all his son's documents. It would be enough to pry open some of the rest. Port Smith Development, by the way, doesn't own a single bulldozer or truck. It subcontracts everything. The subcontractors do their financing at the Port Smith Commercial Trust Company."

"On Merchant Street," Leland said.

"I said that there were thirty-eight principals. I didn't bother to list all the sons, daughters, wives, parents, and so forth. These people have enough confidence in this to set up everyone in their families."

"Our client doesn't know a thing about it," Leland said.

"There's a reason for that. I'll get to it. The subcontracting—the actual construction—was outside MacIver's province, but there is some information in his files. First, the financing at Hanrahan's bank, where the loan interest goes back to Rainbow in public relations fees. Second, the purchase of materials. Rainbow apparently never buys anything unless one of its own gets the sales commission. If a seller isn't willing to do business on those terms, Rainbow goes somewhere else. The commission on the sale of a thousand refrigerators may seem petty in relation to an outfit dealing in millions, but that commission to one man will buy a car, or pay for a year of a college education. There are two or three letters in MacIver's files to indicate that Rainbow has used salesmen's commissions as a way of paying off."

"How did MacIver get to be secretary of Port Smith Development?"

"Joe, at different times MacIver was vice-president, secretary, treasurer, consultant, or public relations man for most of these companies. He was a charter stockholder in all of them. He was the salesman—for a commission—in a dozen deals. He was an accountant, sure, but when he died he had three clients, a grocer, a small stationery firm, and a provisions dealer."

"How did he get involved in this? Who was he to Rainbow?"

"It was his idea."

Leland stared.

"That's right," Mike said. "Colin MacIver made Rainbow come alive."

Leland had to wave him off and look away—down at the table,

not out the window. For a second he seemed to lose control of what he was doing. Once before he had felt something like it, after the war when Karen had driven the LaSalle through the red light. It was like that, rising out of the seat and hitting the rear-view mirror, having no control. He moved away from the window and scratched at the back of his hand. He sat still, as if that would help in sorting things out. There was something underneath it all, a hurt. He felt victimized. He wanted to think that it had to do with telling Norma, but it was nothing like that. He had already told her that the man she had married had cheated his first wife in at least two ways. Leland would never say to any woman that this was worse. It was to him, though, in spite of himself. He could see it, he knew where it went and the circumstances of the people it hurt.

Mike said, "The correspondence goes back six years. For some reason MacIver wrote his first letter to Herbert Davis, asking for an appointment to discuss—I'm sort of quoting—certain aspects of Public Law such-and-such. I can't tell if Davis actually saw the letter and directed his staff man to act on his own. In any case, Davis was protected then and he's protected now. There's no record of participation by him in any part of the corporate tangle of Rainbow. What follows those first three or four letters is a series of invitations to individuals the staff man knew. There were meetings, apparently private, informal, and noncommittal. The next letters were written by MacIver. They were offers to sell participation, on the basis of the previous discussions. What follows are the organizational papers of the first corporations. I would assume that some of them were fraudulently drawn up—that the meetings reported never really took place. That would be impossible to prove. After that, Rainbow was off and running. There are gaps in MacIver's information, but what's there relates to the mechanics of finding people to do the actual work. That required contacts, which MacIver didn't have. He came in with so little, in fact—some money of his own and, naturally, the idea—that it has to be some kind of tribute to him that his partners didn't ace him out altogether."

"All right," Leland said. "This is important to our client. How much was he able to put into this?"

"Twelve thousand, at the start."

Leland told him that MacIver had been married to his first wife at the time and had borrowed money from his mother to handle the divorce. He had even been a college student at the time Mike gave for the start of Rainbow.

"I knew he was married," Mike said. "There is some correspondence from that period, including some stockbrokers' reports that were addressed to a post office box in MacIver's name. That wasn't hard to figure out. The reports explain his money, too. At the beginning of the year before, he put a little more than two thousand in four strong issues, a pretty fair investment, assuming he had little in cash reserves. I had Joan check on them in my own books. By that summer he had made a few hundred. At that point I don't know what he did, because the papers are missing. There is a report for December of that year, and he had nearly four thousand. He probably heard something about a particular issue. Anyway, from there I have to go to a newspaper clipping that he had with a later report. The clipping was dated early in January and had to do with a communications outfit. Joan checked that one, too. It went up forty-three points in the first three-quarters of that year. MacIver probably bought in when he read the item, but he sold fifty shares in July, one hundred in August, and fifty in September. I get that from a note he wrote to himself, so I don't know if he had more of that issue. He could have, and a cash reserve, too. The twelve thousand was only the first installment. He went in for another five the following April, and then twenty in October. He was getting his first returns by then."

"You've done a hell of a job, Mike. You and Joan."

"I worked out my time. And Flo's. I went on this on Wednesday morning and I've been with it straight through. You should charge our client four days for me and two days for Flo. That's up until today, anyway. With your time, eleven hundred, plus expenses."

"We'll see. I want to know what it comes to."

Mike hesitated, regarding him, then he nodded. He said, "MacIver's codes coincide chronologically with the formation of the Rainbow corporations. I had the feeling that the codes came out of the left-hand language he had to use in the correspondence. For instance, there was a Lewis Street Realty Corporation, and it appears in the books as 'Blue Lou.' "

" 'Blue Lou' is an old swing tune."

"I didn't know that. The numbers are more difficult. In one case, they were substitutions. Four and two made thirty-six. Four turned out to be nine; two, seven; and thirty-six, sixteen. In MacIver's own personal record, he made the entries backwards. Fifty thousand became a five preceded by four zeros. Instead of reading from left to right and adding from right to left, you had to read it from right to left and add from left to right. The column on the left was the units, the second the tens, and so forth.

"Now, the other thing you have to know is the way MacIver participated in Rainbow. You'll understand why his widow doesn't know anything about it. The way he handled the stock issue that took off gives a clue to the way he wanted to work, and maybe the fact that he had no holdings in Rainbow at the time of his death helps establish that he did kill himself, but even on those assumptions you still have no progress—I mean, while I worked on his books and papers I knew that I was in the presence of a bright and almost pathologically wary man. His letters show that he didn't care about being friendly with his partners. His sense of humor worked into the letters, but I thought I saw that the recipients would misunderstand rather than laugh. What he did for fun was for his own private fun. He didn't give a damn about the others. I had a picture of him but it didn't go anywhere. He stayed the same—brilliant, timid like an animal, lonely like an animal in a cage."

"There are cracks in that armor," Leland said. "He was devoted to his wife and some people would say that that would have to take more than an average effort. He had an unabashed appetite for the expensive things of life. His car is in the parking lot, if you would like proof. There is his war record. But we're seeing the same man, there's no question of that." He told Mike of their client's impression of MacIver when he had come to work in her office. "He never did discuss his girl friend with his first wife. It seems clear to me that he borrowed that money from his mother to conceal the money he had accumulated on the market. This is what I wanted to ask you: on

484

those lists of yours, are there any women who don't belong—single women, married women whose husbands aren't part of the scheme?"

Mike shook his head. "I don't follow you."

"I'm trying something. A man can be quiet most of the time, but not necessarily always for the same reason. Suppose he cared for his girl friend and felt guilty over the way it turned out? You know what I mean. His reaction was so quick that night he came home bleeding, that you could believe that he had expected something bad. So he tried to make it up to her another way."

"There's no one like that on the lists, Joe."

"You're looking at me as if I had lost my mind."

"She almost killed him. Why would he want to make anything up to her?"

"I said that I was only trying it. Suppose she didn't know he was married? Suppose she did and he had led her to believe he was going to divorce Betty and marry her, and then changed his mind? That would make the best kind of woman act badly. That's the thing, the kind of woman she was."

"There's no evidence of her anywhere. I think you ought to forget it."

"I know how he felt about his wife. He was capable of just what I'm saying."

"You think you know how he felt. How can you be sure? Some of these people in Rainbow have moved their operation into Clausen County. There are letters alluding to that. He started it. He had to expect it to spread. *That* was the kind of man he was."

"I've been hearing things about Clausen. And there's the possibility that it's going into Manitou. Karen overheard a conversation on Monday. But I do know that stuff—how he felt." He looked at Mike, wondering what he thought. "She's not simply the nice kid she seemed to you." He stopped. It was too general, too subject to misinterpretation.

"Look, Joe, don't make the mistake of projecting yourself into the case. You may be the sort of man to feel guilty about driving a woman to attack you. I think you would want to make it up to her. That's you, not him. All right, he had an attractive, interesting wife and a taste for luxury. Anyone could share those things. But I know how much time and effort he put into Rainbow. It isn't something he toyed with. He was close enough long enough to know as well as he knew his name that it came down to stealing from his country, abusing the poor, and thwarting the hopes of honorable men who thought the law could work. He kept at it in the face of all those things. Bear that in mind. As I began to get the idea of the thing I was so dazzled I was envious. He was smarter than I am. I had to stop and put it in perspective. There were the cartons of evidence of the labor he put into a way to steal. Don't place yourself in his class. He was something quite apart. I didn't want to think that, but it's true. You know me. He was something very different from the rest of us. I had to face it."

Leland did not believe him.

"You look upset about something."

"No, you were telling me something I had to know."

"The way MacIver handled the stock that took off illustrates the way he protected his interests in Rainbow. I didn't want to believe it; I spent quite a bit of time checking to see if he wasn't somehow making his money work harder. The answer is no. MacIver methodically sold himself out. He couldn't have been afraid of losses. He knew the layout of Rainbow better than anybody. He knew what his investments could realize. The letters show that some of these people are in it on their faith in their friends. He always sold his interests to one or another of his partners, and toward the end, he was doing it faster and faster. This year, three new corporations were formed and he wasn't in on any of them as a stockholder. Two paid him consultants' fees, and he was supposed to have done a survey for the third. He bought a considerable amount of insurance—"

"I know, all of it covered by the two-year suicide clause. Only a fraction paid off."

"The rest went into blue chips and government bonds. There is some undeveloped real estate in Clausen, but there is nothing to show that it fits into any of Rainbow's plans. That's not saying that it doesn't."

"How much would you say he lost, playing it as he did?"

"At the most, a million four. That's not accounting for a lot of unknowns. He might not have gotten the same breaks from his partners if he had not established a pattern of selling. Nine is a better figure. MacIver lost nine hundred thousand in his own scheme."

"There's nothing to connect Herbert Davis directly," Leland said.

"That's right."

"What about Wendell Roberts?"

"He goes back to the announcement of the Suffolk Street Houses. He's on the staff of a psychiatric clinic on Baxter Avenue, in the Suffolk Street neighborhood. In one letter he says that the staff members take turns at the various responsibilities of managing the clinic, but he's seemed to have grabbed the Suffolk project as his own. He was chairman of the clinic when the project was proposed, and he steered the clinic into becoming one of the sponsors. All these projects have sponsors—organizations, schools—and that's part of what makes Roberts' position so difficult to assess. The other sponsors seem to have only a perfunctory interest—Roberts was absorbed in plans, design, and so forth. In several letters he professes ignorance, but then, in the last, he lists seventeen design objectives, things I never thought of, window placement, ventilation.

"The other item that makes his relationship to Rainbow so curious is that MacIver had no right or reason to possess any of Roberts' letters. I told you that MacIver and Roberts were remote on the table of organization. The only explanation for the letters appearing in MacIver's papers is that, at some time or other, MacIver created opportunities in his partners' offices to go into their files and steal them."

"There's nothing in the letters but this unusual interest," Leland said.

"But it is unusual," Mike said.

"Blackmail is out, anyway," Leland said. "A man doesn't turn his back on nine hundred thousand dollars and then blackmail his neighbor."

"Maybe it wasn't a matter of money. You know more about it than I do."

"They had a good relationship," Leland said. "It was MacIver who decided to buy the house next to Roberts'. He told his wife that he thought Roberts was a civilized man—he wouldn't be knocking on the door every morning. Roberts spoke well of MacIver to the insurance investigators. They had an occasional beer together. Discussing sports, Roberts says, but that's a lie. Did you see anything on MacIver's last few days?"

"Yes. As I told you, there were the three corporations formed this year. MacIver sold the last of his older holdings late last year. His correspondence and appointment book show that he was continually involved up to the end—meetings, lunches, telephone calls, introductions. On his last morning he called a man in Rainbow for an employment interview for the son of the man who did the electrical work on the Palmer Street job. The boy had been graduated from the University of California in June."

"MacIver went there before the war."

"The appointment was set up for the following week. There was no friction. MacIver was in the same good spot he had been from the start. Better. He was in a position to do people favors."

"What about our client? Why doesn't she know about all this?"

"He received a letter from a man who was coming in as an investor. The man wanted to know the same thing. MacIver answered by saying that he was only recently married and the setting-up of a new household took time. He intended to bring her in, he said."

"But he didn't," Leland said. "I should have told you to take a look at the souvenir book and the insurance file."

"I did, last night. Florence brought them up. All I can tell you is that I didn't see anything that contradicted what I found in the papers."

"Let me have those lists," Leland said. "I want to try them on the client." He put the papers, unexamined, in his inside pocket. He knew what was coming and now he knew, too, that he had been groping for a way to avoid it.

Mike said, "The man to see about Hanrahan's conflict of interest is the U.S. Attorney. We're going to have to protect ourselves—we should have copies of everything we turn over. I think we should go to the newspapers, too. You know better than I do that we can't take the chance of letting these people learn that we know about them without putting on the appropriate pressure. They'll be after us whether we make them suffer or not."

Leland sat forward. "The client was told that she would hear first of any evidence of a crime. I'll handle that. I don't want to get sandbagged. If we go to the U.S. Attorney and then find out that the newspapers won't handle it, we'll be in even worse shape than if we didn't see the newspapers at all. It would get around that we have a story nobody wants. The people in Rainbow will feel that they can grind us out like cigarettes. Last, as you point out, the material we have doesn't tell everything. The Hanrahan thing may be enough for the U.S. Attorney to go around the city snapping locks on everybody's files—but only maybe. That's not the important thing. Go back. MacIver went to people telling them they could be rich if they could raise fairly large amounts of capital in a hurry. For that reason—if no other—you can figure that there are silent partners. I don't want to go up against them without knowing more than I do. I want to talk to some people. My father, for one. Maybe Warren Johnson in Manitou."

"You're right," Mike said, but he was disappointed. Leland did not want to look at him. There was nothing now that his father could tell them about the trouble in Port Smith. Who the U.S. Attorney in this district was and how one went about dealing with him. The matter of protection was as Mike had said: copy everything.

It was the client who stopped Leland. She had to be told, but he could not help thinking of how she would react. What would be her attitude toward her money now? He knew what she had been through, what she hoped to become, and what the money meant to her.

Roberts was in more terrible trouble than he could possibly imagine. A man could hit low when there was something to protect that he thought was good, that was easy to understand. Roberts knew enough about marriage to have been able to see that what he said would eventually have its effect on Karen, too. Because of his anger, Leland was willing to believe that Norma would have no problem putting Roberts in proper perspective, but Norma had gone a long way with Roberts, far too many years. It could not be that simple.

"What kind of shape are we in at the office?"

"All right," Mike said. "It's quiet."

"You take the next flight back to Manitou and start assembling the material for photographing. We have to have her approval for the expense. When I have it I'll call you at my apartment. I don't think we can go beyond that for now." Mike looked unsatisfied. Leland honestly did not know what more could be done until he had talked to Norma, but his thoughts about Roberts and her made him want to counter criticism that could not even occur to anyone else. "I'd better stay here. Karen and I had tentative plans for the weekend, but I think we can rework them. Would you call her, tell her that I'll check us into a hotel? The Regent. Tell her to wire the Regent about the flight she and Steffie will take, and so on. If she seems hesitant—well, she won't. Forget that. And I'll be here at the airport to meet her."

"Okay."

Leland looked for the waitress. While he had been talking he had remembered that he had told Mike that he would be in Manitou on Saturday. He could not be sure that what he had just said about "tentative plans" did not contradict that. And now Leland was thinking that he had been urging Karen to come to Port Smith since Monday. Confusion between Mike and her this afternoon would not simplify unscrambling what had happened over long-distance last night. Leland knew what she would say, how upset she would be, but he was not going to take the opportunity now to use Mike to avert a situation. As much as anything, Leland did not want Mike knowing these things about them. The waitress was coming.

Downstairs, while Mike checked the flight schedule, Leland realized that he could not remember what he had told his mother about Steffie staying over. He simply could not remember. There was a pattern to the disorder he had drawn around him, as if he had made a kind of desperate try at telling every side that he was all right—*I'm swell, my old self, recognize me?*—when he was toying with crack-

ing his life
think abo
was so e
The fur
still wa
had s

her
cl
f

found out what had happened to them. Supp
Wendell Roberts is in this up to his eyeballs.
from Roberts where the papers are. No on
by the way, and the management of the
that kind of contact to the police. W
anxious enough to break into a n
word of a man in Roberts' positio
papers are safe in the crawl s
That didn't happen. So at the
became immensely confide
have something. There
of the woman who did
"Here is wher
me from my own
for Norma's sa
like you to a
told him th
over hi
party

The rea
while. So it was a
thing. A psycho is out simp
make a mess, but the man I spoke
the thing in stride. We do have knowledge tha
of value in the office that morning. Norma told me tha
down there because she hadn't been able to sleep. Of course
didn't tell anyone—anyone. No one knew that the office would be
empty. Okay?"

"I suppose."

"We don't know for certain, but it would seem from the evidence that none of the people in Rainbow would have known of MacIver's coded books. But suppose someone became afraid of what would happen to the things MacIver had a right to have—the letters, the documents. So that someone broke in, found the office empty, broke into other offices to cover what he had done. If you were afraid of those papers, would you have stopped there? You would have

se for a moment that
Our anxious party learns
I talked to was contacted,
building would have reported
would know about it. A man
mber of offices doesn't take the
—look at the deceit of it—that the
ace of a garage. He goes after them.
end of it you have a man who suddenly
nt. He didn't have the papers. He had to
s only one thing left—a working knowledge
have the papers.

I come in. By sheer accident Roberts knows of
Port Smith days, and after first asking me to go easy
e, he bludgeoned me with a personal matter. I would
ccept my word that he went as far with it as he dared. I
at I would think about it. Since then, I've been falling all
. He's called me, invited me to a party—that's right, a

"I see. He did have a motive. MacIver had his letters."

"That's the part I don't understand," Leland said. "I know
Roberts and how he handles himself. I know a few things about
MacIver. In any case, I have no doubt that it was Roberts—or someone he put up to it—who broke into MacIver's office. Probably he did
it himself. His own office was close enough."

Mike wondered if Leland had considered the possibility of outsiders—professionals. Leland told him how professionals would have
made a murder and robbery easier on themselves. Mike nodded.

"And the garage wasn't disturbed," he said. "It's inconceivable
that anyone else would go as far as the office only to give up." He was
staring through the windshield. "The question is: do you think
Roberts is capable of murder? Or of living with it?"

"I don't know." Leland slapped uneasily at the rim of the steering wheel. "He's a great actor, that's sure. I'll tell you one thing. He's
not going to get the opportunity to show me what he can or cannot
do."

From the airport Leland drove to Norma's, and while he was getting his clothing, she went over the four lists. She had been told nothing. When he came downstairs again she was waiting. From the sofa she handed up the lists, silent. There were four checks against the first list, none against the second or third, and two against the fourth. She had checked her husband's name. The other three on the first list, she said, were men who had telephoned him at home on business. There was nothing that she could tell Leland about them. She was fairly sure that two had called more than once. She could remember having thought that she would have regarded the men who called him at home as pests, except for their courtesy. Courtesy? Yes, they were unfailingly polite. Could she remember any names that did not appear on the lists? She did not think that there had been any other callers.

On the fourth list she had checked Wendell Roberts and a man she had met at a neighborhood party, barbeque—she might remember if she had the chance to think. All she could tell Leland now was that the man was thin, bookish, musty-looking. He was a college instructor or the husband of one. Leland said that it would be a simple thing to clear up. He folded the papers and put them back in his pocket. She clasped her hands.

"Aren't you going to tell me what this is about?"

"One more question. What did you do the night after you cleaned out your husband's office?"

"The night it was broken into, you mean? I was here. Wendell made the funeral arrangements. The body had to be recovered from the Clausen County authorities. That was done the next day. It's very confused in my mind—do you have to have this? I'd have to work on what I remember."

"You were here alone, that's the thing," Leland said.

"No, not alone. People from the neighborhood came over. You know. Some girls from my last job. I made calls that afternoon. They were here, and the neighborhood people. I stayed here in the living room and other people ran my house, made coffee, answered the telephone and the door. I hadn't seen some of them in months and months. People can be awfully nice sometimes."

"When did you find out about the funeral arrangements?"

"Wendell called. I didn't have to go to the funeral parlor until the next afternoon. He had done everything. You're trying to divert me, Joe. Are you going to tell me what you learned?"

"Not right now." She had not seen Roberts the night of the break-in. "I'd like your permission to photograph some of the things Mike has been working on. He's already gone back to Manitou. He'll be waiting for my call."

"Joe, you can't expect me to be happy with this."

"I know. And I'm sorry." He took out his cigarettes.

"Do what you have to," she said. "You told me that you'd be going to a hotel if your wife came down for the weekend. I guess that answers the other questions. At least you and your wife can talk. After last night—well, I won't say it."

"That's right. I thought that we weren't going to discuss it today."

"Not this part, another. You and *me*." She shook her head and looked at him. "Are you trying to kid me? I can't live with liars. I thought I told you that."

He turned to go. "I'll call you."

"Why are you doing this? I can't play games. I don't want to." He had stopped. She was getting up. "There was a time when I thought I was finished with playing games. Please, Joe."

"You're not willing now to believe that I do understand. But why do you think I'm leaving? There is this job to do. It isn't finished. I'd love to stay—and stay, and stay. Would you like me to start fooling with you, after what you said on the telephone, before I've looked my wife in the eye? We haven't talked, she and I. Mike is carrying a message. I'm afraid of you, I—"

Her skirt needed adjusting and her slip showed in the area cut out for her stomach. She had the chance to show him how weary she was of this. Instead she ran her hand through her dark hair and smiled. "Go on. You say things and you think you mean them, but if I tried to start something now you would see through it and get angry. You wouldn't stay. You would want to leave, as you do now. So you'd better do it while we're still nice."

He extended his hand to her. He wanted to touch her. "I won't take that seriously."

"You want a kiss," she said, stepping toward him. Her eyes were bright until he closed his own. "Go on," she said, kissing him again lightly. "Call me."

CHAPTER TWENTY

■ ●

THERE WAS A LEVEL ON WHICH HE HAD NOT LIED TO NORMA. HE
felt that there were things he could do—before he told her about
Rainbow—but they seemed to depend on how well he could organize
his mind. There was a direction, a current, just beyond his reach. He
was not more tired now than he had been yesterday, but he found
himself looking ahead in terms of his strength, as if he could see what
he had left, and as if it really could be meted out.

He took a tower suite at the Regent. He telephoned for a light
lunch and had the bellboy come up for his laundry.

While he ate he called his mother. It did not please him to hear
her ask at once what time he would be leaving Steffie with her. He
answered that it would be before dinner; he could not tell her more
because he did not have the flight information. He asked if his father
was asleep.

"He isn't here, Joe. He hasn't come home yet. He called after
midnight to say that he had to stay one more night and that he would
be here this afternoon, but I'm still waiting for him."

"He's getting his rest. I saw him early in the evening."

"I know, I saw you. On television. You could use some rest
yourself. Was Karen able to reach you?"

"Oh, sure. Don't worry about me getting rest, either."

"I won't. You're a ham, you know."

"Pop wanted to say that. Wait a second. Do either of you have
any thoughts about that? Serious thoughts—about me being on television?"

496

"Thoughts? You mean opinions? No, of course not. Is something wrong?"

"No, no. As long as I'm thinking about it, did you ever hear anybody—ever—say anything about the stories in the newspapers or anything like that?"

"No. Why? Did something happen?" She decided not to wait for an answer. "I've never heard anything, Joe, and to my knowledge, neither has your father."

"Okay. It's not important. I'm going to try to get hold of Pop. I'll see you later."

He had tried to get busyness into his tone. He stared at the telephone. It was impossible to imagine how he had sounded to her. He prepared another cup of coffee and sat back in the armchair and looked out the window. There was a view of the bay and Bay Slope and for miles beyond to the mountains. Years ago, it had been the style for newlyweds to check in at hotels downtown before going on to the resorts, and he and Karen had heard about the view. He imagined that the rooms themselves had not changed much since those days. The carpets had to be new. They were thick, sculptured broadlooms, green in here, rose in the bedroom. The furniture in both rooms was mahogany and plush brocade—irreplaceable today, for all he knew. The place was beautifully cared for. It gave off a warmth of color and polish that would delight anyone. When he had told Mike the Regent, Leland had not thought of any of these things; he had seen a chance to do something different. He had not remembered the honeymooners until he had registered for "Mr. and Mrs. Joseph M. Leland," and then he had had a reaction, an eerie and unpleasant physical sensation. He felt as if he did not belong, and as if he were not fooling any of the people he passed. He had not asked himself when exactly he had begun to think of the events of the war and the years after, but he knew now that they had been touching him for days. As he had ridden up in the elevator some of those events had come on him in a rush. By the time he had closed the door on the bellboy they had been suppressed again, but now he could not deceive himself about the push they had given him. He had been working steadily since he had arrived. Unfinished coffee to the side, he reached again for the telephone.

His father was in his office.

"I would have called you, if I knew where you were." He sounded as if he were sick. "You showed up here too soon, yesterday. Maybe you wouldn't have done what you did in front of that camera."

"What happened? Are you all right?"

"I'm fine. Let's do things in order. Yesterday you came in to have a talk. What was on your mind?"

"That was yesterday. What's going on?"

"No, no, no. I'm going home in a few minutes and the last thing I want to do before I leave is get this off my chest. Do things in order. Did you hear from Karen, by the way?"

"Yes. I had more to do after I left you, that's why she had trouble getting me." He said he wanted a favor. He wanted to talk to the man who had reported the barroom conversation relating to the subject they had discussed Wednesday morning. Captain Leland remembered. He took his son's number and said that the man would call him. What else? Was there anything solid on their old neighbor who had been mentioned Wednesday? No. Would the Internal Revenue Service be interested in him? Possibly.

Leland changed his tone and hoped that his father would understand. "I'm thinking of starting a branch office in Port Smith. Somebody suggested that I go to the Port Smith Commercial Trust Company of Merchant Street for my financing. What do you think?"

There was silence. "We can have a conversation about it. There'll be something you can work out. I'll talk to you."

"Let's hear what's happened to you."

His father took a moment. "Scanlon's gone. He's at headquarters. Your old friend and I had a series of arguments until late last night. What the hell, I don't know. I'm trying not to think about him, anyway.

"They were treating Scanlon all right, I had no complaint about that. They had him cleaned up, they gave him his dinner. He had rest and they were questioning him in a civilized way. But by midnight it was obvious to me that they weren't going to get anywhere. I said that

498

to Schoenstein and he brushed me off. There was something else. I thought I could see something the matter with Scanlon. There was no life in his eyes. On the three occasions I was in to listen—you know how I am—he had to get up to use the bathroom four times. I asked about it, but Schoenstein thought I was up to something and didn't give me a straight answer. Well, I hemmed and hawed, then I called headquarters. Spoke to one of my friends. We had a sick man here. My friend said that it wouldn't be easy to get an outside doctor— that's what I wanted, I wanted a witness—for that kind of work at that hour, but I was getting worried, and I said there should be two, to avoid mistakes. He called Saint Elizabeth's, and one of the residents and another guy, a specialist—he just happened to be there— came over. Endocrinology, that's what it was. That was at two-thirty. I'd been getting some rest off and on, but by then I was too interested in Scanlon. I sprung the doctors on Schoenstein. By that time we couldn't speak civilly to each other and I knew what he would have done if he had known. He did it later anyway, he called one of *his* friends at headquarters and had Scanlon moved.

"When the doctors came I called Schoenstein into my office and told him who they were, and who had authorized them to come over. Schoenstein is no good at concealing his reactions, but he went out and stopped the questioning so the doctors could get a look at the man. I heard the resident say, 'Oh, Jesus'—I'm not kidding. Later I got the specialist in my office and he told me as well as he could what they thought was the matter with Scanlon.

"He has some kind of heart damage. Either he has a degenerative disease or he's had an attack—a lot of people have attacks and never know it. He has a prostate condition. That could be the degenerative disease again or something separate. They have to run tests for syphilis, and Scanlon isn't showing any of the common symptoms of the third stage—that's the final phase and it can come twenty years after infection. Scanlon doesn't know if he ever had syphilis. In any case, they didn't think there was any brain damage. And he's suffering from malnutrition. The doctor told me that he could have come up with that part of the diagnosis over the telephone." Captain Leland coughed. "Then I asked him if any of it would interfere with bringing Scanlon to trial. He told me to forget about a trial.

"He told me to forget all about it," he said after he had cleared his throat. "First, he said, Scanlon would be dead from one thing or another within a year, maybe a lot sooner. Then he said, 'Your man is already on the long, slow slide toward insanity and death.' My mouth fell open, and not because I've never looked at a man—say a cancer victim—and thought, 'You'll be dead in a week or a month'; I have thought it and felt afraid and ashamed afterward. It was the way the doctor said it, and what he said next. He said that this kind of decay and collapse, a faster and faster spin toward death, happens a lot to old maids living alone and these rootless, homeless men like Scanlon. It's as if nature itself were attacking them, as if it had been waiting for them to get within reach. The stragglers, he called them. I said, 'That doesn't help Mary Shoftel's parents.' And he said, 'They should have been more careful.' I didn't like that, so I tossed the pictures of the girl's body at him—they came in late last night. They didn't bother him. She was torn on the thighs and the lower torso— ripped. Scanlon must have gone at her with his bare hands. She had the body of a baby. The pictures didn't bother this guy a bit. He was off on something else. He looked at them and said, 'Don't misunder- stand me. He knew that he was doing this.' I said, 'You'd think that it would have made him stop.' 'No, he had gone too far.' Then he said that maybe Scanlon wanted to prove to himself that he could still get it up. He would be able to say yes or no to it—he thought. 'He won't tell us that,' the doctor said. 'He'll shrug it off. At this arraign- ment the judge will order him examined, and by the time I could see him again'—the doctor didn't know how that side of it works—'Scan- lon will have disintegrated that much more. He won't be able to an- swer me. It will be like watching a guy die in slow motion—just slid- ing away. When he went after that baby, he was trying to show that he was normal, but the act itself had the effect of driving him further away. He knew it was wrong, he never thought it was right. It was just more important to him, trying to say he was alive. It was almost an error in logic.' But he was fighting another kind of logic that we don't live by. This doctor said that the only way he could live with

500

things like this was to go take a walk in the woods and look at the violence there. Things slashing at each other. If there's a respect for life there, we aren't capable of understanding it. But we are following it, he said, by hounding Scanlon now, and saying that he has to die. We really don't know what we're doing, and what's worse, we don't care. We just want to get rid of him."

"I don't get that at all," Leland said. "It's not as complicated as all that. And if Scanlon is insane, better-qualified men than this one will say."

"I started on the same thing," his father said. "He asked me to define insanity. We talked about the rule of law that determines sanity, knowing right from wrong. Everybody knows that that's no good, but you can't get a consensus on a new rule. So then he said, 'Suppose we're not looking at it the right way? Two things govern us, birth and death. They're the basic rules we have to go by, with everything else the stuff we make up.' Then he asked me, 'What about the time between? We know a little about what we are—not what we need, like love and so on, but what we *are*. We're cruel and violent without giving it a thought. It's not just birth and death, but life, too—three things—' "

"It sounds like he really had his fun with you," Leland said.

"Ah, no, nothing like that. He said he'd stake his professional reputation on what he was saying about Scanlon. He works with the glands, which are supposed to have a lot to do with what we do and feel, but as much as they do, they don't enter into what he was trying to describe. He wished they did. Then he could settle the question with a needle.

"But while he was talking, Schoenstein was on the telephone arranging to continue to try for the confession before Scanlon collapsed completely. He's not just under pressure, he's aiding and abetting. That's who you talked up, a politician using the case to advance and ingratiate himself. I'm an old man. The trolleys were being pulled by horses when I was a kid, so what should I know about this stuff? He *does* know. He has the opportunity to advance the public safety. A little, anyway. That's the great thing about being a cop, isn't it? But that's not the point."

"What is?"

"Scanlon. Maybe these things can't be prevented. The doctor made a big thing about the difference between our needs and our nature. What a cruel, selfish thing a man can become. I'm going to go down to that hearing, if Scanlon lives long enough. I want to look in his eyes. I won't forget this past night and I want to be sure for my own sake. I want to see it."

"There's nothing the matter with that," Leland said. "And don't start calling yourself old. You're doing better than Dave Schoenstein."

"That isn't hard. But he makes me wonder what I've spent my life working for. I'm very depressed, Joe. I'm very unhappy with the way this has gone."

"Come on, forget it. No disrespect intended, Pop, but a good night's sleep wouldn't hurt you."

"You're right about that. We'll discuss it another time. I'll have that man call you. The other thing hasn't slipped my mind, either."

Leland put down the receiver and sat back with his coffee, which felt cold through the cup. His legs were heavy, a sign to him to get up and move around, but he stayed still. He put the coffee down and scratched the back of his hand, careful not to break the skin again. It felt no better today, he was only getting used to it. He was beginning to think of the coroner's inquest in Clausen County; a transcript would contain names that could provide another crack at Rainbow. Even if he had to go through his friends at Manitou Life to get a transcript without attracting attention, it would be worth the trouble. No one would worry about the request if an insurance company let on that it was doing battle with the man's widow. Leland would have no problem safeguarding against a double check on that story.

Leland called Florence at the office. She had not yet heard from Mike. Leland told her to forward the message that they had the approval to go ahead with the photographing.

He did not want to leave the telephone. He did not even want to pick it up to have room service take away the lunch tray. The sense of defeat—and deception, for he had not made a substantial move—was settling upon him. He could look out the window; he had a sense of the cold outside; he felt like a child wishing his winters away. Now the telephone rang.

It was his father's man. He had had to go to his notebook, then sort out and collect his thoughts. Leland wanted to hear everything he had to tell. The man had stopped at the bar after an overtime tour to relax and watch a particular television program. When he had left he had made the entries in his notebook, and on the next day he had reported the incident to the Captain. The last time he had thought about it, months ago, he had decided that the man had been repeating something that he had heard, and had known no more about the trouble in Clausen County than the Port Smith Police Department knew already.

The conversation had been substantially what Leland's father had said. The man had been drunk and running off at the mouth. The officer told Leland that he had tried to pump him, gently, but the man had refused to identify himself, his position, or the source of his information. Leland asked if there had been mention of any name at all. No. Any specific place or location? No. Leland wanted to know what the man looked like. Early forties, five-nine, one-eighty, thinning black hair, blue eyes, heavy beard, thin, small nose, and the beginning of jowls. He had not seen the man since, but his notes had refreshed his memory and he was sure that he would be able to identify him if it ever became necessary. Leland said that it just might, then he expressed his gratitude and said goodbye.

He had never believed that the man in the bar had been Mac-Iver. At no other time had MacIver become drunk or talked indiscriminately to acquaintances. The incident in the bar had not been within his capacity.

Leland's father was next, calling back with the information about Hanrahan and the Port Smith Commercial Trust Company. There were two separate, unconnected things to tell. Two years ago, Hanrahan had been made a Knight by the Pope. He was acknowledged to be the leader of the laity in Port Smith, and an important contributor to a wide range of charities, including the Police Athletic League. During the war he had been active in relief and refugee work, and Captain Leland could remember seeing him on the dais at the dinner at which he, the Captain, had heard the first suggestions of the truth of what had been happening to the Jews inside Nazi Germany. That was Mr. Hanrahan.

Less widely known was the history of his bank. Port Smith Commercial Trust had been founded in the twenties, when the regulation of banks had been minimal, if not for sale. The original directors had been known associates of bootleggers. Leland's father had been a patrolman at the time; he had been given the information as he had moved up the ranks. The personal files of men now retired or dead indicated that the Port Smith Commercial Trust Company had been created by the bootleggers through their "associates" for the purpose of providing a depository for the large amounts of cash that their businesses had accumulated. Captain Leland had been told, too, that the bank had been used as a facility for the disposal of the coins collected from slot machines. After suppression of the slots in the thirties, the bank had faded as an object of interest. It was known, of course, that the bootleggers and slot machine people had gone into dry cleaning, hotel supplies, and jukeboxes, among other things, but their activities could not be specifically related to the business of the bank. Captain Leland had nothing more recent—he had been kept aware of the bank only by the movements of Mr. Hanrahan. It was not to be assumed that Mr. Hanrahan was directly, intimately connected with the mob—although it would be interesting to check on the bank's other officers. Hanrahan was a devout and faithful man. Captain Leland could not explain that in relation to the history of his bank, but it happened to be true. If his son had anything on Mr. Hanrahan or his bank, it had better be good, because he was dealing with elements of enormous power.

Leland thanked him, said goodbye, disconnected, and checked his watch. Two-thirty. He called room service. If he wanted, he could call for a public stenographer and begin to draft a report for Norma. At the least, he could outline what remained to be done—he wanted to do that; the case was becoming too complicated and diffuse to be worked out of his jacket pockets.

There was one piece of business that outweighed all others: telling Norma. He could still do it without having to explain why he had avoided it before. If the prospect of her reaction distressed him so much, he could do it by telephone. And he could have another telephone brought in, if he did not want to tie up his line. It was not a question of not being able to think. He could put together any number of arrangements.

The telephone rang, long distance from Manitou, collect. It was Karen.

"I'm in my office, Joe. It was easier to reverse the charges than fill out the forms for a personal long-distance call at the end of the month. I was just talking with Mike. Did I understand him correctly? You want us to come down there this afternoon?"

"That's right. I want to see you."

"Mike said that it was serious. He mentioned that package in the closet."

"That's a precautionary measure. I don't know what's going to happen."

"You were serious last night," she said. "You couldn't talk"

"Within limits. That requires an explanation. Let it go for now. Can you make it? Can you do this for me?"

"Is it a test? Is that what it is?"

"No, I want you here. I wouldn't let Mike in on a thing like that, he'd run home and tell Joan. I've already made arrangements with my mother for Steffie. It's no game."

"I may be late. It's a good thing I can get a message to Steffie. The information about the flight will come later. I'm going to be tired, Joe. I didn't sleep well last night, and I'm not saying that to needle you—" The door buzzer sounded. "What's that?"

"Room service. I had my lunch up here."

"Oh—why? You don't like hotel rooms—is something really wrong?"

"No—no. You'll see."

"You want to do some talking," she said.

"Yes, but don't worry. Don't worry, just get down here safely."

"I'm not supposed to worry, but I'm supposed to carry that thing down there. Okay." She was gone. In all the years he had been on the Port Smith Police Department, she had never put her hand on either of the two revolvers he had owned. He had demonstrated them and he wanted her to have one in her house. But he knew that she moved it in the top of the closet by pushing it with her fingertips. It had to be cleaned regularly: she always arranged to be in another part of the house when he set out the tools, cloths, and oil on the kitchen table.

He was not going to do anything until he saw her. When he was not thinking clearly he wanted to blame the members of Rainbow for the death of Colin MacIver; he wanted to take them down, individually and together. Wendell Roberts was another matter.

Leland got up and stood at the window and tried to fasten to his memory the scene flooded with winter light. He wanted to dream. Karen's secretary called. He took the information. He thought of calling Norma, not to tell her of Rainbow, just to talk. The idea made him uneasy. He checked the time again. Finally he made another call, long-distance, to Manitou.

Karen and Steffie came down the steps, Karen carrying the shopping bag at her side like a knitting project, Steffie bearing the other package against her breast. She looked to the left and right as she came across the apron to the gate; she was plainly tense. She kissed her father on the cheek, then stepped aside to let her mother kiss him. He took the shopping bag.

"We have to wait for our luggage," Karen said.

"There's no rush."

"I'll hold onto this until we get a taxi," Steffie said.

"I have a car, honey. I'm sorry if I fouled up any plans you had made."

"Oh, no."

"She was going to the movies tonight," Karen said. "Florence met us at the airport with that bundle—scared us, too—and asked if there was anything she could do, but I told her no. I think she had my weekend shopping in mind. She couldn't call Steffie's girl friends."

"We can do that from the hotel," Leland said.

"I thought she was going to your mother's."

"We can stop. I said there's no rush." They arrived at the luggage pickup. He said to Steffie, "I wouldn't have done this if I hadn't thought it was necessary. It won't be a bad weekend for you."

"You don't have to call anybody." She tapped the package. "What is this?"

"That souvenir book you found for me on Monday. And my man's life insurance file."

"Did you know him? Is he dead?"

"I shook his hand once and, yes, he's dead."

"I can't help being a little scared."

"No, you don't. None of that stuff. I've always been very careful, your mother will tell you that. I intend to see my grandchildren. It won't be long now, you know."

She nodded and looked down, satisfied but embarrassed. He felt Karen touch his elbow; he knew why. He turned to Karen and they exchanged a husband-and-wife glance. It was supposed to serve as an asterisk for later conversation. "How do you feel?"

"All right."

"I'll take that from you in the car," he said. "I'll run Steffie up to my mother's. We'll drop you at the hotel and you can rest for a while."

"I have Mrs. Kaminsky's employment record. She registered as a substitute teacher four years ago, but she was dropped from our list that first year simply because she was never available. She was used the next year and since, but she has begged off much more often than she should, and there are two notations of her having lost control of junior high school classes. The second time, she ran out of the room in tears. She's been used in elementary school exclusively for the past year and a half."

"How could she run out of a classroom in tears?"

"It's easier than you think. The kids are brutal when they sense an advantage. Still, it's a terrible thing on a teacher's record. Can you tell me what we're doing tonight?"

"I'm not sure. We have to do some talking. I've done nothing since I talked to you but wait for you."

"I see." She looked over his shoulder to Steffie. He understood what she was asking. He had meant that he wanted to discuss the case with her, but she had taken it for something else. There was no way of getting it right without worrying Steffie. He cast his eyes in her direction and said to Karen, "I think about that once in a while, don't you?"

"Once in a while," she said, and looked ahead. Whether she understood or not, she was willing to wait. He had meant grandchildren. The first of the hand-trucks was coming in.

Outside, he put the suitcases behind the driver's seat while Steffie and Karen got in on the passenger's side. He put the shopping bag, empty, on the rear seat and then got in the car, closed the door and locked it. "Karen, there's a box of shells in the glove compartment."

"You have them there. I made sure I didn't forget them."

"They're over a year old." He turned on the map light and extracted the pistol and holster from the canvas bag. The bag went on the floor. Karen held the open box of shells until he was ready. He inserted the shells quickly. When he finished he put on the safety and buttoned the holster closed. He took off his belt and worked it through the holster slits, then positioned the holster against his left side, forward of his hip bone. He threaded the belt through the loops of his pants, fastened the buckle, adjusted the holster a last time, and finally buttoned his jacket. He shifted in the seat. The pressure of the gun felt like a bad bruise.

Karen asked, "Are you all right?"

He nodded. For a moment he had let himself relax and think of Steffie's plans and the weekend all of them could have had. If they had not gone to Canada after all, he would have put in a few hours' work, taken them out Saturday night, and probably again on Sunday. He started the car.

At the hotel he summoned a bellboy and instructed him for Karen. When he told her that he would hurry back, she turned without nodding and went inside. As he drove away, he caught himself reacting to her coolness. It was not fair. Steffie turned on the radio; the noise was a welcome diversion.

He knocked on the door. It felt strange, knocking on what was his own door.

"Who is it?"

"Joe."

"All right." It took a moment, a snap of the lock and the clatter of the safety chain. She had her shoes and stockings off. "I wanted coffee," she said, walking away. "You said on the telephone that you had your lunch sent up, so I thought that there'd be nothing wrong in having a little room service of my own." She had ordered a club sandwich, too. She sat down in the armchair to finish it, her bare legs positioned under her carefully, the way her daughter was doing these days at parties. He took off his coat and hung it in the near-empty closet. He could feel her presence all around him, and not because she was comfortable. Anything but. When he turned again she looked away from him. He saw that she had sampled the view; the blind was reset. The darkness pressed against the windows; from this side of the room, he could not really see the distant lights.

"I didn't have much of a lunch this afternoon." She was paying attention to licking mayonnaise from her fingertips. "This is the way I'm going to have it. You only need one exposure to this kind of attention to get hooked." She extended her foot and wriggled her toes. "Do you know, I could have someone come up and paint my toenails? Well, I could have a pedicure, anyway." She nodded to the serving cart. "There's a cup for you."

"I was beginning to wonder."

"But you have to wait on yourself." She leaned back and ran her hand through her hair. "Your mother called, after you left her place. Suppose we start there. Hm? She said that you looked more tired today than you did last night when she saw you on television. That's true. This morning I had my own thoughts. And you do look worse this evening."

He sat down on the sofa. "I'll get my rest. There's a lot to do, but I'll delegate some of the work, I promise. I may have to pay for it myself, though. We'll see about that."

"Yes, we'll see. Your mother is worried. She minds her own business, you know that, but she had to speak to me about you. She added something interesting. She said that you asked her if she or Dad had any opinions about your appearance on television. What was that supposed to mean, Joe? What made you ask a question like that?"

"Something that happened last night at—her friend's house. Norma's doctor—he's her friend. There was a woman there, a sick woman. Among other things, she said that I took advantage of things like the Shoftel case to project myself into the public eye. We all saw the interview together. I had no idea that they would use the film. When I had come in—after I finished working—I had told her that I was in the insurance business. What I was doing was Norma's business. So, over the air, they made a liar out of me—maybe they were trying to give my business a plug. She went after me. She was after me anyway."

"What did Mrs. MacIver say? Norma, I should say."

"It wasn't her problem. Don't worry about it."

"What about her friend? Her doctor? Didn't he do anything?"

"No. He couldn't. Don't worry about it, Karen. It's not that important."

"He's some doctor. What's his name?"

"The woman isn't his patient. She attends a clinic where he works. He knows her father."

"Oh. What did *Norma* say afterwards? What did she say to you? They owed you something."

"She explained it all to me." He drank his coffee. "You're getting cute with her name. Is there something you want to say?"

"Why am I here?"

"I wanted to discuss the case with you."

"You're lying. You know you are. Joe?"

He put the cup and saucer aside. "Whatever you say."

"Look at yourself objectively, will you? On Wednesday night you call, miss me, then make no effort to get me later. Steffie told you that I wouldn't be long. The next day, yesterday, you were in Manitou and called my office twice, the second time cursing my secretary. We discussed that. But then you lost interest. When I finally did get you down here, you didn't want to talk to me. I know I was upset, but you couldn't even give me the right time."

"*You* hung up."

"You know what I mean. You didn't want to talk."

"All right, I was wrong," he said. "I was also tired. I was tired Wednesday. And as for trying to get me last night, I was working—as I said—and Norma was in and out of the house all evening."

"Norma, Norma." She stood up. "You're having *your* fun with her name, too." She started into the bedroom.

"Where are you going? What do you call this?"

"I'm going to take a shower, I think."

He sat there. He had not had to be told that Norma was on his mind. There was no forcing anything now. Why was she here? The way he felt offered no clue. He simply did not know.

She came to the door, her jacket unbuttoned. "Two questions, if you don't mind. What is this case about? Why did you have me bring you your gun?"

"I told you that it was a precautionary measure. Mike had to fly down here to tell *me* what the case was about. MacIver was a thief. I will tell you about it, but I'd rather—I don't know. Forget that."

"Don't you see that you're not helping? Just talk to me naturally. You're trying to be precise. Do you have any idea of the things that went through my mind when I saw these rooms? How many times have we spent more than fifteen dollars for a place to stay? Twice, that I can remember."

He had to understand that. "I did it on impulse, Karen. I felt like it."

"All right." She waited. "Is there any reason why you didn't tell me his name?"

"Whose?"

"The doctor's."

"I didn't realize that I hadn't."

"You hadn't." She took off her jacket. "Well?"

"Well what? What difference could it make?"

"None, I suppose." She was watching his eyes. "Joe?" He had to turn away from her. "What is his name, Joe?"

"What could—" He had to stop that. He drew a breath. He did not want to look up and see her still waiting. "Wendell Roberts."

"Oh." Then, "Oh, dear God." Now he looked up. She was already frowning. "You don't know him."

"Yes, I do. He told me."

"Told you? How? Why?"

"He was trying to make me go easy on the case for the sake of his ex-patient. He said. Don't worry, it isn't that simple anymore."

He had been trying to show her that he was all right, but now it seemed as if she had stopped listening. "He hurt you that way? He brought out that old stuff—he did that to you?"

"Stop it. I'm more concerned about you."

"Did you see Jerry Palmer? Is he in on this?"

"No. No, I didn't see him."

"Are you sure?"

He could not blame her for not believing him; he had all but forgotten that she did not know about Palmer. "No, Karen, I didn't see him."

She threw her jacket on the sofa and went to the serving cart, but did not attempt to pour another cup of coffee. "This makes everything a lot clearer. You've been having your nose rubbed in it. I'm sorry, Joe. I'm very sorry."

He got up. He had never felt so guilty in his life. "I wanted you here. Not because of anything. I wanted you here."

She nodded. He put his hands on her bare arms. She shook her head. "Not now. Just no—please?"

"Relax. There's nothing that we have to do tonight. We can do what we want."

"That's right, we can. Excuse me." She pulled away. "Leave me alone for a few minutes." She returned to the bedroom and pushed the door closed behind her. He had not been able to see her face. Her first words had sounded as if she had said them through a handkerchief. He could not imagine what she could be thinking. He knocked on the door.

"I don't want to see you, Joe."

There was no light around the doorframe. He went in.

512

"I'm sitting on the bed. You don't have to see me doing that."

"What is it? What's wrong?"

"It took me a minute to remember things and put them together. Norma. I'm not a fool. Norma, for God's sake. Jerry thought that his friend Dr. Roberts was the finest man he'd ever known. Jerry Palmer told me stories of the things that Wendell Roberts did to help people. Including him. Jerry made a pest of himself with Roberts over me. He told me that. Roberts never complained. This is a man people trust. They go to him. Now you try to tell me that he hurt you with what I did. He had a better reason than the one you said. You gave it to him. You gave him a reason."

"You—"

"Don't tell me a story. I saw her. We talked about what she was, remember? I told you that she'd make a grab for you. His ex-patient? His friend. He saw you move into her house. What else did he see?"

There was no answer.

"I'm not the person I was, Joe," she said. "I did it to you worse than this. But I thought we were past those days. Do you remember last weekend? Do you? And Monday night? Tuesday I slept alone and it wasn't easy. I wanted you. You can be a bastard when you want to be. You left me high and dry for months after you caught me with Jerry, even after you knew I wasn't seeing him. This time, you saw something that interested you and you were gone. You couldn't wait. Oh, *sure,* you were married this week, but it wasn't to me!"

"You calm yourself! It was before you went to bed Tuesday night that Roberts brought it up. I was in Manitou most of that day. I hadn't been in Port Smith five hours. He told me that he was assuming things from *her* behavior, but I have reason to doubt that, too, now. He tried everything else first. I wish you could ask him. He's involved with men who may steal fifty million dollars in the next ten years. It's no game, Karen. They have twelve, fifteen million already. Colin MacIver started it, organized it. And before he died, he went around stealing letters that Roberts wrote to other members of the conspiracy. Mike has the letters in Manitou. We don't know yet what everything means, but we do have the stuff to get some of the people. I know what Roberts tried to do to me. Don't give me the swell guy business. Until this is over, just don't give it to me." He had almost said that he had had it from Norma, too.

"Jerry was never wrong about people," she said. "That was one good thing about him."

"What the hell are you talking about? He was wrong about you. You said that yourself long ago. He was wrong about me. Roberts had some beautiful ideas about me. Don't give me anything about Jerry Palmer, either."

"I won't call him," she said. "Don't worry. I don't know what you've done to our marriage, but you don't have to worry about me calling him. He's had enough of me."

He stayed quiet.

"What is it?" she asked. "I can see you there."

"I don't want to talk anymore. I'll be in the living room."

"What is it? What did you do? Did you see him?"

"No."

She followed him. "Joe, look at me. I want to know what happened. You lied to me before. It was in your tone. You saw him."

"You just said something common. You didn't have to bring him into this."

"That isn't it. All right, it was common. I've been common before. There's something wrong."

"Leave me alone, Karen. Please."

"Do you want to marry her?"

"What does that have to do with it? I'd have all this behind me. If I ever thought of it, I'd have only myself to blame."

"Don't talk like that if you don't mean it."

"Wouldn't I? Wouldn't I have it behind me?"

"Yes. Do you want it?"

"Sometimes. I do now. Defending, protecting you—I hate that. I'm happy when you're yourself. Doing things. *Not* worrying. That's the way you were on Monday in the Flamingo. *She* noticed it. Anybody can see it in a moment. I don't mind catching the odd minutes with you, between the trips to schools and all the paperwork. I almost don't mind waiting for another child—"

514

She had been very still. "What do you mean, defending and protecting?"

"Roberts. He tried to project himself between Palmer and you. And me. He started giving me opinions."

"That wasn't what you meant. You meant now. How are you protecting me?"

He shook his head. He was willing to believe that he had steered them toward this, it had come on them so quickly. It was an embittering thought; a man hoped that he decided such things. If he told her, he would have to put away the entertaining thoughts of Norma. Once past this, he and Karen could almost coast to an understanding. It seemed to be true. He could not hurt her if he was going to continue to harbor other ideas. It reminded him of MacIver and he did not like it. The decision turned on so fine a point as this moment, this moment only, and he did not like that, either. If he thought it through again he would begin to look for ways out.

"Karen, Jerry Palmer died last year."

She stared.

"Roberts told me. It was cancer."

She nodded and turned to sit down. "Tuesday? He told you this Tuesday?"

"Yes."

She rubbed her forehead. "Why didn't you come home? Why didn't you just call me and come home?"

"Don't attack me. There were many good, legitimate reasons to stay."

"I'm not attacking you," she cried. "Did you tell me the truth? Did he do all this Tuesday?"

"Yes."

She got up. "I don't know what to say." She waved her hand at him to keep him from talking. "I don't even—I guess the fact that you called tells me what I should know about us." She started inside again. "He must have thought some nice things about us. Jerry, I mean."

"He blamed me. He was still a stupid man."

515

"Misinformed." She looked back at him, her eyes wet. She held onto the doorframe. "Remember how I lied? *I* do."

"Don't do anything to yourself. You aren't responsible."

"I know. Don't stay there, Joe. I want to sit in the dark, but I don't want to be alone. Put up with me a little longer."

"Don't talk like that, either." He closed the door. She sat on the bed.

"I didn't love him. I love you."

"I know."

"Do you love me?"

"We've known the answer to that for a very long time."

"Stuck with me," she said. "It's a secure feeling for me."

"I want some changes, Karen. I have to have them."

"I guess you do. At this moment I feel very sick. It's like an echo. Nothing like the old stuff will happen again, I know. I'm plain too old. I stink as a wife. That little drip is a better wife in her fingernail." She sniffed. "There's something the matter with you, Joe."

"You're not talking to me now. Stop it."

"It's been a while since I've talked this way."

"I'm still tired of it. I'm tired of you hurting yourself."

"Sit by me, please. I'd like you near me." She lay back and watched him. "He *was* a stupid man. It's no insurance, is it?"

"No." He put his hand on her stomach. Slip, no girdle or panties now. Her stomach was flat. She tried to relax under his hand.

"You know me," she said.

He did not want to talk.

"I want to make love," she said. "I won't get much out of it, but I want to. Now. I want to take some chances." That had a special meaning for them. She turned her head away. "I get afraid, Joe. I'm afraid of death—still. There's no point in thinking about it. I know that. I'm almost forty and I'm finally getting smart."

He pushed up her skirt. "Keep talking like that and I'm going to do something cruel." It meant something, too, but she misunderstood.

516

"Did you do it with her?"

"No."

"You did do things."

He looked into her eyes. She was very frightened. She watched him. "What do you want to hear?" he asked. "I love you. You know that."

"I feel so helpless. I don't know what to do."

"Stop asking questions. Stop worrying. Please. Even now I think I want to go home more than you. We're both getting whipsawed. We'll be all right, if we can keep our door closed."

"Whipsawed?" She touched his sleeve.

"We've both heard from Roberts. At least I saw that you did. You're worried about her, although you shouldn't be. And I have the case."

"Roberts is involved in it?"

"I think so."

"Jerry loved him, I swear."

Leland rolled onto his back. He stared at the ceiling. Karen got up on her elbow. "I had to say his name," she said.

"That's not it. The letters put Roberts very close. His behavior settles him right in the middle. I was willing to bet anything that he broke into MacIver's office. I had him—I want to get him, put your money on it—but the more you say, the tougher it is to hold him. I want to see all these people in jail. They've been hurting everybody."

"Did you tell the client?"

"Ask me another."

"Don't be flip about it, Joe."

"Roberts warned me off. You can blame him."

She put her head on his chest. He could smell her hair. "We aren't going to make love," she said. "It's becoming difficult even to discuss things."

"We're tired," he said. "You were going to take a shower."

She began to sit up. "I can't stop thinking that I'm helpless. I want to help. But this seems to be up to you."

He wanted to kiss her, but he knew that she would think that he was trying to prove something that he did not really feel. She looked at him.

"I can't stop my mind from working. I saw her. It hurts, Joe. It hurts terribly."

"You saw Anne," he said.

"You and I were separated. I was separated from everything." She smiled unhappily. "I *can't* stop thinking. I know now why you didn't want to talk to me last night. You're tired all right."

"Nothing like that."

She put her hand on him. "You're tired."

"I'm reacting to my wife."

"Your wife," she said after a moment. "If we made love now, I wouldn't use the diaphragm."

"This isn't the way you want it."

"I'm not sure of that."

"It wouldn't be right when you thought back on it. We'll make our try in our own home, our own bed, and cold sober. We'll know we're trying. You wouldn't be afraid to think back on that."

She kissed him on the mouth. Her skin was warm. "Don't let it go too long. I'll get afraid. I will. Joey, I still get scared sometimes. That's what happened to me Tuesday night. I got afraid of dying." She put her leg over his body and held him tightly. "I want to cry and I can't. That's what happens."

"When we get home, you and I. You'll see." He rocked her. He locked his arms around her chest.

"I'm all right," she said, pushing away.

"What is it?"

"The gun. It was pressing against my hip. I'm going to take my shower and get into bed. I wouldn't mind company. No guns. No clothes, either."

"A watch?"

"*I'll* wear whatever is necessary." She was up. "We'll do what you say. No thinking. Into the shower, into the bed. You don't have any hickeys, do you?"

"Of course not, I—"

She pinched his nose, hard. "Of course not. You told her not to make marks. I don't want to see you, anyway."

"Are you serious?" He had never thought of hickeys, but obviously she had—once—and it had a blunt, numbing effect on him. He stood up. "Do you want me to wait outside?"

"I was teasing, but I do feel sweaty. I'd rather you didn't see me—what's wrong?"

"I think you hurt my nose just so you would have an easier time of confusing me."

She stepped closer. "You look hurt. How can a man your age be so sweet? You are." She kissed his nose. "I should have pinched something else. You know me, all right. A few minutes and you have me hurrying to get ready." She kissed him again, he patted her, and she hugged him. "A few minutes," she said.

In the living room he removed his belt and shoes and untied his tie and opened his collar. He had to find the souvenir book and the insurance file. The material in the souvenir book was as clear to him as his memory of his own experiences, but he did not want to trust himself. He could not work on the facts. He could not move around the facts for new perspectives. One thought: he could go back to his own beginning in the case and force himself to remember everything he had seen and done.

He spent a longer time than necessary looking at the old portrait of MacIver. There was no doubt of it, he could not remember him from the war. He tried to imagine MacIver as he had been moments before and after he had sat still for the photographer. How had he carried himself? Leland would have no more interest in him today than he had then. MacIver's had been an unpleasant, unfriendly face. Cheerless, unpromising—and secretive? Leland still had the option of calling Matthews, the wingman, for what he knew, but while it seemed like a better investment now, Leland continued to lean away.

He felt himself continuing to lean toward the old mistakes. He caught himself thinking that he was looking at the face of a thief and a suicide. He put the book aside. Of all the people he knew, the only one who had ever seemed close to self-destruction was Karen. And years ago, not now. There had been a time when death had been able to make her cry. It was still never far from her thoughts—a hideous burden; it only occasionally occurred to him. She was the one who had forced him to see death as a way to escape. When he thought of how her problems had pressed on her, he had to wonder how close she had come, or even if she had actually tried it. The terrible thing was the ease with which a life could be taken. A step off a high place. With a gun, a contraction of a finger. If the idea had courted a man, if a man had been afraid of it for years, then all it took was a kind of suck of curiosity. Leland got up and crossed the room to his belt, moving quickly. It took one second to get the pistol out of the holster. Two, three seconds at the most to cross the room and get out the gun. It was infinitely easier to tweak the life out of oneself than to rip it out of another.

"What are you doing?" Her voice filled the room; it was the way she disciplined Steffie. He turned to her as he put the gun away. She held a towel up to herself.

"I was running a test. I wanted to see what it took."

"When were you going to stop? Do you have any idea of how close you were?"

"I *had* stopped. It doesn't take anything at all."

"You had the gun pointing toward yourself, Joe. You had your finger on the trigger." She came toward him, then stopped.

"The safety was on," he said.

"That's the way accidents happen. I hate that thing because of that. It's just waiting to kill somebody."

"Take it easy, Karen—"

"Don't tell me that! I want to slap your face, you stupid man! What's wrong with you?"

"I'm all right," he said. "What did you want?"

"What do you think?" She stepped back. "Forget it, now. I couldn't do anything. Let me get something on. Get away from there. I'm not kidding. Sit in the chair until I get back."

She was going overboard, he thought, but he did what she wanted. She came back wearing her slip. Her face was pale. She sat on his lap. "Give me a cigarette. What were you thinking of?"

He told her to pick up the souvenir book. He put his finger on MacIver's picture. "The client has a more recent shot of him. The more I look at this, the more incredible the other becomes. Toward the end, he was a handsome man—very handsome."

"So? We were all on high-starch diets during the war. Everybody looked awful. Some of us—including you and I—had been eating badly for years."

"How long did it take us to lose that?"

"We've always tried to put the best we could on the table. We could look at our pictures and see. A year or so, I suppose."

"His first wife met him right after the war. She described him as the handsomest man she had ever seen."

"Who had ever paid attention to her, more likely," Karen said.

"No, no. She was very emphatic. Handsome. She said it several times."

Karen looked at the picture again. "Not within a year or two of this. Not possibly."

"What do you think of him?"

"I think he's loathsome. He could have been unhappy in the service. That twists a person's face. You've seen it in me—and I've seen it in you."

"He had a fine war record. It was consistent—" He wanted to stop; he felt as if he were knocking on a door. There was something in his mind.

"Why did you run that test?" she asked. "You haven't answered me."

"I made several mistakes this week. One was in trying to believe that I was thinking like him. I was living in his car. I even ate his breakfast, bacon and eggs. Betty Kaminsky pointed out that I was probably the only person alive who knew both his wives. I caught myself thinking, 'Well, he did this, he felt this when he was in this car on days like this.' "

"If it was a mistake, why did you take it further? Something could have happened."

"No. Absolutely not." He rubbed her leg. "We had things in

common, he and I. I liked both his wives. You wouldn't, Mike wouldn't, but I did. I liked his home. I have an allergy to cars, but there's something awesome about this one. It's fun. I thought that I was getting a sense of his life. I was in it, sort of. I was in his territory. I enjoyed the weather from where he saw it."

"It's still a mistake," she said. "*You* aren't a thief. You haven't killed yourself. You aren't him."

"Being a thief enhanced him. He moved with important people. It gave him a good home and set him up with a good wife. It doesn't add up to putting an end to himself."

"Don't you see that that's your opinion? You liked his first wife, but he divorced her."

"The thing is, I think I know why he did that. When she's not going well, she's a demanding, irritating individual."

"So am I."

"Demanding, but never irritating. She wears thin quickly. You've always been an exciting, interesting person to know. A man has to tolerate her bad times. I'd get bored. I'm never bored with you."

"I'll remember that," she said.

"He put up with her as long as he could, then he made up his mind to get rid of her."

"Didn't you say he had a girl friend? That isn't putting up with anybody."

He kissed her arm.

"You know it's a mistake," she said. "You're still making it. You're seeing him in terms of what you would feel. He did something completely sneaky and underhanded. You've never done that. If I had been on the ball this week—well, this week would do things to any man."

"That's what I mean. Any man. That's as far as I want to take it." He massaged her back. "You might as well grab that nap. The man went off the roof of a racetrack, he was dealing indirectly with people who have been known to kill. He had information that would make them kill."

She wanted to know about that. He gave her an outline of the conspiracy and asked her what she remembered of the conversation she had heard at the Flamingo.

"They were engineers. One of them said something about test borings. There are faults in the rock."

He sneered. "Well, it might have amounted to something."

"Joe, you still aren't seeing Wendell Roberts correctly. I wouldn't lie to you about him. I came close to meeting his wife and him on two occasions—"

"She's dead, too. Mrs. Roberts."

"That's horrible! Jerry said so many good things about her. Oh, that's awful, Joe. It must be so bad for him. They weren't young when they met."

"I know." He was thinking of the meaning of MacIver's possession of the letters. He was fighting to keep himself from going in circles. Karen kissed his forehead.

"I'm not doing anything for you," she said.

He was thinking—at last, he had to reflect—that he had moved too suddenly for Roberts on Tuesday night, getting the papers to Manitou. Roberts would have prevented it, if he could have anticipated it. The idea led back to the letters.

She kissed him again, stood up, and put the souvenir book in his lap. "I'm going to bed. You wake me."

"The more I think of it, the more possibilities I try, the more I'm convinced that it was Roberts who broke into MacIver's office."

She raised her hands in the air.

"Somebody did it. It happened. It wasn't a coincidence. If it were part of a larger professional job, the people involved would be sitting in a car at the bottom of the bay. I've checked on him; he was making the arrangements for MacIver's funeral. You can do that from a pay phone for a dime, that's how much time it takes."

The telephone rang. Karen was still looking at him. "We know who that is," she said.

"We don't know at all," he said. "I'd like you to take it. If it's somebody from the office, I'll talk to him. If it's the client, tell her I'm out on the case."

"Why are you ducking her?"

There was no reason that he wanted to hear himself say. "Would you do this for me, please?"

She went to the telephone. He picked up the insurance file. She did not call him. He looked to the souvenir book, thinking again of the things that Betty Kaminsky had told him. Karen hung up. "It was her. She would like you to call her when you come in. She sounded upset. She sounded unnerved when she heard my voice."

"Did you ask her what she wanted"

"Yes, and she said that it wasn't important." She turned to the bedroom. "I may call you to help me," she said. "I'm going to disconnect the extension in here."

"All right."

If she wanted something more, he did not know it, because he was not looking up to see. The door closed firmly—she would argue that it had not been slammed. He tried to get his attention on what was before him.

He could have moved faster. Or he could have been more thorough, drawing up a chart of the evidence and the testimony so that his eyes could see what his intellect dictated was true. There was nothing wrong now with his ability to deal with the facts. Working carefully, concentrating, almost anyone could remember what he had seen and done during a preceding week. Leland could remember the face of the waitress who had served him coffee on Tuesday morning, when he had turned up his collar against the cold on Wednesday night, the faint, unpleasant odor of Phyllis Reynolds. It was clear now that no one had lied about matters of fact, however inadvertently. No one. There had been instances of bad judgment, but none of them ill-intentioned. If anything, this case was strewn with good intentions. None had been of any help to Joe Leland.

He went to the telephone books first, the white and the yellow pages. His hands were shaking; he had to think of pacing himself. He looked for one name—it was not listed. He had known that in advance. He could check with the county professional association, but there was an easier way. A local call. He had to look up the number. When he had his information, he hung up on the man. This was no time for pleasantries with someone he could not abide in the best of circumstances.

He called Florence at her home and gave her a rush assignment. He told her that he wanted her to handle it because he simply did not have the patience for what could only prove to be background. He would be tied up for a half hour or more. She could do the job in ten minutes, if it could be done at all.

Then he told her to call Mike. It was six-thirty now and time was working against them, even accounting for time differentials. After she repeated what she was to tell Mike to do, she asked Leland if he wanted them to telephone their results separately. No, she was to collect the information and relay it. He did not want to talk to Mike, but he did not tell her that. He did tell her that he was not expecting much from them; he knew what he had to know. It was a question of getting a little extra in the bank.

When he hung up Leland was nearly sick to his stomach. Just talking around the thing had done it. Even he could recognize that it was not something that he could shrug off. *Why didn't you come home?* He had to ask it himself, now. He could wake up Karen, show her what he had learned, they could leave in the morning. She would see it, she would believe him. They would return the lady's money out of their pockets and forget everything. A lot of people would say that it was a closed issue. Nothing would be accomplished by staying with it. There would be no need for Mike to know. It was obvious that no one else could ever learn it on his own.

There was one more call to make, long-distance. The thing he had would remain a theory without what he would get on this call.

It did not take long. There was a little distress at the other end and he had to apologize for apparently breaking a promise. From there it went well. He had not misremembered anything. He had the feeling that he could take the conversation in another direction, but that was like thinking of people who were going to go away. In a sense, they were. They were going to be changed. It was like watching an old movie on television and thinking of the person you had been when you had seen it the first time. And in that way it was like talking to a movie. He heard himself feign nonchalance to set up the framework for the question he had called to ask, ask it, and hear the astonished answer he had anticipated. Then, very quickly, thanks very much, goodbye.

He sat there with his teeth chattering like a child not sensible enough to come in from the snow. There was a way to stop it. Wake her up, tell her, let her take Florence's call. Let her take over entirely. Probably what stopped him was the pity that Karen would feel, the gush of sympathy that she would be unable to control. It made him ashamed. He had to think of his own welfare; waking her was the sane thing to do, but the thought of it made him recoil in self-disgust. He waited quietly for Florence to call him.

Forty minutes. "Mr. Leland, I don't know what you wanted, but we asked the questions you gave us. Mr. Petrakis drew a complete blank. The only way to get a transcript of a former student's record at the University of California is for the former student himself to request it in writing and pay a fee to cover the cost of photocopying."

"I was afraid of that. What about you?"

"I found Mr. Matthews. He doesn't live in Vineland anymore, but he is in the same county—same directory. I told him that Mac-Iver was dead and he was sorry to hear it and so on, and then I told him that MacIver committed suicide for reasons unknown and that he, Matthews, might be able to help me. He didn't know how, he said. He sounded like an old man, Mr. Leland. He sounded more like the First World War."

"It says in the book that he's four years my junior. If you figure out what happens to people, let me know, will you?"

"Don't wait, Mr. Leland. This was really no fun for me. I asked him if MacIver ever talked about his personal life, his background, or anything that happened in college, as you told me. He said that MacIver had been very quiet about himself. He remembered that clearly. I asked what else he remembered. MacIver was friendly enough, he said. He liked to go out. He went to London and Paris whenever he could, with anybody who would go with him. When he was out he loved to have a good time—I'm not quoting; I think if Matthews ever said a word like 'love,' he'd throw up. MacIver would talk to strangers, he did say. Walk right up. Especially girls. He did very well with the girls."

"Then you don't have the feeling that Matthews held anything back because he was speaking to a woman," Leland said.

"No, I don't think so. One more thing that Matthews remembered was that MacIver said that being in Europe, seeing it, was the greatest opportunity an American could have. I said that he, Matthews, had been quoted in the souvenir book as saying that MacIver had been a brave man—words to that effect. He said, 'Well, we came in at the end of the war. We really didn't see much action.' Then he said, 'We shouldn't have been in that war in the first place,' and he went on to remark about Roosevelt and Truman. I kept my ears open, as you said, but I couldn't hear anything unusual in that, for what it was, any hostility toward MacIver. It was strictly political."

"That's right. You did a good job."

"You can't tell me," she said. "Ah, yes, would you answer a question for me?" Her tone was strained. "My *mother* is standing here and she wants to know who is going to pay for the telephone calls."

He sighed. "You know what to do. Have the operator give you the charges. Make out a bill and then add five dollars for your mother's trouble."

"That's it, you have the idea. Thank you, Mr. Leland."

"You'll be paid, too," he said.

"I don't have to be told. I'm sorry that Mr. Petrakis and I weren't of more help. He told me to tell you that for him, too."

It doesn't matter, he wanted to say. *The reasons aren't unknown anymore. I know.* He said thanks and put down the receiver and wondered what would have happened if he had said what he had wanted, how far he would have taken it. His eyes hurt—just hurt. It would be possible to sit in the chair and let the strength he had left evaporate. As it was, he waited a moment too long. When he got up he had to push against the arms of the chair. He felt very heavy. He moved across the room as if he had fallen asleep with the light on. It would pass. If a man took a nap every evening after dinner, he couldn't move during that hour on the night he couldn't nap. It passed. This was the same thing.

Karen rolled over as he opened the door.

"I'm sorry," he said.

"I wasn't asleep. I started thinking about the things they did to you, Roberts and that woman." She pulled the blanket up under her arms and moved her legs to give him room. "They thought they knew you. They don't. They couldn't. It's happened to you before in other ways."

"You shouldn't bother with that."

"I thought of other things. I heard you on the telephone. I heard your voice, but I couldn't make out what you were saying."

"You should have listened in."

"I couldn't." She pointed to the extension telephone on the dresser. It had been on the night table. "I wasn't awake enough, anyway." She folded her hands in her lap. "You didn't talk to her."

"That's right."

"I would have only heard the dialing. Not your voice."

"Detective's wife."

"Your wife, I hope."

He was quiet. He had thought that he would get to this and stare at her until he precipitated another scene, more confused and wild than the last, but something inside him was going again. In the past his bad ideas had come upon him with fanfares of emotion; when he had been lucky they had turned sour before he had tried to put them to use. The good ideas had appeared quietly, like men looking for work. He had seen their faults at once. He had been able to measure their effect. Now he was thinking, trying something as in a rehearsal.

She put her head back on the pillow. "Do you want to marry her? You never did answer that question."

He shook his head. "We settled it. *I* settled it, calling you and having you come here."

She rubbed the blanket with the palm of her hand. "If you wanted to, really wanted to, I wouldn't argue. I was thinking about it, along with everything else. You'd be able to start fresh. No scars. It would be a wonderful feeling."

528

"It isn't possible. I'd be trading in old scars for new. I won't even take us into account. If I did anything, if you showed you could take it, it would break Steffie's heart. You know that. She has her dreams. She has some idea of what goes on between us. She has faith in us. She's watching to see what will happen."

"She's watching *you,* now. She was upset with your remark about grandchildren. Don't you know that you're the king? It will be a while before she outgrows you."

He was thinking of something else.

"Joe? You look so unhappy."

"You'll find out why soon enough."

"What did you say? I couldn't hear you. Joe?" She moved toward him. "What is it? Are you all right?"

"Look—you heard me on the telephone, didn't you?"

"Yes. You made several calls."

"I was working, that's true. I learned something. There's one more thing I can do. We. I can't do it alone. I don't know what it will lead to, but I have to go with it. I have to see. Karen, I'm asking you to do something for me without knowing why. I want you to trust me. There's a very good reason why I can't tell you about it now. You could succeed and I could fail. It could go nowhere. I've never asked you for anything like this before and I know how unfair it is. Let me have my way for a few hours—until we've made our try."

She sat back a bit. "We've told the truth about her, haven't we?"

"In what way?"

"You and her. What you did with her."

"Forget that. Please."

"I want to. I'm trying to. But look at you. *I* can't say it. Look at you."

"I didn't sleep with her."

"And you don't *want* to sleep with me now. That's what I mean."

"I thought before that we were going to make love. You came out to the living room at the wrong time."

"The right time," she said.

"What are we able to do when we're like this? We should know it by now. Why do we even have to talk about it?"

"You're right. I should know, you mean."

He shook his head again. "No, I don't really mean anything. I shouldn't have said it. You don't know what's wrong. But be still for a moment, please. I want to tell you something else. You have to believe it. When you came out before, when I had the gun in my hand, I didn't know what I know now. I was running a test, exactly as I said. Do you understand that? Get it straight in your mind now, so you don't *ever* get confused. I did that first, as a test, and then I went through the papers and made the calls."

She searched his eyes. "You didn't need the gun, did you?"

"There are people in the background. I was thinking of them, no matter what I said to Mike about Roberts. I was very upset. That's no confession. You knew it when you looked at me. You have to trust me to know whether I'm upset or not now. I'm not, I swear to you."

"You should see yourself, Joe. You should have seen yourself when you came into the room."

"I can explain that. The question is control—if I have it. I know that I do."

"You're being careful with your words again. Precise. Okay." She looked tired. She swung her legs to the floor. "What do you want me to do? Are we going out? Do I have to get dressed?"

He put his arms around her. Her skin was warm from the blanket. She did not respond to him, but, finally, she rested her head against his shoulder. "I don't want *any*thing to happen to us now. We've come too far."

"I know. There'll be no danger."

"Then you'll be leaving the gun here."

"No."

He could feel her body stiffen. She tried to control her voice. "I want more of an explanation, Joe."

"I can't give it to you. Not now."

She turned to him. "You are testing me! You're terrorizing me!"

530

"I need your help, Karen. Please." He could not attempt to say more. Unless he told her everything, she would think that he was going out to shoot someone. He was right about what he knew, and there was no danger there, but he was very afraid of what was still hidden to him. If he told everything, she would try to keep him from finishing. He was not sure himself why he wanted to take it further. It was his view of what had already happened that had him believing that he would find something more.

"If I do this for you, what are you going to do for me?"

"What do you want?"

"We were talking a little while ago. You said things about the way it would be. I want that. I don't want to have to worry anymore. I want to know that we made a decision here. I want to be taken care of, me, who and what I am."

It was no kind of a trade. She wanted something that was more than an assurance. "All right, what we said."

"And no more of this—what happened here in Port Smith. I don't want to be deceived, either. I mean it."

He said all right, and she asked him what it was that he wanted her to do. He said that he wanted her to help him to steal something.

A streetlamp down the block cast a set of faint lines on the ceiling and it was all he needed to find his way around the room. There were many more cabinets than he had imagined. He had to go to the window, take a key off the ring, then return to the cabinets to try it. He was going as quickly as he could, but he felt depressed and empty. The man was out of reach. Earlier, someone had brought in the news that James Scanlon had confessed to the rape-murder of Mary Shoftel. The attention had focused on Leland. In the confusion of remembering what his father had said about Scanlon and relating it to what he himself would be doing before the end of the night—this— Leland had had to think that people lied terribly about the amount of television they watched. It had seemed as if everyone had seen him. What his father had quoted the doctor as saying about Scanlon slipping away and disintegrating had reached out to Leland and grasped at his own mortality. It had made him see the frailty of his own orderly life. It made him feel a fierce, spine-freezing fear from which anger had seemed the only escape. The anger was still receding, weighing heavily. He was working steadily, evenly, sanely, but he had the feeling that he could hold the object of his search in both hands and not be able to see it for what it was.

There should be a folder. With MacIver dead, it could have been moved to another location, but what Leland knew said no. The number of file cabinets supported him. Nothing was ever thrown away. Nothing was put beyond arm's length.

At ten minutes to four a Port Smith Police Department prowl car cruised beneath the window. Leland did not see it, only heard it. He stayed still until it was gone. Manitou was using the same cars, six-cylinder automatic Fords, and Leland would recognize their tubercular exhaust note anywhere. He was a quarter finished and he had not seen MacIver's name. He knew that he had had no right to expect an easy time, but he was already fighting with a sense of failure.

He was going through a sheaf of folders at the window when something flicked in the corner of his eye. It was impossible to see the sidewalk below without adjusting the blind. He examined it carefully. There was a different light shining on the edges of the slats. He put the folders on the desk and tried to dampen the sounds that he was making. He could hear his breathing and heartbeat. In a quiet room, in the darkness, the movement of a shirt inside a jacket could sound like a ship collision. He had not forgotten the sound-absorbent ceilings and the deep pile wall-to-wall carpets in the public areas outside. This case had been a study in disadvantages. There was a switchplate in the hall outside the door; Leland had not checked it. He stepped back from the desk, drew the gun, braced his elbow against the cabinet, and sighted down his arm. He could see the door clearly enough. A short-barreled pistol was hardly better than a zip gun at a distance greater than a handshake, but not everyone knew that. There was a soft, smothered creak just outside the door. Sure enough, the lights came on. Leland put his free hand above his eyes to minimize the shock. The doorknob turned silently, but then the door swung wide open.

"Hold it right there. Hold it or I'll kill you."

Wendell Roberts said, "Joe, you're going to be sorry you came here. You're going to regret the day you were born."

CHAPTER TWENTY-ONE

■ ■

"DON'T GIVE ME THAT," LELAND SAID. "GET IN HERE." HE MOVED around the desk. "Push the door closed—don't turn your back to me."

"I was hoping it wouldn't come to this—"

"You'll never hear the shot, Wendell. You'll bounce off the door, but you won't know that, either. All right, with your left hand. Come on, come on. Unbutton your shirt. Now arms out straight. Turn around to the door and get up on your toes. Fall forward, hands flat on the door, your weight on your hands."

"I've seen this in the newspapers, Joe. I'm not carrying a weapon."

"And you were talking sports, too. I know all about it. You have nothing to tell me. A warning, mister. Make a bad move and I kick the legs out from under you. You go straight down on your chin. Don't try to get your hands under you to cushion your fall. Nobody reacts that fast. You'll break your arms as well as your jaw."

Billfold, key wallet, neatly folded handkerchief, small change. Leland clutched the items to his chest and took a step back. "Okay. Again with your left hand—undo your belt, take it off, and throw it in the corner." He waited, breathing hard. The lights were supposed to be soft, but the place looked like any other doctor's office. Nothing more. If a patient ever lost his fear in here, it was because of the doctor, not the furnishings. Leland had expected better. "Open the button. Hold your pants up with your hand."

Roberts' legs were shaking from the strain. "You don't know what you're doing. This is just humiliating."

"Not at all. Turn around. We won't have bad trouble if you have to hold onto your pants." Leland moved back behind the desk. "Sit down. In front of me." He put the wallet and keys on the blotter. Roberts eased over the arm of the chair, afraid to get too close to the gun. Leland spread the contents of Roberts' pockets across the desk. "You had another set of keys."

"You stole the spare set. I had my regular set in my pocket. Look, will you put that away? At least let me button my pants."

"You have all the freedom of movement you need. Relax."

There were keys for the drawers of the desk. Leland would get to them. He sat down in Roberts' contour swivel chair. Roberts was wearing a dark gray suit and a blue tie. For a man who had just hosted a very crowded party, he was in wonderful shape. He had had a drink in his hand any time Leland had looked at him, but his eyes were as clear now as they had been at the start of the evening. Leland said, "You know why I'm here. By all accounts your friend should not have been your patient, but he was. I assure you that I know exactly why. Now I want that file. We can be nice about it or I can take this place apart."

"Let me clean my glasses." He leaned forward to catch his handkerchief as Leland tossed it to him. "You can't dictate. What do you call it, breaking and entering? Plus assault with a deadly weapon? You aren't going to shoot anybody, Joe. I could get up and walk out of here—"

"Don't kid yourself! You made your use of MacIver in spite of what you, a doctor, knew about him. Maybe you didn't put him up to it, but he worked hard for you. Maybe he even finished the job, getting the letters you wrote. I figure that that sacrifices at least your professional privilege, not to say your license to practice medicine. If you don't think you have to deal with me—"

"Just a minute. He had letters I wrote? He had letters I wrote to the people he knew?"

"I think my partner said that there were twenty of them. You'd have a hell of a time proving you didn't know."

Roberts sat back. He wiped his mouth with his hand. If he was not surprised, he knew what to do to fake it. Leland pressed. "As I say, you'd have a time proving you didn't know."

It was a hint of weakness and Roberts seemed to go after it. "Does your wife—Mrs. Leland—know what you're doing? When she covered me for so long, did she know that you were upstairs stealing my keys?"

Leland nodded. Now he had to wait.

"But she doesn't know why you wanted them," Roberts said.

"She will. I promised to tell her."

Roberts looked to the ceiling. "Maybe the sanest of us is mad. How could you think this through? Is theft, burglary, and threatening my life sane? You're headed toward disaster, and you're dragging her with you."

"You don't know her."

"We had a very intimate conversation—"

"I know. You *don't* know her. On the way to your place she told me that she would tie you up by talking about Jerrry Palmer. She wanted *me* to understand that it would be in trying to get the job done. I saw the expression on your face. She frightened you and she did it intentionally."

Roberts nodded. It was as if he had not realized that he had gained an advantage a moment ago. "There were times when she seemed to struggle. I didn't understand that. You can't expect me to admire it—or you, either. You're gloating, you know you are."

"There's only one way you understand a thing, Wendell. You have to have it held up to your face. My wife is stronger than you think—she may be the strongest person I know. Even assuming that you aren't involved in Rainbow, I couldn't go to you with what my evidence showed and expect you to be reasonable. You would have never conceded that I had a say in this. Or that Norma did, too. I had to break in here, get what I could, and stick it in your eye—"

Roberts looked away.

"Norma showed me," Leland said. "You figured that she was going to break down and revert to her behavior as a teen-ager. You gave her credit for nothing—"

536

"Figured? She told me herself that she was afraid of it. No figuring at all. She's been coming to me almost every day—that is, until the day before she went to Manitou with that insurance fellow, what's-his-name. She was afraid then that you wouldn't give her a hearing. She was afraid that you would cheat her. You don't know *her*, Joe. Did she tell you the things she's been thinking?"

"You know that I've heard about her background. She wants to go on. She came to see me, didn't she? She wants this thing resolved. It's all to the good and you know it."

"It would be, if the truth were not something that would hang over her head for the rest of her life. She takes pride in her understanding of men. You can see how she would come to that. You struck the right chord in her. Even Phyllis Reynolds saw the rapport between you. You've been getting the best that Norma has to offer, so don't think that you know her. She could love you, Joe. You could solve her problems." He leaned in. "But you know that, don't you?"

Leland stayed still. There was no point to trying to lie.

"People with Norma's problems don't actually change, Joe. When they've done their best, worked their hardest, they've only gained a partial kind of control—never complete, never one hundred percent mastery of themselves. They'd be the first to tell you, if they really trusted you."

"The way she trusts you, Wendell?" He went for the keys to the desk.

"You listen to me!" His face was flushed. "You hear what it's like, fighting genuinely irresistible urges. You couldn't know what compulsion is. She had a boyfriend who taught at the University here—did she tell you about him?

"She mentioned him."

"Mentioned him. She received a letter from him after Colin died. It was all she could do to keep from inviting him back to Port Smith. She had never cared very much for him, but she couldn't think. She fixed on 'the missed opportunity,' she called it. It took her weeks to stop fantasizing and realize that she was looking for a place to hide.

You should know what a battle it is for people like her when the pressure is on. You have one in your own family—"

"That's enough—"

"You *know* her? She knows herself! We had quite a little talk, she and I. The strongest person you know? Perhaps because she's become so conditioned to the punishment she's inflicted on herself. She knows exactly how to respond to keep her balance. Your wife is an extraordinary woman, I knew that before I realized that she had tricked me, but she's precariously situated—you know that. After she told me what really happened when she was seeing Jerry Palmer— and she did tell me, although I had had an idea all along—I asked her how she was doing now. Better all the time, she said, which I don't doubt, but she added that she still has her moments, which the two of you managed to keep in the family. Those are her words. But then— this is the thing—Norma came by, and, Joe, it was interesting to see your wife. She watched Norma the way I'm trying not to watch that gun. It's something for you to think about—one thing among many. For another, no matter what you do in relation to Norma personally, even if you suddenly decide to change wives, nothing, nothing will protect her from the damage she will suffer if you pursue the case. Forget what MacIver did years ago. Just Rainbow.

"But I'm assuming that you're an honorable man. Jerry Palmer told me that things happened to you, too, during the war, that she— Karen—learned long before you told her. That's over. The war did terrible things to everybody. I have children seeing me now who were born during the war. Suppose you stay with your wife and pursue the case to the end. You're going to have to continue to see Norma. There'll be no way to avoid that. Karen felt threatened tonight, whether or not you told her anything to give her cause. What possible assurance can you offer next week or next month, after she knows the emotional charge of the thing you've uncovered?"

Leland's wrist was aching. He rested the pistol butt on the top of the desk. Roberts could not fail to see. Leland moved his finger to the forward end of the trigger guard. He had not been touching the trigger since he had sat down, but Roberts did not seem to have seen that. "You don't know us, Wendell."

"Now just one more minute," he said. "No matter what you tell Norma or reveal to the newspapers, even if you limit your report to Rainbow alone, you're going to have to tell your wife why it was necessary to steal my keys. That is, unless you go back tonight and tell her that you were mistaken from the start. I want you to think, Joe. When MacIver was at his worst, just before he did the thing that affects you so personally, that time of his life coincides with the time of your wife's collapse. I saw it when she told me what she had done, picked up men in bars and so forth. She'll know that at once. She'll realize that it was only chance that kept them from running into each other. You'll as much as force the idea upon her. She's right in believing that she's past a relapse in those terms, but she's in a weakened condition now, no one could miss that, and the more you see of Norma, the worse she'll become. You go on, and you'll have her reliving the whole experience in more grotesque and degrading terms than ever. She'll wonder how close she came to sleeping with Mac-Iver, what he was and what he was about to become—"

"You're a filthy son of a bitch. You'll use anything."

"At least you're not trying to deny the truth of it."

Leland shook his head unhappily. "I was going to come to you and give you a chance to explain your position in this. People think the world of you. I thought that I would get some common sense. You want to continue to fox around."

Roberts held the arms of the chair. "I didn't think my position was important. This is the first I've heard of Colin having my letters. You check on me, check my records. My house is mortgaged, I'm still paying my share of the debt contracted here. I'm solvent only because of my wife's life insurance, which is in the bank, untouched. You check on that, too. No safe deposit boxes, no special savings accounts. You check on me, I want you to."

"Why did you break into MacIver's office?"

"You know that I did that?"

"It wasn't hard. You made sure that it wouldn't attract attention to him, but you didn't think of someone already interested, someone trying to see into it. If you didn't know about the letters, why did you do it?"

"Colin did something here—against my better judgment—that made me believe he might have written something. A statement. Call it a confession, if you like. I was thinking of Norma. In the wrong hands, it could have led to anything. He was trying to extricate himself from Rainbow, if you didn't know."

"I know," Leland said.

"You had no trouble with his codes."

"My partner said that breaking them took organization and imagination."

"I never had a chance to see them. They probably would have been helpful to me. Toward the end, they embarrassed Colin. They were adolescent, he said. When he started keeping them, he was in a very confused state of mind. Was there anything in his papers?"

"A confession? No."

"Then how did you find out? He thought that he was safe. The further along he went, the more convinced of it he became."

"While he was alive, he probably was. He didn't reckon on his importance to the people around him—you, Norma, even Betty Kaminsky. I saw her, but you guessed that."

"No, I wondered."

"You'll never be a cop." Leland looked at the revolver, turning it over to the left and then to the right. He put on the safety. Roberts did not relax. Leland said, "MacIver didn't reckon that Norma would want answers and seek help. If he had stopped to think, he would have seen that she would have come to me. They had a conversation about me. There are private detectives in the yellow pages, but it stood to reason that she would come to the one she knew by name. You wouldn't have stopped her—he would have seen that, too. I didn't know him, he knew that, but he might have realized that I could get hold of a picture of him. It dated the scar on his neck— established that he had lied to her. His life insurance file closed the other end, after a fashion. It was in error, honest error, and I should have suspected it right away, but I didn't because I worked for the company once, and I know what a slave it is to accurate records. So I saw lies and distortions where there weren't any. I even gave up trying to resolve the conflict because, among other factors working on me, I couldn't help liking and trusting the people I was dealing with. That is, all except you.

"I don't think you could have done anything but draw attention to yourself. You were trying to protect Norma—you said. You thought you knew me and it caused you to make mistakes in dealing with me. You believed the lies Karen told Jerry Palmer and took me for some kind of egoistic authoritarian—"

"As a matter of fact, Joe, I felt sorry for you. I thought that you weren't as unyielding as she had tried to make you appear. I remembered you from the war. I read about you in the newspapers. But Tuesday night, you presented yourself as single-minded, belligerent—worse than egoistic—"

"Wendell, you still have misconceptions about me. You aren't responsible and they aren't important. Norma's dependence on you frightened me. I don't know a lot about psychotherapy; the relationship between doctor and patient is beyond my understanding. You tried to get me to go easy. Maybe that's part of your role as a doctor or maybe manipulating her and violating her trust in you was the only chance you had to squeeze through this, but I had to take it for what it seemed. She never did believe that stuff about talking sports, but she—and Karen—assured me that it was impossible for you to treat your friend and neighbor. I had no choice but to believe it. There was still the missing hour every day. MacIver left his house at eight-thirty and didn't get to the office until ten o'clock or later. When Norma learned that, she thought that he'd had a girl friend."

Wendell Roberts sat back. "What did you tell her?"

"That it was very, very unlikely. He would have left her. He had shown the capacity for divorce."

Roberts said, "He loved her desperately."

"I know that, too, now," Leland said. He explained how Mike's information about MacIver's papers had led to the conclusion that only Roberts could have broken into the office.

"I wrote some of those letters years before Norma introduced us," Roberts said. "I was interested in the housing program. It wasn't until I began to learn something about architecture that I realized how sterile and ugly the designs were. It was Colin who told me that the program was a fraud. At first he saw nothing wrong in it—it was the way of the world. Of course we didn't argue. In those days he was much too close to the calamity that finally befell him to be tampered with. He talked of suicide a lot more—you'll find out.

"He offered to get the letters, later, when his attitude had changed. He had grown, but he had learned more about his associates, too. A few were hoping to get closer to the people who control the narcotics in this city. *They're* more in public life than you could imagine—"

"You mean like Herbert Davis?"

"No, that pompous fool. He is a thief, he has his bagmen, he may be the biggest thief in the state, but he's very, very careful, and he has himself wrapped in a cloak of morality—he gets things done when he steals. Never mind him. Colin told me that his own life would be worthless if he tried to do anything sudden, but that he could make sure that I would be free of trouble if there was a scandal. He assured me that there would be no risk to him, but I said that I would rather have things as they were. It was one of the chances you took with life. I made a mistake, that's clear now. He wanted to show his feeling for me; I wouldn't let him. I should have, at that stage. He was one of those people who are held to life by baling wire. At the time, I saw his problem only from one side. We pay for the mistakes we make, even when we don't know that there's anything at stake."

"Yes, we do," Leland said quietly.

"I've been trying to protect you, too. You believe that, don't you?"

His face had sagged when he had realized that his remark had had to hurt Leland. But now Leland was on his guard again. By accident or design, Roberts had nearly disarmed him. He was going to be more watchful, but he could not fail to recognize this as the second opportunity that Roberts had mishandled.

Roberts said, "The last thing that Colin wanted, the thing he feared most—more than death—was being discovered. He was apprehensive about becoming a father. He was certain that he would have a son—he didn't want to fail him. It was on his mind on August twelfth, I'm sure of it. He was a man of subtle humor and deep, reflective moods. It was hard to tell what he felt from the things he said. Way down, he was still a very young man. Once he told me that he could feel the youth being torn out of him—he was aging. Still, he approached some things with the hopes and expectations of a boy. That car you've been driving. He laughed at it for being excessive, but just as much he hoped that it would be something for him."

"Norma told me how he was when they met," Leland said. "He fell asleep in her arms on their second date. He was glad to have found her—found that she was what she had seemed. He let down his defenses."

Roberts stared at the desk. "He—there were *times* when he was sure that he—or the weight of what he had done—would drag his family down." He sat there tiredly, his hands in his lap. "I know why he killed himself—why he had to. His fears weren't a primary cause. If I had been smarter, he might have made it—he would still be safe."

Leland shook his head. "The letters only gave me an opinion of you that made coming here easy. It was the hour every day, the insurance file, and what Betty Kaminsky told me. You know that he cheated her in their settlement, don't you?"

"Yes."

"She doesn't. It took more than a casual secrecy. If you had to find a reason for it, you would have to say that he planned to divorce her long, long before he spoke up.

"There were too many elements that I couldn't put together. The hour. He had to be in therapy with you. Not anybody else, because then he would not have been afraid to discuss it with Norma. If she couldn't understand it, no one ever will. It had to be something special—special enough to cause you to violate a rule so cardinal that neither Norma nor Karen could even consider an exception.

"That part of it figured into his death, too. A man could have been on that roof with him, thrown him off, and made his escape through the press box. But I found no evidence and no real motive. MacIver wasn't being blackmailed, he wasn't blackmailing you, there was nothing in his files to indicate that he had antagonized Rainbow.

There was no evidence that anyone thought his death anything but a suicide. The Clausen police panicked when they saw the business cards in his wallet, sure—perhaps there was something important in it. It doesn't matter. Even if you were the frightened hypocrite I took you for—you'd steal, maybe, if it was a remote kind of stealing—you wouldn't have let your friend and patient die for nothing. You would have done something. You would have tried."

"Thank you for that much."

"Wendell, you're going to have to face the fact that I didn't have much of a choice in what I thought of you. You showed me that you would protect the interests of people close to you at the expense of others. You didn't hesitate to hang it on me when you thought Norma was in trouble. All right, you were protecting me, too, you say, but I had to go on what I saw. In any case, there's no way you can justify your position with Jerry Palmer. You aided and abetted when he was trying to break up my marriage. You were willing to see Karen socially. Like it or not, a few people would put that on the same level with committing an abortion. They wouldn't touch you with a stick."

Roberts did not like it. He shifted in the chair and crossed his legs.

"The insurance man's name is Fred Miller," Leland said. "I talked to him tonight on the telephone—about Dr. Kelleher. Did MacIver know about Dr. Kelleher?"

"Yes. He told me what happened."

"I wasn't sure that he knew. Not many people remember Fred Miller, by the way, but there isn't anything about insurance that Fred Miller is likely to forget. I'd seen that shaky handwriting in the file at the beginning of the week. No one wants to look at an old man's palsy. It didn't occur to me to wonder how old, weak, or blind Dr. Kelleher could have been. The file indicated that he had died or gone into retirement not long after he managed to get the scar onto the record. MacIver had a new doctor after that.

"He showed up at all his insurance examinations but one. A man either delays and postpones so that it takes years to process his applications, or he's like MacIver, treating those examinations like

544

appointments with the draft board. MacIver bought insurance as though he had an honest respect for it. I didn't learn from his file that he saw it as the cheapest route to a large estate, but he did. So much is in the record of his business dealings that one could overlook the simple fact that he wanted to be rich.

"Fitting it all into place was the thing that kept getting away from me. I wanted to think that the information was coming in too thick and fast for sorting out. I did a lot of legwork—I thought I had been to a lot of places that I wouldn't have cared to see. You've never met Betty Kaminsky, have you?"

"No. Colin had a snapshot of her when we met. This was before he and Norma were married. Betty was a beautiful girl."

"She's a beautiful woman now, but there are marks—she's not healthy and she knows it. She remembered me from the newspapers and she's had some contact with Karen. In some ways the legwork was done on a treadmill. I saw myself wherever I went. I'd been reporting to Norma right along. I do that with all my clients; they want to be told that we're working. This was different in that, in spite of his secrecy, I never really tried to put it all together, one item against another, so that I could see it and go back and say that he was doing this, or that to the best of my knowledge he had stopped doing one thing before he had started another. He was still in college when he began on Rainbow. There were years between the time he had begun to cheat his first wife—of her money—and the night he told her that he wanted a divorce. I never tried to present it that way to Norma—the way it had happened.

"Betty Kaminsky helped all she could. I was the one who told her that MacIver was dead. It was a blow to her, don't doubt it. She thought that it had to be suicide, too, but for the wrong reason—it turns out. His mother had nothing to say to me, in case you're interested."

"Not really. Not about her, no." Roberts had been listening intently.

"On two different days Betty gave the same approximate date for the neck wound. You know that that date conflicted with the one I could deduce from the file. I saw her first on Tuesday, by the way.

On that day I thought that she was just repeating the lies she had told her present husband. Thursday was something else. She talked in depth about how they had lived, what she had felt and thought. She went a long way in the desire to help. So finally I put it down to honest confusion.

"I began thinking about it again when I took another look at the file and I realized that I wouldn't be able to double-check. That's when I began to try to put things in order.

"Tonight Fred Miller told me that Dr. Kelleher had been in his late seventies when he had died, after a sudden illness, five or six years ago. Miller had been to the funeral and could look up the date if I wanted. Kelleher had seen his last patient about a week before, MacIver within the preceding six months. Dr. Kelleher had been a very old man in every way, brusque, crotchety, and probably a little senile. He'd taken to carrying unwrapped sandwiches in his pocket, abusing patients, sending his reports in late. And, yes, he had worn glasses."

"Colin told me that Kelleher never did examine him that day," Roberts said. "He appeared as if he had been asleep before Colin came in. 'Come on, I'll get you out of here,' he said, and went down the form, checking and asking questions. His hair was uncombed and his suit was covered with stains that looked to Colin like pea soup. Colin got his copy of the form and the old man said that he would see him next time. He never did look up. Colin saw right away that Kelleher had written 'None' next to 'identifying scars and marks.' Colin got up and walked out and kept on going. He told me that his heart pounded, he had to gasp for air. He knew very well that the record was in error. The next time he saw Kelleher, which was the last time, too, the old man gave him a real examination. Many old men undergo changes—set their own rules. There's nothing terribly wrong with carrying sandwiches in your pockets if you guess that you won't live long enough to wear out the suit. An old man gets a rare pleasure from buying clothes—they're his bet on the future. Kelleher might have anticipated something. His wasn't a true senility."

Leland nodded. He had never thought of it. "I tried to remember what Betty had told me. I went through the file one more time, and there it was. I happened to think—consciously, because it must have been in the back of my mind all the time—'I know when that was.' I thought that I was going to be sick. She hadn't said it, but she had even given me the day of the week. I knew what was true before I worked it out—that the day was right, the time was right. It answered all the questions. Betty would not have forgotten the thing in the file. I called and asked her. 'Did he cancel an insurance examination the Monday after he came home bleeding?'

"And she said, 'Yes,'" Leland concluded, and picked up the desk keys. "Now let's have that file." He tried the first key. "I've played square with you—"

"There is no file, Joe."

"What are you talking about?"

"We share a single receptionist here, and two girls who take our dictation and do our typing. We know that they talk among themselves. I tried to keep a file on Colin, but there was so much that I had to censor that it did more harm than good. I couldn't review the case in the normal way—I'd put things out of my mind and then find myself needing the reference points to bring them back. I had to put the whole burden on my memory."

Leland got to his feet. "It's too late to play games, Wendell. You would not have come here if you didn't have something to protect. You would have called the police—"

"I'm telling the truth, Joe, if you'll just listen to me." He could not stop glancing at the gun. "Let me finish. There is something. I thought that you understood that from what I've said. Colin was deathly afraid of a relapse. He wanted to think that he was afraid of what it could lead to—again—but that wasn't it, not a second time. He was afraid of the thing itself, a relapse, even if he wouldn't face that, and he took steps to guard against it. You know what I'm talking about; your wife told me that she moved to Manitou to give herself a new start. It helped. 'What would these people think of me?' She kept repeating it. Once she wrote it down on a slip of paper that she carried in her purse. 'What would these people think of you?' She had drawn a line. Some people would say that she had built a prison. The important thing was that she wanted to do something; that was

547

her best way. It wouldn't work for everyone—Norma, for example—but it worked for your wife and it worked for Colin."

Leland had not known about any slip of paper.

"Colin's interest in horse racing was a device along the same line. He threw himself at it, made it an outlet—he could have quit at any time. He deliberately set up the pattern of withdrawing from Rainbow projects. It was supposed to be obvious to the others, eventually. He hoped to get his life in order—"

The telephone rang. It had a muted bell. Leland reached for it. "Who knows you're here?"

"No one. I didn't talk to anyone."

Again. Leland thought of the police, checking the light in the window. "You stay where you are." A third ring. "If you have to do any talking, you come straight to the front of the desk." Leland picked up the handset. "Who is this?"

"Joe? Is that you?"

Karen, and she sounded upset. He said, "That's right. What's up?"

"I called to warn you. Dr. Roberts isn't at home—"

"Too late for that. How did you find out?" He was watching Roberts, who was listening and probably able to guess the identity of the caller.

"Norma," Karen said. "She's downstairs—that's right, here at the hotel. She came to see you. She said she went back to Roberts' house but he wasn't there. She couldn't sleep, she called him, went across the way, then decided to come here."

"What did you tell her? How did she seem?"

"Are you talking about Norma?" Roberts asked. "Where is she?"

"I'll tell you," Leland said.

"Dr. Roberts is there with you?" Karen said.

"On the other side of the desk."

"I don't understand. You're behind the desk? You have that gun. Is he all right?"

"Perfect. A little embarrassed, but in wonderful shape."

"Joe, what have you done? You said you'd tell me what this is about."

"Answer my questions first." He caught Roberts' eye, but it was a mistake. He had to motion to Roberts to stay quiet.

Karen said, "She's all excited. She didn't say why. I didn't tell her that you were out, just that she had to wait downstairs. It's almost five o'clock. I know I have to let her come up. What do I tell her?"

"I'm working on the case. You don't know where I am or what I'm doing. You don't know anything about Roberts. Try to keep her calm, do you understand?"

"Joe," Roberts said, "I wish you'd let me talk to her."

"Just a minute, Karen." Leland held the handset away from his mouth. Karen would be able to hear. He told Roberts that Norma was in the hotel lobby. "I'm going to have Karen keep her at the hotel—at least until I can call her back." He spoke into the telephone again. "Honey?"

"What is this about, Joe? I won't do anything until I know what this is about."

He sat down again. She said, "I mean it."

"I know you do." Leland looked again to Roberts, who had recognized the change in Leland's tone. "Where are you exactly?"

"In the living room. You know that. I'm in the green chair by the window. I'm wearing my nightgown, too—okay?"

She would regret having said that. "Colin MacIver killed Theodore Leikman," Leland said. "There's no mistake. Roberts is here and he knows. I got the wrong man."

She was quiet. "Not you alone," she cried. "There was Dave and Danny Curran and all the others."

"I know. I didn't want to say 'we' so that it seemed to include you." Roberts was staring; he did not understand. Leland looked away from him. "Now you take it easy," Leland said into the telephone. "I've known since early this evening, so you've seen that I'm all right. I don't want you to worry about me."

"Now I know what you meant when you said that you had the gun out first. Before you made the telephone calls. You want me to keep her here?" She sniffed. "You want me to keep her calm," she said.

"That's right."

"Don't worry about me," she said. "Or her. I won't tell her. I won't think about it. Did he tell Dr. Roberts? Is that how you learned?"

"Yes and no." She would understand. "It was the scar. Leikman did it with his fingernails. There were no accidents that night. Mac-Iver left things just as he wanted us to find them."

"What about Tesla? What about him?"

"He saw the body when he came back to the apartment. The way we questioned him, he could have guessed what we wanted. He had his own reasons for confessing. We didn't pump it into him. We thought we had him."

There was quiet. "Why are you at Dr. Roberts' office?"

"For his file on MacIver. You did a perfect job, honey, don't worry about that. Roberts has had sufficient cause to be wary of me all along. Let me call you back."

"There is trouble. I want to know what you've done to him."

"I bounced him around a little. Frisked him. He's all right, believe me. He thinks he can go on playing games—"

"I'm not playing games, Joe—"

Leland acted as if he had not heard. "Listen, Karen, I'm sorry I brought you into this. Do the best you can with her. You don't know where I am, you don't know when I'll be back."

"Joe," Roberts said. "Colin made a confession. I have it here."

"I heard that," Karen said.

Leland looked at Roberts. "What do you mean?"

Roberts stood up and fixed his clothing. "He was afraid of a relapse and he took steps to guard against it. I was explaining that to you when the telephone rang. He couldn't write a confession and he certainly couldn't have it drawn up by someone. He made a recording, a tape recording, that I was to use if anything happened, if he did anything."

Leland regarded him. "Karen? Did you get that?"

"I'm not sure. I think I did."

"Let me off the telephone."

"All right. Be careful."

Leland put down the receiver. "Back in the chair. Where is it? You wanted me to hear it?"

Roberts moved cautiously, taking the arm of the chair before he sat down. "I had to try for an understanding. You'll find the reels in the bottom drawer on the right side. Joe, when I saw that you had come here I knew that you would find it, key or no key. I had to try to reason—"

He stopped because Leland had looked down at the revolver and had begun to heft it in his palm. He put it away. "The safety was on," he told Roberts. "Not when you came in, but I put it on."

He nodded. "I don't know anything about guns. I've been scared to death."

Leland glared at him. "I've never shot anybody in my life like that. I don't feel that *I* ever had much to do with it."

"Joe, people are afraid of guns. Jerry Palmer told me what you were like when you were angry. He telephoned you once, remember?"

"I remember." He waved his hand to silence him. The thought of hearing MacIver's voice was frightening. Leland could not explain it. He knew that he could not feel the full impact now; it was something opening and spreading before him. For some reason he seemed to push himself at it, imagining MacIver's voice in the room, in his ears, as if the man could be touched.

Roberts' chest heaved. "He wanted me to 'have something on him.' If he ever tried to quit therapy, started another thing like Rainbow, or began showing signs of reverting to the patterns that led to the Leikman murder, I was to use the recordings in any way I chose. I never had to—I'm glad I never had to think of it. He didn't simply make the recordings for the reasons he thought. She told you of the night I met him? I called her the next day; it was all I could do to keep from calling her every day thereafter. The conversation that first night worked around to psychology and psychiatry. He steered it. This was a man under terrible pressure. He was tense, putting on a performance. She couldn't have recognized it; it was the kind of thing

551

that takes training to see. The use of his eyes and hands. His inflections. He was concentrating on too many things; what he was saying, the way he was saying it, how he carried himself. He was asking for help—whether he needed it or not. There was nothing in the conversation to indicate what could be troubling him, and frankly I was afraid—for Norma's sake—of suggesting a meeting between him and me. He called the next day and came in the following afternoon. For Norma's sake, I thought, I had to give him all the time he wanted. I was going to refer him, of course. But you can't refer a man until you have an idea of what you are referring him for. Also, because of Norma, I had to be sure that the lines of communication stayed open. Some men I would have had to consider him for would not have discussed him with me. This is a strange and difficult profession. Some of the best men are the most secretive and uncooperative. Colin talked about his first wife, his mother—whom he hadn't seen in years. We were at an impasse until he asked how I felt about my professional privilege. I knew right away what he meant, but I thought—rightly, it turned out—that he had done such a good job of concealing that he could lie to me about what was bothering him, I would believe it, and he would slip away. Do you understand? He could have said that he was an embezzler? I told him that I believed that I had no right to reveal to anyone what a patient told me in the effort to help himself. Then I cut the hour short and sent him out.

"In a little while he called back to invite me to lunch. I said all right and in the restaurant he tried to pick up the conversation where we had left off. He became very nervous. He spilled a glass of water. Finally he asked if I remembered the Leikman case and I said I did, vaguely. He wanted to know if a man like Tesla could be so far gone as to confess to a crime that he hadn't committed. My memory of the case wasn't clear and I couldn't be sure of what Colin was leading to. Later he said that at that point he was trying to stop himself, but he couldn't. He couldn't stop talking. He said, 'I know that Felix Tesla didn't crush Leikman's skull because I did. It's as simple as that.'

"I had no doubt of it. I was looking around to see if anyone else had heard. Later, because I am a doctor, I did go to the library and read the newspaper accounts. They corresponded. There were things that Colin told me that were never mentioned in the papers, only suggested—the mutilations, the condition of the bedroom.

"We didn't get out of the restaurant for another half hour. I had to be sure that he had calmed down. I had a class, but I skipped it, took him here, and gave him a shot to relax him. Referring him was out. I didn't think that he could survive the ordeal."

Leland unlocked the drawer. There were papers, folders, and a frayed, bulging manila envelope, soft as old money. He set it on the blotter and unwound the string. He had not seen such a closure since his days with Manitou Life.

Roberts said that the recorder was in the closet. Leland motioned to him to get it. There were two black and white laminated paperboard containers, without gummed labels or India ink identifications. Roberts must have looked around to see Leland examining the containers.

"I've never played them, although I've kept them since his death, in part, for his voice. I don't know of any other recordings of his voice. There are a lot of reasons why I haven't destroyed almost the last of what is left of him." He swung the recorder onto the desk. "I don't have any children of my own, no brothers and sisters, so no nieces or nephews. Even if I marry again, which I doubt, the woman almost certainly will be past childbearing age. I know that I saw an opportunity in Colin and Norma—I was very pleased when they told me that they were going to have a baby. We had a fine thing, the three of us, due in no small part to him. He worked hard to separate our work together from our social relationship outside. He was always kind to me—because he knew that I was working with him, not because his difficulties compelled him to be kind to me. He was a subtle and complicated man."

Leland had not moved to help him. "You tried to talk him out of marrying her, didn't you?"

"You don't really understand the nature of my work, if you mean a thing like that." He had untangled the power line and now he went to the wall for the baseboard outlet. "I work in the world of the possible. Of course there are value judgments. I believed that their relationship was beyond my influence. I didn't want him to marry anybody, but if I had attempted to impose myself, I would have lost him, perhaps she would have lost him—she wanted to test herself as a wife, remember—and I would have lost her. There was no chance of success. It was not a calculated risk. He wanted her, he wanted to marry her—you'll hear him say it. He did not die with the opinions he expressed here, please remember that. I came to like Colin. I admired him for the struggle he made. If it had gone the way I would have had it, we would have worked for ten years. I never said that to him; it would have defeated him. I was the one who was hoping to live long enough." He sat down again heavily. Leland looked at him.

"I'm going on the assumption that you want to handle the tapes yourself," Roberts said.

"That's right." Leland rose.

"He was not trying to apologize for himself," Roberts said. "He thought he wanted these records for the reasons I've already given you. He told the truth as well as he could see it. By August twelfth he had come a long way. Some people would argue that he was only being more honest. It was that he was *capable* of more honesty. I wanted you to hear these, Joe. When he made them, he was a man still not really sure that he would ever take the reins of his life."

Leland nodded. He had heard him; but he was thinking about other things that Roberts had said, too.

"All right?" a voice in the speaker asked.

"Go ahead," Wendell Roberts' voice said. Leland felt a start; the first voice had been MacIver's.

"My name is Colin William MacIver," the voice said, with the inflections of Manitou. The letter *r* had been as clear as a man could hope to pronounce it. A young voice, very clear, not a voice one heard on the radio—a true, young voice. "I'm thirty years old and I live at Sixteen-ninety Paley Street here in Port Smith. I'm reasonably sane and I'm making this record not because of any pressure." There was a pause. "I want it to be a record of certain things that I did and that have happened to me." There was another pause, a longer one. Leland sat back and started to light a cigarette, his first in hours. His hands were wet and much too warm.

"I killed a man," the voice said. "I killed Theodore Leikman—" He stopped and there was another long silence.

Roberts said to Leland, "He was in difficulty and I reached for the microphone. He pulled it away."

The blank tape continued to run through the machine. There was a sigh. "My father died when I was in teen-age and my mother undertook the job of raising me by herself. I don't think she ever tried to remarry, but I don't know. I've always resisted looking into that side of her personality. If she had the desires and frailties that I find so attractive in other women, she never showed them to me. I don't think that I would be able to accept them now. She was a busy woman but not a popular one, and she did not show me the kind of warmth that would predispose me to kindness to her today. She put limitations on my activities as a child so that, in fact as well as feeling, I was different from the others. They sensed it. I knew that there were girls who liked me, but they tired of my helplessness with them and had to dislike me; and in gym when the football coach had everyone in the class take certain tests and he thought that I could be made into a halfback or end, my mother forbade it. It was more than feeling the opportunity close up in front of my face. The coach was unable to conceal his unhappiness and disgust with me. He had to settle it in himself in some way but I didn't know that at that time. I came to hate him in return—which put me more on the outside, because he was one of the most popular men in the school—and when I got away from there I pushed the incident so far down in my mind that whole years went by without me thinking of it."

The tape ran silently a few seconds and Wendell Roberts asked, "What do you think of it?"

"He wasn't telling the truth. Did he think that he was kidding you?"

"He wasn't looking at me."

"Dur-during those years after my father died my mother went through my closet and my dresser and even removed the lock from the bathroom door in the effort to keep me from doing those things she thought all boys did when they were left to themselves too much. I was jealous of my privacy; and she was as clumsy as she was obvious. For the fun of it I would leave corners of harmless magazines sticking from my drawer or the shelf of the closet. Often I wanted to leave a note for her and once I thought of drawing a huge nude on my ceiling to see how long she would snoop around below before it caught her eye. I would like to think that her dirty curiosity as much as anything inside me goaded me into experimenting with myself, or going outside the neighborhood for girlie magazines—ah, I'll say it: until I left college before the war, I was a habitual masturbator. I would hurry home from high school to do it. I never thought that she would catch me at it. One afternoon I was in the bathroom and she came home too quietly for me to hear. Perhaps when she saw the bathroom door closed she tried to be quiet. She opened the door and whooped, 'Oh, you horrid boy!' and began to hit me with both hands. It was really funny. I'm sure it was as much her shock at the size of me as anything, because she kept hitting me, not saying anything, just hitting until she drove me out of the bathroom down the hall to my room where I was able to hold the door closed while I fixed my clothing. She didn't speak of it later; and for several days afterward she left me alone. For myself, I forgot about the fact of having been caught and concentrated on my memory of the sound of her voice when she had opened the door. I paid no attention to anything she said from that time on. For weeks I thought about her reaction if I used it on her—raping her, I mean. Not for the pleasure of it—I thought at the time —but for the satisfaction of hearing that 'Oh!' again. It demolished her. She demolished herself when she opened that door.

"In the fall of 1942 I went out to the University of California, at Berkeley. That was her choice. I had no choice of my own, and my grades had been good enough for any school in the country. Things went wrong. Even today I don't know what happened exactly, but I felt as if I had started on the wrong foot. I didn't know the routine, I didn't know where I belonged—"

"He's telling the truth now," Roberts said.

"I know," Leland said. "I went to college."

"—a girl in one of my classes. I learned when we went out that she was two years older than me. I know now that she had absurd views of the world and men, and at the time, me in particular. She wasn't a subtle lover, to say the least, and she had her own ways of indicating what she wanted and whether she thought she was getting it. 'Come on, will you?' she would say, or 'This way,' or 'Put your hand here,' and she would shift her body under my hand. Her body was a shock to me, there was nothing delicate about it. I was appalled by the hair and the sweat and the odors, all of which she was aware of and, after she saw my reaction, she thrust at me. She saw that I was inexperienced and it amused her; she called me 'boy,' and emotionally, very quickly, lost interest in me. She made me chase her and finally she put me off completely. The whole thing lasted no more than a couple of months but it left me demoralized. I had made a fool of myself. I had kept calling her until all her friends knew it. I couldn't get it into my head that I really didn't want her. My actions certainly didn't indicate that, I know, but it *was* true. I had been repelled by our lovemaking. There hadn't been enough of it for me to have gotten through the newness of it, and I went away from her after a few times actually disgusted. If it had gone on longer, I would have thought about extricating myself—I don't think now that I would have been able to go about it, but I would have wanted it. I would have had to wait until one circumstance or another did the job for me."

There was a silence, and then Wendell Roberts' voice said, "You don't have to continue."

"He shook his head here," Roberts told Leland. The tape ran on while Leland waited more and more impatiently. It was hard to believe that Norma had been drawn to him for his sensitivity and kindness to her.

The voice began again, closer to the microphone, quaveringly, more strained. "The travel restrictions and priorities of the war made it impossible for me to get home for the winter vacation of 1942–43, so I arranged to go on one of those collegiate skiing trips. I was alone. There were two buses from Berkeley and, when we arrived at the resort, more from Stanford, L.A., Bakersfield, and the other places. The rooms were assigned and a lot of people were dissatisfied and there was switching back and forth. I was with another fellow's friend so when they asked me to change I agreed. I'll never know if they knew more than they were telling; I used to catch myself thinking that whether they knew it or not, they changed my life, but that isn't true: everything would have happened just the same anyway, for if there were events that shaped the patterns of my life, they happened earlier and made me ready for what happened at that resort; and by the same token I've spent a good many years looking for someone on whom to fix the blame, my mother, father, not to mention my ex-wife, but never myself, and for a short while I believed that I could have protected myself if those fellows after they had made the switch had only warned me, and even today I want to believe that they knew, did it deliberately, and acted out of nothing but maliciousness, not thinking that the person they were dealing with already might be in trouble. There's no way to tell all the things that they did.

"I went back to school five days later feeling a curious euphoria and a mounting shame, because just as much as I knew that what I and my temporary roommate had done was hopeless and wrong, I was glad and relieved that we had done it. I felt myself returning to reality and into society. He had been sensitive and in some ways much more feminine than the girl I had been seeing at Berkeley, and while I hadn't admired him I had liked him, but I found myself sneering at him and disassociating myself from him. It hadn't been his first experience and I condemned him for that. I became more ashamed, and when his letters arrived I threw them away, so help me, without reading them. I became more and more afraid of being found out and I watched the girls especially, and even thought that they knew—intuitively, or by a secret communication system men have no knowledge of. It was impossible to go on that way, so after a while I began to believe that at least I had had a complete sexual experience and that because of it I was more mature. Supposedly I was better equipped to deal with other people. I didn't have the maturity to go with my experience, such as it was, and either the more sophisticated girls I wanted to attract saw through me or the others would drop me—I still don't know why. I went to dances and tried to date every girl I took home, but after the first or second dates, if there were any, I knew better than to call again.

"I had to get out of there. Everything gave way to despair and I had to quit living so many lies. I had convinced myself that I was trying to maintain the appearance of normality for no reason at all. I don't know how I came to enlist in the service. I could have put it off for perhaps another year. It became the best thing I could have done. The work and traveling made me forget. I met women and had honest relationships with two of them. There were others, but there were those two with whom I shared at least honest sex. I didn't think about what had happened, and when I went into combat I handled myself without trouble. I take satisfaction in having done well. It isn't really possible to separate that from the fact that I killed people in the process, but I do it anyway and I suppose other men do the same thing."

Roberts asked Leland, "Is that the way you feel about it?"

"I don't think about it at all, unless I'm reminded. It wouldn't change anything, help anything. I didn't have a good time in the war, Wendell."

Roberts wanted to answer, but MacIver's voice had started again.

"—I met Betty, my ex-wife, at Jefferson. In many ways I was still fighting the war. I wanted the pace and excitement to continue and I tried to live as if they were. I was a college student again, but I was other things more than that—ex-GI, ex-fighter pilot. I wasn't chafing in the situation; I loved it. I had some of the polish I had needed and I was full of hope that something would turn up. I can't define that any better now than I could then; it was something I believed and carried with me. Something was going to turn up. I suppose it was Betty.

"She was more ready for me than I was for her. She was young and she was a lovely girl, more than she knew, but it wasn't ignorance about herself coupled with good looks that made other girls stay away from her. She was quiet, diffident, and humorless, but most of all she was high-strung. The men who knew her thought that she was suspicious and self-impressed when she was trying to be pleasant, patronizing. There is some truth in it, because I saw it. She didn't know how to deal with people. She was timid with me, and I had to wait a long time before I found out how attracted to me she was. She never did really overcome her timidity, her seeming diffidence. I was always a little on edge, wondering what she thought. After we were married and I found myself in deep trouble, I wanted to think that I had made myself the victim of my own puritanism, but the truth was that my own problem was only part of what was wrong. I didn't know how to bring our relationship to an end, that was true—still true. But she took everything I did, took it all. I was deathly afraid of her becoming pregnant, because the price of getting out would be that much more. It took a murder to end our marriage, and I had to blame her as much as myself. She was never interested enough to find out what was going on, why I did the things I did in her presence. I broke dishes and so forth, and she never asked why—what was really on my mind. At the end, the lack of change in her attitude—she was like a sponge; there was no amount of punishment that she wasn't willing to absorb —that lack of change made me want to let what could have been neat and clean deteriorate into a series of vicious arguments. There was something that I was trying to prove—that I was right, I guess—but because of what happened I couldn't honestly pursue it. She never tried to see that divorce could be the best thing for her, too. She was getting the same opportunity—better, because she didn't have so much over her head—she was getting at least the chance to correct the mistake. I knew that she would marry the first man to come along. She thought that she was in love with me, but she never knew what love was. I was just a thing that satisfied her. As long as I wanted her, her ego was soothed. That was it, her ego. The whole thing ended far more bitterly than I could have imagined. Accusations back and forth, spite, cheapness—when I told her that she would remarry quickly, I knew that I was being terribly unfair, turning it into a challenge. That was the way we both wanted it—she went into long, savage harangues about why I really wanted a divorce.

"We were married quickly because she had given over all power to make decisions. Neither of us knew what was really happening. We thought we were happy. The misgiving that I had let me see our chances objectively and I thought that we did have a chance at a reasonably happy marriage. I didn't take into account that it could be different from my expectations. We were living in a dream, and I hold her responsible for never honestly facing it. I tried to change my expectations of her. Her expectations of me never changed, and as long as that circumstance prevailed we were crippled—but honestly I thought that it would improve and that we would work it out.

"She didn't realize that living with her forced me to see her as something different from what she had been when we had been going together. She thought that I should be attracted to her in the way that I had been, but the things that had attracted me no longer existed. Sex was no consolation for not having real money and being without the prospect of having any, or for the thought of all the education I had ahead of me, of having to meet our obligations after her parents died. I couldn't be excited by her twenty minutes after she had been doing some dirty job in my old shirt and a torn pair of shorts. Because it had worked once or twice it was supposed to work every time, but of course it didn't. I wasn't able to tell her. That was my failure. But at that time I put value on her learning it for herself. The final effect was not just that there was no respite from the pressure that I felt, but that the one area in which I should have found some relief was actually the one that was the most difficult—my relationship with her."

His voice stopped and the tape ran on soundlessly.

"She *was* timid," Leland said. "She told me that she was afraid of him."

"He realized that before he died."

"He hasn't said anything about cheating her, either," Leland said.

"He will."

The tape ran on and Leland could hear MacIver's breathing, short, light, hurried. "—didn't take long. It didn't take long," he repeated to correct the flaw his loss of voice had made. "I couldn't say how many months, five, six—not eight, that would be a lie. I don't remember how I started thinking about it. Every day I must have gone by things similar to whatever started it, so I must have been predisposed when I encountered it. I wasn't thinking about just what I had done at that skiing resort, but how pleasurable it had been and how much I wanted to do it again. I knew that I wasn't a boy anymore and that this was different from what happened then because I wanted it, I was willing to go out and look for it. The mechanics were simple. Betty and I had been to Joytown and I had seen the homosexuals making pickups. The closer I came to doing it, the more frightened I became. Then it was the only thing I could think of. It terrified me. I did want it. I couldn't resist it, I swear that that's true about the way it was at the start. I made a plan about telling her that I was going to the library one night, and I drove downtown. I was almost sick by then. I went to different places and walked around for hours until I saw someone—I don't know, I had to talk him into it. He wasn't interested in me. We went to his apartment.

"I—I had a shattering sense of relief—and anger and despair. I hurried home. She didn't notice anything. We even made love that night. I thought about it the next day and the day after. But by then I had convinced myself that it had been something that I had had to do once. I tried to forget it. I determined to make a better effort in my marriage. I looked for the things about her that pleased me. It went along well for a while. When it started again I didn't know what to do. I didn't want it to happen to me—I didn't want to be a queer. A fairy. I still hate them. It was only eight or ten weeks after the first time, that's all. I never thought of going back to the first one. I tried to fight it. For a week or more I could feel—things. I don't want to talk about that. But I went back there, downtown. It took hours of going around into bars and restaurants. It was a wonder that none of our friends, who went there as often as we did, ever spotted me. I was physically exhausted that night from the strain and I remember thinking of the insanity of it, but I couldn't quit and go home. I got home at two-thirty after I stopped off for a couple of drinks so I could tell her that I had done that and had lost track of the time. I was supposed to have been at the library. I always told her that. I made her think that I didn't want company, so she never came over to meet me.

562

"We didn't make love that night, after the second time. I couldn't. I can't describe what I felt like—not human. I did know that I was quieter again, and I couldn't help thinking of the implications of that. I hated it, dreaded it, but I wanted to sleep, hide, run away. I didn't like myself, my body, anything about myself. If I could have, I would have cried. I would have done anything if I could have purged myself of what I felt.

"She had no idea of what was happening. Looking back on it, I see that all she knew was that I had become more violent, more hostile. I couldn't help it. I saw that, and tried to control myself but I couldn't replace my behavior with something good, something good for her. For her sake as much as mine she shouldn't have allowed me to abuse her in all those little ways. I wish that she could have showed more self-reliance.

"There were times when I forgot or went for days without thinking of it, and there were times when I thought of nothing else, looking for reasons, solutions. I thought of giving up school and starting a family, but I didn't have the courage to change my life like that, or maybe I didn't believe in it enough. But for weeks I hid in the idea. There was nothing to stop us from having a family, but we never discussed it. I could have gotten a job. Now I suspect that she was just as afraid as I was, for her own reasons. There were none of those drunken, passionate celebrations our friends joked about, nights when we would forget to use the diaphragm. Yes, once, but that was after. She was afraid *with* me.

"She didn't see changes in me that I saw myself. It was more than that I wanted to stay away from other people, normal people; it was that I was frightened of them, afraid that they would see what was wrong with me. I was afraid of the men as well as the women. The furtive, dirty process of picking up—" He stopped. "No homosexual can mistake another. It's more than the mincing walk and gestures; it's something in the eyes. It's in the eyes of men who don't mince or wave their hands and I was afraid it was in mine. On three occasions I caught myself in gestures that were homosexual and I knew that if it had gone that far, perhaps I could no longer control my eyes, so I was afraid—of people. Of what might happen. What could be said.

Betty never suspected. Our sex life had undergone subtle changes, but she asked no questions. We forgot about other things, and I knew that the arguments were on the surface, away from the real issue, which was what was the matter with me; it was that that had goaded me into starting an argument in some other matter about which I had some minor complaint. Petty complaint.

"The thought of turning, involuntarily turning, into one of those pansies sickened me. The only thing I had left was anger. I could just go so far before something happened, something gave way. I saw a lot more of my real nature than most men would be able to stand. Whether I thought I stood it or not, I was irrational. I admit it, I was irrational. I know it now because I can hardly recall most of the things I did that winter. I have a good memory. She told me later about things I said; I don't remember them. I've gone to movies that I thought I hadn't seen. The memory was blotted out to me. I felt like myself. I felt as though I were in control. I don't know how a court of law would decide it. I knew right from wrong, but that just wasn't an issue.

"It was the first warm weekend," he said after a pause, and stopped again, and Leland felt himself respond. He remembered everything. "I didn't think that anything unusual would happen," MacIver said. "I didn't plan to go out. I never wanted to. I gave up and told her that I had work to do. Even outside I tried to convince myself that I wasn't going to do anything. That had happened before; I'd go out and walk around and think about it, even talk to people. I didn't feel anything deeply, although my senses were very alert. I felt normal for the circumstance, that's what I wanted to make clear. Later I was able to go back in my mind and put together everything I had done.

"I met him in one of those bars. He was a little drunk and on the make. He played coy and cute—that twisted idea of what it means to be feminine. He was a good-looking boy. That was important to me. It still is, as if prettiness makes it less of what it is. I've caught myself clinging to that. It's comic. He was a loathsome individual. I didn't want to think of that when we were in the bar. He told me that he had a roommate he was trying to get rid of who might still be in the

564

apartment. I was willing to take that chance. He described the roommate condescendingly and he only hesitated slightly to show that he had no taste for me, either. By then I was too far along to stop. The roommate wasn't in the apartment." He stopped. Leland pictured the apartment as the police had found it later that night. He was seeing how close he had come to MacIver, at least in time.

"He asked if I wanted a drink," MacIver said slowly, quietly. "He wanted one. There were stale drinks near the phonograph from earlier in the evening. The roommate drank soda pop, he said. I sat down and smoked. He gave me a drink but I didn't want it. He saw that I was impatient and it amused him. I never had anything to say. He wanted to find out about me, to see how uncomfortable he could make me. He asked if I was married and I told him no. That's very, very common, married men going with them. Finally I got up; it was going to be bad but I wanted to get it over with. I went into the bedroom and didn't turn on the light. He followed me and turned it on. I turned it off. I always wanted it off. I was near him and he reached—reached to put his arms around me. Some of them like to kiss. That disgusts me. I told him. He insisted and I shook my head and pushed away from him. He had some kind of cologne on him. I've never smelled it since, but I can remember. We undressed. He talked all the time, glib, not crude, but brutal, cruel. I tried not to hear him. I kept my back to him. He turned on the light once more, then turned it off again, laughing. I didn't face him until I heard the bed jounce. He was still talking. I felt little and helpless. I always felt like that. Like a woman, or what I think a woman feels like. I wanted to be a woman. I wanted them to take the initiative and I wanted them to know what I wanted. I got into bed, I—we started to do things. He smelled of liquor, too. I let him kiss me on the cheek. He thought it was funny while he did it. He tried to twist my mouth around to his. 'What's the matter?' he kept asking, but only to amuse himself. Then he got up and went into the bathroom. I wanted to leave, but I couldn't. I smoked a cigarette. I had just put one out. He came back. He had a tube of ointment. That—that's not what I liked, but sometimes I did it. I thought I was going to be sick. Oh, not because—I can't explain it. He kept talking. I wanted him to be quiet.

I thought I could pretend things. He started to move, and before I realized what he was doing—I mean I went along with it well enough; I was curious about what he was trying to do—he was under me, his legs pulled up, like a woman. It was horrible. I hadn't thought it was possible. He laughed at me and locked his legs around me. The horror wouldn't stop. I could feel his genitals pressing against my stomach. He grabbed my head and pulled my mouth down on his mouth. I could smell him. As I tried to pull away I could feel something like a gunshot, an explosion in my head. I hit him. I thought of doing it before I did it. I decided to do it, that's what I mean. My knuckles smacked against his temple. He jumped up and pushed me away. 'You madman!' he said. The stink was still in my nostrils. He was almost off the bed and my second punch bounced off his back. He screamed, 'Get out!' He still had his composure under his anger, that loathsome way of his, and it just made me worse. He got the light on. The sight of him made my stomach heave. I didn't dare look at myself. 'Are you crazy?' He leaned toward me and I lunged and swung again. It whacked his cheekbone and he fell off balance against the closet door. I was glad. I had never thought I could hit anyone like that. I had avoided fights as a kid, more than I can count. He couldn't move fast enough for me. It was almost too easy. 'You better get out,' he said. 'You better get out of here.' I wanted to hit him again, but I didn't move. I was afraid that he would shout if I came after him. 'Come on, get off the bed,' he said. He was trying to talk me out of it. I wanted him to fight back. When he got close I swung again and he went, 'Ooh!' as he realized what I wanted to do. He saw it before I did. I knew then that if I was going to do it I had to go after him and I was off the bed faster than he could get to the door. I still couldn't believe it of myself. I got him against the closet door but he wouldn't let me hit him. He kicked at me while I punched at his shoulders and tried to protect my groin. It was terrifying, fighting in the nude. I banged him against the door and he ducked under my arm. I grabbed his wrist and tripped him and twisted as he fell against the dresser. His back hit it full force and it hurt him badly. There was no backing out then, I knew that. I had him against the wall beside the dresser and the pain had taken the fight out of him. I tried to get at his throat. He was afraid now and whimpering and crying. It came to me, exactly what I was doing. I didn't dare stop but I couldn't get my thumbs against his larynx as you see in the movies. His thumb and fingernail dug into my neck. I felt the blood and looked down but all I saw were our naked bodies. I punched him with both hands to make him let go of my neck but he wouldn't. He wouldn't look up, he wouldn't stop. There was a piece of bric-a-brac on the dresser and I grabbed at it. He saw me. He started to let go. I had the thing the way you hold a softball and I crowned him with it. His eyes glazed. He was really hurt. He let go. He watched me hit him again. The third time he was just leaning against the wall, sort of tired, watching the thing come down again. His arms were against his sides. I was in close and the weight of my body came down with the thing. I could hear his skull crack. He started to slump down. Seeing the life going out of him made me panic. I tried to hold him up. It was too much to do and as I let him slip to the floor I kept hitting him. When he stopped I hit him two or three times more. His blood was on everything, including me. I dropped the bric-a-brac in his lap. I could see my heart pounding through my skin."

He caught his breath. "It seemed like a dream. I didn't want to believe that it had really happened. I was sure that I would be caught —it didn't seem fair. It was over so soon. It was just something that had happened. I had to get away with it and I knew that the only way was by keeping my wits about me. I went into the bathroom to see if I had been cut badly enough to have dripped blood. I was able to locate the light switch without handling the wall. I pushed up the switch with my elbow. I was still bleeding, but I didn't think it was very bad. I wiped what I could with toilet paper and then tucked the paper between my neck and shoulder. I realized that I had to dress, so I went back to the bedroom and did that. My stomach felt very weak. I was in a hot, prickly sweat even as I put on my clothes. I couldn't keep the toilet paper on my neck, so I just pushed it under my undershirt. I went into the bathroom again and took as much fresh paper as I could handle. In a way I was following my instincts. Using the paper to absorb my fingerprints, I turned off the light in the bathroom and closed the door. It had been closed when we had gone by it earlier. I was careful not to disturb the areas I hadn't touched. I went through the house and picked my cigarette butts out of the ash trays. I put them in my pocket because I remembered a case in which the police took evidence out of the toilet trap. I had handled the ash tray in the bedroom. I wiped it with the paper just a little. I knew that I couldn't wipe anything too clean; it would create suspicion. I didn't know what to do with the piece of bric-a-brac. Finally I moved it out to the entranceway where the first person who came in would pick it up and damage or ruin it as evidence. I was thinking of something else then and I went back to the bedroom.

"I could see bits of my skin and blood under his fingernails. I knew that they couldn't be washed. There didn't seem to be any other way; I didn't dare leave things as they were. I couldn't escape the idea that the roommate was going to be suspected. I couldn't let that stop me, if I was to get away. I got a steak knife from the kitchen. He smelled like the icebox in a butcher store by then, so much drying blood. I did it as quickly as I could. It didn't make sense, the way I was leaving it. There could be only one reason for what had been done, the reason that had motivated me. Even if the police couldn't trace me, if it were published that they were looking for a man with a wound, someone, even Betty, might connect me with it. I was going to tell Betty one lie or other. The only answer was to keep the police from thinking that the killer had been hurt at all.

"I didn't understand the psychopathology of such things. It had to follow a kind of logic. What I thought of seemed to be right, so I did it. I never touched it. I used the toilet paper. I wanted to take it with the fingers, but finally I couldn't; I threw it across the room. I put the knife in my pocket. On the way out I threw the bolt of the door so it would stay ajar. Anyone passing might walk in and start handling things. I wanted that. I closed the door as gently as I could and just walked down the stairs. I didn't look back. I kept walking. At the corner I stopped to light a cigarette. Felix Tesla turned into the block at that moment, on his way to the apartment. I didn't know his name, but I knew right away who he was. He gave me that appreciating slow glance. My neck was down in my collar; he didn't see that. It was the best thing that happened to me," he whispered. "If I hadn't seen him

I might have felt sorry for him, but he was another one, like Leikman. I knew him."

"He swallowed several times here," Roberts said.

Leland said nothing. MacIver coughed and cleared his throat. "I walked around a while, then went through Lewis Park to the bay. I found a piece of lead pipe and shoved the things into it and plugged up the ends with the toilet paper. I threw it as far as I could out into the water.

"I stayed out another hour while I tried to settle on something to tell Betty. For all I knew, I had slipped up anyway and the police knew what Leikman had done to his attacker. I couldn't tell an elaborate lie that could be broken down easily. I decided to wait until I saw her. She would believe what she wanted, so I would wait for her to tell me what that was. I headed home.

"She woke up when I was in the bathroom. I told her to stay in bed but she wouldn't. She came out to see and I didn't want to talk to her, just as I don't want to talk anymore now. I had had enough, but she shouldn't grasp that from the way I looked and acted."

Roberts motioned to the machine and Leland got up. "I remember that very well," Roberts said. "He sat there for almost five minutes before he realized that he was finished for the day. I let him rest for the remainder of the hour. I asked if he wanted anything to help him sleep, but he said no. All this was before he and Norma were married, so I didn't see him that night. The second tape is short, as I recall it. When he came in the next morning he was in a very agitated condition."

Leland was thinking of the ash trays in the Leikman apartment and the steak knife that had not been missed and the toilet paper that had been taken from the bathroom. He could not even remember if the roll had been empty. It might have helped. There never had been a solid explanation for the condition of the ash trays. The perfect murder was not so rare, Leland knew that, but it did not help him. The case should have been solved. He blinked; his eyes were wet. The second reel was on the machine and he turned the switch.

"My name is Colin MacIver. Yesterday I made a recording in which I related certain events in my life that occurred four or more years ago. Because—perhaps because of those years, it doesn't tell all I had hoped it would tell, or nearer to the truth, it doesn't give me the feeling I had hoped for in making—a recording."

A moment passed and he coughed. "I had thought that I wanted to tell about the murder, but I spent more time than I wanted on circumstances, the condition I was in—I might as well get used to saying it aloud—my homosexuality. I don't pretend to understand the relationship of cause and effect in the human personality, which is to say that I don't know why my background produced the weak and willful individual that I know I am. I'm having trouble now over this. I don't want to think that I know what constitutes homosexuality. During the war I never really felt that the labels 'officer' and 'fighter pilot' fit me; so even though I killed a man, I try just as much to shake off the name 'murderer,' and the same applies to 'homosexual.' I'm an ordinary man, that's what I know and want to believe.

"I know that I'm afraid to face what I did. I don't mean the murder. Probably because of our moral system, the moral equation by which we live, it feels no worse to be a murderer than a homosexual. There are a thousand ugly words for a homosexual. Is it so terrible? I'm convinced that it is. I—it's futile and it's dirty. I mean both of those things literally. There's something else. They're all the same—we're all the same. Even with a woman, a man doesn't fully retain what we call the male role. It isn't in the nature of sex for one partner to let the other go unsatisfied, unrelieved. The importance of satisfying the other varies in people, but a man who goes to another man does want to feel that he has made contact—it's disgusting. He wants to believe that he hasn't failed."

"He lost his composure here," Roberts said. "There'll be nothing for a quite a while. He told me later that he wanted to say something about curiosity. When you were young, a teen-ager especially, didn't you continue with a girl out of curiosity, even after you had stopped caring about her?"

"No."

"You were one of the very few," Roberts said. Leland was looking at the machine.

"I had an easier time of adolescence than most people," he said.

"I was nineteen when I met Karen. She—" He stopped. He had been going to say, "She was my girl." He felt hurt and battered enough to be drawn into talking, which he did not want to do. Even as he hoped for a measure of control, images of those days, of her, of how she had looked then, filtered through his thoughts. He knew that he was feeling sorry for himself, but the phrase "my girl" and what it had meant to him over so many years had to stay with him. Earlier, when he had told her on the telephone what he had wanted, he had not entertained a second's doubt of her carrying it out; but now he could not help worrying about her—it was Norma whom he could not trust. He did not want Karen hurt. He looked up at Roberts, who had been watching him. He had been thinking, too. If Roberts knew him at last, and Karen, too, from what had slipped out, Leland was past the point of caring.

There was a sound from the speaker of the recorder.

"I didn't have to wait long to learn that I would get away with it. In the days immediately afterward it took all my strength to keep relatively calm. I thought of dozens of things, so many directions—I can't remember it all. It was the most amazing period of my life. It was as if years and years of pressure were taking days and days to ease. There was a constant flow out of me. Somehow I was able to push the murder itself out of my mind. It was like starting all over. I had so many things to decide—some of the decisions were made on impulse. I couldn't keep away from Betty. It was a kind of small, wild hope. I'd never be able to tell her anything, but I thought that we could establish something on another level. Too much had happened —I made a mistake. During this same time I began to make some money. I concealed it from her. A year, a month before, I would have brought it home and put it on the table. My situation was all wrong— our situation.

"There were a lot of things wrong. Our sex life. She couldn't anticipate me. She never could initiate, and after a while, if she had tried it, she would have been out of character. She had a good mind. Sex was just not an area in which she could thrive. Emotionally—I want to say that she refused to develop emotionally.

"I can't say things about her sexual inadequacies without being more honest about my own failures. I said something a moment ago about one partner trying to satisfy the other. It may be true, I don't know. In my own case, I wanted to be the woman. It's that easy. I wanted to be the girl. I did it often enough."

He took two, three deep breaths. "When I was going out, walking, I would see police cars and patrolmen and I would rarely think of getting caught. Or about blackmailers. Both dangers were there, but even in my most clearheaded moments I would push them away. I heard stories about arrests and blackmailers but I wouldn't listen. I can hardly believe that I behaved that way, because I knew at the time that I was doing it for a reason, flirting with disaster. I could have wrecked my life in the most inconsequential twinkling—it took a disaster to bring me to my senses. There is a thrill to fear, I know that. But what good is it to know that I sought it out? Or that more than once I drove myself through something, knowing in advance that I would come out afterward feeling dirty and ashamed—bathed in self-loathing?

"One night while I was still living with Betty—this after Leikman—I began to feel the desire to go out again. I swear it. You have to see the madness of it. Betty was visiting a friend. I went into the bathroom and tried to make myself throw up. I gagged, but that was all. Finally I undressed and went to bed nude. My idea was to make it as difficult as possible for me to go out. I would have tied myself down.

"I did want things between Betty and me to work out. There were good things about her. I don't want to lie about myself. The idea of wanting it to work came and went. Sometimes I would be very interested in it. But something would happen, she wouldn't respond—out of inertia, it's all I can think of—or I would make the mistake of expecting her to do or say something that she didn't have in her. I would feel whipped and angry—very angry. It was all futile. She never understood, made a guess, tried to guess. Perhaps because she didn't try—try—I took a lot of it out on her. I'd break things that I knew she was fond of. Then she would show that she was concerned with her own position. She let that out in other ways, in little threats. When we were still talking about divorce, she said that she wouldn't let go, that she would call my clients. Before we were married, she said similar things to tease me, she thought. It was possessiveness. She was going to ruin my reputation, she said, if I didn't marry her. It frightened me, but I thought—I thought less of it than I do now.

"Her guess was that a woman had cut my neck. I let her think so. There was no perverse satisfaction in that for me; I kept waiting for her to say, 'All right, something went wrong with us to make you do that. Let's find out what it is.' That never happened. She nursed her wounds. Even before, arguments didn't end unless I ended them. Afterward, when it should have been obvious to her that my life had come apart, there was no reaching from her. She made halfhearted, ill-timed gestures; there was never any strength to them. I had to hate her for it. She will always believe that she was right and I was wrong, but at least there is the satisfaction for me that I knew her better than she knew herself."

Leland said, "She told me the same thing. *She* knew *him* better."

"What does that tell you?" Roberts asked.

Leland was listening again. "—my mother accused me of not knowing what I wanted from life, and on the face of it, that was true. First I married, then cheated on my wife; I was attentive, then I wanted a divorce. It seemed that I was going around in circles. The truth of it was that I really was. I was going in circles, but on a level they didn't know about.

"I've wondered about why I did the things to her—Betty—with the money. I did feel guilty about not letting her know that I had it right along. And I wanted to shock her into some kind of maturity— I'm not sure of that; I'm still bitter enough to want to punish her again."

"It was also a test," Roberts said quickly. "He wanted to see how long she would punish him, taking money from him that he seemed to need."

Leland was trying to get away from that part of their relationship.

"When it was all settled I became afraid," MacIver said. "I didn't trust myself. I thought that more things would happen. In Reno

I never left the motel room and when I got back to town I stayed out of certain sections—neighborhoods. For months I lived like a man the police were watching. I stayed up through the nights reading. My mind had to stay clear of the things that could upset me.

"Betty wrote to me, but I didn't answer the letters. I could guess what they said before I opened them. If I answered them she would have come to see me. Before she married they came again. Suffice it to say that her husband will never know she wrote them. But she married him, that was the thing.

"I've had a lot of time to think. I live a kind of secret existence even now. There are people who don't have it in them to understand what I've done—clerks, ministers, civil service workers, bankers, clubwomen. They're the true fanatics, the firing squads, the movie censors, the women who teach prejudice to their children. They feel nothing and understand nothing; they're without imaginations. And they have it easy in life, never suffer or have to think about the consequences of their own meanness. Before Betty agreed to the divorce, I would feel bitter and mean; I would try to stifle it, but it was as if little acts seeped through.

"Betty and I knew a girl who slept with any man who knocked on her door, salesmen, strangers who had been given her name—before she married she told Betty that she had withheld herself from her fiancé and then had played the virgin, complete with tears. She could hardly wait for her husband-to-be to cool off, so that she would not have to sleep with him again—or with any man, if she chose. She knew that she was ill, she was willing to say that she was, but she was determined to go ahead with her plans in the face of that. I put men who keep mistresses and continually use prostitutes in her class. How can they live with such dishonesty?

"I don't consider myself the equal of Norma. That isn't to say that she hadn't gone against her grain in the past. When she's drunk she doesn't care what she does, and I think that if she ever had the idea I had done something willful that hurt her, she would repay in kind, or worse. But it isn't a small percentage of what she is or wants to be. She's honest. She tries to make good use of herself. I don't

574

think that she would understand what I've done. What happened to her had nothing to do with perversion or degeneracy. We've never discussed the subjects. I'm afraid that she has a respect for herself that wouldn't let her continue with someone like me. She could see our relationship as another instance where life has betrayed her. She doesn't deserve it. As much as is possible for me anymore, I'm in love with her. Being with her, letting her be herself, is a scary, beautiful thing. I need it. I've seen people who have forgotten that they passed through what could approximate a nervous breakdown. I've read accounts by drug addicts and alcoholics in which they speak of their feeling before the first fix or drink; scared to death and mouths watering. It's all the same. I'm sure the girl Betty and I knew in college—" Karen had said a similar thing, years ago. She had said that she understood alcoholics. "—I went too far," MacIver was saying. "Something gave way the night I killed Leikman. There was that sense of relief. I was safe and warm as long as I went about my business. I was in a trance no alcoholic or addict has ever felt. I felt the rest later. The fools in the world would say that my conscience had begun to bother me. Those people kill all my repentence. In another world I would want to atone, but not in this. I can't think of all the terrible people in this world. I have to keep to myself. I never would have been a gregarious man. I regret that. I'll never do the good things that I dreamed of as a child. Children have to suffer before they become adults. Childhood is really stolen from people." Now there was a rustle, as if he had moved. The tape went on for just a moment.

"You see, there is something that the censors and executioners of the world will never face, although it comes out in them the most. That's that most of us—the most of us all—hate life. We hate being alive, we hate the life we have to live, the people around us, and finally, really, ourselves. We all have it, a bottled-up, screaming, clawing hatred—everything about life is punishment, death the fitting end. There's nothing left but fighting back and getting revenge, punishing all the things we hate, including ourselves. I never saw him before, but when I killed Leikman, I was really glad."

"That's it," Roberts said. "Later, as he went along and examined the things that he had done, he came to a better understanding of Betty. Neither of them had been ready for marriage, and she had had no more insight into that than he had. Words like 'timid' have only a surface meaning. Her behavior—like his, yours, and mine —was created in earlier situations. I could see no evidence during my work with Colin that she tried to expand her consciousness while she was married to him, so in that sense she bears a responsibility for what happened to him—and Leikman. Colin had had only one brief homosexual experience before marriage—his marriage to her. I have yet to see the situation in which the wife did not bear some responsibility. Her parents were 'little' people; she grew up in that sort of oppressive atmosphere. Her expectations of Colin were unrealistic.

"His expectations of her were impossible. Contrary to what he said, he had never had a good relationship with a woman. Only in retrospect were his affairs in wartime 'good.' He failed to appreciate or understand the women when he knew them. He mishandled the relationships and they terminated unsatisfactorily. In one instance, the affair fell apart because he failed to write to the girl. There was no reason for not writing, no external reason.

"He wanted a wife who was inexperienced so that his performance as a husband couldn't be judged—not because he had premonitions of disaster, but because he had reasons to believe that he would suffer in a judgment. He was not equipped to deal with the problems of his adolescence objectively, and if he couldn't approach his problems except in an emotion-laden way, no one else could, either, he thought. Because he was ashamed, he thought that others would be derisive. An inexperienced girl—a virgin—would be easier to control, and the faster he married her, the safer he would be.

"Just as much, he wanted a wife who could care for him, who would smooth over his instability and immaturity. That implies a certain authority, but a neurotic wouldn't account for that. Still, he was unconsciously prepared to be afraid of her, dislike her, scheme against her in the same way he schemed against his mother.

"Colin lived a vivid fantasy life. He realized that, too, before he died. You can see how it would have come about, the death of his

576

father, who had not been a very satisfactory father, his frustration and feeling of exclusion during adolescence. Colin admitted that he had hoped—fantasizing all the way—to teach Betty how to be his lover. But he had picked—intentionally—a girl who was singularly ungifted for the part—and had further handicapped her by forcing her into a circumstance in which no woman can function as a lover.

"You don't have the training to understand all that Colin had been attempting in his pursuit of men. He liked pretty boys, but chose the role of the girl for himself. There was a good deal of infantilism in the acts themselves. You heard him say that he was aware of the social condemnation he was courting. Courting is the word. These things are never simple. He hated what he did, yet used it as an escape valve, hated himself afterward, and went home and projected that hatred onto his wife. Dealing with me, he wanted to say that he would have had the crisis whether he had married or not, but I'm not sure. As I said, these things are never simple. Through his childhood, Colin had been drummed with his mother's concept of morality—anti-sex, anti-male. He rebelled against it, but he didn't stop believing it. Like all rebels, he couldn't walk away. Like all rebels, he was deathly afraid of the thing he was rebelling against. Deathly afraid. He honestly believed that he wanted to be married and make a success of marriage. That meant not cheating. By going with men, he wasn't really 'cheating.' And more, he was satisfying a deeper, older need related to his father. The social condemnation enters into it, too. Colin knew that he was a failure as a husband and a man. Each foray into homosexuality was an admission of failure. Until the night of the murder—an accident; the accident of two thwarted men coming together—until that night, Colin was working his way deeper into a twisted, tormented pattern of failure, self-punishment, and despair. The acceleration of the pattern made a collapse inevitable. Colin was an extremely bright man. I'm not sure that he didn't anticipate the impending collapse. The murder was a disaster designed to stave off another. Of course he was striking out at himself. You heard him identify with homosexuals. He killed a homosexual. He mutilated the body; no matter what he thought he decided, the mutilations had a meaning of their own. He felt an intense relief after the murder. He was attempting to kill something in himself.

"The events of his childhood smashed his chances for a normal life. He had glimpses of a normal life, and he wanted it very much. He worked terribly hard here. Some of that work—as I hope you can imagine now—was agony for him. He was a man of tremendous personal assets; intelligence, insight, wit, desire. Once in a while he would talk about what he would do when he had his life straightened out. He was looking for an investment he could participate in. He wanted to be an ethical man."

Leland said, "I want to know about Rainbow." Some of the things that Roberts had said had raised the memory of what Karen had endured. Leland had closed his mind years ago to what she had had to think, what she had had to feel about him, to do what she had done. He had convinced himself that it was not his business for as long as she wanted to be his wife.

Roberts said, "The housing law was passed while Colin was in college. A political science professor used it to make a point. Colin had absorbed a lot about real estate while his father had been alive and he saw the loophole right away. He pointed it out in class. It was too complicated for the other students and probably the professor as well, and the professor lost his patience. Colin did his term paper on it and gave it the subtitle, 'An Opportunity to Subvert the Public Interest.' It was a brutal paper that indirectly attacked the professor. Colin was given a D in the course. Later, when he determined to change his life, he saw Rainbow as a shortcut to a better social and financial position. He couldn't explain his need for that beyond indicating a sense of well-being that he felt in the finer homes and better restaurants of the rich and powerful. Some people moving up never feel at ease in such places."

"I know where he lived before he moved to Collegeville Road," Leland said. "It's an ordinary neighborhood, almost run down. He could have done better there."

"It suited his purposes," Roberts said. "He wasn't ready to venture fully into legitimate society. I told you that he forced an interest in racing. He did it because he felt that he had discovered a need for an outlet. He was trying to understand and help himself. He believed that he had to challenge the attitudes and opinions that continued to order his life. Before he had gone into the service, for example, he hadn't done any social drinking. He was never able to forget having been in a bar and feeling a faint but genuine fear. The experience served as a guideline. There were his social and racial prejudices which were broad and very deep. Before the war, casual heterosexual contacts—pickups—had frightened him. He had an unrealistic concept of women—in spite of his hostility, he couldn't account for liars or connivers. He saw that he had never exercised any serious caution or reserve in dealing with women. Just before he met Betty, he had begun to get the feel of the 'game' of society, and when he picked it up again he remembered and had to ask himself if he had not tried to run away the first time. After the divorce, he used prostitutes, many of them. He told me that he had a need—or desire—for female companionship on a level he could control. It wasn't all illusion, he said about dealing with them. Even here he had not come very far in his understanding of the way other people are; he thought that he had to convince me that it was possible to have real relationships—that kind of money had been of little interest to him and he had treated the girls decently. It stood to reason that he would have gotten along with them. Nevertheless, he regarded those months as a 'sordid' period of his life. He was very busy with Rainbow, there were different girls in the apartment for days on end. Before he died he was able to say that no one had been hurt, that it had done him some good. His first marriage hadn't accomplished that much. Still, until the end, he regretted the failure of the one and the success of the other. He hadn't come to a true realization of his capacities and limitations at the various times of his life—"

The telephone rang again. Leland turned to it, letting the bell sound a third time, then picked up the handset. "Go ahead."

"Joe?" She was whispering.

"What is it, Karen?"

"Are you all right? Can you talk to me?"

He looked at Roberts. "Sure. Where is Mrs. MacIver?"

"In bed. She went to lie down. She's all right. Joe—"

"Just a minute." He said to Roberts, "Karen put her to bed."

"No, I didn't," she cried softly. "Not really. I suggested it because of her condition—I don't know if she's asleep. She is all right, Joe. I didn't tell her. Joey, she beat my brains out. She told me things that you said to her."

He hesitated. "Like what?"

"About you. About what's really happened. You told her about me during the war. And that you really haven't done the things you've told me. You had no reason to lie to her about that—like that. You told her the truth."

Roberts leaned forward. "What is it, Joe?"

Leland could not speak to him. He waved Roberts away. "Karen—Karen? How did she get started on it?"

"Little things that happened at Dr. Roberts' house. She thought that I disliked her, resented her—I don't know. It made her angry. She said that she wouldn't have mentioned them if she hadn't had to come here, if she hadn't been getting a runaround since I arrived. She's become convinced that you aren't on the case, that you've been too busy handling me. Handling," she repeated.

"She can't hear you," he said.

"No, that telephone is disconnected, remember? Joe, she's in love with you. She wants to marry you."

"Did she say that?"

"No, but—"

"No buts. She'll be all right just as she is and she knows it better than anybody. Dr. Roberts here assures me that it's the way she is—"

"You don't expect me to believe that," she said.

"I don't want you to worry. Do you believe that? I don't want you thinking about it."

"Joe, I want to help you," Roberts said.

"Be quiet! It's not your business!" He tried to turn away. "Karen—are you there?"

"Yes."

"She guessed some things from what happened between Roberts and me. You can't lie to her—I didn't want to," he said quietly.

"We've been through that. It's settled, I hope. Do you care about that? I don't. I want to forget it. I was wrong."

"Never as wrong as I've been. Why did you do it? Why did you tell me those things when they weren't true?"

"I don't know why. As well as I could guess, they were what you wanted to hear. You seemed to need them."

She was quiet. "You let me do that to you?"

"It wasn't important."

"I thought you were just as bad. I told Jerry what you said about Scotland. I even convinced myself that I wasn't the first to cheat. I was the only one, wasn't I?"

"There was Anne, Karen."

"We were separated. Joey, when am I going to know the last of the things that I've done to you?"

He tried to clear his eyes. "I wanted you. You were that important to me. You changed my life. I wouldn't have known anything, thought anything. I love you. You're that good, Karen. You've been that good to me."

"I'm sorry, Joe."

"I'm not. You—remember that."

"Are you all right?"

He nodded. "Yes."

"Joe?"

"What is it?"

"Do I know you at all?"

"Of course you do. You know everything there is to know. I never thought that this was important."

"It was to me. I had to see you in apartments I didn't know. A life of your own. Not thinking of me. It gave me something."

He wanted to stop her. "You be yourself. I told you that tonight. You be yourself and do the good things you want to do."

There was silence. "Did you find recordings?"

"Yes."

"You heard them? Can you talk?"

"Yes, I can talk, and yes, I heard them. I was wrong about Roberts, he was trying to help the man. The tapes have everything you would want to hear. I still don't understand it all. MacIver was on the way. She was a good wife to him. They were going to have a baby."

"You don't know what you're going to do," she said.

"I've been putting it off—putting it off. I haven't thought at all. There are so many people involved—his wife, his first wife, his unborn child. All the men I worked with. Steffie and you—"

"Don't think about Steffie and me," she said.

"Are you telling me what you want me to do?"

"No, I can't. I don't know. Don't think of anyone else, either. His wives had their chance. So did Dr. Roberts. If they want to cover themselves with guilt that's their business. You think of yourself. Being a policeman is a job like any other. Doctors make mistakes, people die, the responsibility is clear, the doctors go on. You did your best. MacIver let Tesla die, he could have done something—"

"Just a minute." He looked to Roberts. "What was MacIver doing when Felix Tesla went to the electric chair?"

"He was still living with Betty. He wouldn't talk about that. He couldn't."

"I heard," Karen said. "I'm sorry this happened. I want to protect you—that's all I've been saying. I don't really know what to tell you."

"Don't tell *her* anything—that still stands. Can you stretch out on the couch? I want you to get some rest."

"I think so. I'll be all right."

"Are you all right? That's the important thing."

"Yes. Anything you do there—you know. Do what *you* want."

"I'll call you," he said.

"Don't be long. You have to sleep, too."

He hung up and turned to Roberts. "You made a mistake. She's worried about me."

"It's too soon. She hasn't lived with it. I won't argue the point. Not now. You told me to mind my business, but I want you to know—your wife, too—that I wouldn't participate in anything that would hurt you. If I can help you in any way—without violating your privacy—you have only to say so."

Roberts had begun to labor over his phrasing, which Leland took as evidence of sincerity—he had had to say it; he had not thought in advance of the difficulty. Leland got up and started to rewind the tape.

"Were you listening to what I said?"

"I heard only your half, Joe. It's obvious that I don't know much about you or your marriage."

"I didn't mean that. Why did MacIver kill himself?" The tape went through the machine. He removed the reel, boxed it, and put it with the other in his jacket pocket. He went back to the chair. "You said you knew. I want to hear it."

"He talked about it a lot more a few years ago. August twelfth was a sudden and—no, I wasn't shocked. His death was always a possibility. As time went on I felt that the possibility was more and more remote. He led me to believe that. He believed it himself.

"I don't know if you can understand this, Joe. You've said that you've had an easy time. It would not seem that way to some people, but I think you mean inside, with yourself. But you have had insights into the trouble that others can have. Some people don't have the opportunity, and their minds stay closed forever. Colin was right in that. Still, there is a line of experience you have to cross, to feel it, to gain an emotional understanding. For me it happened when I had to come to the conclusion that preaching the gospel as my father had done could not fulfill the quality of my desire to serve—serve in the ecclesiastic sense. I spent years recovering from the shock and coming to an understanding of what had happened. I lost the faith I'd had. It takes a terrible honesty to face yourself no matter who you are, that much more terrible for people like Colin. Colin killed a man. In time he came to understand why, and why he had made a bad marriage, why he had made it worse, and even why he had schemed against his mother. A man doesn't have to have a rigid moral upbringing to feel a sharp disappointment with the apparent baseness of the impulses that direct the neurotic life. Colin did have that rigid morality and his disappointment was that much harder to control. He had come to it before he met me, from what he had been able to work out for himself. He never gained complete control—no one ever does;

it isn't even wise to think about. He had fantasies—homosexual fantasies—fought them and felt them pass within a month of his death. He had dreams—nightmares, if you want—and he worried about saying and doing things in his sleep. He was a bright man. He could see into others, not exclusively homosexuals, but people in flight from themselves, unchecked sadists, others. It wasn't hard for him to project his disappointment outside himself, to other people, to history, and life itself.

"The basic condition stays the same, he said. Not just for him; for everybody. He saw that his prostitutes were a substitute for the fantasies, and that the gambling was a conscious substitute for the girls. The condition was the same wherever he looked. The important thing about the gambler wasn't the repressed inversion, the escape from sex, or the philanderer his uncertainty. Colin saw those things on his own, to his credit. He wondered how often the compulsive gambler could make love, and about the emotional depth of the experience of the philanderer. Colin saw that the promiscuous woman was his sister and the alcoholic his cousin, but not because of the kinship of sexual collapses. Sex is something that people are, not a carnival game they pit themselves against—that's his phrase. The differences between men and men, or women and men, sick or healthy, are not as deep or important as the emotions they share. Absolutely. The thing that Colin believed bound neurotics together was the consuming, overwhelming, often delicious hatred he spoke of, the hatred born of frustration and despair. Psychiatrists' files are full of reports of women wanting to drown their children, men like Scanlon raping and killing children. A woman can do a more terrible job of taking her life than any man, defiling her sex organs and maiming herself—"

"I've seen the photographs," Leland said.

"Colin read somewhere that rats foul their nests and kill each other when they overbreed, not for food or in the way a bitch will eat a puppy she has no nipple for, but in the furious, frenzied pursuit of self-destruction. They succeed in destroying the colony. No one knows why they do it. No one knows why it is in the nature of men to hate and destroy as a result of frustration and arrested development.

It *is* natural, natural as laughter—another thing for which there never has been a satisfactory explanation. Colin thought that his despair had validity. His conception of death was infantile, his fear of death was one of the results of his childhood difficulties—he knew that. And he knew that it was also a device of self-hate; that alcoholism, drug addiction, and the social scorn courted by the homosexual were, in their turns, equations for childish conceptions of death. He could not help seeing all of life as we know it as a mad fantasy. With his own child still seven months from birth, he wondered about the sense of bringing it to life so that it could suffer, age, and die."

"Karen has thought of that."

"And?"

"She cried."

"What do you think?"

"I don't know. Someday I'm going to die myself. No one knows anything about it."

"That's right, and no one intelligent reconciles himself to it, either. It's put aside, out of mind. Colin couldn't make that trick work. On the day he died he was very depressed, more than I had thought. He lost his hold on the things that could bring him up from depression—his marriage, his love for his wife, and his anticipation of fatherhood—and it was over far more quickly and easily than ever he could have foreseen."

"You saw him that morning," Leland said.

"Yes. Did you talk to Norma about that day?"

"And the night before. There was an incident after dinner. In the parking lot outside the restaurant. He seemed upset, but not more than other people might have been."

"Norma repressed it, you know. I was afraid that she would focus on it and want to know why he had reacted so violently. So far, she hasn't looked at it from that side."

"Norma remembered when she was with me on Monday," Leland said. "What did he tell you that morning?"

"At first he didn't want to discuss it. It had taken him twenty minutes to remember, earlier, when he had awakened. He came in in an agitated condition, but eventually he talked freely. He talked about what happened afterward, between Norma and him."

"She gave me an idea," Leland said.

"She's so honest and forthright. It worked a magic on him. She knows better than anybody that sex is a thing you are. You look distressed. Psychotherapy isn't conducted in a drawing room. As you said, if Norma wouldn't understand it, no one would. I knew from my work with her how their private relationship would develop. Her attitude might have been the best thing that happened to Colin. She likes to talk and play. He had had only glimpses of that kind of sex, that loving forthrightness." He looked at Leland. "You don't want to hear this, do you?"

"No."

"He left the office on a positive note. He was aware that he could have been anybody the night before; that he hadn't acted abnormally in the way he had gotten the boys out of the car. The boy who spat on him either acted on his own sudden impulse or because he had said something to the others that he had to back up. Colin and I went on from there. We talked about what he and Norma had done earlier, parking down on the Point. It may seem ordinary to you. Something like that had been one of his fantasies, and bringing it to reality had given him real joy. The turn of events pleased him—the beautiful girl in the car had turned out to be his wife, pregnant with his child. He thought that she was beautiful, but then, you do, too."

"I *know* that she is," Leland said.

"That's where we stopped," Roberts said. "We had discussed the qualities of memory long before, that he could dwell on what he chose. In the course of the hour I had asked about his plans for the day, and they didn't amount to much. I wanted him to see that he could go home, arrange his plans to suit himself, if he thought that it would profit him. If it occurred to him—it had before—he didn't say it. I doubt that he thought of it. I don't think that he really knew that he was in that kind of trouble.

"Something else may have happened after he left here. We'll never know. Norma told me that his secretary hadn't noticed anything unusual. She isn't a perceptive woman; he kept her on because he wanted to be left alone.

"A mood could come up on him like a sea squall. It must have happened that afternoon. It may be that he found himself thinking of the goodness of his marriage and contrasting it with what he thought of himself at that moment. It came up once in a while; I was afraid of it, but not enough. If he felt hatred, it was for himself. He killed himself in despair. I'm as certain of that as I am that he was not in the grip of vivid homosexual desires—he could run from them; he was familiar with them. When he had knocked the boy down the night before he had said to him, 'I could kill you now, you know.' It was not a threat; it was a statement of fact. In the office here Colin saw that he had considered his words. He never felt real remorse over Leikman or Tesla. If you don't understand that, we may as well stop now—"

"Go on."

"Colin wanted me to understand something about the things he felt. You heard him say that he was glad when he killed Leikman. That's not quite correct. By then the consequences of the act were moving in on him. He only glimpsed the unconscious relief that rose to the surface later. He felt something else: the residue of the sick thrill he'd had at the prospect of killing a man. The fight took less than two minutes, as he reconstructed it. When he saw that the one sure escape from the consequences of hitting Leikman was in killing him, the thrill, the morbid, twisted thrill, was in him, like that, as fast as the thought. He wanted me to understand that. It was the key to his despair. He killed Leikman because it would satisfy him, no matter what he could see intellectually about the meaning or the penalties for doing murder. He made me understand that he knew in advance that killing Leikman would be difficult, that he would have to hit him time after time, literally beat the life out of him, and that the result would be the horrible scene that you found—remember, Colin looked at it, too. But before, while the fight was still on, while he was in the act of murder, he wouldn't let himself think of all that. If anything, running away from the thought made him act faster and more decisively.

"It was the logical extension, he said, of the homosexual acts. After the experience in California, he knew all there was to know about homosexual 'love.' The anticipatory thrill—the sick thrill, he called it again and again—overrode every deliberative, intellectual consideration, every image of it he could—or wanted to—call up in advance. It couldn't stop him. I asked him once, only once, if there weren't some emotional satisfaction in relating to another human being. He said no. It was a sordid, furtive negotiation, an exercise in animalism, thoroughly devoid of feeling. And he believed that all homosexuals really knew it. Still, the anticipation, the sick thrill—a rare, supreme kind of pleasure, he called it, too—drove him on. There was pleasure, pure pleasure, in doing the thing he hated most."

Leland asked, "Would you believe *me* if I said that I don't know if I understand that? I just don't know."

Roberts nodded. He ran his hand over his head. "Colin was honest enough to acknowledge that there was physical gratification in any contact of the sex organs—this from a man whose childhood had been surrounded by a ponderous sexual mystique. He saw no reason to concern himself overmuch with why *he* came to believe that homosexuality was the lowest of man's behavior. He knew that there were alternatives to our culture, that homosexuality had been practiced by the elite of other societies—just as, by the way, your wife told me this evening that she knew that there were women who thrived on the kind of life that had been destroying her. The thing that astonished and dismayed Colin was that additional, anticipatory sick thrill in what he found himself choosing to do. He said that he could have stood on a crowded trolley, played with himself, anything, and achieved the same physical pleasure—but it wouldn't have been the same. It sickened Colin, not the capacity for self-destruction, but the absolute, undeniable appetite for it."

Leland had been thinking of what he had said about not knowing if he understood the pleasure. Karen had said that she had been looking for romance. Was that in any way the same? Leland could remember returning from the war and realizing that his wife had been to bed with another man, and not being able to stop himself from making love to her again—he had wanted to stop. She had not loved him in the way he had loved her. It was all changed now, but tonight, at this moment, he could reach out and touch those days with his hand.

"I had to be afraid of marriage, where Colin was concerned," Roberts was saying. "Not just because he had failed in one attempt. With Norma, he had to have a far better chance to succeed. The life he had lived before he had met her had been the best for him. A lonely life, but it had allowed him to grow. Marriage makes its own great demands—people are afraid to discuss them. What happened to Colin was precipitated by the pressure of marriage—the same with your wife. You know it. And both of them wanted so badly to do well—you know that, too. In spite of what he saw in his parents, or what he did himself, Colin believed in marriage. No work, no personal accomplishments compare, he thought. A little while ago you said about him that there was such a complexity to his financial affairs that it was easy to overlook the fact that he wanted to be rich. When he and I were talking about marriage, he said that we lived in such a welter of change and confusion that it was easy to miss the point that marriage is the most important fact of our life on earth—"

"A doctor who looked at Scanlon last night said that there were three things, birth, death, and life itself."

"And marriage is what we do with life, Joe. Or try. We regard it as our crowning achievement. Colin reminded me of that. It isn't the first time a man's sorrow has turned a light on something good."

"I think that the doctor was asking questions about our taste for misery," Leland said. "He frightened my father. My father had a high school education and the doctor talked about Scanlon going mad—that it was happening before our eyes and there was nothing we could do about it."

He had said something, too, about the man being out of reach, as if dead, like MacIver. Leland had not been out to the cemetery. He was going to do that. He was going out and see MacIver's stone. Norma did not seem like one for visiting graves. All the funerals a man went to, all the biers and corpses with rosaries or crosses or

Bibles—everyone knew that much about it. It was enough of a burden for a man to bear.

"Listen to me a little longer, Joe. For Colin, for your wife, for all the people so badly prepared for taking their places as adults, marriage is like a machine made in hell. It tears them apart. You saw what happened to Karen. You helped her help herself."

"It was an accident," he said. "Pure acccident."

He could not help thinking of the flight to Manitou—the way he looked at it these days, he had deserted her. But he rarely looked at it, except in fear, which was true of her, too. They had come this far because they had been afraid to let go of the bits and pieces they had found of the thing they had thought they had destroyed. They were both to blame. Maybe like Betty Kaminsky he had not known enough, and maybe he had expected too much: he had gone home those nights before the war with his head filled with visions of Karen Widener. Had he ever thought of her as someone other than the girl who had had so many good things to do?

"Joe, the despair corroded him. Too much had happened. Listen to me. He knew that there weren't going to be final answers. His marriage with Norma was the best thing he did. It was going to be better. He could see it opening to greater depths of experience, new feelings, aspects of feelings. He loved it, and he loved her more and more as time passed. But for him there was the prospect of a day-after-day struggle for insight and understanding. The good mind continues being mischievous and inventive; he would have had to fight himself to the end of his life. There was nothing to be gained. He had seen himself—he had worked very hard. He was tired. He didn't have the energy to give to it any more."

Leland had heard him. He was too far along even to think of turning around. Manitou seemed like a very far place. The snow falling, Thanksgiving in six days, the air clean, and the Christmas lights strung across Senapee Street. If he let himself, he would feel the snow swirling against his face. Roberts was watching him, hands in his lap. Leland had to avert his eyes. The telephone—he could call Karen, talk to her again, but he did not dare. He had had to know: he did not know if it had been that urge that had brought him here or the simpler, simple-minded falling back on his training as a policeman. If he marched it to the end, there would be no calculating the unhappiness.

The widow of the late admitted murderer Colin MacIver gave birth today to a seven-pound, six-ounce son . . . Mrs. MacIver and the boy, who will be named David, are doing well . . . something like that. A long item would remind newspaper readers that it had been the investigation sponsored by Mrs. MacIver that had uncovered the tape recordings in which her late husband had confessed to the six-year-old murder of Theodore Leikman. Readers would not have to be reminded of her police record. Herbert Davis and his office would settle that. The way things were done in this country, the newspapers and their Sunday magazines would never let her forget what had happened—or had been decided here. She would learn that she had another, public personality. Perhaps that, too, would be determined by Davis and the members of the conspiracy. There was no question of whom he would go to bat for. It had always been the same, the indignant, hysterical name-calling, the righteous posturing—many had suspected, but Leland was as close as any to knowing. Leland had won the previous battle, but he ached with the thought of bringing Davis down for good.

No one in this office is a thief. Where did he stay the first week he was in Port Smith? Check on that. He hasn't lived with his wife in years, everyone knows that sad tale. Look at what we have, a bitter, ten-cent keyhole peeper taking advantage of a slow-witted young woman who never had a day of luck in her life, all for some psychopathic vengeance for a case he alone botched years ago.

Davis would do better than that. He had a staff of specialists.

"You want me to forget it," Leland said. "You want me to walk out of here."

"Yes. That's what it comes down to."

He swung away from Roberts. The ash trays had been crying for attention and every cop in the world knew something of the patterns of homosexuals. MacIver had fooled them with the mutilations. Just a little imagination. Leland was sick with the thought of the ease of it. It revealed a vein of deceit and dishonor in everything he had done since that pursuit across the beach: Tesla had scrambled; that had been enough to convict.

Karen told me to think of myself.

In another moment he did not know if he had said it aloud. He brought his eyes back into focus. The desk, the carpet. There was a glow coming through the venetian blinds. The contents of the tapes would make their way into the newspapers. The district attorney would respond to pressure or someone in his office would be willing to be greased. There was too much money to be made. One of Roberts' colleagues would try to promote himself by challenging Roberts' use of professional privilege. No matter how clear the record, Roberts' connection with Rainbow would be smeared.

"Karen told me to think of myself," Leland said.

Roberts waited.

"If I do as you say, if I go and tell Norma some lie, the only one I'll be *able* to think of is myself. Do you understand?"

"I don't think so."

"I've never taken a dime. When I was with the Department, I never even took a bottle of liquor or a bag of groceries. Do you understand that? I've always done my job."

"No one is asking you to be a thief."

"Where do you draw the line? Why should I draw a line at all? I could be happy with Norma. I might be a grandfather in five years. A honeymoon, a new marriage, would make me feel like a baby again. I'd change jobs, situations, I'd be a quarter of a million richer. It would be a whole new life. I'd love to take off with her. Who wouldn't? Why shouldn't I? Some things would be behind me forever. And I could make her happy, too, and that would be good for me."

"You equate that with street-corner graft," Roberts said. "It's the same thing to you."

"No, I'm just saying that if I do the one thing, I may as well chuck it all and do everything else. I'd be turning my back on my wife—I wouldn't want to look her in the eye."

"I don't understand that."

"You had the conversation with her. She told you about the secrecy of the life she lived. She was too afraid and ashamed to go for help. It would have meant telling me. I wasn't supposed to understand. I didn't, anyway. I do now, or at least better than before, and I couldn't hope to be honest with her again if I went home and tried to give her a true account of this and then said that I had decided that most people would never understand what had happened to MacIver, that it was better to forget about it. Karen is a woman who wants to leave something good with everything she does. I'd be telling her that that time of her life was just worthless, that no matter what she thought, she really lived it for nothing. That's what I would be turning my back on, just when it was clearest to me. I wouldn't want to look at her; I wouldn't want her to look at me."

"You're dealing with other lives as well. I think she would understand that."

"I know she would. But she would wonder how long I would be able to stay on the tightrope. I couldn't tell her that a thing was worthless and then accept it as part of my life. She would wonder when I would start thinking of the other opportunities I had passed up. I could figure some way to keep them open, too. And I would start thinking, she would be right. No matter who would be helped, no matter how much suffering would be avoided, if I went to Norma to lie, the important thing to me would be the edge I'd taken for myself. I wouldn't be where I am today if there had been no Leikman case. Because of it, I make more money than I know how to spend. If I do this, I'll go back to the beginning and retrace every step, but this time around I'll take every dollar and shake every hand with the knowledge that I conspired against Felix Tesla, that I knew he was innocent all along. There isn't a man I call my friend who wouldn't feel the same way. Karen told me to think of myself. You tell me how I could go on building a life with her. You tell me how I could draw another free breath."

"So you'll go to the police," Roberts said. "That's why you'll go to the police."

"Colin MacIver murdered a man. If I had found evidence at the time, I would have arrested him. I'm not a law enforcement officer now, but the license I have was issued on the condition that I would turn over evidence of crime. It was explained to Norma. She understood it."

Roberts stood up. "There's no arguing with that. The law is a century behind society. If you can close your eyes to that, I can't open them. Joe, under that belligerence of yours, that swaggering attitudinizing that seems so attractive socially, is a very immature personality. You broke the law when you came here and now you want to cite it in defense of the course you hope you can take—you want to take it because you're faced with a genuine decision here, and you want to fall back where it's really safe, to what you can understand."

"You've said enough." Leland got up.

"You will understand if I go to Norma and explain my part in this," Roberts said.

"You bet I will. Maybe you won't exactly set her against me, maybe you will try scrupulously to be fair, but you know now that she'll start off believing that you've been right and I'm going wrong. You don't have to be told how she'll suffer before she gets it untangled. There is the chance that she'll surprise you, that she'll want to go to the authorities. You're the one who's wrong. You don't know what you believe—you don't even see it. The sterility in the housing programs can be traced directly to the thievery going on within it, but you're going to stay quiet. A man committed a murder for which another paid with his life under a system you oppose, but you're going to stay quiet about that, too. I'm beginning to see where you've missed the point. Marriage is our crowning achievement? A few years ago you aided and abetted a man who was trying to break up my marriage. If you really believed what you said, no matter what you knew about us, or what you thought you knew, you should not have acted. You should have respected our marriage for being *a* marriage. Even if you thought it wasn't an honest try, which it was. You saw only a public part, and because of your training you were able to gain an insight into the way it was inside, yet you still helped Palmer, just as you want to forget about Rainbow and be quiet for Norma's sake about Colin MacIver, all because you can't help seeing the way people live as a kind of battle. You said game, but you really mean

594

battle. It was Palmer against me, wasn't it? One man's needs set against another's. Now it's Norma's against mine. Breaking into your office didn't frighten me because I had faith in your ability to understand my position once I explained it to you—I didn't think about it. I didn't believe I had to. I told Karen the truth, I didn't know what I was going to do. I swear to you that I can see no alternative—I'm no fool, I'm not going to run down with this to the nearest patrolman. I have to protect my client and myself. There is a way that you can help. Tell her why you thought you were right, then tell her why my position is different, why I'm right, too. She'll have her best chance if she stays with this, if she acknowledges her continued support of what I have to do. Certainly she'll be criticized—but by people she doesn't care about, anyway. No one will dare humiliate her—Herbert Davis would, if she withdrew and condemned me. He could get to me if he could show that I hurt her. He'll go for her throat. You can show her how this will protect her—"

"I could confuse her while she denounces her late husband and the father of her unborn child, if that's what you mean."

"She has a score to settle with these people. They had an effect on his death; they made money on his trouble—"

"Stop it, I've had enough." Roberts came to the desk and gathered his wallet and keys. "Keep the other set. You're here against my will. I'll make the decision about pressing charges after I've seen what you've actually done. I wouldn't be surprised if you finally came to your senses." His hands were shaking. "Perhaps if you thought again about the ramifications—" He went to the corner of the room and picked up his belt. "If you thought about the suffering you would cause. What about her when this is over, all over? Where will she be? She's going to have a reaction, and you'll be far away." He put on his coat. "Are you coming with me?"

"No. You do see it as a battle, not of self-interest, but of self-preservation, which is worse. Your patient first, one patient at a time. We could work together, you and I, get something started. I've been around; I know how ugly it will be and how little, in the end, will be done. You want to tell her not to project her real self into it, just as you've been telling me. You wanted to protect me, and now that's no longer possible, you want me to help you to continue to protect her. It will tie a knot in me, but that's all right, you can help me untie that later. You say you're against the death penalty and against high-powered theft, and here is your chance. Sure, you're on committees and do public service, your body goes in a chair and your hand waves over a checkbook, but that's not the same as putting your self, the real you, on the line. Here is *your* chance, but the way you really see things, not what you say at all, has you moving in the other direction. A little accommodating, a little compromising, Norma is safe—and so are you. Just figure that Colin MacIver was a patient you lost. You can tell Karen that you think she suffered for nothing. We understand it now but we're not going to lift a finger to change things for the future. MacIver showed you how near we all are to the face of death, but you haven't learned a thing; you're content to go on your own way, cheering us up, one by one. Maybe we can stop thinking about it. We'll forget about the dead, too, and we'll let the children fight their own battles. I don't have any answers for you, Wendell, but you certainly don't have any for me."

Roberts regarded him a moment, then turned and left.

Leland was still ahead of him. He went to the windows and adjusted the blinds so that he could see down to the sidewalk. The street was blue with the day, and quiet. MacIver's convertible seemed even larger than it was. Roberts had parked his car around the corner. It reminded Leland that Roberts was not stupid, either. The bars were closed at this hour, he would have extra difficulty locating a telephone. Leland had perhaps a few minutes more to conclude his business and get out before Roberts decided to call the police. Roberts came out on the sidewalk now, hands in pockets, walking away quickly for a man who had been awake all night. Leland had to feel a little sorry for him, because he was sure he was right and he was about to get a very bad time. Leland returned to the desk and brought the telephone before him.

Karen let it ring only once.

"Yes?"

"It's me. Is she still asleep? I don't have long to talk."

"Go ahead."

596

"I'm going for it. I have to. Colin MacIver committed murder, and that's what counts. Roberts has left, on his way to you, to see Norma. When I hang up, call the desk and tell them you don't want any visitors. Describe Roberts. You don't want to see him under any circumstances. Try to get the house man. Tell him you're Joe Leland's wife, and if that doesn't help, have him call my father's precinct to check on us. You want Roberts arrested if he tries to get through, do you understand? Let the house man know that this is important to me, and that I'll take care of him. Okay?"

"I'll do what I can," she said.

"Next, call Mike—that's right, knock him out of bed, tell him to get Hugh Thoms down to my place to watch MacIver's papers. The authorities may be after them very soon, and they're not getting anything without the proper documents and until we've copied it all, from beginning to end. I want Mike down here. Don't tell him why, don't say it over the telephone; the house man may put the switchboard onto us. And we want Florence. We need a secretary. We need records from here on out. We need two top-quality tape recorders and a half-dozen reels of the best tape. Maybe the hotel can supply them, but I don't want to wait until nine o'clock. I want you to call my father, anyway, I need his advice about who to see and how. I might need him in dealing with Mrs. MacIver, Norma. I think she'll listen to him. For her sake, I want her to go along with us. I have to turn this in, Karen. I have to."

"I know."

"Roberts is afraid of reactions and delayed reactions, that's why he's on his way. I can't do what he wants. Do you think you can help me with her? It's asking a lot, I know. There won't be any other trouble—"

"I haven't thought of it."

"Are you sure?"

"Yes. I'm not worried."

"All right. After the calls, wake her. I'll be almost there. Don't tell her anything but that I've been on the case and I'll be wanting to talk to her. Order breakfast for us all. She won't be eating much once I start telling her, but at least I want it to start well."

"You want me to be there?"

"Yes. I want it out in the open as fast as possible. The sooner she sees the reactions of people like you and Mike and my father, the better off she'll be. We'll see. Are you ready, Karen? It's going to be a rough time."

"I will be. I'll be ready."

"This will probably put me out of business. More people than Roberts will want it. It may even be worse. What's left will have to go to Mike."

"I was thinking about that," she said.

"You have a voice in it. We can stop."

"No."

"Are you sure?"

"Yes. I have thought about it, Joe. I know you. I do know you."

He was leaning against the desk. "It isn't going to be just the way we planned. We aren't going to be the same people."

She said, "It's getting late. We'll have our time, Joe."

"Yes," he said. "I'll see you."

About the Author

RODERICK THORP lives in Manhattan with his wife and his seven year old son. He is the author of one previous novel, *Into the Forest,* published in 1961. As an undergraduate at City College, he won the coveted Theodore Goodman Short Story Award. He is presently at work on a new novel.